ANNOUNCEMENT

Toward the Morning is Book Three, following Books One and Two, *The Forest and the Fort* and *Bedford Village* respectively, each part of a long North American historical romance, wide in scope, deep in implication, swift in story. The entire narrative, comprising five books, will eventually be published in a comprehensive two volume novel: I—*Sylvania,* II—*Richfield Springs,* under the title of *The Disinherited*.

Since both the preparation and the publication of such a major work are inevitably difficult in these times of world disturbance, and necessarily require considerable time, the publishers have adopted the plan of offering the various parts, in which so sustained a piece of historical fiction naturally falls, as separate bound books under individual titles to be published as occasion best serves. Each book is a full novel, in itself a vivid and satisfactory story; each is a complete panel, a whole part of a larger tapestry.

Toward the Morning, therefore, follows, in time, narrative, and sequence, the other volumes of the series already published, namely, *The Forest and the Fort* in 1943 and *Bedford Village* in 1944, both of which are available among current publications.

Toward the Morning will be followed in turn and in order of plot and narrative by *The City in the Dawn,* as previously announced.

For readers who begin the series of *The Disinherited* with *Toward the Morning,* the prelude to this volume embodies all that is essential of past reference in order to follow the narrative.

The Disinherited

BOOKS BY HERVEY ALLEN

Prose

TOWARD THE FLAME: A WAR DIARY
ISRAFEL: THE LIFE AND TIMES OF EDGAR ALLAN POE
POE'S BROTHER (WITH THOMAS OLLIVE MABBOTT)
ANTHONY ADVERSE
ACTION AT AQUILA
IT WAS LIKE THIS: WAR STORIES
THE FOREST AND THE FORT
BEDFORD VILLAGE
TOWARD THE MORNING

Poetry

WAMPUM AND OLD GOLD
CAROLINA CHANSONS (WITH DUBOSE HEYWARD)
THE BRIDE OF HUITZIL: AN AZTEC LEGEND
THE BLINDMAN
EARTH MOODS AND OTHER POEMS
SONGS FOR ANNETTE
SARAH SIMON
NEW LEGENDS

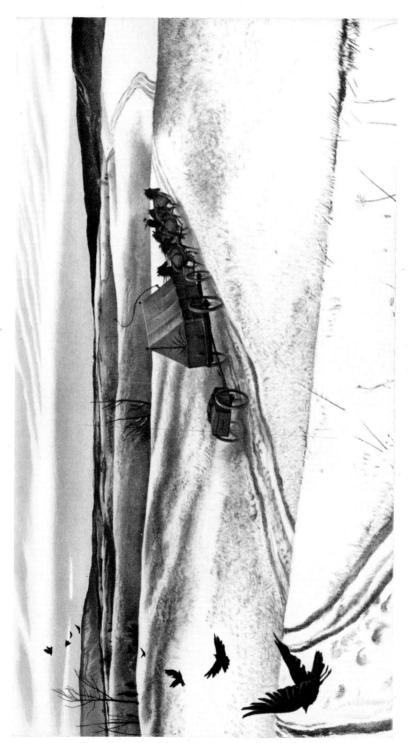

"Pennsylvania was beginning to moan and turn white under the lash of winter."

(The ark on its way eastward in November 1764.)

HERVEY ALLEN

TOWARD THE MORNING

Toward the Morning

New York · RINEHART & COMPANY · *Toronto*

TABLE OF CONTENTS

v

TOWARD
THE
MORNING

Prelude on an Irish Harp

THE DARK OUTLINE of the heavy wagon and its cart trailing a long shadow, the stark silhouette of the two outriders, one behind and one before, passed in slow procession through the bare trees, plodding eastward along the rocky Pennsylvania road between Fort Bedford and Fort Lyttleton.

The man and woman on the driver's seat now sat silent, leaning forward slightly. They had exchanged places some distance back, so he could take over the reins. It was a rough road, dangerous in places. They had gradually ceased their talk. The excitement of departure and farewells at Bedford village already lay many miles behind them. For a while they both felt inclined to be drowsy and to keep to their own thoughts.

The dawn glittered in their faces. The first level rays of sunshine streaming over the crest of the mountains blinded them. That fine elation of high spirits which had overtaken them only a mile or so behind, and a few minutes before, when the softly tinted promises of day first played across the stars, had deserted them as suddenly as it had come.

Now the sheer, white flatness of the growing daylight proved overpowering. They were forced to shade their brows with their hands in order to look down the road, which here led directly into the fiery eye of the rising sun. Even the horses blinked. The deceptive simplicity of night had vanished together with the smoothness of darkness. A thousand small details and difficulties now resumed their familiar shapes, bringing with them a renewed conviction of the arduous journey ahead and the inevitable hazards of the way.

Consequently, they had withdrawn within themselves for a space, each pondering his own particular problems of the past or of the future, as they journeyed eastward. Neither the jogging of the mounts nor the jolting of the wagon had, in either case, disturbed this half-sleepy, early morning reverie. Until, all at once, they mutually seemed to discover loneliness again and their common need for company.

The man and woman sitting on the driver's seat of the wagon instinctively drew closer. The two outriders closed in, finding they should have a word together. The driver handled his reins and shouted at the horses, which had taken advantage of his absent-mindedness to slow down to a walk. Over a brief space of smooth road, the double team settled into their collars and began to trot together, until four horses pulled as one.

After them, the heavy tent-covered wagon with the green, frosty canvas stretched tight along its ridge-pole, and the caisson-like cart trundling behind, rumbled down a succession of precipitous slopes into a dark ravine where the shadowy rear-guard of night still encamped. Here the six horses, and the six wheels, of the entire procession spattered and clattered over the slippery boulders and through the cold, shallow water of a rushing mountain brook. One of the leading team slipped and floundered in the ford, only to rise drenched, and whinnying from the icy shock.

A frantic mountain echo answered back with the shrill neigh of a stallion. And to that every mare in harness replied ardently.

But even this apparently good-natured flirting, the amorous morning banter of the hills themselves, scarcely served now to fetch a smile from its briefly passing human audience. The silence that followed seemed overpowering, and but too onerously familiar. It was the lonesome forest and the silent hills that resumed. Their spell had not been broken. Yet it was that dark brooding menace which, one and all, they were most anxious to leave behind.

The whip cracked.

The horses, nervous for a moment, again surged forward in their traces to make a steady pull against the slope ahead.

They came up slowly out of the chill gloom of the shadowy ravine, onto a rise. There the light smote them once more, but not blindingly. The new day now opened out before them.

From a burnt-out clearing just over the crest, an interminable prospect of wooded vales and hills, of forest dales and rises rolled horizonward; misty; smoking with autumnal haze, flaring into life, as patches of belated shadow fled before the sun. Into this perspective, scarce a half mile below, the narrow cut of the road disappeared like the prism of a neat canal through the forest.

Here by general consent they stopped for a few minutes to breathe the horses.

The wide inflamed nostrils of those curiously shaped beasts smoked like the snouts of smooth dragons in the crisp November air. The black range of the Tuscarora lay ahead, draped like a wall of crape; looped from one high knob to another along the eastern sky. Westward and behind them, the long, rigid rampart of Tussey's mountain broke into a fiery smile.

The sky blazed sullenly.

For a moment there was something sinister about it, a hint of the inferno from reflected scarlet fires. And it was a curious instant they now experienced together, a kind of failure in the flow of time.

They found themselves waiting with the hills for the final event. They felt they must somehow be lost, hesitating fatally; faltering in limbo along a road leading to eternal punishment.

No one spoke.

But no such mood of hooded mystery could last. Wide-awake common sense and natural humour were bound to reassert themselves against so much lonely sensibility. It was Edward Yates, the wise little Scotch attorney sitting in the driver's seat, who laughed. Twisting the reins together in his hands, with a vigorous piston-like motion of his forearms he pulled the heads of the lead horses back into the road again, and swore heartily.

The heavy wagon lurched downward. The day's journey really began. Arthur St. Clair, who had faithfully kept the rear ever since leaving Bedford, now rode forward with Albine.

Yates and the Irish girl beside him watched the dark figures of the two horsemen gain distance before them down the road. There they cantered ahead of the wagon a hundred yards or so, or they led it at a brisk walk. The bright steel of Salathiel's rifle sparkled cheerfully and constantly through the trees. St. Clair began talking to him, gesticulating earnestly while they rode along. The tail of his grey gelding and that of Albine's roan mare switched comfortably together. The sunlight smiled through the forest. The morning gradually became more friendly and intimate. The big man with the rifle was replying gravely to his companion, but with more earnestness than animation. He kept his eyes on the road ahead and his long, double-barrelled piece ready in the crook of his left arm.

Yates had no doubt that they were seriously discussing the lie of the land and the advantages of settlement. He could see St. Clair pointing out the more desirable farmsites. He was familiar with those optimistic and persuasive gestures. He could even guess at Albine's laconic replies. He smiled to himself.

This was all as it should be. Everybody—everything, including the wagon, its assorted domestic cargo, and the cart behind it, seemed to be coming along nicely. Good! He would do all he could to keep the wheels greased for the rest of the trip. That seemed to be the attorney-like function which had been naturally conferred upon him for the journey. However, he instinctively shied a glance at the Irish girl riding beside him.

Trouble, if it came from anywhere, might come from her.

But he saw nothing in the countenance of Frances Melissa O'Toole to disconcert him. On the contrary, she looked, for the moment at least, extremely happy; for once quite contented. Beautiful!

Yes, she was lovely this morning, prettier than ever. But a bit fey, he noticed. Yates noted these facts with satisfaction, as a man might, but calmly.

Melissa sat there like a dreaming sibyl, or a brooding young witch, with her unearthly blue-black hair hanging loose. She rode along drinking in the landscape with hazy grey eyes. Her gaze seemed to be fixed. Miniature reflected clouds moved across her widened pupils in a private sky of her own. Her lips whispered as if in prayer. Or perhaps it was a wild Irish spell she was muttering. He wondered; he smiled to himself again.

But let well enough—let women and their dreams alone! he thought. A man must be more practical. He turned and set himself to a stint of careful driving, watching for the boulders; for the ruts and sloughs in the rough, dirt road.

It was not that Edward Yates was unimaginative or unsympathetic. He felt vividly and understandingly. But the loss of one eye forced him to concentrate on what lay next ahead; focused his single-mindedness, as it were, on what was immediately going on. Just now it was four horses and a difficult road. A very real business to negotiate. And, in common with the two other men riding ahead, the neat young lawyer with the black patch over his left eye had already mentally registered the splendours of the dawn of this particular day as yet another natural phenomenon: as the weather accompanying November the fifth, 1764. Already it had become for him, like a case that had been satisfactorily settled, a pleasant but a closed entry on his precise calendar of the past.

Only in the sensitive face of the Irish girl, who sat contentedly, although worlds apart, beside him, did both the infernal and the celestial glories of that fine mountain morning continue to be reflected and to show themselves in moodily drifting changes of her expression, as though on the misted surface of a mirror of thought.

The magic medley of the play of sunlight on the clouds and silent hills, the massive chords which the glittering fingers of the sun struck from the taut harp-strings of the mountains, these had sunk deep into her being and still reverberated there through cavernous depths of mysterious feeling. In a flow of unpremeditated words all this silent music now surged to her lips again, re-embodied in lyrical whispers and the natural poetry of her race.

It is in such a mood as hers, indeed, that portions of the past can sometimes be *re*-membered and glimpses of the future *fore*-seen by some people. But it was the present that now preoccupied Frances Melissa more entirely. Her eyes saw everything, and her self followed everywhere with a magnified, yet with an intensified awareness.

From the valley below a questing hawk sprang into the sky.

She mounted with him. She identified herself completely with the dot in the blue which he rapidly became. But he did not seem to have receded from her. On pinions borrowed by the mind she followed and towered with him far above and over the hills. For a brief moment of sustained vision she caught hold of the wings of the morning and looked down upon the land beneath.

Behind the higher peaks, which, like prophetic gnomons in that landscape, still projected their shadows pointing westward, huge fantailed ribs of light streamed upward from high, mountain pastures to thrust themselves at divergent angles through a level rack of clouds.

For what seemed to her to be a moment of eternity rather than an instant of time, the whole countryside of dim translucent valleys, shimmering between parallel ranges of bright mountain crests held rigid north and south—all of it assumed within her trance-like and ecstatic dream an exalted, an apocalyptic aspect. The country lay beneath her like a giant, stringed harp lost by careless cherubim; mysteriously abandoned in the sky. Here and there a lone and lofty knob on the far golden rim of the instrument shone out with a sudden crested halo or coronet of light.

Across these mountain ranges, bright strings of vibrant glory, and straight over them, as though indifferent to all but their own interests, V after V of dark wild-fowl were streaming southward. They fled away like notes of music wafted from the harp itself. The low distant beat of their wings lingered as a memory of rumbling summer thunder; like the thud of the pulse in the blood; died away in aeolian overtones. That, and their eerie swan cries, while marshalling themselves for the day's flight, were the sole sounds in the brown and frosty landscape ever widening now in the onrushing light of the windless morning.

The sky lightened. The blue overhead became more intense. Underneath, molten veins of creeks and rivers emerged in a design of silver branches amid the dark rolling forests.

Like a pattern of lines and moulded plumpness in the palm of a tremendous hand, the hills and watersheds spread out below her in a wrinkled form that proclaimed plainly some huge, ancient, and unhuman meaning. But the meaning and the form were equally contained within each other. They were not to be separated. Not even by the mind of a weird-woman riding on the wings of a hawk. She felt baffled. Her vision darkened.

Yet by means of some gigantic palmistry she still yearned to prophesy about that land, to strike new music from the strings of its mountains, and tell its fortune in a noble song fitted to the harp. How plainly in her mind its waiting strings were stretched across those hills! What troubled her was that it could never contain them all; could not even give them a boundary. It was too small an instrument. The hills and the rivers slipped away under its rim beyond, and beyond. They lay afar off like clusters of mysterious folded flowers tucked away into space, colourful, eternally blooming.

How say it? How tell what all that land might mean beneath the sun? It was too much for words. Yet it weighed heavily on her mind. She sank under it. Her poetry was not enough. It had failed her. And yet her children would be living there in days to come!

"Sure, and what would they be after telling one another about it?" she cried aloud.

Yates looked at her in astonishment. Then, seeing she was only talking to herself, he turned away again.

She spoke aloud no more, but her yearning thought of the future still continued to trouble her. Her mood became now an inextricable tangle of wild angelic sorrow and mad human joy. She grieved divinely with the foolish angels who had lost their harp; left it on a peg of the mountains, silent in the halls of heaven. She rejoiced as a woman to think that already her man, riding ahead there, had fulfilled her greatest human desire; had completed her. She hovered over him an instant on swift invisible wings. She overarched him with avid, enfolding tenderness.

They had mated like eagles. He was in her blood.

New life crawled within her today. She was sure of it. It ran like a white-hot trickle of the lava of pleasure-in-pain. There was a palpitation that seemed, as she rode along on the hard wagon seat, to be something that surged up into her out of the very ground itself, a quaking that rocked her and the hills too; that quivered up into the sky until she was dizzy. Her breasts tightened and ached intolerably. The ground heaved under the wagon wheels. There was a universal, intolerable, breathless shuddering. She couldn't catch her breath.

She held it.

Then the whole horizon seemed to tilt, to fling her out and upward.

She gripped her breasts with crossed hands trying to contain herself in her own arms before she was flung clear and sheer into heaven.

My God! How beautiful it was!

If they could only know what she was feeling and seeing; the strange, sorrowful, painful, delicious ecstasy that suffused her; that melted her; that dissolved the world. And then the moment of sight, the majesty of exalted vision.

Ascension!

She could overlook everything beneath her. The two horsemen, and the wagon, and her own bodily self riding in it behind the four horses along the road. No words for it. There was a great rushing past her of all sights, of the pictures of everything from trees to clouds, a gliding-by over her protruding eyeballs. It seemed to be coming from behind her eyes, the world, and all its reflections, washing over and tumbling together as the rim of the cup that contained them tilted up—and up.

And then spilled it all out. Everything.

Everything went down over a grey misty waterfall into a sickening, dizzy abyss of the space of nothing-below.

And she was left there in the sky, alone, hovering.

Horrible!

She might fall. She was going to. She must get up, up! Seize on something.

That hawk there. That single black dot circling upward; flying. Flying safely. Her mind clutched it.

It was she.

That was how and when she had seen the hills of the Western world and the lost harp of the angels laid across them.

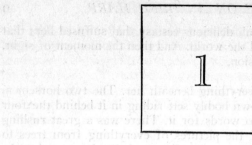

1

A Mountain Approach

AS TO JUST EXACTLY what Melissa did see that morning, it would be hard to say. The trouble is there was nothing familiar with which she could compare her experience afterward. So she could never explain it to others. Indeed, she could never fully understand it herself. It was something queer and lonely, out of the ordinary run of things. A fit of seeing-everything-at-once, sometimes a peep ahead through the glimmering spokes of the wheel of time. Or so she thought.

That was particularly troublesome.

It was especially terrible to know afterward that certain things were bound to happen. To be sure of it, and yet not be able to get anyone to listen to her. But of course not! If things were going to happen, then no talk could turn them aside, no warning. Her warnings even made things happen. They became diabolically a part of the fated happenings themselves. The Father of Evil was in that.

"Sure the devil was in it somewhere," she would say.

She always remembered that morning on the wagon seat, when she first felt certain that she was with child, as the original of these spells, as the first complete experience of an hour of exalted sight and strange suffusance. It began with a feeling of uncontainable triumph, of having overcome the universe and beaten down Death himself. She could not use all the life that kept welling up within her. It flooded, fountained, spurted, a prideful joy that rose and cascaded over the walls of her mind. And then she felt, she *saw* everything, all at once. Became part of it. Could look with the eyes of a hawk.

Afterward, long afterward, it became harder and harder to find her way back again out of such spells. It was her self, then, that she was searching for, her self lost in the world within her, a world without end. Men were to say in other years that Frances Melissa had "gone out of her mind". That is the easy way men put words together about such things. You can nod knowingly at their sage explanations.

But to Melissa the exact opposite seemed true. She did not go *out* of her mind. She lost herself *in* her mind. She couldn't find the way out of it. She wore out the hinges of her wings trying to find her self in there; and where the gates were. She walked and walked in circles, looking for a door. But the flaming walls kept going away from her, disappearing over the horizons of silence. Until she was left lost within, abandoned by God, and alone. Sometimes, a drink would let her out into the world again, where other people were. Sometimes, all of a sudden. She was to try that liquid key too often; to wear it out in the lock.

When?

Oh, years afterward, after all her children had been born.

But this morning on the wagon seat was the first time the thing had happened to her completely. There had been only a few fiery glimpses of it before, when life had been especially full of terror, when things were very bad. After the murder at Frazier's it had been that way. But that was different. This morning there was a great joy about her vision. And she was honestly curious about it. Not frightened at first. She was flying high. The more she saw, the better it was, she thought. Perhaps she ventured too far.

Afterward, she couldn't remember all that she had seen. Or she didn't know how to tell about it. Probably it was best not to talk about such things at all. People would look at her patiently, at best. So much had happened in so little time, all at one time as in a dream. She couldn't possibly tell half of it afterward, not even a tithe of it. Only a snatch here and there. "Up there" she had seen everything going on at the same time.

But people travelling in a wagon along a road, for instance, came across things one at a time. They bumped into a series of unexpected events. And if she told them what she remembered having seen, beforehand, they laughed at her. Pretty soon, when they came across what was coming their way, they were annoyed at having been told about it. They made a joke of it to protect themselves. And she was it.

Ah, it was only too true that they laughed. At best they smiled. She found it so the very first morning that the thing happened to her. She tried to tell them a little, when she came back again to the wagon seat, just a few glimpses of what she had seen going on—of the rivers flowing away through the hills underneath the sun, of the harp, and the road—the road that lay across the mountains from east to west.

After all, there was nothing so strange about her seeing all that. The harp came with her out of Ireland, out of the past. And she had been over that road coming west with old man Frazier only a few years before. Now she would like to see what was going on along it.

It was easy, while she had been "up there". She had just leaned eastward on her wings into the sunrise and left the wagon behind.

The road below snaked-it along through the forest, climbed and fell, made a ribbon through the trees that tied the East and the West together.

She saw four grey wolves chasing some elk through the forest. Their pace was swift and ruthless. They must be hungry to hunt and howl so in daylight. The day had not stopped them. But it was lonely country. All the farms lay deserted, lonesome little burnt-out clearings as far as the last mountaintop.

She went over that final mountain range like a swimmer over a wave. Up! She was flung up again into the sky.

On one side of the Tuscarora the chimney pots of Fort Lyttleton smoked white in the morning shadow of the mountain; on the other, at Fort Loudon, the smoke floated upward like black wavering scarves in the yellow sunlight.

She could see clear up the valley to Aughwick, a hazy patch in the forest. She could see the Susquehanna glittering on the rim of the harp, with the blue horizon beyond. And the roads, the people, the small houses among the trees! This was as she expected it to be, as she had remembered it. In this valley the people were still there. They had not gone away, leaving their cabins to the wolves and stars. Hope in the dawnlight was still bright down there. There were ploughed fields. Frequently there was dust along the road. Travellers. A great dust, a flashing of sunlight through a yellow cloud of morning haze lay along the road leading down from Carlisle.

She leaned eastward again into the full daylight, easily, curiously.

But she was sinking now, falling rapidly. Her speed was intolerable. Dizzy. She was flying nearer the ground, yet everything was swimmingly confused. A town she remembered vaguely—a night of trouble there with Frazier. The millwheel in the flashing race. And she was over it, and by, skimming along the road into the dawn. Sickened, afraid, falling. Ashamed of something, she remembered. Of something hidden in that great dust cloud rolling slowly westward there.

That pillar of cloud by day!

What people were these on the march through the wilderness? Who were coming west into the savage hills; into the Garden of Clouds, where the rivers rise out of the earth to walk down to the sea? Who were more terrible than the red devils that dwelt in the garden? Who feared neither their cruel hatchets nor the wild wolves? Who laughed at kings? Who would inherit the earth without meekness, to spoil it in days to come? Who but the ancient enemy of her race? The Sassenachs. The harp haters. The long-beards with the low Scotch accents. They who had forever moved into the sunset, implacably armed. The old ocean ploughers, the hill and valley ravagers. It was they! They were on the march down the long road from Carlisle in the morning sunlight, headed west for the mountains, with the pillar of cloud by day rolling behind them.

A man of God, a grey-bearded prophet of Jehovah, was leading them, going on before on a great piebald horse that stepped into the west, one iron shoe after the other, possessing the road behind him slowly like due notice. Her heart failed her at the sight of him.

Had she not read about that steed, and the other horsemen, in the English Bible at Frazier's cabin, secretly at night and by firelight? It was the forbidden Book that would wilder the minds of the laity, the Book the good nuns had warned her about over their embroidery at Cork. The Book was in the bag strapped over the saddle-bow of the prophet, along with his axe and rifle. She knew it. She had read it. And now her mortal sin was overtaking her. The remembered glow of the firelight on the page now enveloped the crowding, seething images of her vision.

The sun flashed through red clouds of dust smoking up from the road below. There was a glimpse of white upturned faces, of moving white wagontops. A dismal bellowing from the horned cattle driven along behind came like the braying of war horns through the smoke. There were shouts, and the sound of cruel blows with sticks. The rifle barrel on the saddle-bow of the prophet sparkled, caught fire, blazed. Ah, the terrible face of him under his grim hat, the straight, firm lips! He spoke. Flames came out of his mouth now, fire and brimstone.

The whole seething, revolving vision billowed up into heaven, leaning away from her as though a whirlwind were lifting the dust up along the road for miles, and everything else with it. Out of the cloud came the thunderous, stony noise of wheels rolling away into the future, a tumult and distant shouting as of hosts unborn. Dark faces of cloudy angels, their thick cheeks swollen with whirlwinds, looked at her angrily and slowly veiled their eyes.

She shrank back amazed, terrified into thought again. She was only a hawk, a small helpless bird. They might bring her down. Only a bird—was she? Who was she? Holy Mary, her mortal soul! Remember it? Frances Melissa O'Toole. But where?

There.

As from a great height she caught sight of herself riding on the wagon seat. Her head was sagging down towards her knees and her hair hanging into her lap.

A hag. Dreadful!

She came down out of the sky like a stone.

She seemed to telescope into herself in darkness.

Smash . . .

The shock whipped her back against the seat-rest. Out of darkness the road ahead gradually began to glimmer under her eyelids. Her heart beat till it nearly burst the veins in her temples. Then her eyes cleared slowly on familiar scenes. She was back. Thank God!

But was there no one to pity her?

She began to cry out bitterly. She began to call on the name of the man who had brought all this trouble upon her. Why, she had nearly died up there! Almost—she had not been able to come back again.

Yates turned towards her in blank amazement.

At that instant she clutched him violently by the arm.

"Sal, Sal!" she kept calling distractedly.

He pulled the horses up, dropped the reins, took hold of her and shook her. She was rigid, as tense as iron.

"Melissa," he shouted. "Wake up! Look at me!"

Why, the girl was beside herself! The pupils in her eyes were distracted, wide, and full of strange lights in darkness. Weird! He shrank from her. Not his girl, thank God! Salathiel's!

If he only had some cold water. Anything!

He rose and whistled shrilly through his teeth, beckoning for help to the two riders ahead. They turned and looked at him inquiringly.

"Trouble!" he shouted. He waved his hat impatiently.

"Aye," whispered Melissa, "trouble, trouble it was!" She clutched the hair back from her forehead, threw it behind her over her shoulders. She looked at him through her fingers.

"Did you see me that way, Edward Yates?" she demanded of him suddenly.

"I did," he admitted, still looking shocked.

"Never a word of it, then—not to him!" She clutched his arm again anxiously.

"Very well," he muttered. "You tell him."

He gathered up the reins, still watching her thoughtfully. One of the horses began to paw the stones.

From somewhere she produced a comb and began to use it with swift, skilful strokes.

"I'm no hag now, am I?" she asked, and looked at him suspiciously.

"No, no," muttered Yates uneasily, "of course not!"

Damn the girl, he thought—the wild woman! She was actually smiling at him now. Her eyes had cleared and were a beautiful hazy grey again. Pretty! And yet only a minute ago . . .

The swift beat of hoofs and the creaking of saddle leather approached. Albine and St. Clair rode up, to dismount anxiously by the halted wagon. They looked puzzled. Yates had obviously been much excited.

"Better look after this girl of yours, Sal," he said. "She gave me a bad turn just now. Looked quite ill a piece back."

"You take the mare, then," replied Albine instantly.

"How d'ye feel now, my dear?" he asked, climbing up on the wagon seat and putting his arm about her. The long rifle-gun fell unnoticed between them.

"Better," she said, clutching two stray black locks, one in each hand, and looking up at him. " 'Twas a bad spell, Sal. Sure, I've got something I want to say to you."

"I'll be right here," he said, and gave her a reassuring squeeze.

"All right?" inquired St. Clair. He raised his hat deferentially to her as he spoke.

"It's all right I'd be, if aither of you two gintlemen on the fine harses would provide me a drink."

Yates looked at Salathiel sitting humbly on the wagon seat and laughed. "There's a keg in the wagon," he said. "Garrett's best, I believe. Now we *gentlemen* on horses . . ."

But Arthur St. Clair drew a long silver flask from a saddle pocket, unstoppered it, and offered it gallantly.

She applied her moist lips to the neck of the metal bottle and gulped. She leaned back in proportion as the angle of the flask tilted higher. Her throat rippled.

"That's brandy!" exclaimed St. Clair at last.

"Brandy it was," she replied, wiping her mouth, and finally tendering him the flask, which sloshed emptily.

"Thanks to you, Mr. Arthur St. Clair, maybe I'll be able to kape meself on the airth," she said. "Did ye ever fly off on the wings of a hawk?" The colour came back into her cheeks, and she laughed with relief.

St. Clair looked puzzled. It was Yates who replied.

"Horses, horses, my fine lady, are what we ride on, with four feet on the ground." He touched up the mare until she pranced about the wagon eager to be off. St. Clair strapped his flask back in place, mounted without comment, and the two rode off ahead up the road together.

"Now, I never saw anybody in my life change so instantly," remarked Yates to St. Clair. "You know, I found myself all of a sudden riding along with a stranger. That girl looked like—" He choked back the word "hag", remembering his promise to Melissa just in time.

"Haggard," said St. Clair.

Yates nodded.

"And I know what that really means," insisted St. Clair. "There was an old nurse once took care of us at Thurso, came from the Islands. James Stuart would have had the boots tried on her in his day. Now, take this Irish wife of Albine's—" He grew reminiscent as they jogged on, and the conversation flourished between them. Yates was glad of the change from the wagon to horseback. No one could be more interesting and absorbing when he wanted to be than Arthur St. Clair.

Back on the wagon seat Melissa sat contentedly and quietly finishing the braids in her hair. She sat there without looking at Salathiel or saying anything. There seemed to be nothing the matter with her whatever. He could not help feeling somewhat annoyed. Yates and St. Clair had already disappeared around a bend ahead.

"Well?" he said at last, looking at her inquiringly, and wrapping the reins around his arms.

"It's high time you took the reins into your own hands, Mr. Albine," she replied tartly and unexpectedly. "Maybe there's more in this wagon than you think."

"Everything in the world is in it for me, Melissa," he replied simply and gently.

She relented at that and laid her head against his shoulder.

"One thing is in it that isn't in the world yet. But it soon will be," she added. "It soon will be!"

He gazed at her thoughtfully and gave a low whistle.

"So it's that way with you already, Melissa?"

"It is," she said. "I know!"

To her delight he looked thoroughly pleased.

"A boy?" he demanded inevitably, and without thinking.

"Now, how would I know that, Mr. Albine? How would I be after knowing that yet? But get on wid ye, drive on, and belike I'll be telling you something else you'll meet on the road ahead."

"What more could you have to say?" he replied, and slapped the rawhide reins triumphantly along the backs of all the horses at once.

The wagon rolled down into the woods with sudden speed. There was a straight stretch across the valley here passing north of Sidling

Hill. The teams began to catch up with Yates and St. Clair. The wagon dogged them steadily now, until they remarked the new pace and pushed on more rapidly. Neither the four horses in the traces nor the girl on the seat had any doubt that a man who could have his own way with them was driving. She sat content with the local present now, warmed by a pint of brandy and the reassuring presence of her man. The horses stretched to it. Sixteen hoofs clattered and smacked a constant staccato tattoo. The heavy wheels trembled and rumbled. The little cart danced to see such sport—its wheels spinning.

Afterwhile, above the roar and clatter of the rocky way, Melissa began to try to relate, somewhat breathlessly as they rolled and pitched along, the more salient portions of her "dream". He could see that she had been frightened by it; both troubled and impressed. But he put that down to her condition, always something mysterious to a man.

He listened and made his own silent comment. Doubtless, they might meet with wolves. Wolves were coming back into the deserted country desolated by Indian raids. And he had heard about the Scotch-Irish gathering at Carlisle. But it seemed unlikely they would be making west for the mountains so soon. As for the hawk and the harp, and flying over the hills—and her fall—why, he was quite used to her wild turns of speech and Irish twists of fancy by now. He liked them.

He put his arm around her and laughed encouragingly.

He wrapped her in a warm shawl, because she was still shuddering a little. Presently she stopped talking and lay back against him, breathing deeply and easily.

The forest road slipped past into the west with every turn of the wheels. It gradually began to slope upward, winding away amid the steep rolling foothills of the Tuscarora, towards the dark main ridge of the mountain itself. Somewhere up there, guarding the pass, Fort Lyttleton watched from a broad shoulder of the mountain. The pace became slower, a long, steady, wearing pull. But he kept the horses at it. He whistled and he clucked to them encouragingly.

This was the last barrier. On the other side of that high cloud-tossed ribbon lay the long-settled country that stretched to the sea; the people in the dawnlight, farms, towns, and the city. Ships! For how many years now had he longed to see them, to return to his own!

Somewhere on the steep road ahead sounded the mournful hunting howl of a grey wolf, replied to by his companions—and a whole pack of echoes. Let them hunt, let them go by. Enough of that! He glanced impatiently into the steep wild glens and forested ravines that now began to lie behind and far below him as the wagon slowly but determinedly mounted towards the clouds on the range above.

Think of it, tonight they would be at Lyttleton; tomorrow night over the mountain, and safe at Fort Loudon! And then . . .

He pondered earnestly the face of the woman leaning against him, curled up and asleep on the wagon seat, draped in a many-folded shawl.

She looked as though she really had fallen from the sky, as though something eerie up there had lately had its way with her, and she had not awakened yet to the ways of earth. Undoubtedly, there was something disconcerting and mysterious in her expression. Her mouth trembled and was drawn in when she breathed. The helpless curves of her body concealed in the shawl appealed to him. He pitied her. He felt small. He felt poignantly that she was being used without her knowing it. She stirred faintly. Suddenly he remembered the sensitive white creature he used to find in a river mussel shell. When its lid was torn off it withdrew slowly into itself. Too much light in the wide-open world. He leaned over and kissed her softly on the mouth.

Come what might, he meant to stand by her in the days ahead. He began to wonder about the house he would have to be making for her soon. What would it be like? Where would it be? Unconsciously, he began to drive more carefully.

2

A Warm Welcome

WINKING FIRELIGHT reflected from the mountain wall just beyond, many deep voices singing together, sudden glimpses of clustered lights and huddled buildings—all this roused them at last, after a steep haul up through owl-haunted ravines, to invest eagerly such welcome signs of human settlement with the hopeful anticipation of a comfortable night. Indeed, the forest seemed to fall away before them as the road emerged now onto the grassy flats and level clearings of a broad shoulder thrust out from the main ridge of the Tuscarora itself. Its final crest still towered black and forbidding just above and beyond.

Here, though, were wide open fields with calm constellations overhead. A stockade and a string of wayside cabins loomed up along the road before them. The singing grew louder. Owls and croaking night birds had been left behind in the wooded hills and thickets below. Song and comfortable firelight at least foreboded a companionable evening.

But just then the men's deep voices paused in their chorus. Dogs howled. Showers of sparks rose abruptly from fires behind the black wall of the stockade and drifted out slowly across the stars. The constant clatter of the wagon wheels and iron horseshoes was curtly hushed by an unexpected stretch of mossy turf. They drove on intently and more smoothly, but a certain furtive quiet now resumed. The two horsemen cautiously drew nearer the wagon. The road itself seemed to be conspiring to keep their close approach to the fort a solemn secret.

On the wagon seat, Salathiel fumbled in his waterproof pouch for his cherished silver watch and held its white-enameled dial over the faint glow of his stubby stone pipe. He puffed intently, studying the spidery Roman numerals. Rank forest tobacco and killickinnic had so far had to comfort him for lack of supper during the unbroken journey up the mountain. Frances Melissa had slept comfortably most of the way, leaning against him, wrapped warmly in her shawl. Yet for him the steep stony drive had seemed a long and intricate climb, winding up through the winter darkness, and he was surprised to see that, actually, it was only a quarter past eight by the watch. Its fine Geneva works kept excellent time, but, in any event, it would never have occurred to Albine to suppose that Captain Ecuyer's timepiece could ever be wrong.

No, on the whole, he thought, they had made confoundedly good time on their first day's journey, considering both the road and the season. Not even a horseshoe had been cast. And there was no snow to speak of in the mountains, as yet. Tomorrow they should be over that last cloudy mountain wall ahead. It was only a couple of miles away now! And after that . . .

He slipped the watch back into the pouch thoughtfully. It was keeping *his* time now, and with Frances Melissa beside him. He clasped her hand in the darkness and felt her fingers respond sleepily. Luck ought to hold for a while, he felt. Fair promise of good weather was in the air tonight. It was a clear, starlit mountain evening with moonrise coming on, frosty and deathly still. He gathered the reins firmly and brought the tired teams to a trot, and together—for the last stretch of road to the gate.

The wagon swerved sharply to the left with its escort. It finally pulled up at a walk along a level stretch of meadow under the pointed log walls of Fort Lyttleton. They watched the black edge of the log parapet slide like the teeth of a saw across the glare of firelight from within—and stop.

The fort stood about sixty yards back from the road, set on the level crest of a small rise, and in the midst of a flourishing peach orchard. Its "ramparts", Yates noted casually, while dismounting stiffly from his saddle, were scarcely ramparts at all. Certainly, they were not to be described as "frowning", he thought. In contrast to the more formal military works of Fort Pitt or those at Bedford, there was something homely, even hospitable about the domestic expression on the simple face of Fort Lyttleton.

The fort was essentially nothing more than a large stockade set in heavy fieldstone foundations. It was a "burg", in the ancient and primary meaning of that term, a fortified farm in the forest. The provincial authorities and scared neighbours had erected it frantically eight years before, during the notable troubles following Braddock's defeat. They had hastily enclosed within its stockaded area the sturdy

log farmhouse, barns, and outbuildings of one William Patton. His
ample new home,* with its cold, unfailing spring in the cellar, thus
served as military headquarters when there was a garrison in the fort,
and always as the centre of news and hospitality for all that western
side of the mountain and the road through the Tuscarora gap.

Locally, the place was usually called "Patton's"; or sometimes
"Sugar Cabins", after an insignificant settlement of log huts in a
maple grove situated a short distance eastward on the last flat before
the final, steep zigzag of the road to the summit began. Fort Lyttleton, Patton's, or Sugar Cabins—by whatever name—everybody
agreed the place smelled sweetly of fragrant maple sugar boilings in
the early spring, of rare summer clover, and of the perfume of peach
brandy from William Patton's copper still in the fall.

William, on his part, had consented with alacrity and a certain
canny zeal to assist the authorities in turning his inheritance into a
tower of refuge and an ordinary of entertainment for the not in-
considerable population of a long-settled neighbourhood. Patriotism
and profit were thus for once honestly made one. His defensible farm
was the logical place for the neighbours to "fort-up" in during Indian
raids. In fact, the fencibles of the district always assembled there on
militia days. Provided with a stockade, a few riflemen and light field
guns, as "Fort Lyttleton", Patton's commanded the western ap-
proaches to the Tuscarora; and with Fort Loudon on the eastern side
of the mountain, it controlled the pass between, detaining all and
sundry who travelled the road through the gap either way. Hence,
there was much civil sense and some military strategy in its being
where and what it was. And if, as Bill Patton observed, more peach
brandy were consumed in the face of the enemy than when his back
was peaceably turned, no one, not even Mr. Patton, need be the
loser thereby.

'Twas merely the dividends of time and of family foresight that
he now so generously shared with others, he averred. Was it not his
grandfather, Isaac Patton, who had so sensibly first built the old log
house over the spring in such a fertile, sheltered, and convenient spot
on the old Glades Path?

It was.

And it was William's father, Elder Ensor, or "En", in short,
Patton the elder, who had fetched the first seedlings from Peach
Blossom Creek in Maryland together with a reluctant Quaker bride
from old Easton Meeting near-by. Bride and trees had both been
transported with Calvinistic faith, and bodily, into the high mountains. Both had blossomed and proved fertile. They matured in

---

* The original Patton cabin had been burned in a raid and replaced by a more
ample dwelling.

favour with God and man, while Elder En purveyed hospitable piety in the odour of peach brandy to the Presbyterians in Path Valley and the Big Cove, year after year through the long easy seasons before the French and Indian troubles began. Those hopeful, plentiful old colony days!

Then came wars, battles, regiments marching; the new military road, fortifications—and fortune! Every raid and rumour had brought the local customers of brandy and safety in crowds to Patton's.

And in 1756 William had inherited it all—the goodwill embaumed in the orchard, the stout log dwelling over the spring, the fine copper still, and the natural monopoly of respectable refuge.

Along with all this went a certain austere levity of family disposition and a zeal for innocent innovation. His memorable concoction of maple water, birch bark, spices, and peach brandy with a hot poker was smooth, fiery, and salutary. Quite morose characters, even fiery "independents", had been known to be altered for the better; actually mellowed under its influence. Or so it was said.

Probably such improvements in character were specious rather than specific and permanent. But specious or not, Patton's, Sugar Cabins, or Fort Lyttleton, any way you considered it, was a place that no longer required a green bush hung over the front door to advertise its genial reputation.

Perhaps, it was more in keeping with the convivial fame of Patton's than with its military reputation as Fort Lyttleton that the big gate facing the road was found to be standing invitingly, although carelessly, wide open, when the wagon and its cavalcade finally drew up silently before it, long after nightfall on the evening of November the fifth, 1764.

Puzzled by the total lack of anyone at the gate either to give the alarm or to provide them welcome, it was Arthur St. Clair who had held up his hand and given the final signal to halt. Whether he was more upset by the dangerous failure of the garrison to post even a single sentinel or by the absence of appropriate ceremony to mark the occasion of his arrival, it would be hard to tell. An overweening sense of his own importance was ever the besetting fault of this otherwise amiable and able Scot.

At any rate, St. Clair was sorely disappointed after a hard day's journey by this anticlimax of no welcome whatever, and he now sat his horse, halfway through the neglected gate, where he had brought the wagon to a silent halt, gazing at the wide interior of the stockade with an expression of indignant chagrin.

The view through the gate, however, was ample and unimpeded

—and why no one came forward to receive them was immediately apparent even to St. Clair.

The bright interior of the fort was awash with firelight from several bonfires: only the gate lay in dense shadow. And Guy Fawkes Day was being observed inside the stockade, not only by the Royal Highland garrison, but apparently by everybody else; by the neighbours from near-by Sugar Cabins, and by all the other Scotch-Irish settlers, farmers and hunters, gathered in from miles about.

In short, despite the ugly danger of the frontier, Patton's was obviously celebrating with traditional enjoyment and abandon the ever-memorable escape of King James and his Protestant Parliament from the papist gunpowder conspiracy—and not without a certain native ingenuity and flair for local innovation, at that.

Immediately across a much worn and rutted "parade ground", and before the long whitewashed log cabin of the Patton house, which boasted the unusual feature of a wide and neatly railed and roofed-in porch, stood a dense crowd of wild figures, men and boys, massed about a shallow pit, where some large animal was being roasted whole over a bed of intensely glowing hickory coals. A bank of their intent white faces with deep shadowy eye sockets under shaggy coonskin caps gazed raptly into the fire, as though fascinated by the shifting visions in the incandescent cavern of the pit. But there were other and even more potent attractions.

Set to one side before the porch were four rum kegs and two whisky barrels, one with its head stove in, over which a transparent blue flame hovered and hesitated like a tremulous spirit of the night. These also were the centre of constant attention, and much passing to and fro—especially from a company of about a dozen already lugubriously jovial souls who sat to one side, singing determinedly, about a select bonfire of their own. They had only to rise and kick a few curs out of their way in order to reach the kegs. Yelps, therefore, were fairly frequent.

However, these occasional howls from outraged dogs served to punctuate rather than to interrupt the more continuous lyric efforts of their masters' chorus, which, to be just, did at times achieve melodious crests. Before the choir stood its leader, a gaunt and rail-like personage, in a coat made exclusively of patches. What its original fabric might have been, it was impossible to tell. His voice, a deep bass, seemed to be hiccuping from inside a bucket, and he kept waving a large empty toby in one hand to mark the funereal time of a ballad concerning a maiden's virtue undone. Its lyric statements were either infinite in length or purely circular by nature. The chorus relentlessly repeated,

"So she married a house carpen—ter,
And they say he's a ni—ice young man . . ."

kept coming around again and again, as a maddening anticlimax
wrapped in a wail of husky bathos. Then there would be a pause, and
precisely on the following chord, one that was minor off-key and depressing, a notable assemblage of curs, mostly of the hound variety,
put their noses in the air and howled dismally.

To Mr. Yates, who had dismounted by the wagon, and was now
impatiently holding his nag's nose to keep her from whinnying, there
was something so incongruous and so unnecessarily fatuous about
the peculiarly indigenous scene before him that he could scarcely
restrain a great silent laugh in the back of his mind from being
echoed aloud by his lips.

"So she married a house carpen—ter,
And they say he's a ni—ice young man . . ."

reasserted the chorus, and this time howled like wolves together with
the dogs.

Shouts of self-appreciative laughter and catcalls followed. The
gaunt leader began to make a mock speech, standing before the kegs.

What was there about the New World, Yates wondered, that
made most of its native denizens seem so often thus to be staging a
drama that was a mockery of something else, a caricature of something better only half remembered, a colonial byplay of whose great
original they were somehow bashfully ashamed. He had seen so
much of that kind of self-serving clowning in the colonies, but especially on the frontier. Tonight there was no doubt of the mock
operatic quality of the scene before him. But it was always like that,
at once as natural and as artificial as a play got up by children. Its
parts could be created only by showing off. And, ye gods—the lines!
Quips from bedlam or the pigsty, scabs of humour picked from
sores of thought! Dignity was the victim. Let a man inadvertently
become adult and serious—instanter he must defend himself against
being thought frailly human and begin to turn cartwheels like a
clown. As for the women, they watched silently. Perhaps the trouble,
then, was in the audience? Or perhaps it lay in the overpowering
magnificence of the so-extensive scenery of the theater itself? It was
a stage set for gigantic mimes. Gods in buskins might do well here
with thunderclaps for lines. Men could only mimic them childishly.
He glanced up at the black flange of the Tuscarora from behind
which the moon was soon going to appear.

Now, *there* would be an entrance it would indeed be hard to compete with! And how attain a balance of acting in support of that? Possibly the men in the stockade were taking the only way out. Lunatics! Maybe only the moon could shed a fitting light upon it all! But tonight there was going to be human competition in illumination, at least, to judge by the piles of tar barrels and lightwood that stood about ready to be kindled.

The chorus came round the third time. The dogs howled.

"No, you don't, my fancy lassie," said Yates, squeezing his horse's nose like a sponge to prevent her whinnying. "I'll gie that horse-laugh mysel', when the time comes." He sensed that his companions were in sympathy with this; that they were watching, too. Their astonishment at so unexpected a scene and a certain creepy feeling of approaching crisis in the firelit drama before them had served so far to keep their attention fixed.

For, watched secretly even from a short distance, there *was* something naturally compelling and even sinister about the bright interior of the stockade set in a frame of starry darkness. And this was especially true of the centre of interest, the crowd of dark, fur-capped figures and lean, long-eared hounds clustered around the glowing pit with the liquid firelight washing over them. Above their heads, dimly visible against the moon-etched mountain beyond, towered a vague pyramid of piled combustibles crowned by a shadowy gallows! From that in turn dangled a long helpless figure whose feet alone could be plainly glimpsed, and then only when they swung listlessly and let the yellow firelight play on them from below. It was plain, however, that those feet were shod in a pair of fine, new, beribboned scarlet mules. Nothing could have been more extravagant, more unexpected—and fatuously real.

"Belike 'tis an image of the Howly Father they'd be after burnin', the foul Orange traitors!" exclaimed Frances indignantly. "And the new, red shoes—reft from a good Catholic, I'll wager!" She was now thoroughly awake and aroused.

"Hush, for heaven's sake, ma'am," said St. Clair. "Let's stay oot of it all, and watch!"

Salathiel chuckled, remembering how dearly St. Clair's caution had been bought.

Frances subsided temporarily. For a while all in the wagon party were content to be unobserved and uninvited spectators. All felt the furtive satisfaction of their purely private view. Albine jumped down from the outboard to hold the heads of his team. Frances Melissa stood up on the seat and craned her neck, delighted with the bright novelty of seeing a crowd of people again.

Two men in fringed shirts began to shift the carcass roasting on the fire. It was lifted up sizzling. Someone shouted loudly for "Leftenant Grant".

The door to the farmhouse opened and an ungainly redheaded officer in a Highland bonnet and flaming tartans came out and stood leaning over the railing. A tall impassive Indian wrapped in a dirty blanket followed him and leaned back against the whitewashed wall. Over two streaks of white paint on his cheekbones his eyes glittered. He had the face of an old hawk. Two women in linsey-woolsey, and a ragged little girl, several small boys, and a tall smooth-faced man with iron-grey hair appeared; then a couple of black women, a squaw, and some young Highland officers—the porch rapidly filled up.

"So Patton's enterteenin' the Grants," muttered St. Clair.

"Maybe he can't help himself," said Yates, "there's fully half a company of Highlanders here. They must have marched over from Loudon lately."

St. Clair grunted.

"We'll see," he said.

The big redheaded Scot on the porch held up his hand. The noise about the fires died down.

"Men," said he, "I've high hopes there's none amongst ye but will find the enterteenment provided the nicht—gratifyin'!"

A reassuring shout with a ragged attempt at a grateful cheer followed.

" 'Tis a braw bricht Protestant nicht the nicht," shouted a little man, evidently a Welshman, poking fun at Grant's Scotch accent. There was a good-natured laugh here and there.

"Aye, onyway it's a' that!" continued Lieutenant Grant, unconsciously banging the porch rail for emphasis with a large pewter mug that he held in one hairy fist. "An' I'll no deespute wid ony of ye the nicht aboot the hard feelin' goin' the rounds in these hills o'er some o' the late measures of goovernment. But, howe'er a' that may be, I'm sure in these parts ye will no want ony new people crowding in on ye to make land trouble. I can promise ye the garrison'll see to that. And as for the Injun traders—"

"Aye, wot about 'em?" a tall hunter shouted.

"Why, as for them, it's only the traders licensed by goovernment, only the treaty goods goin' forward to Mr. Croghan, the king's Indian agent at Pittsburgh, that we'll let pass."

"No, No! No more hatchets for the damn yellowbellies. Leave that to us!"

A general growl of assent followed this reply from several in the crowd. Grant made a deprecatory gesture.

"Aweel," he said, "it greets me sair to hear o' them that would sow trouble between his Majesty's loyal subjects and his faithful troops. So we'll let a' that go by the noo. And noo," said he, drawing himself up to his full height, "noo I'll gie ye the toast for the nicht. Wha will no join me in it?"

He leaned over the rail suddenly and filled his mug with whisky from an open barrel. Then he stood up again.

"The king—the Protestant suc-ceesion, no popery!" he bawled.

Everyone, but a few of Mr. Croghan's Irish on their way to Fort Pitt, sitting sullenly apart about their own fire, roared a hearty reply and crowded forward to fill their mugs and leather botels at the barrels. A stream of people with brimming cans soon began to return to the pit fire, where two hunters with flashing tomahawks and knives were cutting up the smoking meat. Men snatched hot pieces of it and tossed it briskly from one hand to the other as they made off.

Yates, who was especially ravenous after the long supperless haul up the mountain, would have ridden forward at this juncture to claim a share in the feast. But he was restrained by St. Clair, who laid a hand on his arm.

"Bide a wee, Edward," he said. "Tarry for the main event. If I know my cousin Wully Grant, yonder, we shall have a fiery spectacle worthy of Vauxhall Gardens, the nicht. 'Tis not for nothing Mr. Grant was known at home as 'Whuzz-Bang Wully'. Goonpowder is his forte, Indja rockets and Chinee crackers his delight. Him and Guy Fawkes, indeed! Aye, now, did I no tell ye! The pyrotechnic illumination begins!"

Yates laughed. His belly hunger was real, but not so overpowering that he could not pause to enjoy a bit of irony and humour at the expense of an eccentric relative of St. Clair's. And the illumination was already proving to be startling.

Somewhere behind the crowd a Catherine wheel began to sputter. A fiery glare from a row of bonfires, which a young coloured boy now ran about kindling with a torch, soon blent into a genial ivory glow, one in which the entire interior of the stockade suddenly stood out against the deep shadows in startling relief. A large tomb-shaped stone magazine and several other whitewashed buildings emerged starkly and rigidly from the darkness, providing instantly a bold background with a formal and monumental design. Behind the crowd at the roasting pit, someone lit a tow cresset, and a sparkling and sputtering of powder fuses began.

"Hold your nags, Albine," cautioned St. Clair, anxiously. "Wully Grant is up to his old tricks wie goonpowder. We'll hae some braw fireworks—"

"And trouble," added Yates. "Look at Croghan's Irish over there by the forge shed. They've a keg of their own stuff, private. But they look sullen. Some Quakers amongst them. I think I see broad hats."

"Aye, they'll drink, but they'll no sing nor fight," replied St. Clair.
"This is a Scotch-Irish cove in the hills, and the Presbyterians do
swarm. Losh! What did I tell ye?"

A large rocket took off with a swish, soared over the parapet,
missing it narrowly, and dropped into a field beyond, where it exploded. A sudden apprehensive silence gripped everybody.

Two Catherine wheels burst into a frantic whirl of glory. Another rocket followed.

Someone lit the pyre underneath the gallows. A sheet of flame
leaped up, revealing the lank figure dangling from the crosstree.
Draped in an old bedgown arranged in churchly folds, even though
its paper triple crown was more like a fool's cap than the bishop of
Rome's mitre, its meaning was plain enough.

An appreciative roar and din went up from all the Protestants in
the crowd. The flames crackled and licked the red-shod feet of the
"Pope".

From the porch a child's voice was heard crying out frantically,
"My red shoes, they're burnin' up! My red shoes! Stop! Stop them,
Aunt Tibby. You promised! Oh, oh, my red shoes, my dear red
shoes . . ." The door opened and the child was hustled off the porch.
Inside the cabin, she could still be heard shrieking hysterically in pro-
test. The house dog began to howl.

From her point of vantage on the wagon seat, Frances spluttered
indignantly.

"Stolen! I said so—and from a little girl at thot! Sure, it's a
sorry Orangeman's jape at the true faith your cousin Wully Grant
would be after makin' in the wild woods here, Mr. St. Clair. Bad cess
to him, I say. And will ye do nothing about it? Must the whole world
take fire to warm your Scotch heart! But for that matter, 'tis the
wonder of the world the fightin' Irish by the fire yonder stand so
peaceably by. And with an image of the Howly Father himself,
danglin' in the flames from a gallows before their very eyes. *Ochone!*
'Tis a disgrace to the awld sod they are. Belike, if I trip over and give
them a bright burning piece of my mind now!—" She climbed down
from the wagon seat impulsively, her eyes shining and her face aglow
under her bonnet.

Salathiel put a restraining arm about her as she passed him,
where he was holding the heads of the lead team.

"Now, now, sweetheart," he said, "Mr. Croghan wants his Irish
to keep the peace and watch the trade here. He'd sack them if they
lifted a hand. It's peltries and not the Pope he most cares about."

"Ah, the black fuzzy heart of him! Croghan and his everlasting
furs!" exclaimed Melissa. But with Salathiel's arm about her, she

grew calmer and eventually stood quiet, while he held her with one arm and the horses with the other.

"Besides," chimed in St. Clair, anxious to compose matters, "all this foolin' over Guy Fawkes Day is only a joke now in the New World. Wha really cares? No, they forget. Maybe it's *not* the Pope dangling over the flames yonder. Maybe it's Guy Fawkes instead they mean to have sport with. Guy Fawkes! Dinna ye ken him? The mon that told King Jamie to his verra face the goonpowder was to blow all the Scots in England back to Scotland."

Melissa laughed. She was not taken in by St. Clair's well-meant fibbing.

"But there's not enough powder in the world to keep the Scots in Scotland, is there, Mr. St. Clair? You and Mr. Yates are both livin' ividence of thot!"

They all grinned into the darkness at her retort. Yates began to say something feelingly about supper, and to lead his horse through the gate. The rest prepared to follow him, when circumstances and gunpowder combined in a flash to stop them all in their tracks.

For it was just at that instant that something went horribly wrong with the elaborate pyrotechnic arrangements of Whuzz-Bang Wully Grant.

The only warning was a young coloured boy in a thin white shirt, who dodged through the legs of the crowd like a scared rabbit and streaked away into the night. Whether it was prophetic insight or a bad conscience that so moved him, no one ever knew.

Before the faces of the crowd, and between them and the porch, there was a blinding arc-like flash, and a clap of thunder.

A cloud of pungent white powder smoke, dense as morning fog, rose on a wispy stalk from a burning powder chest and collapsed like a rotten mushroom over the heads of the crowd. In the midst of this half-luminous mist, the spectral forms of men and hounds could be seen madly careening, milling about, shouting and howling as though in a bad dream. The chest glowed with renewed energy and began to vomit fire like a small volcano.

Rockets, whizzing Catherine wheels, squeegees, signal grenades, and partigoes banged, streaked, and sizzled through the scattering crowd. Something like a bomb hurtled into the heart of the fire under the gallows and blew the pyre and the figure over it to smithereens.

A rain of flaming wood embers and fizzling powder sparks showered the now madly deploying company with a fine catholic disregard for their Protestant sentiments. Coonskin caps blazed, racing across the night like meteors. The beards of patriarchs threatened to become burning bushes. Fiery-edged holes widened like wildfire through the folds of old blankets and greasy shirts. A tall Highland sergeant was briefly glimpsed racing for the well, emitting a column of smoke from under his kilts.

The crowd dissolved madly in all directions.

Left alone in the middle of the parade ground in a self-illuminated panic, a large shaggy dog, mysteriously on fire behind, chased his own tail with hideous clamour.

The air cleared slowly . . .

But against the clear yellow glow of the remaining bonfires, dark figures could still be seen rushing wildly about, beating their caps out on their knees, the sparks out of their clothes, and each other on the back with oaths, roars, stampings, and bursts of cursing.

All this finally swelled up into a single hilarious chorus of sheer relief and grim human triumph, when a tidal wave of dogs, evidently mistaking their hysterical tail-chasing comrade in the centre of the scene for the cause of all this calamity, fell upon him en masse, furiously, and then upon one another. Dogs took over the spectacle.

A mound of worrying curs, a hell of squirming fur from which proceeded a continuous growling roar and fugue of despairing howls, was now the only worthy focus of attraction. Everyone's attention, even those smarting with burns, was inevitably fixed upon it. The outcome was predictable. It was a conflict to the death. Men watched. Their voices died away. The snarling worrying sound from the mass of squirming animals completely prevailed.

Leaning against the whitewashed wall of the cabin, the old Indian on the porch had undergone a bombardment of firebrands, flying embers and sparks, alone and with unchanged attitude. During the worst moments he had raised his blanket before his face, but his expression behind it probably remained the same. The flying sparks that fell on his blanket were quenched by its ammoniac reek. He had not deigned to brush them off, and he still stood there like a carved figure, impassive as ever, an unmoved spectator..

It seemed quite likely to Edward Yates that it was this old redskin who must make the final comment on the elaborate trouble and tumultuous catastrophe so artfully arranged by the white man, he who had unleashed chaos with his clever key to the cupboard of lightning. And Mr. Yates was not disappointed.

As the dog fight began to disintegrate into its component parts, its cause forgotten in its own agony, a modicum of decent silence resumed. Both the victors and the vanquished removed themselves painfully into the shadows to whimper in self-pity and lick their wounds. Finally, only the dead remained.

A pause in both sound and events ensued.

It was during this apparently normal interval, when ordinary natural desires might again be satisfied, that the hawk-faced old red-

skin on the porch wrapped the folds of his blanket about him with all
the dignity of a Tully, stepped indifferently over some still-smoulder-
ing débris on the porch steps, and plunged his head and shoulders into
an open whisky barrel. There he remained for some time, resting his
hands on the rim, like a thirsty traveller drinking from a deep spring
in the summer.

At this point Frances returned to the wagon, giggling.

St. Clair struck his hands together in ironic sorrow. "Ah, Wully,
Wully," he said, "how sair thy subtle plans hae gone agley!"

Yates gave a low whistle to his friend Albine, and together they
led the still-sweating and nervous horses into the stockade.

Even then no one seemed to see them. Except for the old Indian
with his head still in the barrel the place appeared suddenly deserted
and devastated.

"Aweel," St. Clair said deprecatingly, "ye canna say we've no
had a warm welcome, Edward."

"I *Will Grant* you that, Arthur," replied Yates, grinning. "Your
cousin is a blithe original."

"Losh, mon, losh!" exclaimed St. Clair, instantly on the family
defensive. "Is there naught human or divine you will no quip and
make a poon aboot? The Grants are a perseestent race, bound to
leave their mark wherever they go."

"Undoubtedly!" said Yates, pointing to the scorched circle in
the grass, where the chest of fireworks had exploded.

The two ascended the steps to the Patton house together, still
arguing. Salathiel was left holding the horses. The door to the
house, he noticed, still remained discreetly closed.

Presently a barefooted little girl with tear-streaked face peeped
out and let the gentlemen in. The door closed again.

Albine stamped impatiently. It was decidedly cold and he was
very hungry. The day should come when he would not be left just
to hold the horses. What in the world was going on in the house
there? he wondered. Some people would rather talk than eat.

Inside the wagon Frances lit a candle and tied on her best bonnet
carefully. She sat waiting for Salathiel to come for her. She was
going to be respectable, and respected. He would have to remember
they were a family now. Manners—manners were what counted
most in the world, and they were in the world now, leaving the
forest behind them. She sat peering into Ecuyer's little field mirror
as though into a crystal, with a comb held in her hand.

Finally she peeped out. Salathiel was tying the two riderless
horses to the porch rail. The moon had risen and was peering with a
wry half-face over the mountain edge, pouring a grey light into the
stockade. Curious people were closing in now on the wagon from

all sides. There were surprised whistles, and excited voices calling. She gave a final touch to her hair. She tied the strings under her homemade bonnet even more primly, and sat waiting.

Outside, drawn up before the porch stoop, the long wagon faintly glimmering with candle shine stood ghostly and alone in the moonlight. It seemed suddenly to have materialized out of nowhere, along with the big man with the rifle who stood watching over it at the head of the double team.

The breath of the horses ascended regularly now. They were too tired to be impatient. The man with the rifle began to stride up and down.

My God, would they never get done talking in there!

He stopped suddenly.

The house door began to open, throwing a widening fan of cheerful light across the floor of the empty porch.

3

Levee by Firelight

WILLIAM PATTON, a plump smooth-faced man with iron-grey hair, followed by Edward Yates and a couple of Highlanders, came out on the porch. For an instant before the door closed behind them again, Salathiel caught a glimpse of a crowded tavern room with leaping flames running up the chimney, the glow of candles, and a flash of brass buckles and gold buttons winking through tobacco smoke, where shawled women moved about serving. The door banged, and Mr. Patton came forward hurriedly to greet his unexpected guests.

Yates nodded reassuringly to Salathiel, pointing out the two Highland soldiers who now came down the steps, one to watch and the other to lead the tired teams off to the stables. As soon as the horses were gone, Albine walked quickly to the rear of the wagon, where he was introduced to Patton, and was thus on hand to do the honours quite satisfactorily for Frances Melissa herself when she finally came tripping down the ladder out of her boudoir-on-wheels with a certain mincing air. She made a deep Dublin curtsy to Mr. Patton, one that summoned forth his best bow in reply, and also produced an instant change in his attitude towards Salathiel, upon whose tall, gun-nursing, half-Indianlike presence he had been apt at first glance to cast a respectful, yet a decidedly quizzical eye.

The appearance of "Mistress Albine", for as such she had been presented by Yates, had, indeed, hastily forced Mr. Patton to revise his social estimate of his guests upward. Anyway, he thought, he never had been able to be sure about people coming downcountry. They might be anybody to whom anything had happened on the wild frontiers. Inevitably, they would bring back *some* bizarre impression of the savage wilderness upon them. He had even seen

33

white men returning tricked out in feathers, earrings, and copper paint; staid commissioners at that! But Mistress Albine's bonnet, her neat shawl-draped bodice, and her black gloves, picked up by a stroke of feminine luck at Pendergasses', were not alone respectable but somehow fashionably genteel. At least she contrived to wear them that way. For Frances Melissa O'Toole had not only the charming Irish gift of being a natural actress but also the full sense of an occasion. She instinctively thought herself into her parts, and her native interpretation made them real.

Salathiel, Yates noted with satisfaction, was already learning to support her in her dramatic rendering of various little episodes of life, as a sensible partner should. He had handed her down from the wagon with a pride and tall proprietary affection that were impressive in a man of his size and obviously troublesome potentialities. Six feet four inches in flawless buckskin, with a double-barrelled rifle-gun—and an ancient tomahawk peeping with a curved smile from its smooth sheath at his belt—all that, and the implacable, impassive countenance of a Roman standard-bearer minus one ear, tended to provide Melissa with what might be termed a positively sombre impact of protection, yet one which overshadowed her gratefully like the loom of a giant sycamore falling across the white petals of a flowering dogwood tree.

Despite his initial confusion about the Albines, few implications in either the appearance or the manners of his guests were lost on William Patton, whose rôle of a professional host had necessarily long taught him to look upon all newcomers with both a wary and an appraising eye. And he was far from being impervious to an arch smile and limpid grey eyes under a deep bonnet. Not many such came his way. Ladies travelling to or from the frontiers were novel and rare attractions, not only to him, but to everyone else. Indeed, by this time the scattered crowd was again beginning to gather full of eager curiosity about the distinguished newcomers, the fancy lady, and the big illuminated "ark".

So far as Lieutenant Wully Grant of the 42nd Highlanders was concerned, it was probably an exceedingly fortunate thing for him that the wagon had driven into the stockade at Patton's precisely when it did. The arrival of so sumptuous a vehicle, for such Ecuyer's "flying camp on wheels" appeared to be to the backwoods inhabitants, the emergence from it down a rear ladder of a neatly dressed and comely young woman in a fashionable bonnet and black knitted gloves served instantly to fix the whole curiosity of the crowd on the novelty and to pose a topic of conversation and speculation of more immediate and paramount interest than even the devastating

failure of Mr. Grant's late fiery spectacle could provide. The fireworks were over; the wagon was standing before the porch, *now*.
It seemed to have materialized mysteriously out of the moonlight.
To learn that it came from the west, from Bedford, only lent a
touch of the incredible to the mysterious. Most miracles on wheels,
or otherwise, in that remote part of the country came from "the
City".

It was only a few minutes, therefore, until the crowd, which had
been so thoroughly scattered, was again packed more densely than
before and in larger numbers before the porch at Patton's. Even the
suspicious and timid who had betaken themselves to a more than·
safe distance during the fireworks now returned. Women and small
children from the quarters now pressed in freely amongst the men.
There were whites, blacks, and reds, since Patton's boasted quite an
establishment, including indentured servants, a few Negro slaves,
and several families of dependent and permanently stranded Cherokee Indians.

Both St. Clair and Yates were familiar to a large number in the
crowd, from former visits. St. Clair, in particular, had passed
through Fort Lyttleton when he had been in the army and later,
during several trips to and from Philadelphia, while perfecting his
cherished venture of bringing new settlers to his lands about Forts
Bedford and Ligonier. He had already thoroughly identified himself with the interests of the western settlements, and both he and
his business were highly popular. Few either remembered or cared
about his late dabblings in Indian trade.

Yates was favourably known as a legal and personal agent of
the Penn family, and not a few recalled that he had been at Patton's
only the summer before on business connected with the running of
the new southern boundary line that was to settle at last the long
conflict over land claims between adherents of the Penns and of the
Lords Baltimore. The young attorney's affability, his undoubtedly
good-natured adroitness at law and at cards, were vividly recollected
by several who, although they had paid smartly for their professional
experience in both fields, still admired him. These old acquaintances
now came forward eagerly, others crowded at their heels, and all
desired to meet and to talk to the Albines.

Now, it was Mr. Patton's intention to take full advantage of this
new and helpful twist in events to forestall, if possible, any complaints by disappointed and aggrieved participants in the recent
disastrous celebration of what some people might now be inclined
to regard as "Wully Grant's powder plot". Considerable finesse
would undoubtedly be necessary to avoid resentful questions or angry
recriminations by badly singed or startled neighbours. In the new-

comers Mr. Patton now thought he beheld his opportunity, and in his suddenly elaborated plan to shift all attention to the strangers, he felt the consuming curiosity about the wagon to be a godsend, and the restraining influence of the presence of a lady, salutary.

So it was that with much more than ordinary ceremony and formality Mr. Patton finally placed Melissa's arm ostentatiously over his own and led her up the steps onto the broad whitewashed verandah. There, instead of escorting her immediately into the house, he turned to face the crowd, and began to hold forthwith what might be termed a kind of firelight levee on the verandah, with Melissa as the principal attraction, Salathiel the guest of honour, and Yates acting nimbly as the master of ceremonies.

Thus commenced a deal of scraping and bowing with "your humble servant, madam" and "honoured to meet you, sir"—which required a quick summing-up of the remembrance of things past in regard to nice manners on the part of many a good man in homespun or fringed deerskins, farmer or trapper as the case might be. St. Clair was quick to take an active part in what now seemed, even to him, to have been a well-planned reception for the distinguished visitors *he* had brought.

In short, the affair soon became an integral part of the evening's festivities, a social and a genteel success, in which the late rude fiasco of the fireworks was a triviality that good manners and refined local pride must be bound to overlook; only the rude and ignorant could still harbour resentment. Perhaps the final touch was the inclusion in the reception line of several of the embarrassed but delighted married women of the settlement. Thus the explosion in which both the "Pope" and his red shoes had so violently disappeared was gently passed over and conveniently overlooked.

Lieutenant Grant, on the other hand, was *not* summoned forth, and from a sense either of frustration or of canny Scotch caution, he had the rare good sense to remain indoors. His rebuffs and ill luck ever since he had been commandant at Fort Loudon had been notable, even savage. He did not know they were to become historic. This, he muttered, was merely a minor instance of the damned barbarous manners of the bloody back-inhabitants. With the door carefully closed, he sat inside and alone at a small side table, apparently playing a close game of dice with himself. He rolled and swept up the cubes again, peering at them in his big, hairy red fist as though he were practising and hoping for greater skill in future bouts with Fortune. He looked glum, but he said nothing, not even when Yates bounced in to lead Mrs. Patton out on his arm in order to join the festivities on the porch.

"Lawks!" said she, throwing an India shawl about her. "What's agoin' on out there?"

"A sudden reception, ma'am, a levee, a veritable rout," replied Yates, gaily, "and Mr. Patton wants you with him *immedgit!*"

"Well, I never!" she exclaimed, catching sight of her husband with Frances already making her twentieth curtsy beside him. "Now, how long has *this* been agoin' on?"

Yet from the very first there developed an active sympathy between Frances Melissa and Matilda Patton. Mrs. Patton saw intuitively that night that Melissa was acting for the men, but in need of feminine comfort and understanding. From certain strained shadows about Melissa's eyes she even suspected her condition, and it was not long before she had made her excuses to the women neighbours and ushered Melissa off the porch and back into the warm room—not, however, without a few tart asides to her spouse about "using up a poor tired young wife—and where in Goshen was the hospitality of the house and his common sense gone to?" "I do avow I'm consternated! What the deil's got into you, man?" With such remarks, some of which were evidently barbed for Mr. Albine, she swept Melissa off the porch in an indignant but competent motherly way, leaving Mr. Patton, St. Clair, Yates, and Salathiel to hold the fort there with what cheer they might maintain, for men alone.

But that was not now so very difficult. Much manly talk, hearty eating, and drinking were under way. Everyone helped himself. The only exceptions were the host and his newly arrived guests, who were once more compelled to defer their long-anticipated supper. Others were luckier. Few in that mountain locality needed to be urged twice to help themselves at the open liquor barrels or to sample hunks of the roasted elk, which was now being rapidly cut up and generally distributed. Tall fellows in buckskins with strong breaths, a dripping bone politely clenched in the left hand, still crowded onto the porch to shake hands with the strangers. St. Clair, who already cherished local political ambitions, was more than affable. Yates had a deft word or a personal quip for everybody. His forte was remembering names and places. He kept bringing more people Salathiel's way, although a crowd was already standing about him and Mr. Patton.

It was some time before Albine fully realized that he was the centre of much genuine interest and cordial curiosity. But when he did it was a helpful surprise. He had managed at least to snatch one mighty pull at one of Mr. Patton's barrels, that which the old Indian had lately been unable to empty, and it had warmed him through and through. Hunger, fatigue, and his usual phlegm and passiveness vanished. In many of those who now came to shake hands, he recognized brother Masons. Some of them, James Collier, William Duffield, Captain Alexander Culbertson, and the McDaniels he had met in the lodge at Bedford a year before. Sid and Cal McClanahan had come over from Conococheague, and now wrung his hand and said "how". It went well. It was pleasant beyond expectation thus to find himself launched into the world, travelling in a far country, yet still among friends.

It was going to be all right with him, he concluded. He had really broken with the wilderness. Here he was successfully crossing the bridge. He was coming over amongst his own people, and they had received him. They were even proud of him. His fame, it seemed, had spread clear over the mountains.

Men wanted to meet "the lieutenant of Captain Jack". They spoke of the affair at the Salt Kettles, of the big fight at Pendergasses'. They asked him questions about his double-barrelled riflegun. They even knew its name was "Twin Eyes". He was particularly pleased at that. They were roughly congratulatory and humorous about Melissa. They looked at him towering there beside Patton, they tested his grip. They liked him!

Suddenly, he found himself talking with great ease, responding to so many so naturally that his Indian reserve and taciturnity vanished. He no longer felt inclined to be laconic or briefly ironical. He was not even ashamed of his size. For the moment, he felt its advantage. His handclasp became warm, even formidable. Several felt the pain in their knuckles and numb fingers for days afterward. They remembered they had met him.

Perhaps Yates was the only one who did, or who could, understand how important this evening at Patton's was to his friend. Probably that was why he kept stirring it up quietly and making it go. It was, Yates knew, for Albine the step over the threshold of the mountains into the world beyond. For his own reasons, too, it was important to make it go. It was better to present the lion in Salathiel than the bear. Bears were sulky and people were inclined to bait them. On the contrary, lions . . . so Yates thought.

At any rate Salathiel never forgot that evening at Patton's, neither the scene on the porch nor later on in the room inside. Long afterward he could recall with singular vividness Melissa standing there beside Mr. and Mrs. Patton, curtsying in the light of the bonfire and the winter moon. He remembered forever the long whitewashed front of the house with red firelight winking from the lower windows and a low still candle or two upstairs; the wagon and the trundler in the moonlight, surrounded by a crowd of curious men and boys, with the kilted sentry leaning silent against the big rear wheel, smoking a pipe. But above all there remained the warm sensation of welcome, of having been received as somebody in this world; himself standing on the porch, towering above the others—himself suddenly warm-hearted, "married", and Frances safe in the warm house behind. Here he was welcomed, believed in, blood kin!

Perhaps it was foolish; to him it was much. Now he was going down into the plains to be one with the People of the Dawnlight. It seemed as though his initiation at Bedford was confirmed that evening at Fort Lyttleton, informally, to be sure, and roughly and heartily. But for that very reason made real.

Patton's—Lyttleton—how much happened there! How many apparently trivial things occurred that evening, acorns of the future that grew slowly into oaks that overshadowed his whole life— Yates's, too.

Years later he was almost superstitious about that evening, when he chanced to recall it. How casually things had got under way. Just a small shift in the current, a tiny twist of the paddle of Fate in the rapids of Time. Then it had seemed nothing. He had simply stood on the porch and shaken hands; felt happy and been confident. Why, he had felt he was coming home! And in the big room afterward . . .

Ah, if he had only known how much was on the cards in there!

4

An Empty Hand Is Extended

MORE THAN SATISFIED, indeed genuinely relieved by the general trend of events since the arrival of the strangers, Mr. Patton now saw fit to put an end to the gathering on the porch, and to invite those of his friends who still lingered there in close conversation to further entertainment within.

His little ruse of delay and distraction had worked well enough. The crowd as a whole was now engaged in hearty enjoyment of both the liquid and the solid refreshment so amply provided. To these Mr. Patton now reinvited his guests' undivided attention. He broached another keg of hard cider, as a further pledge and reminder of his hospitality, and left amid the cordial clamour of those who had lined up to drink his health.

Raucous-voiced demands for explanation from Wully Grant had long since died away. Indeed, seeing their betters and most of the substantial characters of the settlement gathered on the porch to greet the strangers—this sight had daunted even the more morose and determined troublemakers from voicing their irritations aloud. Those who still felt inclined to make trouble for dear distraction's sake itself looked at the tall man with a tomahawk in his belt, now standing alone on the porch, and refrained. They turned more easily to the immediate satisfactions so close at hand.

The scattered bonfires were built up again. Here and there convivial singing in a minor key was resumed. Croghan's Irish, it was to be observed, had retired during the late bombardment and were now assembled with their own whisky keg and some smoky lanthorns in the exclusive shelter of a wagon shed at the far end of the yard.

"Hell's janglin' bells!" exclaimed Cooney Patterson, one of Captain Smith's men from Conococheague, and a "Black Boy" by

natural inclination, " 'tis the same old story these days! Let a damn
fool king's officer bring fire and trouble amongst peaceable settlers,
and all the gintry and the well-to-do will take him in and cherish
him and cover him up. But the day will come . . ." Mr. Patterson
rubbed some bear's grease into a scorched patch on his arm to finish
off his prophecy with proper emphasis.

"Tush, mon, 'twas always the same both here and at home,"
replied his Scotch friend soothingly. "Mon, what should ye naturally
expect? Birds of a feather . . ."

"Someday it will be different here," averred Mr. Patterson. "I'd
change it now, if I had my say," he muttered. "Had ye had your
own cabin burned by the magistrates, for bein' out of proclamation
bounds, MacGregor, ye'd talk more like a native son than ye do."

"At Sugar Cabins Squire MacDowell says we're well east of the
new proclamation line."

"At Burnt Cabins, long ago, we'uns got fiery news of how the
Penns and the Quaker government of this province cherish the
salvages. And now with the new peace there's this new line. Line!
Line! What line, and who drawed it?" growled Patterson. "The
God-damned royal proclamations! How the marchants and gintry in
Philadelphy all love the yellowbellies and in Lunnon too." He spat
contemptuously. "An' if I were you, Mac, I'd keep a close watch on
Croghan's Irish. They're like to slip away with their Injun goods to
Pittsburgh most any night. Maybe thot's what the hul show has been
got up fer this evening," he said, his eyes narrowing. "Do you see
what I'm drivin' at?"

"Aweel, aweel," sighed MacGregor, "ye may be right, my guid
whiggamore friend, but I'd be verra carefu' who I jealoos or make
surly talk aboot. Yon shaver, for eenstance, is no the mon I'd pick
to prefer me ain complaints to." He pointed with his thumb at
Salathiel, whistling plaintively. Mr. Patterson's reply was diplomati-
cally muffled by a succulent piece of elk.

Albine had not gone into the house with the others. He was
uneasy about the wagon. Everything he and Melissa had was in it.
And there was still a considerable crowd of the curious, youngsters
and others, gathered about. People peered inside and kept trying to
peep and pry under the canvas. It would be just as well to have a
word with the Highland sentry, who had shifted post and now sat
like a wooden man with his arms folded, looking cold and glum on
the lower step of the rear ladder. There was something familiar about
him, Salathiel thought. Probably he was a veteran, but it would do
no harm to rouse him tonight to a closer watch.

So thinking, he descended the steps in a few sudden strides, and lighting one of the old whale-oil lanthorns that had come from Fort Pitt in the side chest, he flashed it in the face of the half-stupefied sentry and motioned for him to accompany him inside. The man followed awkwardly but willingly enough.

In the wagon it was very quiet and exceedingly snug under the canvas. There were two comfortable bunks laid out with thick feather mattresses and grey trade blankets over the great-chests on either side of the middle aisle. The chests were lashed down through ring bolts set in the tongued-and-grooved wagon-bed. That sturdy floor was solid as the deck of a ship and covered with a buffalo robe. At the forward end Ecuyer's old camp desk, still provided with his small framed mirror, had been taken over by Frances Melissa for her brushes, combs, and sewing articles. These, with a small brass night-lamp, whose clear little flame reflected steadily in the mirror, lent the interior an unexpectedly luxurious and domestic touch. Captain Ecuyer's swing chair was still suspended from the centre pole, just as the old sailor at Fort Pitt had rigged it for him. The row of side lockers, let-in drawers, and chests were now painted blue, and seemed to pout with small iron padlocks down either side of the vehicle.

Salathiel had kept the ingenious and elaborate ironwork of his cherished "ark" well furbished. Even the broad heads of the wrought-iron studs and bolts were now sanded bright. With much ingenuity he had lightened up the interior, after he and Melissa had once taken over the wagon at Bedford, by painting the canvas roof a clear white inside. Also he had made side sockets for two big artillery lanthorns acquired at Bedford from a venal quartermaster. There was a leather sling on the ridge-pole for his rifle-gun, and a couple of "Brown Bess" muskets stood in a stand under the driver's seat, one on either side of the desk. Powder horns, axes, knives, and even a few large iron forks and spoons were strapped against the upper panels of the sideboards or held firmly in nicely finished leather sheaths. Everything was strapped, lashed, or bolted down to hold it firm and to keep it from banging and clattering, so that the wagon would go silently over the "highest waves" on the worst of mountain roads without shifting a single item of its cargo.

It was this effect of everything handy, and of everything in its place, of neatly knotted cords, new leather straps and bright iron stanchions; of fresh paint, clean boards, and white canvas, all arranged with a canny economy of space that accidentally, but inevitably, suggested the interior of a yacht's cabin to anyone who had ever seen one. And to the curious settlers of the frontier "the ark", as they called it, presented an unheard-of convenience of living, a degree of comfort that seemed to them to be either magically elegant or sumptuously sinful, or both. In any case, they, and everybody else, upon first looking into the wagon were astonished, and with right good reason, for it was not at all like whatever anyone might have been expecting to see.

Salathiel was proud as the devil of his wagon. In his own mind it peculiarly marked his status as a white man. It was his rolling estate on wheels that he had inherited from Ecuyer. It, and the sturdy trundler behind, contained all his worldly goods and chattels, everything he had accumulated since he had ceased to live like an Indian, except Enna, the captain's mare, which Yates was riding to Carlisle for him. Thus the wagon was a substantial and tangible measure of his personal progress. Possessions, he had soon found, were one of the things by which his civilized friends measured him. And the farther east he went, the more important property became.

If only he owned the four wagon horses, too! Enna was too light for anything but the saddle. He needed the two draught teams. But they were not his—not yet. They had been lent him by Stottelmyer as a great favour, and he was simply taking them over the mountains to be turned over to that lusty wagoner at Carlisle. Perhaps he might be able to strike a bargain with Stottelmyer himself when he came back from Fort Pitt. He must manage it somehow, for he had grown very fond of the big capable greys. But what would bargaining with the "Dutch" at Carlisle be like? he wondered. He had a few furs on hand, but only a handful of coins. Ah well, he would wait, he would see . . .

Meanwhile, the wagon with Frances Melissa in it was house and home. She had added what was now the most unexpected thing about it, for it was a huge and heavy contrivance, a touch of the daintily feminine. Her clothes and personal things exhaled a vague odour of orange water and lavender, parting gifts from Mrs. Pendergass herself. Poor Captain Ecuyer's verbena was no more. Lavender now vaguely pervaded the whole wagon. It was very much as though a grim and mustachioed artillery sergeant had been found at inspection wearing a fragrant lilac instead of a pompon on his hat . . .

"Verra deeferent from the days o' the guid captain," said the Highland sentry, grinning, while sniffing the air tentatively, and gingerly sitting down on the edge of a padded chest to look about him.

Salathiel peered at the man more closely, as he notched up the small lanthorn before Melissa's mirror.

"Dinna ye recollect me, Mr. Albine? I've watched this same chariot for ye before. An' through the wee sma' hours, too. At Ligonier it was, the nicht o' the fire, before they hanged the puir ree Irishman."

"Oh, so it was you, then," said Salathiel. "I thought I knew ye,

Mac. You're one of the several Alexanders in Ensign Erskine's company, aren't ye?"

The man settled himself on the chest more easily now for having been recognized.

"Sax we were, but sax we be no longer," he said dolefully. "Kenneth and Donald niver marched back from the Muskingum. Nor the wee wanthriven drummer wi' his sharny trews and duddy polony and no hair on his pow. Do ye mind him? Puir laddie, he couldna surveve bein' scalpéd twice."

"Bad, heap bad!" said Salathiel, assuming the Indian. He remembered the little drummer with the head like a ghost mask, vividly. "But I do rejice that ye're still here to be recognized, my friend."

"Noo, Mr. Albine, I take a walth o' satisfaction in thot masel'. I'm glad I'm still here to take a wee nip wi' ye to the memory of puir Kenneth and Donald, and the wee tonsured laddie—and to watch your bonny auld hurley-hacket."

A flask passed silently between them, and the red spots came out over the high cheekbones of the Highlander as the good Cumberland rye took fiery hold.

They sat talking for some time about Bouquet's march into the Ohio country and old times. Half an hour passed—and so did the flask . . .

"An' so ye're a married mon, and a' thot," continued the Scot, as Salathiel seemed inclined to linger and poured out a further ration into a mug. "Tell me noo, how *did* ye iver find yoursel' a bonny hempy lass like yon pratty one in this green desert? Ye maun well be a mighty hunter before the Lord to do thot."

"I found her lurking from Injuns in a coal mine," said Salathiel.

"Noo, did ye!" replied the Scot, genuinely intrigued. "Then you maun be a luckier mon than I am, for I've worked i' the coalheughs at Newcastle as pit boy, and I didna fare nearly so weel. All I got was a skelpy-limmer and a ripple-dose gudlin i' the dark."

"Bad, heap bad," grinned Salathiel. "Happen I'm more prickme-dainty than you be, Alex. Or more chancy." He put the flask back in his shirt-flap this time, indicating the evening's amenities were over.

"Aye," sighed Alexander, reminiscently, "but thot was no humdudgeon, I'm tellin' ye."

"Well, at least keep your eyes open this time, won't you? I mean keep a close watch on the wagon," admonished Salathiel as he descended the brief ladder in the rear.

"Thot I will," answered the Scot, and then stuck his head out to shout, "You'll find the wagon safer wi' me than your lassy is wi' all the rantin' officers in there, to say nothin' o' Whuzz-Bang Wully."

With this negative Scotch assurance ringing in his ears, Albine made for the porch—and it was then that in the moonlight a curious, and to him an unnecessarily memorable, thing happened.

As he started to mount the steps he found himself weirdly confronted, about chin-high, with a grey-coloured hand held out like a cup at the end of a long thin arm. Both the hand and the arm were withered as if they had once been in the fire, and the fingers seemed at once to warn him away and yet to threaten and to beseech him to put something valuable immediately into the hollow of the shadowy palm. All this he saw and felt as *one* thing, instantly, before he saw the man behind the arm.

Seated in the black shadow of the porch pillar, with a foot thrust out into the moonlight on either side, was a dim bundle. Salathiel became aware of a head on it with bright eyes and flesh the same colour as the moon shadow, of a vague mouth from which came a whispered whine.

As he mounted the steps, the hand continued to mount with him, until, as he stood on the porch level, it was finally thrust up at him out of the darkness about waist-high, propped from its elbow set on an invisible knee.

The voice continued in a strange accent to ask him for help. The fingers wriggled persuasively, desperately, with sharp nails clutching inward, asking, demanding like the voice.

The words were a travesty of English. But more shocking to Albine than either the strange accent or the depressing tone was the smell that rose from the bundle. It was undoubtedly a white man's smell, "wolf-stale in hickory smoke".

Now, Salathiel had always taken it for granted that begging was purely an Indian prerogative and convenience. But here was a white man and necessity in one stinking bundle. He stopped, half from surprise and half from chagrin, detained by the hand. He could not get past it without thrusting it away.

"Who and what might ye be?" he exclaimed impatiently.

"Some call me 'Taffy', your honour," whined the voice from the shadows. "I ply the western road. I take what little charity there may be betwixt the mountains and the dape salt say." The figure wriggled like inky flames. "In Philadelphia I fell among Christians."

"Well, you've come to a good place here," said Salathiel. "They're givin' both meat and drink away down there around the fires to-night." He made as though to step forward. But the hand remained. "What more do you want?"

"Money! Tomorrow will be another night. 'Tis coin alone will always do the trick."

Salathiel continued to stand, pondering this. He remembered he had some of Ecuyer's gold, some loose shillings and pence, a couple of scalps he had traded for a bad beaverskin, a twist of killickinnic, and a copper medal of George I in his pouch. The watch, he now recalled with a twinge of uneasiness, he had left hidden in his bunk. But, after all, the wagon was well watched.

"Look you, you are tall and mighty," whined the voice. "Give me a Portagee joe, a pine shilling, an old Bermudy hog piece, any-thing—anything round and hard. Look at me pore feet." He wriggled them in the moonlight.

They were bad.

The moccasins were tied with strings and old rags woven into the rotten openwork of what was no more now than mouldy leather lace. Through the holes peeped the chilblained bunions and calluses of one David Ap Poer like white fungi growing on a rotting log.

Yes, the feet were bad. But the hand was worse. And that was all of the man he could plainly see.

On a swift impulse that was not quite anger, he fumbled in his pouch and smacked something into the hand that snatched at it.

"There's a cud of comfort for ye," said he, and tried to pass on.

The fingers clutched the brown twist of tobacco, and crushed it.

"God damn ye," said the whine, now in a rising key, "God damn yer big carcass! May the fever get ye and wither yer prat into a long bony point like the arse of a frog."

The voice continued to come out of the shadow, but the hand had withdrawn into it.

Salathiel laughed, and strode across the porch towards the closed door. There had been something eerie and disconcerting about the incident—but he would give it no further thought. What was going on now in the big room? he wondered. Had he talked with the Highlander too long?

The door opened with a round brass knob, and that for an instant halted him, too. It was a new kind of latch, iron. He got the knack of it, entered, and closed the heavy panels quietly behind him. His first sensation was that the ceiling was so high that he need not take off his fur cap. He removed it, however, and leaned back against the door.

The big iron lock clicked.

Outside in the shadow of the log pillars, the unfortunate descendant of a long line of Cambrian bards and chieftains sat cogitating his sorry predicament. Ages of old European oppression and half a lifetime of new North American misery were concentrated in him personally. He had come too far west. After this Lancaster should be his western limit. Begging and petty thievery needed many people, excess and luxury to flourish on. A big, bad town. There was only one place like that in all the colonies. And, as a matter of fact, he did better along the waterfront at Philadelphia than anywhere else.

He must, he *must* get back out of the wilderness. In the hills near Wilmington he had some Welsh relatives. But how to get there—that was the question. Money, something to swap for food and rest at night must be had. The tall man with the pretty woman—he had watched them, peeked into the wagon at her. And what he *had* seen! A gift was in order. But nothing—a twist of tobacco!

How long before the Highlander in the wagon would doze? he wondered. He spat down the steps thoughtfully several times.

Finally, he gathered his ragged blanket-coat about him and slipped into the darkness around the shadowed corner of the house. The drinking might go on for a long time here and there. But not all night. Already the crowds about the various fires and empty barrels were beginning to break up. Nor was it likely that any hounds would bother him. He hated watchdogs like hell, all curs. Fleas were the only thing he and they had in common. But the dogs had met a mighty defeat tonight. They had literally devoured one another. He stopped to laugh silently at the remembrance. A cloud drifted across the moon slowly.

He'd wait awhile. It was cold outside in the corner of the big chimney under the loom of the wall. But cold quieted fleas. Even the lice in his hair might stop crawling. Yes, he would wait. No one but Croghan's men knew he was at Patton's, and they were going west tonight.

Well, he would not be with them.

5

A Pair of Moccasins and a Bowl of Duck Soup

THE LOCK CLICKED behind Salathiel, and he looked eagerly about him. The ceiling was high, and it was a big, long room. The red firelight winked through shadowy yellow candle-shine, itself suffused through a veritable fog of tobacco smoke, in which the candles shone here and there like fixed stars. To his right, and at the far end, a frame of double-tiered bunks filled with fresh straw ran clear across the chamber. Here was evidently the main sleeping accommodation for ordinary travellers. On them several young Highland officers had already spread their plaids and cloaks and lay sprawled out amid a dim blur of colour, dozing, or playing cards sleepily in the folds of their blankets; observing, hoping fervently that the rest of the company would soon retire.

But apparently there seemed to be small chance of that. There were no less than six square tables scattered throughout the room. Around three of them a number of local personages in neat buckskins or butternut suits, friends whom Mr. Patton had invited in from the porch, were still engaged in various stages of eating and drinking, smoking, and more or less lively and earnest talk.

Squire MacDowell, the local magistrate, was listening, evidently with some choler, to a clanging dispute conducted by a couple of his neighbours, who appealed to him constantly for legal confirmation of their political opinions. He looked as though he were trying a difficult case. The argument was about a new tax soon to be levied on legal papers, as far as Salathiel could gather. How did Mr. MacDowell stand, and would he try to collect it? Would he comply and buy stamped paper, if the bill passed? People were leaning forward eagerly to hear his replies. Loud assertions about Parliament, the royal prerogative, the rights of English freemen, and the king's new ministers were being exchanged, and not always respectfully. The squire's learned jargon scarcely seemed an adequate answer or even a sedative to so much emotion. The argument grew more heated.

Why, Salathiel wondered, were a few penny stamps on legal papers so interesting? And why was there so much bitter feeling about them? He must remember to quiz Yates about such matters. That fool Virginian at Fort Cumberland had been excited about taxes, too. He yawned and felt enormously indifferent about papers and penny stamps. Supper would be much more to his mind. There were others who evidently felt the same way about it.

Over in a corner a couple of Highland sergeants, with a platter of smoking venison collops on the side, were playing draughts and making moves between bites. "I'm in your king row, MacPhearson. Mon, dinna ye see? Croon me, croon me!" Sergeant MacPhearson swallowed a hunk of venison thoughtfully, and reluctantly complied.

Two bored young ensigns wrapped themselves in their tartans and crawled back into the recesses of the straw bunk. They lay down as far away as possible from a red-faced Highlander with a bagpipe tucked under his head. From time to time he emitted short squeaking snores, plaintive wheezes that might have come from his pillowed instrument, whose pipes rose out of the straw behind him and seemed to look down reproachfully into his face. All that end of the room was now a sombre blaze of colour with the plaids of the huddled sleepers smouldering in the firelight, their claymores and glittering harness hanging from pegs on the wall.

"A verra wild and warlike scene," Whuzz-Bang Wully Grant suddenly remarked in a loud voice to Yates, who with a calculating squint was leaning back in a chair near-by, watching him throw dice. Mr. Yates nodded.

"Like a huntin' lodge in the Heelands," suggested Lieutenant Grant.

"Precisely," said Mr. Yates, "all but for the trivial absence o' bonny Scotia herself."

"Ah, ye ken the blue lochs, then, the long shinin' firths, the bracken i' the wild glens," sighed Lieutenant Grant, a boyish look of patriotic cunning overcoming his habitual scowl.

"Loch Lomond's long been me ain dimpled favourite," replied Yates.

Lieutenant Grant pondered this as a possible basis for fellow feeling, for some time. He was a man who always thought everything over carefully, and was usually wrong. "Hoo would ye like to pursue some sma' game wi' a fellow Scot to pass the nicht awa in this brutal wilderness?" he asked tentatively. "Just twa homesick Heeland bairns oot togither wi' a handfu' o' siller for a peep at Fortune's twinklin' behind."

Mr. Yates pondered this alluring prospect, too. "After supper, sir," he said finally.

Wully Grant gave a deep disappointed grunt. He was not going to let pass what he felt to be an unexpected opportunity for recouping himself for the disappointments of the evening. "I'll cast wi' ye for the supper," he cried impulsively, rattling the dice box in his red fist as a challenge.

"Done!" shouted Yates, evidently quite unexpectedly to Lieutenant Grant, and so saying, he shifted deftly into a chair opposite that gentleman at the same table. "The best out of three wins, and I'm damned hungry," he added.

Grant passed him the dice cup, wetting his large lips anxiously with the tip of his tongue.

Salathiel, standing in the shadow by the door, grinned. He had seen people cast dice with Yates before. Unconsciously, he still lingered by the door and thus delayed to discover himself. The tipple in the wagon had warmed him and he was in a gently glowing mood, capable of enjoying the incidental dramas in the room before him quite thoroughly. But even more arresting was the domestic end of the establishment, where much cooking was going on and the Patton family and their favoured guests were gathered about the hearth. For several reasons the scene at that end of the apartment seemed memorable.

The chimney was huge and the fireplace recessed into a cavernous ingle-nook, where an old Negro woman in a flaring white turban and glittering eyes sat in the flame-wavering shadows like the Spirit of Darkness herself. She held a lithe hickory switch poised in one hand. A battery of spoons, ladles, forks, knives and skewers were disposed on an iron rack before her. Pots on spiders, pots hung on adjustable hooks and chains, kettles on swinging cranes, hooded roasting pans, gridirons, hinged baking moulds, and two spits driven by springs and weights, all ingeniously and conveniently disposed, completed the equipment of her culinary arsenal.

Pewter plates were stacked high on warming racks, and three sweating black youngsters tended the main blaze and the many little fires of heaped coals underneath the pots and simmering dishes, where a hand bellows was frequently applied. Their faces shone with sweat, soot, and apprehension.

The crackle of the flames and of hot fat, the sibilant directions of the old woman, the hiss of frying, and the frequent swish of her switch all blent into a kind of melodic whisper. That, together with the sighing of the chimney, the creak of the turning spits, and the hum of steam kettles provided an undertone and continuous accompaniment for the illuminated drama in the smoky cavern, where the old black witch presided and her dark sprites tended the fires. This musical whisper rose and fell with the hum of conversation, and like the firelight itself beat against the walls.

As for the rest, some fanciful comparison with the interior of a small theater was inevitably suggested to all but the rude or stupid by the accidental design of the room itself. For the whole spacious hearth-space and the recess of the ingle-nook were panelled and framed-in by the oval sweep of a proscenium-like arch, the main feature of an ample wooden mantel intricately carved with acanthus leaves, delicately moulded, and supported by classic pilasters. This magnificent mantel was indeed the masterpiece of William Patton himself. On many a long winter evening he had worked with skilful hands and infinite patience over cherished pieces of seasoned wood, and from the best design books he could obtain from the City. In five years he had achieved the mantel and panelled-in half the room. And it was in this finished part of the room, garnished with some of Mrs. Patton's cherished Philadelphia furniture, that the family now lived and the more genteel guests were entertained.

Over the high mantelshelf, and flanked on either side by shield-shaped silver sconces, hung an oil portrait of a florid-faced worthy in a periwig and the blue naval uniform of a captain in his late Majesty's service, casting a quarter-deck glare of disapproval at the bare log walls still visible at the opposite end of the chamber. In the painted prospect behind him was a ship careened on a tropical beach, where brown natives under palm trees danced about a black cauldron. It was a good portrait of a powerful man, Richard Norris, Mrs. Patton's grandfather, who had been among the first English mariners to winter at Tinian with the hospitable Spaniards.

Quite accidentally and for practical purposes alone, but as though especially designed to lend depth to the foreground under the captain's ample red nose, two all but semicircular, high-backed oak settles extended ten feet out from the wall on each side of the broad chimney, enclosing within their firm embrace, like a pair of crab's pincers, a large oval space and a small round table set precisely midway between the pincer tips. On this, set off by a snowy linen cloth, were displayed with obvious pride a pair of really impressive candelabra and Mrs. Patton's enviable silver tea service.

Here quite literally was at once the family circle and the centre of domestic affairs for both the tavern and the household. Cut off from cold draughts even in the winter by the high-backed settles, and basking in the genial glow of light and warmth from the hearth, the family and its pets, children and grownups, sat, ate, talked, entertained their chosen guests, and even said their family prayers in a kind of public-privacy and familiar but decorous ease year after year.

Here somehow, with a bit of worn but spotless French carpet, and the chaste disposal of a few pieces of fine furniture, silver, and her even more precious china—somehow by dint of feminine art-magic, Mrs. Patton had achieved to an astonishing degree an effect of comfortable elegance, good taste, and settled ease in the midst of crude disorder.

It was this particular part of the room at which Salathiel was now gazing, feeding his heart and mind with the food of satisfaction and slaking the hunger of long-delayed desire. This was the kind of thing he had come far out of the forest for to see. Beside it, his physical hunger for a more material supper was temporarily stilled. If there was still something of avid curiosity and of savage wonder in his examination of a scene, it now served only to lend the bright magic of eternal novelty to his view. Everything seemed new to him, pristine as the candlelight reflected from the silver.

But there was no longer any fear, none of the awe of wary ignorance in his examination of his surroundings. It was not like that day when as a boy he had first peeked out over the cliff on the Monongahela and looked down at Fort Pitt—a lifetime ago! He was no longer embarrassed or confused. Just a bit shy, conscious of the more than six feet of himself.

This evening, for instance, he still stood by the door doubtful of just exactly how to introduce himself into the magic circle, where Melissa was obviously already so much at home. A happy omen, he hoped, of things to come. Momentarily he was content merely to savour the atmosphere, leaning back against the door. Something would happen; someone would see him. Meanwhile, it was by far the most civilized bit of human landscape he had ever glimpsed. The colour and the smell of it was grateful to his eyes and nostrils. He watched, and breathed it in, content for the instant. Certainly it was a very human view.

Behind the high backs of the settles the squaws passed to and fro, carrying the food and drink to the tables at the far end of the room. They appeared and disappeared through the shadows on silent moccasins, with only a faint shuffle. At one end of the left-hand settle Mr. Patton and Arthur St. Clair were having a glass and a hearty man's conversation. Mr. Patton was slapping St. Clair's silver buckled knee in a very ecstasy of appreciation of a joke so subtle and so arrestingly humorous that they had both stopped drinking a moment just to laugh.

Suddenly Salathiel saw Arthur St. Clair in an entirely new light, that of a good fellow out to enjoy the fruits of prosperity in ease and affability—but always in a comely way. A good companion! It seemed strange now that he had not thought of St. Clair that way before. What if he was a bit pompous at times! How natural and happy, with what kindly blue eyes and fresh boyish cheeks, he sat there tonight. And undoubtedly Mr. Patton knew how to tell a sly story.

Directly across the circle on the opposite settle two results of that ridiculous act—about some aspect of which Messrs. Patton and St. Clair were no doubt laughing—two babies only three or four years old slept with their arms about each other and a half-strangled puppy, ravished, but almost crushed by so much unconscious affection. Beautiful as young angels in a church window by moonlight, when asleep, these two young sons of Mr. Patton were little Saxon devils when awake. As yet neither time nor America had left any visible imprint upon them, although they were of the third generation born away from "home". They were still atavistically blond, sweetly merciless, and English as hell.

Albine looked at them, and thought of himself. Had he once been white and gold like that?

Sweat broke out on his forehead.

In the dark forest of dreams where his first memories began, and were lost, he saw his mother's face leaning over him against the green light of leaves; heard the soft tones of her Irish voice, talking to him, saying something vastly important . . .

He strained, listening inwardly. And then came the wait, the fierce tension of fear, waiting, waiting for her to scream . . . not tonight . . . thank God!

No one but he knew how the sight of sleeping children moved him, and why. He remembered the dead child with yellow hair he had buried near the burnt cabin nigh to Fort Pitt. Shades of himself and Captain Jack! And the red baby playing with the bright beads in the sunlight. *Ah—ha,* young snake! His hand closed around the small neck . . . clutched . . . the smooth handle of his tomahawk . . . and brought him back to himself in time to stifle the war-whoop rising in his throat. He seemed to be tumbled back into the room again, sweating.

By God, when he had his own house there would be no damned Injuns sitting by *his* hearth!

Like the old chief there, for instance, the survivor of the recent bombardment and the hero of the barrel, who was now sitting precisely midway between the two settles with his back to the fire, wrapped in a frayed red blanket and frousting himself. A turkey feather hung down out of his hair into one eye. A jest? But there was no sign of life in the furrowed and wrinkled bronze countenance behind it. None, save the pits of an ancient smallpox. A great man of the forest fallen low and stupefied.

The chief heard and saw nothing. On the wings of firewater and tobacco he had been transported back to the Great Smoky Mountains of his fawnlike youth. Now and then out of the folds of his blanket one hand crept tremblingly to his nose-haunted mouth. His writhing lips sucked at a stub of a stone pipe, and throwing back his head until his eyes showed like two china moons, he slowly emitted a cloud of incense. The smoke curled easily about his head and then, descending from heaven in a back draught, eddied along the floor.

It drifted slowly towards the hearth.

At the same time the bristles on the neck of the largest dog Salathiel had ever seen would rise, and his black lips quiver, exposing a glimpse of white fangs as the big tawny English mastiff snarled silently at his unconscious tormentor, with whom, stretched out and relaxed in every fibre, he was reluctantly sharing fleas and the grateful warmth of the fire.

Evidently he was an innkeeper's dog, for he alone had noticed when Salathiel had come in and was still aware of the stranger standing by the door, but yet did nothing more than look at him warily from time to time, his head between his paws. He was not asleep. He watched.

The boys slept. Melissa and Mrs. Patton talked, fast, intimately. Anybody could see that already they liked each other; were deep in gossip—much at home. Salathiel was delighted, but also somewhat astonished at what he now discovered and overheard going on.

It was Frances Melissa, of course.

Melissa sat at the extreme near end of the right settle, Mrs. Patton in a winged chair only half facing her. A low table with the remains of their recent supper and some untouched covered dishes had been pushed aside so that Mrs. Patton could draw up close. But that was only incidental to something else.

Seated in Melissa's lap was a small brown-eyed girl in a long woollen nightgown. She might have been anywhere from five to seven. Already she was "old", a mite of a woman. Her glossy brown pigtails fell gravely to her shoulders. There were traces of recent tears on her face, but she now leaned back against Melissa, pressing her head ecstatically against her bodice, and now and then bringing up her feet to gaze rapturously at a pair of pretty moccasins decidedly too large for her—moccasins which Salathiel recognized he had once made for Melissa at Cumberland. But there was no doubt to whom they belonged now.

In the candle and firelight the matronly Mrs. Patton in her white cap, Melissa calm now but still starry-eyed, both of them sat there basking in a tide of warm comfort that seemed to flow from the little woman in Melissa's lap. Well!—Lord, he hoped it *was* prophetic! He had a sudden revelation: What women wanted was children! The moccasins twinkled again, and the little white legs gleamed.

"Laws-a-mercy," Mrs. Patton was saying, "you've won her body and soul with your nice pat gift. Says I to Mr. Patton when he come aborrowin' those red slippers— 'You don't know what you're doin', Wee-um!' And he didn't. 'Those mules are a gift from that nice Leftenant Francis of the Sixtieth, him that brought the child in naked from the wilderness.' And then I showed him the letter that Mr. Francis writ Bridget from Philadelphia. The script of a scholar and a gentleman. 'Bridget, my love,' was the very words he writ, 'here's a pair o' red mules for milady's wardrobe, a little large, but you can skip in them until you grow up. And Mrs. Burd is sending you on some other nicknannies, drawers, and petticoats, and a bib and tucker from Lancaster.' Now, wasn't that downright nice! Mrs. Colonel Burd's my own cousin, you know, she's a Shippen . . ." Mrs. Patton's voice made genuflection. She actually paused—but went on.

" 'Deed, I don't know how we'd ever have clothed the child if it hadn't been for Cousin Sarah and Leftenant Francis' sendin' the little red shoes and things upcountry by an express. But don't think *that* stopped Mr. Patton and Wully Grant from borrowin' the shoes, and havin' their Guy Fawkes night chivaree, and nearly blowing up our stockade. Serves 'em right," said Mrs. Patton, jabbing her thumb in the direction of Lieutenant Grant's table. "He's daft over rockets and such fizzy truck, tetched, you might say. Politics it was, 'tryin' to rally the loyal sentiment,' they called it. *Ha-haw.* Men do beat all. It's cost Wee-um a pretty penny tonight. *He's* well burnt, I'll be bound."

"They burned my red shoes," cried the little girl, sitting up straight, her eyes brimming with tears.

"*Sh-sh*, mavourneen," said Frances, "now nivver ye mind that no more. You've got new mules for your paddies, and Mr. Albine will be after making ye another pair that will fit your little fate, before he takes ye on to your gran'ma."

The child still lingered on the verge of tears.

"Bridget," said Mrs. Patton, "you'll soon be ridin' to Carlisle like a lady in the great wagon with the fine grey horsies. And you'll be seein' your own grandma there. Now, what do you think o' that?"

"I'd rather stay with you," replied the child doubtfully, and hid her face in sudden embarrassment against Melissa's shoulder.

"Sure, I'll be the one to take you along, nivver fear," replied Melissa, slipping her arm about her.

"My, but it's the soul of kindness of you," continued Mrs. Patton. "I've been that put to it to look after her. Not that she ain't the most helpful young creature alive, and a domestic little soul, but there's been no one I could trust her to on the road with so many wild and half-naked captives goin' downcountry to Carlisle. If her grandma hadn't writ in and all I'd keep her. Seems McCandliss was her pa's name. Virginians. All took by the Injuns. All of 'em . . ."

At this juncture Mrs. Patton was interrupted by the harsh voice of Whuzz-Bang Wully, who began ordering supper for two in broadest Scotch. He wanted it served hot, lots of it, and instanter. There was a note of tipsy triumph and unnecessary urgency in his manner that was most exasperating.

The impossible, it seemed, had happened. Yates had lost throwing dice, and Lieutenant Grant was now insistent upon a glorious supper to celebrate his Scotch victory, a meal that should do both himself and his vanquished countryman full justice. Mr. Yates was also buying the wine. He had lost there, too. No one in the room was allowed to miss the point. Grant fairly clamoured. He barked out his orders. Everybody stopped talking to look at him, and Mrs. Patton finally arose indignantly to direct the flustered servants.

It was in that way that she first saw Salathiel standing by the door. Realizing that he must have been left there unnoticed for some time, her patience broke.

"I swan, Mr. Patton," she cried, "what's come over you? Here you be gossiping, gossiping like an old gaffer in a warm corner, and your guest leaning up against yon door until belike it will fall in with him." She approached her husband closer and said something in a low tone that made his face burn.

Whatever it was, Mr. Patton made sudden excuses to St. Clair, and betook himself rapidly to subdue the now vociferous gloating of Lieutenant Grant. Between him and Yates the redheaded Scot eventually subsided, and supper was decently served. A faint "Thank God" in a sepulchral tone coming from the straw bunk at the other end of the room caused Lieutenant Grant to stride in that direction viciously, and to survey the row of his apparently slumbering subalterns indignantly.

"Leave him to me, Patton," whispered Yates, while Wully stood with his back turned. "Bring me your card-box directly after supper. I'll give you the nod when. And tell Arthur and Sal to be ready to join me in a brisk hand."

"Good," said Mr. Patton, who had not been enjoying himself. "I'll tell 'em! And I might say I have one kag of powerful old peach brandy on hand. I'll contribute some of it. But watch it yourself," he warned, and winked.

"I'll watch it," grinned Yates.

Lieutenant Grant returned, having received no reply to his threats but snores and other unmilitary noises.

Meanwhile, Mrs. Patton had, with much clucking and tut-tutting, led Salathiel by the arm into the "family circle" and insisted upon seating him nowhere else but in her own wing chair. Nothing would do but he must sit in the place of honour and have his supper out of the covered dishes which she had been saving for him.

"What in the world delayed ye so long?" demanded Melissa.

"Oh, the wagon. And I was lookin' over the room a bit," he answered sheepishly. "I hear I'm to make a small pair of new moccasins."

"Ah, so ye heard that," replied Melissa, tossing her head. "But will ye?"

The child also was regarding him gravely with her level eyes.

"It's a promise, isn't it? It's what *you* want?"

"It is," she said, and smiled tenderly at him. "Bridget, me love, say your manners to this gentleman, he's my—me man!"

With great dignity and complete self-possession the little girl climbed down out of Melissa's lap, placed her feet carefully in the right rehearsed position, took hold of her long flannel nightgown, and made him a deep curtsy.

"I hope ye find yourself in prime health, sir," she said, smiled, and swept a pigtail out of her eye.

Mr. Albine arose and bowed as Captain Ecuyer had once taught him, straight from the waist. He felt he could do no less.

"It's my great good fortune to be meetin' you, Miss Bridget McCandliss," he said gravely, and took her small hand in his own. For a moment they looked at each other man to woman, steadily.

Then Bridget retreated with sudden embarrassment into Melissa's lap.

"He knowed my name!" she whispered.

"Sometimes he's highly intilligent, me love," said Melissa. The child nodded, still looking at Salathiel.

Mrs. Patton put her hand to her mouth, but was nevertheless seriously delighted at the proceedings.

Years later Salathiel was to recollect that what he had first said to Bridget was probably the most unconsciously prophetic sentence that ever came out of his mouth. But all that was in the acorn now.

At the moment Arthur St. Clair, who felt left out, came over to sit beside them. He was followed by the big mastiff, which lay down a few paces from Salathiel and regarded him doubtfully.

"Bran," said St. Clair, "this is the renowned Mr. Albine."

Bran growled.

Salathiel selected a bit of broken meat from one of the used supper plates and offered it carefully to the big dog. It was hard for him to realize that Bran was a member of the family and not a wild animal. He was big as a wolf.

The dog accepted the offering thoughtfully. Presently he swallowed it and wagged his tail. Everyone laughed, especially the child.

"Now that you've all met one another," said Mrs. Patton, "I hope you'll let Captain Albine have his supper. It's high time. He must be starved." Mrs. Patton conferred a military title as easily as she whisked the lid off the waiting platter. A mound of turkey, ham, roasted chestnuts, and yams still steamed fragrantly with a tang of sage. Mrs. Patton began to draw tea.

"Thank ye, ma'am. I *am* a bit hungry," admitted Salathiel, and fell to.

The taste was new. This was high Pennsylvania cookery, he understood from the first bite. He minded his manners and used his knife carefully, but the mound on the platter disappeared like a haystack in a spring flood. St. Clair looked on with considerable amusement and not a little envy; Melissa, with some apprehension.

"Sukey," cried Mrs. Patton to a sloe-eyed squaw who came shuffling out of the shadows, "bring 'em heap soup."

"Well, my boy," remarked St. Clair—"*Captain,* I should say now, I suppose—I opine you must know you are almost over the mountains now. The Shawnees don't cook like that down the Ohio. In the City, Mrs. Patton's family sets a famous table."

"The Shippens," murmured Mrs. Patton, closing her eyes.

At this juncture Mr. Patton came and sat down, having left Lieutenant Grant and Mr. Yates in the midst of hired plenty.

"I was just saying you were a wise and lucky man to marry into a family of famous cooks, Patton," continued St. Clair.

"Now, I admire to hear ye, Mr. St. Clair," cried Mrs. Patton. "It's comfortin' now and then to be rightly esteemed." She glanced at her husband meaningfully. "Wee-um, I fum! I hope you won't ask me to put up with the vagaries of your bosom friend, Lieutenant Grant, any longer. I wish he and his hungry Scots would clear out and stay over at Fort Loudon. It's doin' our reputation no good in this neighbourhood to have them here. Some people will be wonderin' whether you're a Whig like your pa, or not."

"Wife," replied Mr. Patton, "you know right well Wully Grant's no bosom friend o' mine. I admit I was o'erpersuaded by Squire MacDowell and the commissioners to see that Croghan's Irish got through to Fort Pitt with the government trade goods. But you know there's been lawless doings in these parts lately with the Black Boys, a great stir amongst restless and feckless newcomers and burnt-out settlers. 'Twas MacDowell's idea that by fetching a detachment of Highlanders here from Loudon we could give protection to Croghan's men this far, and then let 'em sneak off to Pittsburgh themselves, quietly and with no trouble. They have the whole season's supply o' treaty trade goods for the western frontier. It's no mere matter of merchandise. Croghan, you know, is the king's deputy agent to the far western tribes under Sir William Johnson. Well, what could I do but agree? They count me a loyal man, and the province has a legal claim to use this fort for havin' helped to build it. You know that."

Mrs. Patton sniffed. "That's no reason Wully Grant should be bellowin' at me like a bull o' Bashan in me own house, and you standin' by," she said. "He's a zany. And the fireworks—they blew up!"

"Aye," said Patton, "I *know* that! But it was his idea to improve on the occasion and rally the loyal Protestant sentiment of the countryside, being it was Guy Fawkes Day. And there was some sense to that. We figured by the time the liquor died out, Croghan's Irish could be quietly on their way without anybody bein' the wiser, or only maybe feelin' a little foolish the next mornin'. If it hadn't been for the damned fireworks!"

St. Clair laughed. "It's not the first time Wully Grant has burned his fingers with goonpowder," he said. "I could tell ye a tale of a fancy affair in Scotland soon after he came back from Inja. Him and the English Congreves and the Galts. 'Twas at 'Flowerbanks' on Creewater one night it happened. Rockets rocked and rocketed. But Wully's verra sensiteeve aboot it a'."

"No doubt he is—sensitive about himself, but no one else," cried Mrs. Patton. "That's the way with men like him. Now, I swan! What's happened to that lazy Sukey and poor Captain Albine's soup?"

She stepped briskly over to the hearth to hurry matters along.

"Listen," said Patton, leaning forward and speaking in a low tone, "the Irish will be leavin' in the early hours o' the morn. Tomorrow, please God, they'll be gone! Now I want to get Grant and his garrison men off the place, too, and safe back to Loudon. I don't want any more trouble here. There's enough hard feelin' in the countryside as it is, and I'm an innkeeper and no backwoods politician. Now, Ned Yates is goin' to take Wully on at cards tonight, and he wants you two to sit in on the game and take a hand. You know Yates can riffle the pasteboards cleverly. If Grant loses, he won't be able to pay, and he won't tarry long with us creditors."

"*If* he loses," laughed St. Clair. Salathiel grinned, too.

"I'll supply the brandy," said Patton. "Watch it though. It's powerful big medicine laid up in 'fifty-two by my pa. Are you as one on this?"

Both of them nodded happily.

"Good," said Patton, "good! We don't go in much for play in this house, but this will be a righteous exception. Only *after* the neighbours have gone, you know. Private!" Just then he happened to catch Yates's eye and winked, letting him know that all was arranged.

The growing intensity of an appetizing odour at this point caused Bran to sit up and wag his tail hopefully again. Sukey arrived with a large crock-tureen full of steaming black soup. "And hoe cakes are comin'," said Mrs. Patton.

"Madam," said St. Clair, sniffing, "if that's the same delectable duck soup I had a short while ago, I beg to be allowed to jine Mr. Albine in another bowl—and to drink the health of the company in it, too. For it's nectar—or is it ambrosia? Both! It's food and drink alike."

Mrs. Patton naturally enough flushed with girlish pleasure under her matron's cap at so high-flown but earnest a compliment. She began to ladle out the thick black soup to both Albine and St. Clair with the ceremony it now seemed suddenly to deserve. She tested it daintily with her little finger and gave a nod. *"Not* scalding," she said.

St. Clair raised his bowl and looked at the two ladies across its rim. "May the well-disarved plenty of this household be presarved, Madam Patton"—he paused—"and continued into your own, Mistress Albine."

To that both he and Salathiel drank.

The soup was so good that not even praise could spoil it. The tang of an aromatic spicy odour married to a substantial rich meaty taste filled Salathiel's throat and nostrils with a promise of belly satisfaction, one which he found was instantly fulfilled. He drank the whole bowl and saw that everybody was looking at him. Before he could have any more he realized that he must say something. He winked at Mr. Patton.

"Melissa," said he, "it's this kind of soup that will keep a man from ever wantin' to leave his bride."

"Belike in our house the trouble might lie the other way," she flashed back at him. And they all laughed happily together.

"Good soup," said Mr. Patton, and patted his wife's hand, "good soup, Matilda, and for nigh twenty years past."

"Two and twenty," insisted his wife.

"My God, how *do* you make it, Mrs. Patton?" demanded Frances Melissa, her eyes twinkling as she looked down into the face of the child now asleep on her lap. "I'm after thinkin' I'd best have the receipt of such a love potion to carry home with me, wheriver that's goin' to be."

Mrs. Patton, being practical, took Melissa literally. "I'll tell you, Mistress Albine," she said. "But mind ye, it's not only what you put into soup, but how you make it stick together, by rilin' it up and smoothin' it down. And then there's the seasoning, too. The very best pottage can be naturally flat. It takes taste . . ."

"Yes, yes, Matilda," said Mr. Patton, "but *this* soup now?"

"Oh! Well, ye take a brace of fat ducks, an onion, and some wild rice, and ye kiver 'em up with hard cider—some prefers white wine. And ye stew 'em all slowly a long, long time. Then you lay 'em aside and let the whole mess cool. Next you take the ducks and bone 'em. Bones is the only thing the matter with ducks. You chop up the shredded meat with hearts, giblets and all, real fine."

Here Mrs. Patton closed her eyes, remembering.

"Next you put all the meat back in the original liquor with a dash of sage, a lot of chopped parsley, a bay leaf, and a tetch of marjoram, yarbs, you know. Then you just add a little water accordin' to how much soup ye may want, and then you stew that a long, long time again until it's all smooth. But you don't skim it. You let the duck fat stay. At the last you thick it up with 'Mudian arrow-root flour, and it's then you put in your salt, pepper, a bit of mace or nutmeg, and three thimbles of rum—*so, so!* And simmer for a minute or two . . ."

"My goodness, whativer's the matter with that child?" she exclaimed suddenly.

"She's havin' a bad dream, a real bad one," said Melissa. "Wake up, me love, wake up, Bridget."

The child, who had been twisting and whimpering on her lap, suddenly opened her eyes wide with terror and shivered. She looked at the old Indian sitting by the fire. And, then, before Melissa could stop her, she dashed over to Salathiel and clung to him.

He lifted her up and held her close. "He'll not hurt you," he said. "I'll never let him." Her arms went about his neck, and he felt her small heart beating violently against his own.

"Will you always stay close?" she whispered. "I'm afeared. You know what of. Please! Promise!"

"Always," he replied, "always"—and so it was.

He got up, and going over to the old Indian, took him by the shoulders and started him for the door. "Out," said he.

"Do you suppose she remembers . . ." began St. Clair.

"*Sh!*" said Mrs. Patton. "Now it's high time every one of these sleepy children was in bed. Sam! Rodney!" she cried, and went over to shake up the two boys.

"Yes, ma, yes, ma." They unwound themselves from each other and the puppy, yawning, while the pup barked. Bran growled.

"And you, too, you little tail-waggin' varmint," cried Mrs. Patton. "To bed with ye, off to bed with you all! Rodney, don't let that pup piddle the sheets. I'm tired changin' your trundle bed."

"No, ma," said Rodney, "but it ain't me."

"I think I'll retire myself," said Melissa, holding out her hand to Bridget, "if the gintlemen will koindly permit. And I hope you'll not mind sleepin' alone in the wagon for once, Mr. Albine. I'm to have a fine dape fither bed all to myself, says Mrs. Patton, and I find 'tis a superior timptation this evening. 'Twas a long hard drive today, you'll remember."

"Aye, it's best so tonight," agreed Salathiel, "but I'll miss ye . . ."

"*Coo—coo,*" said St. Clair.

Melissa flashed them a brief bow. Bridget copied her, but with formal curtsy, as though her nightgown had a court train. She smiled at them through eyes still troubled with sleep and her bad dream.

The men and the mastiff watched the pageant of the women, the three sleepy children, and the scampering puppy disappear through the door in the corner. The soft swish of skirts and the patter of feet died away up the stairs. Bran put his head back on his paws again.

"It's a funny thing," said Mr. Patton, as the pad-pad of small feet passed briefly overhead and then died away, "but *that* sound always seems to come runnin' out of the past and to be gallopin' away somewhere into the future. A house without it—well, you just keep listenin'."

" 'Faerie horses,' " remarked St. Clair, "was what mither called it back hame. I jealoos the old house at Thurso *is* pretty silent now." His expression grew thoughtful and remote with the far-off eyes of an exile. "*Hum-m,*" said he.

The good nights of Mrs. Patton and the children seemed also to be an understood signal of departure for the neighbours and friends of the family who had earlier been invited into the room, following the evening's entertainment. Squire MacDowell and his argumentative cronies adjourned their debate on the powers of Parliament, thanked Mr. Patton warmly, shook hands with his guests, and stamped out.

A general exodus of everybody who was not lodging in the house followed.

The two Highland sergeants left their draught pieces on the table and crawled into the straw next to the snoring piper.

As the door had opened from time to time to permit exits, Salathiel noticed that the yard outside had quieted down. The bonfires were burning low. Only a few figures still sat about them, and some of these were already prone. The dark bulk of the Highland sentry could be seen silhouetted against the canvas of the wagon which glowed faintly from the pallid lanthorn light within as though a titanic firefly had settled down before the door. The moon rode high.

Probably Alexander was asleep, thought Albine. But he was *there*—and comfortable enough, no doubt. Well, let him wait. Afterwhile, when he was ready to go to bed himself, he would give him sixpence for his trouble—no, a shilling! Just for old sake's sake. One of the garrison at Ligonier and a veteran of Bouquet's expedition deserved a kindness. Probably it had been a mistake not to give that Welsh beggar a penny or two. He wondered if he had gone. Or was that hand still hanging in the air out there in the moonlight? No. He remembered now. When the door had opened the porch was empty and bright clear over to the steps. Pshaw! What of it? Tobacco was all right. A good gift. Unconsciously, he began to rummage in his pouch in order to fill his pipe. He rose to get a coal from the fire— and found that Patton and Arthur St. Clair were filling their pipes, too.

"The weed goes well on a full belly in front of a fire at night," said Patton in low tones, as they lit up, passing the coal on small tongs amongst them. St. Clair relaxed, stretched out his sleek legs, crossed one fine boot over the other, and blew a cloud of fragrant smoke into the air contentedly.

Suddenly the big room seemed quite empty and silent. Even the servants had vanished. Only Yates and Lieutenant Grant still lingered happily over their wine. There were a couple of empty bellarmines before Wully and he was peeling the wax and wire off the neck of a third. Yates was talking in a confidential tone, but in the quiet room it was impossible not to follow what he was saying. An occasional snort or sigh from the sleepers at the far end of the apartment punctuated rather than interrupted his remarks. They sat listening contentedly. The three pipes glowed.

6

Conversation

YATES WAS TALKING about the difficulties of running the new southern boundary of the province of Pennsylvania:

". . . Jerry Dixon's thought to be better with his instruments than Charley Mason, but they're both careful men, and if we don't get anything else, we'll get a true line east and west between the quarrels of the Penns and the Calverts. But the rub is that nobody knows just how far west to go before establishing a cornerstone to turn north. Probably, they'll compromise that—eventually."

"Thought they'd run the line clean west to Redstone or the Ohio," said Grant.

"The Ohio runs north from Pittsburgh, then west for a bit, and then south," grinned Yates. "They might have to go right on into the sunset. That would seriously annoy our friends, the Virginians, and cross their western claims. And then there are all of the Indian treaty tracts, the Iroquois presarves, and a' that. And did you ever read the strict words of the Penn grant? According to the amiable King Charles, the western boundary of Penn's province is supposed to wag its happy tail through the woods somewhere in the west, exactly as the Delaware River does on the east, curve for curve. Now staking out that wriggle really would be a notable mathematical task. No, the best thing this present line will do is to settle the age-old quarrels between the Penns and the Baltimores. But soon there'll be new quarrels with Virginia about the western lands south and west of Pittsburgh." Yates laughed.

"You know," said he, putting his hands behind his head and leaning back confidentially, "now that the monsieurs have gone, this whole continent would soon be hatching a snake's nest of petty wars between the colonies were it not for the home government, the regulars on the frontiers, and the king's ships."

"Noo, there ye spoke wi' a' the lair o' Solomon!" exclaimed Wully. "Take this verra mountain-*i-ous* neighbourhood, what's it but a mare's nest o' dawky Scotch independents and ramstam Irish snotters, dimocratic rascals that would play neevie-neevie-nicknack wi' the pearls i' God's croon. They make the life o' a royal officer tryin' to do his loyal juty in these dismal woods a verra torment and crucifixion o' daft insults and petty mischiefs. Sometimes I do think it's more than I can abide."

"*Montani semper liberi,* you know," smiled Yates, "but I wouldn't suggest you'd get too much out of it for your trouble, Wully."

Lieutenant Grant snorted. His red hair seemed to rise and bristle. "A wee pittance, the pay of a puir subaltern, wi' the prospect o' Edinburgh garret lodgin's i' the Grassmarket on Scotch half pay for me old age. And the Grants are no well-heeled like the Hamiltons, I can tell you thot, Edward *Hamilton* Yates. Most of them at hame are rejuced to mere bonnet lairds. It's lang syne a retired gentleman o' our ilk could live wi' honour in a tumbledoon castle on a loch in the west Heelands wi' a piper and a few gillies, on oats porridge and cold haggis. Mar's Year and the 'Forty-five put an end to a' thot—and mauny anither proud dream, too. Puir auld Scotland!" sighed Wully, and tossed off a glass from the new bottle.

"I should think ye'd do much better to stay over here and seat yourself on a new plantation, half pay and all," replied Yates.

"Aweel," sighed Wully, "noo thot's preceesely what I *do* plan for to do. Wi' the help of Cousin Jeemes Grant I micht find masel' a snug seat i' the wilderness, and some belly comforts, too. Cousin Jeemes has been verra forward-lookin', not to say canny, in takin' up land grants here and there. Hoosh! He's a wise mon, is Jeemes."

"Cousin James?" inquired Yates, raising his brown silky eyebrows. "You mean Major James Grant that was defeated on the hill nigh Pittsburgh in Forbes's time by bangin' the drums and playin' the bagpipes too early in the mornin'?"

"Aye, the verra same!" replied Lieutenant Grant proudly. "If there hadna been a wee bit too much whusky i' the camp the morn, maybe Jeemes wauld have taken Fort Duquesne from the salad-eaters before puir Johnny Forbes could get himsel' carried thot far west. And what a fine feather thot would have been in the war bonnet o' the Grants! But as the deil would hae it . . ."

"Oh, I see," said Yates, leaning forward with growing interest. "And so—now that Cousin James, according to the gazettes, has got himself appointed governor of East Florida by his gracious Majesty,

I suppose all the more he's still the hope and mainstay of the Grants, and of the land grants likewise, eh?"

"Noo, Yedward, you put it *verra* preceesely, poon and all," admitted Wully, glad to talk about his family at any price. "You see, Cousin Jeemes and masel' started oot from Inveravon aboot the same time. In 'forty it was. He studied law and later on was commissioned i' the Royal Scots, while I went oot to Madras in 'forty-three as a gintleman-writer, a kind o' cadet-factor, ye ken, for the Honourable John Company. Sir Jeemes St. Clair was our guid patron. But he was a far better patron for Jeemes than for me, as it turned oot.

"I wint oot on the same ship wi' young Bobby Clive, and the gales drove us to Brazil, where we spent nine mortal months. Clive picked up the lingo, and I got something else equally native, but not so usefu', which, as God would have it, was the way me ain luck always seemed to rin, even after we both got to Madras.

"Aweel, ye ken how Clive met glory at the siege o' Arcot, and I was near to findin' me ain fortune, too. For I was made trade agent to the Raja of Tanjore, His Highness Sharabhogi, whose father had been deposed, and the company was restorin' young Sharabhogi to the throne of his ancestors. A' for the most pious reasons, ye ken. So there was I, the luckiest o' the Grants, the main factor, at a fine sumptuous new coort in the walthy auld town o' Tanjore, where the rivers Cauvery and Colocoon rin togither—and a whole ordeenance factory wi' goonpowder galore, and a troop of trained elephants, and scores o' black sarvants at me disposal. Losh! What an opportunity."

At this point, for some reason or other, Yates was unable to keep from laughing.

"Aweel, ye micht well lauch," said Wully sadly. "All I'd to do was to sit still as a pillar of the restoration and rit me prat. But it was then that auld Reekie himsel' led me to experiment wi' rockets as a means o' scarin' off the irregular Maharatta horse employed by the French. I made sma' fire rockets wi' a hand rest to fasten on the saddle-bows o' the raja's cavalry, and bigger ones to be loosed from wee cohorns mounted i' the elephants' howdahs. And a' went weel, till the celebration of His Highness's glorious restoration coom aroond."

"Fireworks?" asked Yates.

"Aye," replied Wully, looking wilted.

" 'Twas one o' the grandest pyrotechnic spictacles ivver arranged, the one I set up in the raja's gardens, and a' the world an' Tanjore, too, was there to see. The first star-burst was magneeficent! Unfortunately, the fortified howdah on the leadin' elephant took fire from some flyin' sparks. The rest was awfu'! The big beasts panicked, and while rockets and star-candles went hizzin' and streakin' higgledy-piggledy into the Hindu crowd, the elephants started to trample the fugitives, all tryin' to rush down to the river Cauvery for to quench thimsel'. And the warst of it was that in their unseemly haste they trod the raja's uncle himsel' into the mud. A high Brahmin he was, brought low, and like to lose caste, which is a terrible thing for a heathin mon."

"Terrible," cried Yates, "just terrible!"—and snapped the black patch over his blind eye, which seemed to be weeping.

"Aweel," continued Wully, "I lost caste masel', ye micht say; that is, at the coort of Tanjore I was *persona non grata,* and like to be pelted wi' mud i' the streets if I so much as stuck me red pate oot o' the palace to go to the bazaar. So when I was called back to Madras, I was sorry to go, but happy to leave, if ye ken how thot might be. The goovernor at Fort St. George was annoyed. He disliked Scots, onyway. And there were ither minor deefficulties, the usual debts, and fevers, and a'. So after bidin' a wee to see how the trade winds would blaw, I took the offer o' a guid Scotch ship's captain to transpoort me back to Lunnon, jist for handlin' his bills o' ladin' and company accoonts. And I was no nabob when I landed, I can tell ye, for I had only aboot eighty poonds starlin' more than when I went oot. Thot is, I had aboot eighty poonds.

"Aweel, say I was soon hard oop, and I was thinkin' o' walkin' back to Scotland and of settlin' doon to croftin' and to scones and oats, when one day I met Cousin Jeemes at the Cocoa Tree, whar mauny of us puir Lunnon Scots used to gather o' mornin's. Jeemes was havin' a cup o' chocolate and burnt sugar wi' Sir William Congreve, who was just up from Suffolk. And after I told me sorry adventure at Tanjore, what did Sir William do but invite me to come back hame wi' him and experiment wi' rockets! So I did, and afterwhile between us we burnt his auld coach-hoose doon.

"Noo, I'll no go into the ins and oots of a' we did and undid. But we finally had a verra effective explosion nigh the Galt place at 'Flowerbanks' on Creewater the next summer. The river ran wi' dead fish. And thot was aboot a' we proved. But masel', I'm still convinced that explosive rockets wi' a revolvin' brass carcass would be warse than mortar shells. Hoosoiver thot may be, I was blown oot into the world again.

"Noo, Cousin Jeemes Grant had been visitin' wi' the Galts at 'Flowerbanks' when the wee mill on Creewater where we ground the powder went oop. He was a captain by that time, havin' been aide to Gineral Sir Jeemes St. Clair at both Turin and Vienna. He was coomin' oop fast. Sir William Congreve gave me a letter sayin' I had a latent talent for manipulating goonpowder, but he would no have me foolin' at the royal arsenal at Woolwich. Gineral St. Clair, when he read thot letter, said mine was the kind o' talent had best be left wrapped in a napkin. And Cousin Jeemes suggested it micht be safer to hide it i' the colonies. They both said they would see what could be done. And aboot this time auld Aunty Jane Grant o' Inveravon died, leavin' me and Jeemes to share a wee legacy between us—and the resoolt of a' this was that I found masel' wi' a commission i' Montgomery's Heelanders. 'A dangerous mon safe i' the army' was the wry way Cousin Jeemes put it."

"And now?" asked Yates.

"Ye can tell me a' the rest yoursel', Edward Yates. I was lucky, I suppose, to find masel' an officer amongst auld friends in a famous Heeland regiment. Then came the French war, and we were sent to America, and a'. But I've had only one promotion and been kept here in the backwoods most o' the time. Last nicht was the verra first chance I've had to take me talent oot o' a napkin. Losh, I'm like to rust away with it here."

"You haven't lost a battle yet like Cousin Jeemes. What do ye expect?" grinned Yates.

"Noo, I wauldna poot it thot way," replied Wully. "Jeemes Grant is a mon o' real pairts, for a' thot. He made a brilliant retreat in the Carolinas from Fort Loudon there, and greatly disteenguished himsel'. And he noo has more powerfu' friends in the War Department at hame, and in Parliament, and on the Board o' Trade. Ah, he's forward-lookin', as I said before, even in a retreat."

"Doubtless he'll look after you, then, since you're of his own ilk," suggested Yates.

"He will, he will thot," said Wully. "To tell the truth, there's always been a guid understandin' between us. And then Jeemes still has me wee legacy from auld Mrs. Grant in troost. Why, I've a letter from him only the noo, came by the last express rider twa days syne, writ from St. Augustine hardly a month past, and his fine proclamation aboot East Florida enclosed. Have ye yet seen it? It's a' the talk."

Yates shook his head.

After some wrestling with his own bulky person, Lieutenant Grant produced from under the complicated folds of his tunic a well-sweated piece of officially printed paper, and tendered it to Mr. Yates, with a light in his eye. Yates read it slowly, holding his hand over his black patch:

A PROCLAMATION by the *GOVERNOR* of His MAJESTY's Colony of *EAST FLORIDA*

St. Augustine
7th October, 1763

... And whereas, it may greatly contribute to the speedy settling of this His Majesty's province, to inform all persons of the healthiness, soil, and productions thereof. I do in this proclamation, further publish and make known, that the former inhabitants lived to great ages. His Majesty's troops, since their taking possession of it, have enjoyed an uninterrupted state of health. Fevers, which are so common during the autumn in other parts of America, are unknown here. The winter is so remarkably temperate, that vegetables of all kinds are raised during that season without any art. The soil on the coast is in general sandy, but productive with proper cultivation. The lands are rich and fertile in the interior parts of the province, and on the sides of the rivers, which are numerous. Fruits and grain may be raised with little labor: the late inhabitants had often two crops of Indian corn in one year, and the breeder here will be under no necessity of laying up fodder for the winter, for there is at all times sufficient pasture to maintain his cattle.

The Indigo plant remains unhurt for several years, and may be cut four times in a season. Wild indigo is found here in great abundance, which, with proper cultivation, is esteemed in the French islands to be the best. From the great luxuriance of all the West India weeds found in the southern parts of this province, it is not to be doubted but that all the fruits and productions of the West Indies may be raised here. Oranges, limes, lemons, and other fruits, grow spontaneously over the country. This province abounds with mahogany, and all kind of lumber for transportation or ship building, and the conveyance of the commodities will be attended with little expense, as there is water carriage everywhere ...

Yates finally looked up and nodded. "It reads uncommon well," he said.

"Hoots!" said Wully. "You'd better conseeder comin' doon under the palms to jine me in a planters' paradise on the St. Johns. It's a braw big tidal river full o' fish, and the land wi' a grand lush climate. You can make your fortune in indigo alone. Five hundred pounds bounty a year is bein' offered. And there's plenty o' neegars and contraband rum to be had cheap. It's a bonny new colony their Lordships are plannin'. It, and West Florida. I hear of a Dr. Turnbull, a rich man in Lunnon, plannin' to transport immigrants from the Mediterranean by shiploads. You might better yoursel' conseederably, Edward Hamilton Yates. You maun try it."

"I might," said Yates, "later on, I really might."

Wully seemed more than usually pleased at Yates's serious consideration of his schemes. He grew confidential and in his excitement spilled some red wine on the proclamation extolling Florida, that still lay unfolded on the table before them.

"Noo, I'll tell ye something," he said, "but in streectest confidence. If ye'll come and settle doon on the St. Johns, I can put ye in the way of gettin' some parcels o' the best seated land cheap. De Brahm, the government surveyor, is a guid friend o' mine." He looked as mysterious as he could, and leaned forward earnestly. "You see noo that Cousin Jeemes is a royal goovernor, it would never do for *him* to be holdin' great tracts a' in his ain name. So he's turned over some o' the land to me, in troost, and had the papers transferred to my name."

"All in the family," said Yates.

"Exactly," said Wully. "But not a' in Florida. There's aboot two thousand acres in New York on a lake in the Iroquois country. Jeemes, and George Croghan, and Hardenburgh went into it togither with the goovernor of that province and some ither canny folk some years ago. Since then Croghan's been livin' up there on his ain land in a cabin, with an Indian squaw. It's at the south'r'n foot o' a lang stretch o' shinin' water the savages call Ot-see-go—or how do you lay your tongue to it? But it's magic country, Croghan says, bonny as the Lochs o' Killarney in Ireland, or a broad blue Heeland domain, but untouched, fresh as Adam's paradise on the first Sabbath, swarmin' wi' fish, flesh, furs, and fowl, and handsome squaws, too, if you like 'em. You know Sir William Johnson's a squaw man. What a canny Christian tactic it is to prevail by marryin' the enemy and lovin' them like yersel'. It maun poot them a' at conseederable disadvantage."

"Not necessarily," said Yates. "It's always difficult to keep a savage peace, you know. And then, I confess, I'm delicate about unbelting. But, Wully, could you not dispose of some of this idle land for Cousin James, now?"

"Aye, a stock o' siller would come in handy the noo for the goovernor. He has ower much land, ye micht ken. And a sma' salary wi' prodigal expenses at St. Augustine. As for me, a fistfu' o' hard money for me ain sma' claims would no be a savage insult, richt noo." Wully licked his lips thoughtfully. "I'll no mind tellin' ye, Ned, if the wee cubes had gone agin me here the nicht, I'd have had to borrow to pay for the twa suppers. Me last pay's a' but gone, and there's no news of the paymaster at Fort Loudon yet."

"I'll think it over," said Yates, "and talk to ye tomorrow. But it's the northern land I do like most."

"Palms or maples, ye can hae your choice. A few poonds doon . . ."

"What are the papers like?" asked Yates.

"Direct grants from the royal goovernors or from the croon itself. You canna do better. All in order, all registered, surveyed, and the fees paid. I'll show 'em to you when we get back to Loudon."

"Agreed," said Yates. "Maybe St. Clair will be interested, too."

Wully's face brightened. "Noo, that's well thought of, Edward. You maun go into it togither."

"So we might," said Yates, "but *tomorrow*"—and leaning back again he managed to catch Mr. Patton's watchful eye, and tipped him a wink.

"Well, let's join the others over on the settles there for a glass or two and a pipe before bed. I'll be glad to offer you some of Patton's best peach brandy. Seventeen-fifty-two he says."

"Noo, I'll no argle-bargle wi' ye aboot thot," said Wully. "And it's been a braw supper we've had togither, even if you . . ."

"Pshaw," replied Yates, "you never can tell how any man's luck will run."

"No, but I'm tellin' ye *I'm* a verra lucky mon at a' kinds o' games o' hazard, Mr. Yates. It runs i' the family. The luck o' the Grants, ye ken." Lieutenant Grant rose proudly, if a little unsteadily, from the table. "No doobt you can see that much wi' *one* eye," he added, and gave a great open-mouthed guffaw at this delicate bit of Grantian wit.

He followed Yates over to the fireside, like a lamb.

7

Cards

YOUR TRULY great troublemakers are either finally squelched or
effectually banished. After all, there are traditional and well-known
ways of taking care of them. Sometimes pardon and the turning of
a new leaf are the best ways out. But with small offenders, your
human gadflies, wasps, or mosquitoes, it is quite different. Their ill-
conceived instinct for inveterately coming back, and humming while
they sting, includes their own tragedy. Nemesis herself is at last
aroused, and it is for thus having been trivially annoying for a long
time that her traps are so often irrevocably sprung; dropped, so that
a man is left hanging in some ridiculous noose which he has blithely
been tying about his own neck as a scarf of distinction. The temptation, the humour, inherent in the situation of certain self-gratulatory
sleepwalkers, is often too much for wakeful people to withstand.
Someone is bound to spring the trap, somehow, somewhere. The details of such tidy takings-off are purely coaccidental; to the spectators, amusing. For there are certain types of personality that attract
the mischiefs of their fellow men, even as a lone pine too long upright and successful on the bare savanna draws summer lightning.
Take Lieutenant Grant, for instance:

Whuzz-Bang Wully had, of course, no idea that his little joke,
over which he was still chortling as he sat down confidently on the
settle beside Arthur St. Clair, was a double-edged jest that might
cut himself, his heirs and assigns, forever out of about three thousand
acres of some of the most fertile land in North America. Yet such
was the actual potential of his devastating wit. Everyone present had
in fact been electrified by it, and the ways and means of his ambush
from then on seemed genially to arrange themselves. Indeed, the
whole affair that evening unfolded so good-naturedly, the drift of

72

events seemed so spontaneous, that to his dying day Lieutenant Grant, natively suspicious as he was, was never able to conclude whether— as in the case of rockets—he had been or had not been the innocent victim of irrational chance.

For as soon as he sat down on the settle by Mr. St. Clair that courteous gentleman rose and drew up a chair more comfortable for a Grant to sit in. By this means Wully found himself facing the small round table on which Mr. Albine's supper had so recently been served. And who should remove the remains of it now but Mr. Albine himself? Scarcely were the dishes gone, when Mr. Patton, that excellent host, replaced them with two decanters of peach brandy, golden with the preserved summer of 1752, and four appropriate glasses.

Mr. Albine proffered Lieutenant Grant his tobacco, and Mr. Yates filled his pipe. Mr. St. Clair lighted it. All joined him in a toast to bonny Scotland—to the king—to her Majesty, that good woman! To the ladies upstairs—to ladies downstairs—to ladies everywhere. To Governor James Grant—to Sir James St. Clair—to the whole damned Penn family, widows, children and all. Mr. Yates knew all their names. And none of them were taken in vain.

The dry searing brandy went down more like liquid light than fire; and ascended, mixed with the fumes of previously imbibed potions, to enlarge, tickle, confuse and delight the otherwise sombre brain in Mr. Grant's thick skull so covered up by red bristles, until naked Good-Nature herself came out and swam in the cold melting pools of his wintry eyes. The halcyon golden light seemed to have escaped from the decanters and to be suffusing the room.

What a select company, he thought. The kind he deserved to find. He even felt fatherly now towards those young devils of subalterns snoring away at the other end of the room, oblivious to the staggering social triumphs of their kindly commanding officer. He took a long deep friendly breath in unison with them, *ha!* What boon companions he had found, what sympathy and understanding!

Mr. Yates was on his feet, starting to say something, and with a brandy glass in his hand. He waved it. Another toast—a toast to Wully Grant? How extremely gratifying!

> *"To the lucky Lieutenant Grant. May his fortunes mount like a rocket, burst into heavenly glory, and scatter a few stars amongst us poor dwellers on earth."*

Why, what a noble sentiment, how apt, how fitting!

With a Scotch mist before his eyes Lieutenant Grant tried to rise now to reply with adequate feeling. But he was not *quite* able to do so. His Scotch became too thick for his own tongue. His knees quivered under his kilt—and all the others as one man motioned him to sit down. Perhaps, there was something more they had pleasantly in view for him? Undoubtedly.

Mr. Patton was opening a brass-hinged wooden box, beautifully carved. Out of it came an oblong object wrapped in blue Bristol paper. Yates opened it, and a torrent of white seemed liquidly to pour through his hands. Suddenly it arranged itself in a neat rainbow before him, laid out on the table in an arc. A brand-new set of crisp, block-printed cards. No limp, greasy pasteboards these! They were the kind they used at White's, glossy linen with a starched spring and a snap.

"What shall we play, gentlemen?" asked Yates, quite deferentially.

"Bezique," suggested Lieutenant Grant. "Loo," demanded Mr. St. Clair. "Irish loo," rumbled Salathiel.

"I never play in my own house. It's a rule of the tavern," announced Mr. Patton, gravely. "But I'll be glad to keep tally." Out of the convenient little box came a neat framed slate with pegs and holes down the sides.

"Agreed," said St. Clair.

"Irish loo has it," announced Yates with finality. "What's the loo?"

"Five shillin's a round," insisted Salathiel, "—and the same stake, with the fool left out. He retards the play."

All nodded their agreement. Lieutenant Grant was much relieved. He was afraid St. Clair might have suggested guineas for the stake. He knew St. Clair carried them.

At the last minute, looking a little sheepish, Mr. Patton decided to play a hand.

Might he?

"Of course . . . of course . . ."

"Gentlemen, the cards," said Mr. Yates, as was customary.

He fed them about him in a complete circle for all to see. Somehow they were all neatly arranged perfectly by suits. He withdrew the jester.

"Let's play," cried St. Clair, impatiently. "Mr. Grant with his active commission has the first deal, and leads."

Yates shuffled and handed Wully the cards. Lieutenant Grant reshuffled, cut twice, once with those on each side of him. He dealt swiftly and with an obviously practised hand that only trembled a little, throwing five cards face down around. He deposited the stack and turned up the top for trumps. Diamonds. Being Irish loo, no "miss" was dealt.

After five rounds with several passes and forfeits, mostly on the part of Yates and Salathiel, who were looed, there was a sizable sum at stake. It finally fell to St. Clair and Grant to play for it. St. Clair drew a five-card flush, and was already smiling at having looed the board, when it appeared that Wully had four cards of the same suit and "Pam", the knave of clubs. This was high and took everything. Grant had won. His face flushed and his eyes sparkled.

A really phenomenal run of luck now came the lieutenant's way. During the next five rounds when hearts were trumps, the knave of clubs seemed never to be out of his hands. Even when Yates laid a five-card flush with ace of trumps and the king, Wully was ready with "Pam be civil," and Yates had to pass the trick without revoking. Pam in the hands of Lieutenant Grant forced everybody to loo again and again. "Pam be civil" became a kind of war-cry on his lips, out-trumping everybody. Indeed, Wully seemed to be exemplifying the words of Mr. Yates's toast literally. His fortunes rose like a rocket, and burst into a shower of glory when at the final fifth round, again between him and St. Clair, he emerged with twenty-five pounds and fifteen shillings cold. Wully was triumphant. Everyone had had his five deals, and he demanded settlement.

Arthur St. Clair was not a little chagrined. He passed out five good guineas for the company, the extra shillings in which just covered his last loo, and prepared to retire with more dignity than profit. He felt that somehow Yates had managed to deal Pam to Wully an unconscionable number of times. Mr. Yates would, of course, have been the first to deny any such sleight of hand, and Mr. St. Clair knew it. But he still felt that he had been asked to subsidize a forlorn hope and to keep quiet about it, too. Well, it was now long past midnight of an expensive evening. He pressed his lips together firmly and began to bid the company a decent but rather curt good night.

At this, although it was still much too early in the morning to announce the dawn, Wully Grant began to crow. He really looked and acted like a red male chicken, wattles and all. His luck, he felt, presaged a better day. He had five red guineas in his fist and the brandy flooded the roots of his being with the very ichor of confidence. Seeing that St. Clair was definitely out of it, Wully began to rally Yates and ended by triumphantly chanting over him like a small boy:

"I beat you at dice, sir,
    I beat you at loo;

I lay I can beat you
At baccarat-two."

The rhyme had occurred accidentally, and Wully was enchanted with
it. He repeated it again, quite offensively . . .

"I lay I can beat you
At baccarat-two."

"I'll lay thirty pounds sterling to your five and twenty you
cawnt," drawled Yates, and nervously twisted the patch on his blind
eye, always a sign of tension and that he meant business.

Grant hesitated a moment. Despite the brandy, his native Scotch
caution reasserted itself. He cocked his head to one side like a puzzled terrier considering. But it was irritating to have the potency of
his family luck still doubted and—Yates had oiled the bait skilfully.
The extra odd pounds in the hazard offered finally made Wully plunge
again. He handed the cards to Yates as the challenged party, contemptuously bade him be banker, and impatiently signed for him to
shuffle and deal.

St. Clair sat down again to watch the play. He now thought he
began to see some strategy in Mr. Yates's tactics. Mr. Patton erased
the tally for loo, set up the new bets, and ruled the lines for baccarat
on his slate. He solemnly announced the wager, his voice cracking
with excitement. He then gave Yates two more packs of new cards,
and snuffed all the candles.

Yates "milked" the three packs together and began to deal. The
evening entered upon its second and final phase, a trial by battle between champions.

None who watched the play that evening ever forgot it.

Cards are an old and strictly human accomplishment. When not
too simple a gamble, they frame-in a fascinating miniature analogy
of life itself; skill and memory in action blending with pure chance
in a technical match of character—and with the future mathemat-
ically in doubt.

"Baccarat-two," as Wully rudely called it, *baccarat á deux,* or
two-handed baccarat, is a fine, ruinous swift game of hazard. It has
a tremendous interplay of chance and skill, where skill can sometimes
predominate. Its rules were ingeniously elaborated in the palaces of
perpetually insolvent majesties whose royal rate of losses accused the
tedious utterance of their mints, whose every coin bore a portrait in
miniature of the sovereign cause of bankruptcy himself—palaces
where the raddled estates of nobles and the impounded revenues of

provinces were whisked across the clinking tables every candle-lit night. Baccarat is, therefore, a kind of royal alembic of lottery and noble catalyst of bankruptcy not to be lightly engaged in either by very civil and solvent or by merely domestic persons.

Nevertheless, the play between Lieutenant Grant and Edward Yates, Esquire, began. Both were playing for much more than either of them had, and both with great but traditionally different skills.

Lieutenant Grant had been grounded in his methods in India by certain card-devoted, bored, but careful servants of the Honourable East India Company, and he had later perfected his play with brother Scots in many a garrison club of Great Britain and the colonies where no one expected to lose. Mr. Yates, on the other hand, was a graduate of a school of baccarat that long flourished about the Inns of Court. While reading law and eating his dinners at Lincoln's Inn he had also innocently played baccarat. Finally, he had been asked to sit-in at what was then called the "Lord Chief Justice's Bench", a scandalous but enduring memorial of the gay days of mad Lord Jeffreys, with an appropriately merciless tradition. And he had done very well there, quite well indeed.

In a little less than half an hour the game of baccarat, which afterward affected so many people's lives, was over. Fortune swung back and forth. The pattern of betting repeated itself, and the stakes rose ever higher, with Yates acting as the imperturbable banker. From Yates's standpoint, the danger was that Grant would cry quits at some moment lucky for him and walk off with the bank. Yates's strategy as banker was therefore to make the prize so tempting that his opponent would always come back for one more deal. Twice Yates doubled, and lost. To cover that, and still to keep Grant hankering for more, was a heavy risk. Yet it was a certain swagger that Yates now developed which kept egging Wully on. Between avarice and caution, Lieutenant Grant was sweating. Probably, after a certain point, it was the brandy that really kept sustaining him. Or it may have been that there was so much at stake, it was win all, or ruin. The sum on Mr. Patton's slate soon registered one hundred and thirty-six pounds.

But a prime factor in the play now became progressively important. Memory. The winning of each hand now depended more and more on recollecting exactly what cards out of the three packs in use had already been played. Yates's meticulous memory now stood him in good stead. He could have called precisely all the hands that had been played that evening. Evidently Wully also could remember. But Yates felt that as the brandy began to die out Lieutenant Grant's memory might become dimmer. Yet so might his courage to stick. There was the rub. It was necessary, therefore, to seize the exact moment for the grand temptation, the instant when Grant would have only enough courage left to play one hand more. To be sure, the risk in doing this was ruinous, but that was the risk. And Yates determined to strike when he thought the instant had come.

He had a brief run of luck, and then he deliberately lost. Wully grinned and placed his hands palms down on the table, resting, and looking quizzically and triumphantly at Yates. The three onlookers were transfixed. It looked as if the evening were over. Then Yates doubled the stakes. It was a comfortable little fortune, at least from a colonial standpoint, that he now offered. Everyone knew it must be the last hand that could be played. Grant hesitated and closed his eyes. Then he slowly raised his hands off the table and took up the cards.

They played through—and Lieutenant Grant lost. Four hundred and sixty-seven pounds sterling.

Wully shot his legs out under the table and sat stricken, breathing like a bull after the first stroke of the maul.

After a moment or two Yates took the patch off his blind eye and looked at Wully, stone pupil and all. This gave more satisfaction to him than having won. There was no doubt that even Wully got the point.

"Wh-o-o-o-o," he said, his breath whistling. "I might have known better than to play wi' a Hamilton. Losh! I'm ruint! Sell my commission? 'Twon't pay ye. Those queens, the jades! All the coort was there, when what I needed was jist twa pips. Aweel—" His arms slid out on the table slowly before him, and he laid his head down amid the welter of bright new cards.

All of them looked at one another and at Yates.

It was one thing to win, but another to have reduced a strong man and a fine brutal officer to tears. No one knew exactly what to do about it.

At last Salathiel got up and walked over to the table. He looked down at Wully and then shook him by the shoulders. There was no response. "He's not weeping," he said, "he's sleeping!"

"By God, so he is," cried St. Clair, much relieved.

And indeed it was not sounds of grief that came from between Wully Grant's arms but the wheezing of a man asleep with his nose pressed close against the table.

Yates got up and snapped the black patch over his eye.

"I suggest we all make our little settlements with one another to-morrow," said he, and looked significantly at Grant.

"Good night, gentlemen," said Mr. Patton in a kind of awed whisper. "It's late indeed, but 'twas an eventful evening." He smiled deprecatingly. "I don't think I'll disturb our sleeping friend here, though 'tis truly a scene of ruin where he has laid his head." Apparently no one felt inclined to insist upon helping Lieutenant Grant to bed. Mr. Patton handed St. Clair and Yates their night-lights. "First chamber on the right after the turn on the stairs," he said. "Try not to wake the pup." He and St. Clair disappeared with their small-lights into the cavelike darkness of the stairs. Salathiel and Yates looked at each other and grinned.

"What happened just at the last? I couldn't quite follow it," said Salathiel.

"Too many court cards, and then Wully forgot that it's better to make eight with two cards than nine with three," replied Yates.

Salathiel yawned. Only the steady glow from the great backlog now threw a dim radiance through the room. Yates and he stood a moment by the table, listening to the subdued chorus of the sleepers in the straw bunks at the far end of the room and to the steady wheeze of the gentleman with his face on the table.

"Will you ever get anything out of him?" queried Salathiel. "You know, Yates, if *you* had lost, he would have hounded you to the grave. And for a while it was a near thing."

"Close as a hound's ear to his head," said Yates. Just then the pad-pad of a child's feet passed suddenly overhead. Instinctively, they both looked up.

"Sounds like young Bridget," said Salathiel.

"Listen," said Yates, taking his friend by the arm as they walked towards the porch door, "I'll collect something out of this. Tomorrow I'll get his note of hand in acknowledgment for the total sum, with witnesses, before he leaves. And this fellow boasted to me that he is a landed gentleman and his relatives well-heeled. We'll follow him straight through to Fort Loudon. Leave the rest to me. I'll make him dig up his land-office papers there. It may take a day or two, but it will pay to wait. And we'll see what we'll see.

"How would you like to join me, Sal, in bringing in settlers to the lake country in New York, or to the new colony in Florida? I rather fancy the northern lochs. Hamilton Manor, a Highland domain! And only the wild loons to laugh at us patroons. Why not? We could make a go of it there together. You won't always want to be working for St. Clair." Yates was so earnest and eager he went clear out on the porch with Salathiel. "It's a dream of mine, you know. And in this country such dreams often come true."

"I'll be with you, if you can get the land," answered Salathiel, after a little. "Iroquois country or not, you can count on me. What's a feud but a fillip? But I *must* see Philadelphia first. I want to do that, you know—and there's Melissa now."

"There'll be plenty of time for the City," said Yates. "But if the time ever comes I'll count on your promise—no matter what."

"Count on me, then," said Salathiel—"no matter what!"

Standing on the porch in the waning moonlight, they shook hands on it. Perhaps the summer of 1752 had been even more salubrious than they thought, its distilled cordiality overwhelming. Yates's candle blew out, and he teetered a little as he turned to go in.

"Damn it," said he. "Now I'll have to grope my way up the stairs in the dark." The door, however, closed quietly behind him.

Salathiel stood for a moment on the top step looking out over the interior of the stockade quite steadily. The moon was going down. A kind of grey half-light streaked with mist lent a false distance and mysterious perspective to everything. Except for the heavy breathing of Alexander, inside the wagon, an unearthly stillness and the biting chill of high mountain country in the earliest morning hours gripped the little fort. The bonfires had gone out and their ashes lay grey and still.

Evidently Croghan's Irish had departed. For some reason they had left behind them a lighted lanthorn in their shed. He could just make out its dim smoky glow. But they and their pack horses and wagons were gone.

Well, let them! he thought. To that extent Lieutenant Grant might be allowed to be successful. In another hour it would be dark as the hinges . . . he yawned at the sinking moon . . . a man did need some sleep.

He swung himself down the steps and into the wagon, wakened Alexander, and gave him a drink and a shilling. Even in the middle of the night the Highlander appreciated both.

"I'll take over now," said Salathiel, "and mind, when you go in you don't bang the door. They're all asleep in there, even Wully Grant." Alexander departed quietly after the final nip, feeling it and his shilling.

Except for unbuckling himself and throwing his pouch and tomahawk on the floor beside him, Salathiel did not undress. He crawled into his blankets, moccasins and all, and dropped off instantly. He was tired.

But "they" were not "all asleep in there", as he had said.

Upstairs some minutes before young Bridget had suddenly trotted into Melissa's room and wakened her by crawling into bed.

"I want ye, Melissa, I want ye," she whispered. "There's something awfu' going on downstairs in the darkness. I know there is. I just know it. I don't want to leave you alone with it."

"Now, darlint," said Melissa sleepily, while moving over to make room for the frightened child, "just lay your head down here and come to sleep. It's too late for any pillow talk." She put her arms around the small shivering body and comforted her.

"But, you know," said Bridget, "*I* came to take care of *you*."

The last moon shadows lengthened eastward over Patton's. The place lay locked in deep slumber. All save one poor beggar, who was still miserably awake.

8

In Which Salathiel Takes Too Clever a Hand

THERE IS AN old saying that misery loves company. But this, like so many other popular and antique versions of the laws of average human conduct, is a general statement, and there have always been special and particular exceptions to it. Actually, only *some* misery loves company. For instance:

Old hounds frequently prefer to die alone, and a wounded lion resents the vultures to the last. Hermits, who are usually quite miserable, still cry out against intruders, while the stricken rich man is seldom comforted even by the jovial company of his expectant heirs. But that misery which likes most to be alone is desperate and criminal misery. In every companion of its dangerous lot it suspects a potential Judas.

Mr. David Ap Poer, *alias* Taffy, was no exception to this last sad item in the sorry anatomy of misery and loneliness. There were times when for his own particular and peculiar reasons, no matter how miserable he was, he found it not only expedient but essential to be alone.

If fate had been kinder, Taffy in his native Wales might have been entitled to be addressed as "mister", since his father was a respectable and learnéd man who drew rents. But since Fate had been a veritable bitch to Davy, the *alias* which had been humorously conferred upon him in America was seriously earned. Not the least fitting part of it was that no one who casually addressed him as "Taffy" had any idea how genuinely appropriate his nickname was.

For "Taffy was a Welshman, Taffy was a thief"—granted. But he was not only just that. He was a skilful, an inveterate—and an ecclesiastical thief into the bargain.

David Ap Poer's specialty was robbing churches of such hansable articles of communion paraphernalia as either their rich or their royal donors had seen fit to bestow upon a prosperous and faithful congregation. This consecrated swag he invariably deposited in the grave of some departed member of the flock in the churchyard near-by. Then he himself discreetly vanished from the neighbourhood—where apparently he had never appeared—until the agony, the perplexed recriminations, and the confused hue and cry died fitfully away. And he stayed away until the mystery became as mossy as the stone under which the subject of it lay hidden.

Afterward, in due course of time and usually on a moonless night, Taffy returned with a bag. He then exhumed the reward of his dishonest labours, took it home, melted it down; and after adding a judicious amount of leaden alloy, cast it into passable counterfeits of sundry current coins.

Thus it was, first, in the judicious choice of the initial hiding place for his cache; and secondly, in his careful patience in deferring his immediate enjoyment of the proceeds that what must be conceded as, in a bad sense, the virtues of his professional methods lay. As to the first, the mortuary architecture of the period was in itself helpful; family vaults, and even solitary box- or table-graves were, for Taffy's purposes of temporary concealment, ideal. And whomsoever the bereft congregation might suspect, or wherever they might search for their vanished candelabra, chalices, and pyxes, they were not likely in either case to suspect one whose sins were long forgotten, or to look behind a door upon which a list of honest virtues was incised in stone.

So far, then, so bad.

But connected with the estimable rose of safety that the temporary deposit of his wages with the dead undoubtedly supplied, there were certain prickly disadvantages and thorny difficulties. To say that in this way, although in this way alone, Taffy undoubtedly evinced a touching trust in the discretion and honesty of by far the majority of his fellow men would be beside the mark.

For he was often hard put to it to exist in the long intervals between his thoughtful denudation of churches, to say nothing of his delay in realizing on the proceeds afterward. Only the bitterness of past harsh experience and his fond expectation of those periods of affluence and respectability which followed his final coining of opportunity provided him with the necessary will power and patience, indeed with what may be termed the essential stamina of criminal character, to persist in invariably following out his all but foolproof plan. Frequently it was hard and bitter going. But not so hard as prison, whips, or the gallows. And there were, of course, mitigating circumstances. Yet the zeniths and nadirs of his fluctuating fortunes were necessarily extreme opposites and consequently hard to survive. And, then too, in the process of rendering unto Caesar the things that were God's, still another transformation was involved.

For the transmutation of some solid and holy knick-knack into the more fluid metal of baser coin was always the prelude to a corresponding metamorphosis in his own personality. Once the new-minted money was in hand, Taffy visited some relatives in the country while he grew a delicately pointed beard and two wispy mustachios. He cleansed himself, powdered his hair, and attired in conservatively sombre yet obviously fine clothes of a genteel cut and intriguingly exotic pattern, he took ship or horse, and appeared next at some distant point in another colony, where, bandboxes and all, he put up at a fashionable inn.

Once creditably established at a respectable ordinary, it was not long before he was invited, as the genial custom then was, to leave his tavern and to visit at some near-by country seat. And as soon as the news got about of the presence in the vicinage of this eccentric but gravely charming foreigner on his literary travels, a round of hospitable invitations left him only the further choice of those local personages and mansions with whom and at which, for his own purposes, it was most expedient to stay.

For the most part he cultivated the acquaintance of those who were members of the locally established church or of the Catholic persuasion. His social accomplishments were modest but sufficient to prolong his welcome. He played chess brilliantly, cards conservatively. He never danced, but he talked well. He attended church and affected the society of the learned and the clergy, without seeming too especially to associate with the latter. He gave out that he was an Estonian nobleman of minor rank and modest estate from the island of Oesel, on travel bent while writing his memoirs. This accounted at once for his elaborately cloudy accent and his gratifying curiosity about Protestant theology and church customs, as an Orthodox Greek. Also he bore an alleged passport, containing an icon of a Russian saint for a seal, whose text was composed in an engraved script that looked like a still life of a nest of frozen worms. On the whole, his assumed character was a good lay. No one knew anything about Estonia, except what he chose to tell them. And his chance of meeting a genuine Estonian traveller in America was about the same as that of encountering a mermaid climbing a persimmon tree.

True, all this was bizarre, but it is the record rather than the enacting of it that seems improbable. Brought to life in the character of the man who played Anton Berg of Estonia, it was not only plausible, it was consummately real. For Taffy in his own mind *was* Berg of the island of Oesel. Temporarily, he had no doubt whatever about his other self. All that he did was easily in character. Consequently, no doubts were stirred in the minds of any of his temporary friends.

Perhaps—perhaps there was something intellectually strange about all this? Just enough of the convincing genius of a zany at play to take neatly the necessary tricks. Yet it was by no means completely irrational, for the cup of David Ap Poer had so often and so plentifully overflowed with misery that there was a constant compulsion upon him to become, at least temporarily, somebody else.

The person he chose to be was affluent, romantic, happy, naïve, and totally unexpected. In short, a great pleasure to David, and to everybody else. Yet it was David who cunningly planned and skilfully contrived the practical means for sending Anton Berg on his literary travels—and for his eventual return. For as Taffy he always came back later on—although secretly.

But no one, literally no one, in any of the several English colonies where Anton Berg had appeared and departed—no one who had smoked a churchwarden over a bottle of old port with him, won at cards, or been beaten in a round of chess by that brisk little foreigner had ever the remotest idea of connecting him with the inexplicable disappearance of the altar plate from St. Anne's or St. John's or the Catholic chapel, which, if they had only noticed it, invariably followed his departure by only a few weeks. And even if they had, it would not have quickened their suspicions, for always it was Taffy, poor miserable ragged Taffy who returned, both to steal and later to exhume his swag.

Four times since his arrival in America, some ten years before, had David, for purposes of enlarging the circulation of the currency, levied upon the church. Three times Anton Berg had set out for South Carolina, Virginia, and Maryland respectively, and three times had Taffy returned successfully to Philadelphia. But his fourth church robbery had in some ways been an exception, and in several of its aspects a mistake. He knew that now.

Sitting cold and forlorn, with a greasy blanket wrapped about him, in a corner behind the chimney of the north wall at Patton's, David Ap Poer had had more than enough time to consider the quirks of fortune. He muttered a little as he chewed indignantly on the last of Salathiel's bitter shag. He spat and silently cursed. Probably it had been an error to show himself at all to that tall gentleman in buckskins. No one else besides Croghan's Irish wagoners knew he was at Patton's. He had seen to that. But he had managed to reconnoitre the Albines' wagon thoroughly and quite unobserved when it had first drawn up before the door, and the prospect he saw in it was alluring. Yet he had really hoped that the tall man might give

him some money and thus save him further trouble. But no, no! Only
a handful of tobacco! And he was hungry already.

The Irish took an unconscionable time to get quietly on the
move. With a sentry in the wagon, however, that was just as well.
Above all he feared being dragged to the frontiers by those mad
Irishmen. It was lucky they had to sneak off. They would never dare
look for him now. And afterwhile no doubt the Scotch sentry would
go to sleep. Also there would be no dogs. That at least was a distinct
bit of help. So he waited and shivered, peering around the corner
of the chimney from time to time to see if the light still burned in
the big wagon. Lord, it was getting cold!

And that fourth robbery, what a fine botch he had made of it!
Oh, he could see that now. But it had been a great temptation. It
was the old Swedes' church at Wiccaco, a hamlet that was so near
Philadelphia it was really in the City now, a part of Southwark.
And thus so near home that he had not thought it necessary to go
through with the usual preliminary part of Anton Berg. Besides he
had been too poor. He needed new money. So he had just walked
out one day and looked the place over.

It was a fine old brick church with plenty of lonely ground about
it, on a neck of land near Hay Creek south of Gloucester Point. A
good many of the original Swedish settlers, all Swansons, still held
the land about there. The new stone parsonage was near-by, and it
was there that the pastor of the flock removed his church plate every
Sunday evening—and brought it back every Saturday night to
prepare for the services next day. These Swedish Lutherans had a
high ritual. Among the altar furnishings were some particularly
fine chalices and a gold cruse presented by Queen Christina herself
to her subjects in the New World, years before.

These and other particulars Taffy picked up from a garrulous
ancient named Nils Gestafson, who could remember when Philadelphia was a forest, and almost everything which had happened there
since. But he was now blind, and so Taffy talked freely with him as
he sat in the sun at the corner of his farm lane.

The result of these conversations was that late one Saturday
night Taffy left his cellar in the old cave-house on the waterfront,
where he usually slept, with a large pedlar's bag over his shoulder.
This time he intended to bring the loot back with him directly. There
would be nothing to connect him with the robbery, nothing at all.
And he was in desperate straits. It was so easy, he wondered he
had not thought of robbing the Swedes' church before. So near
home! All he did was to walk over to Southwark, pry open a door,
and fill the bag with the altar furniture.

And then it happened. He was almost taken.

Someone was returning to the church. He saw the lights coming up the lane just in time.

It would never do to be found with the loot on his back. He skipped out, pried up the flat table-stone on the grave of the relict of one Sven Schute, dropped the bag in the walled-in space, and let the stone fall back in place. Then he lit out. But the pastor's damned little Pomeranian tike took after him, and he had to brain it. He heard them shouting "Stop thief!" behind him.

And he heard more about it next day. The news was all over the City. They hadn't found the stuff. But he was badly scared, and it would never do to be seen around the Swedes' church now for months yet—maybe never. So he would just have to let the stuff lie there, a treasure without use.

In his desperation he hired himself as a waterer to Croghan's wagoners, who were just leaving town, and set out with them for the west. He meant to give them the slip at Carlisle and pose there as a returned refugee, but the Irish whisky got him. He was stone drunk at Chambersburg, and when he came to, the wagon was already halfway up the mountain and being escorted by Highlanders.

The confusion of the celebration that night at Patton's was his last chance to nip out. Without pay, of course. That was why he had risked begging from the tall frontiersman, and why he was now sitting so disconsolate at the base of the big chimney, shivering, and waiting for the light in the wagon to go out.

In a drawer in the chest at the head of the wagon there were some loose shillings. Taffy had seen them when Frances had been primping that evening just before she went into the house. She had opened the drawer to take out her comb and only partly closed it. He remembered that distinctly. He knew exactly where the money lay. Not much, only a handful, but in this God-forsaken spot it was his last, his only chance for any coin.

So he waited.

He was still waiting when Yates and Salathiel came out on the porch together. He watched Salathiel get into the wagon and saw Alexander leave. Then he waited for Salathiel to blow out the light. But there he was disappointed again, for the light was only dimmed. After a while, though, he was sure the tall man inside the wagon must be asleep.

The stockade was unearthly silent. In half an hour the moon sank behind the shoulder of the mountain and the stars blazed. The wagon still glimmered ever so faintly in the darkness. A fox barked somewhere, but no dogs replied. Now, if ever, was the time.

He moved out from the loom of the chimney slowly, painfully, but soundlessly on his rag-wrapped feet.

It had been a long and active day, a momentous evening, and a night filled with anxiety and excitement. Even the iron frame of Salathiel had succumbed to the demands of nature. The big man in the wagon, where the small whale-oil night-lamp burned dimly, slept profoundly, undisturbed by its feeble rays.

Exactly what awakened him he never knew. He had had no dreams. But suddenly—it seemed to him instantly—he was wide awake, every muscle tense, and a quivering sense of threatening danger and of someone hostile near-by an unarguable conviction in his mind. With it came the instinct to keep still. He opened his eyes only slightly. He was lying on his stomach with his head pillowed on his left arm, on the left side of the wagon.

Nothing inside the wagon had been disturbed. He could see from one end of it to the other. The hind flaps were tightly closed just as he had left them. The canvas sides were intact. His belt, tomahawk, pouch, and leather harness lay beside him on the floor, where he had thrown them. His watch ticked under the blanket. The small dim light before the mirror at the head of the wagon cast a curious fan of gold rays on the canvas roof that seemed eternally motionless. Melissa's brush, comb, and poor little fineries lay waiting on the chest-top as though they had been left there by a woman who was dead. In the mirror the reversed interior of the wagon hung suspended in grey ghost-land. Peace, silence, soft light, stillness—and the presence of . . .

Now he could smell it. Wolf-stale and hickory smoke, salty, strong, nauseously aromatic. The man must be standing almost beside him just outside the canvas wall towards the head of the wagon. He smiled grimly and relaxed. He knew who it was. He waited . . .

At last a sound. The faintest of rasping on the left wall of the wagon. The drum-tight canvas trembled slightly. Immediately opposite Frances' chest and the small flame of the light, the blade of a small knife appeared through the canvas, sawing gently to and fro, cutting the fibre thread by thread. It was about three feet from Salathiel's head, where he lay watching it. He smiled again.

The brief tension of apprehension and fear of the unknown had completely left him. Curiosity, even a certain grim amusement, had taken their place. It was not yet plain to him exactly what the beggar was after. He did not know of the shillings Melissa had left in the chest drawer. Why was the fellow cutting a hole just opposite the light?

Surely it was not the small brass lanthorn he was after. What, then? At any rate, he would make him pay dearly for the rip in the canvas. Damn him for *that,* almost six inches of a vertical cut now.

The knife was suddenly withdrawn as it reached the wooden top strake of the wagon-bed. The pupil of a brown eye gleamed for several seconds at the hole, examining what lay before it. Salathiel lay quiet, breathing slowly as though in a deep sleep. The eye disappeared.

Swiftly and silently as a swallow, Salathiel's right hand dipped behind him into the deep shadow close to the floor and disengaged Kaysinata's tomahawk from its sheath. He held it firmly on the floor with the blade up, and with his whole arm extended straight behind him.

A hand—*the* hand, which only a few hours before had hung in the air so persistently before him, yellow fingers, dirty nails, blue veins and all, came through the flap in the canvas, and, as though it had a life and intelligence of its own, began to feel its way carefully across the top of the chest.

The arm that followed it was long, thin as and twisted like a leather rope.

The hand crept across the chest directly under the light. The fingers explored before it, they stopped to set Melissa's brush and then her comb aside. Once it picked up a ribbon, fingered it, and laid it down. Presently the fingers went over the chest edge, grasped the knob of the small top drawer and slid it forward. Then they groped for some time in the darkness. There was not a sound. But they were picking up, busy.

There was something entirely uncanny about this. Salathiel felt that he was looking at a disembodied hand. A thing acting of and by itself. He entirely forgot the man behind it. In the fierce concentration of the moment he thought and dealt directly with the hand alone.

It began to withdraw after a while, a long while, it seemed, clutching something. It began to slide cautiously backward after the arm and across the streak of light. Now he understood. It was a hand full of shillings, several of which obtruded edgewise between the fingers and flashed briefly under the light. The hand was almost to the canvas now.

At the precise instant when the wrist was on the wooden rail of the wagon strake, he struck.

His arm and tomahawk flashed a complete arc from floor to rail, a blow of fearful force instinctively calculated. Steel bit through the bone and quivered in the wood. He let the hatchet stand there. It seemed to Salathiel as though the carved bone handle ought to hum.

But the astonishing thing was that, except for the single thud of the axe, outside for a long time there was not a sound, not a squeal or a whimper.

He was standing up now, ready for anything, listening . . .

Finally came a gasp. Then the swift pad-pad of muffled feet— and they were gone.

That was all. He reached forward and pulled Kaysinata's little axe out of the wood.

Then he went swiftly to the rear of the wagon, untied the flaps, and looked out.

Nothing but starlight and the white rime of a new frost on the grass. He bent down and examined the ground close by the wagon. The frost by the left side had been considerably disturbed. A trail of blurred patches in the grass led around the corner of the house. The man had been running, leaping apparently.

Strong enough for that, eh? he thought. Well, the fellow would have something to occupy him besides coming back to make more trouble. There was blood down the side of the wagon, but little or none he could find in the darkness on the grass. He wiped the side of the wagon off with some tinder rags. Tomorrow the trail in the frost would be gone. It would vanish in a few minutes, in fact. Nobody need ever know. Much better for Melissa not to be worried by this. He would just keep it to himself. But he would speak to her about keeping that chest drawer locked. Shillings were not so easily come by as all that! Hereafter . . .

A vixen yapped twice from a thicket down the road.

And so—that stinking white he-fox would have robbed the wagon, robbed Melissa of her little stocking-gift!

A rabbit shrieked—or was it a rabbit? He stood listening a moment, and yawned. Time for a little more sleep yet. The owls were still hunting.

He stepped back into the wagon—and saw the hand looking at him from the side by the rail, poised on the flat chest-top like a spider in the lamplight. The fingers had contracted. It was standing up now. It must have moved!

Damn that crab out of hell! Away with it.

He turned swiftly and dropped it into the salt box. Covered it up, out of sight.

Salt was expensive, but Melissa must never see a thing like that, not in her condition. He wiped off the top of the chest carefully, put the scattered shillings back in the drawer and looked about him. Ah, yes, one thing—one thing more.

He got out his darning kit and carefully and neatly stitched up the rent in the canvas.

Now, by God, that *was* all!

It was sleep now or sit up until morning all alone. It would be light soon enough now, he thought. He blew out the lamp and crawled in under his blankets gratefully. The last thing he heard was Captain Ecuyer's watch eating time under his blanket-roll.

It was a full hour later when some dogs far up the road at Sugar Cabins began to bay. He never heard them at all, nor the roosters crowing a little later for false dawn.

Sunrise comes late in November. The year is near its close.

9

Correspondence and Farewells

WHEN SALATHIEL looked out of the rear of the wagon next morning he realized that he had done what he had seldom done before, overslept himself. The sun was already over the top of the mountain, coming up out of smoking wreaths of mist, and even as he watched the whole place was a mad glitter of light.

"Never saw anything like it, did ye, young fellow?" said Mr. Patton, who was standing on the porch smoking his morning pipe, with one hand in his pocket and surveying the interior of the stockade with an air of proprietary pride.

"Thar's been a first-class dew-freeze. Hoarfrost, they still calls it, downcountry. Best one I ever see."

Salathiel whistled with polite surprise. Everything on the small plateau or shoulder of the mountain where Patton's stood looked as though it had been embossed in a glaze of silver and pearls by some mad magician during the darkness. Every grass stalk, leaf, and flower stem, all the trees, the rim of the stockade itself, and the peach orchard beyond the gate were crusted with billions of twinkling diamond points. The wagon, especially the wheels and hubs, was a thing of indescribable silver beauty. A small thicket half a mile down the road blinked and blazed with the flashing arcs of innumerable prisms. The buckets and barrels, every domestic article—no potentate had ever possessed their like. The pearly roads and paths winked.

" 'Twon't last long," said Mr. Patton. "Must have been a cold wester crept down the ridge this mornin'. But it's going to be a wonderful day. And no snow yet! There hasn't been a season like this since 'fifty-eight. If it keeps up they're like to have St. Martin's summer in the vales below till pretty nigh Christmas. I've seen it that way before. Look, she's changin' already."

Even as he spoke the magic silver frosting began to fade. A cloudy blackness seemed to pass here and there over the grass, everything trickled and ran. The woods smoked. Only in the cold shadow of the house a small patch of the silversmith's handiwork remained, outlining even the clover leaves with water pearls. The wagon still glittered.

"It's a fine place you've got here, Mr. Patton," said Salathiel. "You must have been here a long spell for all the stumps to be outen the fields."

"Some of it was natural glades to begin with," replied Patton, "but we've been here nigh five and thirty years come next May Day. Granddad came in with the Chambers brothers to Falling Spring in the valley below. Yes, sir, 'tis a bit of Eden we have here through Path Valley, Amberson's, and the Coves. They were settled early by determined and discerning people. Your friend, Pendergass, came in a long time past, you'll recollect. But there was Marylanders with stone houses here long before him. If it hadn't been for the Injuns—" Mr. Patton sighed, and blew a cloud of smoke into the morning air.

"My folks came in with Garrett Pendergass," said Salathiel.

"Now, did they!" exclaimed Patton. "Oh, yes, I did hear you was carried off. By the Shawnees, wasn't it?"

Salathiel nodded.

"Well, Bouquet has settled accounts with them, I reckon," replied Patton. " 'Spect we won't have to have garrisons here much longer. Times are comin' when a man can really farm in peace, maybe." His clear blue eyes seemed to look far into the distance over his pipe, almost as though he saw palm trees on the horizon.

Salathiel looked about him again. It was amazing how different Patton's looked by daylight. Except for the stockade, the military features of the place now seemed to be nil.

It was quiet. The crowd had vanished. A few of the coloured servants and an old Indian or two stalked back and forth between the farm sheds, feeding the horses and stock. A squaw came out to the suck-pump to draw water. White smoke ascended from the chimney of the house into the calm morning air, until the sunlight struck it through and through high above the roof. It spoke of breakfast and all the comforts withindoors. The only reminder of the frontier was the big shed at the far west end of the enclosure, where the platoon of Highlanders were gathered about a large kettle getting their oatmeal porridge. Some were playing leapfrog, happy and exhilarated in the high mountain air. They shouted like boys. The fevers of the Indies were far behind and long forgotten. Their tartans flamed bravely as they leaped. How incongruous their presence here seemed. For the first time they looked foreign to him. This was a farm. Roosters crowed, and horses whinnied and stomped in the big stone barn. The lanthorn in the shed, where Croghan's Irish had left it, still burned behind a sooted glass.

"Yep," said Patton, "they've all gone. Must be pretty nigh to Bedford by now, or even past it. Well, that's a damn good riddance. And glory be, liken our friend, Wully, and his hungry Scots will be lightin' out for Fort Loudon sometime early today. They eat us out of house and home, and besides they're slow-payin' king's men," he shrugged his shoulders. "But come in, come in and have a bite yourself. I'm blattin' away like an old gaffer, as the missus would say, and you're young and hungry."

"I am that," admitted Salathiel. "I'll be with you directly."

He strolled over to the pump, pulling his shirt off, and began dowsing his head and bare shoulders in the stream of cold well-water that dashed from its spout. What a clever thing a pump was! He'd have one. He looked through the bright drops of water at the cheerful sunshine and the mountain rising steep and green before him up the road through the gate. The last short haul! That was all he had to make and he would be out of the woods. He paused a second. He thought he heard an echo of someone calling his name . . . pshaw! . . . God, he felt fine, glowing all over. Melissa must see the wagon before the sun struck it. The top was beginning to run off now.

He sprang to the door and opened it, "Lissa, Lissa," he called, "come out and see your silver chariot—hurry! And here's a posy for you all covered with pearls."

From where she was sitting sewing by the fire with Mrs. Patton, Frances rose smiling and, followed by young Bridget, ran lightly out onto the porch.

"Look," he said, "look," pointing to the wagon and trundler that still glittered like solid silver with the fast-fading frost. "And here, look at this!" He reached down and plucked a spread of clover that grew about the Pattons' porch.

"Fawncy now," said Melissa, her grey eyes veiling with pleasure as he slipped an arm about her waist and held her close—"fawncy, a set of shamrocks and all covered with pearls!" She fastened them in her belt and smiled up at him. "Fit for the Queen of Ireland," she whispered. "Fit for you," he said. For an instant a rainbow in the clover leaves winked as they looked down at them. Then suddenly the leaves turned black and the droplets of water ran down over her skirt like tears.

"Sure, 'tis a fairy fraud you've wished on me," cried Melissa, and laughed ruefully.

"Never mind . . ." he began.

"Hello, big man, hello," insisted Bridget, grasping him about the leg. "I'm here, too. And I'm agoin' to Carlisle with you, in the big wagon with the bells and the grey horsies."

"Are ye now, *are* ye?" asked Salathiel, a bit doubtfully, looking at Melissa.

"She certainly *is*," cried Melissa. "Come in and let Mrs. Patton talk to you about it. We're sewin' on her things and packin' 'em up now."

"Kind o' seems to be settled, then," laughed Salathiel.

"I'm a lady, and I'm goin' to help ye," insisted Bridget. "I kin make the beds, I kin. All but the big bolsters. An' I know how to sew. I'm no poor squaw."

"I believe ye, little one," said Salathiel, picking her up. "You're a useful piece."

"That's what the McQuiston said when I was with Lieutenant Francis and her," said Bridget.

"*Uh, huh,*" said Salathiel, wondering at the familiar names.

They went in together, and Mrs. Patton looked up smiling from putting a hem in a small skirt.

Old Bijou, the coloured woman, was frying something in deep fat that crackled. The flames leaped and snapped cheerfully.

The lower part of the room was already hazy with morning tobacco smoke. The subalterns and sergeants were finishing their breakfasts. Yates and Wully Grant were laughing together over a table, apparently with the greatest of good nature, as if nothing at all had happened between them the night before. St. Clair sat leaning back, much amused, evidently with a full breakfast under his vest, upon which he jingled his watch fobs and little keys. Premonitory sobs and squeals from the bagpipe, which the piper was furbishing and adjusting, brought occasional answering low howls from Bran. Between-times his tail kept knocking a constant tattoo on the floor in a rhythm that somehow expressed for him, and for all the rest of the company, the general air of satisfaction and good morning cordiality that now pervaded the place.

"Sit down and have your breakfast, 'Captain' Albine," said Mrs. Patton. "You've had a good sleep, I hope. Land, but you men were late last night, weren't you?" Her eyes twinkled, "But sit while I draw a dish of tay. You like it? I've got somewhat to talk to you about. It's the new member of your family. I mean"—she nodded towards Bridget—"at least she will be for a while. You'd best know all about her that I can tell you, so you can pick up her folks later when you get to Carlisle."

"Sukey," shouted Mrs. Patton, "some crumpets, hominy, pork

chops and potatoes for the captain. Tell Bijou to look alive." The squaw shuffled off. "Here's your tay, sir. No, no, pour it in your saucer." She laughed, a little, embarrassed at correcting him. He drank the tea off gratefully. It was real Bohea.

"Just before you begin, Matilda," interrupted Mr. Patton, "I thought we might ask the Albines to stay over a few days with us. Over the Sabbath at least. You know the Reverend McArdle is holding a stump preaching up at Aughwick, him and his reverend helper —what's-his-name, the garrison clergyman from Fort Bedford. If they stay that would give you and Mistress Albine a chance to catch up on the youngster's clothes here. And we'd like you to stay . . ."

"Thanks, thanks," said Salathiel somewhat hurriedly, putting down his saucer of smoking tea. "But we must be getting on. I once sat at the feet of Mr. McArdle somewhat extensive, you might say. He's a powerful preacher," he drawled. "I didn't know he'd been ridin' a woods circuit. Many people rally in to hear him?"

"Crowds from all over. Wagons when they kin or just horseback. The spirit sweeps 'em." replied Patton.

"Hm," said Salathiel, genuinely disturbed to hear that McArdle was so near. What would he say if he saw Melissa? No, no, that would never do!

"We'll be pushing on this morning, sir," he said finally. "Mrs. Albine is a Catholic, you know—and we'd best go down the mountain with the troops as far as Loudon, seein' they're goin' back that way. Thar's always a chance of a war party, and that when you least expect it. I won't feel cocksure till I get clean to Carlisle."

"Reckon that's good sense," said Patton. His wife evidently agreed. She was disconcerted at hearing that Frances was a Catholic. She might have thought of it, she told herself. Old Ireland!

"Bridget is a Presbyterian," she began quite unexpectedly, and then bit her lip with vexation.

"Madam, I'll *never* lift a finger to unsettle her faith," exclaimed Frances Melissa, her cheeks flaming.

A general embarrassment fell on the company. Bridget sat wide-eyed on Melissa's knee. She knew well enough she was being talked about. Yes, indeed she was a Presbyterian. Her ma had said . . .

"Darlin', run out with the boys and play on the porch, and take that pup along. He's a-badgering Bran," said Mrs. Patton. The child departed gravely, looking back once or twice.

"She's that biddable," continued Mrs. Patton, "but little pitchers, you know. Poor baby! About all we can make out about her is that her folks must have been gentle people, lived somewhere down in the valley, Shenandoah country, though what fork, of course, I don't know. Well, it's the old story. Her pa was ploughin' one day when the Indians burst out on him from the woods. 'Pears that he and some of the nigger boys put up a fight in an old tobacco shed, but they burned that over their heads. Mrs. McCandliss and young Bridget and a baby boy were dragged off west through the woods. Seems that all the poor woman could do was to snatch up the baby and a Bible from her burning house. Delawares, I hear they were. Maybe a mixed party of frontier scum. Anyway, they later put the little boy to the hatchet, and Mrs. McCandliss was terrible hurt trying to save him. She must have been dying, for she gave the Bible to young Bridget and told her to sneak off down the stream when they made camp that night. Bridget was to keep on wading in the branch as far as she could. Then she was to go through the woods in the direction where the sun came up the first morning, until she found white friends. She told the child she would certainly find friends on the third day.

"I reckon that's about as far as she thought the child would last, anyway. Or maybe she had second sight at the last moment and prophesied. The really wonderful thing is that a little girl so young as Bridget was then would understand and do exactly as she was told.

"It was just a little while after the fight at Bushy Run when it happened, early fall, if I remember right. And sure enough, it seems it was the third day after she ran away from those red devils that Lieutenant Francis found her when he was bringing downcountry some of the first of the freed captives from Fort Pitt. That Mc-Quiston gal he carries on with was riding with him, all tricked out fine as a London lady, when she looks up and sees a wisp of dress caught in a blackberry patch on the side of a hill near the road. 'Twas no more than ten miles west of here. And there that baby was, half the clothes dragged off her by the brambles and her poor little body all scratched like she had been flogged, and her face smeared with blood and blackberry juice, but still clutching her little Bible.

"But do you think she'd forgot her manners? No, sir, when they washed her off in the stream and the McQuiston puts her shawl around her and pops a bit of biscuit dipped in wine into her mouth, the first thing Bridget says is, 'My ma said you'd come. She's Mrs. McCandliss, and she wishes to thank you.' And I'll swan, if she didn't make them a curtsy, and then fall down.

"All Bridget knows is she kept coming through the woods after she left the branch she waded down the first night, and she spent two more nights and climbed a little tree each time. She said she saw beasts with eyes that burned in the night. Well, I wouldn't doubt it.

"I will say, too, that the McQuiston was mad about her and wanted to take her on to Philadelphia. But Lieutenant Francis wouldn't hear of it. Not that he wasn't soft about the child, too.

But he as much as said that the house he was setting up for the McQuiston in the City would be no place to nurture a young child in, and would I please keep her until he could find out who her people were. He said he felt sure they were gentle folk.

"And then there was that Bible with the family names in it. It's the smallest Bible I ever saw," remarked Mrs. Patton, rummaging in the basket of clothes before her and pulling it out. "Here you are, but you can't make out much about people just from their names."

"Oh, a good deal more than you might think, Matilda," said Mr. Patton. "It does take time, but Lieutenant Francis was pretty clever about it. He advertised Bridget in the list of captives being returned from the frontiers by Colonel Bouquet to Carlisle, and sure enough he found the child's grandmother. She seems to be a pious and decent woman and must have come all the way from Boston to Carlisle to search for the child. But judge for yourself. Here's her letter Lieutenant Francis sent on only a few weeks ago. I writ her, of course, and she must have mine by now. Jim Fergus carried it back."

Salathiel took the neatly folded double-paged letter in his hands with considerable curiosity and feeling. It amused him to think that Bustle McQuiston had taken a fancy to young Bridget first—and now Frances Melissa was eager to take her to Carlisle. It might be just as well if those two girls never met. He could sense trouble in that—over the little one, of course. He grinned.

But they were looking at him. They might think he couldn't read . . .

Carlisle Prv.º Penn—Sylvania
3rd Sept'mb'r—1764

To Mr and Mrs Patton at Fort Lyttleton on the Glades Road beyond Chambersburg.

’Tis the maternal grandmother of the orphan child, Bridget McCandliss, who ventures thus to address the charitable Mr and Mrs Patton at the behest of the Honourable Lieutenant Francis of the Royal American Regiment, mutually and favourably known to us all.

Dear Sir, and dear Madam,

Oh, may the blessings of Charity and Mercy which you have so liberally and tenderly bestowed on this, I fear motherless lamb, be returned to you seven-fold by the same Divine Spirit that prompted your noble acts.

I would that I could anticipate on Earth the reward which will be yours in Heaven, my dear Sir and Mistress Patton, but I am a poor woman, old, a widow these many years, and I have nothing to send you but my fervent blessing and the request that you send the child to *me*. And what little is left of my small competence, after the dreadful expense of coming here to Carlisle from Boston, shall be lavished upon the care of this babe, the last of all the sweet little ones of my blood, saved it seems as by a miracle of the God of Mercy himself from a living death with the savages.

'Tis now ten years since my pretty young 'Dosia married handsome young John McCandliss of Port Tobacco in Maryland. They removed from that place to the Valley of Virginia six years since. The news of the calamity which hath overwhelmed this little family flew to me on cruel swift wings, as the news of evil doth, but it was many a long day before a word of hope followed. Had I not seen a chance copy of the *Pennsylvania Gazette* by the good offices of one of my neighbors of the numerous Franklin family here, I should never have known of Bridget's salvation.

I sold my small house and came to Carlisle where I met and have talked with that gay and comfortable gentleman, Lieutenant Francis. I know he hath writ you of our meeting. And now this is to beg you to send on the lost lamb that was found with all the speed ye may. For I am laid up here by an aggravated stiffness in my lower joints and cannot endure the cruel joltings of waggons no more, or I would fly to her; so I beg of you, delay not as soon as you can find some fitting company to care for her this way.

And I will do the rest, and bless you all my remaining days and bear witness for you hereafter amongst the elect. But haste I beg you, good Mr and Madam Patton, haste, for my poor pen doth much o'er leap my fond anticipation and, I fear, the bounds of courtesy too, in the urgency of my affection. My eyes overflow when I think of you and how I am so near my little Bridget and yet so far as is. Your humble much gratified and obliged servant,

Theodosia Larned

p. scriptum—A mighty company of the captivated from the western frontier set free by that good soldier, Colonel Bouquet, are gathering in this place. Here are daily and hourly incidents would wring tears from a stone. Can you not send me Bridget by one of the now frequent downcountry convoys? Provisions be mortal scarce in this town. Inquire for me at Mr. Campion Honeywell's on the Commons. Send there also. This rides west by Jim Fergus, his kindness.

Now, as he read this, an astonishing thing happened to Salathiel. Tears flowed down out of his eyes. At the words "living death with the savages" he was touched to the quick, and he neither cared nor tried to conceal his ungovernable emotion. It now seemed a miracle to him that he also had escaped this living death, but how nearly! He would show his gratitude to his Maker by kindness to this child. He now recalled his light promises to her of the night before with a glow of satisfaction. "Always" was what he had said, and now he was glad and hoped it would be that way. Looking down into the basket of little clothes the women had been preparing so tentatively for the child's departure, he understood how much hung on his decision—and looking up again he saw how all of them were equally touched by his own emotion and respected him for it.

"Make ready," he said huskily. "I'll make her the new little shoes. We'll take Bridget to her grandma. And when I raise the new rooftree, we'll make a place at the hearth for her, too—won't we, Melissa?"

"Sure and I knew the great heart of you would find room for her," said Melissa, hugging his arm in happiness. "Maybe, she'll be a playmate for our own soon," she whispered. So it was settled.

He rose from the bench suddenly very happy and with all the good feeling of doing right. Mr. Patton came over and shook him by the hand.

"No words can thank ye," he said. "We've had Bridget here for nigh two years now, until she's like one of our own. It'll be a sore loss for Matilda, but we have no right to keep Bridget from her own flesh and blood. Now you'll write and let us know, won't ye? Our hearts will follow after you downcountry."

"I'll let you hear, sir, you can rely on it. And you'll be seeing Bridget again, I opine."

"I have little doubt of it," said Patton. "We'll pay ye a visit when ye get well settled. Ye'll be findin' many of the brethren in the city, and I'll come down for the Grand Lodge when I can. I'll write the Worshipful Master." They gave each other a fraternal clasp. "Matilda," said Mr. Patton, "call the child in now. This company will soon be goin'. The time has come."

"Aye, Wee-um," she said, and went to the door to bring the children in. They heard her calling from the porch, "Sam, Rodney, Bridg—*et*," and on the last name her voice broke.

Whatever was the nature of the conversation that had been going on over the breakfast fragments between Mr. Yates and Lieutenant Grant, the result seemed to be mutually satisfactory, for Wully Grant now rose up, apparently reassured, his usual callosity of temperament restored to all its normal overconfident, red-cheeked vigour, to judge by the bull-voiced and overbearing tones in which he now began to bellow directions to his subalterns to get the damned detachment lined up and prepared to leave for Fort Loudon.

Yates passed a wink of amusement and reassurance to Salathiel as they went out together down to the barn to look after securing the horses.

"You would think," said Yates, "that it was the subalterns who had been delaying Wully. For their part, they would rather have marched hours ago. If the news of the Irish having slipped west with the trade goods gets about this neighbourhood before the troops leave, there may be trouble. They would be better off at Loudon."

"What conclusion did your Grace, and his Majesty's representative in these parts arrive at in the matter of the little affair at cards last night?" demanded Albine.

"Oh, Lieutenant Grant is quite willing to settle his gambling debts with his cousin James's land. He gave me his written acknowledgment. And I let him keep the guineas he won from St. Clair. It may result in broader acres for us later on. Hard coin is a' that matters wi' Wully."

"Did ye now!" said Salathiel, astonished. "You really want that land bad, don't you?"

"Yes," said Yates, "and I'll bear down hard when it comes to making the papers out at Loudon. No compromise then!" He smacked one hand in the other. "Land grants are my speciality, you know."

"How will he arrange the matter with Cousin James?" inquired the curious Mr. Albine.

"I know not, nor do I care," said Yates. "That's strictly a Grant family affair. If Wully can transfer valid title, that's all I need to know."

They met Alexander and still another Alexander emerging from the big barn with the wagon horses all rubbed down, glistening and prancing in the bright sunshine and the brisk mountain air.

"Glad to do your Honour a sma' favour any time," said the big Highlander. "I hope I'll be watchin' the wagon for you again. I thought maybe you might hae a wee doch-an-dorris wi' me and Andrew before this severe march doon the mountain begins. The horses have had a bit more oats in their drench than the landlord himsel' might have measured ye. Fine grey beasties they be," said he, smacking the neck of the leader, which laid back his ears at the stranger's hand.

"There goes the pibroch the noo!" exclaimed Andrew. "Whuzz-Bang Wully will be awa at last."

The sound of the bagpipe skirling from the front porch for the assembly made the horses uneasy and inclined to rear. However, with the assistance of his two Highland friends, Salathiel soon had them harnessed to the wagon.

The rawhide harness had been newly oiled and the big brass buckles and brazen hearts, which each horse wore on his breast strap, had been brightly polished. The reins, rubbed pliable with neat's-foot oil, coiled easily through Salathiel's hands as he drew them through the brass rings on collar and dashboard. So much early-morning solicitude on the part of the two Alexanders deserved to be rewarded. He coiled the four pairs of reins over the runnels to avoid untimely snarling, dashed a few buckets of water from the pump over the wheels and the sides of the wagon, thus obliterating the last possible traces of the affair of the night before, and after snaffling the bridle of the off leader to a ring on the front rail, invited the two Scots into the wagon for a parting drink.

The jug gurgled generously several times. Pure white, but aged and smooth, the corn liquor set their hearts aglow. They drank to luck. Then a silent one, standing, to the memory of "the little captain" (Ecuyer), and a final swallow to meeting again. Then with many a "good fortune to your honour, and guid faring wi' your bonny lassie" they leaped out of the back, their kilts flying, to run nimbly and take their places in the ranks, as the detachment formed-up facing the porch awaiting the final appearance of Lieutenant Grant and the word to march.

Salathiel looked at these Highlanders fondly. He had been through a bloody siege, frontier forays, and night and day life-and-death affairs with them. It seemed strange that, after all, he was not going to be marching off to Fort Loudon with them today. The life of garrisons had for a long time been tangled with his own. Nothing could ever erase the respect and affections of the past.

There they stood silent, impassive, a long row of kilts and bonnets, claymores and gorgets glittering, brown Besses grounded. The spontoons of the two young officers rose like silver fleur-de-lis above the heads of the rear rank. The piper stood, pipes slung and mouth ready, two paces to the right on the flank. Grants, Campbells, Mac-Donalds, and Grahams blazed and glittered in the morning sunlight of the Alleghenies, *Caledonia invictrix*—a living sword of the British crown.

Given good leaders nothing would stop them. With them at Bushy Run, Bouquet had broken the ring of savages; broken through forever into the country where the rivers ran west. And now they were using these soldiers to keep the people from settling the frontiers. What was wrong? he wondered. Didn't they know what they were doing, these men in London, trying to make a hunting preserve of all the huge country west of the mountains—a park for the fur trade with these soldiers as gamekeepers; when the people, when everybody in the colonies was hungry for land?

That was where real trouble might come, as he saw it. There might be a fight someday about that if they kept on. As for these stamps the lawyers were talking about, he'd have to inquire into that matter a little further. It seemed a rather trivial affair. Maybe it would all blow over. Lawyers and politicians always talked hotter than other people. And then, there was one thing that was certain. There was endless land. What a pity, then, to be using these fine fellows as bailiffs, and making them unpopular. He shook his head doubtfully at so perplexing a drift in events. No doubt, too, certain people had high and mighty attitudes that were irritating . . .

The door opened and the strident, overbearing tones of Lieutenant Grant, making life miserable for Sergeant MacPhearson, robbed the air of peace and the morning sunshine of its happy promise. Whatever the sergeant had done, it was probably not a crime, and no man should speak to another man like that.

In the end it simply proved to be Wully Grant's harassing way of giving an order to march. "Back to Loudon, awa wi' ye," he bawled, and came out on the porch red-faced, his claymore clanking—only to find the detachment already drawn up and waiting.

Most of the people on the Patton place had gathered to see the regulars depart. About twenty persons, men, women, and children; Indians, Negroes, and whites of various kinds and degrees, stood back a little distance from the porch and watched silently. The Pattons and their guests came out and stood along the porch rail.

Wully mounted his shaggy nag, lurching indignantly into the saddle. "I'll see ye at Loudon the morrow nicht," he said to Yates sullenly. He saluted Mr. Patton a mite morosely, and roared a command.

The line wheeled into column of four, the pipes skirled. Bran sat on his haunches and howled. The crowd watched without moving and without comment until the last file, white knees flashing and kilts flaunting, rounded the corner of the stockade gate. "Bluebells of Scotland" piped its way eastward up the road towards Sugar Cabins and the ridge. Now and then wild bursts of the shrill music came back more clearly, but always more softly and with the fading melancholy of lengthening distance.

A sudden cheerfulness and lack of tension seemed to flow back into the stockade. The king's men were gone! Everyone turned and went about his business. The children commenced to play. The work of the day began. After all, Patton's was a farm.

Two young Indian boys began to help load the wagon with Melissa's little horsehide bag, the willow basket containing Bridget's clothes, and sundry small packages wrapped in woven grass mats containing the offerings of Mrs. Patton and her family: brown eggs, clover honey, a loaf of maple sugar, hams, and a leaden canister of London tea.

"Way-gifts, way-gifts," said Mrs. Patton with tears in her eyes, refusing to be thanked for them.

Salathiel found her standing on the steps with Frances Melissa, who had pushed her bonnet back on her shoulders and was looking up earnestly with a clear sweetness of expression, listening to Mrs. Patton's last affectionate torrent of well wishes and good advice.

Bridget stood by, holding Melissa determinedly by the hand, her long heavy brown braids coming out of her fur hood. She was wide-eyed with suppressed excitement at leaving, but was also finding the parting with the Pattons an unexpected misery. In fact, up until now she had thought of it scarcely at all. Now she was leaving them— going away! Only her grey kitten would go with her, only the cat out of all the warmth and comfort that she had known and taken for granted for so long.

Even that young animal, wise in its own way, sensed the threat of imminent change in its surroundings, and the strength of fate. Thrusting its head out of the hole in the top of the small woven basket in which Bridget was carrying it, it mewed piteously, laid back its ears, and scratched.

Young Sam and Rodney, balanced precariously on the porch rail, wriggled in nervous misery. "Sis is goin' away. Sis is goin' downcountry," blubbered Rodney. "Our sis is goin' away!"

"Shut up you—you little . . ." Seeing his father's eye upon him, Sam didn't dare use the work *raca* to his brother, which the Scriptures forbade. Instead, he fell off the rail onto the porch floor and lay there crying miserably. Bridget stood shaking now, her brown eyes brilliant with tears.

"Good-bye, Sammy, good-bye," she whispered. At that Sam took his head off his arm and looked up at her and smiled.

"Good God," said St. Clair, "do they take to each other so young as that? I'd forgotten."

The mounting emotion indeed was now uncomfortable.

Mrs. Patton gave Melissa a peck on the neck. The Irish girl suddenly snatched Bridget up, kitten, basket and all, and turned her back on the porch to let the child see the wagon.

"Look at the brave horses, me love," said she, "look at them standin' there lookin' wise with their blinkers on them, all leanin' forward a bit ready to go."

She whisked Bridget towards the rear of the wagon, glancing up at Mrs. Patton with a swift tender smile as she passed under her. There were tears in the older woman's eyes. Frances thrust Bridget into the wagon, and once inside herself, pulled the rear curtains across. The two sat together in the half-twilight under the canvas, listening.

"If that's money you're fumblin' in your pouch for, young man," said the grave voice of Mr. Patton, "I'll have the hide offen ye, big as ye air, if ye even show it to me. What kind of people do ye think we be?"

"Oh, the best in the world," said Salathiel, dropping his louis d'or back amid the scalps, and suddenly taking Mr. Patton's hand and crushing it.

"Enough, enough!" cried Mr. Patton, wringing his fingers. "I'd not be able to make change for ye now."

St. Clair and Yates laughed.

"We'll see you in Philadelphia come June, then," said Yates to Mr. Patton, as he and St. Clair mounted.

"Yes, I think I'll come to the City with the missus when Bouquet marches downcountry in the summer. Maybe he'll march earlier. Maybe it'll be April or May, if the rumours hold true."

"Until then—" said St. Clair.

The two gentlemen rode forward to the rail and both took off their hats together to Mrs. Patton.

"Madam," said St. Clair, "I'm mortal obleeged to ye for a more than royal entertainment."

"In that sentiment," said Mr. Yates, "I wish to jine, but for a native entertainment, for a Pennsylvanian—nay, for a Philadelphian welcome. It was worthy of the City itself."

The two gentlemen leaned forward slightly in their saddles, and replaced their hats.

Mrs. Patton, her face shining with domestic pride justified, swept them a low curtsy from the porch as they galloped off.

Quite unexpectedly the wagon teams pulled loose and bolted after the two horsemen across the green parade.

Shouting a decidedly less ceremonious farewell, Salathiel leaped after the thundering wagon, and with considerable difficulty managed to vault into the seat and take over the reins. Luckily the turf was smooth and the curve to the road gradual. As it was, the trundler skidded and grazed the gate of the stockade. The big portal post cracked, and the splinters flew.

"Mercy, mercy me, Wee-um," cried Mrs. Patton. "I'm not sure you were right after all about those people. Look at that!"

"Time alone will tell, mother," said Patton, putting his arm about his wife as they turned to the door and went in. "You know, I'm never *plumb* sure about anything. But I still think we've done right."

"No, no, Mr. Patton," said his spouse, a little breathlessly, "you never was an obstinate man. I never did say that."

She sat down and wiped her eyes on her apron. Bridget was gone. She had always wanted a daughter, and her bowels yearned after the child.

Bran came and put his head in her lap. She wondered if he knew. Would they stop to see her cousin Burd at Lancaster? She hoped so. Colonel Burd had married a Shippen. She would like Bridget to see a great house like theirs. The Burds were so rich, and so very, very, very genteel.

10

In Which an Obstacle Is Surmounted

WHAT WITH ONE thing and another it had been nearly ten o'clock when Wully Grant had finally given the command for his Highlanders to march. It was half after ten when the wagon had so unexpectedly flashed out of the stockade gate—and a full five minutes later before Salathiel got the bits out of the teeth of the two lead horses, by dint of much jaw sawing, and the whole cavalcade settled down to a regular and decidedly chastened trot.

He had used the whip on the outside leader, the big gelding that was half a stallion yet, it seemed. He blamed him for bolting. That horse would still bear some watching, he thought.

> Two black feet and a yellow eye
> Let the lash come ever nigh . . .

He hummed this snatch to himself, one he had picked up from the wagoners at Bedford, with considerable satisfaction at having directly confirmed it.

What a start! And he had meant to be *so* careful. Luckily the road was all turf and moss here, and a steady upgrade straight through the brown-leafed woods so quiet now in the lee of the big ridge that loomed just beyond.

Already it was beginning to get unseasonably warm, a fine Indian summer day. Sugar Cabins should be just ahead, around the next shoulder. Probably St. Clair and Yates would wait for him there. How they did ride when they cut loose!

All this he kept telling himself just to put off looking around into the wagon behind. He wondered how Melissa and the child had come through the wild start. If anything had broken loose back there in the wagon—if one of the big chests had shifted . . .

And then he heard Bridget laughing, a steady, amused, giggling laugh, with long ripples of pure childish merriment in it like a small waterfall tumbling over pebbles.

"God bless her," he said, and turning about, raised up the canvas and looked behind.

Bridget was sitting in Ecuyer's swing chair, kicking her heels. As she surged with the slow motion of the wagon, the cat, shut in its willow basket, emitted a series of growls punctuated by an occasional sharp feline explosion. It was such a miniature rage that somehow it was side-splitting. Melissa was laughing, too.

Just then he caught her eye. For an instant she frowned at him. "*So* you let them get away from you at the very start, Mr. Albine," she said severely. "And wasn't I after tellin' ye only yesterday 'twas high time you took over the reins? And now *listen* to what you've done."

A fizzing yowl worthy of a small panther came shrieking out of the basket.

Young Bridget dissolved, the corners of her eyes turned upward like twin moons. Frances leaned back and joined in. He grinned at the sheer silly happiness of it, much relieved.

"You see what you have done," said Frances, swiftly moving up from the chest where she had been sitting and throwing her arms about his neck. She pressed so close to him that he was now forced to handle the reins blindly.

"Sal," she whispered, "I'm terrible, awful happy today! You did nearly spill us out, and you might have cracked the captain's mirror, if I hadn't caught it in the very wink of time. But it didn't crack— and I'm not alone in here any more. I'll be ridin' inside most of the time now. Just get us to Carlisle safe. That's all I ask now. But do keep the reins in your own hands. Maybe 'tis follerin' after the two gintlemen too close that makes trouble. Did ye ever think o' that? It's ourselves now—*and her*. Ourselves alone, if I'm to be like a wife to ye, Mr. Albine." Their lips met.

He turned to his outside view of things again and let the canvas fall behind him. But he pondered what she had said for the next half mile, letting the horses walk slowly up the ever-increasing ascent.

"Ourselves alone", eh? Well, that was a fine brave Irish thought. And he was going to make things right for Frances Melissa—and for young Bridget, too—and the little one when it came. Yes, they should have all that his strength and skill could bring them. He would do everything, and anything. But "ourselves alone"? He wondered.

So far what would he have done without friends and their advice, a man like himself raw from the forest? Where would he be now without them? Even McArdle had helped, had really saved him alive in the old days. He shook his head as though he had caught his hair in a thicket and would shake the leaves out of it. Could it be that Melissa was speaking of Yates—and St. Clair, and almost everybody else? Some white women, he noticed, wanted everything just for themselves—for themselves alone. And he had seen bitches that ate their young. They started to lick them all over as soon as they were born and just went right on through with it, and swallowed them, too.

But Melissa was not like that, he felt quite sure. She was just in the early mating stage, he decided, and didn't want anything, not even the shadow of something strange moving outside to fall across the entrance to the den where the young were. Also, evidently, she was afraid she might lose him. No, that wasn't it exactly. She seemed to be scared she might get lost herself! Sometimes she acted like a person who had been lost in the woods and then rescued, but wasn't sure of it yet. Take that spell yesterday, what was it she had seen, where had she been?

Bridget, he felt sure, would never grow up to be like that. Already she knew exactly who she was and what she wanted. She'd certainly make some wild leg-clutching boy into a good steady man someday and keep a warm fire burning on the hearth for him, too. But Frances Melissa? Well, he couldn't be sure. There was something mysterious about her.

In fact, you could never tell from one day to another just exactly who Frances Melissa was going to be. Sometimes she took the last ounce of strength out of him. Yet he could never tell just what it would be like next time. And then she always seemed to be asking him for help, trying to get him to hold her even closer; to find herself by being one with him. How curious! He had never thought mating could be like that. But maybe that was why he loved her so much. And then there was the wonderful stray way she looked, sometimes, so strangely beautiful.

Certainly he was tangling his hair in branches high over his head with all this thinking about women. He still had a sneaking feeling he never would have much luck with them. He had told Melissa about Jane Sligo, that lost girl-wife that a thoughtless boyish passion and McArdle's obstinate theology had wished on him. Melissa had laughed at him. Now, what could he say to that!

Where was Jane Sligo, he wondered, and what was she like? She was no girl any longer. If she ever turned up, if McArdle tried to be troublesome about her again! Well, he was no boy any longer, either!

And he would protect himself and Frances against them both, and the whole world, too.

Hadn't he set out to find his wife again, and come back with Frances Melissa? She was his wife now, no matter what any preachers might say. It must have been meant that way or he would never have found Frances as he had. What McArdle had written on the piece of bark when he and Jane were married was only a boyish promise, something wrung from him by surprise. He had tried but he hadn't been able to keep that promise.

But the remembrance of the bark writing and the ring that Jane had kept often worried him. He hoped that she had lost it, and the ring, too. It was a bad-luck ring, the one which the sick woman had provided that afternoon when they were trying to sneak into Fort Pitt. Well, he was glad she had died. That was one witness gone. The whole forest marriage on the wild island down the Ohio came back to him vividly.

He hoped the other woman who had put her name on that piece of slippery elm bark would die, too. Nothing but trouble had come out of that affair with Jane. And how hard he had tried to find her! He rubbed his ragged ear thoughtfully. Sometimes it made his head ache, and it always itched. It reminded him of trouble—maybe of trouble to come.

If so, so be it.

At any rate he would take this much of Frances Melissa's advice. He certainly *would* handle the reins himself. And as for his friends and other acquaintances, and the various affairs he would have to undertake in the world on the other side of the mountains, he was going to be the judge of all that for himself. He would take Yates's advice, or St. Clair's, or that of anyone else who seemed to be a wise counsellor and a clever trader or hunter. There was something to be said for the way the redskins managed such matters. All the squaws did for the council fire was to bring wood for it. The men lit it, smoked their pipes there, and made big medicine.

Much comforted by this profound conclusion, the inadequacy of which he had as yet no means of guessing, he began to handle the reins more briskly and once more forced the horses into a lumbering trot.

Some of this cogitation about his personal problems and his resolutions as to the future had been unconsciously suggested to him by the sight of three steep zigzags in the road ahead. These and the pitch down over the rocks on the opposite slope were known to all unhappy wagoners as the "Stoney Batter". The Stoney Batter rose suddenly out of the forest and climbed up over the comparatively bare rocky ridge only about a mile away now. By sheer propinquity it was now forced upon his active attention, both as a physical fact and for what it signified in the life journey he had undertaken for himself and for those behind him in the wagon.

At the top of that ridge he would, so to speak, be looking down into his future. His past in the forest would lie behind him, hidden amid the mountains. The backbone of the main ridge of the Tuscarora, which the road just barely managed to negotiate on three steep boulder-piled inclines, was the final ridge of the Alleghenies eastward. Here was the actual physical frontier, definitely marking the end of the mountain wilderness, one which even the wild game had learned slowly to recognize and the Indians now reluctantly confessed.

Below were the foothills, the valleys and plateaus of the long-settled country, the hard-won birthright of the English dwellers in the dawnlight, the domain of the paleface, where chimneys smoked, wheels rolled, and ploughs bit deep through open country conquered by the rifle and made good by the axe. There Europe had been brought over in ships and was flooding westward into America, dammed up for a while against the mountains.

To Salathiel the ridge of the Tuscarora was thus of much greater import and significance than would even a national frontier ordinarily be to a usual or casual traveller. For him, it was the barrier he had always dimly felt and often heard about, one he could now plainly see; a wall between him and all those things from which he so bitterly felt he had been cruelly disinherited. Now—now after years of hope deferred, struggles, and lonely yearning, he was about to surmount it and to go on down into the country beyond.

At the very top of the ridge the sun glittered on a mound of black wet rocks piled there either as a marker or as a point of survey by the first military engineers at the very top of things—mighty high! That would be his milepost, he thought, the marker between his youth and his manhood. Yes, he would make it so, a mark in time.

One more steep haul then, one more wild scramble. Over the Stoney Batter! Those boulder-piled zigzags were narrow, stony, and steep. More like a landslide with a path on it than a road. It would be close going and a last desperate scramble with the big heavy wagon and the trundler. He might need help. He hoped Yates and St. Clair had not gone over the crest after the troops, ahead of him. He thought they ought to stand by to help with the two extra horses. Hadn't it been understood that they were going to wait at Sugar Cabins? By the way, what had become of that sweetly named place?

He came up out of a shallow swale where a small branch began trickling merrily westward through the forest, and halted to look about him in what had once been a considerable clearing. This was a place where people had evidently dwelt in peace "before the late troubles began". There were several empty cellars. A dozen or so hardy apple trees still survived. Some had a little, high red fruit that even the bears had not been able to get. Yes, a small settlement must have been begun here. Probably it was at the road's end then, in the years just before his late Britannic Majesty and the Most Christian King of France had so notably fallen out. He thought he could see the people leaving the day the news of Braddock's defeat came, the mad panic and the frantic flight. Or had the news come in the night, he wondered; struck silently with a painted face? That was ten years ago or more. Now the forest had come back. All but for a rosebush and a few red apples hanging highest on the scraggly bough. God, what a lot of trouble this country had seen!

He started the teams forward again, and following a curve that skirted a rocky shoulder, he found himself, almost before he knew it, in the midst of Sugar Cabins itself.

Its most notable civic feature just at that moment was a runny-nosed boy in a coonskin cap and shaggy fur trousers, who stood forlornly holding the heads of the noble steeds of Messrs. St. Clair and Yates. This youth scowled at the wagon when it drew up, and gave Salathiel a painful cross-eyed stare. His embarrassment at having to exist was patent, and he answered questions bashfully and slowly, blushing every time.

The two gentlemen were over yonder at Hank Laughlin's cabin, "jawin' with pa and ma"—it appeared. As to where "yonder" was, it was quite impossible from the double direction of the boy's eyes to guess with any accuracy. Salathiel, therefore, looked around for himself.

Four or five miserable log shebangs, evidently the remains of shacks once inhabited by Colonel Burd's road workers, lay scattered about through a fine open grove of sugar maples, containing some of the largest and oldest trees of the kind Salathiel had ever seen. There were many old holes and scores in the bark of their trunks, the sole evidence of industry that marked the settlement, unless a few pigs rooting listlessly in the autumn leaves here and there implied some modicum of care in their behalf. There were no windows in the cabins, and the slab doors were grimly shut. No one was about, and sullen silence was the only noise.

Salathiel spat over the wheel in disappointment. What in time could St. Clair and Yates be stopping to jaw about here?

"Got a chawr?" asked the boy.

"Yes," said Salathiel, "hev you?"

"No," said the youth, "nothin' but sassafras." He spat some green juice.

At this brilliant turn in affairs, most of the horses blew their noses as a sign that they all recognized one another.

"*Haw!*" said Salathiel at last, feeling the equine friendship was being overemphasized.

"The macaroni with one eye said ye was to tarry for him," said the boy suddenly, remembering Yates's message.

"We be," replied Salathiel.

The boy considered this for quite some time.

"I know ye be," he said.

"Good!" exclaimed Salathiel, and resumed silence. He heard Frances giggling again inside the wagon.

"While you're awaitin', big man, kin I come up and set there beside ye?" asked young Bridget, unexpectedly sticking her brown braids out from under the canvas.

He reached down and swept her up onto the seat beside him. She sat swinging her too-large moccasins and looking down at the youth holding the horses.

"'Low, Hank," she said.

"'Low, sis!" the boy managed. He blushed to the roots of his hair, and then gasped out, "Be ye goin' downcountry in that *thar* contraption, sissy?"

She nodded happily. "Yes, I'm agoin' to Carlisle for to find my old granny."

"Thought she was took off by the Injuns," said the boy, wiping his green mouth with the back of his hand.

"Not she," chirped Bridget, "she's from Bosting Town, and they don't have Injuns there no more. The Injuns give up and cleared out."

"Wal, we've still got 'em here," drawled the boy.

"I know," said sis. "At my house—at Patton's, I mean," she corrected herself, "I don't live there no more. But Mr. Patton's Injuns do be tame."

"Maybe," said the boy, doubtfully. "But arly this mornin' comes a little Welshman crawling up to Cousin Finney Laughlin's door with his hand cut clean off. And he says the Injuns done it to him just a piece up the road from here."

Salathiel looked about him quite unconcernedly. But he understood the silence and the complete lack of any sign of life at Sugar Cabins now. The houses themselves seemed to be listening for the war-whoop. He laughed a little at this unconscious tribute of respect to his former playmates. It was the kind of joke the "Shadows" would have appreciated.

"Did ye hear what that boy said, Sal?" cried Frances from inside the wagon, a piercing note of anxiety in her usually soft voice. "Belike some of your friends of the Long House are after followin' ye up. What are ye goin' to do about it?"

"I'm just agoin' to drive on over the mountain, Melissa, whar the people of the Long House won't care to follow. We're like to catch up to the troops before we get to Loudon, halfway down the hill. Besides, it doesn't sound a very likely tale to me. If they was Injuns, they'd hev taken this man's har instead of his hand. But here come St. Clair and Yates, and we'll hear the gist of it from them."

(The salt box, he thought, the salt box! He must get to it before Melissa prepared the next meal.)

Yates and St. Clair were coming from the nearest cabin, where a woman stood peering out the door after them apprehensively.

"Hank, you come right back in here," she screamed at the boy, who scarcely needed the warning. Hardly had St. Clair slipped a couple of pennies into his hands before he let go the horses' bridles and made a bolt for the house. The door slammed behind him. Both the gentlemen smiled.

"Injuns?" asked Salathiel.

"Oh, I don't think so," replied St. Clair. "Not a war party, anyway. It might have been a prowler or a renegade."

"Looks more like highway robbery to me," said Yates. "I can't make head or tail of it. There's a poor devil in there with his right hand cut off clean as a whistle just behind the wrist, nigh dead from loss of blood and terror. He's a stranger to all of them here. Crawled in last night, it seems, with a thong wrapped round his arm. The dogs found him first. He's clean out of his head now, talking in Welsh about a Swedish widow with a gold cup buried in her coffin. At least that's all I could make out of it. I've small Welsh, though. The Laughlin woman called us in to help rebind his arm as we rid by. Arthur and I have done the best we could. And I left a little money with Mrs. Laughlin t' encourage her to take care of him, or to bury him decent if he dies."

" 'Twas too much, Ned," said St. Clair. "They're not used to gold in these parts."

"It's all I have with me now," replied Yates.

"Aweel," sighed St. Clair, " 'twas a charitable impulse we both had."

Salathiel stood listening to this gossip somewhat impatiently. "It's nigh noon," he said at last, "and I want t' get me to Chambers Mills before nightfall. Wully said the road down the mountain has been new worked lately and is in good shape. But I'd like to get on now. This talk of Injuns has made the women anxious, and the sooner we're on t'other side and away from it all, the better. But I guess I'll be needin' to borrow both your nags for this last crawl to the summit. It does look like a bad hazard."

"All right, Mr. Orator," said Yates, "as Wully Grant would say, 'Awa wi' ye!'—and, of course, we'll see ye over the crest."

The reassembled cavalcade took off forthwith, with a clatter of hoofs and wheel rumblings that must, if anything, have been reassuring to the scared inhabitants of Sugar Cabins, who viewed its departure cautiously through their respective loopholes.

The deep-rutted road wound for a few hundred yards through the temple-like sugar maple grove, dipped into a soggy stretch bordered by scrub white oak, and then seemed to fling itself in one last level stretch through a hemlock thicket straight at the face of the granite ridge. At the very foot of this cliffy wall was a narrow rim of sleek green meadow grass, evidently much frequented and cropped close by herds of deer.

Rising sheer and swiftly above the tops of the hemlocks, the road seemed to leap in what looked like a man-made stroke of lightning traced in three zigzagged inclines to the crest of the mountain, about three hundred feet above. It was by far the most ambitious and artificial piece of construction on the whole of the "Glades Road". At the foot of the first boulder-piled ramp the heavy wagon and the two horsemen accompanying it came to a well-advised halt for mutual consultation. Frances and young Bridget emerged to look fearfully rather than hopefully at the goal so high above, and no one had any doubt but that here was an obstacle which it would take skill and determination rather than mere brute strength and a merciless whip to surmount.

"Bejasus," exclaimed Frances, " 'tis a bit of the Giants' Causeway let down out of the sky." At which, as if to confirm her comparison, the front of a thin cloud began to drift across the top of the ridge, pouring down over the summit a sinuous river of mist and veiling the cairn of black rocks at the crest in a bright halo of sun-streaked fog. A light pearly rain began to fall like dew on their upturned faces, and at that instant Bridget gave a little gasping scream of joy. For the sun, which was now almost directly overhead, and whose bright disk could still be traced as a golden glow above the vapour, suddenly threw an intense and complete circle of rainbow against the oncoming mist above. In this the half-veiled cairn of dark stones seemed to mark the precise centre and to point like a hand.

It was almost as though the face of an apocalyptic clock had been revealed to them pointing to some prophetic noon in secret spiritual glory amid the mountains, and the child was by no means the only one whose feelings were mysteriously touched. All of them stood

gazing upward, their damp faces fixed in a quiet astonishment of delighted wonder. But seconds on that airy clock bled its colours white.
The vision dissolved. The cloud fell in a shower of tinkling rain over
the tops of the hemlocks behind them. Standing startlingly clear
against the blue sky on the very crest of the ridge, they now saw the
dark body of an elk with cloudy antlers staring down at them.

In the same instant Salathiel had covered it with his rifle. He fell
down on his back behind the trundler and rested the muzzle of his
long piece on the iron rim of the big artillery wheel. It was not a long
shot, but it was upward, a high angle. He was just beginning to
squeeze the trigger when Frances Melissa snatched the gun from his
hands. It was so unexpected, it left him staring up at the sky, and
into her face, blankly.

"Would ye be after bringin' Death into the middle of our good
luck?" she panted. "Sure an' is the sign of the rainbow to be wasted
on ye entirely?"

He rose slowly and stood looking at her, grim and white, shaking
with anger. She gave him back the gun, which he slowly shifted to his
left hand. The elk had gone. Salathiel stood there. She, and all of
them, stood breathless, waiting for him to strike her . . .

In a curious and serious tone the voice of Yates reached out and
seemed to take hold of the scene. "Brother," he said quietly, "it is time
to turn your face towards the east, whence enlightenment comes."

Then, as the red mist cleared, Salathiel heard him, and remembered.

"Go back into the wagon, Melissa," he said hoarsely. "You've
fouled the finest shot God ever sent me."

She took Bridget by the hand, and together they walked over to
the wagon and got into it without looking back at him. Bridget was
quietly weeping. She too had been badly scared. Melissa sat down and
crossed herself. She felt she had acted the fool, but she had also felt
a draught as from cold wings pass close over her neck. Her lips moved
and her fingers flew. Bridget sat on the big harness chest, kicking her
heels and watching. She did not approve of the way Melissa was saying her prayers. There was something strange and elaborate about
it.

Outside, the three men did not discuss the incident. They turned
earnestly to solving the problem of how best to drag the heavy wagon
up the steep inclines and past the home of the clouds where the elk
had vanished in the mist.

The method of their passing the obstacle was this. Yates and St.
Clair unsaddled their mounts, which were temporarily fitted with two
spare collars from the harness for an extra team carried in the trun-

dler. That sturdy two-wheeled cart was unslung from the wagon and the two idle horses hitched to its shaft. Aside from sundry spare parts and harness and an extra wheel on the back of its caisson, the trundler was not heavily laden. Most of its freight consisted of peltry, beaverskins, fox, mink and others, which Salathiel had either shot, trapped, or traded in for a long time past. Actually, this "cargo" constituted most of his ready capital, since furs were always salable at some price. But he had carefully forborne selling them on the frontier in order to reap their greatly increased value when he should get farther east. Their weight, however, on wheels, was comparatively light. Thus one team was able to haul the cart easily, and it was simply driven up the road to the summit and left there standing by the big cairn with its shaft in the air. St. Clair and Yates returned with the horses. The main difficulty, the wagon itself, of course, remained.

There were two sharp and short curves where the road reversed direction at violent angles, and it was a nice question whether the teams, as they swung around these, could keep the wagon moving. If it once halted it might indeed be difficult, if not impossible, to start it again on so steep a slope. Most of the surface had worked off the road, exposing the heavy conglomerate rocks, of which the fill, contained in a crib of logs, consisted. Actually, the grade had here been constructed to pass the heavily laden wagons going westward *down,* rather than up, for most of the wagons going east were empty.

After some discussion, it was decided to hitch Yates and St. Clair's mounts in tandem, that is, one behind the other, before the lead team and to ride them at the same time to the top. Yates was to go first on Enna, the spirited little mare. Some drawing power would thus be sacrificed, but the gain would be in letting the two leading horsemen pick the way carefully and set the pace, thus permitting Salathiel to give all his attention to his double teams from the seat of the wagon.

It was nearly half an hour later, nevertheless, before the change of harnessing, which the new arrangement implied, could be completed. Nothing was left to chance at this point, for a loose buckle or an unhooked or broken trace chain or leather might bring disaster. At this point Salathiel was especially glad that he had fitted his teams with blinkers at Bedford. There was considerable controversy about the use of blinkers at that time. But the argument that what a horse couldn't see was not liable to scare it seemed hard to beat. At any rate on this hazardous stretch his nags would not be able to see anything but the next horse and a small bit of the road ahead. And he hoped that this would prevent any shying at the steep curves.

At length they stood ready to breast the first ramp, Yates and St. Clair mounted before, the two teams and the wagon stretching behind. They made a couple of wide circles over the grassy sward at the foot of the cliff to get the horses used to the new order, and then at a good fast walk, Yates headed for the first incline.

Each of the ridden horses snorted as it felt the unwonted drag come on its collar, but each was kept steady by its rider. The first team put their shoulders into it, feeling the urge of the reins, the second followed, straining together as one, the big wagon tilted skyward and was dragged upward slowly, rolling, bumping from rock to rock, its driver standing up, the reins like so many nerves in his hands, whip ready.

Twice one of the team horses stumbled and was almost lifted to its feet by the strong arm that pulled its bit and head upward by the reins. The thing to do was to keep them all going, all pulling together steadily like one thing straining forward and upward without pause and without panic. The rippling necks of the big greys, the swing of their giant hip muscles from side to side, the line of backs all pointing forward was wonderful.

Yates swung around the first curve without mishap, and the climb for the second steep began. It was longer, but not so steep as the first.

Salathiel now began to talk to the horses, calling them by name, cheering them, and urging them onward. The second curve was so short that the two lead horses could do little hauling, and the whole brunt of the load came on the four beasts in the teams. They struggled here, straining fiercely, their hoofs clattering and slipping in loose stones. The ugly off leader, as the wagon almost came to a stop, humped himself for a kick. Salathiel saw the ripple of mutiny begin at his shoulders, but before the big back leg could slash out behind, the whiplash flicked his rump with fire, stung him into a surge forward that jerked the wagon around into its place facing the last slope. Once straightened out again, all six horses strove together. They moved slowly upward.

Two hundred yards more, Salathiel judged. Yates shouted something about the road getting smoother now. He began to spur his mount. The last effort was necessary. The whip leaped out from the wagon seat. It cracked. Then it stung. At the lazy off leader it bit again and again. Laying their ears back and struggling forward frantically to escape the mysterious searing pain, the six scrambling beasts seemed to pull the wagon loose from the force that was holding it back, and like a single many-legged monster writhed forward to the summit.

The iron of the wheels rang as the ark rolled out onto a wide flat space of bare table rock and came to a halt almost at the foot of the black cairn, where the trundler stood poised at the very edge of nothing.

Salathiel stood up on the seat and looked—eastward.

11

Pigtails and Horse-Chestnuts

EXPECTATION and Performance are difficult steeds to drive in a team as yoke mates, the former so easily outpaces the latter; and so Salathiel found.

He had fondly hoped to be in Chambersburg before nightfall, but it was well on towards nine o'clock of a clear valley evening, shortly before moonrise with the stars still burning brightly, when he pulled into that little settlement, better known locally as Chambers Mills. Here, only a generation before, Benjamin Chambers had established his plantation, a fine grant of four hundred acres, and his grist- and saw-mills, both at the mouth of the Falling Spring branch on the then clear and swiftly flowing Conococheague.*

All about lay gentle and fabulously fertile limestone and slate country, Pennsylvania fading away under the blue mist eastward, and southward into Maryland. Northward and westward, the walls of the mountains marked the barrier of the wilderness, preventing and fending off the sweeping blasts of winter. Chambers Mills basked at their feet in sunshine and a more salubrious climate, just beyond the blue shadows of the hills. In the remote past some vast conflagration had swept through the forests along the base of the mountains. Consequently, this section had been transformed into miles of natural open meadow luxuriantly grassed, with a few scattered trees and patches of hazel bushes, wild plum, and crabapple. The piedmont in this vicinity was thus a kind of rolling prairie country, the first great break in the western forests. A man could start to plough here without spending the best part of his years and honeymoon strength cutting down trees and burning out stumps. And from the very first,

* All the old settlers pronounced it *Conny-ca-jig.*

with the fecund momentum of a natural paradise to start with, Chambersburg had flourished signally.

Travellers who then approached it from the westward were given a grateful and premonitory welcome to the place by experiencing the first bit of consistently level, well-drained, and soft dirt road through open country east of the Alleghenies. In contrast with its former perpendicular performance, the highway now proceeded to ramble on gaily from one easily tilting crest of the eastward sloping piedmont to another. The tremendous lurching and grinding, the straining and panting of tired beasts, the slow jolting down with fearful bowel-wrenching jars from one round boulder and bare rocky ledge to another, while descending the final Stoney Batter, were over and left far behind.

Hence, the comparative silence of the wheels and the rapid rate of level progress suddenly achieved seemed incredible. People breathed easily as the clutching fear of Indian ambush relaxed its hold. They spoke loudly, and, later on, they could even laugh again as their native good nature revived under a tonic of returning confidence. As Frances Melissa remarked, "Sure, their skins grew smoother." Certainly, the furrows of fearful care tended to disappear from their brows. Trotting along between young apple orchards and the relatively numerous farmhouses encountered as they neared Chambers Mills, eastward bound wagoners and pack-horsemen were wont to break into song.

For the mysterious and overpowering gloom of the menacing forest lay behind. The sun shone out unexpectedly and delightfully. A rapid blue river meandered, gleamed, and glanced amid the hills. This, then, was Penn's peaceful province at last; subdued land, open fields and long meadows, with good company, kindly folk, more and more of them ahead to look forward to.

So it was to come "downcountry" and to escape suddenly from the mountains. Everybody felt the relief and happiness. Even the horses pricked their ears forward expectantly and inhaled grateful breaths of fragrance from the clean mown pastures and good drying hay. And so it had been that November afternoon with Melissa and Bridget and Salathiel as they came "down into the province" and rolled, really rolled for the first time, along the level stretches of road leading towards Chambersburg. This, it seemed, was what a wagon must have been built for.

Once they had left the precipitous chute of the Stoney Batter behind them, and emerged by way of a rocky gorge from the cold shadow of the mountain wall itself, their journey seemed all at once to assume a more casual and habitually pleasant character. They were no longer oppressed by silence and their own loneliness. This was long-inhabited country. They passed the road fork to Black's Mills,* where Captain James Smith lived, without stopping. From there on, cultivated country began. Crows cawed cheerfully across wide sunny fields. Now and then they met people along the road and exchanged cheerful greetings with them and neighbourly bits of news. Settlers who had been driven away by the raids of the summer before were already coming back. They heard about this and that family of farmers returning from Carlisle. Chimneys long left cold were smoking away again. Cattle were being driven home to familiar pastures. There were even a few enterprising pedlars about.

Only two miles west of the road that led briefly north to Fort Loudon they met one James Speer in a wagon piled high with goods, tools, and provisions, his decently kerchiefed young wife, Elizabeth, sitting demurely beside him.

St. Clair seemed to know Speer well. He was a sturdy, blue-eyed and broad-shouldered little Scot, who ran a small trading post in a wild and lonely side-glen halfway up the rocky gorge, just at the foot of the Stoney Batter. Two years before he had been driven away to Lancaster. Now he was coming back again with a new wife and a full wagon to open up his small trading store in one of the two log cabins by the mountain spring in the glen. St. Clair, it appeared, was interested in the establishment. Either he had lent Speer some money or recommended him for credit to Philadelphia merchants. All brother Masons, probably. At any rate, cordiality and fraternity reigned as birds of local rumour and broad Scotch flew cheerfully about.

While Mrs. Speer sat blushing under her India kerchief like the young bride that she was, listening to Yates's compliments and Melissa's soft accents, her husband displayed his new trading stock triumphantly to St. Clair, and from a small spigoted keg behind the wagon drew them a shallow pannikin each of as fiery a mountain beverage as ever started a slow Scotch heart beating under sturdy ribs.

"Thar's a whole bale o' prime beaver pelts in this sma' kag a' by itsel'," averred Jamie, patting the small fat barrel affectionately. "Say what ye will, mon, whusky's the ile o' frontier trade. And thar's no a painted savage beyond the tumblin' Tuscarora but would trade the har o' the best beaver i' the wilderness for one more panfu' o' this native heatherbrew. Aye, some o' the feathered chieftains will hear the tails o' heavinly beavers slappin' oop a starry dam across the Milk-maid's Way, wi' a zany oopside-doon moon lookin' on, after only a half mug and a sip. And then how their askin' prices do tumble! I

---

* Now Mercersburg. One William Black settled and built a grist-mill here as early as 1729-30. The old road passed to the north of it.

dinna ken how lang 'twill be before the wild hunters begin to slip back across the ranges again for a bit o' secret trade and a wee nip o' flamin' dew wi' honest Jamie, but 'twill no be so verra lang! And thar's a brisk commerce wi' the settlers aroond aboot coomin' into view. Times do be lookin' oop again, Meester St. Clair! Dinna ye think so?"

"I believe they be," replied St. Clair. "There's a new independent stir abroad in a' the colonies from Georgia to Massachusetts. Talk is a' o' growin' trade and commerce and o' more people comin' in. The frontiers will soon feel the pulse of life renewed, now that Bouquet has at last put the king's peace upon the western savages."

"Aye, thar's a braw grand fightin' mon!" exclaimed Speer. "I do hope the croon remimbers him."

"Perhaps," said St. Clair, "but 'tis more important just now that the Parliament should forget us. For a' thot though, Jamie mon, ye should do right well here even in your lonesome glen. Yon's a fine resting place for the thirsty gangin' o'er the pass westward, and the country this side is bound to fill oop wi' well-heeled farmin' folk. I hear Colonel Chambers has been layin' oot a bonny new town on his ain side o' the river this summer."

"And mauny a guid family from Antrim and the Land o' Cates, Campbells, Findleys, Wilsons, Langs, and MacAdams wi' their Eves expected shortly, all guid pious Presbyterian stock. 'MacThis and MacThat', as they say," grinned Speer. "What I'll soon be needin' masel' is a couple o' brisk young Macs a' me ain to help tend the counter and till the farm. But ye ken leave that part to me, Arthur. The pleasure will be a' mine. I'll attend to it a' masel'." And with that Mr. Speer chuckled and began to pat Mrs. Speer affectionately, instead of the keg.

A stick of barleycorn sugar for Bridget and a pair of red Carlisle stockings, which Salathiel bought for her on the spot without stopping to bargain for them, made perfect for all members of the company, great and small, the bland air of the bright Indian summer afternoon for a spell of roadside gossip. They lingered on, chatting together for almost an hour, and it was nearly half after three when the two wagons finally reluctantly pulled away from each other to resume their several journeys in opposite directions.

Bridget sat swinging her smooth scarlet legs and big moccasins from the wagon seat beside Salathiel. A look of dreamful satisfaction lingered in her wide brown eyes as though she had just glimpsed a vista of paradise, and the landscape of that country was still reproduced within. "Big man, will you make me some new red shoes, *too?*" she asked afterwhile, hesitantly.

"I will that," said Salathiel emphatically, and then responded him-

self to the wriggle of complete satisfaction, one of happiness sur-
feited, which his brief and blithe answer produced in Bridget. The
child sighed as if new shoes were almost *too* much to contemplate.

For that matter, Salathiel was feeling fairly well satisfied himself. Perhaps it was Jamie Speer's mountain cordial. But not altogether so, for while the others had been talking with the voluble little
Scot, he had managed to slip back into the wagon and extract the
severed hand from the salt box. It now reposed in his rifle pouch,
wrapped in a rag and a modicum of crystallized salt that still en-
crusted it. But if it now rested securely in his pouch, it was still not
contained so surely in his mind.

What constitutes a moral problem differs greatly in both substance and degree with various individuals and between races. To
Salathiel, the ultimate disposal of the severed hand forced him to face
the question of whether and to what extent, in certain situations, he
would still instinctively feel and act like an Indian. Or, to put it another way, how far had he actually succeeded in casting off the habits
of his forest life? Had he really been kidnapped from his own people
irrevocably? The situation was explicit.

There was the hand, heavy in his pouch and still damp. What
should he do with it?

He intended to be honest with himself about this affair. He would
act as he actually felt, and no shamming. Moreover, he would ask no
one else's advice.

As for the swift blow which had severed the hand from Taffy, he
had no regret for it. That act was not in itself a part of his problem.
The hand was. It was the hand of a thief, one who had tried to rob
him in the night, and as such it was a tangible proof of swift justice
and of right action. So he thought. But—it was also the hand of an
enemy, and from that point of view a souvenir of victory. So he
felt.

Now, among a certain forest people it was customary to preserve
and even to adorn oneself upon ceremonious occasions with portions
of the remains of one's enemies. Scalps, for instance. To be sure,
scalps could be turned in to the commissioners for a bounty. They
could be changed into pounds sterling, and pounds into goods. But
just now he was not thinking about the profitable aspect of the matter.
No, the hand was different. It was a memento. How did he feel about
keeping it? The ordinary white man would probably bury it by the
road before it festered. That would be simpler, too. Yes—but he did
feel it would undeniably give him a curious, a profound, and even an
upbuilding self-satisfaction to keep it. Secretly, of course, that much
he would concede to the white man. But the secret itself seemed to be

peculiarly his own and an Indian one. Hence, when he got to Chambers Mills, he decided, he would smoke and cure the hand.

Having thus settled this manual question of morals satisfactorily with his own conscience, he dismissed the subject peremptorily, and, leaning back in the seat, whistled through his teeth to the horses and slapped the reins.

St. Clair and Yates had gained considerably upon him, riding ahead. Apparently they were still hopeful of catching up with the marching Highlanders. But there was little chance of that, he thought. They had lingered too long gossiping with James Speer. And Wully had been in a hurry with the troops. He would have marched fast. The sun was nearing the mountains already. He saw he would never make Chambersburg before dark now. But what of it! This was a pleasant road, and he was in the dawn country at last.

He called back to Melissa to come and join him and Bridget on the driver's seat. Already he had forgotten what it was like to be angry with her. But she hadn't. She came forward to sit with Bridget between them, secretly happy and relieved to find herself "forgiven", as she thought; actually, it was simply to take her usual place. The child hummed a wordless, happy little song, leaning up against her. The horses were going at a fast steady trot. Salathiel was smiling contentedly.

Suddenly confidence and the sunny calm of the Indian summer afternoon, as the shadows of the trees lengthened slowly across the fields, filled her with peace—while James Speer's sustaining drink still warmed her comfortably. Putting an arm across Salathiel's shoulders, she began to sing in a rich contralto a ballad, which, with her roguish Irish lilt and shaded irony of phrase, proved irresistible. After a couple of staves, they all sang it together over and over again. Bridget picked up the words like magic:

> My name was Captain Kidd
> When I sail'd, when I sail'd,
> My name was Captain Kidd
> And so wickedly I did,
> God's laws I did forbid,
> When I sail'd, when I sail'd,
> When I sail'd.
>
> My name was Captain Kidd
> All around, all around,
> I sail'd from sound to sound,
> And many a ship I found

And them I sunk or burned,
And my evil name I earned,
When I sail'd, when I sail'd
All around.

My name was Captain Kidd,
When I sail'd, when I sail'd . . .

The captain's final taking-off at Execution Dock in Wapping—
and his noose-strangled farewell in the last stanza were peculiarly effective, and young Bridget was much moved thereby. Her shrill little
soprano died away to a quaver. Luckily one of the horses neighed as
though in sympathy, and they all laughed together at the ridiculous
effect, while the pebbles battered and clicked against the spokes and
the dust rolled out behind under the trundler.

And it was thus that Yates and St. Clair, who were waiting impatiently at the Loudon crossroads, saw and heard the big wagon, as
it came trotting ponderously but gaily down the road. Salathiel drew
up and looked at them inquiringly.

"We've missed catching up with Wully and his kilted retainers by
nearly an hour," said Yates. "They're probably back in barracks by
now. But it's only a mile or so from here to the fort. Now, Arthur
and I have been talking things over, and—"

"Ned thinks it will be best if we follow up last night's little affair,
and strike while the iron's still hot," interrupted St. Clair. "You
see—"

"I'll garnish the papers off him now, and settle for what land we
can get," continued Yates. "Either that, or probably we'll never get
anything. Arthur and I think possibly we can manage the affair ourselves. Amicably of course, amicably! But it might take a day or so.
Wully will be fairly savage."

"That arrangement will suit me," said Salathiel, seeing he was
not needed. "I can manage alone for a bit. We'll wait for you to overtake us at Chambers Mills. At the Davisons'—they've moved to the
Mills, you know."

"You'll stay *there?*" said Yates. "All right, but . . ." and he
looked significantly at Frances.

"Well, wherever we may be stayin', you'll soon hear of us, I warrant," said Salathiel.

"And if you'll be after needin' a lion to chase your unicorn, you
can send down for this one," added Melissa, patting her man's arm.

"A lion? He's only a big bear," replied Yates, "but I think our
unicorn will be a pretty tame one after tonight. Anyway, we'll try to
bring back a piece of his golden horn, without asking for help."

"Here's to it, then!" exclaimed St. Clair, and drew out his long silver saddle-flask. "The only thing I got oot o' the game last nicht was a fill o' Patton's 'fifty-two peach brandy. You'll remember why *this* was empty, Mistress Albine." He looked at her, his blue eyes twinkling, as he shook the flask.

They all remembered, and laughed at her.

Nevertheless, as the flask went around, she tilted it up again at a high angle. After the first gulp, Salathiel snatched it out of her hand.

"Just like you did with the rifle-gun," he said, and grinning, handed the flask back to St. Clair.

She sat breathless for a minute, and then began to laugh. "Ye damned spalpeen, so ye'd snatch the drink out of me parched mouth, would ye? Sal, I guess we're even now," she whispered.

He patted her hand, and they drove off suddenly.

"We'll be stayin' at Nathan Patton's house, nigh the fort," shouted Yates. "Wait for us at the Mills until Monday, at least."

Salathiel waved a paw that he understood.

"*So,* we'll have to get along for a few days without the two noble gintlemen," said Frances, philosophically. He grinned and slipped an arm about her waist. "Yes, but *we* will miss them more than Wully ever will."

She tossed her head.

The way for the most part was now a gentle downgrade. He put his whole attention on tooling the horses along and maintaining a good steady clip. The big beasts seemed to know they were going home, perhaps the scents along the old road were familiar. The steady rhythm of their hoofs was seldom broken. But it was over twelve miles from Loudon crossroads to Chambersburg. He was determined to get there that night, and it would take about all that the horses had. So he nursed them.

From a curve of the high road going over a long crest, they caught a glimpse of Fort Loudon looming up some miles away to the west near Parnell's Knob. Even at that distance they could make out the Union Jack flapping in the wind above the stockade. Smoke poured merrily from the barrack chimneys, and there was a twinkle of steel along the parapet. Then the slope of the land and a bit of woodland intervened.

"I hope Nathan Patton will be as hospitable at Loudon as his cousin William was at Lyttleton," Salathiel remarked half to himself.

"I doubt it," replied Frances. "Mrs. Patton is an uncommon foin woman. Bridget, has Mr. Nathan Patton a wife?" she asked.

"She died last Christmas Eve havin' two little babies, and they both died, too," said Bridget.

The best reply to this was silence.

Four miles farther, and just before sunset, they passed a long train of pack horses. It was a convoy of supplies, winter clothing, and light ammunition going forward to Bouquet at Fort Pitt. Salathiel nodded to a young ensign of the Royal Americans, who headed the mud-splashed string with a lone corporal, but beyond that he made no acknowledgment to the storm of "howdies", shouts, rude questions, and ribald advice that greeted him and the wagon as he passed down the road. He saw no familiar faces among the riders, but many a loutish one. One little brown man with a beard did look vaguely familiar, but he had his hat pulled down over his eyes. A sergeant and two mounted men from the old 60th brought up the rear. Their familiar scarlet and buff-white gave him a homesick turn. But they were strangers all. Replacements probably. He cracked his whip and drove on faster to get out of their rolling dust.

"Buckey" must be pretty confident of himself, he thought. Five men to escort fifty horses! Last year there would have been half a company at least. He doubted if the country were really as quiet as all that. But maybe it was? Bouquet probably knew. Too bad Ecuyer couldn't have lived to see this. He might be going home now to Geneva. Lord, how he missed Ecuyer, and blessed his name! He remembered his wholehearted admiration for Colonel Bouquet. "By far the best officer in the colonies" was what the little captain had said. "And if you are ever in difficulties, go to Bouquet. He's a man who remembers when you have once done him a service."

Well, he was in no difficulties now. Quite the contrary. But he would like to talk to the colonel. Where now was the list of Indian captives McArdle had given him to take to Fort Pitt? he wondered. It was just the kind of thing some ignorant clerk would mislay or destroy, because it was written on bark. But that list might be very helpful now to the colonel, since Bouquet was rounding up every one of the captivated from all the tribes at Carlisle. It would be mighty good medicine as a check on the chiefs' stories. How they would lie! The Injuns loved many of the adopted captives, and some captives would hate to leave them after years of wilderness life. Many would have gone permanently wild. It would not be easy to separate them. Then he remembered where one copy of the list was. It was in his own mind!

He began to say it over to himself, hearing his old singsong half-Indian, boyish voice recapitulating the names to McArdle, while he lay sprawled out on the floor of Kaysinata's lodge. Malycal used to join in. Yes, he could still "sing" them all. Lord, how well he remembered! And all the dim old ways of the forest, the deer browsing on leaves, all those beautiful wild islands down the Ohio—what a life it had once been! Unconsciously, he sighed.

Probably it was the oncoming of evening that had thus given a sombre cast and a retrospective twist to his thoughts. The twilight was beginning to deepen. Bridget and Melissa sat silent by his side. The horses trudged on monotonously. He was letting them walk part of the time now. The peace of the countryside, the grey light over the low hills, and the reflected glow of the dying sunset from the other side of the mountains were well-nigh unearthly. He liked this time of evening—in a peaceful land!

They splashed into a broad but shallow ford, and in the middle of the stream he pulled up the teams to let them have a drink. Their long necks arched down towards the flowing water. They sniffed it. They made sucking and sipping sounds, drinking with the bits in their mouths. The stream gossiped happily, whispering in the last glow of the sunset, as though it were practising a musical prelude for moonrise. Just around a curve in the thicket ahead, a liquid voice seemed to be talking with a continuous quiet excitement in an unknown tongue. It was telling a story he ought to remember, he felt.

"What's that?" he demanded suddenly. Instinctively, at a strange sound, his hand groped for his rifle-gun.

They listened. It kept coming closer.

"Sure it's the sound of cowbells," said Frances. "Cowbells! Someone's after bein' late drivin' the kine home this evenin'."

He had never heard cowbells before. There were three of them. Two that clanked, and one that tonked.

Presently at the other side of the stream the herd appeared with white mottled faces and stubby horns. They halted for a moment at the unexpected sight of the silent horses standing in the water, and then began slowly to cross. There were about thirty of them, cows, calves, and one small, shaggy brown bull with a broken horn. Salathiel fingered his whip. But they passed quietly on, stopping for a brief drink, and lowing softly. A dog of the long-haired Scotch breed burst out of the woods and began harrying his charges along. He paid no attention to the wagon whatsoever, but swam through the ford, and rounded up the stray calves and heifers on the far side of the little river like a competent thunderstorm herding small clouds before it. Bridget was delighted with this expert performance and clapped her hands. The herd took off down the road with the dog yapping behind, when an obviously excited boy on a newly broken-in colt showed up. His yellow curls flowed down from under his raccoon cap almost to his shoulders. Seeing the wagon, he drew rein on the riverbank, looking both startled and disappointed.

"Lost your chance to show off, didn't ye?" called Bridget.

The boy looked at her for a moment, horrified at having his thoughts read. Then he put his fingers to his nose and gave them a twirl. "You've got eyes like horse-chestnuts," he retorted. At that he began to cross over. "Pigtails!" he remarked, as he came opposite the wagon. Frances put her hand on Bridget's arm as the little girl began to bounce in the seat indignantly.

"Look here, young feller," said Salathiel, "didn't ye ever hear about loutin' your cap to the ladies?"

"Yes, sir," replied the boy sheepishly, measuring the distance between him and the whip with careful round blue eyes, "but this yere colt don't like fer to stand in cold water, and takes both hands."

"Hold him, then!" said Salathiel.

The boy did so and managed to remove his cap, too. A further cascade of curls drenched his shoulders.

"That's a handsome scalp ye got, sonny," remarked Mr. Albine. "If ye ain't right keerful somebody's liable to lift it for ye."

"I know," said the boy, clutching his locks with evident embarrassment, "but I'm bound out, and the mistress won't let me nor her Jim cut our hair short. It marks us, she says."

"It does that. Who might ye be workin' for?"

"Mrs. Shaemus McKinney. Her old man was took off in the raids of 'fifty-six. But I'm none of hern. I'm Roy Davison."

"Kin of Arthur at Chambersburg?" he inquired.

"Cousin," replied the boy. "But my pa won't hev no more truck with hisn. They fit like bobcats when uncle moved his tannery to Chambers Mills. Liken you folks might tarry the night with us, maybe?" said Roy, looking at Bridget. He smiled at her archly. "Hit's a *big* stone house, and hit's half empty." Bridget wriggled. "And hit's nigh five miles from here to the Mills at the Falling Spring," he added, hopefully.

"Get on with ye, Mr. Albine," said Melissa. "There's no time to tarry here jist for these childer to fall in love."

Why not? he thought, remembering Phoebe. Somehow the boy had reminded him of her. Probably it was his name. But he looked at the sturdy youngster on the colt sympathetically.

"Good night, son. We'll have to be drivin' on," he said. He spat a disgruntled "giddap" at the horses. Just why he was irritated, he didn't quite know.

The boy sat watching the big wagon disappear down the road into the gathering twilight. He was late with the cows this evening. Mistress McKinney would wallop him well. But pigtails and horse-chestnuts for Mistress McKinney! He stuffed his gold scalp locks back under his cap and whistled softly, looking after the wagon disappearing down the road in the blue dusk. Suddenly a light shone out through the canvas behind.

Frances Melissa had taken Bridget off the seat and was putting the little girl to bed. Afterwhile she lay down herself on the long clothes chest. It was getting dark outside now, and it would be another hour, with the tired horses, until they got into Chambersburg.

Bridget lay looking up at the white canvas ceiling, her kitten beside her.

"Did ye like him, Mama Lissa?" she whispered.

"Who?" answered Frances, teasingly.

"Roy—Roy Davison." She kept repeating the boy's name over and over.

"Yes, of course, I fell in love with him, little silly. I niver saw sich hair, and the sunny smile of him. Oh moi!"

Whether it was Bridget or the kitten that did all the purring now, Frances couldn't tell.

Both she and Bridget were fast asleep when Salathiel finally rumbled over the timber bridge into Chambersburg a little before the late moonrise and began to look for a place to stable the horses. He listened to the deep breathing of the sleepers with a curious mixture of apprehension and satisfaction.

Only the kitten came out to rub itself against his gaiters and demand supper in its own way. But where and how would he get supper even for a cat in a place as dark and lonely as Chambersburg seemed to be?

12

In Which the Little Turtle Laughs Like a Loon

SALATHIEL LOOKED about him as he stood in the starlight, and he could see very little. The overpowering impression of Chambersburg was a dark velvet silence poised against the continuous rushing of falling water. Evidently the sound came from a dam and mill-race not far to his right, where Colonel Chambers's mills stood in a dark cluster, and the first beams of moonrise were beginning to shimmer on what appeared to be the metal roof of some large building. A little farther up the stream was a notably heavy clump of cypress, black against the starry sky. One dim light, and one only, showed feebly some distance to his left.

He left the wagon alone unwillingly, although the horses were too tired even to stamp, and walked towards the light across a field full of muddy wheel ruts. As the moonlight brightened, he gradually made out that he was crossing a large public square, where four roads coming together traced a rough cross. Here and there in the lots around the edges of the common the roofs of houses now began to show above the trees. The light came glimmering from a long building with a platform before it like a low wharf or a roofless porch. Now and then the feeble radiance flickered and blinked. It seemed to be filtering through the panes of the largest window he had ever seen. Over a sliding door towards the far end of the platform was a store loft, where a gallows-like loading beam with a hook and pulley jutted out. There was also a swinging sign near the window. The light fell faintly on one side of it. He could barely make it out:

> Will Somerfield
> Domestic Merchandise
> &
> Choice London Goods
> Household Sundries
> Victualler & Vintner
> (Licensed Prov. Trader)

Will Somerfield, eh? Probably the merchant prince of Chambersburg. But where was he?

He turned to peer through the wavering squares of glass in the big boxed window. It was the first shop window he had ever seen. Inside, several bolts of fine figured cloth were unrolled for display, and there was a clutter of minor metal articles that appeared to be cutlery. The light was certainly dim. He pressed his forehead against one of the better panes and squinted beyond. Curiously distorted, the interior of a general store sprang dimly into view.

Somewhere around the corner of a long cavelike room, a log fire was flickering. He could not see the fireplace, but its reflected glow discovered numerous rows of shelves lined with shadowy merchandise. At the far end of the place on a broad wooden counter dangled the weighing pans of a pair of brass scales in the light of two thick candles stuck into jugs. Barrels and kegs were everywhere about. Seated on one of them before the counter was young Arthur Davison talking earnestly to a kindly looking old man in a leather apron.

Lord, how Arthur had grown! He was a tall youth now. He had his sister's regular features, her wide brow and her provocative mouth. Close beside his head, the candles suffused the boy's face, cameo-like against the darkness, with a smooth porcelain glow.

Inevitably, for a sick and tender moment, it was Phoebe and not Arthur, that Salathiel's eyes beheld again. Phoebe, lost Phoebe Davison!

He weakened down to the soles of his feet again, just as he had that day at Bedford when he read her farewell letter. The strength ran out of him, even as it had left the iron limbs of Samson. He closed his eyes. But he could hear her voice and her shy feet passing up and down the stairs by his door. Why, why had he so carefully hunted up this old agony for himself again?

Why? Because he meant to face the music; to bring his hopeless dream of her face to face with reality.

Yes, he must know about Phoebe. He would never see her again. But he could *hear* about her; find out, for instance, if she were still alive. And then, equally important now, he meant to take care that Frances Melissa should never learn about Phoebe. Instinctively he knew that it might be fatal; that it would be entirely different from Frances' knowing about Jane.

So he must carefully warn young Arthur. If necessary he would . . . Pshaw! That *was* an Indian thought. The boy had always liked him. He had taken him on his first deer hunt. Maybe he'd remember those days. He gave a certain shrill whistle they had once used as a signal at Pendergasses'.

Arthur looked up startled and with an incredulous expression of happy surprise. He listened . . .

Salathiel tapped on the glass, and whistled again.

An instant later the door by the shop window flew open while the small customers' bell tinkled violently, and Arthur stood there gazing into the night as though he couldn't believe what he saw: the huge bulk and familiar outlines of his friend, nursing his long gun as usual, and towering up mysteriously into the darkness.

"It's you, Sal! It's *really* you, ain't it?" the lad exclaimed.

"Heap much me it is," Salathiel replied, crushing the boy's fingers.

"*Ow!*" cried Arthur. "It's you, all right! But, good God, Sal, that's the curiousest thing. I was talkin' to Mr. Somerfield about you when I heard your whistle. What do you think of that? Mr. Somerfield," he called to the man at the back of the store, "here's the very feller I was jes tellin' ye about, and he's got that rifle-gun, too!"

"Bring him in," said Mr. Somerfield, leaning forward with both hands pressed flat on the counter in frank curiosity. "Bring him in, son, and let's have a look at him."

"This is him, sir," said Arthur, "Sal Albine."

"Well, well, speak of the devil!" exclaimed Mr. Somerfield, shaking hands over the counter cordially. "Ever since Arthur's been clerkin' for me here, I've been hearin' a lot about ye. We all have. If there was as much goods went over this counter as gossip, I'd be a rich man. Happen ye didn't come downcountry to dispose of some peltry?"

"Wal, now, I have *some*, Mr. Somerfield," Albine replied. "Arthur and I might show it to ye tomorrow. I'll be right glad to. But I'm on my way to Carlisle with my lady and a little girl in the wagon. They're asleep out there in the common now. Happen ye might know where I could shelter the wagon and four tired horses for the night?"

Mr. Somerfield pondered. "You're right welcome to my sheds in the paddock behind the store," said he, still considering. "But then my back lot's full o' a sight o' poultry, and old lumber and plunder.

Tell ye what ye do, Arthur. Wake up St. Clair's nigger. He's been eatin' his head off here jes doin' nothin' but waitin' for his master. Get him to watch Mr. Albine's wagon while ye walk him around to Colonel Chambers's. Liken the old man will open up the mill stockade for ye. Ye'll find *that* safe enough, and lots o' shelter for the horses in the big sheds. It's the building with the lead roof, the one where the whole neighbourhood usen fer to fort-up. Some folks call it 'the castle'. No one lives there now, but the colonel keeps the place in good repair."

"Sounds just elegant," said Salathiel, gratefully, "but I didn't expect a castle."

Mr. Somerfield looked embarrassed. "Now, sir, I'd take ye in here ifen I could," he said, "but Effie died nigh four years ago, and ever since I've been livin' all alone. I've got Arthur here in the store, and a couple of old niggers for gineral yard help. But there's not even a private decency with a sand box here fit for a lady, let alone comforts for a small child."

"Now, now, ye're bein' mighty kind as it is," drawled Salathiel. "I've no doubt Colonel Chambers will be able to put up one of Captain Jack's old band o' rangers for the night. We can all sleep in the wagon, anyway. It's only yard room I want."

Just then Arthur reappeared, followed by St. Clair's Negro servant, his eyes still heavy with sleep.

"Remember me, Jed?" asked Salathiel, shaking him awake good-naturedly. "Say, can ye still turn hand springs like ye did on the mound at Shawnee Cabins?"

"Do Gawd, sah," exclaimed the sturdy little Negro, shaking with apprehension. "Yah ain't gwine fer fetch this fellah back ter de Injun country, be yah? Marster say stay hyah. Wait! Him come back soon."

"Yes, your master will be along in a couple of days, Jed. And he's aimin' to take ye back to the City with him then. So I've not been sent to get ye. All I want you to do now is to watch a wagon for about half an hour. Cheer up! No widow's son-of-a-gun would carry off a good boy like you to sell to the Injuns."

Jed looked greatly relieved by this news. But it was still with evident reluctance that he now accompanied Albine and young Davison out into the dark square, where the wagon loomed up impressively in the moonlight. The horses and kitten made it plain they thought it high time their needs were taken care of. Despite the mewing and the shaking of harness which greeted the appearance of the party, however, Melissa and Bridget remained sleeping soundly. Salathiel determined he would not disturb them, and cautioned Jed to be quiet and not to discover himself on any account, as Melissa was nervous about black boys; he left him holding the horses' heads and returned to thank Mr. Somerfield.

"Why, it's nothin', brother," said the old man. "After you see Ben Chambers and git settled down, come over to the store and we'll have a snack over the counter out o' one of the fish barrels. I'll keep the fire goin'. By the way, Colonel Chambers is right active in the lodge here. Thought from somethin' ye just said that news might interest ye."

"Why, it certainly does, sir," Salathiel replied. "I'm obleeged for the information, and I'll try to drop around for a bite later on."

The old man looked pleased. "Don't forget, it's *Somerfield's* at the corner o' Front and Queens streets," said he, proud of his establishment and of the newly named streets in the new town. "But Arthur will guide ye. Now git along and try to see Ben before it's so late. Everybody ain't night-owls around here like me and young Arthur. Still, that was kind o' lucky for ye."

Salathiel agreed that it was. And taking Arthur by the arm, they started off to find Colonel Chambers.

"Old man Somerfield's begun preparin' me for the first degree," said the boy proudly. "I'll be old enough fer first questioning pretty soon."

"That's fine," said Salathiel. "You couldn't do better. Your grandpap Garrett would rejice to know it." He felt the boy glow under his approval, and came to a swift conclusion.

"Listen, Arthur," he said, "do you remember that buck we shot near Naugles' at Bedford a long time ago?"

"Why, it was my first! Of course, I remember. How could I ever forget?"

"Wal, the Injuns, least ways the Shawanees, think that when an old hunter first bloods a younger one that way, the twain are kind o' bound to be a huntin' pair afterward, and to keep a tight lip about what they happen to know about any huntin' grounds shared between them. Now, would ye kind o' play Injun that way and buck me up?"

"Sal, ye know I would. Dang I wisht I had ye for a brother-in-law instead of . . . Oh, well, but that *was* the damnedest thing, wasn't it? Phoebe just cried her eyes out. We used to sleep in the same room, you know. Don't think I don't miss her awful special, too. She was more like my ma than a sister to me. But now I hear she'll soon have a young'un of her own. Say, didn't ye meet Mr. Burent in that pack train ye must have passed? Ye couldn't have missed him?"

Then Salathiel remembered. "Has he got a beard now?" he asked.

"Yep, and a gold watch with a big thick chain. But his beard's come out grey, for a wonder, instead of bein' brown."

"We must have passed each other. I guess he knew me," said Salathiel, "but I didn't know him. Happen I did kind o' think one of the riders looked familiar."

"Well, Mr. Burent's been here for a week past, stayin' with my folks down at our new tannery. Pa says they're doin' right well with the cooperage at Pittsburgh. And sis is expectin', come March. They didn't waste no time doin' it, did they? But you've got a youngster in the wagon yourself now, didn't ye say?"

"Her name's Bridget, and she's about seven years old," drawled Salathiel.

It took a second or two—

"She's *what!*" Arthur blurted out. He came to a halt from sheer surprise. "Now, how *did* ye ever manage that?" he demanded.

"That's what I want to talk to ye about," replied Salathiel.

He had determined to save himself as much anxiety as possible by taking the boy fully into his confidence. He felt he had lost Phoebe at Bedford by keeping his mouth shut too carefully, and he didn't want to lose Frances Melissa the same way.

Standing in the darkness at the entrance of a lane that ran down to the river, he told young Arthur Davison the whole sorry story: How McArdle had married him off. Why he had lost Phoebe, how he had set out to find Jane and found Frances instead. He did full justice to McArdle's "meddlin'", as he termed it, and of how determined he was to do the right thing now by Frances Melissa— and young Bridget, too, if it came to that.

"*So* that's how it was," said Arthur. "Oh, I'm glad ye told me, Sal. Nobody likes to think they've jes been fooled, ye know. Do ye want me to tell sis sometime?"

"I'm goin' to leave that to you, Arthur. Yes, I'd like her to know sometime how it really was. But whatever ye do, don't make trouble for her. She's got her own family to think of now, and I've got mine. And we'll be miles and years apart. Maybe you'll understand it all a little better when you come to get married yourself."

"I can understand it now," the boy said firmly.

"I believe ye can," rumbled Salathiel. "Course the main thing is that not a word of this should ever get to Frances. Everybody thinks she's my wife. Naturally, I ain't goin' to be the first one to deny it— and it won't be healthy after this for anyone that tries to throw a spoke through the wheels of my wagon. We're havin' a baby early next summer."

"If it's a boy, name it after me, will ye, Sal? We'd both know why, and nobody need ever say a word. Lord, I'd like that."

"Now, that's mighty fine of you, youngster," Salathiel exclaimed, greatly relieved at this unexpected but happy turn of affairs. "Tell you what, ifen we're settled down by then, I'll write ye upcountry and let ye know. And ye can come down and visit with us."

"Suppose it's a gal?" said Arthur.

"Wal, then it will be one," replied Salathiel, laughing. "Still ye might like to come downcountry anyway, and I'd like to have ye for a while, just for old time's sake."

"Lordy, it'd be like bears' grease and tree sugar," chuckled Arthur, "seein' the City! Lord—*ee!* Don't ye forget now! Send to Mr. Somerfield at the store here."

"Oh, I'll let ye hear," Salathiel promised. "Now just where does our friend, Colonel Chambers, hang out?"

"Phew, I'd plumb forgot him," cried Arthur. "Come on!"

He led down a lane past a bare-boughed orchard. On an alley that ran between the mill-race and the river stood the small but comfortable log dwelling of Colonel Chambers just at the foot of his son's vegetable patch. From a shed in the rear came the rays of a lanthorn and the sound of chopping.

"Thought I'd lay in a bit of kindlin' for the night," said he, dusting off his hands, and giving Albine a keen glance and a nod. "Well, Arthur, what is it?"

"My friend, Sal, here, sir. Mr. Somerfield thought . . ."

"I'm Sal Albine, colonel," said Salathiel, stepping forward, "one of Captain Jack's men. Maybe you've heard of me from James Smith or some of his boys up the Connycajig."

"Heard of ye! Of course, I have, sir. Dang, if I didn't spot ye as soon as I laid eyes on that double-barrelled enjine of destruction you're fondlin'." They shook hands while Arthur looked on proudly.

"Come down to the house," said the colonel, carefully resuming his coat and wig, "and meet Ruhannah, my daughter. Mrs. Chambers is off visitin' at Shippensburg. But Ruhannah's here. She's married to Dr. Colhoun, but he's away tappin' fer dropsy and she's lookin' after her old pa agin for a while. Arthur, bring in that axe and the kindlin', will ye, son? But whar's your folks, Albine? Be ye alone? Where are ye stoppin'? Maybe ye'd like to look over some of the lots in the new town plot I'm layin' out here, eh?"

"I'd like to consider it," said Salathiel, "but just now I'm intendin' for Carlisle and the City. I've got my missus and a young one in the wagon—and four horses—all waitin' up on the square. Brother Somerfield thought you might let me hut-up for the night in your castle yard. I think that's what he called it."

"Somerfield's a good guesser," replied Chambers. "Of course, ye kin. Arthur, fetch a lanthorn, and the key to the stockade gate from the cabin. It's the big key behind the front door. You'd best show your friend the way over the mill-race. Mind the little trestle bridge, it's loose at the far end."

"I know, sir," said Arthur, delighted to be found so importantly useful. "And I'll go and fetch the wagon for ye, Sal. Jed and I can bring it down here and pick ye up on the way. We'll lead the horses most careful."

"All right. I can have a word with the colonel, then. Try not to waken the women. And, Art, be sure to bring that kitten along. I'd be scalped if it gets lost."

Arthur hurried off after securing the key and the lanthorn.

"Spry youngster, that," remarked Colonel Chambers, holding the cabin door open for his guest. "He certainly spread your fame and glory in these parts. He's Burent's brother-in-law, the cooper at Fort Pitt. Know him? Mighty clever man, and the best cooper in the province, they all say."

"He's a mighty good man," agreed Salathiel, making a wry face inwardly. "Now, I wouldn't want to keep ye up, colonel. It's right late."

"Ye ain't keepin' me up, I'm doin' my accounts these winter evenings, but I do like a fire and warm hands and feet while I'm clerkin'. That's the reason we're stayin' in the cabin here. The big house's cold as a barn, unless you keep twenty fires goin'. I've a sight o' children used to do that, but they're all married and live out, every one of 'em; Ruhannah, who's just visitin' here, Jim, Ben, Bill, Jane, Adam, Joe, and Hetty. Yes, sir, I hev to call even my little Hetty 'Mrs. William Brown' now. Scarcely seems natur'l, but really it's natur'l as time." Here the colonel produced a jug from under his desk and, slinging it back of his wrist over his forearm, poured a jet accurately into two noggins without spilling a drop.

"I suppose you got practice and learned to handle your jug liquor that way drinkin' birthday toasts to all the children," said Salathiel, admiringly. "You've got nigh as many as Garrett Pendergass, I reckon."

Colonel Chambers laughed. "No, that's only the old Connycajig twist on a jug. Speakin' o' childer, I was really just tryin' to tell ye why the big house is so empty now, and how it comes I can't take ye into the cabin here like I'd hope to. I built the stone house in 'fifty-six and put a lead roof on it later. Just to keep off Injun fire-arrows. Some wits laughed. But the old place contained their jests and kept the har on their heads through many a raid. Afterwhile, for all my follies, I was appointed justice of the peace and made a colonel of the line. So I mounted an old cohorn and a blunderbuss and made a kind of fort out of the house for the militia. My court and the blue lodge still meets there. I'm lettin' the house stand empty, but I'm keepin' it up. All the ginerals mightn't prove so clever as Bouquet, and we might have raids here again. It's pesky nigh the mountains, ye know. Now, if you and Captain Jack would only settle down here, that'd be like a permanent regular garrison. Tell ye what, you and your missus come over to the cabin and have breakfast tomorrow mornin', and bring your little one. I'll tell Ruhannah and she'll set some extra batter for ye. Now, don't say no, it's all right, and I want to ask ye a lot of things about Captain Jack. He's an old friend o' mine. Well, 'here's powder in your horn, and good huntin'!' That'll warm ye! It's about ten years old."

"I feel that much younger already," said Salathiel. "It's powerful stuff."

The colonel looked up, listening.

"That must be your contraption comin' down the lane now, I guess," said he. "Sounds like artillery wheels. Have ye feed fer your nags?"

"Plenty, sir, and I do want to thank ye."

"Now, now," said the colonel, "you jes come over tomorrow mornin', and we'll really give ye somethin' to be thankful for." He followed Salathiel to the door and said good night to him.

Arthur was coming down the lane with a lanthorn, showing the way for Jed, who led the tired horses gingerly.

"They're still asleep in there," said Arthur. "And I found the kitten a fish head and put her in the seat-chest. It's only about a hundred yards or so to the castle. This here's the bridge now, the one the colonel said to be keerful about."

They were at the foot of the lane by this time, and the sound of running water filled their ears. After crossing the short bridge over the mill-race without mishap, they came out on a perfectly level piece of ground, with the mill-race on one side and the river on the other.

"The dam lies a bit farther down," said Arthur. "It's the spill-way ye hear so loud. But here we be!"

A stockaded log wall lay directly across their path. It was at the gate of this that they now halted, while Jed held the lanthorn and Arthur worked the big key in a huge and rusty padlock. Finally it gave, a bar tumbled, and the double leaves of the gate swung inward.

Salathiel stood stock-still for a moment from sheer surprise. The space ahead of him seemed to end in nothing but a field of stars. It looked as though only a few hundred feet farther and they would fall off the edge of the world.

Arthur laughed. "It does kind of get ye at first by night," he said. "You see, this here's kind of an island we're on, and you're lookin' out over the dam at the lower end of it. The house is over this way."

"Guess I'll get it clearer tomorrow," said Salathiel, "but let's get the horses bedded down. They're near done in."

"Yas, sah, in a jiffy," replied Jed. "Dah's de sheds now."

They drew up in a deep-sodded stable yard surrounded on three sides by sheds and penthouses in solid array. The side of the yard next the riverbank was occupied by Colonel Chambers's stone house that stared stolidly in the moonlight. All its windows were tightly boarded with heavy oaken shutters pierced with loopholes. The lead roof, wet with heavy dew, seemed to be molten under the moon and to be dripping hot metal over the eaves. A flight of white stone steps led up to its massive but extremely narrow door. The effect was strangely unpleasant, even formidable. The house at night bore the expression of a merciless fanatic showing his bared teeth in a bad dream.

This, however, was only incidentally to be noted by a side glance at most. It would have taken a great deal more than a dubious architectural welcome to have repulsed the tired travellers. They intended to spend the night and to find rest and refreshment in the very face of the frowning mansion. If nothing else, its eerie aspect was practically helpful in causing the young Negro Jed to develop a speed and concentration in getting his work done, which no one had particularly noticed as being characteristic of him before.

Something in the sound of the rushing and gurgling waters, the unexpected angle of owl-flights slanting through the moonlight, the angry silence of the grim house guarding its dark island domain so implacably, convinced Jed that *this* was a place where it was not healthy for a young person of colour, only recently removed from Dahomey by slavers, to tarry in. Nor did the rugged profile and menacing outlines of the big white man, who was detaining him, tend to sooth his African spirits. It was all frightfully strange, and the moonlight in America was cold. Consequently, Jed shivered, but his fingers flew all the faster.

The horses were unharnessed in a trice. Arthur led them to the sheds, and Salathiel bedded them down. He gave them plenty of dry straw to lie on and a generous supper of corn with a dash of precious salt as a special donative for their patient day's work. Tomorrow they must have a rest and a good going-over by a farrier. No one could get horses over the Stoney Batter without casting a few shoes. And most of those remaining were worn or working loose. The harness was laid out for a careful going-over on the morrow, and then all hands turned to, to give the teams a good rub-down and currying.

Thus, "in a jiffy", everything was suddenly done. Jed stood waiting hopefully, not daring to leave until Arthur, who still held the lanthorn, should be ready to go.

"You won't have a snack up at the store, then, like Mr. Somerfield said?" inquired Arthur, who had visions of a night of talk and forest tales by Salathiel, before the fire.

"Not tonight, young'un," laughed his friend. "You forget I'm not alone like I used to be," and he motioned towards the wagon.

"Shucks," said Arthur, "I'd jes forgot. But kin I see ye tomorrow?"

"Sure ye kin. I'll come over to the store, say about noon, with a bale of peltries I want fer to do a little hawse-tradin' over with old man Somerfield. You and him can paw them over first. And I guess any clever clark that brings in beaver to trade gets a bit of sugar on the side."

"Golly!" exclaimed Arthur. "Gol—*lee!*"

"Jed," said Salathiel, "you're a good man, and I'll tell your master as much. But listen—"

"Yas, sah, both ears am pintin' yuh way."

"I'll give you something right handsome when *you stop bein' scared of me*. Now, close the gate when you go out, and don't lock me in."

"Yas, sah."

Salathiel stood watching them depart as long as he could see the lanthorn sliding along the mill-race among the willows. Suddenly it ceased to show at the corner of the lane.

Actually, *he* wasn't body-tired at all. Driving was wearing, but it gave him small exercise. Colonel Chambers's drink still made him glow. And it was luck to be alone again in a safe place like this, sequestered from all strangers. The moon was beginning to sail high, and there was a heartening touch of frost in the night air. He had no words to express his sense of triumph at having arrived thus in the dawn country. It was a feeling only, a sensation of satisfaction. Indeed, the refreshing but monotonous rush of water had scoured all thought-in-words out of his head. Like a savage, he once more gave himself up to pure sensation and to being still and happy within. Time lapsed. This place *was* good, a fine grassy level surrounded by a hedge of trees, washed on all sides by living water. It was like some of his islands of refuge down the Ohio. Only one thing troubled him. He still smelled of horses and the dust of the road.

Twitching a blanket off the wagon seat on sudden impulse, he slid out of his clothes and walked to the river's edge. The cold air seemed to tighten about him. He tingled. He stood looking out over the black pool, where the stream backed up into a deep lake behind the dam. Somewhere, farther up, he could hear the roar of the falls where the Falling Spring branch dived into the Conococheague. Below, the dark roofs of the mill buildings rose vaguely above the dam. One seemed to be only half finished. But there was no one about.

Two or three night-feeding waterfowl were moving in the shadow of the opposite shore. The moony water flashed where they dived. Loons, probably. Winter could not be far behind. He gave the low chipping-cluck of their private night language, and watched them begin to edge over towards him cautiously. Then, suddenly, he sprang forward in a wide clean arc and flashed into the dark depths. As his head emerged, he gave the long weird laugh of the loon.

Two of the startled birds answered him, their wings thrashing violently as they took off into the night over the dam. The whole place rang with a raucous burst of wild demoniac laughter. In the face of the haggard moon, the Little Turtle pranced and capered on the riverbank, wringing the cold water out of his long hair, and dancing violently to dry himself off. He just felt fine. He glowed like a house afire.

Presently, he flung his blanket over his shoulders and ran back to the wagon. He crawled in stark naked, and squirmed under the covers on his bunk. He heard Frances stirring uneasily.

"*So* you're back again," she said.

He reached over in the dark and took her hand, pressing it to his lips and fondling her long soft fingers. Lord, it was good to find her here.

"Howly hiven," she whispered, "whir in God's beauteous world have ye taken us now? Are we on land or at sae? Hark to the rushin' of tireless waters! And what was that wild fleerin' laughter passed overhead jist now like a family rally o' banshees? Did ye meet up with them in yon empty house, in the quiverin' moonlight?" She sat up suddenly, badly scared by her own talk, and staring into the darkness.

"Lie down, sweetheart. Turn over on your easy side and sleep. I was jes talkin' with a flock of loons. You're safe on Colonel Chambers's mill isle, with the river and a fence all about ye. No one comes here but night fowl to feast on the eel grass. And tomor-row . . ."

"Yis," she said, "tomorrow?"

"We're to take breakfast with Colonel Chambers himself and his new-married daughter, in their nice little cabin up a grassy lane."

"Ye do well by us, Mr. Albine. Ye're a right clever man."

"Handy to have about?" he chuckled.

"Yis," she whispered, and softly withdrew her hand. "I think I'll be wearing me new blue linsey-woolsey and the yellow snood ye got fer me at Cumberland, the morrow for breakfast."

"Wear somethin'," he said. "But I do like ye best with nothin' on at all!"

"Sal, you're a woild man tonight! I can feel it," she whispered. "Come over and let me soothe that little red tartle that's always gnawin' at your heart. Maybe it will lie quieter on mine."

The night and the sound of the flowing river surrounded them. They drifted as one down an ever faster moving current, until the music of the real river's thoughtless monotone was lost. Then they went over the dam together—but not the one Colonel Chambers had built to turn the wheels of his mills.

13

Morning Transformation

BRIDGET WAS UP with the dawn next morning. She had heard her kitten scratching and mewing in the chest under the wagon seat and got up to release it. It emerged, growling, with the remnants of the fish head, and laying back its ears promptly disappeared into the grass.

Under the fading stars the child felt herself entirely alone, but she was pleased by this rather than frightened. Like her cat, she felt inherently able to fend for herself, provided she was not helped too much. And she also had a secret country that was hers only, one which she knew much better than to try to share with anyone else. It was, in fact, too delicate and subtle a place of magic to suffer the slightest interference. It concerned herself alone—but nearly, dearly, and sustainingly.

Bridget's private realm was always near-by, yet it could be found only by way of a kind of ghostly hide-and-seek that she played with herself. For there was a certain ritual and tomfoolery of mood-invoking conjuring that she had discovered by experiment was necessary to re-create her world successfully. Wild, lonely, and beautiful places, especially if they were mysteriously green, helped. Indeed, since they reminded her of her lucky escape through forest solitudes, they usually suggested her play to her. It was a game she called "Finding Mrs. McCandliss".

As she stood listening to the river that morning, she heard familiar voices talking to her as though they were only a short distance away; just around the corner in a recoverable past. All she had to do was "to go back". Undoubtedly, then, this was a good time, and certainly here was the kind of place in which to find Mrs. McCandliss.

Ga-trip, ga-trip, ga-trip, scuffed the loose moccasins on the small feet, tripping and scraping over the wet grass. Across the lonely front of the grimly staring house the small figure passed rapidly, skipping, holding her skirts out, now this way, and now that.

She rounded the corner of the dooryard and came out onto the wide open lawn that led over to the riverbank on the far side of the mansion.

The light grew, the house shifted its grim shadows and slowly began to smile in the growing light. The small figure in the centre of the lawn skipped faster and faster. Around and around she flew, saying

"Mama, I did,
Mama, I did."

She kept saying it over and over again. Then she leapt nimbly out of her big moccasins, leaving them close together on the grass, and began to whirl on her bare feet, her arms and her pigtails flying outward. All at once she stopped . . .

The rim of trees with their bare, black branches that grew thickly all about the verge of the island, with the morning mist flowing through them, kept whirling about her in a rapid circle. Gradually, the misty ring slowed down. Suddenly it stopped, too. Her vision cleared. She pressed both fists against her temples, hard. She stared . . . She knew she would find her . . .

"Hello, Mrs. McCandliss," she whispered, "hello. Be'ent you kind of cold in a wispy nightgown?"

The reply, whatever it was, brought a confident smile to the child's lips, which blended perfectly now with the bright promise of the first glance of morning sunshine.

While the sun rose small and redly-round out of the river mists down the distant valley, and then began to glitter like molten gold, Bridget stood as though rooted, passive, with round, wide eyes, engaged in a long and mystical conversation.

It was not the kind of talk that can be overheard, listen as closely as you will. It occurred neither in space nor in time. It went on in Bridget's head.

But that was not the way it seemed to her. Her lips moved when she talked, and moved also to shape the words of reply. She spoke and was spoken to. She saw, and she heard again things that were comforting and familiar. She remembered completely again exactly who she was. But she couldn't tell where she was.

Wherever it was, she couldn't stay there long . . .

. . . afterwhile she found herself standing wide awake, looking out over the lawn and the roofs of the mills below the dam, into a patch of especially clear blue sky.

My, but it was going to be a pretty day! And it had been *so* reassuring to find Mrs. McCandliss. Of course she would mind what her mother told her to do, even if Mrs. McCandliss did have a hole in her head. She felt quite confident again.

Her kitten came to her through the damp grass, mewing piteously. She picked it up, and, although it still smelt of fish, let it snuggle against her. Talking nonsense to it softly, she walked back to see if her new folks were still asleep. As she neared the wagon, the cat jumped out of her arms.

Salathiel was up, stripped to the waist, and busy about the sheds, watering and feeding the horses. That was good, now there would be somebody lively to talk to! She began to skip again to a fine old skipping tune:

> "Mind your manners and say your prayers,
>   Keep your feet on the heavenly stairs.
>   Troubles will come by threes and pairs,
>   But mind your manners and say your prayers."

"Here she is, Melissa. I told you so," shouted Salathiel, "and the kitten, too. They've just been out for an early morning traipse together."

Frances poked her head out of the back of the wagon, reassured to find Bridget had not wandered away—and just in time to see Salathiel toss her up on his shoulders and gallop off with her into the sheds, where with much noisy merriment, laughter, neighing and pounding of hoofs, the horses were roused and turned loose into a small pasture behind the sheds.

Nothing is more ponderously ridiculous than a full-grown horse rolling with four iron-shod feet pawing the air, while it looks at you skittishly from the corner of its eyes, its head upside down—nothing, except when it scrambles to its feet again and kicks out gaily behind like a colt, with heels dainty and trim as a watersogged mop. The snorting and other noises accompanying such performances are always superb. Bridget could scarcely laugh hard enough to suit the occasion, as the four horses squirmed and rolled about in the paddock.

And it *was* an occasion.

As soon as the horses had recovered from their astonishment at not being led out and hitched to the wagon for another day's desperate haul—as soon as they had begun rolling and cavorting in the paddock from pure animal spirits, it was as plain to Bridget, as it was to them, that on this particular sunny morning a holiday had been declared. It was going to be like a Sabbath day, only it was to be merry. To her, at least, it remained in memory as a wonderful day. For from the very beginning of it, from her standpoint, remarkable things continued to happen.

"Hurry, you two," called Frances from the wagon, "if that's Colonel Chambers's cabin where I see smoke rollin' out of the chimley, they're already up and gettin' breakfast. 'Tis with our best foot forward we'll stip over their honourable threshold this foin mornin'. Heat me a kettle of hot water, Sal. And come here, Bridget! I'm going to dress you fancy and do your hair."

Nor was fashion that morning to be confined to ladies only, as Salathiel discovered when he sat down as usual to clean and polish his rifle-gun. While the small fire he had kindled to heat the water was doing its work, Melissa looked out at his languid activities and became unexpectedly emphatic.

"Sure, and it's yerself ye might be furbishing instead of pamperin' your rusty musket," she began pointedly. "Did it iver occur to ye that ye won't be needin' to nurse Twin-Eyes at your breast any more? With five mountain ranges and the king's royal armies betwixt you and your troublesome friends, you can wean your iron baby and lay her up in her cradle. And, Howly Mither, how I wisht ye would! Ye might even put on some dacent clothes, and do your lanky hair with a bit of a bow behind, and sweep the bristles off your craggy chin. What's the use of our haulin' a valet's kit over the high mountains if you won't use it in the lowlands? Do ye think I'd be after callin' it macaroni to visit Colonel Chambers with ye in a deerskin shirt and a turkey fither in your hair? How would ye like me to riprisint you in me ould butternut kersey, bare fate, and no shtays? 'Twould be a grand bow we'd be after makin' to your foin friends in that fattle. Look, the pot's boiling! So get out your razors and a bit of pomade."

"No wonder it's bilin'," said he. "All the time you've been droppin' hot coals onto it over my head. Liken I might bile over myself, if ye keep on."

"Go long wid ye," said she, "and make yourself into a gintleman. It ain't like ye didn't know how," she added.

"Oh, I know *how*," he replied.

"But the question is do ye know *when?*" she countered.

"Looks like it's goin' to be this mornin'," he admitted. He stoppered his rifle thoughtfully, and giving it a farewell polish with his deerskin sleeve, laid it away carefully in the slings under the ridge-pole.

So all the time he had been heating the water for himself!

Secretly, he was delighted. How many times had he looked forward to what he was going to do this morning. He took the kettle off the fire, got out Ecuyer's case of razors, and for the first time in many a long day brought out Johnson's valet kit and looked it over. Afterwhile he unpacked his best blue serving suit from Fort Pitt and considered it carefully.

"What day is it, Melissa?" he asked.

"Sure and it's Saturday," she said. "I don't know what saint's day it might be. I've forgot. But why would ye be wantin' to know a mere trifle like the day o' the week?"

"Oh, I thought I might as well begin right, if I'm going to be shavin' regular from now on," he replied, and picking out the captain's razor marked "Saturday", he began to strop it vigorously.

Melissa was so pleased she had tears in her eyes.

She had a plan for getting on in the world and holding her head high. Now she felt she had a partner in the scheme, one who would not only act but was going to dress properly for his part. She had not always been sure of it before. Sometimes she had wondered just how it would go in the City if he walked down the street, Twin-Eyes on one arm and she on the other. This was only going to be a rehearsal this morning, to be sure. But it might be an important first appearance, too. In all the country about, up and down the Conoco-cheague and the Conodoguinit, Chambers was regarded as the most respectable family.

Now if Bridget only had her new red shoes!

Indeed, if it hadn't been too much to ask, Frances would have liked to have had Salathiel get out the peruke-curling irons and heat them up to do a little primping on her own hair. *That,* she decided, however, had best come later. She sighed, but happily. Some things could wait.

Nevertheless, it was a decidedly respectable and pristine, if not a fashionable trio which emerged from the old stockade gate about an hour later and took the path along the mill-race towards Colonel Chambers's cabin.

Melissa had not only put on her new blue linsey-woolsey and yellow silk snood, but had also seen fit to wear a broad wool shawl and a small straw beehive bonnet besides.

The shawl was deep blue, with a looped fringe knotted from heavy white linen cord, and had heavy scarlet flowers, roses probably, embroidered on it in concentric rings. Both the fringe and the roses Frances had contrived with her own skilful fingers. And Bridget, too, had profited by her ever-flitting needle and deft shears.

In the early morning hours before leaving Lyttleton, Frances had reshaped and stitched together a small butternut dress packed in Bridget's basket, one that the much-harassed Mrs. Patton had been working on for weeks. It was not hemmed yet, but if the bastings would hold, it would do, Frances told herself. She had only four pins to her name, and she had "borrowed" those from Bella Pendergass at Bedford.

This butternut dress, however, with a small white kerchief about her neck, pigtails tied with black bows, the new red stockings, and her brown rabbitskin hood gave Bridget a feeling of utter elegance, a conviction which even the big moccasins tied especially tight this morning with deerskin thongs about her small ankles, could not disturb.

She therefore tripped along, occasionally stubbing her toe, but otherwise daintily, carrying a large calfskin reticule with adult dignity. In this hairy maw reposed the badly battered and paint-blistered head and torso of an old wooden doll called Queen Alliquippa.

Alliquippa was Bridget's chief secret treasure and darling child. And her mother was now revolving maternally what might be done in town for improving the lot of her offspring. All that Alliquippa needed was everything. Thus there could be no doubt but that she was quite like other people's children. In fact, in the back of her mind, Bridget had already resolved that her Big Man could easily accomplish the desired rehabilitation. And why not? Look what wonders he had done for himself this morning! Indeed, except for his permanent size, his hawklike face and mangled ear, Bridget hardly knew him as she trotted along, looking up admiringly and holding his hand.

A white linen shirt, a leather stock, Johnson's carefully refurbished deep-cuffed Osnaburg blues with tails, a waistcoat, and small clothes to match; long black military gaiters and brass buckled shoes, these, and a low-crowned beaver hat, which any macaroni in London would gladly have given ten pounds for, were the plain but none the less potent elements in a carefully pondered and long-anticipated transformation; one for which Frances Melissa, if she had only known it, had but to give a sign to bring about.

Actually, he had long waited for a proper opportunity to burst thus from his sombre forest cocoon. Not that he fancied a butterfly of fashion would emerge, but he had often dreamed of the day when some of the valeting skill he had so painfully learned at Fort Pitt to practise on others might be decently applied to himself.

Well, this was the morning! Melissa had certainly said "when" —and the long-closed chests of the erstwhile meticulous Johnson had magically opened up.

Pomade has a powerful way even with lanky hair. He had now combed it back, oiled it, and tied it exactly as he would have for a bag-wig. But he had not powdered it. He had not done that, because he remembered he was neither a soldier nor a servant. None the less, the pomatum had set firmly. As a result a certain grim aspect of wildness in his appearance had inexplicably vanished. It was replaced now by a kind of formidable formality. This effect, it so happened, matched the cold grey of his eyes and plain pewter buttons quite well. And it was further reinforced, somewhat ponderously perhaps, by a heavy oak stick with a half-pound iron ball on it. This "cane" he carried as a mere trifle under his left arm, remembering how Ecuyer had handled his Malacca stick. But light as this weaver's beam was, its heft served to confirm him, and was at hand at all times ready to encourage others, in the firm opinion that there was nothing whatever but what was most becoming and absolutely to be taken seriously in every item of Mr. Albine's sartorial form and style.

Thus newly tricked out and fortified in his own opinion, he made his way along the mill-race path, despite the hisses of Colonel Chambers's flock of green geese, like a cock o' the walk, with Bridget clutching his left hand and Melissa leaning upon his right arm. The morning sun glistened, and the huge roses on Melissa's shawl bloomed. If they were a little enormous, they had been created thus hopefully for great occasions. And who, if he had met the three of them there that bright morning coming along the willow-lined mill-race, would have had the heart to stop Bridget skipping or Frances smiling, by saying so.

"Mind your manners and say your prayers,
    Keep your feet . . .

"*Ow*," exclaimed Bridget, "my toe!" and sighed a little breathlessly, for Salathiel now began to stride along more eagerly, as they crossed the small bridge over the mill-race and turned up into Colonel Chambers's lane. There the smoke still rolled quite reassuringly out of the chimney-top.

Mistress Ruhannah, no doubt, was busy making ready. From a large and hospitable door the leather latchstring could be seen hanging out.

They were only halfway up the front yard path, however, when the door was jerked violently inward and a shrill heart-stopping scream that died away into sobbing groans and agonized gurgles stopped them in their tracks. It was a woman shrieking, and she was in the house. The voice of pain continued, although more subdued.

"What the devil?" grumbled Salathiel, regretting his rifle.

"Jasus, sweet Howly Babe! Belike the colonel's married daughter has burnt the hoe cakes. And here we be all dressed up only for a family shindy." Frances began to turn away bitterly.

Salathiel put a restraining hand on her arm—but, indeed, as the crying in the cabin continued, the placid tenor of Colonel Chambers's domestic life did seem to be in question.

Then a tall ungainly woman, holding her face with one hand over her mouth, stalked out of the cabin, moaning. Blood oozed through her fingers. She gave the strangers a brief agonized glance, turned, and fled up the lane towards the town, her white mob-cap bobbing.

Bridget began to whimper.

At that Colonel Chambers came out on his door-stoop, and seeing his bidden guests standing at the gate huddled together, called out reassuringly. Plainly he was somewhat nonplused, if not embarrassed by their appearance.

"Rat-me, if I knew ye at first. Well, well, beaver hats, new bonnets and all! I'm delighted to know ye, madam. What a sorry welcome you've had! But you mustn't mind it. That's just the way things do happen around here. Poor Mrs. Flannery! It was a turrible wisdom tooth she had. I often say to folks like her when they come to me for comfort: 'The worst turn an affliction takes may be only a blessing in disguise.' Now, if that tooth hadn't bealed as turrible as it did, I'd have had to use the horse pincers instead of the door. As it was, it popped out jist like a loosened bung. All it needed was a stout cord and a firm jerk."

As proof of this gentle proposition, the colonel picked up a large trine-pronged tooth that still lay on the floor and dropped it into a black bag. This he now shook, listening to the clicking of many teeth within, with obvious professional satisfaction.

"There's more agony laid to rest in that bag than in most grave-yards," he remarked. "But I *do* wisht they wouldn't come around moanin' like Grief bewitched, before breakfast."

No one in the company was inclined to disagree with his emphatic comment—on the contrary. But the scene of dental carnage was soon forgotten as they looked about them at the genteel furnishings of the cabin parlour.

In one corner was the colonel's desk with the jug under it. In another stood a spinning wheel with a treadle, and a small tambour frame with some bright half-finished embroidery. A banjo clock clicked on the wall with a faint echoing hum from a loose bell spring each time the pendulum swung, saying "I'*m* domestic, I'*m* domestic, I'*m* domestic."

"Ruhannah," called the colonel, leaning through the door into the kitchen wing, "Mrs. Flannery's gone with all her pain, and here be our visitors. And mighty pretty they look," he added. "You'd best put off your check apron."

A merry-looking young blonde, dressed in stays with waist puffs and a wired skirt, came through the door, hastily rearranging her kerchief over her plump shoulders.

"My daughter, Mistress Colhoun," said the colonel, proudly. "Mr. and Mrs. Albine—and?"

"Miss Bridget McCandliss," murmured Frances.

Bridget's deep curtsy set a prim standard of manners. For a moment or two there was enough bowing, bobbing, scraping and murmuring of politenesses to make even Frances Melissa happy.

And certainly it was obvious that the Chambers were not only impressed but more than pleasantly surprised. For a while there was a certain formal tenseness in the air, something which Frances loved. It was the necessary prelude to respect, she felt, and squeezed her man's arm. She combined this signal with a little dig in his ribs, as they went into the kitchen together, to call his attention to the fact that her plan for getting on in this world was working.

He thought so, too.

They found their places naturally, the three females standing together at one side of the table. Colonel Chambers raised his grizzled leonine face and looked at the ceiling.

"O Lard," said he in a tone of reverent conversation, "bless these good victuals to our use. May we remember the labour of Thy servants in bringing them to our mouths, that health in humbleness, grace in plenty may be ours in serving Thee."

Whatever stiffness had once starched the atmosphere for a moment in the other room now limbered into good-natured ease and hearty enjoyment, as they all sat down to breakfast.

14

Breakfast

ALE IN THE MORNING is a positive social emollient, and the colonel's was of the best from his own brew-house.

Much to Salathiel's satisfaction, there was no "coffee soup", and so far Mrs. Colhoun had made no motion towards employing her mother's pewter tea set, the large urn of which smirked complacently from a table in the corner. There was small-beer for Bridget, however, and since the colonel laced the ale with a bit of brandy, tongues were soon loosened, while heavy feeding and light conversation flourished.

Mina and Tina Oister, mother and daughter, two coloured women with Nanticoke blood,* who looked Moorish, with brass earrings, yellow head cloths and wadded gingham gowns, lent an almost buccaneer air to the broad, low kitchen room, padding back and forth in their rag slippers from the fire-in-the-wall at one end of the ell to the family table set at the other.

Fried hominy mush in quantities, cornpone fingers, tree-syrup, a platter of trout from the Falling Spring, sausages, scrambled eggs, and a cold venison ham reposing in the centre of the table were the principal gastronomic topics discussed, along with local news, personal anecdotes by the colonel, politics and Masonic confidences; while the domestic chatter and gossip of the women, in which the two Oisters occasionally joined, encouraged by Bridget's appreciative giggles, overlapped the deeper voices of the men with recurring ripples of comment frequently breaking into laughter.

Out of all this the grand purpose of the occasion gradually unfolded. Like Mrs. Flannery's tooth, it was triple rooted: First, the colonel was anxious, as the head of the tribe of Chambers, to enter-

* Weslager, C. A., "The Nanticoke Indians in Early Pennsylvania History."

tain and to impress all worthy and distinguished strangers who passed through his bailiwick, either to or from the frontiers, with the genuine warmth of heart of himself and his people. He was a successful man of the world that embraced two fertile valleys, and proud of it. Secondly, he sought not only to entertain but also, if possible, permanently to detain promising visitors and travellers as settlers in his new town laid out only the summer before, namely, Chambersburg. And lastly, Colonel Ben had long ago discovered that the end of making a living is to live; in fact, that short of dying, living is inevitable and you might as well make life, when opportunity served, as pleasant as possible. And this was an opportunity. It was Indian summer; mild early November. The sun shone with a kindly warmth reminiscent of spring. The harvest was in. The Indians were quiet. Mrs. Chambers was away.

As the morning grew warmer, the colonel, without interrupting himself, threw open the doors and wedged up both the windows. Outside in the carpenter shed, Jed, who had developed the eye of a connoisseur for the quantity and quality of smoke rising from prosperous chimneys, a talent much whetted by the parsimony of his master, sat on a wooden horse with his feet in the deep shavings, and from time to time received a platter from the kitchen, piled high with fragments of the feast and occasionally garnished in serving by a smacking testimonial of affection from Tina Oister.

Inside the cabin, talk, the kind of talk out of which almost everything human emerges, flowed naturally onward. That is not to say, however, that it was entirely desultory. Like the river he had dammed, Colonel Chambers was also inclined to monopolize and direct any loose stream of conversation into useful channels, those which might eventually turn the wheels of his grist-mills.

Perhaps it is unfortunate that some of the kind of talk the colonel was indulging in could not be overheard or by some means have become audible to several influential gentlemen who were also talking in more fashionable but equally provincial accents in the halls of Westminster in the distant valley of the Thames.

To be sure, the colonel was conversing in a flat-toned Scotch-Irish idiom, one which almost amounted to a dialect, with certain local frontier peculiarities. But for all that, it was a very ancient form of plain English, and he was saying the kind of things that have always most concerned the folk who use the English tongue, subjects which it is well shaped to deal with. He was talking about people, politics, and the land; how they could be brought together and best formed into a livable future. The colonel was much concerned with such matters, whimsically sometimes, but always consciously and carefully. For there was one thing peculiar to him and his kind in their time and place, they were fathering a commonwealth, and they knew it.

Colonel Chambers was anxious to have Albine and Captain Jack, and some of the others of his rangers, if possible, come to settle in Chambersburg. It was high time they were settling down, he indicated. And where better than here? For his old friend, Captain Jack, the colonel would do much—everything! As for Salathiel, he would give him a lot on the square in town with full five years to pay for it, and also advise him in choosing and help him to take up some of the best of the "slate-pine lands" along the base of the ridge. Now, the colonel insisted, was the time. In a few years the land east of the mountains would be full of people. They were coming! He was certain of it.

Two congregations, nigh three hundred and fifty souls, mostly Marylanders but all Presbyterians, were on their way west from Carlisle even now. Rumour had it they were bound for more southern regions, however. Somewhere far south and west in the back country of Virginia lay their promised land. If so, they would turn south at Chambersburg on the old trace to Hagerstown, and then go on down, edging towards the sunset, as the mountains marched inland, to settle eventually about the sources of west-running rivers whose courses and ends only a few men knew.

"I swear," said the colonel, "if I was younger I might go with them." The thought of it evidently excited him. "Sometimes I wish I could live three lifetimes jist to find out what the tarnal place is like tother side of the big blue hills. But drat me, what am I sayin'! I'm gittin' along in years, and what I'm goin' to have to do is to try to argue some of these good Presbyterian folk into tarryin' on here. Maybe you'll jine me in that?" he suggested, smiling hopefully.

"That's what I'm doin' now, sir," replied Salathiel. "I'm to go and wait for a spell at Carlisle, until Arthur St. Clair can get a parcel of his new settlers together for me to lead over the mountains to Bedford and Ligonier. He's got land thereabouts, and permits for settlement. There's a new plantation laid out in a circle at Ligonier—or Loyalhanna, as some call it. I'm promised to St. Clair for that service for a spell, and he's payin' me a bit, meanwhile."

"Only a bit, I'll bet," grinned the colonel, who was obviously disappointed at this piece of news. "But later you might like to bring people this way for my town, maybe?

"Now let me tell you somethin' about this country around here," he went on, "I mean the Connycajig and Conodoguinit valleys. They're all one really, just a kind of nat'ral path over the neck between the Potomac and the Susquehanna. So this country ain't so spang new around here as some people think.

"There were English traders came up this way from the bays, and Frenchmen down from Canady at least a hundred years gone, and maybe more. You see, it's only a mile or two of a portage between the Connycajig and the Conodoguinit, so you kin come up the Potomac this way from Virginia or Maryland and cross over the watershed to the Susquehanna by way of our two handy streams. That way you can git all the way north and nigh to the big lakes, almost without takin' your canoe out of the water. And that's a mighty help, especially if you've got heavy trade goods or bales of furs to carry.

"The Injuns knew all about this carry-over, of course, and there was trade this way long before there was any white traders. That's the reason the English found French goods, knives, kittles, hatchets and sich on the Cheeseapeek even when they first came over. The tribes traded 'em down south all the way from the coast fisheries in Canady. I've no doubt of it, else where did the steel hatchets come from? The Dutch and Swedes got their northern furs by this path, and quarrelled about it around the river mouth before the English came in.

"Oh, it wasn't all peaceful, not by no means. This trace was a warpath, too. It was down this way the Five Nations came to strike the Susquehannocs. Did ye ever hear about that tribe? Giants they were, all over six and seven feet tall. There's no Injuns left like 'em any more. They lived here in the midnight o' time on the fat o' the land, when this country was all a great deer park, swarmin' full of elk and shaggy buffalo, wild nut-trees, and fat sassy bars. And the river ripples creamed every year with schools o' shad and salmon. Somethin's happened to the salmon and sich. It ain't like it was for fishin'. Too many dams—lower down, I mean! But the time I'm talkin' about was long before even the Shawanese came pokin' in this way, and the Delawares still lived peaceably, all to the north and east.

"*Hi-de-do,* I'd sure like to have seen it then! Yes, even though fightin' giant Injuns with a snap-haunce by turnin' a wheel to strike sparks, while they filled ye full of arrows till ye looked like a porcupine, mustn't have been so natty. No, it's the rifle-gun we owe this land to, and the Pennsylvanians perfected that. Riflin' was a clever German refinement on murderin' irons. The Quakers always relied on prayers and treaties, and the slow English just stuck to their old smooth-bore muskets. Friends would never have moved the Susquehannocs.

"An old Baltimore trader once told me the Susquehannocs went in for steam lodges, and rubbin' and sweatin'. And they were especially fond and fancy about genderin'. The squaws ran the tribe and showed the girls how. At the big summer full-moon corn dance, when everybody was fatted-up and slick with bar's grease, they went to it with the young warriors, while the drums and bull whistles and rattle gourds kept *tunkin'* and *swishin'* and *bunkin',* and not to no idle tune, let me tell ye!

"Potency, you might say, was their tribal god, and they carved his big totem all about here on the flat river rocks, and wherever there was a broad piece of nat'ral slate to put down what was much on their minds. If ye know where to look, ye kin still find them signs. There was an especially notable one at Standing Stone up above Shirley. In the end, though, it didn't keep the tribe from perishin'. The Long House struck 'em sudden in the night.

"The story is the Susquehannocs were to jine the Delawares, but they kept on havin' a war dance on the night the big battle was foughten. After that the Delawares were put in skirts,* and what was left of the Susquehannocs was a miserable remnant. Firewater finally did for most of 'em. And the last of 'em, if I hear right, were murdered off at Lancaster jail last December, when the Paxtang boys settled with the rump of the Conestogas. There's been an awful row about that in the City. Guess you'll hear a lot more about it when you git downcountry.

"No, sir, it ain't so prime and spang-up new around here as some folks now comin' in to settle like to think. It's old and disputed ground. The Marylanders, them that came in first, found the Injuns had burnt off the forest to make open huntin' lands, and they liked that. Some of 'em built stone houses and settled down along the portage trace, doin' a bit of fur trading and easy farmin'. But 'twas the huntin' they liked best and lived by mostly. They brought some nagurs with 'em to tidy up. It was a grand easy life for many years before the French and Injun troubles came on. It was secret and plentiful. Time kind o' stopped for 'em up here on this plain and in the valleys round about. Just the days and seasons went on. When the southrons needed somethin' they couldn't make, they sent down the Potomac for it with a few prime beaver pelts for currency.

"That way they used to hear a little news from the world now and then. But it was always too late for 'em to do much worryin' over it. There were no taxes or ground rents here, not a shillin'. And so country politics was nothin' to them or riyal wars over the water. They just claimed to hold under Lord Baltimore's grant, shot wild turkeys, and tried to keep the deer out of their young orchards. They had a few cows lived on the tall buffalo grass and some horses. The pigs bred wild, thrivin' on the chestnut and acorn mast. And acorns do make a fine kind of hominy, if ye know how to leach 'em

* Weslager, C. A., "The Delaware Indians as Women."

out and dry the meal. No doubt ye do. The Shawanese was especially good at it, come to think of it.

"But I guess the main reason the southrons abode here so well was they didn't try to grow too many artificial things. They just took what they needed out of the woods. All they wanted, but no more. Well, in a way it was too bad their time couldn't go on. I opine it was kind o' too easy and too gentle to last. Anyhow, that's what we mean by 'old times' around here, when some of us elders git talkin' about the 'old colony days'.

"I can still recollect a few of the family names of the early Marylanders, and so kin my brothers. The Oisters was one family. They left their nagurs here. But none of our children kin recall them, or care. The old Maryland people are forgotten. But they allers liked to be private. They even had their own family graveyards that are all gone to Jimson weeds or second-growth thicket now, and in some of them the trees are pretty big. As for their stone houses, when the Injuns burned 'em down in the raids, they just turned to heaps of white lime. The grass is a little greener there, if ye know where to look. Just a little greener, that's all."

Out of regret for vanished Eden, Colonel Chambers now inverted his formula for enduring sorrow and laced his brandy with a little ale. A toast without words, but apparently to the good old days, followed.

"How did ye happen to come into this country so early, colonel? I hear you and your family made some of the first tomahawk improvements along these branches and back streams," queried Salathiel.

"Tomahawk improvements! A little better than that, I guess! We did a lot more than just blazin' the trees and callin' it ours. I'll tell you," continued the colonel, leaning back and putting his heavy boots on another chair, while filling his pipe.

"There were four of us Chambers brothers, myself, Jim, Bob, and Joe. We came over from Antrim to Philadelphia, in 'twenty-seven, and we all believed in three things"—the colonel enumerated them on his fingers—"in the Westminster Confession, in stickin' together, and in ownin' land with a good millsite on it.

"At that time the Penns were gittin' pretty anxious over the Marylanders' movin' in here. They didn't admire to hear it none. They were afraid the southrons might eventually filter clean acrost the watershed and claim up into the Susquehanna valley. At least they might have made good the Calvert claims along the border, and they were certain to interfere with the fur trade. So, although the Penns hadn't boughten the land from the Indians yet and the Pennsylvania land office wouldn't sell any tracts west of the Susquehanna, still the proprietaries themselves made very temptin' promises of large grants later at easy quit-rent terms for smart people who would move in and make their own bargains with the Injuns, and settle.

"Well, we had already settled at Fishing Creek back east and had built a mill there and were doin' well when your old friend, Captain Jack, who knew all about these parts, told me about the wonderful millsites up and down the Connycajig and the Conodoguinit. I was jist turned one and twenty then, and feelin' my oats. And I talked so much about this country and what the 'Half Indian', that was what we called Captain Jack, said about it that brother Jim took fire too, and went to Pennsbury and saw his honour, Thomas Penn. That was what did the trick for us. Seein' we were all millwrights and strong and likely lads, and there were four of us, the governor made us mighty favourable promises, and we came west and searched out all this country like the Promised Land, lookin' for likely town- and millsites.

"Jim settled at the head of Green Spring near here, Robert made his nest at Middle Spring nigh Shippensburg, and I came here with brother Joe at the mouth of the Falling Spring. I soon set to and built me a house and brought my first wife upcountry, her that afterward died.

"Well, sir, that was the first regular hewn log house with lapped shingles and clapboards on this branch. But it didn't stand long! One spring I went to Harris's to trade, and while I was away, bedanged if a worthless pelt hunter didn't burn it down jist for the iron nails. When I come back, he said he was right sorry, but he kept the nails. After that I went in for stone whenever I could.

"It was pretty hard goin' at first. Joe stayed with me for a while but gave up after a spell and went back to the old mill at Fishing Creek, where he had a girl. But I didn't quit, not even when Mrs. Chambers died havin' her first baby and left me to bring up young Jim alone. I made firm friends with the Injuns. I warned the old Marylanders off, and I got a few spry young fellers to come in and settle here. The trick was, I put up a saw-mill, and we could rip boards out for the new houses. After quite a few more families moved in, I built the grist-mill. Water keeps runnin' downhill all the time, and it does help a settlement mightily when you kin put it to work for you. The proprietaries liked what I was doin'. The Penns finally bought the Injuns out, and in 'thirty-four I got my grant confirmed, four hundred acres right here where the town and mills now stand.

"Naturally, it wasn't all easy like clearin' the blood with tansy and boneset tea in the spring. The Injuns were more than a nuisance sometimes. They always liked to loaf in our kitchen, and finally we had to stop it. Once they tried to steal a nagur wench and young Ben's watch, one day when we were hayin' in the broad meadow below the dam. But I took after 'em with the coon dogs and gave 'em an all-night chase acrost the river that finally brought 'em to time. Still, that warn't nothin' much, and we never had any real bloody troubles till just before Braddock's time.

"The truth is we did pretty well here. We kept the wanderin' rum traders out. One summer I rid down into the valley of Virginia and married me a new wife. She was a Welsh pastor's daughter. She filled the house with pretty children, and taught everybody the old-time psalm tunes. A good many people came in in the late forties, and the Marylanders felt uneasy and kind o' gave up arguin' with us Macs. That tickled the proprietaries. They allowed me a magistrate's commission and later sent me over to England to testify in their behalf in London about our south boundary. That was in the big chancery suit they had with Lord Baltimore.

"While I was over there, I took the opportunity to visit home to Ireland. The main thing that struck me was how turrible poor people were, how small everything seemed, and how there wasn't a chance for a man to git an acre of his own. I guess I talked wild turkey and sweet chestnuts, and free land and liberty, better than I thought. Anyway, a whole parcel o' folks listened and decided to come after me out of Antrim. And most of 'em came right here to the Falling Spring.

"Well, I never heard any of 'em were disappointed with Pennsylvania, not even when the Injun troubles came. No one that I knew of ever went back to Ireland. They saw their children could git ahead here. Even in the worst years they never forgot that. Some was pretty skeered, but they all acted as if it was much better to have grandpap scalped than all the grandchilder skinned for rack-rent, till kingdom come."

"I once thought of goin' back to the old country myself with one of the officers of the Sixtieth," said Salathiel. "Thought I'd like to see London and Paris and Switzerland, and the fine life that goes on over there, for a while. I've been readin' about it in whatever books I could pick up, and Major Trent had quite a few at Pittsburgh."

"You!" The colonel laughed. "You'd be a curiosity to 'em over there. There ain't room enough for ye. The chairs would break when you tried to sit on 'em. Freedom's dyin' slowly o' greed and new macaroni refinement. Nobody cares for anything but his own little trade, whether it's bein' a duke or a saddler. If you don't inherit, and can't git, you're liable to end up in prison for debt. It's the London Whigs and big marchants who are in the saddle now.

Now that Great Britain's licked the world, they're out to make England a tollgate. Everybody will have to pass through it, and everybody will have to pay. England's goin' to be the eye of the needle that sewed the empire together, and trade will have to be the pack-thread that follows through the eye."

"Maybe we'll be a kind of thimble over here to keep 'em from stabbin' their own thumb," grinned Salathiel.

"Liken we might," said the colonel, quite seriously.

"You see, they've got a way o' thinkin' about this continent as a kind of mine you kin dig things out of to put on ships and take away. It's really the same with the British as it is with the dons. Gold with the Spaniards in South America and the Indies; furs and everything else in North America with the British. All of Europe's the same about the colonies. But this here habit o' thinkin' of America as the place where the tree with the golden apples grows; that it was planted there to be shook by Hercules and baskets of fruit carried home by the lucky to the old country—oh, that's an old story! But suppose Hercules gets tired makin' trips back and forth, and just decides to settle down and tend his own orchard. I'll bet they'd find it was agin the law," chuckled the colonel.

"I ain't heard of Herquelees," admitted Salathiel.

"It's jist an old heathen story," murmured the colonel, knocking out his pipe—and refilling it. "Ye ain't read all the books yit. A lot o' 'em have been left behind over there, all except the Good Book. It keeps catchin' up with us even here."

The colonel's pipe now began to glow, and he puffed a cloud of smoke that rolled slowly out the open window.

"Now look a-here, young feller," said he, "you're agoin' downcountry to the City. And you're goin' to hear and see a sight o' things. I kin see you're keen on that, and I don't blame ye. But don't ye go too far. What I'm indicatin' is to advise ye to stop at the edge of the big water. You was born on this side. I wasn't, but just the same I found I couldn't go back when I went over again. They wouldn't let me. Just one look at you would do. You ain't tame, and they don't like that. You'd larn the rules, but you'd break 'em. I do guess."

The colonel paused for a moment to press his fill down for a final draw.

"Now this is jumpin' a lot of fences and cuttin' acrost claims from what we've been talkin' about, but it's part o' the same story, too. What you'll be needin' to be doin' is to find out how best to get along in Pennsylvania. And there's a sight o' different people and interests in this province. There's more kinds of people here than in any other colony. There's Germans, Welsh, Irish, Scots, Scotch-

Irish, Dutch, Swedes, and Injuns and nagurs. And there's the
English-English that holds 'em together and speaks the old sovereign
tongue and makes the laws, bein' as they brought the law with 'em,
not only in their books but in their minds and ways of doin' things.
Well, that's one thing.

"Then there's all kinds o' Christians in Pennsylvania; Quakers;
Anabaptists of many peculiar German sects, Lutherans, Moravians,
Dunkards, Mennonites; Presbyterians o' the auld kirk of Scotland
and seceders; Church of England High and Low; Methodists; and
a few papists, to say nothin' o' hermits and queer Protestant monker-
ies and nunneries. And on the frontiers there's the naked heathen
makin' medicine in the wild woods. You'll meet 'em all, and you'll
hear 'em and see 'em. And ye kin make up yer mind which path is
the best one to take to heaven or the nighest stairs to bring back
the kingdom of God to earth. Ye kin find out what makes the most
music for yer own soul. And nobody will hinder ye. Ye've got the
legal right to be damned yer own way, for that matter. This is the
only province or country on the face of the earth where you'll not
be fined for not thinkin' jist one way, or taxed to pay for some
monopoly and patent on salvation. Jist step over the borders in any
direction out of Penn's grant, and ye'll find out.

"William Penn's plan is the best one there is, I do believe. But
I will say it does play hell with Pennsylvania politics with so many
different opinions as to how best to bring heaven down somewhere
between the Delaware and the Allegheny. Maybe paradise will just
keep slippin' west down the Ohio. There's an old story about heaven
lyin' westward that the poets have always told. Meanwhile, I'm
waitin', but I'm strong fer the auld kirk, and I think the Masons
have somethin' important to keep quiet about in all this babble over
ways and means for inheritin' the kingdom of heaven.

"It's like all great secrets, it's old and it's plain. It's so patent, it
gits overlooked. It's like this I say: Pennsylvania ain't heaven, and
it ain't goin' to be. We have to pass our sinful days in it. But it ain't
hell either, and it don't need to be made to resemble it. One of the
best ways of preventin' hell on earth is fer a few sober men to
remind themselves regular of the everlastin' presence of the Ancient
of Days, to remember where enlightenment comes from, and how
the seed must die first to bring the harvest home. It's easy to forgit
how to plough when everybody wants to be a harvester. At any time
it's only a few men that kin remember that secret well enough to pass
it on to a few others. Whatever ye do, don't forgit it. There'll be
a mighty harvest here, but there's also got to be a mighty plantin'
and replantin'."

At this point the colonel seemed to be talking to himself. His pipe had gone out. The two Oisters were gossiping with Jed in the back yard. In the front room the voices of the women suddenly became audible again, as the colonel ceased. They were talking about needles and pins.

"You can get a whole paper of the best brass pins at Somerfield's store, and blue Bristol needles in beeswax, and fine linen thread," said Ruhannah Colhoun, evidently addressing Frances. "Somerfield's just brought up a couple o' stogies loaded with London goods from the City. I slipped over early this mornin', and, my dear, he has some of the finest sheer paduasoy I ever took between my finger and thumb. Old Somerfield's stockin' up now that so many are usin' the Glades Road again. I'd buy now, if I was you. I'd buy before all those Macs camp here waitin' to go south. If you don't, you'll find everything high as a steeple when you git to Carlisle. Better lay in here, I advise ye."

Here the colonel rapped his pipe out three times, and looking at Salathiel, smiled knowingly, nodding towards the front room.

"They've got half the secret," he said in a low tone, "but they don't know it. And it wouldn't do to tell 'em all of it. You'll see what I mean if some of those stump preachers come around and start to git the women excited. It takes men to remember God ain't love alone."

Salathiel nodded as if he knew and agreed. He was not so sure he understood the colonel fully. But he felt he was learning a lot, that it was big medicine and an honour to smoke with a chief personage and a colonel of the Pennsylvania line. As for Frances Melissa and her pins and needles, he would certainly buy her some at old man Somerfield's, and maybe some paduasoy, too—whatever that was—if the colonel would only give him a chance. It was getting pretty late!

A burst of laughter came from the yard and the happy voices and exclamations of Jed and the two Oisters.

"That's that smart City nagur of St. Clair's out there," said the colonel, apprehensively. "If you don't keep your eye on the blacks, they drop work and talk the mornin' away. Now, what I was leadin' up to was a little politics.

"In Pennsylvania it's hard to tell where tradin' and religion begins and politics leaves off. Ofttimes they're the same. But as I see it just now there's three parties in this province: there's the Quakers and proprietary interest; there's them that would tax the Penns' holdin's and appropriate for the military but who want the crown to revoke the charter and send over a royal governor; and there's the Presbyterian independents on the frontiers.

"And then there's a whole world o' poor folks, runaway redemptioners, mostly young'uns, in these western woods that have jist gone on their own and really don't want no government at all. They've jist gone hog-wild, you might say. They want free land, free huntin', and wild livin' *ad lib*. They don't even want neighbours very nigh, and they're death on the redskins. As near as I kin tell, they want to kill the Injuns off and then live like 'em, and forget everything else. They're native as rattlesnakes, and they're pisen to all but godly and orderly thinkin' and right-livin' folks. The truth is they're half heathen. Your friend, James Smith, is one of 'em and kin always whistle up a gang o' Black Boys for any slick mischief he has to do. He's a kind o' Robin Hood around here. I guess that makes me a kind o' Sheriff of Nottingham, only I ain't so easily fooled.

"The truth is there's a kind of civil war gettin' under way in these parts. The Black Boys are makin' it hot for the regulars for tryin' to enforce the proclamations, and they're out to stop all western trade. They're down on town marchants and debts. Of course, this king's man, Wully Grant, up at the fort is a natural-born damn fool, instead of a help. He's goin' around the country arresting folks without warrants and takin' their rifle-guns away from 'em. And that's agin' the law, too. Liken he won't play the tyrant very long. I wouldn't give 'im more than a few months at most before he'll be hee-hawin' for help to Colonel Bouquet.

"The trouble is the proprietaries are helpless when it comes to quellin' violence. The Quakers are no help to them there, and all the frontier Presbyterian riflemen despise 'em. Last Christmas when the Paxtang boys marched agin' Philadelphia to finish off murderin' the Moravian Indians, it amounted to a regular uprisin' of the frontiers agin the authorities. It took Ben Franklin to arouse enough spunk in the Philadelphians to put it down.

"I'll give Franklin credit for his common sense in preventin' bloodshed and coolin' down the hotheads. But Ben's always led the fight in the Assembly against the Penns and the Quakers. And now the legislature has sent him back to London at a good salary as agent for the province, and to try to git the new Parliament to revoke the Penns' charter and set up a royal government here like they have in Virginia. I'm not for that," said the colonel, smiting the table. "No, sir, not by a dang sight!

"I'd much rather have John Penn for governor, like we have now, and the old charter o' liberties and godly government, Quakers and all, than havin' some hack o' the Ministry or a court favourite set o'er us for governor with a Church of England council to throttle our lower house. I don't see that the king and Parliament and the Lords of Trade are going to be any easier masters than the old proprietaries, who ain't really tryin' to be masters at all. Ben Frank-

lin's a smart and clever fellow, I do agree, but maybe he's startin'
somethin' that just Poor Richard's common sense can never finish.
Poor Richard always sounds mighty Yankee to me. You know,
they say his mother came from Nantucket island, where the main
business is lancin' big whales. I wonder sometimes if it mightn't end
up here like William Penn said in his book, 'no cross, no crown', and
with Poor Richard talkin' in the State House at Philadelphia. Might
be," said the colonel, "might be!"

Thus it was, connected with serious doubts and a cloudy prophecy, that Salathiel first heard of Benjamin Franklin.

"Tarnation!" exclaimed the colonel, getting up indignantly.
"Dang if the nagurs haven't gossiped the mornin' away out there,
and the breakfast mess still settin' on the table. Mina," he called,
"send that pert city boy out of the yard. Don't ye know better than
to let a gentleman's town jockey like that tickle your daughter?"

"Kunnel, suh," replied the older slave woman, pausing in the
door and solemnly shaking her earrings at him, "you is a mighty
knowin' man. I listen to yuh about de Lawd, but ye can't tell old
Mina nothin' much about men. Suh, I'se wintered 'em and I'se
summered 'em, and when they ain't they is, and when they is they
ain't. And that's de God's trufe about 'em."

At this bit of perky wisdom, the colonel laughed heartily, and led
the way into the front room, where the ladies were discovered showing Bridget how to read the future in tea leaves: The women seemed
to be quite content with the present, Salathiel thought. After a dish
of tea and a few amenities were passed, he and the colonel departed
to get the day's work under way. There was a lot to be done that day
in Chambersburg.

15

Saturday Afternoon Amenities

CHAMBERSBURG—just to be in it was to be elegant, or so Frances Melissa thought. Mrs. Colhoun was that correct; so well dressed and agreeable; she was such a clever needlewoman!

The conversation that morning in the "clock parlour" of the colonel's cabin had been one of the most pleasant Frances Melissa could recollect. The talk had been pitched naturally; flowed without suspicion as between one respectable housewife and another. It was almost like being at a respectable wake, where dear Grandmother Past was lying in peace, with nothing but her virtues to be celebrated. Not that there was anything funereal in the atmosphere. Just the peace of complete decorum, and Frances' own secret sense of assistance in laying her own past to rest—all but the best of it. Possibly the faintly fragrant although invisible presence of Lady Ale and Sister Brandy and the liquid sunlight flooding the rag-carpeted floor were more than usually consolatory and illuminating guests. Certainly Bridget's being there was a visible and solid comfort. She gave a restful and assured family tone to everything, moving plumply about the room, helping competently with the tea things, and playing sedately in general at being grown up in miniature. Or was she playing?

Holy Saints, Frances prayed that things might just keep going on this way! To find her more delicate feminine qualities not only being appreciated but also being taken for granted and reciprocated gave her a sustaining self-confidence in the present and a streak of sunshine to follow into the future.

As she sat there in the little parlour that morning while the clock ticked, the seconds fell like timely manna into her lap. For Ruhannah Colhoun was not just being kind. She *was* being nice. But what was more important, Mrs. Colhoun obviously felt that nothing less than her own best manners were called for in the presence of so refined and respectable a guest. Of course, Mrs. Colhoun was still very young. The doctor must have been a great surprise to her. He might still be.

Nevertheless, Ruhannah's naïve yet wholehearted and sisterly courtesy was veritable balm of Gilead to Frances' much-bruised but still gallant soul. The bitter years and blows of slavery on the Hogendobler farm, the horrors of her escape from the madwoman, and much else were lulled to rest by the healing elegancies and amenities of the quiet feminine present.

Nor was this evidence of small-things-observable trivial or unimportant. Unwittingly, but none the less ardently, Melissa shared in the general urge of her age to become refined and elegantly artificial. But final success in this bore for her the peculiar stamp of personal necessity. Her need to become dainty and delicate was dire. Indeed, her individual salvation and integrity were now dependent upon what elements out of her past she might be able to mix as alloys in the running flux of events, in order totally to recast her future and renovate her personality.

How fortunate, then, that she had the fine feminine capacity of attaining a white heat of emotion over apparently trivial things. A hot flare, indeed, was needed to reduce much of the refractory material of her past experience to the ore of present and everyday use. A sad heap of the black stones of adversity, the cold white ashes of poverty, and not a little of hell's own irreducible red slag was to be picked over and sorted out for what residue of usable metals still remained. And in her case what was to be firmly rejected was equally, if not more important than what she might be discriminating enough to retain.

That process, with the furnace and alembic of emotion in full blast, was now under way in the little parlour of the log cabin at Chambersburg. Apparently Frances Melissa was simply sitting in a rocking chair, rocking and talking amiably with a friend. So she was. But invisibly, a thousand other things were busily going on. Both her past and her present were melting together in her mind into an elaborate amalgam. Instinctively that morning, she had sensed the passing over of an important threshold, and the necessity, as she had already pointed out to Salathiel, of putting her best foot forward.

Consequently, with what amounted to a desperate and yet an admirable womanly sagacity, she now boldly recalled a hundred details of her odd life in the fashionable house of joy in Ireland, as a child, and ingeniously adapted them to the more respectable exigencies of her present situation. Certain memories of childhood, her deep religious feeling, and her native sharpness of taste and wit— such gatherings and her brief tutelage in morals and sewing by some charitable nuns in Cork were the chief nuggets of the past which she now found available, as she fumbled for what lucky gold there might be in her former experience. The rest, if it was not entirely dross, was at least not immediately usable.

In one thing, if not in many others, she had been fortunate. Her pasts had been many and various; and her experiences in them were not only wide but deep. In this she actually held an advantage over many of the more staid but purely provincial women with whom she saw she must now match herself, and she was beginning to suspect as much.

Enlightened by native Irish wit, however, she was able to extract not a little enjoyment from her ironic situation and even to ponder with a certain cynical relish on the indubitable fact that most of what she knew of graces in both manners and speech had been taught her by a gelded French nobleman.

He was a prisoner of war on parole, to whom she and Maggy Magee used to bring chocolate upstairs in the morning, while he lay recovering from his wounds in her "aunt's" notable establishment in Cork.

Recovering?—

The term was doubtful, although it was, so to speak, the crux of the whole matter. For the reason Monsieur le Vicomte de Q had taken such a debonair and yet purely paternal interest in his two virginal pot girls in Cork was that he had lost the more vital portions of his manhood in a brief but bloody brush with an English corvette off the Scilly Isles, when balls and oak splinters flew. Weather had eventually driven the French prize into Cork, where the twin fact of his disablement was officially known.

And yet, once on parole, he had gallantly chosen to recover, in so far as he could, in an Irish Catholic bordello rather than virtuously to languish in an English Protestant hospital. How French, and yet how sensible! And, under the circumstances, how very innocent, she thought. Yet here was a situation which Mistress Colhoun, for instance, would probably *not* be prepared to understand.

Frances smiled to herself, looking dreamfully out the window, and far over the dancing water to Cork, as she sat rocking in a cushioned chair, listening to Mistress Ruhannah's pleasant chat and the clock insisting upon domesticity.

Perhaps some of the Monsieur de Q's prophecies were actually coming true. "You'll be ladies yet, fit partners for any bully of an English milord," he used to say to her and Maggy. "But to be graceful graduates of my forlorn Irish school of love, you *must* be gentle, my darlings, and learn how to act as heiresses of great refinement. *Doucement!*" And then how he had rehearsed them, those two little pot girls.

First, they must learn how to chair themselves, i.e., how to sit down and how to rise up gracefully; next how to enter a room charmingly and depart airily; then how to appear severe, touching, arch, and simpering. And finally there had been merry lessons in how to languish and dally, and the nice art of being coyly provocative with a bustle, the silken toe of a slipper, or a fan. Above all, he had taught them polite worldly phrases; what to say in a hundred critical little situations, and how to look when you said it—with convincing gestures. Heavens, those gestures! How she had had to practise them. There was the trick of looking thoughtful and being impressed by putting your chin on your hand and gazing soulfully; and five different ways of seeming to listen to what another person had to say. (How he had laughed at her and Maggy when they seemed to be listening to him.) Afterwhile they came to understand what monsieur was really laughing at. Poor man, the technique of blandishment was all he had left to impart.

Man?

Well, this much was certain; before his accident Monsieur le Vicomte must have been a very ardent gentleman. His ship had borne the reputation for the most finished and exquisite amateur theatricals in the French navy. And afterward? Afterward, he was certainly the politest eunuch on parole in all Ireland. As such he had had nothing but fine manners and a little chocolate to give to his pupils. Luckily for young Frances and Maggy, no doubt.

Where was poor Maggy now? Frances wondered. Was she still working for that fat old glovemaker in the City? She looked up to see what Ruhannah Colhoun was taking out of her sewing basket.

Ruhannah was hémming baby napkins out of smooth old linen. "They have to stand constant bilin'," she said. Dr. Colhoun's baby was expected in April. It occurred to Frances that she might tell Ruhannah about her own. Then they could talk babies and baby clothes together. This passing inspiration proved to be most fortunate. Not only the Chambers and Colhoun households, but the rest of the town opened up like a lid on a linen chest.

Half the women in Chambersburg were having babies. Pregnant conversation thus, as always, was open-sesame to the town's ever gravid sisterhood of anxiety and hope. Before noon Frances Melissa had been in and out of five different neighbours' houses. She had had sympathetic bundles of dry herbs and green bottled embrocations forced upon her. She had whispered with Granny Boggs, heads close together, over the shocking shortcomings of midwives, while sipping elderberry wine. And she had been shown how to knit a small cap over a hoop with long fringes to keep the flies off a new baby's face in the summer, by Mrs. Lang. She and Ruhannah had both been warned against cats crawling into neglected cradles and sucking the baby's breath. As to when and how to wean a child, there were two parties in the village, and pretty firm about it, too. There were the two-year and the three-year advocates. It was rumoured by Mrs. Vance that ladies from Philadelphia, uppity people like the Shippens, sent their children out to the German villages to be suckled, and some of the gentry kept slaves for wet nurses—the great big lazy things! Mrs. McClintock averred that squaws knew a thing or two about yarbs, and the best way to strap a baby on a board. Mrs. Culbertson, who was given to twins, had once had a Delaware hag come and foment her breasts with hot sassafras when she didn't come in strong at the birth—and the sassafras worked.

All of this Frances listened to gravely, with her chin on her hand. And apparently gratefully, which ensured her immediate popularity. For who so welcome a visitor as she who listens to the recital of fellow female ills? By midday all those expectant ones whom she had not yet called upon were prepared to be slighted if she should not visit them in the afternoon. Ruhannah, however, undertook to take care of that. Her father had practised physic and dentistry on all who came to him in the past years of the settlement, and she was now married to a licensed surgeon-barber from the City. No one of immediate clinical interest was, therefore, omitted. And on the whole no round of calls could have proved more interesting. With those who are in complete health it is difficult to be personal, but with fellow sufferers the intimate introduction is ready made.

Dr. Colhoun himself rode into town about two o'clock, over from Fort Loudon, where he had tapped the old garrison storekeeper for dropsy for the third time. "It's near the end now," he said, cheerfully. He didn't believe in bleeding when the patient's blood turned to water in his veins. Otherwise, he bled heavily. St. Clair and Yates had sent messages. It seemed they would be coming through Chambersburg "not later than Sunday".

"*Sabbath* you mean, George, don't you?" suggested Ruhannah hopefully, as she presided with great dignity over the noon meal. Dr. Colhoun laughed. He was not only a surgeon but an Episcopalian. He was even known to play cards, when he could find anybody who wasn't afraid of losing his soul during the game. He and Yates, it developed, were by way of being cronies. Frances could see that the doctor was a wise young man and enjoyed a bit of gentlemanly wit. Archness with dignity was called for, she thought—and it sufficed during luncheon.

He took a fancy to Bridget, who brought him a coal for his pipe, as he sat down for a much-needed rest in the colonel's chair. Bridget asked his advice for Queen Alliquippa. The doctor diagnosed that played-out female at a glance. "Sutures," said he, "sutures are the only thing that will recompose her constitution," and he proceeded to sew on a loose leg with a catgut, and to bind a flapping arm back into place. For the Queen's appalling baldness he could do nothing. "That has gone too far," he said. "There's nothing but bare ivory on which to glue her crown. Surgeons are no good at that. You must apply to Mr. Yates."

Bridget pretended to understand, a little disappointed. Still Alliquippa was *so* much better, so much better composed than ever before! She was now all in one piece, poor thing.

After the meal, from which the colonel had been absent, they all took a brief nap, the doctor in his chair, with a handkerchief over his face. Later the women and Bridget went over to the store.

Their departure was well timed. Mrs. Colhoun heard from Jed that both her father and Salathiel were at Somerfield's and that a smart piece of trading had been accomplished that morning in some remarkable triangular deal. About the nature of this deal Jed was not clear, except that Salathiel had given him a half-joe.

"Come on, my dear, we will both soon be having children to clothe," said Ruhannah, laughing and giving the doctor a hopeful look. But, as usual, her husband seemed to be asleep when money was in question. "But there's faither," whispered Ruhannah. "Faither will remember how it is."

Frances hoped so. If there had been a deal, she thought she could count on her man. (And maybe old Somerfield might have a dash of the hot Jamaica black on hand. Just a dram.) Ale was so bitter in the afternoon. The doctor had not offered any wine.

"Alliquippa's naked," said Bridget, putting her favourite back in the cowhide bag. "She ain't got a single thing to wear."

"That's the way they come," remarked Dr. Colhoun under his handkerchief, but not until the women were well out the door.

There was quite a crowd hanging around outside Somerfield's. Much to Melissa's surprise, the wagon was standing before the loading ramp, but without the horses. A crowd of noisy little boys were pitching pennies around the platform, and the minister himself had just entered the store. Something was going on, something important. "Come on," said Ruhannah again. "Come on!"

The women raised their skirts with both hands and started to run.

Things happened a great deal faster in town than along the road through the forest, Salathiel discovered. He was reminded of those days at Fort Pitt when he was serving the captain and there were scarcely hours enough from dawn to dark to get his work done. He had liked that. It kept him from brooding. The experience now stood him in good stead. He had a lot of things to accomplish at Chambersburg that day, and to tell the truth, he had been not a little impatient with the colonel, who had talked the morning away from eight until half after nine o'clock, if Ecuyer's watch was right; and, of course, it couldn't be wrong.

Also, he reflected, this was Saturday when all work stopped at sundown. Not even cooking would be done in this Presbyterian town after dark. At sunset the Sabbath began. He was even surprised to learn from the colonel that there would be a lodge meeting that night. Something special, probably. He hoped Yates and St. Clair would ride over from Loudon in time to be there and pass in with him. He didn't care to visit alone. And then there would be the kirk tomorrow. A sermon, which, for some reason, the colonel was quite insistent he must hear. Dang! Melissa would have to be there, too. It wouldn't hurt her, he reflected. She might for once just keep quiet about being a papist, since she wanted to be so respectable. He hoped they hadn't noticed her crossing herself after grace at breakfast. He would speak to her about it. She must remember to watch things like that.

All this ran through his head as he walked with the colonel back over the little path along the mill-race that morning. They had left the women gossiping happily in the parlour and set out for the mills. He brought Jed out of the carpenter's shed with a shrill whistle and bade him come along for a little light work. This pleased the colonel, who was meanwhile full of explanations as to the necessity of setting up two new English millstones Somerfield had packed in for him from Newcastle—and a pretty penny they cost! Salathiel would have to come down and see them.

He promised to do so later, and then managed to leave the colonel at the stockade gate, where he and Jed now turned in on the morning's work. In the new mill below the dam, a continuous din of hammers could be heard above the roar of the falls and the crashing of planks. The open framework of the mill roof, rafter by rafter, was going up rapidly.

Jed was quite a different being by day. Merriment had taken the place of sleepy fear. And he was not only amazed but proud of the transformation in the appearance of the big white man, who was his master's friend, and who no longer looked like an Indian.

"Sah," said he, "this fellah ain't gwine be skeered of yah no moh."

Salathiel remembered his promise and promptly gave him a half-joe. Rather too much, he thought, but then it was a poor coin and would not pass for full face value. Yet it accomplished his purpose that morning. Jed was ravished by sudden riches into sudden labour.

They fell to on the harness together, furbished it, patched it, and even renewed some worn links in a piece of doubtful trace chain. They cleaned out and made up the interior of the wagon, putting everything in place and locking all the chests and drawers, ready to go. Then they caught the reluctant horses, hitched them up, and drove over, trundler and all, to Somerfield's store. It was going on towards noon when they got there—but not too late for trade and for a delighted welcome from young Arthur, who had begun to wonder what had become of his tall friend. He looked at him in his new guise, but said nothing. If only sis could have been here, he thought.

The trundler gaped, and from it Salathiel took out what he considered to be his best bale of peltry. It was a motley collection, he knew. But there might be some good skins in the bundle, and it would be just as well to turn them into money now; coin, if possible. He was beginning to realize that what the Welsh thief had said about money was true.

Arthur carried the bale in proudly, mentally calculating his promised reward, while the deerskin wrapping was removed and the thongs untied in the back room behind the counter. Here there was considerable floor space before the open chimney, a place Somerfield reserved for his widower's cooking, conviviality, and his more important transactions with fur-trading customers. Through the back door, beyond in the store yard, two long, blue Conestoga wagons just in from Lancaster could be seen drawn up together like a couple of canvas-covered barges, which they much resembled in both shape and size. These had been unloaded only that morning, which accounted for the overflowing stock of merchandise that now inundated the war-depleted store with barrels, crates, and bales; that crammed the shelves which had seemed so bare only the night before. It was, in fact, a prodigal consignment, and just in the nick of time.

Mr. Somerfield was rubbing his hands. It had taken considerable finesse to get this fine bill of goods so far west with all the merchants clamouring for everything, at any price, at Lancaster and Carlisle. There the troops would soon be paid off. There refugees, claimers, released captives and their families were gathering—and such a crowd of camp followers—idlers, sharpers, swindlers and harpies— as had seldom been seen in the colonies. Trade was only waiting for Bouquet to march eastward; for the final winding up of affairs after a long Indian war. Yes, it was almost like finding treasure to have two wagonloads of choice imported goods sent through to Chambers Mills at such a time. But the Philadelphia merchant that Mr. Somerfield liked to refer to as "my city factor" kept his promises. He was a Quaker, and Friend Japson's word was as good as his bond.

In view of his good fortune, therefore, it was with considerable complacency and with something less than his usual urge to clip the last penny that Mr. Somerfield now turned to view the skins of sundry small animals laid out by Arthur upon his kitchen floor. There were one hundred and twenty-nine pelts in all, and as various an assortment as he had ever seen.

"Looks like that naturalist's plunder, the man from Philadelphy—what's his name?—old Bill Bartram, that came through here in Forbes's time after lookin' things over around Fort Pitt—only ye ain't got no dried shrubs and birdskins in your pack," remarked Somerfield, as he began to finger and turn over the pelts.

Salathiel grinned from the barrel where he sat overlooking the proceedings. "Maybe so," said he. "I ain't a pelt hunter, ye know. This here is jist what I could fetch out of the woods at off times when I went out with Twin-Eyes and did a bit of barkin',* or whenever a stint of private trade came my way. But there's a right smart lot o' beaver there and a few otter and plenty o' black squirrel. Squirrels o' that kind be mighty scerce south-away. I got 'em north of the Conemaugh, where most people have never been."

"But they all look like summer coats to me," objected the old trader.

"Spring, airly spring," said Salathiel, "when the coat's thin, but new and prime." He laughed at his own blarney.

Somerfield grunted. "Wisht there was more mink," said he.

"I never had the patience to trap the little varmints," replied Salathiel. "But there's a white fox pelt from Canady once started a riot at Bedford, and the big brown painter that stinks so persistent, I knocked down with a hatchet. He ain't so bad. Captain Jack never knew I skunned him."

---

* *Barking*—it was the custom to stun a squirrel by hitting just below it on a limb, thus avoiding a bullet hole in the pelt.

Somerfield grunted again and sniffed. This was certainly a powerful bale, if nothing else.

"Tell ye what ye do, sir," suggested Salathiel. "Just figure it up and make me an offer for the lot."

"Reckon that's the only way," said the old man. He got his slate and, sitting down with Arthur, went through the assortment and jotted his decisions down with a constant squeaking of the stone pencil. He took nearly half an hour, and towards the end Mr. Somerfield seemed to be having trouble with his arithmetic.

"Thirty-six pounds, eighteen shillings, and four pence," said he, looking up at last. "And I don't say you mightn't git more for 'em in the City, but you'll have to allow me my cut for handlin' here."

"What kind of money?" asked Salathiel.

"Some coin, and the rest province script."

"Tell ye what. Call it forty pounds even, starlin' value; take out twenty-five pounds in trade goods, and give me the rest in coin. Maybe you kin make a bit for yourself on the goods that way. But the coin's got to be weighed, good pieces, copper or silver, and no paper."

Mr. Somerfield scratched his ear with his slate pencil, considering. Then he went over to the till and unlocked it. "All right," he said, reluctantly, "but I do hesitate to part with the hard pieces. Even with tradin' it takes metal change."

However, he shook hands on it. And while the coins were being weighed and considered one by one, Arthur, who was in pocket five Spanish dollars, put the furs away to be pegged out on stretchers later and given a good going-over. Mr. Somerfield knew a trick or two when it came to slicking up pelts.

It was strange how the news of a deal going on got around town. Perhaps Jed had something to do with it. About two o'clock, the colonel himself had dropped in. By that time, exhilarated by a can of watered penny blackstrap, Jed was doing cartwheels before the wagon on the loading ramp.

A crowd of small boys gathered. Jed's half-joe, minus the drink, had somehow turned into several smooth old coppers, and a noisy game of pitch penny was soon under way, interrupted from time to time by the arrival of the boys' parents, for it was Saturday afternoon, and the news of the new goods at hand had been noised about. Then the women began to gather in force, even those who could not buy came to stare through the window and to finger the samples. They all knew what good weaving meant.

By three o'clock young Arthur had his hands full, measuring off cloth on the brass nail markers on the counter, tearing it across or cutting to the line, biting his tongue as the shears closed, with one eye on Mr. Somerfield, who he knew would hold him responsible for every inch.

But trying to be a grocer and calender all at once finally proved too much even for the willing Arthur, and he was allowed to call in his friends, the Culbertson twins, to help. The twins, after assuming leather aprons, turned in behind the counter to weigh out tea and loaf sugar, or to ladle out molasses, rice, and rum; or open barrels of salted and smoked fish.

Such a boot scraping, such a flashing of unrolled cloth, so many dashings back and forth to make entries; a busy coming and going of people, women mostly, with cans, buckets, bundles and bags provided a pleasing air of excitement and bustle. Young darkies called at the door with notes for "marster's purchase". They were never allowed inside. The shuffle of feet in sawdust, the clink of small change, the murmur and babble of gossip and bargaining gradually grew in volume. So lively a Saturday afternoon Somerfield's had not seen since long before what people were already beginning to call "Pontiac's Rebellion".

"Bless me, I'd no idea so many of the back-settlers had come home," said Mr. Somerfield. "Look at the farmers' nags tied up in the yard. And half with pillions. Only last August the whole county was a desert from here to Lancaster. I guess if you gave a warwhoop now they'd all light out agin for Carlisle. But don't do it, don't do it," laughed the old man, mopping the sweat of labour and satisfaction off his brow, while he and Salathiel worked on the ramp, loading part of the agreed-upon goods into the wagon and trundler.

The game of pitch penny swarmed under, in, and about the loading porch. It unrolled amid the wheels of the wagon with shrill shouts of excitement and occasional fights and tears. The horses stamped and switched impatiently, shaking their hides and the new yoke chimes.

"Dang, if that ain't a harsefly," exclaimed Somerfield. "It's the warmest November afternoon I can ever remember," he said, lifting up his face to feel the grateful, unseasonable sunshine. " 'Tain't like to last. It jist naturally cain't. I heard loons late last night, and whenever ye hear 'em here, there's cold close behind. Loons is the laugh of winter comin' on."

"Thought I heard one myself," smiled Salathiel. "Say, Mr. Somerfield, have you got a good smith around here? Speaking of the horses, just take a look at their shoddin'."

"Flannery's the only man can do it right since old McCormick was scalped. But the question is, will he? He's a retired army farrier, and he has all the tools and the skill, but his half pay is half too much for him. Mostly he's skittled. Owes me a pretty penny on his store slate. Tell ye what . . . But bedang, here comes his old woman now! Wants a bit of an extension no doubt. Maybe you can work on her, and if ye do, remember me."

Salathiel looked up to see a tall ungainly yet familiar figure with a kerchief binding up her jaw approaching the store thoughtfully. He raised his hat to her as she turned in at the door, and she stopped from sheer astonishment. So huge a gentleman had never lifted his hat to her before.

"I do hope the misery has abated, Mrs. Flannery," said he. "You may recall we met at Colonel Chambers's door this morning. He said he'd seldom seen so large a wisdom tooth, one with three roots! I'm certain you're much to be commiserated."

" 'Deed, it must have been turrible," said Mr. Somerfield, shaking his head.

The look of suspicion faded from Mrs. Flannery's tired blue eyes. She felt herself at once condoled with and flattered. Under her bandage and sunbonnet she tried to smirk with a kind of grimace that somehow reminded them both of a wrinkled cabbage.

"Now, it's sure uncommon kind of ye to remember my misery," she mumbled.

"Is Jim engaged today?" inquired Mr. Somerfield, innocently.

"*Him!*" she exclaimed. "He's got his bloody rope 'ammock out again with the warm weather. 'Twas a bad 'abit he brought back with him from the Havanner, along with the tertian fever. And there he lays swinging in the breeze, and the forge gone cold."

"Maybe between shakes he could be persuaded to make the sparks fly again—for a few Spanish dollars," suggested Mr. Somerfield. "Then you could git some of the things you want, mistress."

"I've four horses much need to be reshod, ma'am. And I'm willing to pay well for an honest stunt," urged Salathiel solicitously, for much depended upon her answer. The next smith would be at Shippensburg.

"It's poppy drops and a pair of new cloth slippers I need," muttered the woman. "Me old shoes are like a cheese drain."

Mr. Somerfield nodded. "Wal, ye kin have them, if you want," he said.

"Happen ye have a nagur can tend the bellows?" she asked.

"Here's one," said Salathiel, reaching down and pulling Jed out by the heels from under the porch.

"Go 'long with this good woman and do what she tells you," he admonished the young Negro sternly. "If you've lost any pennies, I'll make 'em up to ye." Shrill shouts of triumph and the sound of quarrelling over Jed's abandoned hoard came from under the platform.

"I'll follow with the nags in a few minutes, ma'am," said Salathiel—"and there may be two more horses," he added, as he just then caught sight of St. Clair on his grey, and Yates on Enna, riding across the square. Between them was the boy with the yellow scalplocks, mounted on his awkward colt.

Mrs. Flannery nodded in agreement, albeit grimly, and seizing Jed by the left ear led him off with a determined and dragoon-like tread.

"Yah nigger, yah, yah," shouted a young scion of the clan McClintock, sticking his red head out from under the porch. "Finders keepers. Got yer winnin's after all!" Unfortunately, the boy's uncle just then chanced to be going into the store.

"Is that so?" said the irate farmer, catching the boy by the scruff of his neck and heaving him out from under the porch and across a convenient barrel with one jerk. "I'll larn ye to gamble with idle black boys, ye young cockchafer!"—and with that he began to try to splinter a barrel stave on his nephew's behind.

The impressive silence under the platform that ensued during these painful proceedings was so effectually cancelled by the roars of the victim over the barrel that the other devotees of pitch penny escaped all notice.

"Hold," said Mr. Somerfield, "enough! That's a youngster you're manhandling, McClintock."

" 'Tain't nothin' to what his pa would have done to 'im," replied the lad's uncle, tossing the stave aside and walking into the store.

For a few moments the boy continued to lie over the barrel, sobbing. Finally he got up, still clutching his pennies in one hand and rubbing himself with the other. He stood red-faced and whimpering.

Yates, St. Clair and Roy Davison had ridden up and dismounted just as the affair of the barrel occurred.

"Is it awful bad, Tom?" asked young Roy, sympathetically. The sufferer nodded, tears in his eyes.

"Go down to the tannery and sit in the wet tanbark for a while. It does take the sting out," said Roy.

The men burst into a laugh. "That's a new one, youngster," said St. Clair. "How'dja know?"

"Ifen you worked for Mistress McKinney, you'd soon find out," replied the boy, grimacing. "She uses taws."

"They're bad," said Somerfield, sympathetically. "I remember. But your friend ain't really hurt. The McClintocks are an upright race, except when someone has them over a barrel. But you can't get the pennies out of their fist by working on their behind."

St. Clair laughed, appreciating the wisdom of the storekeeper.

"Somerfield knows the family traits of all his customers," he said. "If you expect to collect your quit-rents about here, Yates, you ought to consult him."

"I have," said Yates. "How are ye, Mr. Somerfield? I'm glad to see you again. And you, Sal!" His eyes grew wide as he contemplated the marked change in the appearance of his friend. "Glad to see ye dressed up," he added. "We're about due for a celebration. Yes!" said he, touching his saddle pouch, "I've got the signed papers here from Wully. Land, my boy, land!"

"Anybody see that nigger of mine?" interjected St. Clair. "How's he been behavin'?"

"I've jes' sent him down to the farrier's to work the bellows," explained Salathiel, "and, by the way, if you two want your horses reshod, you'd best send 'em down now with the wagon teams. I've made workin' arrangements with Mrs. Flannery."

"With the old woman, eh? Then you're like to get results," said St. Clair. "Where's Flannery set up his smithy now?"

"I know, sir," exclaimed young Davison eagerly, "and I'll take the horses around for ye, all six of 'em, if this gentleman will let me talk to his little girl. I rode over this afternoon jes' for to see her, hopin' you'd still be here," he added, addressing Salathiel alone now, but most earnestly. "Look, I brought this along!" He pulled a toy canoe out from under his jacket. "Hit's for her, for Pigtails!" The blood rushed to his face. "An old Injun made it. I thought maybe ye might let us swim it in the race together." At the thought of so much happiness, his voice died away and he appeared flushed and embarrassed at having disclosed his fondest dreams.

Salathiel looked at him gravely. "Take the horses around to Flannery," said he, "and then you kin come back and talk to Pigtails. Her name's Miss Bridget McCandliss, by the by. Ye'll have to find out yourself whether she'll go swimmin' canoes with ye. And don't forgit your cap this time."

"No, sir," said the boy, removing his rakish ring-tailed headpiece there and then. A rush of golden hair inundated his shoulders. "Damn hit," said he, and bit his lip with vexation. "I allers forgit about them long locks. Here, sir, please keep this for me while I take the horses around." He handed Salathiel the canoe as one man to another, and then began to cut the lead team out of the traces like a veteran.

Yates grinned at the droll sight of his large friend sitting on the platform with a toy canoe solemnly resting on his knees. "That's a sacred pledge you're holding there, Sal," said he. "I hope ye take it seriously. Your Pigtails has picked up a fiery young Romeo. He rid over from the ford with us and discoursed of love all the way. St.

Clair was like to split, but promised his good offices. He's your Phoebe's cousin, ye know. By the way, are you stayin' at the Davisons'?"

Salathiel shook his head. "No, I managed not to," he said, and put the canoe upright in his pocket for safekeeping. "But I've had a good talk with young Arthur about certain matters."

"That's wise," replied Yates. "Melissa can be easily upset, if I'm not mistaken."

"She ain't goin' to be," said Salathiel. "But let's go in the store now. The colonel's in there and will be wantin' to see ye." As he rose, the surreptitious sound of pitch penny once again getting under way came through the platform.

"Gambling's a hard thing to stamp out," chuckled Mr. Somerfield, as they went into the store together. "Even in this godly village it goes on under the feet of the elders."

"What's that?" inquired Colonel Chambers, coming through a crowd from behind the counter, eating a sour pickle.

"I was just explainin' a curious fact," said Somerfield. "But here's Mr. St. Clair and lawyer Yates fresh rid in from Loudon."

"How's Wully and his fightin' gurls?" demanded the colonel. "Did Croghan's Irish get through all right? What's the western news? Any riders this way from Fort Pitt?" All five of them made their way to the rear of the store, where barrel chairs were pulled out before the hearth, and questions and answers and heavy repartee lightened by a touch of fiery blackstrap, which made St. Clair cough, went around.

Behind the counters out in the store, Arthur and the Culbertson twins flew about nimbly, with many a "What do ye lack, ma'am; what do ye lack?" and a "Thank ye kindly" as a shrill chorus that accompanied briskly the march of trade. Presently Mr. Somerfield left his guests in the back room and joined his clerks, slate and pencil in hand. He began to unroll some of the more flamboyant of his cloth for display.

Outside, the abandoned young devotees of fortune, taking courage from their ever-growing numbers, had come out again from under the porch. Tom McClintock, his trousers well padded now with damp tanbark, had returned to the scene of his late downfall. But he was now losing what remained of poor Jed's half-joe to young Roy Davison, a penny a pitch. The language of both the red and the golden-haired cherubs smoked.

The Reverend Mr. Muir Craighead, just then in from Rocky Spring, Old Church, to preach the morrow's sermon, had no opportunity whatever to rebuke the young sons of Belial, who literally gambled about his very feet.

He was having a terrible grim battle trying to moor his obstinate and powerful jack mule to Somerfield's lamppost and to keep his remarkable clerical bag-wig on his pate, all at the same time. It was literally too much for one Presbyterian clergyman to do. So violent were his exertions that the white powder flew from his wig, and some Biblical language got mixed with the dust of what looked like defeat. Had any of the orthodox been listening, they might have been scandalized, for even a layman would have instantly gathered from Mr. Craighead's remarks that he now included mules in his views on the doctrine of predestination. The question was temporarily settled, although only temporarily, when the good man drew back for an apostolic blow and smote his mule on the side of its head with righteous indignation and a heavy black bag containing a big leather-bound Bible, two hymnals, a Westminster Confession, and a green ham. The jack staggered, sobbed like the brazen trumpet that shattered the walls of Jericho, and dazedly permitted itself to be bound to the lamppost.

"Ahaz, Ahaz!" exclaimed Mr. Craighead, while settling his wig, "bray on, unwilling bearer of the abused servants of God. Thou son of Jorham; Ahaz art thou rightly dubbed!" Nevertheless, Mr. Craighead's saintly arrival had good effect.

Roy Davison and Red McClintock had ceased scrambling ignobly in the dust for lucre. They were both upright boys now, gazing at Mr. Craighead, dumb with respect and admiration.

"Good evening, my venturesome young friends," said the minister, glancing at the pennies and smiling benignly as he stepped into the store. "The Lord be with ye."

It was precisely at this juncture that Ruhannah and Melissa, coming down the street with Bridget, had picked up their skirts and started to run.

They were, of course, in plenty of time. There was over an hour till sunset yet, and, in any event, the doctor's wife and her genteel visitor were not going to be neglected by a man who knew his custom as well as Mr. Somerfield. But despite that, owing to the pleasing excitement of a purchasing adventure, they were both in a hurry, and neither of them noticed that Bridget remained outside, where someone had something to say to her. They turned headlong into the store and made their way breathlessly to the rear counter.

"'Tis some of your best new drygoods we want to look at, Mr. Somerfield," said Ruhannah, as the old man swept a place clear for them on the goods counter, and leaned forward to take their commands. "Imported goods," she whispered, looking about her apprehensively, but smiling, too. "Paduasoy!"

"There *is* that," said Mr. Somerfield, turning about and summoning Arthur. "And also there's Irish linen, silks from Lyons, English lawn, Bedford cloth, Scotch tweeds, and stout Osnaburgs, all recent imports by the good ship *Gilbert* of Lyme Regis, my city factor informs me. And the chiffons," he said, knowingly, "good lack, you never saw such chiffons!" As he spoke, he began to pick out choice bolts of cloth from the shelves and to assemble them.

"Arthur," said he, "show these two ladies everything they want, and git old Timba to come and hold a candle so they kin see the weave and the quality. And, mind you, no drippings git spattered on the cloth. This is Mrs. Albine, your friend's wife, you know, and, of course, Mrs. Colhoun." The lad looked at Frances so searchingly that she dropped her eyes. But that was only for an instant.

Soon neither of the women was conscious of the young clerk at all, except as a pair of hands that unrolled before them beautiful waterfalls of cloth. This they not only saw but heard. They heard the ripple and swish of it. But above all they felt it. Innumerable generations of women were now concentrated in their fingertips. Ruhannah was all sighs and envious hopeful little exclamations. Frances was silent. Young Arthur was disturbed by the far-off misty look in her grey eyes as she fingered the cloth.

How different would any place be if seen through another's eyes. What strange, unexpected, and perhaps insupportable revelations would ensue? The literal might perish of astonishment, and the imaginative die of boredom, if lenses could be mixed. And so, wisely, unto each his own pair of precious spectacles, lest anarchy and madness ensue.

To any of your great oneyers from London—or Philadelphia— Somerfield's would have been a poor, crude, rude and bucolic little establishment, picturesque perhaps, with its loading platform, lamppost, and two shading maple trees; but not to be entered, except out of dire necessity or condescending curiosity, and then only after a tucking in of cuff-lace and a careful stripping off of buckskin gloves, if one perchance *were* forced to come in out of the rain and buy something as a kind of quit-rent for shelter, on the way to the frontier. That even a whisper of the rustling skirts of Fashion could be overheard in such a dull cavern of back-country vendue was unthinkable.

But to Ruhannah Colhoun nothing could be more inevitably right, familiar, and wholly useful than Somerfield's general store with its sociable common counters, its shelves packed with drygoods and exotic comestibles and its small manufactured necessities and amelioratives of the feminine lot in life that made all the difference between her being a woman drudging in the wild woods and a neat lady living comfortably in town. Her pa and old Somerfield—*they* had made Chambersburg. She rather took her father's part for granted, but it seemed amazing to her that any man could remember all the things that everybody might want, as Mr. Somerfield did year after year. That he always remembered what Ruhannah wanted in particular, she took as her gentry due. And then here was a touch of romance and luxury and elegance extended from the world beyond the ocean: spices, tea, coffee, silks, ribbons, and the folding framework of whalebone skeletons for Sabbath bonnets and reticules. So it was to the store that Ruhannah came to be served promptly, and to gossip freely about one of the greatest pleasures of existence, purchasing something for herself which would cause others either to envy or to admire her. At such times her mood fitted snugly into the establishment as though she were slipping into a place that warmed her soul like a comfortable mitten. There was no nonsense or fripperies, but there was everything else, and some sugar and spice, at Somerfield's.

To Arthur the store was the anxious, but yet on the whole congenial scene of his own first really important labours; it was the proving ground of his initial and well-meant fumbles and small successes and failures in the business of life. Being a boy, he was to himself the centre of it, and the store so much scenery about him. But he lived there at night as well as labouring in it by day, and unconsciously he loved it. He throve on its mercantile sociabilities and on his being entrusted with things of value. He liked his status as a clerk who could read, write, and cipher; and being the friend of everybody, one who was frequently asked for advice. He admired the cavernous old shelf-lined establishment from the lacy shade of the maples by the loading platform before it to the bright glare of sunshine on new wagon canvas at the rear door. Every crack and cranny of it existed in his mind probably more vividly than it did in reality. To him the show window was a unique wonder, and a kind of ogling and bewitching eye. He took pleasure in deviously arranging its interior splendours and spent much time watching and speculating as to whether customers would stop and be taken-in by something fancy in the glances of this magnetic eye, or not. On idle afternoons he would sit on his clerk's stool, watching people pass or gather to discuss what was newly displayed. And sometimes, if it came on to rain, he would sip a little rum and feel sorry. True, it could be very lonely at night for an apprentice sleeping on a straw pallet amidst the barrels, where the rats squeaked. But day or night,

it was always familiar—something natural in the order of things—
just as it was to Ruhannah.

In fact, anyone would still have recognized the place as Somerfield's with either Arthur's or Ruhannah's spectacles on, but not with
Frances Melissa's.

Her eyes transfused the small frontier store with the mad Pictish
colours of a smouldering elfin glory. The solid bolts of cloth that
old man Somerfield and Arthur unrolled for her seemed for a magic
moment to be liquid sheets of rippling water streaming from the
walls of a cave and spreading out in a pool of running colours before
her.

She might have been standing in some cavern behind a waterfall,
where the sun barely struggled through, and the old Negro holding
the candles was a gnomelike guide to further treasures in the darkness beyond.

What unspeakable secret treasure she had found. All hers now,
shimmering, golden yellow, scarlet and heavenly blue, powdered with
stars and the creeping viny growths and strange rigid lilies of the
foreign looms. How she revelled and rejoiced in them! For an instant
or two she achieved a passionate immersion and a sense of healing
triumph, as though her sick soul had plunged into the bath of colours
before her and was being restored there. The clerk's hands rippling
the cloth were only the troubling angels of the pool. When she put
forth her fingers to touch the surface dreamfully, and felt passing
finger ends underneath the cloth, it seemed as if she had touched the
tips of invisible wings.

It was a shock to find that they were tingling human hands.
Arthur felt the current, too, and smiled at her in sudden embarrassment.

She must remember where she was; get back into the world again.

She sighed deeply, running her hand down a bolt of crinkling
crêpe. "Paduasoy," she heard Mr. Somerfield saying, "only one bolt
of it. Smuggled! The finest weave out of Italy, and the first I've
seen these many years. Times have been lean, you know."

Lean! Who should know that better than she? Lean as the wolf-
licked bones of a last year's lamb.

"Twelve shillings a yard," said Mr. Somerfield.

Well, she would have it, yards of it! Enough to make up for the
naked past; enough to make herself a dress and a bonnet—and a
bodice for little Bridget, too. She would sweep through the streets
of the City like a lady, a fine lady with a handsome child. If necessary, Sal could sell some of the horses. The best girls in Cork used
to give themselves for less than a yard of this stuff cost. Why, it was
worth it, worth it!

She heard Ruhannah, whom she had entirely forgotten for a while, calling, "Faither, faither." Of course, why not? She would call Salathiel.

The voices of the men in the rear room were suddenly stopped. Colonel Chambers and Salathiel came out to see what it was all about. They looked at the counter and the women and laughed.

"Yes," said the colonel, after listening to Ruhannah, "yes," a little doubtfully. "You know, I have other grandchildren, here and on the way." But he nodded and said something in a low tone to Somerfield. Ruhannah held her breath. Then it was all right. She could see that, and sighed. "Anything in reason" was what her father had said.

"Five pounds," said Salathiel to Frances briefly and to the point. He seemed in a hurry. "Your share out of this morning's trade. Git what you want for the family. Git plenty, git some needles and pins and skeins. I meant to git them for ye anyhow, and," he added in a low tone, "I'd git a little present for Mistress Colhoun, a ribbon or some falderal. You'll know what." He put his arm around her proudly, and drew her close to him. "Now I've got to git along to oversee the horses. New shoes for them. It's been a good day, I opine. The colonel wants us down to supper this evenin' "—all this under the eyes of Arthur, who stood waiting to measure and cut, and kept looking out the door steadily.

"Five pounds!" was all she could murmur. "Oh, Sal—five pounds! But is it sterling?"

"Yes," he said, "five sterling!"—and strode out, calling to St. Clair and Yates to follow him and get their own nags at the farrier's.

Five pounds, that was more than she had got for a whole year's work when she was bound out at Frazier's. She turned to the counter proudly and began to buy.

It was getting dark now. It would soon be six o'clock, and the Sabbath. She must hurry. But old Timba still stood like a statue of carved mahogany holding the candles. The wax dripped away onto the floor, drop by drop, like passing minutes. Still there was light and time enough to buy paduasoy.

She and Ruhannah smiled at each other triumphantly.

16

Expressions on the Face of Time

DOWN AT THE SMITHY matters had progressed considerably faster than Salathiel had been given to expect. The smithy was an open shed with the inverted bodies of two old army wagons for a roof. There was an anvil, quite rusty now, a fine kit of farrier tools and a portable blow-forge all of which had accompanied Corporal Flannery, involuntarily, as it were, out of his Majesty's service, when the corporal-farrier had been discharged as an invalid from the garrison at Fort Loudon several years before. Flannery's great pride was that he had once shod the chargers of General Forbes and of Colonel Washington at Bedford. The Virginian had paid him, the general had died; but he remembered them both, with equal satisfaction.

Since then life had been a long and constant bout with Holland bitters, poverty, the tertian ague, and Mrs. Flannery. Nor could it be asserted with truth that over any of his opponents Corporal Flannery had come out top man. He had merely managed to exist— in the summer in a hammock—always on half pay—but in the fall and winter, when the shakes sometimes relented, on the proceeds of a little honest work. And very skilful it was. For, although he had lost any ambition to employ it, he still retained his skill.

Now, it was not by firmness of character alone or her two arms either that Mrs. Flannery had prevailed on her veteran husband to resume his place at the forge that afternoon. His progress from the hammock to the anvil had, in a curious way, been due to the moral force inherent in Colonel Chambers's remark to Mrs. Flannery earlier that morning, that afflictions are sometimes blessings in disguise. It had put an idea into her head. She determined to capitalize on her misery.

Looking up at his wife from the hammock that afternoon, when she had first tentatively approached him on the delicate subject of work, Flannery had been shocked to see that her face was in a bandage and that she had lost a tooth. To the best of his recollection, she was entitled to nothing more than a black eye.

"Arragh now, mavourneen," said he, "sure and it was only a family tiff after a bit of poteen last evenin', and I niver did mean for to mar ye."

Instantly, she had him.

She saw that his worst anticipations of himself had been more than realized, and she made hay while the gloom lasted.

" 'Tis a poor frail woman I am," said she, "and no iron anvil for ye to lavish yer brutal blows upon, ye drunken harse-handler. Look upon me! Jasus! Am I always to be put upon and knocked about by a mere bog-trottin' Flannery like yerself? 'Tis not enough that ye should lie there, swingin' in your airy Injun pallet, denyin' me a crust for me famished mouth, but now ye must be after knockin' the most handsome teeth out of me jaw for fear I should ask ye for somethin' nourishin' to bite upon. Git up, ye miserable spalpeen," she screamed. "There's a gintleman like a giant out of Cornwall with four foin harses to be shod, a big iron stick under his arm, and milled Spanish dollars clashing in his pocket. Which would ye rather have rattlin' about yer impty pate? If ye've got a yard of Christian bowels left in your heathen guts, ye'll git up and strike a blow fer yer long-sufferin' wife—and she a proud Fitzgerald linked by the blessing of God, and as the divil would have it, to a poor fever-striken farrier. *Ochone,*" sobbed Mrs. Flannery, "*ochone!*"

Washed out of his hammock by this rising tide of domestic eloquence, the remorseful smith made no attempt to defend himself, but began to assemble his tools in a fit of low spirits humble enough to permit him to accept work as a penance for his sins. It was only when Mrs. Flannery led Jed up to the bellows by his left ear, and began to shout into the other one, that he saw fit to protest.

" 'Tis a profound mistake you're after makin', Mrs. Flannery, to be handlin' another man's nagur boy that way. Ye should drive him to work by the power of words, instead of tryin' to guide him to it by his ear for a handle."

"As long as I have him by one ear and at arm's length, I know he'll never be out of my sight," countered his spouse.

"Only a man who was short-sighted enough to take the king's shilling when he was sober could refute ye," replied her husband, "and I'm that man."

Manhood, good-fellowship, and self-respect thus being caustically restored, Flannery began ringing his hammer on the iron of the cold anvil. It worked. And at about the same time young Roy brought around the first instalment of horses.

Later on, Roy brought Bridget around too, after the last team. The two youngsters sat together, watching the fascinating process of applying red-hot iron to the smoking feet of living horses. Other children soon appeared shyly from nowhere at the sound of the anvil. Surprised but pleased neighbours loitered by, and dogs came and went, waiting to snap up eagerly that greatest tidbit of dogdom, a reeking bit of hoof paring. Seeing himself the center of so much approving attention, Flannery began to take an interest in his own work and gradually, as he warmed up, regained his form.

The unrelenting presence of Mrs. Flannery was also, no doubt, conducive to industry, for by half past five both the wagon teams were done, St. Clair's grey and Enna attended to, and without asking any questions, the smith proceeded to complete his task by shoeing Roy's colt, which had never been shod before.

"Mrs. McKinney will never pay for that," whispered Roy anxiously. "But I guess I can't stop it now." He and Jed helped finish up, after the smith had clipped the shaggy fetlocks, by polishing the hoofs of all the horses with beeswax, soot, and a hard brush.

It was almost dark when Salathiel finally came by to see what the farrier had accomplished. He was well enough pleased with the work, and agreed to pay for the colt's shoeing, too. The wagon horses were led off with instructions to Jed to bring the ark back to "the castle". Jed had a whole shilling this time, and young Roy got back his canoe and permission to go and play with Bridget. As Frances afterward said, "Sal ought to have known better than that." But all seemed in order and the day's work well sped, when something curiously disturbing, because it was so mysterious, began to overtake Salathiel.

It happened while the last shoe was being fitted on the colt. The song of the hammer, the red glow of the forge, the smell and loom of the smithy, began to feel vaguely familiar to him. For some reason or other, he suspected the presence of a big brindled ox near-by. Presently he began to fear that it would certainly appear and sniff at his face.

All this, to a matter-of-fact man like himself, was essentially disturbing. He tried to pay no attention to it, but the sense of familiarity with something seen before steadily grew. He brushed his sleeve across his eyes, and opened them again, sure that there would be no ox, or anything like that, and all would be as he expected. And so it was. The hammer clanged on a hot shoe, the forge fire glowed under the bellows, the stars were coming out in their old places in a clear sky—and then, suddenly, he was *overwhelmed* by the conviction that he had seen all this somewhere, that it had all happened to him before.

It was the same and yet the place was subtly changed. Things were not exactly as they used to be—*and ought to be now*. The man at the anvil should be bigger than Flannery. Much bigger! And he had golden hair, and mighty hands. Oh, yes, they were the hands that had made him his first bow. It was the smell of the hot iron that must be doing this; the small twinkling sparks on the white-hot shoe. He began to understand, he thought. And then the most disturbing thing of all occurred. It completely upset him.

A voice that was entirely familiar in its tones and emotional meaning began to speak. It seemed as though a door had swung open some place in the back of his mind—and he heard people talking.

"It is now past six of the clock, and the Sabbath has begun," said the Reverend Muir Craighead precisely with a slightly nasal and professional twang. "And it is the custom of the Christian people of this town to do no work after sundown, as the holy Commandment requires. I would advise ye to cease."

"To cease instantly," he was saying . . .

Who was this that had come out of the past and yet was speaking now, apparently to Flannery? The smith was gaping at him, his wife stood rigid in the corner. Jed paused at the bellows and looked up apprehensively. There was a tremendous tension in the air. What was wrong?

Now he knew.

Jed ought not to be there at all. No, it was a soldier in a red coat. There ought to be a soldier working the bellows! A soldier? Why . . . Why, this was crazy!

But he knew what to do now. It came upon him as though his muscles were doing their own thinking. He would pick up this canting minister and carry him out. By God, he would throw him . . . heave him through a window! The impulse was irresistible. Now!

He advanced on the Reverend Mr. Craighead with half-closed eyes, and then he remembered about the hands. They must be his father's hands!

Mr. Craighead gave an alarmed snort and retreated backward towards the Flannerys, into the revealing glow of the forge. His wig string, already badly strained in his bout with the mule, burst, and the wig slipped backward and down onto the back of his neck.

Salathiel found himself confronted by an unknown bald man, a total stranger, who was shivering. His hands fell helplessly by his sides, but they still twisted. *His* hands? Good Lord, whose hands *were* they?

Finally, he reached out and lifted Mr. Craighead's wig gently from around his ears and began to turn it about and examine it in the firelight. He leaned over to do so, and by so doing managed to conceal his face until his great confusion passed . . .

"Let me mend this wig for you, sir," said he at last. "I have some skill in the craft, and a machine along with me in the wagon."

"By Jehosaphat, I thought ye were going to scalp me, young man," replied Mr. Craighead, relieved beyond measure at so rational a suggestion. "You wild men from the frontiers, you're so unexpected and impetuous."

"Wal, in a way I have scalped ye," replied Salathiel, able to smile now. "But I'll return your hair to ye with a new drawstring, and all powdered, in time for tomorrow's sermon. You'll have to let me keep it for a while tonight."

Much mollified and still astonished by this offer, Mr. Craighead thawed. His bag-wig was half his clerical presence, and he knew it. His head was stark naked and shone like a looking glass, but for all that he did not believe it could ever serve as a mirror of faith. He looked at his precious artificial locks dangling from Salathiel's big hands, doubtfully.

"You'll be *sure* to have it in dacent time for the morning sermon?" he quavered.

"You shall have it before breakfast," replied Salathiel. "Meanwhile, please, sir, accept the loan of my hat. I owe it to you, ye know, for the fright I just gave ye. I'm sorry. I find for some reason I wasn't myself. Mr. Somerfield's old blackstrap is mighty powerful—" But even as he said that he knew that he lied.

Mr. Craighead cleared his throat. "That does happen occasionally," said he. "I was just on my way down to the colonel's for supper when I saw ye standin' in here. I knew you're bidden to meat at the Chambers' this evening, too. As for the smith's work here, *I* was a bit hasty perhaps. We're strict old kirk in Chambersburg— but, pshaw, 'tis only the last shoe for the little colt. Flannery, you're a papist anyhow. Ye may work on."

So Roy's colt was shod, after all. Salathiel gave the Spanish dollars to Mrs. Flannery as agreed upon, and he and the minister set off down the lane for the colonel's cabin together.

Mr. Craighead was quite curious about Salathiel. It seemed that he had heard something of his past.

"Ye were James McArdle's pupil, were ye not? I've heard him speak of ye with affection. He's a true servant of the spirit, a missionary to the lost and the heathen. He's a man of iron courage, dinna ye think?"

"I do, sir. I'm sure of it. But—he's lately given over, I've heard, to some peculiar and extreme views about matters I do not know much about."

Mr. Craighead chuckled. "I agree," he said. "Learnéd men have long tried to prove that the red Injuns are the lost tribes of Israel. But 'tis *not* Scripture, unless ye read it a bit cockeyed. As for myself," said he, his voice getting more hearty, "I think it enormous nonsense. 'Twill go hard with Mr. McArdle if he comes preaching his faith to those recently snatched from the cruel mercies of his 'Hebrews', at Carlisle."

"Does he plan to come there?" demanded Salathiel, by no means ravished by the news. "Colonel Bouquet will never permit it."

"Bouquet can do nothing about such matters after he returns from the woods to this province," replied the minister. "Every man, even every fool, moved by any spirit is free to propagate his views in Pennsylvania. 'Twas a provision especially made by William Penn in his first charter for the protection of zanies like old James Fox. It was hard, they say, at times to make old Jamie keep his leather breeches on. Now the spirit bloweth as it listeth, but whence cometh the inspiration to make a preacher take his trousers off?" Mr. Craighead chuckled.

"I never knew that," said Salathiel.

"Oh, aye, 'tis an old bruit amongst Friends, but hushed up now. Time covers all things, even the bare behind of a false prophet." Mr. Craighead chuckled again, and this time a little longer.

"By the by, speaking of Bouquet," continued the minister, "your colonel is a colonel no longer. Have ye not heard that the last *Gazette* from London says the king's promoted him brigadier and put him in command of the southern department?"

"That's brave news! That's grand!" exclaimed Albine. "I rejice to hear it. Indeed I do."

"Aye, 'twill be a verra popular act on the part of the crown," commented Mr. Craighead. "I hear the Assembly is busy preparing a resolution of thanks, and well they may, for there can be no doubt but that Bouquet is the presarver of this province, and the best gineral that has ever been sent by the king to war on the frontiers. If he were not a Switzer, they might have made him a baronet. That would have been wise, I think. No doubt he will go south now to complete the occupation of Louisiana into the west. You know, there's many a post up the great inland rivers where the lilies of France still wave. Either they haven't heard, or they're waiting for someone in a red coat to pull them down."

"That country seems far away," mused Salathiel. " 'Tis a pity we must lose Bouquet to it. But many speak now of those rich western prairies, and of the fair twin colonies in Florida."

"Not so far away," muttered the minister. "But ye can easily lose yourself there. It's a world unto itself. I hope you'll not be lured by it. Too many of our young men are wanderers now, and nothing more. And there's a mighty work to be done here."

"I admire to be this side o' the mountains," replied Salathiel. "I saw a sight of the back country yonder. I'll tarry downcountry for a while."

Thus chatting together, they took the final turn in the lane to Colonel Chambers's. Somewhat to his surprise Salathiel found himself much at home with Mr. Craighead, and liking him. Their response to various things seemed to be mutual. The minister was a quiet, unassuming little man, but with a touch of fire under his amiability. And there was no doubt he was a devoted servant of the Lord, with the divine sense of humour also vouchsafed him. They found themselves chuckling together over the same things several times. Oh Lord, if McArdle could only have been more like Mr. Craighead!

"Mind ye now, young man, I'm depending upon you to cover my naked poll for the sermon. 'Tis a pious work ye may well engage in, even on the Sabbath," added Mr. Craighead, laughing and laying his hand appealingly on Salathiel's arm just before they went in the door.

"I'll not fail ye, Mr. Craighead," replied Albine. "Ye shall have your wig returned tonight." And with that they went in to supper.

Salathiel was astonished when he went into the small clock parlour. There were about twenty people crowded into the low-ceilinged little room, while Ruhannah, Frances, the two Oisters, with several of the wives of neighbours were bustling about in the kitchen ell. All cooking was over, but the feast was to be laid, and, it appeared, constantly enlarged.

For it was lodge night. Friends of the colonel and Dr. Colhoun kept riding in. Salathiel caught the air of expectancy pending an important meeting. St. Clair and Yates were busy as usual talking with everybody. Mr. Craighead, with a small black cap, mercifully furnished by the colonel, was the center of much respectful attention and some careful hilarity at his mishap. He seemed only half the man he was without his wig. Seeing that he was really and deeply embarrassed, Salathiel went out to the woodshed, and placing the wig over a small hard pumpkin, began some rapid repairs.

A new main thong, a combing-out and recurling over clothespins, some shavings stuffed into the sagging bag, and a coat of wax, with a new bow on the eelskin pigtail, wrought wonders. The colonel's powder box, hastily called for, completed the miracle. There was no time to send for the irons and forms in the wagon. In a few minutes he called for Mr. Craighead and tied and fitted the wig over his head. The return of the minister redisguised as himself brought a shout of good-natured welcome from the crowd in the small front room.

But Salathiel also was welcomed, and unexpectedly.

The two Callahans were there, leaning against the wall in the corner, where their long rifles also reposed. There was a crowd pressing about them. At first Salathiel could not see why. Then they called out to him, and crossing the room, he saw an old man seated on a chair between them, a big man. His face was bland with the kind of smooth return to youth which senility sometimes ghostfully suggests. His mouth was straight and toothless. It was the voice that had changed most. His eyes were the same. It was Captain Jack.

"My son," said the old man over and over again, with his mouth quavering visibly. "Salathiel, it is good to see you yet again, Salathiel, my son."

And now for the first time Salathiel became fully conscious of having become the accepted heir of the admiration and gratitude for what Captain Jack and he and the Callahans, and other men like them, had done in those harassed days of darkness and massacre, when cabins were fired by night on the deserted frontier. They had stayed, fought, triumphed, and saved the province. Bouquet was the great hero, but he was a king's man. For the rangers, for the native sons and intrepid rifles of the frontier, was reserved the full measure of personal affection by the settlers.

Captain Jack was passing. It was plain to be seen. The change from only a year before was unbelievable. Curiously, he had returned down the ladder of life, and was now again an approximate ghost of the mild and once happy Dr. Caldwell. This, however, was more a physical than a mental reversal in time.

His memory was clear, but at most times not so active. He now tended to recall episodes in his more distant past. His mood was a subtle one of passive contentment and a clinging to all that was secretly of moral and affectionate satisfaction to him, a preoccupation with the people and places he had fiercely and silently loved. The feeling that his work was over, that like his rifle-gun he would slay no more but was laid up to rust away, had cancelled the importance to him of the future. Vengeance satisfied and the ruling passion of his life gone, as it had been since the great Indian slaying at the Salt Kettles, Captain Jack quietly, if not entirely contentedly, awaited his end. Sometimes there were flashes of lightning in the old eyes and a far-off reminiscent roll of thunder in his voice and talk—and then Dr. Caldwell was sitting there smiling. Few remembered Dr.

Caldwell, and none present had known of Dr. Morton, save Colonel Chambers.*

Salathiel, of course, was not aware of all this instantly, and that evening it took him some time to realize it fully. But he was aware instantly that Captain Jack was not able to conceal his respect and affection for him, nor his belief that in Salathiel he saw himself renewed, and so looked to him as a son to carry his mission on.

Certainly, everyone else present that evening had felt the inner meaning of Captain Jack's greeting with the gestures and tones of voice that conferred upon Albine the old man's blessing.

The Callahans talked earnestly to Salathiel, taking all this for granted. They spoke of certain names already well known to him, and of others who were promising candidates for the small group of associators, riflemen, backwoodsmen and rangers, which, if he would agree to lead them when needed, they promised on their part to keep in touch with him and hold ready for his call. That he was going downcountry made very little difference, or even if later on he went to the City. They would pass the word along to him through the lodges and from time to time they would come to see him personally and confer, wherever he was.

This was the gist of the conversation at supper, the general drift of which Colonel Chambers highly approved. And with Captain Jack sitting there between himself and the colonel, it was impossible for Salathiel not to promise to comply. And so he did—much to Frances Melissa's secret anxiety. She was not, in fact, able entirely to restrain herself.

Halfway through supper she suddenly demanded to know Bridget's whereabouts. He explained as best he could, and thus brought the laughter of the entire company down on himself. For Frances upbraided him angrily and brilliantly for letting the two youngsters wander off—and now, please God, what had become of them?

Soon no one present had any doubt but that Sal Albine was a very much married man, and that his wife had an able tongue. But that, fortunately, was the worst and the best of it, for before the last of a still-smoking remnant of venison pie and peach cobbler had been devoured, Roy and Bridget both appeared. They had been swimming the canoe in the mill-race together.

Roy, of course, had fallen in. Bridget hadn't, and had even taken off her new red stockings, which she extended towards Melissa as a kind of propitiatory offering and proof of her responsibility and foresight. Dr. Colhoun sent Roy up into the loft and told him to go to bed, as his lips were blue and he was shivering.

* For Dr. Caldwell and Dr. Morton, see "The Secret Story of Captain Jack," Chapter 6, *Bedford Village.*

"We'll just keep him here till the morrow," said the colonel, "when no doubt Mistress McKinney will be in town inquiring for him, and wanting to warm him proper. The young rascal must have stolen off this afternoon."

"I'll speak to that cold-hearted woman myself," said Ruhannah, tossing her head. "She treats her bound help and the poor niggers she took over from the Marylanders like cattle. Her own flesh and blood, for that matter, is not exempt. And her prayin' louder and longer on Sabbath than anyone else!"

"Yes, it's a sad case of a bitter widow tearin' the heart out of her people and her farm. Young Roy is one of the finest youngsters in the neighbourhood. A very good family the Davisons are. Maybe you'll say a word to Mrs. McKinney," said the colonel to Mr. Craighead, "about a little less cattle drivin', and a little more marcy and gentleness out her way. It would come better from you as a man of God than from me as the law."

"I'll take the first occasion," promised Mr. Craighead. "I'll put it upon her to relent. 'Tis a pity her kind husband was caught out and scalped."

"Aye," said Captain Jack, "but he wouldn't listen to me. I rapped on his door only the night before Logan's raid and told them the Big Cove was in flames and he'd better fort-up."

"The McKinneys be an obstinate clan," said the colonel, reminiscently. "They'd ruther be scalped than harkin' to another man's advice."

"See that the boy upstairs has some supper, Ruhannah, and some comfort for the morrow," he added. "I mind me well going to sleep with the horror of taws in the mornin' hangin' over my young soul. Let the child say his prayers in this house in peace."

Ruhannah nodded. She loved her father for his strength, but above all for his never-failing "marcy", as she called it.

"Ma will be home for kirk the morrow," she said. "But I hope the lodge night supper was what ye liked, faither, especially with Captain Jack here."

"Ye treat us too well, Ruhannah," said the old hunter. "Ye tempt me to come back to live close by ye here in the town, as your father allers wants me to do. But I must go and settle up affairs of mine that I have neglected for half a lifetime and abide the coming of one more winter in my old cabin on the Blue Mountain. There I can smoke my pipe in peace, alone, and before the Lord. Yes, it was a good pie, my dear. Succulent! And venison's a dry meat mostly. An old-fashioned Sabbath baking it was, well turned and juicy through and through."

Ruhannah blushed with pleasure, and looked at Mina and Tina

in triumph that her own directions, rather than her mother's, had been carried out and were being praised.

The colonel rose, said a brief after-grace, and the company, leading their horses, followed him and Captain Jack down to the stockaded gate, where after a careful scrutinizing by some of the brethren, they were admitted one by one to the "island".

Only those who could be recognized beyond all question were acceptable. Word had been passed down from the Grand Lodge for a general tightening up all over the province of Masonic practices in ritual, administration, and correspondence.* Records were to be in form and meticulously kept. Only those who could work the first three blue lodge degrees were to be recognized. The old days of disputed jurisdictions, doubtful charters, and wandering brethren with a confused grip, or a word or two a bit awry, were to be things of the past. The character of candidates was to be more carefully scrutinized and their preparation made more thorough.

A general feeling of a time of crisis to come, when great things would have to be decided and men of ideals and character must be known to one another—men who would not fail or betray the cause of liberty by unseasonable talk or bargains in the wrong places—this stir was abroad in the land and was peculiarly concentrated in the free and accepted lodges.

There was to be freedom, but there was also to be order. New wine from the vineyard might prove heady, and there must be faithful tenders of the vines. "Cowans" could be dangerous. In these meetings by night going on here and there all over the colonies, the people of the continent were becoming conscious of themselves through their mutual problems and interests. Correspondence between men of affairs and influence, leaders who could completely trust one another in the bonds of a fraternal oath, was made possible and was going on. It was only the beginning, the first stir of independence. But it already had the air and the conviction of being a conspiracy for right thinking to maintain and further the general welfare by practical means confidentially employed.

It is curious how the growing intentions of men, the inner meaning of a time, place, and people are shadowed forth and livingly embodied in the ways and manners, the sights and sounds of par-

---

* What "Grand Lodge" it is impossible at this late date to ascertain definitely. It may have been the Grand Lodge of England according to the Old Institution founded in 1751, also known as the Grand Lodge of the Four Degrees. It was from this Lodge of the Four Degrees that Royal Arch Masonry stemmed. More probably, however, the local lodge at Chambersburg would at this time have been under the jurisdiction of a Grand Lodge of "Ancients" at Philadelphia, which was granted a charter June 20, 1764, as No. 89 in England and No. 1 in Pennsylvania. This was not the Grand Lodge to which Benjamin Franklin and other famous worthies belonged. Franklin's lodge was a Grand Lodge of the "Moderns".

ticular and significant occasions, long before the meaning is reduced to words. The living drama, the lively gestures and tones of unconscious yet determined intent show themselves outwardly, become manifest, and are to be apprehended even before the end in view is declared. Such glances from the countenance of time are always fleeting, and neither the face of events nor the expressions upon it are ever quite the same.

So it was with the men of Chambersburg and of the countryside around about as they passed down Chambers's lane that evening in November 1764, leading their horses, talking quietly, and halting to pass through the stockaded gate to the "island", man by man. There were about sixty in all in the small procession.

Some wore the buckskins of the mountain wilderness frontier. Others not. Several rifle barrels borne on the shoulders of rangers moved slowly across the constellations, high above the heads of the crowd. There were many farmers in homespun, leading plough horses, two young officers from the fort in royal regimentals, and a distinguished visitor from the City in the fashionable garb of the town. But they were all one in inner tone and feeling.

The several accents of the different dialects they spoke had all merged in the quiet of the night and with the native language of the rushing stream into a subdued and murmurous tongue of common communication, the slightest intonations of which were significant and mutually intelligible. It was English that was thus being spoken, rude but ample. In it was hidden the reservoir of the past and the fountain of the future.

Yet there was still another language by which the time and the occasion was being automatically described in the idiom of its own contemporary phrases. It could be read aloud in the clumping sound of boots and horseshoes, in the scuffing of moccasins along the smooth mill path, and in the deep growls or subdued laughter of the company as they lengthened out into a single line. It could be read silently in the silhouettes of their clothing and shadowy profiles faintly visible in the cool blue darkness. Even the acrid scent of tobacco, sweet willow bark and sumac from an occasional pipe that here and there illuminated a grey-bearded or a lean-jawed young face for a glowing instant, had something to say. A dim coonskin cap or a cocked hat bobbing against the sparking stars added each its own short syllable of meaning.

For all blent into a companionable and yet a solemn and surreptitious feeling of a dangerous destiny being secretly shared. It was a compound of the common emotions and intentions of the various individuals in the small procession, which, as the brethren filed up the white stone steps and into the narrow door of Colonel Chambers's fortified mansion to disappear one by one, was mysteriously not there any longer. It was almost as though the grim house waiting in the starlight had anticipated the cannibalistic tendencies of time.

How different was this meeting from the atmosphere of suppressed excitement and missionary zeal that had marked the assembling of the lodge at Bedford in Garrett's garret. Salathiel could not help but agree with Yates when he commented upon it. The ritual seemed to flow out of the past as a matter of old memory in which all were letter-perfect. The impression was that of piety and sustained order. The setting was less theatrical and less crowded. Except for a few officers of the lodge in aprons, regalia was at a minimum. The truly huge hall of the fortressed dwelling accommodated all comfortably and yet made a perfect theatre for intimate speaking. Log fires burned at either side in the massive chimneys, and candles at the cardinal points. The squares were chalked and would be erased later. Actually, this was the ruling assembly and moral nexus of the neighbourhood, and of both river valleys up and down. As such, it was so understood and taken for granted. Opinions were openly discussed and policies settled here.

The meeting that evening was an important one. After some of the local and charitable problems of various brethren and their families were discussed, communications from the Grand Lodge and letters from several quarters were considered. Charles Humphreys of the "Mansion House", seven miles outside of Philadelphia, and a member of the Assembly of the province, discussed the understanding which the Assembly had arrived at with Brother Franklin on sending him as an agent for the province to England, and the possibilities of help to be derived from the brethren abroad.

Colonel Chambers made a plea for upholding the hands of the proprietaries in their old policy of toleration for all sects, and read some passages in support of his argument from a poem by Mr. Peter Folger, called "A Looking Glass for the Times, or the Former Spirit of New England Renewed," which had just been brought to him from Boston. It was a powerful plea for liberty of conscience written in old times, but only recently printed. "It is the spirit of the former age which we must continue to cherish," said the colonel.

The Reverend Brother Craighead followed with a scheme concocted by some of the brethren to import and support a decent Protestant schoolmaster. He made an eloquent complaint of the tendency of the new generation to remain illiterate, and of the consequences to the community. Subscriptions for the bringing in of young Mr. William Thomas, the son of a minister from Hill Town, Bucks County, to start a school for boys at Chambersburg were pledged forthwith.

Captain Jack followed with an appeal that "his young mountain rangers" should continue to receive the tacit support of the frontier Masons as they always had in the past. All his rangers had always been sons of the widow. The promptness, secrecy, and freedom from government which they had enjoyed in the past, and which might again be vital should Indian troubles come, he asked to be continued. He made it plain that he was about to disappear from the scene. "My labours and my mission are o'er." And if anyone could have doubted this, the halting eloquence from the now toothless mouth, which made his valedictory sound like language already half blown away by the wind, was in itself the proof of his theme. He ended by pointing out Salathiel as the one best qualified to re-rally the "Fighting Quakers", when the time came. "And that time will surely be upon us in the nigh and onrushing future. Amen," said Captain Jack.

"The mantle of Elijah has fallen upon you, Brother Albine," said Arthur St. Clair.

There was nothing for it, but under the eyes of Captain Jack and the whole lodge, Salathiel must rise and accept. And to Yates's delight, he acquitted himself on this important occasion not only modestly but very well. It was a solemn promise he gave. How reluctant he was to give it, he was at some pains to conceal. The obvious pleasure and affectionate gratitude of his old leader were his immediate and only reward. It was arranged on the side that evening that Captain Jack should accompany him in the wagon as far as Carlisle.

The speech of the old partisan and patriot of the mountains was by far the most moving event of the evening, but not the most discussed. What was most immediately stirring and disturbing to the neighbourhood was the growing hostility of many of the younger men to the downcountry city merchants, and the trade with the Indians, which they roundly denounced. Colonel Chambers complained and warned of the growing lawlessness of the Black Boys. Captain James Smith, the Callahans, and others from Conococheague defended the "taking of necessary measures", short of taking scalps. A number of members spoke bitterly of having their arms seized and their houses searched by "Captain Grant up at the fort". His petty tyrannies were generally execrated.

Nothing very definite came out of all this. It was not something which the lodge could entirely control. It was quite plain that Injun traders, whether licensed or not, were going to have to reckon with the Black Boys. Owing to the presence of Ensigns McNairn and Erskine from the fort, nothing more was said about dealing with

Wully and the royal garrison, except perhaps elliptically by Magistrate McDowell, who spoke of the sins and the folly of rebellion against authority.

Two emissaries from the emigrating congregations then on the way from Carlisle were next heard from, and certain plans for seeing them on their way down through the Valley of Virginia and "cherishing" them through the winter were gone into. There were many Masons and their families amongst them. Certain letters could be written to lodge No. 12 at Winchester, but not in this case to Colonel Washington, who was sometimes inimical to communications from Pennsylvania, it was thought. The lodge was adjourned as usual, except for a prayer by Mr. Craighead addressed fervently to the common Father of all men, denominated by the minister as the "Lord God of Sabaoth". It was late, after midnight, when quietly and with as little disturbance as possible the members dispersed themselves, either homeward or amongst the friendly houses of the brethren in the town.

Meanwhile, to anyone of a full and sensitive apprehension, to someone with a poetic sixth sense, the feeling and meaning of the meeting might have been sensed from the outside by the sight of the deserted ark and trundler drawn up waiting in the deserted dooryard, and by the cracks of yellow light streaming through tightly closed shutters and gleaming like a hundred small eyes from loopholes under the frowning leaden eaves of the forbidding house. A sound of rushing waters, the steady drift of thin flocks of small white clouds across the face of peeping stars seemed to denote the passing of time in a given direction and from a mysterious source, while inside the sheltered house bearded and apple-cheeked men secretly deliberated. There was a hush, a silence, and a note of disturbance in the rising wind from the north. Southward-bound birds with thin urgent cries passed high as the cloud rack overhead. A change of seasons, a certain apprehensive expectancy was in the air.

When Salathiel and Captain Jack finally emerged from the meeting, all this was evident to them and present in feeling, sensitive as they both were to every change and meaning in the weather of the wilderness and the hints in the atmosphere of any natural place. But it was so well understood, and so taken for granted, that neither of them saw fit to comment upon it. They were there; certain things were going on. The world as always, even when it seemed pleasant and contented, was secretly astir.

Captain Jack was to sleep that night in the wagon. Melissa and Bridget were tarrying with Ruhannah up at the colonel's cabin. Women were not expected to be near-by during a lodge meeting, and Ruhannah had especially asked them to stay.

So, except for Captain Jack, Salathiel shortly after midnight, with the grim mansion finally lightless and deserted, found himself alone.

Captain Jack went to bed gladly. He seemed greatly fatigued, indeed all but overcome by the effects of the meeting and the excitement of his farewell speech. After a few jocular comments on the luxurious headquarters bequeathed by the "little captain", and the follies of fighting Injuns from a palace on wheels, he lay back on Frances' pillow, swallowed a measure of old Cumberland rye gladly, and after only a few movements of his lips was asleep.

Salathiel sat watching him intently by the dim light of a single candle. There was the same large frame outlined by the blanket, but as his sleep became deeper the face of the old man relaxed and imperceptibly changed. It was possible now to look back through the mists of years and to surmise what Captain Jack must have looked like when a boy. It was a strange haunting of age by the lost ghost of youth. Perhaps here was the subtle outward evidence of some returning cycle of the spirit, of that ancient inner person which in sleep always deems itself to be immortal. Perhaps *that* was returning whence it came. Nymwha had often spoken of this return. He could overhear very old voices when he fasted, he said, speaking wisely of happy summers spent somewhere long ago. By the solemn and single light of the candle such things seemed possible, as he sat gazing at the old hunter's face in deep silence. There were no traces of trouble there any longer. The countenance was smooth and bland, only a little pitiful about the mouth.

Salathiel breathed deeply, which was as near as he ever came to sighing. He thought over the events of the long day. Finally, he rose and extinguished the candle. He had one thing to do yet, before the day could be called finished. It was the hand.

He walked down the row of Colonel Chambers's sheds until he came to the smoke-house. It was empty, all but for a small pile of hickory chips saved for kindling in a dry corner. A few of these he now arranged in the square pit in the middle of the floor, placing some dry rags amongst them from his tinder box. He struck a few sparks with flint and steel and blew on the glowing patch. In a few minutes the pile of chips began to smoke and smoulder. A blowpipe made from an old gun barrel extended under the sill of the door to the bottom of the fire in the pit. This pipe he now stopped with some clay to regulate the draught until the pile smoked, burning at a slow rate, and exactly satisfactorily.

Unwinding a moccasin thong, he suspended the hand by the wrist a few feet above, and directly over, the smoking pit. The hand spun slowly, barely visible in the faintly fire-tinged darkness. Clouds of pungent smoke ascended like incense about it.

Salathiel took a final look at it, and nodding his head in approbation, closed the door. Twenty-four hours of that steady heat and smoke, and the article would be "presarved".

He went back to the wagon, undressed, and lay down.

"Hickory smoke," muttered Captain Jack, turning over and sniffing. "Ye stink like a Shawanee."

But I'm not one, thought Salathiel, for all that. Tomorrow I'm going to the sermon with Frances and Bridget, in decent clothes, and like a Christian man. The smell of wood smoke shall not be upon me.

In the smoke-house the hand continued to point downward into the pit.

17

The Sermon

VERY EARLY that Sabbath morning Frances and Bridget were back at the wagon. While Captain Jack slept peacefully on, Salathiel slung an iron pot over a small fire and prepared a breakfast of corn mush, roasted potatoes, and sidemeat. This was quickly dispatched, and the two women turned in to primp themselves and each other for the great occasion of the morning sermon. Bridget, to be sure, was not much of a help to Frances, except as an ardent supporter and abetter of Melissa's desire to appear more elegant than anyone else.

Salathiel, however, was content for his own reasons to go along. He was pleased to find that not only was Frances not going to object to taking part in a Protestant preaching, but was apparently determined to make the most of it, at least from a worldly and visible standpoint. Of her motives for doing so, he could only surmise. As a matter of fact, they were rather complex, and she did not undertake to explain them.

Despite her small chance for indoctrination in the orthodox Roman faith, she remained in her own mind an ardent Catholic. Almost her first certain memory was that of being baptized in The Church at Cork. Her instruction by the nuns there, brief and rudimentary as it had been, had yet made a profound impression upon her. It was not easily, therefore, that she was to be persuaded to enter a Protestant place of worship. Above all, she feared listening to the reading of the King James version of the Scriptures.

To the English Bible, as the source from which her Protestant and Sassenach oppressors of whatever sect all seemed to draw their strength and inspiration, Frances attributed a magic potency and capacity for ill. She regarded it as the wellspring of heresy and the prime cause of the downfall of the Irish. Besides the moral fascina-

tion of the Book, which she had experienced while cogitating by firelight in front of Frazier's hearth, there was the entrancing and convincing sound of its language. That wizardry remained indelibly in
her memory, along with the conviction that she had committed a
mortal sin in feeding upon forbidden poetry. To her starving and
avid mind the Book had indeed proved a heady and confusing potion.
But it was the only book in the cabin—and she had read it.

Now, this morning, she was actually dressing and preparing to go
to a Protestant preaching! Well, she couldn't help it. She had been
caught in the net of her own vanities, perhaps. But she *must* get along
in this world, even at the risk of trouble in the next. She must attain
and maintain her respectability, or she was lost here and now. Also
she must bring her fine husband along with her; keep him in his town
clothes lest he go back to the woods again. And now there was
Bridget! Bridget, that young limb and splinter of Presbyterian doctrine. She felt an inborn spiritual obstinacy in her already. She both
sensed it and feared it. How would it be possible to explain to Bridget
why she should not go with all the rest of the neighbours to listen to
the Reverend Mr. Craighead this Sunday morning?

No, it was impossible. She must even risk her soul. Perhaps she
could confess when she got to Philadelphia, and be shriven. There
would be a mass priest in the City, please God! It had been a long time
since . . . yes, she would go this morning and make the best of it, the
very best.

There was one great and consoling circumstance, nevertheless.
As yet there was no chapel in Chambersburg. The service was to be
held in Colonel Chambers's new mill, and the roof was not yet over
it. Only the open framework of the beams was there. Therefore,
strictly speaking, it could not be said that she was going *into* a Protestant chapel.

Thus, with apparent equanimity, and saying nothing of her inner
doubts, Frances continued her own and Bridget's outer preparations
to attend the preaching at the mill, while moving about quietly and
whispering in order to avoid waking Captain Jack. In fact, to get
herself up properly, she had left Ruhannah early and returned to the
wagon, where all her means for primping were more immediately at
hand. And if her preparations of the morning before for Colonel
Chambers's breakfast had been startling and effectual, the final results
of her Sunday morning toiletring were little short of triumphant.
She had worked hard for the result, too.

Defying the danger of being suspected of working after Saturday
sundown, she and Ruhannah had locked the door of their bedroom
the night before, and while the lodge met, they had revelled in the
purchases of the day and contrived between them to cover the bare

bones of two new bonnet frames with rich yellow paduasoy, and a small one for Bridget with black silk. These, with the addition of blue-black ties and hemstitched bows, were such pieces of worldly millinery as had seldom swum before the eyes of the Lord in any congregation in Chambers Mills, or for miles about—and Ruhannah knew it. Alas, there had been no time to make new bodices. But the bonnets!—they would burst on the gaze of the faithful unexpectedly as meteors.

Frances must still wear her dress of the day before, but there was a new grey silk shawl and a neckerchief to match, both with long fringes. And for Bridget, Melissa had borrowed a pair of small cloth slippers. They were not red, but they fitted. This time she had out the hot curling irons, and everything else, for doing her own and Bridget's hair. Bonnets required bangs curled in front, small ones, tight little ringlets.

So Salathiel had most of Johnson's kit in full blast that morning. And it was his best blue woollen suit, good stockings, and no leather stock but a tied cravat that he wore. Short of powdering his hair, he was now willing and even submissive "in going the whole hog" in the proceedings, as he nicely phrased it.

One reason for this was that he had been told that the emigrants were looking for a ranger to guide them south and west over the mountains, and that someone had recommended him to them. They were offering one hundred pounds down and all found, Yates had said so; and said it so that St. Clair could hear him. That was all right, but he, Salathiel, was not going to turn west again, not now! Not even for one hundred pounds and the lure of seeing new country. That he had to admit did entice him. But since it *was* a temptation, he would rather not have to meet it.

So the less he looked like his old self, the better for a day or two at least. The emigrants would be looking for a tall man in fringed buckskins, nursing a long rifle. Let them look, then. He would pass them by in a smooth blue coat and silver buckles on his shoes. He finished by fastening on an old pair that had once belonged to the captain, and giving his small-clogs a polish. He also displayed the captain's silver watch and chain across his best yellow serving waistcoat. But he was mighty glad Captain Jack slept like a babe all through this dressing-up business. So far he hadn't even stirred.

It was half past nine almost exactly when Colonel Chambers, Mr. Craighead, and Dr. and Mrs. Colhoun came down the mill path on their way to the mill and the morning's preaching. Ruhannah's bonnet glowed afar with a fine saffron effulgence through the bare upper branches of the willow trees. Colonel Chambers wore the regimentals of the Pennsylvania line but without his small sword. Mr. Craighead's wig was newly powdered. From the black bag in which he carried his Bible and other books, the ham had been advisedly removed. Dr. Colhoun approached his Maker in a modest grey surgeon's coat with cherry-coloured pantaloons, a black three-cornered hat, and a little beaver muff that hung from his neck on an amber chain. In this he kept his empty purse, a full snuffbox, and both his hands on a cold day. It *was* turning a little cold this morning, he opined, and sermons were usually too long, especially in November in an open mill. He took a small pinch of snuff in anticipation, and said "Pshaw" loudly, as he found himself just balked of a wholesome sneeze.

A small brass bell began ringing down at the mill. The colonel's party approached more rapidly. The Albines were waiting for them. They stood for a moment, regarding one another with mutual appreciation.

Colonel Chambers was especially well pleased. He would appear at preaching today with a most genteel and acceptable company. As the chief personage of the neighbourhood, and the landlord of many in the congregation, he felt properly complemented; his example respectably supported. It was an important occasion this morning. Mr. Craighead had come over from Old Church especially to preach the morning sermon. He was much beloved, and people always turned out in large numbers to hear him. And then there was a certain announcement the minister was to make, one which concerned the colonel deeply and the congregation at Chambersburg, too, for all time to come. The three new bonnets *were* a little gladsome. But then this was no Quaker meeting, and they were nothing to what even the Seceders were wearing in the City. Folks would just have to get used to a little style with a man of substance like himself as presiding elder. Sooner or later he would have in instruments for the psalm singing, too. "Trumpets and psalteries and harps before the Lord"—an organ! There was Scriptural warrant for it in the last psalm. He would ask Mr. Craighead to announce that particular psalm for the benefit of Patrick Vance, Esquire, an elder much opposed to instrumental music as a modern innovation.

"Good morning," said Mr. Craighead, cordially, touching his wig reminiscently and gratefully to Salathiel. His eyes twinkled as he looked over the women in their new shawls. "Some of us, I see, are making the fringes of our phylacteries long," he chuckled, and then led the way along the mill-race at a faster pace. For the bell had ceased clamouring, and he prided himself on being on time—whenever Ahaz would permit.

Under the fluctuating shadow and sunshine of a swiftly passing flock of clouds, the well-satisfied little company made its way towards the skeleton of the new mill, whose bare rafters could be seen rising gauntly above the dam. It would be a pity if it came on to rain, thought the doctor. But no, it would hardly do that. It might snow, if it kept getting much colder. Perhaps the raw weather would hold off until the afternoon? If so, it would still be comparatively comfortable in the sheltered valley below the dam. Indeed, there was a hush in the atmosphere of the place when they arrived there.

A larger congregation than even the colonel had anticipated was awaiting the minister. At the far end of the new mill the elders sat before a table reared on saw-horses on the raw plank floor. The open work of the rafters in the rough Gothic joinery of the gambrel seemed to sketch airily overhead only the bare reminder of a church roof. Beneath, the congregation sat on plank benches or were gathered in close about the new building, as close as they could press on either side and still see over the heads of the sitters from the rising ground about. The curious and continuous alternating of cloud-gloom and bright sunshine was startling and impressive; now everything was bathed in glory, then all was overcast and plunged in gloom.

It would be a hard thing to preach against, thought Mr. Craighead, as he walked up the narrow aisle between the benches and deposited his black bag on the big table. He took out his heavy Bible, leather-bound hymnal and psalter and arranged them carefully and somewhat dramatically, as was his wont. He then put on a large pair of square spectacles. Colonel Chambers sat down amongst the elders, facing his family and visitors, who were now seated honourably on the front bench. He noted with pleasure that Mrs. Chambers was there, just come in on time from Shippensburg. But ready to lead the singing as usual. She *never* failed him. He would like to have smiled at her if he could. But being presiding elder was no smiling matter.

Mr. Craighead turned, faced the congregation, and announced the opening psalm. They began in gloom, but a drench of sunshine suddenly poured down on them. And it seemed to the minister that it was not Madam Chambers, but the river itself with a certain hint of eternity in the hushed voice of its ever-rolling waters that set the pitch of the old tune. Two hundred voices filled the valley with song—

> "Praise ye the Lord. Praise God in
> his sanctuary: praise him in the
> firmanent of his power . . ."

Back at the wagon, Captain Jack knew the 150th Psalm when he heard it. Indeed, he knew a great part of the Old Testament by heart, particularly the more sanguinary passages dealing with vengeance upon the heathen. He was up now, crouching over the remains of Salathiel's breakfast fire, and roasting a bit of sidemeat on a long fork.

> "Praise him with the sound of the
> trumpet: praise him with the psal-
> tery and harp . . ."

The singing of the congregation rose deep and clear, high and eerie over the roar of the distant falls upstream. The meat was turning brown. Captain Jack hummed the next verse with the congregation:

> "Praise him with the timbrel and
> dance: praise him with stringed
> instruments and organs . . ."

He hadn't meant to go to preaching this morning. He was glad the young folks had let him sleep. In the past he had heard a good many sermons. But the taste of the music was almost as strong in his mouth now as the taste of the meat—and he felt the better for both.

> "Let every thing that hath breath
> praise the Lord. Praise ye the
> Lord."

This time he joined in with all his old-time vim. His voice echoed heartily against the face of the old mansion. He looked up to see Yates and St. Clair grinning at him through the yard gate.

"We wondered who was praising God all alone," said Yates. "We're bound for the preaching ourselves, but tardiness always likes company. Won't you come along, sir?"

"Wait till I finish my pork and taters," answered Captain Jack, a bit testily. "An old man needs his morning sustenance, Sabbath or no."

They came over respectfully and sat down by the fire to wait while he ate. Presently St. Clair produced his silver flask, and they all had a brief pull.

"That's better," said Captain Jack. "I don't git immedjit effect from my victuals any more." He raked a roasted potato from the ashes, broke it, and put salt on it.

"What surprised ye to hear a man praising the Lord all alone?" he asked out of the blue.

"Well, now," said St. Clair, "since you ask *me*. Praise by a congregation does sound more convincing. At least to me," he added.

"That's 'cause you're a politician, Arthur," said Captain Jack. "You think everything must be done by committees. That's the way ever since thar's so many settlers in these once lonely and decent parts. But if the chief end of man is to glorify God exceedingly, one God and one man is all it takes. Ain't it?" asked Captain Jack, poising his potato.

"Do you glorify him most by faith or by works?" inquired Yates.

"Oh, I won't quibble with ye, mister attorney," said the old man. "No doubt you're better at splitting hairs in a circle than I be. But kin ye tie a knot in them before ye lose both ends? And let me ask you this: as a man of reason, what did ye ask me to go down to hear the sermon this mornin' for?"

"For your company," said Yates.

Captain Jack dropped his potato, and grinned through his gums. "That's mighty well put, young man," said he. "Still I suspicion, as a lawyer *you're* lookin' for direct evidence. If so, testimony, indirect testimony is all you'll ever git."

"Then I'll be curious to hear what Brother Craighead may have to say this morning," replied Yates.

The *old devil,* he thought. Who would have guessed there was theology in him! To take for granted what he still had to prove! We might have been here all morning!

Captain Jack began brushing the ashes off his buckskins. He wiped his mouth off, too. "We'd better git goin'," he said. "That's the invocation now."

They set off for the mill together.

"Brother St. Clair will feel better where two or three are gathered together," said Captain Jack, a little too casually as they walked along.

St. Clair turned pale and purple under his stock.

"But shucks," continued the old man, "it looks today like we'd do even better than that. It's no rump caucus down there."

There were, in fact, too many in the congregation that morning to hold the preaching in the mill. Everybody shifted to a hollow in the meadow near-by, a place that had frequently been used for field-preaching, weather permitting, long prior to the erection of Colonel Chambers's mill.

And there was good reason for this arrangement. For not only was the ground in the field of a convenient conformation, but there was a memorable pulpit naturally provided. There was only one other pulpit in Pennsylvania that resembled it.* It was the hollow shell of a huge poplar tree, which having once sustained a bolt from

* At Hill Town in Buckingham County.

heaven a half century before, now contributed its convenient remains to echoing forth the divine thunders of the itinerant clergy.

Some rough-and-ready but ingenious axe work on its massive and heavily rooted lower trunk had cut into the solid wood a short semi-circular flight of steps leading to a floor within the tree itself. That in turn supported a rustic lectern. Above this the shell of bark still projected in a prolonged hollow oval and was tied together at the top with old rope and stoppered with tar. A few thin planks extending forward and upward had been inserted towards the roof as a sounding board and hung there by a rusty chain.

Crude as this rostrum accidentally furnished forth by nature might appear to the ecclesiastically sophisticated, it was nevertheless curiously impressive and acoustically effective. For in it the minister stood ten feet above the crowd like a jack-in-the-pulpit; but in full sight of and, what was more important, within perfect hearing of all his congregation gathered in the hollow of the field before him. Furthermore, the pulpit itself, being what it was, served to confine those who used it to its own deeply rooted and earthy style. Any affected discourse echoed from its natural depths would inevitably have suffered the tragic fate of inadvertent comedy.

Yates, Captain Jack, and St. Clair arrived just when the congregation was shifting from the mill to the meadow, and in time to take their places amidst the others without arousing comment. A few open wagons were drawn up towards the side, where some of the farmers' wives and children sat overlooking the heads of the majority, who now seated themselves on the bare turf or on what fragments of logs, planks, and shingles they could secure.

After a short pause for all to get settled, Mr. Craighead, his black bag under his arm, and followed by all the elders, approached the wide-spreading roots of the old tree, and after giving the opening lines of a hymn, ascended the notched steps into the pulpit, while the congregation sang

"Farewell ye blooming youth . . ."

This, if not precisely appropriate, was stirring and popular as the new field-preaching hymn that ran to the same tune as the "Ballad of Captain Kidd." It was therefore familiar to all. Almost too familiar in fact, for Bridget could not restrain herself and was heard on the last stanza prefacing the "Amen" with

"Farewell to Lunnon Town
The pretty girls all round;
No pardon can be found . . ."

until Frances put her hand over her little mouth, meanwhile trying to stifle her own giggles. However, this too passed unremarked, while the elders took their accustomed places in various convenient coigns of the roots below the minister, and solemnly awaited the end of the hymn and Mr. Craighead's opening remarks.

Had it not been that an air of wisdom and dignity, even a certain lugubrious solemnity, were the expected and habitual accompaniments of Presbyterian preaching, the droll appearance of Mr. Craighead in a wig, a square white stock, and a pair of large horn-rimmed spectacles peering from his bark pulpit would inevitably have reminded people of an owl discovered in a hollow tree by daylight, more often than it did. As it was, from long familiarity his neighbours took his appearance for granted and saved their comments for what he might have to say; and this in full confidence that it would not be as solemn as he looked.

For it was not Mr. Craighead's habit when preaching to

> "Draw a wrong copy of the Christian face,
> Without the smile, the sweetness, and the grace."

Nor did he, like so many of his contemporaries, preach by rote from manuscript with a flowing hourglass set before him. George Whitefield was his better original. He spoke by inspiration, timed himself by the mood of his listeners, and chose his text at the last minute by skilful intuition.

Quite often, indeed, he would open his big Bible haphazard and preach from the first text that happened to catch his eye and forefinger. And it was this method that he decided to follow that morning. He rolled his eyes upward—to take a glance at the now-threatening clouds—and prayed silently that he might be permitted to preach without interruption from heaven. Then he opened his Bible about the middle and found his text:

> "Thy people shall be willing in the day
> of thy power, in the beauties of holiness
> from the womb of the morning: thou hast
> the dew of thy youth . . .

Psalm One Hundred Ten, the third verse," said he, and paused impressively.

Mr. Craighead spoke with a clerical accent that had been acceptable some twenty years previously in certain Calvinistic circles in Aberdeen, where the Scots think that excellent English is spoken. His *a*'s were flat but his tones were rounded; his general utterance was both strong and clear. Nevertheless, it is not to be denied that on this particular Sabbath he *hemmed* a little, although without *hawing;* and hesitated, as it were, a trifle in his usual forensic stride. For the truth was that, as God would have it, the text he had blundered upon by divine guidance, taken out of its context, had no grammatical meaning at all.

Now this, as any kindly body who will stop to consider a moment can see, was a very serious predicament for Mr. Craighead. For, unless it rained, he was expected to detain, nay, to edify and inspire the minds and souls of his two hundred listeners for two mortal hours at least with an uplifting discourse on a subject without a theme. Not only that, but both his reputation and his living depended upon it.

Quite hastily therefore, indeed with all the speed of thought, he rearranged mentally the resounding phrases of his text, hopeful that the holy obscurity would clear and a human meaning emerge. But nothing of the kind happened. If possible, the result was even more impenetrable. And it was this which had given the good man to pause.

At the same time Mr. Yates looked up from the wagon wheel against which he was leaning, with an alert and fascinated stare. If, a few minutes before, he had answered Captain Jack's question candidly, instead of preventing it by courtesy, Yates would have had to admit that it was for such moments of intellectual crisis as this that he came to listen to sermons. Alone among those present he fully sympathized with and realized the minister's predicament, and it was his keen curiosity to see how Mr. Craighead might extricate himself that now caused him to gaze towards the pulpit with an all but burning intensity.

Nor was Mr. Yates's curiosity only an idle one. Between the practice of his own profession and that of Mr. Craighead he drew many valuable analogies. Both, he thought, harked back in essence to custom and authority and were dependent for happy results upon persuasive oratory and the turning of awkward corners by neat rhetorical tricks. Such was, of course, merely his professional and tactical view of law *versus* theology. For their common grand strategy and difficulties in proposing to restrain the evil in mankind, he had nothing but deepest sympathy. Hence, he was sorry to see that his good friend, the minister, was in difficulties, while at the same time he hoped to profit professionally by observing the method of his way out. That it would take considerable acumen he had small doubt. For the text had undoubtedly been recklessly chosen. It was a perfect *fanfaradol* of mystical saying; in short, a frightful religious stunner.

No wonder Mr. Craighead had paused. The question was, how in the world could he ever go on?

But go on he did.

Like so many other essentially logical-minded people, Mr. Yates had simply underrated the powers of religion and professional habit. Besides himself, there was no one in the congregation who was aware that morning of anything more than a seemly pause and a little throat trouble on the part of Mr. Craighead just before the sermon began— nothing that a glass of water couldn't cure. The pastor looked at his flock owlishly and benignly, while they quite patiently and expectantly stared back. They waited in faith. Only Mr. Yates leaned forward anxiously. And then the minister began.

"Aleph: Thou hast the dew of thy youth," said Mr. Craighead, and continued. How fitting were the words of the Holy Writ this morning and in this place! This was a new country. There was a rising generation in it, young, bright with the dew of a new day, the precious pearls of God's grace. The question was, would they wear them in holiness or carelessly shake them off? They were the sons and daughters of a God-fearing people, who, to escape tyranny over body and soul in the old country, had made of their lives a living sacrifice to the Lord in the New World; and this in order to attain that freedom of the spirit which only Christians can have.

Yes, the older generation had braved the mysterious and stormy Western Ocean, the loneliness of the forest, ravening beasts and the strange face of nature far from home. They had suffered the wild painted savages more cruel and subtle than the children of demons in hell. And theirs had been an acceptable and sufficient sacrifice. God had savoured the smoke of it and found it good. His people had prevailed. The new land and all that was in it was theirs.

Thus it was a Promised Land, the land of brightest promise in all the world under the sun and stars. Only within the past few years, in the memory of even the youngest who now sat before him, the cruel heathen had been vanquished; the idolatrous and naughty French uprooted and banished forever from the land. But that was not all. They were living in the days of the triumph of His people. How complete and mighty was the fulfilment of God's word! In all the world from one climate to another, and on the land and on the sea, the Lord had sent forth His bright angels of victory to light upon the standards of Great Britain and her Protestant kings. This was God's bequeathment, the opportunity of all ages since ancient times, the inheritance of the new generation.

And the greater part of that inheritance, by far the better portion of it, was peculiarly theirs. America! Here in a greater Britain, a nobler Scotland, a happier Ireland, a vaster and wilder Wales lay the vineyard unto which the new labourers were called. America was like the lost garden that all nations had always remembered. But it was not a dream of the past, it was the hope of the future, a garden set apart from the beginning for the re-enfranchisement of man. What would the new generation do with this their inheritance; how should they finally come to possess it?

In this vein Mr. Craighead continued for over half an hour, until he came to the second part of his discourse:

"*Beth: In the beauties of holiness from the womb of the morning*"—Thus was the land to be possessed forever, and only thus; by righteous living that well befitted an undefiled and virginal continent. For such was the new Eden to which the Lord had led them, a place of new beginnings saved apart, a secret garden kept in the sweet morning of God's thought from whence, when all the rest of the world had gone old and stale and lapsed into twilight and darkness, a new day might burgeon and gloriously unfold.

Where in all of remembered time, save for the incarnation of the Son himself, was there ever such a gift, such a proof of God's providence and love for the children of men, as His merciful withholding of the Western world from the carnal knowledge of Europe and the wicked ancients, until in the fullness of appointed time the seed of the gospel was ripe to be planted, and the womb of the morning ready to receive it?

Was not this, then, the prime prize, the great inheritance of the ages for all the Adams and Eves, who by grace had won their way back to it? Woe unto them that abused the gift. For there was a covenant to be kept concerning it. It was plainly implied and explicitly stated in the words of the Psalmist. What was to be born of the union of the New World and the Old, the good which was appointed to issue from this womb of the morning, must be brought forth in the beauties of holiness. Here in this garden, as in Eden of old, by disregarding the covenant with the Lord, those who had been permitted to dwell in it might bring about another fall of man, and be driven forth by angels with relentless swords. By doing evil they might lose their inheritance.

Arrived at this lofty level of flight, Mr. Craighead maintained himself on the wings of eloquence for some time. High in the rare atmosphere of Christian virtue, he towered like a condor and looked down with passing notice on the heaps of evil carrion with which, he said, it was plain to be seen the garden was already defiled and bestrewn.

Gradually he lowered himself to take notice of the more notable spots of evil in the immediate neighbourhood and of the familiar failings of friends. These he dealt with forthrightly, and finally lit with an indignant flutter of wings upon the errors of the new generation. But it would not do to remain too long or permanently at so depressing a level. Launching forth again upon a rising whirlwind of prophecy, the minister rose again for his peroration and the final theme of the text—

"Gimel: Thy people shall be willing in the day of thy power"— God's providence was not to be balked or turned aside even by the most evil doers. To admit this would be to suppose that Satan was more powerful than the Lord. The Lord's promises *must* be fulfilled, as in the past. Eventually His people would prevail. The day of His power would come to pass and be manifested in the mighty nation that should come forth out of the womb of the morning in the garden of the Western world. Then, in that day, Thy people shall be willing; able and willing to do His will amongst themselves and to execute His righteous decrees throughout the earth. Hence, this people must not disinherit itself by doing that which is evil in the sight of the Lord. Rather they must prepare themselves and their children for the great days of power to come, in the beauties of holiness and the light of Christian freedom. And then the words from the Scripture shall come to pass: *"Thy people shall be willing in the day of thy power."*

The last of the patches of sunshine had passed some time ago. Mr. Craighead, in spite of the glowing predictions of his peroration, was ending in gloom. A brief spatter of rain passed down the valley, leaving a few glistening drops on the faces and clothes of the congregation. The minister looked up at heaven and smiled. His congregation, however, awaited his decision whether to go on with the sermon or not, apprehensively. Evidently the patience of the weather at least was about come to an end. But their anxiety was soon relieved.

"This will be the last preaching of the summer," said the minister—"a summer which has been out of all season graciously prolonged. For many years now we have met in the open, sung His praises and offered our prayers directly under the open roof of the sky. That time has come to an end. I have an announcement this morning that deeply concerns us all.

"Colonel Chambers has made an eternal gift to this congregation. It is the natural garden of cedars lying along the banks of the river in the town. A log church is to be erected there speedily. The labours of the coming winter will be consecrated to it. So, we shall meet no more together like the early Christians under the sky. Since time presses," said Mr. Craighead, peering anxiously upward again, "I shall read the terms of the gift only. Then we will omit the usual psalm singing at the end and depart immediately after the benediction."

He picked up a small piece of paper and peered at it. "The land has been left to you," he said, " 'in trust for the Presbyterian congregation of the Falling Spring, now professing and adhering to, and that shall hereafter adhere to and profess, the Westminster profession of faith, and the mode of church government therein contained, and to and for the use of a meeting house or Presbyterian church, session house, school-house, burying-place, graveyard, and such religious purposes.' May the Lord make us all duly thankful, and bring us at last to come to rest there in eternal peace. And now . . ."

The benediction followed.

Everyone left instantly. The wagons were hastily packed with relatives and driven off. In the grove on the hill near-by a hundred farmers' horses were hastily mounted, and with the women clinging on behind, clattered off in every direction into the countryside. It seemed as if the congregation of the Falling Spring were literally being scattered before the oncoming winter storm. Northward, the mountains were already dim with swirling patches of snow. In the valley, at Chambersburg itself, doors and windows were being hastily closed. Chimneys were beginning to smoke. Indian summer was over. The wind shifted eastward, and driving squalls of cold rain began to sweep from time to time across the vacant open square of the town.

"Ain't it curious," observed Captain Jack, while toasting his shins that afternoon before Colonel Chambers's fire after the midday meal, "how whenever thar's an east wind picks up in these parts along the Maryland border, everybody huts-up and has spiritual rheumatiz, even if their jints ain't begun to swell yet? There's somethin' kind o' lanky-danky and plaguey about an east wind. Hark to the rain beating on the windowpanes now, and only yesterday the weather was smilin' like your genial old aunt."

"Looks to me like we're in for a regular nor'easter," agreed the colonel, taking his jug from under the table. "I can spy winter marching down on us in battalions. Well, it's past time for frost now, and you always pay high for a too mild October. You'll have a foul journey to Carlisle, unless she freezes up."

"Reckon she'll do that," said Captain Jack, getting up to look out the window.

Salathiel was finishing loading the wagon in the rain at Somerfield's. He and Arthur were stowing it carefully for the last leg of the journey, in the yard behind the store, where no one would notice that neither the weather nor the Commandments were being carefully observed. Meanwhile, Frances, Bridget, and Captain Jack were snugly ensconced at the Chambers'. Mrs. McKinney had been prevailed upon to leave Roy Davison, who had a sore throat and a fever, with the Chambers for a day or two.

At the store, Salathiel found he had considerable on his hands in the way of minor arrangements for departure before dawn next morning. Yates had picked up the lame horse he had left at Fort Loudon some months before. It was in fine fettle again. But Enna would now have to be taken care of, and there was Captain Jack's sturdy brown gelding, which the old man would not be able to ride back to Carlisle, if it continued to storm. Despite his protests, it was only common sense he should ride in the wagon, rather than expose himself to driving sleet.

Finally, a solution offered by St. Clair was found to be the best way out. Captain Jack's mount and Enna were to be driven as a third team for the wagon, and Jed was to ride postilion on Enna as far as Carlisle. Adequate harness and a drag pole for the new arrangement were put together that afternoon.

"Wisht I was goin' along," said Arthur several times. He looked wistful.

"Wait till the summer," said Salathiel. "I won't know where I'm goin' to be till then, or how long we'll be tarryin' at Carlisle. You'll be much better off here at Somerfield's."

"I suppose so," replied the lad doubtfully.

Suddenly Salathiel burst out, "Arthur, I jist can't take care of ye now. Thar's no use talkin' about it. And you've got another year to serve with Somerfield, who's your good friend. Also, ye have no idea what it means to have so many mouths to feed. I'd be skeered to take on any more now. What with Jed wantin' me to buy him from Mr. St. Clair, you wantin' to come along, and your young cousin Roy beggin' me to buy his time out from Mrs. McKinney—why, thar's no end to it! And between you and me, maybe Captain Jack will take a little lookin' after, too."

"Roy!" said Arthur. "That young'un! Why, he's uncle Ed's brat."

"But a fine youngster, and our Bridget is much taken with him."

"Thought ye was jes' takin' her to her granny," mumbled Arthur.

"So I am," snapped Salathiel, "but I ain't found her grandma yet, all I know about her is in a letter. And if I do find her, maybe she'll be sittin' at the hearth, too. You can't tell.

"But, there now," he continued, seeing the boy was much chagrined by his irritated tone, "I didn't mean to take my troubles out on you. It's jes' that I've been gittin' a little worried lately about how the family does recruit itself. Tell ye what ye do. You patch up that old family fight with your young cousin. Have him down to the store now and then. Teach him to read and cipher a bit. Try to help him. And when I do git settled in the City, you kin both ride down. Never mind what your pa once said to your uncle Ed. You youngsters ought to stick together like cousins agin the world. *All* the Davisons be fine people! Don't forgit I'm mighty partial to 'em."

They finished the work in silence, but Salathiel could see that Arthur was turning it over in his mind.

Before dark all was in readiness. Only a trip to the smoke-house remained to complete the last item. But the longer it stayed there in the smoke and drying heat, the better.

He and Arthur went over to the colonel's and everybody was there for supper that night. Ruhannah was delighted to find that Arthur was so solicitous about his young cousin and insisted on helping out with him. As for Roy, he was noncommittal, surprised, and secretly pleased. Never mind what my pa said to Uncle Will, he thought.

"Sometime soon I'll ride downcountry and see ye, Bridget," the boy said as they prepared to leave the cabin that night. "Ye'd better git some clothes for Alliquippa, ifen she's goin' to go ridin' in that canoe," he called after her down the hall.

"Yes," said Bridget, and fled.

She and Frances and Captain Jack came over to sleep at the store that night to be on hand for the early start next morning. Yates and St. Clair would ride later, but promised to catch up with the wagon before Shippensburg. The good-byes were brief but heartfelt. " 'Pears like you've been here a month or more," said Colonel Chambers. "We'll be seein' you all again, I'm sure. Here's some muster rolls I want ye to take down to Colonel Burd at Lancaster," he said to Salathiel. "And I've writ him a line or two about ye, won't do ye no harm."

When they left the hospitable cabin that evening it was already starting to snow. There were eight degrees of frost on Colonel Chambers's London thermometer and it was getting colder. Salathiel went down to the mill sheds, put blankets on all the horses, and retrieved the hand.

That night the wind blew with an ever-rising crescendo. In the morning, it was shrieking through the bare branches of Somerfield's maples with the authentic howl of winter, and no doubt about it. Captain Jack was quite content, although he did not say so, to let them hitch his gelding in the lead team with Enna and ride himself in the wagon with Frances and Bridget.

Mr. Somerfield and Arthur saw them off by the light of two lanthorns. The six horses, with Jed hunching forward into the storm on Enna, jingled and jangled through the darkness along the icy road to Carlisle.

18

How They Passed God's People By

THE RUMBLE of turning wheels, the steely clatter of twenty-four hoofs on the hard-frozen road, billowing clouds rolling westward—that morning the whole countryside seemed on the move as they pressed on eastward in the direction of Carlisle. Weather gave the overpowering impression. The entire landscape appeared to be torn loose and flowing.

Stripped trees waved their bare arms in the blast. Long lines of brown, curling leaves scuttled and swung sinuously before the storm, rising here and there into swirling fountains to be instantly snatched upward and away. The day brightened slowly into universal silver gloom.

Along the road from time to time, moving with an all but military front and precision, battalions of sleet and snow advanced swiftly down upon the wagon—and struck. The icy needles of sleet pattered and slithered along the canvas, while dry flakes swirled. The horses neighed and snorted under the recurrent punishment; shook themselves until their new slip bells clanged and sang. Then the flurry would go by and the road open up before them again.

It was a grand nor'easter that was marching down.

At least that was what Captain Jack called it as he sat comparatively warm and snug within the wagon talking, and smiling reassuringly at Frances and Bridget with her grey kitten purring in her lap. The sudden patter of ice and half-hail would drum on the tight canvas overhead—and pass.

Outside the two drivers, one on the wagon seat and the other on Enna, leaned forward into the storm and raised their heads again only when the assault ceased.

Jed, with a battered three-cornered hat tied ludicrously over his fuzz by an old knitted scarf, which covered his ears and flapped behind him with ravelling ends loose in the breeze, sat hunched uncomfortably on Enna, a tattered blanket bound with twine swathed heavily about him. Still he was cold. Riding postilion for Marse Albine was not the fun he had anticipated.

Snowflakes caught and lay melting on his upper eyelids. He looked forward despondently into the advancing storm, squeezing his eyes tight shut as the grim blasts swept down. The mare's hard military saddle galled him. Between flurries he rode stolidly, half frozen, dreaming of the sun-stricken market square at Dahomey and its rustling palm trees.

He gazed at the strange landscape ahead of him despairingly. Pennsylvania was beginning to moan and turn white under the lash of winter. What had become of his hot African town, of the camels lying in the shade of mud-plastered walls, of the empty palmnut-oil jars under the cool arcades, where little girls used to hide with small boys, smooth, naked, smelling of rancid butter? Lawsy! Under the wooden porch floors in Philadelphia it was hard scrabbling and dangerous going after curfew. Oh, Jedu-gawd, if only that fierce bearded Arab slaver hadn't bought him from the chief—a twist of copper wire and a stinking old goat cheese for a thin little black boy. That was all *he* was worth. His sleek mammy had fetched a good deal more, he supposed. She might still be in Barbados. He hoped so. It was warmer there. Poor mammy! Her new baby must have died. A half-frozen tear slid down his cheek—and then, the great bull whip was snapping about his head, cracking like pistol shots.

He grabbed Enna by the mane and looked back fearfully.

The big man on the wagon seat was laughing at him. Maybe *he* would buy him? He was a good *baas* to work for. Marse St. Clair was kindly, but there was seldom enough to eat.

Smack.

It was the lazy horse with the yellow eyes that got it that time.

They were moving fast now. No Dutch wagoner would ever drive like Marse Albine. He didn't seem to care if he killed a horse or two —or a man! He was one reckless buckra. Jed started posting painfully to ease himself as the teams tore forward down a long smooth declivity. Maybe the Albines would let him stay with them for a while at Carlisle, provided he could hold on long enough to get there. Gradually he managed to feel more cheerful, as the weather grew drier and speeding gleams of sunlight showed now and then hastening across the countryside. The snow flurries began to pass like clouds of light feathers as it got colder.

But Jed's difficulties were not so apparent from the driver's seat; on the contrary—

Salathiel was rattling along in high fettle and the best of good nature. He was more than content to be on the way east again so close to the end of his journey. Carlisle wasn't Philadelphia, but it was *almost* there. No matter how St. Clair's scheme for settling Ligonier worked out, it would mean only a temporary wait for him and Melissa at Carlisle. He wasn't going to be balked of getting to the City now. At Carlisle he could lay plans for getting a toe-hold in Philadelphia. He might see Colonel Burd at Lancaster; deliver that letter personally. Why, he could even talk to Buckey himself when he came through. The colonel—no, the brigadier!—would certainly remember him as "Ecuyer's man". Buckey had been so amiable to everybody at Fort Pitt. Now, why hadn't he thought of *that* before?

Well, he would see; wait for a while at Carlisle—pick up something in the meanwhile. He was well fixed to do that, if he could just get shelter somewhere. He'd have to return the horses to Stottelmyer. But maybe that stout wagoner would not be back from Pittsburgh yet; maybe he could still keep the loan of the two faithful teams for a while.

A hundred such alternatives and dim plans and hopes kept running through his mind. The main thing, of course, was that with Frances being with child, he'd just have to get her sheltered. They must settle-in before summer, but how? Where?

And yet he wasn't too worried about the immediate future. He had done well thus far; laid in valuable stock and made friends at Chambersburg. And Frances Melissa was certainly one smart girl; a clever helpmeet, if a man ever had one. Oh, they were going to get ahead. They were going to do well together.

Most of his serious troubles lay behind him, he felt. By comparison the future seemed positively simple. He was escaping into it, he thought. He couldn't help but feel fine about it. The future seemed so full of hope, of free movement, and of happy adventure. A little luck, a little *more* luck now, and . . . The whip cracked merrily.

It was something to have six horses and Jed outriding. How it did make the old wagon clatter along. They'd be in Carlisle that very night. He wouldn't tarry for more than time-out for the noon meal at Shippensburg.

In fact, as the day grew brighter and the wind keener, he felt more and more sanguine. He was warm in an old officer's greatcoat with many capes. His beaver hat was tied down with a muffler over his ears. No one would recognize him now. Twin-Eyes for the first time was not beside him. She rode well greased in the sling on the ridge-pole in the wagon behind. Bridget was laughing and giggling in there again. But who would have thought that he should live to hear Captain Jack sing! Melissa certainly did have a way with her!

Yes, they were all going to be happy together for a while. It was a peculiar notion, he thought, but he saw the past lying behind him like a deep still pool in which only his own memories were clearly reflected. Out of it, like a swiftly rushing river, led the road. It was full of new sights and sounds, full of hope and movement. It flowed on smoothly into the time ahead.

Five miles out of Chambersburg they passed the two empty Conestoga freighters going back to Lancaster from Somerfield's. He fairly flashed by them, bells ringing, his three teams at a rumbling gallop. But getting on! The sleepy drivers, who had left Chambersburg in the darkness hours before, scarcely had time to raise their whips in salutation and give a surprised yell before the big wagon went by, and they were looking at the little trundler flouncing and jouncing behind. Only when it seemed likely that Jed might be bounced clear off Enna's back did he finally pull up again and walk the teams for a spell.

A thick squall of snow came down the road, covered them, lifted—and they saw the long emigrant train on a crest afar off. Men, wagons, cattle, and horses in dark groups of toylike moving figures were crawling westward, pursued, it seemed, by the weather; appearing and reappearing through other snow-flurries ahead.

He determined to push on straight through. He would not stop to hold a powwow with any of them. He would *make* them give way if necessary!

That was what he thought, until he saw they were strung out over a long mile of road, and still coming.

He topped a gentle rise at a trot. In the swale below, in a bowl of meadows, lay a settlement, a few blind cabins stretching along the way. Two miles farther the advance guard of the emigrants, a small party of horsemen, were just beginning to come down the opposite slope. He pulled up for a moment to consider. The settlement lay between him and them.

It would be just as well not to meet these people coming through the village. They would be most likely to pause there and want to talk. Then, either he or Captain Jack would be recognized, and they might try to strike a bargain about leading them westward, and all that. It might take hours, and he was in a hurry. He turned to warn them in the wagon.

"We're goin' to pass the Maryland Old Lights now," he announced. "There's a mighty congregation of them strung out along the road ahead. I don't aim to confabulate. I'm goin' by fast."

"Jist as well," replied Captain Jack dryly. "Reverend Alexander Alexander, their leader, is a powerful detainer and persuader."

"Alexander Alexander, the *riverend!*" exclaimed Frances Melissa. "Him!"

She peeped out across the seat at the column of riders, carts, and pack horses now pouring down the crest ahead. "I told you so! A big man with a beard, mounted on a piebald stallion. A long gun and the English Book in a black bag at his saddle-bow. He'll be ridin' like black Fate to an unholy weddin'. Didn't I tell ye we'd meet up with him and his murderin' Sassenachs?"

She seemed greatly excited for some reason. "I told ye so," she kept saying. "I told ye so."

He thought little of it. Everybody had been talking about the emigrant congregations.

"I told ye so . . ."

"So ye did, so ye did," he finally had to acknowledge. "I didn't think they'd be on the move so soon, and winter comin' on. Well, here they be, and we goin' t'other way!"

He held her hand and talked cheeringly. He knew that for some deep reason she hated and feared these emigrant Presbyterians. "Now sit ye down and hold fast. Don't worry. I'm goin' right through. Just keep your head in. I want no wayside gossip."

She withdrew into the wagon willingly.

"Jed!" he shouted, "hold on! Don't let them stop ye. Lead around if ye have to. Go 'round!" He motioned what he meant vigorously.

Jed looked sick and hugged Enna desperately with his knees. He understood. But he wasn't sure that Salathiel could see what he saw. Just ahead the slope fell away suddenly and awfully into a hidden creek bottom. Oh, Lawdy, Lawdy!—they were off.

The ears of the lead horses disappeared down a steep banklike declivity. The wagon followed with a sickening swoop. The rounds of its rear wheels fitted snugly like coins rolling in a hoop into the curving fall of the road. They ground and crunched on the pebbly stuff of the stream-bank, while the trundler striking a boulder leaped into the air, its wheels spinning. Bridget left her little stomach hanging in air. Frances Melissa clutched her sides. Down, down, down . . .

Jed wailed . . .

Down . . .

The teams were going like mad. They were running away from the wagon now, terrified. It threatened to overtake them. They laid their ears back and galloped, streaming ahead. It was the breathless moment of the journey. Everyone from Jed to the grey kitten felt the sudden free swoop of the heavy wagon and the clutch of panic made palpable by gravity.

They crashed through thin new ice in the shallow ford at the bottom of the hidden glen, a wicked rut that nearly wrecked them. And then luckily—luckily for them—since the teams were now making a frantic bolt for it, the road swung away gently, almost level, and straight before them. It led across flat meadows and on through the settlement.

Down the gentle slope on the far side of the village, the emigrants were beginning to pour in a steady trickle of men and vehicles. They flowed down the road as though a dam had suddenly broken somewhere behind them and its long pent-up flood was now released.

For some distance Salathiel lost control of his beasts entirely. He was angry with himself. It was his own fault, he felt sure. He had let himself go wool-gathering in a fine daydream of the future while the present had slipped his hand. Minding God's business was a dangerous thing. Now the only thing he could do was to let the horses have their silly heads and gallop it out. Sooner or later the cumbersome weight of the ark behind them must begin to tell, and it was uphill not far ahead.

Nevertheless, it was a mad quarter of a mile to the village; more like the wild finish of a chariot race than the decent progress of a respectable wagon with a domestic load. The iron rims sang, the hoofbeats gathered themselves into a regular frantic rhythm. Flecks of foam worked loose from the ends of the horses' bits and spattered back against his coat.

They drove down on the village like a small cloud on the forefront of a gale. They fairly thundered through. Astonishment seemed to close in behind them.

Half the houses were still empty. Only a few belated people ran out of doors to see. Even the dogs were too late. All but one hound. Driven into a frenzy by the thundering of wheels, it gathered itself, even as it coursed them, for a jump at the lead horses' heads. The whip caught it in air as it sprang. It rolled over and over, yelling. The wheels rumbled on. Captain Jack permitted himself a generous cut of shag to comfort his vacant gums. Jed opened his eyes and began to ride upright again. He was still in Pennsylvania!

They struck the beginning of the rise beyond the village. The whip cracked. Marse Albine was driving again. "Golly, golly!" muttered Jed. He was going to take it out on the teams now and gallop them uphill too! The reins tightened and slapped viciously. Jed and the horses settled down to business. Salathiel swore.

Frances Melissa had just said something pretty hot to him under the canvas. A fierce word or two about murdering them all. That, under the circumstances, *was* annoying. As if it hadn't been exasperating enough that he'd let the horses run clean away. That damned *haw-haw* in the road had certainly jarred his equanimity badly. But that wasn't all. He felt an increasing sense of tension, the presentiment of a crisis to be met just ahead in passing the emigrants. It was quite unreasonable and mysterious. He even told himself he was being superstitious. None the less, his feeling of guilt kept growing. It was this:

He could not shake off an unreasonable impression that somehow or other he was going the wrong way.

Swift as the pace had been for the last quarter of a mile or so, and absorbing as the business of restraining the horses was, he had none the less been thinking. And he felt the doubt of the direction in which he was going overtaking him as though it were something physical catching up with him from behind. Perhaps it was because the hidden dip in the road had suddenly and so violently disconcerted his dreamful anticipations; or perhaps it was Melissa's wild talk and his knowledge of her terror of these Scotch-Irish that he now shared?

When you lived with a woman you came to sympathize even with her mysterious hatreds, to share her antipathies against your own will. You couldn't help it, if you loved her. And yet, and yet—*that* wasn't it.

No, it was all *so* surprising, so unexpected, as he whirled along over the next furlong of road. All his life, ever since he had talked with McArdle as a boy, he had been scheming and struggling; hungry to get back to the settlements, to find himself and what belonged to him in the Dawn Country. And now?

Now, by God, he felt an all but overpowering impulse to turn around and drive back to the mountains again. . . .

That wonderful summer, hunting homeward through the secret green-gladed forest back to Bedford; that paradise of careless ease and plenty beyond the Conemaugh, lonely freedom—would it ever be like that again?

Something caught in his throat. He cursed. . . .

Why, he must be going crazy, thinking of turning back to live like an Injun again! Hell's jangling bells! Who would have supposed he was not sure enough of himself to talk to a passel of Macs bound westward? He'd show them, he would! He'd . . .

He'd drive right on through!

That was why the whip cracked again. That was why he seemed to be swearing at the horses instead of at himself, and why Jed felt a blast of hot fury pass close by over the back of his neck as the reins slapped angrily.

Marse Albine was sure damn mad at somebody. Jed hoped he wasn't mad at him. He leaned forward to take the coming rise at a gallop and guide Enna through the oncoming horsemen just ahead. Evidently Marse Albine wasn't even going to slow up. But those people ahead looked pretty grim and he hoped *they* would draw aside. He remembered he was only . . . only worth an old goat cheese.

At that moment a blast of driving snow topped the rise ahead and swept down the road towards the wagon. Jed could just see through it, and that there were other flurries following behind, trailing long curtains of frozen misty weather. Patches of yellow sunshine like small round eyes began to move down the line of the emigrant procession as if someone in the clouds above were examining this people curiously. For an instant the long caravan was spotted like a writhing snake. Then the advancing flurry passed them and closed down over the wagon.

Salathiel drove recklessly straight through it.

When Jed opened his eyes again the lead team was galloping down on a party of horsemen, some in the road and some scattered out in a vague line advancing through the fields on either side, carrying rifles. They were the van of the caravan, young men, the chosen of both congregations, well dressed and determined looking.

Gentlemen, gentlemen, gentlemen, pounded the hoofs of the six horses.

Salathiel grinned, crouching low, and hurling the whip only once. It cracked like a breaking beam and the wagon and its hard-breathing horses burst out of the flurry ahead of the riders like an apparition, rumbling and coming uphill at them furiously.

The young men in the road hesitated for a moment, and then rode aside hastily. They had never seen anything quite like this heavy travelling-machine. One of the king's wagons probably, something royal and massive—yet swift. They shouted a warning after it as it plunged on up the slope. There was a child mildly looking out behind. Another billowing curtain of cloud came sliding down the hill.

It passed . . .

Just ahead now Salathiel could see a company of sturdy horsemen, six or eight of them. From their mounts and their clothes, there could be no doubt but that here were the leaders of the congregations. Good horses, long blue cloaks, Bible bags, and a couple of ministers among them with wide felt hats.

The elders and clergy of the following host rode as the leaders of God's people should ride as they passed westward towards the Promised Land: sedately, grimly, determinedly. They shook the snow-flakes from their capes gravely. In the unearthly racing winter weather of alternating and mysterious gleams and glooms, fingers of sunlight burst through from overhead and played wantonly with the rolling cloud of mist and whirling snow-flakes passing down the road just before them. Here and there a swirling column seemed to dizen into dim white flames and silver smoke, on fire inside. The leader of the host pointed proudly at the phenomenon, and smiled. There was no one in the group behind him who was not solemnly aware of the apt Biblical reference in his gesture.

Out of the pillar of cloud the wagon burst suddenly upon them. It was going like hell.

The Reverend Alexander Alexander held up his gauntleted hand. This strange, rocketing vehicle must stop. It was coming out of the west and he would have speech with its driver about the state of the roads ahead.

He now held his hand up higher, spreading his leather-clothed fingers out like a yellow star on the end of his arm. Neither he nor his elders ceased to advance along the highway or meant to pull aside. He had held up his hand. Like Moses, he was used to being obeyed. In the amalgamated double congregations marching behind him were three hundred and thirty-odd souls. Auld Lichts, sons and daughters of Calvin and the Scotch Covenant. Let all the heathen beware. In the dour personage of the Reverend James McTain, an Aaron rode just behind him. A faithful man, a tried servant of the Lord God of Sabaoth. The Reverend Alexander Alexander stretched forth his hand.

"Go 'round, Jed," roared Salathiel, and gestured, standing up to handle the whip and reins. The Reverend Mr. Alexander and the Reverend James McTain both thought he was going to pull up. The hand sank back to its pommel.

Frances Melissa could not resist peeping out under the canvas. What was it they were going to drive around?

There he was!

She saw him now directly ahead. Just as she had seen him before. The terrible man! His beard flowed down over his breast, spotted with snow-flakes. Under his wide-brimmed hat, which flapped back flat against his forehead, his eyes blazed a cold and horrid blue. He was tall, straight, dour. A grim Jove of a man on horseback. No smile could bend the iron level of those lips. And there was his piebald pacer, too. Its knee action seemed to devour the road; to push the very landscape aside. Oh God, thus and thus had Cromwell rid. Mother of God, have marcy upon us!

She began to mutter and to pray. She saw a look of swift surprise turn into a blaze of red anger on the minister's face. She was that near. But the wagon was *not* going to stop.

She sank back against the side boards, one hand at her pounding heart, white-faced.

"Jedu," muttered Jed into Enna's ear. "Jedu come an' ride wid me on this hyah hawse."

Jed no longer remembered the secret African name of his native duppy. A kind Quaker in Philadelphia had taught him to read a little and to say his prayers. There was the Great Snake, of course; but far away, long ago. Not in these cold woods. Jedu would help. "We's gwine 'round," Jed informed his new white Saviour. "Jedu, we's gwine 'round."

And with that he pulled Enna's head violently to the right and guided the column of galloping horses and the wagon after them off the road and out into the open meadows at the side. It was a shallow ditch—thank God! They described a wide half-circle about the horsemen in blue mantles, and then, with only a minor jar, were back on the road again still going, still going like hell uphill. Someone in the wagon had screamed. Marse Albine was laughing.

The Reverend Alexander and all his elders stopped. They had watched the wide avoiding sweep of the wagon as it hurtled past them, with astonishment. They were not used to being treated so cavalierly. The chief minister was indignant. He turned around to get a good look at the affair. Who was it that had been standing up, driving like Jehu? Up the road the caisson seemed to wag its tail at him, and he saw there, still visible on the box, the fading black arrow of the king.

That might explain it, then.

But he gave an indignant snort as he turned westward again and sternly resumed his way towards the wilderness. For as long as he could remember, he and his fathers had been at either physical or spiritual odds with the royal authority. James or George, it was all the same; Penn or Calvert. In the Promised Land, somewhere in the rolling mists ahead, he and his people should soon be free of all earthly authority whatsoever. They would go beyond such malignancies and live according to Holy Scripture. "You may be king, Alec, you will be king," whispered an unseen voice. "Get thee behind me," muttered the minister, and began to pray that he should not be led into temptation. The devil might follow, but it was a long, long way. And he would wrestle with him; wrestle in prayer, even as Jacob, on the headwaters of the Cherokee River.

Captain Jack had observed the passing events of the last few moments from the back of the wagon with considerable satisfaction. As he saw it, these people were *fleeing* westward. Their rifles were badly needed in Pennsylvania. They were piously deserting their country. As the wagon swung back on the road violently, he comforted Bridget, who had given a startled scream. Frances, he saw, was sitting in the forward corner, the colour of new wool and looking drawn.

"Now, *now*," said Captain Jack, "there's nothin' about the Reverend Alexander and his moss troopers to be so skeered of. Besides, they're takin' themselves clean out of this province. They've bin called by the voice of God into the nether parts of Virginny, or so Mr. Alexander avers. Maybe it was another noise, maybe it was jist the voice of the governor of Virginny they heard. I see by his last proclamation the governor's kind o' assumin' the Almighty. *'We, the Governor'*—wonder what it is makes a man feel so durned plural as all that? Might be tapeworms," ruminated Captain Jack. "I cawn't say, but mawt be." He rose and ejected a long fan of yellow tobacco juice out of the rear of the wagon in the direction of the fading horsemen.

When he turned again Frances was smiling. His old eyes slyly twinkled at her. He and she enjoyed a little turn of wit together. She was a good gal, he thought, a mighty fine piece out of old Ireland. But it wouldn't do for him to linger too long with these young folks. They made him remember what he had to forget—or die of the memory.

"Thar's nothin' but wagons and cattle ahead," he remarked casually, poking his head out, "but we'll git to Shippensburg shortly. And—I think I'll be quittin' ye there. I've bin thinkin' it over," said he.

Frances began to try to persuade him not to leave them, not realizing that it was she and the child that had started him dreaming again of old days. Memory had brought a sudden longing on him to be alone in his cabin by his own hearth, where there was no one at home but himself and the fire.

He would not answer her protests, but kept talking about the wagons they still had to pass. "They're comin' on," he said, "and we ain't goin' so fast now." He was right about that, and she came to look out behind. Dragging the big wagon uphill had finally taken the tucker out of the horses, and they had been glad to fall back into a trot at the first restraining pull on the reins. In fact, they would have walked if Salathiel had let them.

The rest of the caravan proved to be about a half mile behind the leaders. The reason for this was soon apparent; a great many of the wagons and carts were being pulled along by oxen.

However, the first group of vehicles they passed must have belonged to the more prosperous among the Marylanders. It consisted of a string of fine Conestogas, evidently newly purchased for the remove westward, and still gay with fresh paint, new leather buckets, and white canvas. These wagons were all drawn by horses. But the nags were of all kinds and descriptions; farm and draught animals of somewhat plaintive dispositions, to judge by their pace. Here and there, mounted on more mettlesome and respectable chargers, the fathers of families rode beside their wagons, many of which were being driven along by women or young boys.

Yet the string of ten new Pennsylvania wagons indubitably did present a prosperous and impressive appearance. They might at a little distance have been taken for a regular convoy of freighters had it not been for the piles of furniture—chairs, beds, chests, and spinning wheels loaded behind at all angles and in an unconvincing way —or for the crates of drooping half-frozen fowls, lean dogs running underneath, and an occasional favourite milch cow or promising young colt hitched behind and towed along, always, it seemed, with a taut rope kept at an obstinate angle.

Once the sound of a jew's-harp and childish voices singing softly penetrated through the canvas to Frances and Bridget as they pulled past. Children and drawn-faced women, their heads in shawls, peered out through chair rungs, swinging lanthorns, and domestic sundries from the oval canvas opening over the tailboards. They waved to Bridget and Captain Jack, or called some message after them; something which could not be heard over the grinding of wheels and the shrill squealing of axles.

Squeals, indeed, were the last thing they heard from the Conestogas, and such eminent and heart-rending squeals.

The final wagon towed behind it, on a pair of old cart wheels, nothing less than a heavily barred pigpen bolted to a wooden floor. Confined in this dripping coop, a dilapidated sow and her numerous young family lamented in a lively chorus of squeals and contrapuntal grunts their involuntary transit to the western wilds.

Punctuated by the violent bumps of their mysteriously moving penitentiary, the pigs' Miserere at times achieved a shrill fife-like harmony of terror that blent with the piping of the winter wind whistling through the upper branches of pine trees. Then it would die down into a wheezing undertone of tired umbilical melancholy, but never while on the move did it entirely cease.

As the two wagons passed each other, three red-headed little girls looked out of the oval canvas-frame of their house-on-wheels, waving violently to Bridget. They jumped up and down, joining her in a gale of high silver laughter in mutual appreciation of how humanly funny is the audible sorrow of pigs. Captain Jack also was drawn into this humorous understanding and came to the rear of the wagon to look out. Just as they passed, the tragedy of pigdom found its perfect voice.

Moved perhaps by the sight of the east-bound wagon returning towards her old Maryland home, the huge tit-draped black and white sow thrust her conical clownlike countenance halfway between the stakes of her prison, and while her pink muzzle smoked in the frosty air, she achieved for a lyrical interval complete prima donna status as the Calliope of Hogdom. Nor was her expression of sorrow rendered any the less poignant by the fact that, at the moment of her supreme tragedy, her family fell upon her from behind to seek nourishment. The noise of her maternal indignation carried far. If there were any bears hibernating in hollow trees in the neighbourhood, they must have turned over in their dreams, while their mouths watered.

At any rate, Captain Jack had not laughed so heartily for twenty years. "I do aver," said he, wiping the beads of humour from his eyes, "the old gal has more sense than most of the leaders in yon fawncy caravan. She's the most eloquent prophetess of the hul company. It's predestination she's complainin' about, and she's a firm believer. She knows she's got her feet on the downward path and is headed the wrong way."

"What's that?" inquired Salathiel, sticking his head back into the wagon—"what's that about their bein' headed the wrong way?" Frances and Captain Jack laughed at his serious and anxious expression.

"Nothin'," said Captain Jack, "practically nothin'. I was jist commentin' on the wisdom of mixin' a little hog sense with religion." He grinned. "Jist keep on drivin', Sal. You're doin' all right. Jist stick to your last."

From this, since he had not been in on the beginning of the conversation, Albine derived considerable unexpected comfort. Maybe he *was* going the right way after all. The emigrants were certainly headed for a forest of troubles, and he noticed that not many, even of the outriders, were carrying rifle-guns. What kind of people did they think they were going to meet? Quakers?

The shrill lament of the emigrant pigs died away sadly into the distance. A thick gust of winter concealed the white tops of the Conestogas in a pall of snow. Bridget stopped waving. Salathiel drove on. Half a mile ahead he struck the main body of the people of Israel advancing towards the Promised Land.

Nevertheless, they were still in wagons, wheeled vehicles of all kinds. But these moved at a foot pace. Most of them were pulled by oxen, the first in yoke-span Salathiel had ever seen. There were some old army wagons evidently recently purchased from the military authorities at Carlisle, for the king's mark was still on them. Beside them, armed with tall goads and switches of stout hickory saplings, the fathers of families plodded along patiently in cowhide boots, their frosty breaths and those of the oxen intermingling. There were innumerable old farm vehicles too; frail, heavy, four-wheeled, and otherwise, laden like Noah's arks, piled up and obviously overwhelmed with everything that would ride and not disintegrate.

For the most part these sorry carts were covered with old sails or linen mangoes held in place by an agony of amateur knots and tackle, with crazy quilts as often as not stuffed into cracks and rents.

Here, in dismal corners and hollow places amid their sorry chattels, women and children, old people and babies faced westward, freezing but patient; comforted by what small helps their ingenuity could conjure, from cradles to liniments; sustained by their hope of Beulah land and their firm faith and prejudices; cheered along by prayers, songs, hymns, a fife or a solemn flute. But above all, they relied on everlasting gossip and the constant din of their own progress. That indeed was considerable, both human and otherwise.

Yet there was a certain soothing and eternal tone about it, too. Ducks quacked, geese honked, and children chattered; cows bawled and the oxen from time to time lowed softly. A few cherished pigeons in small cages occasionally cooed. Only the wheels and the surging and creaking furniture, only the grating of iron implements and the chains of the harness jangled or complained. All that was living, except the doomed pigs, passed westward with a kind of invincible and visible assurance that hope lay in the direction in which they were bound. It was as if the sun itself, hidden by clouds though it was that morning, was drawing them after it by some magnetic influence rained down from the sky. It was this impression, in fact, that had made Salathiel so uncomfortable. He seemed to be pulling against it. He felt the tension as he passed.

What, thought he, suddenly moved to a bit of classic reminiscence —"What! will the line stretch out to the crack of doom?" It seemed so. Out of the weather still darkling behind them, an interminable line of vehicles continued to come.

It was not often, he reflected, that he would meet a whole colony on the road. He wove carefully in and out among them now, passing them on either side of the road, how and where and as best he could. Or at a walk perforce, or with his tired teams steaming, he waited for them at times to pull aside, which they did contentedly, meanwhile exchanging many a cheerful greeting and kindly salutation with him as they passed.

They were a kindly folk, hearty, but too decent ever to betray their curiosity. There was never a loud laugh or a curse. "Howdy" and "The Lord be with you" rang in his ears. Frances was calling and nodding now to the eager women from behind. She had taken off her bonnet. So it was not at it that they smiled, but at a sister's fair face, and with womanly sympathy.

Now, at last, they were down to the two-wheeled carts, and the strange and ramshackle contraptions on wheels of all kinds that brought up the rear.

Ancient scarecrow steeds and sway-backed dobbins imparted what motive impulse they still had to spare to that which followed them behind. Bony hips and knotted and twisted tails stalked slowly forward. There was even a dilapidated post-chaise, some social derelict of time, drawn by a team of an old mare roped in with a cow. A young boy drove this proudly, his sister, her face swollen with toothache, sitting beside him. "Now, sis," he kept saying, "now, sis, we'll soon git to Colonel Chambers'." Behind him were several families whose draught cattle had perished or who were too poor to own any. There were some who dragged a light cart after them by hand, desperately but as confidently as they could. Only *they* had nothing to say as the wagon passed, and were too tired or preoccupied to gaze after it.

This must be the end, thought Salathiel. This is all that anybody can do with wheels. And in that he was right. But he was not quite to the end yet.

A quarter of a mile farther on he passed the bell.

It was not a big bell, but it was bronze and it was heavy. It was slung from a log tripod on a stone boat dragged by two white oxen. The clapper was roped and muffled. Still, at certain angles, it had a slight play. Now and then when the sledge struck a rock or a deep hole in the road, the clapper swung and the bell hummed, whether reminiscently or expectantly it would be hard to tell. Its strange melodic murmurs reverberated and died away through the astonished woodlands. Two of the minister's young sons drove the oxen, and a younger brother, an urchin with a bow and arrow in his hands, rode upon the sledge with the bell.

Out of sheer curiosity Salathiel pulled up the teams to see so strange an object going past. "Londinium MDCCXI" ran the inscription around the rim of the bell. There was something cast on the other side that he could not see.

"It's from our old chapel at Munster, sir," replied the tallest boy in response to Salathiel's inquiry. "We're takin' it along with us to hang in father's new church at the south."

"It calls the people to say their prayers," piped up the urchin on the sledge, and made a steeple with his hands to illustrate. His fingers looked blue with cold.

"Here's a pair of old mittens for ye, son," said Salathiel, much moved by the child's earnest little face. "Liken they might fit." He reached under the seat-box and pulled out a pair of old coonskin driver's gloves and tossed them to the little boy. They "fitted" half-way up his arms.

"Judas priest!" shrilled the child.

"Bind your blasphemous tongue, Donald, and thank your bene-factor," growled his brother.

"Thankee, sir, oh, thankee kindly," cried the little boy, wiggling his new paws violently. Even the older brother laughed. Salathiel waved his whip and drove on. "Mind the cattle," screamed the youngster. "There's bad bulls among 'em." Another wave of the lash and its sharp report over the backs of the horses replied. Weaving through the caravan had consumed considerable time.

Bridget crawled out on the seat beside him now and put a small arm over his shoulder consolingly. "I'm comin' to sit beside ye," she said encouragingly. "Did ye hear what that little boy said? Well, ye don't need to heed him. There's always more cows in a herd than bulls. And I've not got my red hood on, anyway. It's the brown rabbit one."

"Liken we can git along, then," said Salathiel gravely.

Nevertheless, they came across the herd unexpectedly.

It was in the middle of a patch of half-open woodland, when suddenly there was a dismal bellowing and the sound of cow horns being blown ahead and on all sides, with a constant barking of dogs. Stray cattle began to pass them, running ahead of the drove through the trees. Here and there an outrider could be glimpsed heading them in, with a dog dashing back and forth frantically. A heavy fall of sleet suddenly dimmed the scene before them, coursing in long white lines past the black boles of the trees. The wind moaned and seemed to answer the braying of horns.

In the midst of this, and in a cloud of flying snow, they met the main herd, which appeared to be stampeding away from the storm. A mass of black cattle loomed up on the road on the run, moving solidly. He had only enough time to draw up and stop. The moving mass flowed around the white wagon as if it were an island in a stream. For a moment or two they looked down on a forest of pass-ing horns, lines of black backs streaming past, the inflamed whites of startled eyeballs rolling up at them. They were little cows, a few motleys and some dun-coloured, but black mostly, dead black. They drove past muttering in a constant dismal lowing with here and there the deep bellow of a bull.

The horses stood and sweated while Jed looked into the faces of a legion of black-horned devils. Their horns passed terrifyingly near his shanks. He drew his legs up gingerly and sat his saddle squatting like a Turk. Then there was a tempest of bleating and begging baas, and for a minute the wagon seemed to be inundated by a flock of sheep. Five or six busy dogs, and as many horsemen, sounding what amounted to a kind of fierce fugue on cow horns, brought up the rear. They moved onward with the storm, and a silence that now seemed unspeakably grateful, as the wagon still stood waiting, resumed.

"I guess most of what them settlers own is cattle, property that can move on its own legs," mused Bridget.

"Reckon that's about right, milady," agreed Salathiel, unable to keep an entirely straight face at so unexpected and practical a comment from one so small. It was not an observation which he would have thought of making himself.

"But I like sheep best," continued Bridget. "I like 'em when they're little e-we lambs."

"Giddap," barked Salathiel.

. . . lambs, eh? He remembered the wolves hunting the elk only a few days back beyond the ridges. I wonder how they'll fare, he thought. He stood up and looked behind him over the roof of the wagon. They were out in the open now.

The last flurry of thick weather rolled down the road behind him. The wind came keening and clear, piping out of the northeast. A high whirlwind of leaves and small twigs and branches rose from the edge of the road down which the herd had just disappeared. It slanted forward in a cloud westward, seeming to be following them. Now and then a distant barking, a solemn bellowing, or an eerie note on a horn broke through. Then the sound of the wind swallowed all. The cloud rose higher, the sun looked through. God's people had passed.

He sat down and handled the reins again hopefully. Now that they *were* past, he was glad to be driving east again. He put his arm about Bridget and drew her closer to him. Jed looked back and took courage from his smile.

A mile or so over the distant fields and scattered woodlands, the wood smoke from the chimneys of Shippensburg made a blue hazy patch in the winter air.

19

Swan Song on a Harpsichord

OUT OF THE DARK weather retreating into the distance behind them, St. Clair and Yates came posting down the road and overtook the wagon just as it was entering Shippensburg. St. Clair shouted something to Jed, as he and Yates flashed past without drawing rein. Evidently the two riders were making a race for it; both fine greys paced each other neck and neck down the long muddy vista of the single street of the town. As far as Salathiel could see, they turned in at the same place precisely together.

He watched them dismount and tie their horses to the hitching bar before a stone building, where a cumbersome canvas-covered wagon, its teams lacking, was standing forlorn in the road. Leaning over a fire that had been kindled directly beside it, a man in a black cap was very busy about something. Except for him, there was no one in sight. A light, patchy snow covered the village, and had it not been for the smoke rolling from numerous chimneys, it would have seemed desolate. Certainly it was unkempt.

But there was good reason for that, Salathiel reflected. Most of the inhabitants must have fled to Carlisle during last year's troubles; probably the majority had only recently returned. Some houses were still forlornly boarded up with log slabs. Still, it was the largest town he had ever been in, also the longest. It stretched out for a mile or two ahead on either side of the highway in a loose congeries of buildings, mostly log cabins, but with gardens, barns, and an occasional stone or brick house of pleasant proportions. Decidedly it was a town and not a settlement. It had been there for a long time, he supposed.

Indeed, his nose, if not his eyes, assured him of that. Even in winter there hung about it something of the stale reek of Fort Pitt during the siege. Too many people have lived too close together here

for too long, his nose said—white people and horses; a stale odour
mixed with wood smoke, faintly rancid and sweetly sour, when the
fresh wind stopped blowing in from the fields. He sniffed it and
remembered. Possibly so keen a nose-sense was going to be a considerable cross to bear. As for letting people know that he could best
recollect them that way, better not! But he did, he could—he laughed.
There was a certain advantage to it, too. When that thief had stood
so close to the wagon the other night, for instance.

They were passing a rocky mound on the left of the street now,
with the remains of a considerable stockade on it. Old Fort Franklin
perhaps? He'd heard of it. But it had been abandoned not long after
Braddock's time. Where, then, was Fort Morris? That must be Mr.
Ed Shippen's mansion they were passing now! The finest house he
had ever seen: red brick, tall windows and a fanlight doorway, glass,
glass everywhere. He whistled and pointed it out to Bridget. "Shippen's," he said. She took it quite calmly.

"Marse St. Clair say pull in here," shouted Jed. He pointed to a
low stone building with a parapet, and embrasures in the walls instead
of windows, on the same side of the street as Shippen's. St. Clair's
and Yates's mounts were hitched before it. He now saw that the
wagon standing in the street had only two wheels. The rear wheels
were off and it was propped up. A lot of household stuff had lately
been spewed out behind. Some smashed furniture and pieces of china
still littered the road. Feathers had come out of a pillow and were
still blowing about. The man in the black fur cap—and leather apron
—was putting on a new axle. He had some thin iron rods heating in
the coal fire near-by to bore rivet holes in the wood.

"They're watchin' fer ye in thar," said he, looking up from the
ground where he was lying underneath the wagon, and pointing
with his hammer. "Tell 'em I'm nigh finished, will ee?"

Salathiel allowed he would. It was only as he was hitching the
teams to the long log rail that he realized he was about to enter Fort
Morris. The curious blind-walled stone building with nothing but one
door in its long front was it.

"We're here!" he shouted.

Captain Jack and Melissa came down the rear ladder stiffly. The
old man was carrying his hand-pack.

"Hope Rutherford has a right hearty blaze goin'," he remarked.
"It really does be turnin' cold."

"What's the pack for?" asked Salathiel.

"I've got somethin' valuable in it I wouldn't trust ye with,"
grinned Captain Jack. "Let's go inside."

Bridget was already fumbling in vain with the massive wrought-
iron handle of the fort door.

"That's a tough one for young customers," said the old man. "Better let your pappy snag on."

Salathiel leaned heavily on the lock before it gave. The left leaf of the heavy loopholed oak door swung inward, and they felt the welcome indoor warmth and smelled new whitewash. There was more warmth than light inside, however, and for a moment they stood in comparative darkness, trying to make out the puzzling features of the room.

The interior of Fort Morris was unique, almost cavelike. The floor, the groined ceiling, and its walls were all alike of dressed stone. Inside there was a single huge barrack room, with one tremendous open chimney for the garrison's cooking at its far end. Several ample stone platforms about three feet high rose at regular intervals along both walls, upon which small marine cannon had once been mounted. What windows the place had were deep embrasures let high in the walls like the ports of a ship. But these openings were now in process of either being carefully boarded over or smoothly bricked up.

The ceiling was comparatively low, but it was composed of a series of domes like those in a German wine cellar, and the first impression of the place was that of the flickering flow of shadows and lambent firelight which perpetually washed these inverted stone cups overhead and flowed downward, streaming away in grey wavering lines of luminous shadows along the whitewashed walls. So confusing was this dim home of shadows, after the bright daylight, that at first neither Salathiel nor Frances could make out into what strange place they had come. Then, as their pupils widened, they saw—

The fire, the warm leaping heart of the room; a grey-haired woman in linsey-woolsey standing before it turning two fowls on a spit; another woman standing beside her helping, in a shimmering blue silk dress; the pointed ears and backs of two tabby cats solemnly watching the cooking. On one side, on the stone platform nearest the fire, sat St. Clair and Yates, a bowl of hot punch already steaming on the table before them. On another platform, immediately opposite, three tow-headed children leaned across a table staring fixedly at a cratelike object, as though they were mesmerized.

And so on down the apartment, from the bright glowing hearth to the deep shadow by the door, where they were standing, there were four platforms arranged along each wall. And the platforms were something to see. On them had been piled anything and everything that had once furnished the fort. The entire impedimenta of its departed garrison was still there. Only one platform had turned entirely domestic.

On it was a dirty canopy bed, unmade, and with a tossed trundle-cot beneath. Several broken chairs, a small table, old clothes, a cradle, a boot-jack, a wardrobe, and two covered jordans seemed to be having a smug gossip together over what had transpired the night before. This "bedroom" without walls, clatty as it was, appeared indecent by naughty contrast, for all the rest of the place was swept, garnished, and whitewashed. Obviously the fort was but newly domestically occupied.

Just then, down the middle aisle between the piled platforms, they saw a tall lantern-jawed man in grimy butternut advancing towards them and about to speak.

"*Tut-tut, chuck—ooooee*" . . . an indescribably shrill whistle followed, echoed dully amidst the domes. For an instant they thought it must be the man was making fun of them. But he laughed at their natural confusion and held out his hand to Captain Jack.

"Well, old un, I 'spect ye had a big lodge night over to Chambers's," said he. "Glad to see ye ag'in. None the warse for the trip, eh?"

"Nary a bit," replied the old hunter. "Here be some travellin' folks I brought ye. But jist for the noon snack. They're intendin' fer Carlisle."

"Wal, now, we'll dish them out some kind o' fixin's. Thar's possum stew and praties, if they kin take it. My name's Jim Rutherford, by the way," he added. He extended his hand to Albine carelessly—and winced. "Mr. St. Clair warned me ye were comin'. Some of the congregationers that jist passed through here was mighty anxious to have a talk with ye. They camped nigh us for four days, so we're et out like rats in a corncrib. That's why thar's naught but possum stew. No, the fowls ain't any o' mine"—he nodded towards the woman in the silk gown. "Hern," he said. "That's right. Her and her man hev tarried behind 'cause o' wagon trouble. . . . Turkey-fither gentry!" he whispered, and beckoned them towards the fireplace.

That strange shivering whistle sounded again, and a raucous voice that seemed to be cursing itself swore like a sailor.

Bridget dashed forward and joined the children peering into the object on the table. For an instant she seemed to be enchanted, too. Then she screamed, "Look, M'lissa, look!"

The voice began to chuckle wickedly. Out of sheer curiosity, it was Salathiel who bent down over the table and looked.

Through the bars of a light iron cage with a brass ring on its top, a strange knowing bird sidled away from him on its wooden perch, blinking; fluffing its feathers; flexing one glovelike claw in the air thoughtfully. It was green as the scum on a stagnant pool—

and smelt like it. It gave a low chuckling whistle. But, of course, it couldn't . . .

"Poor Poll, poor poor Poll," it said. He *saw* it talk.

He all but fell down and knocked his head on the table out of sheer helpless astonishment. It couldn't be true. It was like having one of Nymwha's firelight beast tales come to life. Impossible— but a brutal, blatant fact. The bird talked!

All four children broke into screams of appreciation at finding a big man so obviously sharing their happy wonder.

"See!" said Bridget triumphantly.

"Come on over," whispered Yates to St. Clair, "this is bound to be rare. Our large friend is discovering something entirely new."

Everybody now gathered about the table with the cage on it.

The parrot, however, was not entirely pleased at being the centre of so much concentrated attention. He sidled back and forth on his perch, making deprecatory noises. He looked askance.

At that moment, as the devil would have it, Mr. St. Clair decided to act the showman. He offered a small bit of bread to the bird, too confidently perhaps, and chirped at it. Poll now began to strut like an admiral on a quarter-deck during Sunday inspection. He assumed a lofty, aloof, and condescending air.

"Walks like ye do," said Bridget to St. Clair.

Mr. Yates chortled. The bird mocked him. Then it cocked its head at St. Clair and winked, " 'Ow now, guvnor, 'ow now?" it said. " 'Ow's your 'andsome bowsprit?"

Mr. Yates convulsed, silently this time. Mr. St. Clair beat a hasty retreat to his table and hid his face in the punch bowl. His had been a terrible surprise and shameful repulse. It took two noggins of the best hot arrack to restore his equanimity. At least he was left alone to recover. The bird still continued to be the centre of rapt attention. They were all waiting to hear what he might have to say next.

"He's a naughty, nautical old reprobate," remarked a clear, feminine voice, causing them all to look up.

It was the lady in the blue silk dress. She had come over from the fireplace and was standing close beside the table, holding fire tongs before her with something in them that glowed white hot. She was hardly more than a girl, with a grave mouth that threatened to smile at any moment. Her dark hair was a mass of ringlets and short curls. Her blue eyes shone with a tearful lustre, but the lids were red, either from the fire or from recent weeping.

She stood very straight and slight, holding a piece of gleaming stone before her. She was pathetically attractive. They all felt it, and gaped at her.

"Would you mind letting me give Poll what he needs?" she asked gently.

It was Yates who first guessed what she meant. He pulled two of the children away from the cage so she could approach it.

Coming closer, she reached forward with the tongs and dropped the heated half-brick, for such it was, into a small iron receptacle like a box fixed in the bars of the cage under the perch. The parrot moved over and began to fluff its feathers and stretch out its wings in the grateful glow. It croaked happily.

"Well, I'll be double-damned," exclaimed Captain Jack.

"*Hush*," said she in alarm. "You'll start him swearing, and he's just the profanest old—" She put a hand over her mouth. When it came away there was a smile there like a gleam of moonlight, and her eyes danced. "He's very very naughty, but I just love him," she whispered.

"An extremely fortunate old bird, ma'am," replied Yates, bowing ever so slightly. He might have proceeded further, but the big door at the end of the room opened, and he saw the girl's sensitive features freeze.

A thin middle-aged man in the primmest of black suits came walking down the room. He had a grim, determined face, and he kept his hat on. He glanced at the group around the parrot's table indignantly.

"It would be *much* better, madam, if you would give your un-divided attention to hurrying the cookery, instead of gossiping idly with these doubtless—*ah*—very worthy persons," he added, running his eye over the company. "The smith informs me he has all but completed his repairs. As it is, the delay already . . ."

"Can we take the things with us?" she interrupted.

"*Impossible!*" he said icily.

She closed her eyes for a moment and stood perfectly still. Only the sound of the chimney draught was audible. Then she turned obediently and went back to the fire. The fowls were done. Her husband stood looking after her for a moment. His mouth tensed.

"How do you do, Mr. Preston," said Yates.

"How do *you* do, sir?" replied the man, without looking at him. Then he went forward and dragged a small bench and table close to the fire, sat down with his back to the company, and awaited his wife's serving.

"Friend of yours?" inquired Captain Jack sardonically.

"Apparently not," replied Yates. "But I know him." He shrugged and led the way back to St. Clair's table, where Jed, who had ap-peared from a dark corner, was hopefully helping set the board with wooden plates and spoons for all. After the potatoes and meat had been piled into one big earthen bowl, and the punch renewed, Mrs. Rutherford and her husband joined the company, while the children held a noisy revel all their own. Despite that, the parrot went to sleep. The meal began.

"Wal, how's your new venture here afarin'?" demanded Captain Jack, addressing the innkeeper.

"Tolerable good, considerin' the fact that most people ain't acquaint' yit with the fact that Fort Morris's now an ordinary, 'stead of a barrack with a garrison. O' course, thar's feelin' in the town ag'in me on account the garrison left almost before the Injun war-whoops died away. Still, that ain't my fault. Them that really knows will blame Shippy. You can't beat the Shippens. They're right in on the council and blood brothers with every governor. The bargain they made when they built the fort was that as soon as the province ceased to garrison it the building and land was theirn ag'in. And I declare it warn't more than a month after Bushy Run when old Bill Shippen's son-in-law, Colonel Burd, put it up to me about takin' a lease here. We didn't think much of it at first. Me and the missus like Lancaster. But when the colonel himself ordered the militia out, I seen the light. Naturally, we ain't doin' so slick as the widow up the street in the old stone house whar the court usen fer to sit, but we're comin' on, and when the childer get bigger and kin help, we'll jist hum. Won't we, old girl?" He brought his hand down on his wife's back with enough emphasis and enthusiasm to cause her to lose a half a potato, and to sputter.

"Liken we will," said she finally, putting the potato back, "with *our* three girls. And them Old Lights goin' west was a mighty windfall."

"Three hunder and two and thirty of 'em!" exclaimed Rutherford, "not countin' the lovin' couple you see cooin' together at yon table before the fire. They're goin' to have to leave a raft o' fine heavy stuff behind," he added, lowering his voice. "Weak axletree. I'll git most o' it yit, you see. The old boy's in a fix. His young wife do take on. She wants the parrot and *all*. Lordy! But say, do tell me now, Mr. St. Clair, you an' Mr. Yates ought to know, what be the authorities doin' to let so many good fightin', prayin' people like them congregationers leave the province? I thought the Penns wanted the Scotch rifles on the frontiers?"

"Oh, that's another story, Rutherford," said St. Clair. "The people that just passed through here aren't Pennsylvanians. They're a peculiar folk. About a hundred years ago one of the Lords Baltimore brought their grandfathers over from north Ireland and settled them in to keep the Quakers and other Pennsylvania people from coming down into Maryland. They settled at a place they called

Munster, not so far west of New Castle and the new town of Wilmington, a little back from the Swedes on Christiana Creek. It was like the old border troubles between England and Scotland before the Union. These people were to be a kind of frontier garrison, 'moss troopers' for the Baltimores. But Mr. Yates can tell you the rest. He knows all about them. He's tried to collect rent from them for the Penns, haven't you, Ned?"

"Unhappily, yes," said Yates, grimacing, "but it would take a regiment of dragoons and the lord chancellor himself to collect even a widow's mite. You see, these people were Church of Scotland, Covenanters, right out of Cromwell's time. They hadn't been settled so long in Ireland when Baltimore brought them over to keep the marches of what he claimed was Maryland. They did that, but they had small use for the Catholic Calverts, and they despised the snivelling Quakers even more. The result was that Munster, and the pleasant valleys about it, became a fine little Presbyterian realm all of its own. Other Scotch-Irish, all stout Church of Scotland, 'Old Lights', as they call them now, joined the first comers from time to time. In a way these folks at Munster were lucky. The Calverts let them alone so long as they did free fightin' for them and would deny the authority of Penn and his heirs. The border dispute waxed and waned for half a century. Nobody really knew in what jurisdiction Munster lay. It was an enclave in time, space, and politics. The result was, they accepted no earthly rulers. They had none. The only authority they recognized was the voice of God as proclaimed by the minister and by that bell you saw goin' west today. It was a royal gift from Queen Anne. But after good Anna died, they had no sentiment of loyalty left for the new dynasty. Monarchy was conveniently confined to heaven.

"No, that place was an anomaly," continued Yates, shaking his head in a kind of speculative legal dream. "There were no taxes at Munster, only voluntary church tithes. If the ghost of old John Knox had walked down the village street in Munster five and twenty years ago, he would have seen the Scotland he hoped for in full blossom, and not a malignant for miles around. God's people alone abode there, presarved, pickled in their own holy vinegar.

"About the only bad trouble they had was too many children. Their congregation increased mightily, and one minister after another would lead them to the frontiers. Little Munster was like a hive that sent out new swarms with ministers for queen bees, if you'll take the mixed figure. No drones, they! Half the Scotch-Irish you meet in the colonies seem to hail from there. Maybe it's a portent. I've given much thought to it. Theocrats, y'know. Dangerous! Farmers and warriors with John Knox's God. Whew!

"Lately the Penns have tried to persuade them to the frontiers to drive back the savages, and then move German farmers in behind them. It's not a bad policy, but last year the Scotch-Irish frontiersmen came back and nearly overthrew the proprietaries in Philadelphia. If it hadn't been for honest Ben Franklin!" Yates shook his head and continued:

"What finally moved the people we met today was the settlement of the border case and the new south boundary line agreement. They found they were indisputably in Pennsylvania. They would have to pay quit-rent. My first legal task in this colony was to try to levy on the landholders at Munster. 'Twas a hard bare bone on which I was set to cut my new milk teeth. Bein' a born Scot, I escaped violence. But hardly. And I brought no shillings back to Philadelphia. The rents are due for nigh a century back. Now they've gone where no rent will ever be collected by any of the Penns. They were offered lands in the Wyoming valley, if they'd go there and keep the Yankees out from the New Hampshire grants. But no. The quarrel came to a head at Lancaster, and they took the Virginia government's offer to go down south to the headwaters of west-running rivers—over the hills and far away. Virginia claims from sea to sea, you know. But I opine where these people are wending few writs will run for a long time to come. They can ring their own bell and let the mountains echo it back again, without any courts to tell them what it means."

"Kind o' gits ye, don't it, mister attorney?" chuckled Captain Jack—"these poor folks escapin' from sovrains and lawyers and all that. Wal, thot's a lawyer's way o' lookin' at it. But you've pretty nigh left out religion in your legal story. Now, what *I* know is that the Reverend Alexanders have been preachin'—two generations of 'em, father and son—since I was a boy, exhortin' God's people to h'ist the yoke of Phar-a-oh off their gallèd necks and prepare fer the journey through the wilderness. They've got only one book and they've read it so hard, and had it dinned into their ears so long, that they're jist livin' the story o' comin' up out of Egypt over ag'in, until they're more Hebrew than Scotch-Irish.

"Of course, it is kind o' ridiculous tryin' to make the Penns out to be Phar-a-ohs, they bein' quiet gentle people mostly, but thar's always the king to lay it on. And the present Reverend Alexander Alexander lays it on. He's Moses, and he's takin' the tabernacle and the ark o' the covenant and the bell along with him to the land of milk and honey. And the Injuns will be the Jebusites and the Malekites and the Blatherskites, and all the other heathen tribes that once infested the Promised Land. Thot's his story, and they believe him. They *are* God's people in their own heads. And what

I say is, somethin' powerful unexpected is liable to come out of sich divine play-actin'. It's right ticklin' to me, sometimes, to think how all the gintry in the City busy themselves bein' Greeks and Romans, even gettin' republican in their oratory, while the Scotch on the frontiers be carryin' on like the hosts of Joshua. Jove and Jehovah! —what readin' books kin do!" Captain Jack shook his head lugubriously, too, and took a drink out of Mr. Yates's punch mug. "Bein' as all this is at your expense, Ned," he explained.

"Now, what teched off this particular gang fer to leave the land of bondage was a schiz-izzm in their midst. Yes, sirree, the New Lights! They don't hold so strict to not pleasurin' themselves any as the Auld Lichts do, an' they've even durst set up a synod of their own over at Philadelphy to deny the authority o' the Kirk o' Scotland in the colonies. Why, only last year, the Reverend Alexander's favorite daughter, Sarah, up and married her a New Light husband. Her preachin' father cawn't bear to think on it. So he's goin' west, where no more of the children of his loins will be snared into burnin' forever in hell's fire and hev to cry to God in vain out of the tarnal furnace. Oh, to be an Auld Licht, to be an auld Auld Licht! You gentlemen with your reasonable new ways, you forgit. Maybe the forest will quench the auld licht and the new together? Maybe? For I'll tell ye somethin', it's a huge land they're headed fer.

"Not so many moons ago came a young man to my cabin to spend the night. On his way south to Car'lina, he was. Man by the name o' Boone from old Berks County. He said Ben Franklin once arranged a mortgage on his pap's farm.* As fer him, he was danged tired of such lawyerisms, seein' thar's so much empty land no parchments cover, and all he needed was a rifle-gun to foreclose. He'd bin way down the Ohio gittin' buffalo hides, huntin' all summer. Then in the fall the Shawanees took 'em all off him. He kind o' wanted a little advice from me about thot. Well, we talked as long as the pine knots lasted. He sez the land's waitin' thar west of the mountain, big as the full moon, swarming with critters, a dark forest with limestone springs, glades, and succulent grass. Thar's strange, lost rivers thar, too. It's the loamy Eden of God's fresh creation, vargin, wonderful! And he knows a gap through the rivers in Car'lina handy to option. Maybe it's young fellers like him will be the Moseses for that new country.

"Ye know what I sez to him? I sez, 'Don't ruin yer eyes with no fine print, jist keep 'em bright fer gittin' the beads of yer Pennsylvania rifle-gun in line. An' don't let the Injuns holler ye out o' them hills neither. Git the people started, and in one generation we palefaces will outfornicate the redskins five to one. You'll be seized and entitulated into that land by pure force of gism and a

* Nolan, J. Bennett, "Ben Franklin's Mortgage on the Daniel Boone Farm."

little gunpowder and lead.' Thot's what I laid down to young Dan'l Boone, and I wisht to the Lord I could live to see the day, but I cawn't. I've got the call now to an even better country."

Suddenly, Captain Jack shut his mouth like a clam.

St. Clair smiled into Yates's single eye. "I've made that my religion, too," he said.

" 'Let me not to the marriage of true minds admit impediments,' " murmured Yates.

"Oh, the devil with all *that* rantin' stuff, too," snapped St. Clair.

"Look, it's nigh half after one by my watch," interrupted Salathiel, displaying his timepiece proudly, "and it's three long leagues into Carlisle. For myself, I'd like to be gettin' on."

Frances was only in partial agreement with him. While the men had been talking, she had been listening to what snatches of conversation from the couple dining before the fire she could overhear. It was not much, but what she had heard confirmed her in her sympathy for the young wife in the blue silk dress, and she wanted to hear more.

Still, at Salathiel's urging, they would all have left immediately had it not been that everybody else's attention was suddenly focused in the same direction as Melissa's.

Mr. Preston had risen from his chair, evidently in grim anger, and he now announced in a voice that reverberated dismally, "Woman, if I've told you once, I've told you a score of times, we *canna* take the bed with us! That bed! It may be rosewood and cedar, or it may have been Grandma LeTort's bridal bower and death couch too. But 'tis too massive a piece for the axles of the wagon to bear. 'Tis a catafalque with urns carved from massive shittim wood, a four-cornered hearse that needs wheels in its own right and six horses dight with plumes to draw it." Mr. Preston wiped his mouth, and looked at his wife.

"But the spinet, my poor little harpsichord!" pleaded the girl, now openly tearful. "It's light, *it* will ride.

"See!" she continued, in one last attempt to mollify the marble. "Look! It's *very* light."

In her desperation, she went over to the wall and dragged a small spinet out from a pile of furniture, putting it in the firelight where all could see. Its wires sang faintly. They seemed to sigh.

"Hear?" she said. "How can you still listen to it, Andrew?"

"Felice," said her husband icily, "I'll have no sich godless instrument in the hoose. The meenisters will not permeet it. Your profane bird is the only conceesion to balladry I'll make."

"I'll have a last song then," she cried desperately. "And will ye stay to hear it, Andrew Preston? Durst ye listen to a swan song?"

"Aye, I'll hear ye oot," he replied, and folded his arms stoically.

"Candles, madam, candles, if *you please!*" the girl cried to Mrs. Rutherford. Meanwhile, she dragged the little harpsichord farther out across the stone floor to a more central position before the fire, and with the fierce energy of anger. Two candles were brought her by the puzzled Mrs. Rutherford. These she took with shaking hands, lit them at the hearth, and returning, placed them in two small sconces on either side of the instrument. A tense drama of protest informed every motion of her body. Unconsciously, she was making a ritual to express what she durst not fully say.

There was no one, not even her husband, who was not now intensely aware of this. The children stared and were suddenly quiet. Yates and St. Clair stood up the better to see.

She sat down at the instrument, with the firelight behind her and the twin stars of the candles gleaming beside her face. She tossed her curls back, opened the spinet, and looked at Mr. Preston fixedly.

To Salathiel, who had not the slightest idea what the instrument was for, the ivory keys grinned as though a horse had skinned its lips back from its teeth. The first chord that she struck swept him with a shock of overwhelming amazement. He was caught as though in the undertow of a wave and swept into an unsuspected sea of melody. The quills striking on the little wires rang charmingly with small twanging echoes in the inverted cups of the stone ceiling. He sat there drowning in lovely sound. Music finally closed over his head . . .

She ranged slowly upward on the chords of an octave, her voice gaining smoothness and power as it rose. A little husky at first, it was soon clear and lovely again. It was plain to St. Clair and Yates what she was doing. She had lost herself in memory and was prac-tising on the keyboard as a child. Presently she hummed a brief nursery rhyme, accompanying herself. Then quickly, after the ripple of a merry prelude, came the full tide of a song.

It was something about a famous general who always rode a-cock-horse before going to sleep in his mother's lap. In the next stanzas he grew up, became a real soldier, and returned safe from the wars to his bride.

She soared now into the last verse, her voice ringing liquidly, with a little harplike banter on the upper keys—as the soldier's bride replied

> "And who so very bold
> When battles 'round him rolled,
> But that he would that he
> Were even now as we—
> Are now, my love, in arms,
> In arms, in mutual arms,
> Away from war's alarms?"

The voice ceased; the music went on quietly, seeming to relate a wordless tale of ardent melancholy. In the candlelight the girl's face became languidly composed and grave. Her hands slowed from flashing whitely, paused, and roved gradually down the keyboard into the sad minors of an ancient hymn:

> "Sun of My Soul, arise, arise,
> Display thy glory to mine eyes;
> Star of My Life, what e'er betide,
> Lord of My Life, abide, abide."

She closed the harpsichord softly, as though she were saying amen with the covers, and then stood by with her hand on it, patting it good-bye. Tears traced down her cheeks. She leaned over and kissed the dark wood that dimly reflected her. She blew out the candles.

He stood there waiting for her.

"Do you remember?" she asked in a low tone as she passed him. "Do you remember, Andrew, how it was when you first came to the old house at LeTort's Springs?"

"Yes," he said, "but why will ye 'mind me of those pretty times now?"

"Because," she replied, "because . . ." She hesitated for a moment —and then, going over to the children's table, slipped a flannel cover over the iron cage and, taking it by its brass ring with two fingers, stood waiting for him resignedly.

"Come," she said, for he still looked at her with some doubt. "Can't you see I'm ready?"

He came forward then and offered her his arm. "At least I'll have a bird to sing my profane songs for me," she added.

He let her have the last word.

She laid her hand over his arm, and they walked down the long room together, her shoulders beginning to droop. Neither of them looked back.

"Poor Poll, Poll's a-cold," croaked the parrot, as the door swung open revealing the bleak street beyond. Then it closed firmly behind them.

There was a moment's utter silence before they heard the rolling sound of iron wheels commence and then diminish down the street.

"The poor darlint, oh, that poor, poor darlint!" exclaimed Frances, springing up and going over to lay her own hands on the abandoned spinet. "And *him* like an old dry pipe stem. Oh, Mr. Rutherford, will ye not be takin' the best care of her pretty things?"

"For a year and a day, ma'am," replied Rutherford. "For that,

I'm to be paid. Afterwards—who knows? Mr. Preston is a hard case, and no one can be nursing another man's plunder when he will not house it himself." The landlord of Fort Morris turned away to collect his reckoning for the meal—3s 6d, which Captain Jack paid, and 3s for St. Clair's punch.

Captain Jack said nothing, but continued to wait quietly at the table while the company broke up. Presently he beckoned to Frances and began to explain to her that she was to say nothing to Salathiel about his staying behind; and that his horse was to be driven on to Carlisle. He'd made arrangements for sending for it later. "No use of havin' a big set-to now," he said. "I ain't in a mood to take it."

All indeed was now in full bustle for the final departure for Carlisle. Jed was taking the nosebags off the horses and tightening the girth of his saddle. The women went to the jaques and the men to an intimate corner against the rear wall outside. Incidentally, the recent departure of Mr. and Mrs. Preston was casually discussed.

"A sorry manner of departure for foreign parts," remarked Yates.

"Ifen you're movin' west over the mountains, you can't carry *all* your heavy furniture along. It just stands to reason," grumbled Rutherford.

"Mr. Preston is leaving behind a good deal more than his furniture."

"He is," agreed St. Clair. "I'd like to bring the serpent to his knees."

"That would involve you in a coil of difficulties, Arthur," laughed Yates. "Besides, the man's an attorney, and a good one. He has represented the Munster congregations for years. I heard him argue the quit-rent case before Justice Allen. In fact, I was representing the proprietary interest then myself."

"And won?"

"Yes, but as you see, it was a Pyrrhic victory."

"He married him his wife just recently," volunteered Rutherford. "Reckon he needed a young partner for the western wilds. She's a Huguenot lady, a LeTort, grandniece of the old Frenchman that first settled-in at LeTort Springs fer fur tradin'. You'll hear about them at Carlisle. Guess it was mostly *her* old family stuff he's left behind."

"I've no doubt," said St. Clair.

A general buttoning-up followed.

Just then someone passed at breakneck speed riding up the town street at a furious gallop. "Sounds like an express," remarked Rutherford. "They often go tearin' right through here for Carlisle.

Say, did ye hear they say Buckey's started marchin' from Fort Pitt?
Might be at Bedford now."

" 'They say,' " quoted St. Clair scornfully. "What don't *they*
say? The last I heard, Bouquet was due to march east by April at
the earliest."

"Ye can't be sure," mused Albine; "now that he's been promoted,
maybe he's in a hurry to wind everything up."

But none of them thought any more of the rumour. It seemed
unlikely that Bouquet would march his rescued captives over the
mountains in the winter. Besides, they had more immediate affairs
of their own to consider.

While St. Clair stood in the street before Fort Morris, giving
final instructions to Salathiel about waiting for the expected Ligonier
emigrants at Carlisle, Frances and Bridget were inside, saying good-
bye to Captain Jack.

The old hunter was going home to his cabin on Jack's Mountain.
He would not be moved by any argument. He wished no fuss to be
made about it.

"It's jist come over me again," he said, "I must be alone. Tell
yer young man I'll send fer him at Carlisle if I ever need him.
Rutherford's bound boy here knows the trail to my old mountain
shack. Now, git along without worryin' Sal any about me. Keep the
horse till I send for it. 'Tain't any use havin' Sal arguin' with me
at the last. Good-bye, and God be forever with ye, my dears."

Bridget threw her arms about his neck. It was only then that
for an instant or two he showed any emotion. They left him sitting
at the table filling his pipe.

When they hurried out, Salathiel was already in the seat, waiting, and the wagon drawn out into the street ready to move. St.
Clair and Yates had ridden on ahead. They were going to the land
office at Lancaster and were in a hurry. Jed was sitting on Enna,
round-eyed, expounding something to Salathiel.

"Yas, sah, it was sure him, de pastor what preached at Chambers
Mills yesterday. He done pass through hyah on his big jack mule
like hot spit through a knot hole. And he hollers somethin' out to
me real loud. Somethin' about a Marse John Gilpin. When I tell
Marse Yates that, he jes larf like hell. He say he tink de reverend'll
sure git to Carlisle fustest."

"All right, Jed," smiled Albine, "I guess Mr. Craighead's mule
has decided to go back home. Now hold on tight yourself for the
rest of the way, if you want to get to Carlisle, too."

"All right in the wagon?" he called back.

"All set and comfortable," replied Melissa's sweet voice. *"Please* drive easy, Sal. The horses be tired." He had no idea Captain Jack was not in there with the women.

He slapped the reins. The yoke bells chimed faintly, and they rumbled off up the long street of Shippensburg, bound for Carlisle.

It was the last leg of the journey, the final stretch of the western military road that lay before them. He thought of that with a satisfaction impossible to exaggerate. The forest and the fort on the Ohio, where he had begun the journey "long ago" with Captain Ecuyer, lay actually only two hundred miles westward, and on the calendar not so far backward in time. And yet, measured in terms of fruitful experience and the span of his own lifetime, the country behind the mountains and all its ways of life slumbered in the eternal wilderness nothing less than æons behind him. Certainly in terms of his own personality, an entire age away.

He had left old Kaysinata standing in the moonlight on the banks of Beaver Creek. Then he was a callow and savage boy. The Little Turtle had left the Big Turtle behind in the wilderness. He had been given an axe that evening and warned never to eat turtle meat.

This afternoon it was Salathiel Albine aware of himself and his shortcomings as a white man; aware of the past and the future; of God; of the world about him, and of heaven and hell. He could not help thinking of it that afternoon as he approached Carlisle, with surprise, and perhaps a certain justifiable satisfaction.

From Yellow Breeches Creek that rolled to the Susquehanna through the valleys only a few miles before him to the westward-flowing Ohio was scarcely fifty leagues measured on paper maps. But the mountains of a mighty frontier lay between. He had crossed them from boyhood into manhood, from darkness into the dawnlight. He would bury the hatchet of Kaysinata and enter into the inheritance before him. Almost he had been disinherited.

All this, in a kind of grand symbol stamped upon the face of the landscape itself, seemed to be made visible to him that afternoon as he looked north and westward to the twinkling ranges of the Blue Mountains, whose crests rolled like a school of enormous fish leaping along the horizon. They were not really so far away, but in the blue haze of the dying winter daylight they seemed to be withdrawing themselves, travelling away from him, into an incredible distance and a remoter time. The southmost of the big school of fish was the one they called Jack's Mountain, alone, detached, high and forbidding. Some low clouds dragged across it and concealed its crest. That was where the old hunter had his cabin. Pretty soon Captain Jack would be seeing his last sunset up there—but he, Salathiel, would not think of that yet. They might still have some happy and peaceful days together at Carlisle.

Carlisle, Carlisle, tne yoke bells seemed to sing. After Carlisle he would not see the mountains any more at all. They were marching away from him now. They would soon be lost behind the horizon. They would become mountains of mysterious memory only, mountains of the moon. He said a brief silent prayer of thanks and hope.

He pulled the horses up and lit his pipe in the face of the winter wind, and tossed Jed a twist of shag to chew. He liked that genial and simple-hearted character. He needed his ever-cheerful help. He was glad St. Clair had agreed to leave him behind for a while longer. In a way it was palming Jed off for his keep, but in the end St. Clair had been decent enough. He had given him ten guineas as a retainer and pay for the time he might have to wait at Carlisle. If no settlers showed up for Ligonier by the end of two months, the arrangement would be cancelled. That was the bargain, and so far good enough. Hard coin.

He puffed comfortably and let the horses walk. They were a bit tired after the morning's pace. But what was the difference, they were almost there now. Anyway the family would have to sleep in the wagon that night. Yates said there wasn't a house or a hut to be had at Carlisle, not for love, money, or influence. Oh, well . . . But he would miss Yates. He hoped he would catch up with him again soon.

Clear and ever colder the wind swept down out of the northeast. The road, badly rutted by transport, led away straight and steadily over low rolling hills of mixed woodlands and cleared farm lands. The land was bleak, deserted, and desolate. They passed no one coming west. They stopped only once. It was to retrieve a white object caught in the limbs of an old pear tree that leaned low across the road. It was a clerical bag wig, hung there by its ribbons like a deserted oriole nest. This time it would take considerable repairing, and it was splashed with red mud. Salathiel laughed and passed it back to Bridget to lay away.

Then the patient teams began walking forward again.

As the early November twilight dimmed rapidly into the smooth darkness of a low cloud-hung night, a deep red glow burned brighter and ever more widely across the sky above the black outlines of tumbling forest. By eight o'clock they seemed to be approaching an immense conflagration. The clouds ran and slobbered with scarlet.

It was the reflection of a thousand campfires, the united glow from the greatest military base in the colonies and the rallying point of the western frontier. Carlisle.

At half past nine they pulled up in the broad open town square, drew water from the king's well, had a brief bite of supper, sent Jed with all the horses to Stottelmyer's stables, and turned in for the night.

The journey was over.

But Salathiel longed for morning. He was impatient to see what the dawnlight might have to reveal.

20

A Beautiful Whip Changes Hands

"SIX O'CLOCK of a clear winter's morning, and all's well. Fifteen wagons, fifteen to report."

Thus chanted the sentries of the garrison at Fort Lowther and the cracked voices of the two old codgers of the Carlisle town watch, seeming to mock one another in chorus. The watch rattled their staffs and passed on towards breakfast and their senile mendacities about Queen Anne's War, over small beer and scrapple.

It was still dark, but Salathiel bestirred himself. He slipped into his old buckskins more out of habit than design, and popping an iron saucepan on a spider over a charcoal fire, busied himself preparing a hot morning stew. The bag of charcoal in the side-chest with the smith's tools now came in unexpectedly handy.

All about him in the starry darkness numerous invisible people were hunting or trying to borrow fuel from one another—anything, old worm-fence, even the splintered hickory spokes of a broken wheel would do. Obviously the "ark" was not the only wagon on the square, the outlines of which were gradually becoming visible in the oncoming dawn. Presently he could hear Frances and Bridget beginning to stir and talk in sleepy voices behind the canvas. It seemed strange without the horses and no work to do. It was lonely without Captain Jack. Doubtless, Jed would show up soon for victuals, and with news. He could always be depended on to do both.

While he stood, still a bit sleepy, watching the coals glowing under the pot in the morning darkness, he turned over in his mind the possible reasons for Captain Jack's unexpected decision to remain behind at Shippensburg. He had been not a little nettled and disconcerted last evening, when he first discovered that the old hunter was not along with them in the wagon. Frances ought to have told him, he insisted. He didn't relish being fooled like that. But as he listened to her explanations, he finally had to admit that she had probably acted for the best. It would have done no good to have had a painful parting yesterday at Fort Morris. And that was what it would have come to. For no one had ever been able to argue with the Half-Indian. His obstinate whims and moods were his law. Besides, Salathiel knew better than anyone else that when the necessity to be alone overtook Captain Jack, nothing could move him. All he hoped was that it wasn't the "scalp-fever" running in his veins again. But probably not; not any more. No, it must have been a deep longing for the refuge of his lonely cabin that had suddenly seized upon the old man. He couldn't support lively companionship for any length of time. Certainly Captain Jack must have wanted to get away awful bad, when he had just let them drive on, and told Melissa to keep his horse until he sent for it. That was surely a sign he meant to keep in touch. Well, he would use the old gelding carefully. He'd take care of it as a trust. Later on he might pay the old man a visit in his mountain eyrie. But, my, how he'd miss him! He'd counted on still having some good times together with him at Carlisle. How unexpectedly things turned out! Maybe the old hunter just wanted to die in peace. And a body was entitled to do his own dying, he supposed. But he didn't much relish *that* idea. He sat staring into the fire fixedly for a spell, while the grey light slowly dawned in the east. Finally, he shook himself clear of such doleful speculations and looked up.

Sunrise was late that November morning, and yet the dawn, when it did begin, seemed to come swiftly. The details of the scene surrounding him emerged from a mist of wood smoke and fading stars into a firm, clear background of houses, people, roads, and streets.

He was in a wide-open town square, dotted here and there with wagons camping overnight like himself, and surrounded on three sides by dwelling houses; some of them of two or more stories, built of brick, stone, or logs, with ample yards and gardens between.

There were several large public buildings, the most notable of which were a log courthouse with a strong jail, an unfinished town hall already of promising proportions, and churches.

About these buildings, especially at the south end of the square, there was already a considerable passing to and fro of people, a gradual assembling of horses and vehicles, as the business of the day got under way. An incessant barking of dogs and a rumbling of wagons, the lowing of cattle, and the spreading cry of crowing roosters combined with distant shouts, all in crescendo as the dawn intensified behind the eastern wall of the forest, gave the impression of a far-flung and teeming neighbourhood rousing itself eagerly.

The atmosphere was clear. The storm had passed on. A light powdery snow, smoking whitely now and then in the winter breeze, lay in scattered patches on the roofs and ground. Ranks of brick chimneys curled forth blue smoke leisurely.

A convoy of white-topped wagons, lanthorns still glowing yellow in the grey morning light, came down the Lancaster road and gathered waiting before the closed portal of Fort Lowther, their harness bells chiming faintly. Here and there a sow and her brood emerged speculatively into the open square. Somewhere an anvil began to clang. A woman called shrilly and banged a house door.

He stopped stirring the pot and stood up to look eagerly about him. His nose wrinkled. A faint underlying fetid odour and a smell of communal cooking and wood smoke both tainted and savoured the air. He smiled slowly. To him, at least, the general impression of Carlisle was overwhelmingly metropolitan; almost everywhere he looked there were people. And yet, there was something uneasy and confusing about it. He felt that from the very first.

The east end of the square, however, was quite another matter. There the familiar aspects of the western frontier still held sway. In that direction the public square was half pre-empted and solidly occupied by the broad front of Fort Lowther. Its stockaded log walls, over twelve feet high and two hundred feet long, extended across the eastern vista with squat-roofed rifle towers at each corner and a broad portal in the centre still blindly closed. The small postern beside it, however, already swarmed with a gathering crowd of leather-aproned workmen carrying their tools and awaiting admittance.

Officers of the Pennsylvania line in green and regulars in scarlet regimentals began to emerge from their various boarding-houses and ordinaries about the square and to stroll across it towards the fort, buckling on their side-arms, laughing and talking, while the sky lightened overhead. Behind the stockade itself a tentative humming of drums and a muffled tootling of fifes preluded the formation for morning roll call. As the sun rose suddenly out of the forest mists some miles away, a field piece boomed. The shrill music of the reveille squealed and rolled. A prolonged pulsing of drums shivered the air as the Union Jack unfurled into the sunlight. The lanthorns went out. The portals of the fort rolled backward, and the waiting crowd and wagons rushed in. All the town noises suddenly heightened and became more confident. Horses began to trot, and men to walk faster. The day at Carlisle had officially begun.

Salathiel called to them in the wagon to come out and eat. And while the music played "The World Turned Upside Down" and the hoarse shouting of many roll calls filled the air, they had breakfast together under the open sky in the public square.

It is a fair surmise that there were not many other people in the world that morning enjoying their breakfast so thoroughly as Salathiel. The victuals were a plain example of hard-boiled simplicity, but the mood in which they were eaten provided a *sauce piquante* with an ultimate satisfaction that no culinary artifice could have contrived. Circumstances themselves seemed to have melted together into a smooth wine gravy which blent perfectly with his every bite. The tense apprehension of lurking danger had gone. In its place was a calm sense of safety and pride in its achievement. Instead of the doubtful silence of the forest, on every hand now was the confident early cheerfulness of the town. Its morning noises had a bell-like quality of silver and crystal happiness about them. Salathiel filled his pipe, took a long draw, and slowly exhaled through his nose. His eyelids drooped half over his pupils, and he sat looking down like an Indian lost entirely in the present, immersed in a sheer complacency of well-being. After a few minutes, he aroused slowly as the bell before the courthouse began with its insistent clamour to proclaim *all's well, all's well*. He smiled as Frances looked at him happily, her eyes wide and calm.

A few moments later Jed showed up, covered with stable straw, and looking serious and much cast down. The wagonmaster at Stottelmyer's had refused to release the horses to him when he had asked for them that morning. He had had an argument with the man, who had struck him painfully with a bull whip. He ate his mush and bacon slowly, with tears in his eyes. Marse Albine didn't seem to make much of it. Jed supposed he would just have to take it. That's the way things went in this mad world. Marse Albine even seemed pleased. He grinned at everything. Bridget was already demanding to be taken to her granny.

"Afterwhile," said Salathiel—"afterwhile. It may take a few hours to find your grandma."

To Frances' eager questioning as to where they were going to find shelter, he had the same laconic answer. They would find a house "afterwhile". His satisfaction in both appearance and expression was infractible. He ate heartily and was not to be hurried. They had come a long long way. "Afterwhile," he kept saying—"afterwhile."

Afterwhile—he rose and entered the wagon.

So! They had begun by striking poor Jed with a whip! Well, he knew how to deal with people like that. Doubtless Stottelmyer had not yet returned. It *must* have been someone in temporary authority. But—he looked at Twin-Eyes in her sling, and considered. He decided finally to let her rest. Then he slipped Kaysinata's axe in his belt, set his coonskin cap at a truculent angle, and stepped out. When he got Enna again he would put on his town finery with all the fixins. Meanwhile, his present rig was more suitable for what he had in mind to do. Just to make sure of it, he reached down into the ashes of the breakfast fire and smeared his face thoughtfully with a bit of charcoal.

Frances rose with anxiety and laid a hand on his arm. "You be careful, *Mister* Albine," she said. "This is no place for war paint." He nodded and laughed. "Just a bit of funnin', sweetheart, is all I hev in view. Now don't worry, I'll see you under a roof tonight, or I'm a son of a gun!"

"Big man," said Bridget, looking at him doubtfully, "Grandma Larned's a lady. I know she is. You might be mistook in a dirty face."

"I'll sure gentle her," he said. "Now help your ma to look after the wagon. I'll be back—afterwhile. Come on, Jed!"

He strode across the square towards the town hall, with Jed toiling after him, the burn of the whip stinging across his shoulders. The two women stood looking uncertainly after them.

"Now what the divil's got into him?" mused Melissa. "He looks like a Black Boy renegade."

The fifteen wagons that had been called for that morning, and a half score more, were crowded about the new town hall, of which so far only the lower story was in use. Twenty-five competing drivers were trying to crowd at the same time into the bureau of the provincial commissary, a small room off the main hall. In there John Byers, Esquire, the wagon commissioner, was bargaining like mad for his king and country with eight Pennsylvania Dutchmen at once, and enjoying it. A convoy was making up to fetch barrelled beef from Baltimore by way of York. It was eight o'clock already, and so far *nobody* had been hired. Mr. Byers was masterfully roaring them down. His voice was one of the chief bulwarks of the colonial treasury. Salathiel listened for a moment with amusement. Well, if anybody knew what was going on at Carlisle, it would be Mr. Byers, the wagon commissioner, he judged. But the present thunderous moment was not entirely auspicious for questioning him, he felt. He would wait.

He then gave himself over to reading the innumerable notices, old proclamations, orders, and handbills pasted on the walls of the vestibule.

No wonder Mr. Byers had his troubles with wagoners. Just look at that—and an old notice, too, half torn off and fluttering in the wind:

Fifteenth
eenth, Nineteenth
thofe of *Chefter* the Twenty-fifth and
thofe of *Philadelphia* County the Twenty-
and thofe of *Bucks* and *Northampton*, to be alfo
the Second of July.

And for the Convenience of the Townfhips, proper Perfons, living in each County, will be appointed to contract with the Owners of the Waggons, and have them appraifed.

Each Waggon is to be provided with Forage fufficient to maintain the Horfes to *Pittfburgh* and back: and fuch as are ordered to unload at any of the other Pofts, their Surplus of Forage will be purchafed for the King's Ufe.

Each Waggon to be fitted in the following Manner, VIZ. With four good ftrong Horfes, properly harneffed: the Waggon to be complete in every Thing, large and ftrong; having a Drag Chain, eleven Feet in Length, with a Hook at each End, a Knife for cutting Crafs, Falling Axe and Shovel, two Setts of Clouts, and five Setts of Nails, an Iron Hoop to the End of every Axle-tree, a Linen Mangoe, a two Gallon Keg of Tar and Oil mixed together, a Slip Bell, Hopples, two Setts of Shoes, and four setts of Shoe Nails for each Horfe, eight Setts of Spare Hames, and five Setts of Hameftrings, a Bag to receive their Provifions, a fpare Sett of Linch Pins, and a Handfcrew for every three Waggons. The Drivers to be able bodied Men, capable of loading and unloading, and of affifting each other, in cafe of Accidents.

The order dated from Brigadier General Stanwix's time.
Underneath it was pinned an old certificate of the finding of a court-martial, signed—

SIMEON ECUYER, CAPT., R.A.R.

He stopped for a moment and bowed his head before that finger-smeared document. How was it that a mere piece of paper could continue to exist—while the captain . . . ? Oh, where, oh, where was he? Presently his vision cleared, and he resumed reading . . .

TAKE NOTICE
Run away, Abſconded, or Impreſſed

HERCULES

〖Black valet, cook, and proven property
of
Monſieur de Molyneaux of Martinique〗

---

5 ft. 9 in., Large, Muſcular, coal black, ſpeaks
French but ſmall Engliſh; *neat*, plays the
noſe flute.

When laſt ſeen, near Lancaſter, wore a decent
blue fuſtian coat, a fine cambric ſhirt, good
black ſilk breeches, red worſted ſtockings, ſtout
Copenhagen boots, one ſilver earring, and his
maſter's gold watch.

An exceeding valuable, nimble and well trained
gentleman's ſervant. Bears good repute. May
have been loſt, ſpirited, or wrongfully impreſſed
by the military.

Civil Magiſtrates Take Notice:

 £5 ſt'r'ling *REWARD*
And All Fees in Gold

Paid without let hinderance or queſtion to whomſoever ſhall
deliver the perſon of the ſaid man Hercules to his maſter intact
at the London Coffee Houſe in the City of Philadelphia or ſupply
information leading to his apprehenſion and return to the ſervice
of M. Henri de Molyneaux, who, intending ſhortly for St. Pierre,
hath left full inſtructions with his factors to attain and fulfill the
above notice and ſo to offer until further notice.

Apply at the London Coffee Houſe
Philadelphia, Pennſylvania

Nota bene:

Overtakers of the ſaid Hercules will be well
adviſed to proceed circumſpectly in apprehend-
ing him and to ponder upon his name, he being
marvelous luſty and cunning. (Anſwers to
N'Benaithy in the African tongue.

B. Franklin, pinx

Salathiel read this notice through twice and smiled to himself. The sad loss of Monsieur de Molyneaux seemed trivial in view of the contents of some of the other notices. This business of keeping slaves, too—there was something unchristian about it, a lazy fancy, he thought. At any rate, he would catch up with the bully who had lashed Jed. A fine lout, no doubt . . .

The rest of the wall was covered with rewards, and pathetic appeals in script, attempts to get news of or some word to those captured by the Indians. Hope, tragedy, and despair fluttered on the wainscoting, fading, being blown away and trampled underfoot.

And here was the latest printed list, evidently quite a recent one—

LIST of the Indian Captives Being Returned to
Carliſle by Brigadier General Bouquet—

the unclaimed ones, the homeless, over two hundred.

He stood pondering this list of names long and carefully. He checked it against the roll that sang itself in his own mind. Yes, *most* of them were there, but *some* were absent. There might be several reasons for that. But it would do no harm to recite those lost names again to the brigadier. It might mean the salvation of some poor soul, some "adopted" victim. By God, he *would* see the general. He'd sing him a pretty tune, even if he had to stand in front of his tent before reveille. And what had McArdle done about it? he wondered.

Just then a mass of wagoners rushed out of the commissary bureau, pursued by the admonitory roars of Mr. Byers; snapping their whips joyfully—hired! Jed cowered on the outside steps as they passed. The unchosen also departed, but sullenly. Silence resumed its reign unharassed by Mr. Byers.

Salathiel strolled into the commissioner's office and sat down. The gentleman was stuffing a lot of papers into a handle-box, evidently preparing to leave.

"Well, sir, what the devil can I do for you?" said Mr. Byers, looking up at last. He then saw fit to clear his throat respectfully. His visitor rubbed a bit of charcoal off his chin.

"Mr. Byers, can you remember names?" asked Salathiel.

"B'God, I'm ravished in my vargin sleep by 'em," rumbled the commissioner. "Come midnight, a fish-tailed St. Cecilia sits by my pillow and treacles my ears with the dulcet Dutch cognomens of half the blasted wagoners in German Pennsylvania. *Arbeleist, Bendendorp, Reinhold, Hogendorper, Weisenkrantz, Schimmelpfennig* —the damned burly ruffians, never a decent English syllable or native virtue in the lousy lot. God save the mark, his Majesty, and me!"

"Amen to all that," added Salathiel. "But did ye ever hear of one Campion Honeywell"—he drew Mrs. Larned's letter from his pouch and looked at it—"said to live in the square here at Carlisle?"

"On the *square,* and on the *level,* I never did," mused Mr. Byers, looking at his visitor meaningly. Salathiel gave him the sign.

Mr. Byers replied by producing a jug.

"Are ye one of Buckey's new Virginia rifles?" he inquired, after his turn at swallowing.

"Nope, I jist range the woods private with Captain Jack, doin' what good I kin in leafy places."

"Oh!" said Byers, looking a bit startled, "of *that* doughty brotherhood, eh? Maybe you carry a twin rifle-gun, brother?"

"Happen sometimes I do."

They both laughed.

"Now, that's curious odds," continued Byers. "The Reverend Mr. Craighead was talkin' about you and Captain Jack only last night. Better let me see that letter, I guess," he added, reaching out over the table.

Salathiel handed it to him.

Mr. Byers read Mrs. Larned's letter through, grunting from time to time. "Seems maybe the old lady got some of her Boston names confused in this," he remarked finally. "I know of no Honeywells at Carlisle. But, tell ye what, the rider that carried that letter to Lyttleton will know. The old lady must have given it to him. And he's here." Stepping to the door, Mr. Byers roared, "Fergus, Jim Fergus?" in the tones of an irritated lion.

"Presently, sir, presently," replied a pleasant voice.

In another moment a bow-legged little man in a semi-military riding rig came into the room, his spurs clanking. Salathiel recognized him instantly as one of the intrepid express riders who had carried letters between Bouquet and Ecuyer during the siege at Fort Pitt. "The unsung heroes of the frontier," the captain had called them. The recognition was mutual. Fergus nodded pleasantly to Salathiel. "What do ye lack, Mr. Byers?" he said, his eyes twinkling. "Thought I heerd someone depriving a painter of his meat."

Mr. Byers relented. Express riders were privileged people; the survivors among them, few.

"Our big friend here wants to know if ye can recall a certain old widow woman, a Mistress Theodosia Larned from Boston town. Here's the letter she gave you for Patton's some time ago."

Fergus looked at it and the superscription briefly. "Why, sartain, sure," he said, "precious old Yankee grandma with nice bright silver hair. Neat as a new pin. Don't tell me you're bringing her little grand-daughter? She'll be transfigured into Glory at the sight of her. Couldn't talk about nothin' else, poor soul. When I gave her Mr. Patton's reply back from Lyttleton, I thought she'd melt in her own eye-water. Last I talked to her, she was fixin' to go to Manoah Glen's mill at Bilin' Springs in the mill wagon. Not a nook or cranny for her here. It's silver to pewter buttons you'll still find her at Glen's mill. Ye know, I'd clean forgot. Thar's so dang many troubled ones hereabouts keep pesterin' me for letters." For a moment he looked troubled himself. "I'd try to find her today, ifen I was you. Ye kin, ye know, 'tain't far to Bilin' Springs."

"Just drive east past LeTort's old stockade, and take the south wending trace at the first forks," said Byers. "The Springs be about eight miles from there. Ye can't miss the big mill at the ford— and all."

So Mrs. Larned knew they were coming! Still Salathiel hesitated.

Then he decided to tell Mr. Byers about the predicament over having the horses detained, and the probability of Stottelmyer's still being away. He didn't want the stable-boys to raise a hue and cry when he came to take them. "Stop thief"—it might be awkward. He explained at some length.

"Don't let that deter ye," said Byers. "The stable-boys don't own the nags. And I judge you be entitled to 'em until Stottelmyer returns. If they make any trouble out at the stables for ye, tell 'em *I* said the province has hired 'em. I'll put the two wagon teams on the special emergency roll. No use splittin' hairs about it now. 'Tis an errand of marcy you're on."

"That's mighty damn civil of ye," replied Salathiel.

" 'Tain't much," replied Byers, carried away by his own generosity. "Stottelmyer'll probably be back in town with Bouquet in a few days' time at most. Jim here just rid in with the dispatches. They've marched from Fort Pitt."

"Might be pulling out of Bedford now," added Fergus.

"You don't say!" exclaimed Albine. "Now, *that* is news!"

Mr. Byers looked embarrassed. "So it is," he said. "And it kind o' slipped out, you see. I'll have to ask you to put the seal on it. If it gets out too soon, the confusion here will be thrice confounded. There's nigh three hundred strangers waitin' to claim their kin. And crowds of other gentry, none so savoury. Do you see?"

"I'll button my gab tight, my word on it," Salathiel assured him "Now thank ye ever so kindly, and give my regards to Mr. Craighead too. Tell him I'm nigh, and I'll be returnin' his wig directly. I found it hangin' on a pear tree."

"Now did ye?" guffawed Byers, slapping his breeches. "That'll pleasure him. His temper's as bald as his pate at losin' it. Come over and see us when ye kin. It's the small stone house, third down the west walk on the square—have another?"

"No, thanks," answered Salathiel. "I've got sober work to do. Happen ye hear war-whoops up at Stottelmyer's stable, don't turn out the garrison." He winked, and they shook hands cordially.

"Whoop away! I'll just hold my hand on my hair if I hear ye," said Mr. Byers. "All right, Jim. Thanks."

They went out together while Mr. Byers returned to packing up his papers.

"Here's a little somethin' I maunt tell ye," said Fergus, as they walked out. "Thar's an old Injun and his family sort of lurkin' fertive like on Yellow Breeches Creek nigh the Glens' mill. Doctor Scarlet they call him. He's an old yarb gatherer. Digs mandrakes and sich for the Chinee trade. Harmless. One of the convarted. Thought I'd jist mention him. The magistrates are all in a tither since the Lancaster jail massacre, you know. And poor old Doctor John was took off here not so long ago with horrid consequences. So I'd jist say 'how-how', ifen you meet Doctor Scarlet out diggin' 'sang, or buy a little rattlesnake ile off him for old sake's sake, like. It'll make smoother rubbin' fer ye here, ifen you do." Fergus looked quizzically at Salathiel.

"Makeum heap good medicine," promised Salathiel. "And if anything happens to Doctor Scarlet, don't blame me. I'm not warrin' on the Moravian convarts. All my scalps are lifted clean and honest, west of the proclamation line."

"Sure, sure," said Fergus, "I was jist talkin' in case. Say, do ye ever wrestle like ye used to at Fort Pitt? I seed ye there when ye was dandying the little captain. Guess ye miss him, like we all do, eh?"

"Mighty much, Jim," said Salathiel. "You might ride over and have a snack with us when we git to Glen's mill. Reckon I might stay there if I find the old lady, and the miller could put us up."

"Ye might do much warse," said Fergus. "Shelter's mortal scarce in Carlisle. And you kin be quiet at the mill. I know you woodsmen like to be private. I'll track ye down at the mill shortly. Jist now I've got some dispatches for Colonel Burd over at Lancaster."

"Now, have ye!" said Salathiel. "Maybe, then, you can take this letter from Colonel Chambers to Colonel Burd? When ye git back I'll look for ye at the mill." Jim took the letter, and they shook hands warmly. Salathiel had taken a positive shine to the man.

Now to the work at hand at Stottelmyer's stable. He meant to have the use of the horses. And the sooner he got to Boiling Springs that morning the better.

"Come on, Jed," he called. "We're goin' down to Stottelmyer's stable, and I want ye to pint out the bugger that lashed ye."

"Do gawd, Marse Albine, he's one big ornery Dutch *buckra,* dat feller !"

"No !" drawled Salathiel. "Well, I'm only goin' to play a little mumblity-peg with him. Boys will be boys, ye know."

He patted the axe at his belt. It felt smooth and cold.

Jed's eyes protruded. But he trotted along over the rutted road more confidently, the road leading out into the fields south of the town.

There was nearly a mile of stables and picket lines ahead of them before they would come to Stottelmyer's establishment, a place which Jed had found considerable trouble in reaching the previous night. Paddocks and rough shelters for hundreds of horses, a park for wagons and artillery occupied the fields on both sides of the road. Orderlies were coming and going and exercising officers' mounts. A pack train was being loaded at a log warehouse. Stacks of fodder covered with dingy tarpaulins stretched out like a deserted city of dilapidated tents. For the first time it was brought home fully to Salathiel the extent of the English preparations at Carlisle. Evidently the Great White Father in London had been seriously annoyed by his red children in America.

And what were Pontiac's naked-arsed warriors compared to all this? thought he. Poor painted-faced animals, lurking amid the trees . . .

"Take your bows and arrows and haste into the sunset. Tree-men, flee swiftly. Flit with the shadows at twilight. Mountains of rum, hills of powder, bundles of muskets; wagons, cannons, and horses—the king of the world is upon you. Death has come up out of the ocean-sea. He blows westward on the East Wind. Out of rolling clouds the red volleys thunder; the fire sticks speak. Will you answer them by blowing through the hollow bones of an eagle's wing? Outwhistle the White Thunder Bird? Nay, the old medicine is an empty shriek. The dry voice of a dead prophet crackling. Go tell the prairies the Long Knives are coming. The morning stars move westward. The wagon wheels roll. The fire of the dawn light licks over the mountains. The forests wither. The wild deer flee . . ."

He checked himself suddenly. He had forgotten himself. He was speaking aloud in Shawanee. In the old lost tongue, the chiefs' secret language. He had been answering Nymwha. Well, then, he could still feel like that sometimes. Let be !

A staff officer in gold lace and scarlet flashed by on a black

stallion. Salathiel felt proud. Bouquet had avenged Braddock. He
was bringing back the English captives. Suddenly he felt like shouting, God save the king . . .

They trudged on for another half mile.

"Hyah we be," said Jed. "Dem's Marse Stottel's stables. I done
crep' in an' slep' hyah all alone last night in de big log mow."

Stottelmyer's was the largest freighters' station on the western
communications. There was a great log byre down one side; a stable-
shed for fifty horses on the other. Log sleeping quarters for wagoners lay between them at one end. Idle wagons stood in the "off-pen"
between the two main buildings. There was an armourers' shed; a
saddlery and a small smithy, with a gate between.

Thus the internal square made by the establishment was nicely
fenced off and even made defensible, if need be. Everything was
whitewashed and the stables kept clean. A huge pile of manure was
carefully thatched over. A farm down in Lancaster County grew
more fertile every year on the proceeds of the king's fodder. The
war was making Stottelmyer rich. Two of his convoys were on the
western road continually; two resting and refurbishing between trips.
The crown and the province paid for everything. Manure was produced prodigiously. It was a Pennsylvania Dutchman's dream of
affluence.

The chimney of the bunk shed was smoking away lively enough
as Salathiel and Jed pushed open the small hand-gate between the
saddlery and the smithy and walked into the off-pen between the two
main buildings. There a dozen or so wagons waited their turns to
be called out. But at the moment there was no one in the yard.

"Likely him be dar," said Jed, pointing towards the byre.

Like most Pennsylvania barns, the big building on their left had
a broad projection of the upper story on one side that jutted out
along its entire length like a porch roof. The lower portion was
stone; the upper, log. The log story was crammed full of hay. Along
the lower stone section under the "porch" ran a series of small windows and double doors, the latter all tightly closed. It was to one of
these doors near the end of the building that Jed had pointed.
Salathiel opened it very quietly and peered in.

He had never seen such a tremendous roofed-space before. It ran
from one end of the huge barn to the other, with only a few posts
here and there to hold up the fodder stored on the planks above.
Ordinarily, it would have been a stable for cattle. But with no cows
to keep, and ample horse sheds on the other side of the yard, this
room was the storehouse for the wagon base, floored with slate
flagstones, and clean.

Spare wheels, spare canvas tops, extra poles and crosstrees, ropes and hides; wagon parts of every sort, tools, barrels, and axes, all arranged by kind in blocked heaps and piles, took up at least two-thirds of the room with aisles between. Here and there rough open stairs and ladders ascended through the gloom into the loft above.

At the far end of the place, however, a narrow glazed window ran clear across the end wall near the ceiling, and the lighted floor space under it had been kept relatively clear. There in fact was the office of the establishment, furnished with rude pine desks and tables and several bookkeepers' stools. These were vacant now.

But standing with his back to the light, and leaning over a table, with a quill pen in his hand, an open ledger and stacks of small coins before him, was an elephantine, moon-faced individual. He was arranging coins in various amounts and checking the ledger, diligently. Projecting downward near-by on a ladder from the ceiling were the legs of another man. He was evidently busy shifting something about on the floor of the loft. The silence in the place was all but complete.

Salathiel looked the prospect over carefully, and rapidly elaborated his strategy. The part of the room with the equipment piled in it was comparatively dark; the portion where the two men were working, relatively bright. Doubtless the man at the desk was Stottelmyer's wagonmaster, Hans Schmidt. Salathiel had heard rumours of him at Bedford. His name was a byword. He bore a hard reputation even among wagoners, who were not a gentle folk. Salathiel beckoned to Jed to enter and pointed out to him the man at the desk.

"Dat's de man, dat's him!" whispered Jed, instinctively shrinking back against the wall. "Him got a bull whip two rods long!"

If so, Salathiel couldn't see it.

Perhaps Herr Schmidt had temporarily abandoned the whip for the pen? Nothing else about him, however, appeared to be clerical. He was pumpkin-shaped, with a broad rawhide belt for an equator, and colossal arms. He appeared to rest on a pediment and waddled powerfully. As he stood over the desk, now and then lowering his head and looking up again, it was hard to tell whether it was his moon-shaped visage or the fringed top of his bald head that comprised his countenance, so double-faced was the effect. Nor did it much matter, for both faces conveyed essentially the same vacant, brutal expression; that of a malignant baby.

Obviously, here was a bearlike specimen, one with whom verbal remonstrance would be labour lost. Surprise, terror, and threats were called for; wrestling to be avoided. And it was along these lines that Salathiel decided to proceed.

"Jed," he said in a low tone, "will ye trust me?"

"Yas—yas, sah," mumbled Jed, backing a little closer to the wall.

"All right. Now take hold of yourself. I want ye to walk down there to the other end of the place, show yourself, and tell Schmidt your master sent you to git his horses. Be pert!"

"Gawd! He'll take after me sure t'ing, Marse Albine!"

"Sure he will. But don't let him collar ye."

"Jedu, no!"

"Run *this way*. Run back into the shadows. See? Ye kin dive in and hide amongst the plunder—and then I'll take care of Mr. Schmidt. Ye kin jist lead him on and leave him to me."

But still Jed hesitated. He was ashen-grey and sweating.

"De whip," he muttered. "Him cut dis feller clean in two."

"Not *this* time," said Salathiel. "Try it, Jed! Be a bold boy."

"Yas, sah, baas, I's gwine. I's gwine fer to go"—and with that Jed actually stepped out with a swagger, although his hands clutched convulsively in his sleeves, as he walked down the long room. He threaded the piles of matériel on tiptoe, until he came out into the lighted space and stood before the terrible bald-headed white man bending over the table. Twelve feet away he stopped. He stood there, but he was quite unable to say anything.

Hans Schmidt was finishing his payroll. He was deducting small fines and collecting his rake-offs. And it was a full minute before he looked up. His piggish eyes rested incredulously on the shivering blanket-draped figure before him, and finally focused to a gimlet point of rage. He rose slowly, one hand still on the table.

"Du kleiner schwarze Teufel du!" he shouted. "Vas! Haf I not tolt you I vil haf no black turds mixen mit mein good stable manure here? Raus!"

Jed cleared his throat tremulously, "Baas-man say he want dem same six hawses *now*. And wid new hawness," he added, with a certain impish twist of delight at his own inventive daring.

"Du lieber Himmel! Zo! Der vip haf nicht gelehrnet you. Vell, dis time I pop your gottam eyes out." Schmidt came ponderously from behind the table, his thumbs twisting in an anticipatory rotary motion over his fists.

Jed backed away slowly.

The man followed.

He seized a stool and dashed it at the Negro's head. Jed dodged, and darted back into the shadows, running zigzag like a rabbit between the piles of plunder.

He disappeared.

Herr Schmidt followed breathing heavily, waddling alertly on his square toes with ponderous stealth. He knew he had his victim cornered. He hated niggers with an insane animal animosity, such as a gorilla might feel for a chimpanzee. His lips worked and his eyes wrinkled his fat cheeks as he peered myopically into the shadowy gloom of the piled warehouse, trying to spot his dark fugitive . . .

There he was!—just behind that great pile of tarpaulins. Blut und Tod! Der verschreckende Hund. *Now.* His arms tensed, and he groped forward.

And then his hands fell back to his sides.

Something—something was curiously wrong, and yet vaguely and terrifyingly familiar.

Even in the shadows and twenty feet away, he could see that Jed had turned into something else. Was he being hexed? Nein— Ja! The figure crouching before him *was* an Indian. He was leaning forward with an axe in his hand.

Gott! It was even more terrible than that. It was the worst thing that could possibly happen. It was the wild man from Bedford, who had killed men with a table. He had seen him. He was here! Impossible—true!

The terrible man stood up; towered. Schmidt's breath sucked inward with the sound of an unprimed pump. The axe glinted.

"Murder!"

The man was after him.

"Wa-waw-wa . . . waw!" The shivering scalp halloo of the Shawanee rang in Schmidt's ears and unsocketed his soul.

He was lunging like a bogged elk now. The door, the office door! Lieber Jesu, the door! He tripped over the stool he had thrown at Jed, crashed, and blundered on.

Disemboweled? Nein. Castrated! He rolled with the pain, but he rolled towards the door. He was getting to his feet, still going, when the yell burst out just behind him again. He surged forward, plunging.

The man falling from the ceiling struck him down like a bag of grain. That fool had the advantage of him. He had started running while he was still in the air. The door opened. *Whiff*—the fellow was gone. The door closed. It banged in his very face. The bar fell down.

But he crawled, he still crawled for it. And he was just reaching up to . . . when something whizzed, smacked—and he saw the axe standing in the wood, holding the bar in place.

Trapped!

Life was all—and he was *so* young yet.

He caught his last breath, and puked a little.

"Get up, Schmidty," the voice said. "Get up, you big fat bow-wow, so I can tell yer face from yer behind."

Oh, no, he would never do that. He would just stay on his knees. If there was still any hope, he would make the most of it. He started to crawl slowly on all fours towards his tormentor. The man was standing there with a scalping knife in his hand.

So! He'd often wondered: to be bald and to be scalped. How would it be? Ach, Gott!

He put his head down on the floor, with one hand patting his bald spot, his pudgy fingers spread out over it protectively, feeling the beautiful unspoiled smoothness of it. "Gnädiger Herr," he murmured, "let your august eye-shine rest mercifully upon me, lieber gnädiger Herr."

"I'll knot yer hair fer ye, good and right, if ye don't get up," said Salathiel. "Get up!" he roared. The double-faced effect seriously annoyed him.

Schmidt got his hands on a table-top eventually, and after feeling it tentatively, managed with the assistance of his arms to rise and plant his fat fundament on a stool. He was still too shaken and thoroughly terrified to feel even a twinge of shame or resentment. Never, never under any conceivable circumstances would he ever, ever annoy the terrible man who now sat before him with his arms on the table, looking at him, grinning, with the big knife stuck upright in the wood still teetering back and forth a bit on its point, vibrating with disappointment, as it were.

"Look, Big Little-guts," the man was saying, "you struck Mr. Arthur St. Clair's servant with a whip this morning. Do you know who Mr. St. Clair is? Do you want to spend the rest of your goddam life in the jailhouse?"

"Ja," gasped Schmidt. "Ja wohl!" Under the circumstances, so sheltered and permanent an existence as a whole lifetime in a safe prison, where thieves would not break in to steal nor Indians to scalp and slay—why, it was positively alluring.

But horrors! No—it had been the wrong answer. Himmel!

Of course not, if he'd only known whose nigger he was striking. No, no, never again would he use the whip; never again, without finding out first whose nigger it was. Now he'd had his lesson. He'd remember. And, oh, blessèd thought, he was going to have time to remember.

"And," continued the man, "when *I* sent the coloured boy to fetch the horses this morning, the horses Mr. Stottelmyer lent me, and my own mare, you were going to whip him and keep the teams. And to think that I'm still going to let you live!"

The wonder of this, the sheer gracious restraint of it, was too much for Herr Schmidt even to try to comment upon. He sat there in silent amazement. He trembled and he twitched, one great shaking jelly of abject gratitude.

Salathiel could stand it no longer. Some way or other he must return the quivering oaf before him to some semblance of a man. Already the whole place stank with the sour smell of his cowardice.

"Where's the whisky?" Salathiel demanded.

Unable to get the jug himself, Schmidt pointed it out. It was brought to him, and he drank. He gurgled. He set it down at last, and sat feeling the genial warmth course along his limbs; watching the wavering grey outlines of the world gather themselves together. The pain in his groin was becoming bearable now. His hands stopped twitching of themselves. He could even think, a little . . .

What *could* he do for his benefactor? How could he best serve him? He began to purr in a weak, relieved voice, while he rubbed the bruised spot under his belt—"ach"—that verdammte three-legged stool!

He listened . . . ach, what kindness!

He would be permitted to ready the two teams that had been left with him. But *immediately*, and with new harness. He could groom and saddle the roan mare, tie a bag of oats on each wagon horse with three days' rations, and look after the extra little gelding like his own child, until it was called for.

Was *that* understood?

Ja, all of it, down to the last buckle, precisely. But wasn't there something else he could do? Some special token of his everlasting personal regard?

Salathiel looked at him in amazement. Schmidt really meant it. He seemed scared into permanent gratitude for being left alive.

Well, then, yes, there *was* something. He could give the whip, which he had dared to use on Mr. St. Clair's servant, as a present. He could lay it very gently in the black boy's hands.

"Now, get up and get out, and give your orders. I'll write a letter to Mr. Stottelmyer here while I'm waiting, but I won't wait long."

No indeed. *Bitte,* it would be but a few moments, the mere swish of a mare's tail. Only the pain in Schmidt's groin prevented his bowing. He waddled stiffly to the door and shuffled through it. He looked up gratefully at the sun in heaven, and began with a note of chastened authority to give his orders to the stable-boys in the yard.

Only the whip, his marshal's baton as chief wagoner, stuck in his craw. It was such a *pee-u-tiful* vip. A monstrous black bull's pizzle with an elk-hide lash on it, a silver mounted handle and a wampum beaded thong. *Aber,* it would be best to deliver himself from temptation and give up the whip, for he, Hans Schmidt, was a terrible uncontrolled fellow, dangerous when he was enraged. He called a little more confidently now.

Inside, Salathiel finished his note to Stottelmyer rapidly and sanded it at Herr Schmidt's table. When he looked up Jed was standing before him, just where he had been standing a few moments before. They grinned at each other, man to man. Jed put his hand respectfully over his mouth. His smile *might* perhaps be too wide at the discomfiture of a white man.

"Now get out there," said Salathiel to him. "Get along with ye, and when Schmidty hands ye that whip, don't ye be skeered. Crack it, and drive the four horses back to the wagon in the square. I'm goin' to ride Enna this morning myself. And don't ye call me 'master' any more. See!"

"Yas, sah," replied Jed. He walked confidently to the door. Salathiel watched him.

"That's better," he said.

Lord, he was tired of all this slave business. It made cowards out of everybody, master and man. It was no good. If anybody was going to work for *him,* they'd have to do it the way he had worked for Ecuyer. By God, if they didn't, he'd murder them.

Outside, he heard the yoke bells of the teams begin to chime gaily. A whip cracked. The teams departed.

He walked out and mounted Enna. Schmidt was holding her, but said nothing. "Now keep on lookin' after Mr. Stottelmyer's wagons, and don't fail him no more liken ye did this morning," said Salathiel. Suddenly, as an afterthought, he reached down and crushed the man's hand in his own.

Herr Schmidt stood looking after him and gazing at his puffing fingers. Even that man's friendship was painful. Had he really meant what he said? He thought so. He didn't dare to doubt it. Anyway, next time he wouldn't be so afraid of him, and he'd sure let other people's niggers alone. No more jokes that made the world turn upside down. The *pee-u-tiful* vip was all—it was gone.

Salathiel passed Jed at a gallop on the way back. He noted that Jed was managing the tough horse with the yellow eye. Also he was cracking the new whip. Experimentally, to be sure, but with a rapt look.

As he cantered past the long sheds and loading yards of *Boynton, Wharton & Morgan,* Salathiel rose in his stirrups and let the mare go. It was elegant being back in the saddle again. It was a fine clear day, frosty, but not a cloud in the sky. A perfect morning for finding anybody's grandma. Now that he had the horses back again—five of them! And it was only ten miles to Boiling Springs.

21

The Mill on Yellow Breeches Creek

THE WAGON and the trundler, with the king's arrow on it, fading so rapidly now under the action of time and weather, passed through the east gate of Fort Lowther without question and took the road for Boiling Springs.

With good horses and Jed driving, a hard road, and only ten miles to go, Salathiel assumed that he might shortly arrive at Boiling Springs, following the directions given him by his friend, Jim Fergus, the express rider, only a few hours before. At Boiling Springs he confidently expected to find Mr. Glen, the miller, and Bridget's grandma, to whom the miller had so kindly given shelter. And, since Mr. Glen seemed to be such a hospitable man, perhaps under the special circumstances it might also be possible to persuade him to give the rest of Bridget's "family" at least temporary shelter at the mill. Anyway, that was his plan and hope for the immediate future; and it seemed a reasonable one.

He now felt more than ever how important for many reasons it was to provide Frances with a decent and quiet place to settle down in, even if it were only for a short while. He'd promised St. Clair to wait for at least two months over the business of the Ligonier settlers, and, whether any settlers showed up or not, St. Clair had retained him with hard money. He was bound to tarry until early spring.

But meanwhile, he and Frances must live somewhere in the vicinity of Carlisle. That was the rub. For only one night and a few daylight hours in Carlisle had thoroughly convinced him that there was no lodging to be had in the town for love or money; and that camping in the wagon in the public square, day after day in the midst of winter, was not to be thought of. It would be an even greater hardship than any they had encountered on the journey. Besides, it was high time now to put an end to haphazard wayfaring.

What Frances Melissa needed now, with her child coming on, was—well, it was the shining little house he had promised her and that they had both dreamed about. They needed only a modest roof, but a warm hearth, and privacy—some place in which to try the great experiment of living together. What forest wanderers and cave dwellers they had been! No, the next place, whatever it was, would have to be home. Frances would inevitably consider it so, with a woman's sense of reality, and judge him as her provider accordingly.

That was why he was so anxious about settling down now. He remembered the many small household articles and the cloth she had bought at Somerfield's in anticipation, five pounds' worth! He recalled her longing for pretty things; how her hands were always busy over new clothes, sewing, stitching, embroidering, knitting. It would not do to put off too long the hope that all this implied; it would be worse to disappoint it. The latter might be fatal. It would be like . . . oh, it would be like stopping a young dog from burying a bone by taking it away from him. A pup seldom went back to bone-burying again, if he was balked. It prevented the natural habit, he supposed. When a young dog was sagacious, he gave it up. Maybe young women were like that? Not squaws, of course. But Frances Melissa was no squaw just to do as she was told or to follow him about anywhere. He'd better not keep on disappointing her.

And so he was now fondly anticipating their arrival at Boiling Springs, and having Mr. Glen take them in. What could be better than that? He could picture it all now. His and Frances' kindness to Bridget would receive its just reward for bringing her home. Mrs. Larned would be "in heaven", as Jim Fergus had said. Mr. Glen would be gratified at finding Bridget's family to be such respectable people—Frances in a new bonnet, and all. So they could all settle down for a while together. Anything, a room or two in the mill loft, an old shed—oh, he'd fix it up! He'd make himself invaluable to Mr. Glen . . . If not, he must go back to Shippensburg and hire Rutherford to take them in at old Fort Morris. That might do, but it would not be like Boiling Springs with Bridget's grandma. Boiling Springs was the place. He just knew it. He couldn't bear to think of giving Bridget up. No, Boiling Springs was it! It just had to be.

"Get along, Enna!"

He touched the mare with his heels and beckoned to Jed confidently.

Certainly he couldn't expect Melissa to settle down in a hole in the ground like these refugees, the poor squatters, he now saw camped in the fields in lamentable huts and shebangs all about him.

Their miserable "villages" seemed to line the road all the way down to LeTort's Spring. The wagon was a palace compared to such shacks. It was astonishing to see how flimsy they were. Any Injun could do much better with a few bent sticks and some bark. He was not prepared for such abject dirt and confusion; nor the, to him, intolerable stench. Was it possible white men could be reduced to this?

Yet, except for the main hold of the garrison within the stockade at Fort Lowther, where a reasonable degree of order and sightliness was visible in the regularly aligned streets of the encampment —in the huts, tents, neat barracks, and ordnance shops that lined its interior—his overwhelming impression of Carlisle so far was that of a frantic welter of confusion, a pot boiling over into a seething fire. Once beyond the gate, he had expected to find the open country, the fields at least, quiet and decent. But this! All the more reason, then, for pressing on rapidly to Boiling Springs; Boiling Springs in the clean forest, beyond the wall of trees.

Possibly Salathiel was contemplating his arrival at Boiling Springs a mite too rosily. To be sure, "the future blooms out of the past as a rose blossoms from its stem", but then there were some sharp thorns on the stems of the immediate past rooted about Carlisle and Boiling Springs that Salathiel knew nothing about. The ancient saw about gathering thorns with roses did not occur to him. For the time being, then, the wagon went trotting into the rosy future confidently, while some of the thorny aspects of the past were not yet in view . . .

————

Outside the town, beyond the confines of the stockade and the square itself, an animated and blowzy confusion, the effect of a disturbed past that lent at once a battered and devastated aspect to the immediate vicinity of Carlisle, was evident in all directions and for a considerable distance.

What happens to any tract of land, even to a lovely landscape, when many people in great trouble and mortal perplexity moil, trample, and toil over it for many years was as apparent here as the calluses, blisters, and half-healed cuts on an abused and overworked hand—and for much the same reason.

For since nearly a decade past Carlisle had been the much-abused military base, rallying point of forlorn hopes and scared militia, last place of refuge, and scene of warlike preparations by the greatest military power in the world; but for its worst conducted, least successful, and most harassing wars. As a consequence, those itinerant sluts, Defeat, Confusion, and Despair—even Panic—had all picnicked in the pleasant meadows near-by and left their squalid refuse behind them.

It was the country around about rather than the town itself, however, that had most suffered.

The town lay in a gently undulating plateau in the very midst of a cleared circle in the dense forest which had gradually been pushed back on all sides to an average but irregular distance of some three or four miles. Hence, no matter in what direction you looked, from any edifice within the town itself, the dark wall of the encircling trees was still visible at the end of every vista. Only a comparatively brief moat of cleared fields lay between.

Into this open circle of bushy half-cleared meadows, in many parts of which the stumps of forest trees still dismally remained, the life-giving arteries of the place, the roads of the military frontier, converged from several directions, red and rocky streaks, cut like the prisms of veritable land-canals, and by incredible labour, through the all but invincible barrier of the primeval woods.

There was *the* main artery, the principal source of connection with the eastern seaboard, the road that led northward to the islanded ford over the Susquehanna below Harris's, thus tapping the highway to Lancaster and Philadelphia. There was the old southern road to York and Maryland; and there was the new, the all-important "Great Western" road over the mountains to Fort Pitt and the Ohio country. All these land-canals converged at Carlisle, the stomach and the heart of the frontier, for it was both; and along them sailed like so many fleets of barges, the white-topped convoys of Conestoga wagons, or "stogies", those "ships of the wilderness", that seemed to have been providentially elaborated to surmount the waves of the mountains and later on to cross the grassy seas of the prairies themselves.

In the centre, then, of a "lake" or open space in the forest, the village of Carlisle had grown gradually and fitfully about its well-planned and ever-hopeful public square, a common laid out by the colony's surveyors in the peaceful tradition of William Penn. But in '64 a large part of the square was temporarily pre-empted and intruded upon by the loopholed stockade of Fort Lowther, an ugly symbol of the grim troubles of the times.

But it was much more than a symbol. It was the actual storehouse and arsenal of lethal energy, the prime frontier base for a military power, which, under the genius of Bouquet, was now at last manifesting itself abundantly, and for the nonce intelligently, from

Carlisle to the DeTroit. And the fort, the town, and the extensive camps and "deposits" in the country around were vibrantly and hopefully alive.

It had not always been like that, however.

Again and again, Carlisle and its entire vicinity had swarmed and thronged; positively undulated with the high tides of desperate military efforts and the reflex ebullitions of civil despair, during numerous expeditions and defeats. Now the place was in a preliminary spasm of readjustment and rejoicing, a hectic period of bitter regrets and fond anticipations that so often follows closely the end of a long and only finally successful war.

Bouquet's great and unexpected victory at Bushy Run of the year before and his final subduing of the tribes on the distant Muskingum were an inexpressible relief to the long-suffering inhabitants at the base of operations. The intoxication of victory was, to them, something new.

For ten years past there had been few extremities of terror and misery which the patient but determined permanent settlers about Carlisle had not had to endure. Yet in the midst of continual flux and counterflux they had persisted admirably. Some of them indeed had attained, even at the very centre of lamentation and confusion, to a certain degree of affluence and the sordid reputation of being able to wring excess profits from the clammy hands of Defeat herself. But this canny trait was undoubtedly more grumbled about than the facts warranted.

The majority of honest folk and hard-working artisans of the place—if a contemporary military chronicler of their virtues is to be believed—were sustained in their hope of a peaceful future by a prophetic quality of stillness in the countryside, one that needed only a brief piping time of peace to dance with fertility—we are assured—and "by those Monuments of Eternity itself, the Blue Mountains of the western distances," which, according to the local bard, "contemplated, over the shoulders of the horizon, with a constant equanimity, the modest navel in the belly of the forest that constituted Carlisle."

That, of course, is a questionable bit of tompeepery, and no way for respectable Monuments of Antiquity to carry on. Yet that, and nothing less than that, according to the rhymed and faintly amorous diary of Lieutenant Eustace Pomeroy of the Pennsylvania Light Infantry, was what *he* caught the mountains about Carlisle doing on the morning of November 8, 1764—and the evidence of a light infantryman is not necessarily lightly to be set aside. His verisimilitude may, in all conscience, have been less irregular than his verse or the manœuvres of the quite irregular unit in which he served.

But conceding that Lieutenant Pomeroy of the Light Infantry must have had his contemporary moments, then it is all the more the pity that he did not keep his eyes about him in regard to the conduct of the rivers as well as of the mountains near Carlisle. The lieutenant, it seems, was much given to feeding his diarial muse with small scraps of geographical erotica; and yet not a crumb of scandal as to what the Yellow Breeches might have been doing with the Conodoguinit about the same date has been salvaged from the green mould of time.

Yet, undoubtedly, here was a spritely confidence ready for his diary that our military poet missed. For the rivers about Carlisle are as provocative as the mountains, and both the Yellow Breeches and the Conodoguinit are fast little streams. They play around with each other a good deal without ever quite deciding to come together, kept apart perhaps by a prudish lie of the land. And yet they take every opportunity to fall. Now, surely here was a pastoral situation, just the kind of prankish aquatic flirtation going on in the landscape before him, which the classical pen of a Pomeroy might then have so fashionably limned.

But not a whisper of all this got set down in our poet's couplets, not even an innocent aside in his commonplace-book. Perhaps the lieutenant was promoted—many a martial song bird has thus been inadvertently translated to higher things. Or he was evacuated too soon—inspiration is so often like that. At any rate, only the mountains, those blue mementoes of the brief frolic in eternity, observed by the lieutenant on November the 8th, got told on.

For more prosaic yet equally pungent news about the rivers in the vicinity of Carlisle, we must turn elsewhere:

> Very early [says an old historian] the country about Carlisle and LeTort's Springs was penetrated by unauthorized but observant and self-seeking persons. Unknown to the Proprietary, and careless of any interest but their own, they soon pre-empted most of the more desirable mill sites along the Yellow Breeches and the Conodoguinit branches and disposed of the Indian families, hitherto resident in the vicinity, by methods more salutary than those originally advocated by William Penn.

> Once in firm possession, they flourished both by diligence and ingenuity. The hitherto friendly and sportive little rivers found the virgin transports of their headlong currents restrained. And the wild nymphs of the heady springs of the district were soon, for the most part, tamely

and domestically occupied in the turning over of mill wheels for their several petty tyrants.

These millers had been accompanied in their settlement, and in some cases preceded in it, by sundry farmers proficient in the growing of grain. And a certain clergyman of the Church of England, sent out by the Society for the Propagation of the Gospel to reside at Lancaster, having recently imported a new kind of seed wheat from Smyrna, the results were unusually gratifying. The output of fine wheaten flour from that portion of Cumberland [County] augmented annually, and a hundred small, and some quite considerable plantations and clearings along the banks of the rivers, each provided with a busy grist mill, proclaimed alike the fertility of the soil and the unauthorized prosperity of the inhabitants.

It was about this time, *circa* 1750, that the Proprietary Family, finding their just interests set at naught or openly flouted, instructed the provincial surveyors and local magistrates to observe more zealously the reservation of desirable parcels of land for the Penn interests; and caused to be laid out their Manor of Springetsbury and the town plat of Carlisle.*

However that may be, whether the "nymphs of the heady springs of the district," and the proprietary family too, had been outraged or not, certain it is that the numerous rivers and creeks about Carlisle had long been the scene of much milling activity, and that along the course of the Conodoguinit and the Yellow Breeches, in particular, many a snug enterprise had taken root and prospered, each in its own small hole-in-the-woods. And quite frequently a small settlement would begin to cluster about a grist-mill as the market centre of the adjacent wheat farms and the network of grass paths and hauling roads involved.

Boiling Springs, then, was a mill in the forest about ten miles southeastward of Carlisle, situate only a furlong away from the spot where the Boiling Springs branch foamed into Yellow Breeches Creek. At this place there was a convenient ford over the creek, and a wagon track rather than a road crossed the little river at this point and ramified into certain forest trails and traces southward. In times of safety the "mill road" had been considerably used as a short cut

* *Historical Collections of Pennsylvania,* General and Local, Sherman Day, Philadelphia, 1833, pp. 265-270. Also letter of Governor Hamilton, April 1, 1751, "to Nicholas Scull, Surveyor General . . . likewise for Mr. Cookson."

to various places, and the ford was well known. As a site for a mill-dam, the Boiling Springs branch was little short of ideal.

The place had been picked out and settled sometime in the late 1740's by an educated and ingenious millwright, one Manoah Glen, said to have come from the valley of the Mohawk, a "Yankee-Yorker", who, whatever else his origins, inherited the sterling characteristics and good sense necessary to charm success out of a waterfall and to improve upon his luck by marrying a "dame of French Protestant gentility full well endowed". This double heritage of gentle Huguenot blood and ingenious aptitude, he passed on to his two sons, John and Martin. Later on, they were pioneers in erecting some of the most successful iron furnaces of the vicinity, and they both engaged largely in lumbering.

But in the autumn of 1764, the original miller, Manoah Glen, had been a widower for seven years. He was beginning to feel his age, and was much troubled at having to live and conduct his numerous affairs alone and in a deserted house. Both his sons were away from home, temporarily it is true, but absent: John, upon business at Conestoga, and Martin, in the Pennsylvania battalion with the redoubtable Bouquet. And, then, this particular autumn was the end of a long period of strain and anxiety for the aging miller.

For some years past it had needed all the stamina that *Glen & Sons* possessed to hang on to the mill and keep the business barely alive at Boiling Springs through harassing rumours of Indian massacres, frequent defeats, and consequent hard times. Over and over again, the three Glens had been forced to see their little settlement by the ford deserted, when the entire village, except for themselves, fled to the convenient protection of the garrison at Carlisle. Finally the blacksmith shop, the ordinary by the ford, a couple of store-dwellings, and all the near-by farms were totally abandoned in the summer of '63, when the dire news of Pontiac's rebellion and the collapse of the frontier posts had been brought to Carlisle by Jim Fergus.

Only the Glens remained behind, clinging to their mill and the fine "mill house" connected with it, where all their mother's French furniture remained. But they clung to both their wheel and their hearth with a courage whose wisdom was hard to assess at the time. All they had was at stake, however, and there was a good deal of property: grain, flour, buildings, and hand-wrought machinery. So they stuck it out, bored loopholes in the upper log story of the mill, kept the dam repaired, the race clear, and the wooden beams and gears of the "grist 'gin" slushed down—and last, and equally carefully, they kept their two young German redemptioners fast locked up at night in the mill.

It was lonely and dangerous, but as far as living went—more than usually comfortable, with plenty of supplies on hand and only their own work to do.

Prophecies and bets as to their approaching end had not been spared them. But their eventual reward for this "piece of foolhardy bravado", as their quondam neighbours had called it, was to be given a contract to grind flour for the garrison by Colonel Bouquet, and to possess their house and mill in peace and quietude.

For they never saw any Indians whatever, except for poor old Doctor Scarlet and his sorry Delaware family, who settled down on the banks of Yellow Breeches Creek near-by to gather ginseng, sing Moravian hymns at twilight, and beg a little corn meal from the mill every Sunday for "the love of God alone".

The wrinkled old "chief", the escort with a covered wagon from the camp, when a run of the mill was necessary for the garrison—these were all the people and only signs of human life the Glens saw for many a long day. It was only an hour's easy ride to Carlisle, but such was the stark terror of the countryside and the deathly silence that had fallen upon it, they might as well have been on a bayou of the lower Mississippi. Nevertheless, they made the best of it. They worked hard, kept watch, and stood their ground.

Thus primeval peace returned to the small hole-in-the-woods by the ford on Yellow Breeches Creek in the midst of war. The Boiling Springs branch rolled musically over the mill-dam, the blind buildings clustering about the mill grew green moss on their shingles, the wary deer once more ventured out of the forest to drink shyly at the deserted ford.

It was towards the end of this epoch of undeclared peace, during the early autumn of '64, when the news from the west was so reassuring and glorious, that John departed to have new iron-work fabricated at Conestoga, and, although he did not say so, to woo him a wife. Martin, the other son, was at that time on the banks of the Muskingum.

So, Manoah Glen was now left to his own devices and certain cherished memories of his once gay young wife.

She, in the perfect silence of the deserted village, broken only by occasional wild snatches of belated bird song, seemed to the aging widower to be invisibly present, like remembered music, in the lonely rooms of his long empty house. He had a growing subliminal impression that she was there. Yet there was nothing disturbing about her unapparent return. In the evening, especially, she simply seemed to be near him again. And from this feeling of her quiet presence he derived merely a familiar comfort and a sense of sweet companionship renewed. Only an unusually plangent note from the falling water of the mill-dam caused him to glance curiously, if not expectantly, into the corner at her dusty harp.

Otherwise, the pleasing monotony of his daily tasks engulfed him. His sons, of course, would come back shortly. That was the understanding. Their father was simply to hold the fort a while longer, until they, and more prosperous times, might return together.

And this he did quite contentedly with the help of his two young German redemptioners. They were not exactly good company, but they did help him about the mill. They also milked a few of the neighbours' abandoned cows that came wandering in, they cooked after a fashion, tended the two wagon horses, loafed, and grumbled together in guttural tones. That was the serene and quiet status of affairs for some time at Boiling Springs, one that suited the mud swallows particularly well. For the mill had remained quiet so long that it finally fooled them. And they began to build nests in the drying blades of its motionless wheel.

But as the days of Indian summer commenced to wane, and there was no harvest with new wheat to grind, Mr. Glen began to be weary of himself; of the constant sound of falling water, and the grave memories of his shadowy wife. He needed certain supplies, snuff in particular, and above all he longed for a word with his vanished neighbours and news of the doubtful progress of the war.

And that was why, one day at the very end of October, he hitched up the big blue mill wagon and, taking both the bound boys with him, set out for Carlisle.

22

Manoah Glen Drives Over to Carlisle

IT WAS A SCARLET and golden day. The tree-lined road wound through a canyon of blazing autumn colours, and the leaves drifted down singly from half-denuded branches, seeming to coast along the yellow shafts of sunlight that illuminated the forest floor. A few crows cawed through the echoing woodlands. There was no breeze, and it was quite warm. Mr. Glen drove leisurely. Karl and Johann, the two German boys, sat looking backward over the tail-gate behind, one of them playing a jew's-harp. Its monotonous melodic *thrumming* conveyed perfectly the sense of subdued contentment and mild lyric satisfaction that they all felt at going to town in such glorious fall weather.

At a ford over a small stream a couple of miles from the mill, Mr. Glen had Karl lead the team over the water. It was a nasty place. There was an abrupt gravel bank, and only recently a bolt of lightning had stripped the bark from a giant sycamore that stood on the south side of the ford. Horses reared up and carried on here. One of the flour wagons from the fort had been overturned and lay, wheels up, but bogged down in the water.

Mr. Glen didn't know it, but it was only when horses were coming *towards* the mill that they reared up and carried on. He took no chances, however. The place bore a sinister reputation. Several farmers he knew had been thrown and injured. So he had Karl lead the team over the water, with a firm hand on the bridles.

Both Karl and his companion, Johann Krautze, agreed with Mr. Glen. They knew for certain the little ford in the forest was "hexed". Even the English knew that. Jenny Greentooth, the wrinkled old barmaid, who used to live at the ordinary at Boiling Springs, had told them so. And she was an old wise-woman with an evil cross-eyed squint. The south bank of the stream was still covered for yards about with white lightning splinters from the thunder-smitten tree—and the smallest chip was an omen of bad luck that could sour cream or curdle a strong man's blood. The jew's-harp stopped twanging, and both boys shivered as they crossed the leaping water.

As they drove on down the road, Johann, looking out of the rear of the wagon, suddenly saw what it was that made horses go crazy. And no wonder! It was the great sprawling lightning blaze on the bark of the thunder-tree. It looked, in the shadows and sunlight shimmering through the trees—it looked like a ferocious white monster; a griffin; a ghastly hell cat? Du lieber Gott, it was an unholy vampire about to pounce! Johann pointed it out to Karl, as they sat tight-lipped and silent together.

The devil had left the mark of evil at the ford.

Ten minutes later they abruptly emerged from the wall of the forest and looked out across a haze of yellow dust that covered the cleared meadows, to the distant jagged roof-line of Carlisle.

In the middle distance, at LeTort's Springs, was a large military camp. White-topped wagons crawled across the vista along the streaks of dusty roads. Smoke from many fires curled leisurely upward. Over the distant town hung a dusty haze of activity. Lord, it was good to be out of the woods and into the cleared fields again! The German boys started to sing shyly, the jew's-harp twanged away again, and Mr. Glen smiled.

It was between three and four miles from the place where they had emerged from the woods to the outskirts of Carlisle. As Mr. Glen drove slowly along over the red-clay road, with the hovels and thatched "miseries" of refugees growing ever more numerous in the fields on either side, the miller felt inclined to congratulate himself that he had had both the bowels and the good sense to remain living at the mill.

He had not been to town for nearly a year now, and the sight of such pitiful crowding, the squalor and slovenly confusion, was shockingly unexpected and profoundly disturbing to his decent and sensitive mind. It was the kind of existence his father had left London to avoid!

As he drove on, his impression of unease gradually grew in intensity. Eventually it confounded him with surprise and a certain unexpected indignation. After his undisturbed sojourn in the quiet mill house by the ford, rude noises, so many blatant people, and the numerous wagons converging on the town dazed him.

At LeTort's Springs, a mile or two outside of Carlisle, the first complete sample of what the town itself might be like burst upon him.

The muddy crossroads by the camp near the LeTort Springs bridge splashed and churned with noisy traffic. He and the wagon were both thoroughly spattered, and he got tangled with a convoy amid a maze of hucksters' wagons. As for LeTort's itself! Why, he remembered it when it was a serene old place; when the ruined stockade and blockhouse of James LeTort, the first Huguenot fur trader, was covered with coral-red trumpet vines and his friends, the LeTorts, lived next door in their fine new mansion close by the spring itself. But now?—Lord! The whole place was a hang-shutter tenement, a swarming hovel that literally stank—a hive of ragged indigents. Nevertheless, he clambered down to scrape the mud from his person and, if possible, to buy a packet of snuff at one of the many booths.

Almost at once he was surrounded by a crowd of muddy urchins, and solicited, furtively but brazenly, by two young drabs in linsey-woolsey. Both of them, he felt sure, must be runaway redemptioners. He became helplessly indignant, for there was no way to shake them off.

Their nubile and smutted charms left his widower's pulse unfluttered, but their misery and abject begging eventually touched his heart. Finally, he consented to let them climb into the wagon with the two bound boys for a ride to Carlisle, where they claimed to have relatives. "Uncles," they said.

What had become of the LeTort family, he wondered, as he drove off. There was old Madam Anne and her musical daughter Felice. Gentle folk, gone where? He shook his head doubtfully. Of course there had been no snuff. Only rumours of the "gineral's" success and impending return were uncommon plentiful—and good. Well, that was one comfort. The war news was much better than he had expected.

Still, the rest of the way to Carlisle was for Mr. Glen a mile or two of nightmare—although he had never dreamed of anything approaching what he now saw—people, people of all kinds, innumerable wagons, noise, curses, and compounded confusion! Folks from all over America seemed to be foregathering at Carlisle. And in that observation Mr. Glen was correct.

Not many of the frontier refugees had as yet ventured to return to their abandoned farms. Their exodus was just beginning. But the ranks of those who had departed were rapidly being replaced and augmented by other strangers of diverse kinds. They were now pouring into the town from all over the colonies, and for the most various reasons besides the ostensible one of awaiting the arrival of Bouquet and his more recently released captives.

Besides, captives rescued earlier had already been sent down-

country from Fort Pitt and were still encamped in the neighbourhood. The rest were confidently expected, especially those being
released by the Shawanees. Nor was this all, for many others besides
the captivated had been sent back to Carlisle in the summer of '64.
All the matrons, laundresses, sutlers' wives, officers' servants, and
various petty traders and camp followers, those who had followed
the army over the mountains during the months after Bushy Run,
had rigorously been returned to Carlisle from Pittsburgh and all
the intermediate road stations. Bouquet would tolerate no needless
mouths or "fancy persons" on his final advance down the Ohio. He
had issued strict orders. He had swept them, one and all, back to the
base—and no nonsense about it!

These non-combatants in themselves, their hangers-on and de-
pendents, constituted a small "multitude". But they were as nothing
in either numbers or variety compared to the multiplicity of various
other strangers, whom Mr. Glen noticed as he edged his team forward in a press of farm wagons, two-wheeled carts, and stray Conestogas, all indignantly jammed together at the narrow east entrance
to the town. Just at that point a man with two young dancing bears
was giving a performance on a bit of greensward under the southeast
rifle tower. It was precisely where the road narrowed into High
Street and passed on between the stockade wall and the opposite
houses, in a narrow defile that led to the square.

"Ho, ho-haw, ho, ha," grunted the bear-master hoarsely. His
bears ambled and shuffled, now and then standing up, their jaws
slavering in the unseasonable heat. When the cubs sat down to pant,
the man belaboured them with a cudgel. Occasionally they whined
and tried to break away. Frantic horses reared and snorted. The
long line of wagons closing in towards the main entrance to the town
was effectually held up. It was a strategic stance that had thus been
chosen. And the bear-master, a bearded hulk of a fellow in filthy
buckskins, whom few cared to trouble, knew it. He would not budge
until a satisfactory toll was collected. Yet there were few German
wagoners who cared to contribute, even to their own release.

"Ho, ho-haw, ho, ha"—the bizarre dance continued. Whips and
voices cracked impotently. A torrent of oaths and lurid language
mixed with the haze of rising dust at the narrow corner. But no
shillings were forthcoming—and the show went on, while the bears
growled.

Helpless for the moment, Mr. Glen looked about him, waiting
with everybody for someone else to give the metallic password.

Before the east gate of the fort stretched a level tract of greensward hedged-in by extensive lines of abandoned grass-covered entrenchments dug in a time of panic ten years before. Through this

pleasant green ran the old road to LeTort Springs, now used only for an exit. In the course of time the whole entrenched approach before the east face of the fort had gradually taken on the aspect of a small park. Marked by the regular lines of the old entrenchments, it presented an artificial, sequestered, and formal aspect.

Here it was that the better and the more select, certainly the more pretentious people and personages of the town and garrison came to promenade and take the air—in the summer in the evening, after the heat of the day—and in the autumn in the morning, before the hour of the midday meal.

Winnowed out by the guard at the gate according to the understood customs of the time and place, and by the strict standing orders of the commandant, *not everybody* might breathe the air in the "Artillery Walk"; only those who dressed well and were socially entitled to escape from the unclassified rout and common mingling in the public square at the opposite side of the fort were admitted to the lawny precincts of the king's artillery garden. Under the twinkling bayonets of the royal sentries high on the stockade platform, here in this green forum of adjudicated rank—gentility, wealth and distinction, sensibility and fashion itself, made a point of daily renewing its cherished conviction that elegance existed even at Carlisle, and of proving it.

Now, it was about eleven o'clock that morning when Mr. Glen was held up by the bears. The entrance to High Street was along the lower boundary of the east gate plot, and he could look right over the crest of the old entrenchment into the artillery garden. Possibly two score couples, and half as many beaux and bachelors, were walking up and down. Several clergymen in decent black and even a few Joseph-coated macaronis were present.

The royal officers from the garrison with their wives; foreign officers from the Royal Americans with their housekeepers and mistresses; officers of the Pennsylvania line and their ladies of various degrees; rich and well-dressed merchants, a few trim-suited Quakers among them; some of the local landholders and gentry, three or four magistrates, and five or six well-known lawyers, all with their well-gowned ladies in hoops and bustles, shawls, reticules, kerchiefs, and big hats—strolled up and down, turned, stopped, bowed, curtsied, removed hats while white wigs shone, exchanged snuff, gossiped, and pleasantried with an air of gay decorum.

Someone, Mr. Glen could not see who, had brought a sedan chair from Philadelphia. It was carried by four Negro lackeys dressed in blue livery, and reposed now by a neat pyramid of piled round-shot not far from the sallyport. There was a couple seated in it—some great oneyers—possibly one of the governor's council, an

Indian commissioner with his lady, or a great city merchant and his dame. At any rate, the chair was the cynosure of genteel attention, and its occupants were, in effect, holding court.

There was an obsequious crowd that continually changed about the sedan chair. Everyone who came out of the gate hastened to approach it, bowed, was introduced; bowed again, and passed on. The commandant and his wife stood next to it, talking. A thin young man, in bottle-green pantaloons, high-heeled red shoes, puce-coloured satin coat, laced-in until he somehow resembled a frog, hopped about in attendance, with the most minuscule of all three-cornered hats under his left arm. A large Chinese fan, his own or the lady's in the chair, continually fluttered in his right hand. It was he who was the dandy master of ceremonies and the favourite channel for formal introductions. The other macaronis present merely basked in his reflected sunshine. But they also chattered, twirled infinitely slender Malacca canes, looked at their eyebrows and patches in small hand-glasses, and flew about gallanting everybody, like so many male midges dancing in a cloud of perfumed snuff.

It was this dainty group about the chair that especially attracted attention. It seemed wonderful that with the rough log stockade for a background it could dare to exist. But there it was—gay, fragile, and very much alive.

To Mr. Glen, at least, the fashionable agitation about the sedan chair, the chatter and goings-on of the several couples in the park, were of much greater interest and respectable concern than the rude shuffling of the two adolescent bears and the coarse shouts of their savage keeper. In fact, from where he sat, he could no longer see the bears over the tops of the other wagons now wedged in so hopelessly at the street corner. Also, he had no doubt but that exhaustion, indignation, or extorted generosity would eventually break the ursine blockade.

Meanwhile, the human bear garden in the park was undoubtedly more instructive, even if somewhat disconcerting, for he found that he himself recognized many of the people who were putting on the select show on the green. With several he did business, and with others he was friends. It was the size of the rout and the presence of so many strangers, not all fashionable ones, that surprised him and gave him a hint of what a sad levelling of barriers was going on in the town itself.

Indeed, to his old-fashioned and certainly conservative notions, there were quite a few promenading that morning who, to *his* mind, had small reason for being admitted to the walk at all—and this applied more specifically, he thought, to many of the females.

Certainly the taste of the royal staff officers was flamboyant, and the dress of their female companions, exotic. Rouge, ribbons, and feathers! Maybe that was the way fine ladies in the colonies dressed now? But it reminded him of the London trollops and doxies who . . . Well, it reminded him. And some of the females with the Pennsylvania provincials were obviously not of the best provincial families. As for the many bachelors in mercantile rigs, doubtless they were minor merchants, the jobbers, contractors, ambitious clerking catchpennies and leeches which the hope of army business had brought to Carlisle. They must indeed have come from "all over". Northern broadcloth mixed with the nankeen of southerners. There was a medley of high boots and plain buckled shoes. Some of the young men in straw hats, without wigs, looked to be scarcely more than aspiring artisans! Mr. Glen sniffed. There was even a Frenchman there, a Creole, he thought. And he was gay as anybody. Good Lord! He sat looking at them, not altogether approvingly. As time passed, he sniffed several times.

Other people in other wagons, however, who also were being forced to observe the antics of their betters, were not confining themselves to quiet sniffs. The German wagoners, in particular, hooted, vented raucous laughter at the macaronis, shouted obscene observations, and insolently roared. These evidences of contempt and disapproval from beyond the slopes of Parnassus, as it were, were at first disregarded by the nymphs and demigods of the Artillery Walk. Or they affected to suppose it was all directed towards the dancing bears. But the din at last became so considerable, so pointed and prolonged, that the Olympians themselves about the sedan chair were finally touched to the quick.

The annoyed gestures of a gold-headed cane and a doeskin glove from the chair itself brought a sergeant of dragoons on the double from the gate.

Mr. Glen now watched the proceedings about the chair with renewed interest. One of the smallest of the gentlemen's extremely small hats was passed rapidly from hand to hand, the doeskin glove itself contributing. The sergeant, then, in his extremely neat black gaiters, strode off, jiggling the little hat, in the direction of the man with the dancing bears. An expectant and grateful silence instantly accompanied him. The line of wagons stood quietly waiting. Evidently the gentry were going to be of some use after all. The *ho ho humphing* at the street corner suddenly ceased.

" 'Ere," said the sergeant, looking down from the top of the old breastworks at the red-faced man and the tired tongue-lolling bears just beneath him, " 'ere's a 'ole bloody 'atful o' swag for you and your un'oly libours. A 'ole bleeding 'atful!" He held up the Lilliputian headpiece for all to see.

The bear-master put his thumb to his nose, but removed it immediately as the sergeant extracted a new shilling from the hat as a fine for the gesture. "An' if *hi* was you, me bahr-biten friend," he continued, "I'd tike them two 'airy pupils back to the kive of their hawncesters and crawl in arter 'em. For Gineral Buckey, ee'll be back hany di now, and 'e 'ites biby bahrs and halligitors and all sich pets like bloody 'ell. Now, be orf!" And with that, the sergeant poured the remaining pennies, pistareens, and picayunes into the bear-master's eager hands.

What the sergeant had said—the news of Buckey's return—flashed down the line of waiting wagons like lightning. Men now handled their reins impatiently again. The bear-master dragged his cubs across the street into a bricked alley, and the pent-up flood of vehicles, suddenly released, streamed headlong, bumping and clattering over the cobbles along the stockaded street amid a torrent of oaths, volleys of whip-cracking, and an infernal squalling of brakes that almost stopped Mr. Glen's old heart. From doorways and upper windows, women screamed frantically to their muddy brats to get out of the gutter, as the whole medley of clanking wagons and scared farmers on rickety high-wheeled carts hurtled forward, and gushed out into the open square.

Two minutes later the good miller, feeling faint and overcome, and with every thought of gentility swept out of his head, sat wiping the sweat of apprehension from his kindly old face, while he looked about him for a place of refuge in which to tie up his team. Every place seemed to be taken.

Finally, he snagged onto a hitching post near the west gate of the stockade which seemed to be providentially vacated, and after resting awhile to settle a bit of nauseous vertigo, he stood up in the wagon to look about him:

Godamighty!

What was the old town coming to? Whatever could the authorities be athinking of? The place had sure got away from them; the common people had broken loose. Look at *it*—just look at *them*! Or, for that matter, listen! The square seethed in blatant sound. Mr. Glen felt dizzy again, and had to sit down for a moment.

"London bridge is falling down—falling down," sang a shrill-voiced young slattern, tripping homeward, with a wooden pailful of beer that slopped over and foamed on her bare feet. She rolled her eyes up at the fat German boys in the wagon and gave the two girls an unpleasant wink, one that managed to cast a wet blanket of contempt on Mr. Glen as she passed by, with a twitch of one muscle in her eyelid. All the young people seemed to be in a conspiracy against him, he felt. Somehow or other the girl with the beer contrived to show a dirty chapped leg almost up to her—neck! Mr. Glen turned away feeling his nausea renewed.

It was *so* safe and private at Boiling Springs. The old mill house there had his wife's furniture, her bed made up under a tester—just as she had left it seven years before—and outside there was the whisper of trees and the music of clear running water—oh, to be at home again!

He wished the two young hussies in the wagon would find their uncles. Maybe he'd been a bit too kind. Anyway, they still sat in the wagon buck-toothed and dirty-faced, simpering at his two bound boys. What could he do with them? He felt too faint to try to make them leave. And the boys, damn them! For a sad moment he wished that he had never come to town.

The weather was so much hotter than he had expected. It was hard at his age for a widower to put up with all this. But pshaw—he had errands to do. He could find shelter overnight with some of his friends. He stood up again, looking across the stir and confusion to see how he could pick his way, and what to do next.

Godamighty!

Over the familiar roofs of the houses on the opposite side of the square, far far away in the blue distance, the rounded tops of the leaping mountains seemed to be peeping down into the town, observing, perhaps, the navel of the public square. Mr. Glen's view of the scene, while not so exalted, was even more intimate, and the effect upon the quiet and orderly mind of the bucolic old widower was disturbing to the last degree. In fact, the surprising concatenation of sights and sounds threatened to overwhelm him. He stood upright again on the wagon seat, but his legs were trembling. Among other things, a perfect hell of a noise was going on. For a minute he could hardly think without closing his eyes.

Wheels rumbled like the sound of a constant ground swell before a storm; this ground-shaking thunder of heavy wagons ceaselessly rolling underlay all else. A welter and babble of talk, loud, offensive and insistent, reverberated from every part of the square. English, Scotch, Irish, German, Dutch, and the harsh Palatinate dialects—Welsh, Flemish, and even a bit of French relentlessly collided and were mutually misunderstood, until people took to shouting at each other furiously in bad English. Yet it was quite plain that this din, to so many frontier people tired of the grim silence of the forest; and the rich confusion, to numerous vagrants from the eastern seaboard, sick of rigid customs, restraint, and orderly dullness—were equally delicious. At any rate, the square sounded delirious. It frolicked as though at the height of a carnival and seemed to be in love with its own novel disorder. It flopped and squawked in careless liberty and with a fearless, unrepentant, devil-may-care air.

From the open windows of boarding-houses and numerous ordinaries came the fused noise of revelry within; voices and the sound of various instruments blended. Fiddles squeaked and curious folk-contrivances of distant European origin and vintage wailed, squalled, and sweetly twanged. Zithers seemed to echo a bell-like melody from steeples in the Valley of Forgotten Dreams. Liquor flowed. Outside the taverns, people danced and sang, while others wept and prayed. No one paid attention to either, and noisy business swept about them all. At the fort drums were beaten and bugles blew from time to time, speaking out clearly from another country beyond the stockade walls as though military order might suddenly debouch from the gate and impose itself forcibly. But so subtle a threat went unheeded. The square rollicked on, happy in its new-found sense of freedom.

Nothing quite like it, and on such a scale, had been seen in the colonies before. It was the aftermath of a long, savage, and continental war; a universal din of release and relief at emerging from the dangerous past. America was assembled, discovering itself, and enjoying it. Something new was being born, and was making a natal noise. Anarchy was in the air. The excuse for the occasion was morally satisfying and exciting. Everybody, in his own opinion, had come to Carlisle to help release the Indian captives, to do a good deed (as profitably as possible); and, incidentally, to celebrate the victorious return of Brigadier Bouquet.

At the moment the square itself was a condominium of everything civil and military. It was a park for ordnance and surplus supplies. Mounted brass cannon and caissons, the heavier guns, that Bouquet had not been able to take with him, and which were not needed now at the frontier forts, since the French had gone, were disposed in reserved plots under guard. There were also piles of solid shot, shells, and new-cast carcasses, spare wagon wheels and axle-trees ready for transport, the product of the new factories at the fort.

Mr. Glen had arrived at a peculiarly crowded moment, at the dizzy height of activity for the day. Two divisions of empty wagons on their way back to Lancaster and Philadelphia and a newly laden convoy bound for Fort Pitt were trying to leave and cross the square at the same time. The place was therefore a maze of slowly moving wagon-tops edging outward, while the right-of-way was being vigorously disputed with German profanity and blacksnake whips. The dust and din were prodigious.

A thief was being drummed out of camp by the garrison, and Mr. Glen was forced to get one of the boys to hold the horses, while to the shrill accompaniment of the rogue's march, the culprit, his guard, and the jeering crowd accompanying them emerged from the west portal of Fort Lowther and swept past. Evidently neither courts-martial nor the civil magistrates were idle.

In the stocks by the jail a couple of wretches with bleeding backs and blood-caked ears sat groaning and enduring as best they might showers of filth hurled by a swarm of ragged youngsters tormenting them.

Here and there along the edges of the public enclosure, in the very shadow of sedate houses, booths and dilapidated marquees had been erected by the numerous quacks, raree showmen, and sellers of sovereign elixirs and "celebrated" nostrums. Here too were barber-chirurgeons with their bowls, a puppet show, card-fortuners, and sundry drawers of teeth. They were all prepared to decamp instantly. Meanwhile, they shouted, rang bells, and pattered a continuous litany of their own applause.

Hard cider, apples, and doughnuts were being sold by ruddy-faced Germans from high-wheeled carts. Hawkers of tobacco, ginger confections, and pretzels; pedlars and tinkers with pewter plates and copper pans; a man with wooden Yankee clocks on his back and a tray of small cutlery and ribbons; all wandered noisily and at will. Free Negroes sang and chanted the merits of hot pepper-pot and fried catfish. A wagon from Baltimore was selling oysters, three a ha'penny, while it dripped stale sea water, and stank.

Bargelike German wagons from Lancaster, painted with sprays of yellow flowers, covered with a half-hood, and swarming with fat farmers' wives and children, sold scrubbed vegetables, poultry, eggs, cheese, and butter from big brown crocks. These vehicles were strung with links of sausage and displayed loaves of rye bread covered with anise seeds, meat pies, and küchen.

There was a long line of these vending carts at the north end of the square, where a temporary free market had been arranged by the authorities, and everybody, from commissioners to officers' servants, came to haggle. Prices were almost as high as the piles of green refuse that released captives, dressed in shabby remnants of Indian finery, constantly picked over for a bit of cabbage stalk, a beet root, or a sprouted potato to make soup.

Under the shadow of the stockade, and as close to the guard by the fort gate as he could get, one Jacob Moïs, a Sephardic Jew money-changer, come all the way from South Carolina, had erected his booth out of empty ammunition crates. He plied a busy trade in the worn paper currencies of various colonies. Or he made small change—and with such a variety of minor coins of foreign origin as only his delicate scales and the professional acumen in the tips of his fingers could evaluate. Jacob would also write letters, if time permitted, and his olive-faced, brown-eyed daughter Rachel would consent to help.

All this, decidedly, was *not* the kind of world Mr. Glen had expected or hoped to live to see. The possibility of personal refuge and decent privacy seemed, to have vanished from it. Rationally or not, he felt surprised, dispirited, cheated of his just expectations, and duly indignant. There were too many people here—too many kinds of people, and all free, unrestrained, absolutely on their own. What could have happened? What was going on? Unconsciously, the scene itself forced these questions upon him. For the moment he was stopped. He could only stand and watch. His sons were away, and how was he going to deal with so many people, and so many people of different kinds?

"Godamighty, God-a-mighty," muttered Mr. Glen, as though only God were left to appeal to . . .

Well, he would have to leave the wagon where it was and pick his way across the square to Mr. Williams's house on the west walk. There he could at least sit on the porch for a while and recollect himself. He had forgotten exactly what it was he had come to town to do. And he would have to pick his way across to the porch carefully. Lord, he hoped the Williamses would be at home. He climbed down slowly by the wheel spokes and told Johann to take charge of the wagon and to wait. He didn't have the energy to get rid of the two girls. It might mean a row and their impudence. He turned—and dizzy with a buzzing confusion, began to grope across the square towards the other side.

It was not easy. It was about the time when most people, not gentry, were going home for the midday meal. Artisans in leather aprons from the ordnance and wagon shops poured out of the fort gate. Officers and non-coms attached to the garrison, militia and regulars, in bright uniforms of bewildering variety, made hastily for their various quarters and ordinaries, and would not stop to be polite. Washerwomen and matrons officially attached to the barracks, who wore blue aprons and half-leather clogs, sporting the buttons of various regiments as ornaments and personal testimonials of their various professional abilities and female accomplishments, clattered back and forth between the banks of Bonny Creek, where their washing was done, and the quarters and barracks, with bundles and baskets of clothes. They made way for no one and had savage tongues.

A smoothing-shed for the officers' linen just to the left inside the fort gate, provided with a half dozen sad-irons and a charcoal stove, was the cause of constant bickering amongst the washerwomen and the scene of frequent hair-pulling encounters over precedence in the waiting-line. Somehow Mr. Glen became involved with these viragoes and was bumped down the line. He emerged into a crowd of hawkers of pies and carriers of cooked dishes, and was nearly run down by a Negro's hay cart.

He was aware now that something terrible had happened to him, that he was ill on the inside of his head. But he struggled on. The sky over the roof-line on the opposite side of the square had unaccountably turned inky black. Underneath, the houses grinned at him like a line of bared white teeth. And yet, there, infinitely remote now, was the sure refuge of Mr. Williams's porch. He could still see it. He blundered on, his feet unaccountably heavy, while he seemed to be burning up.

White children chased scared pickaninnies back to the refuge of their masters' yards. Coloured house servants of prosperous families, in bright turbans, proud of their masters' colours, elbowed aside the miserably dressed and forlorn redemptioners, whom they despised. Pedlars, townsmen, a gang of chained prisoners under guard, hurrying shopkeepers, and leisurely merchants all flowed past him. A loose colt got in his way.

"Godamighty!"

A grey mist seemed to be closing down on the line of houses just ahead. He walked forward blindly. Somehow, somehow or other, he found himself at last staggering up the three white steps onto the Williamses' front porch. He sat down, the flies dimly bothering him . . .

He was sitting in a big chair fanning himself with his hat, and Mrs. Williams was fussing over him and exclaiming. She gave him a good strong drink. Lord! *That* was a relief! He felt better almost immediately. The world cleared. He could fan himself and enjoy now the cool breeze he made that way. It was splendid to be among friends—and the Williamses were always so kind. Old-time neighbours.

He mustn't move, Mrs. Williams said. He must just sit and make himself comfortable. No one had ever seen such hot weather, and November just around the corner. Good lack! It certainly was hard on old people, and he'd better sit still and cool off. Of course, he could stay overnight. Why, Mrs. Williams wouldn't hear of anything else. She sent a young coloured girl with her baby out to watch him, while she went in to air out the side bed-chamber herself.

Mr. Glen, the coloured girl, and the baby, who was sucking its thumb, all sat on the front porch and stared at one another. He did feel better now, more at ease, strangely relaxed. He felt amiable once more . . .

Presently an old friend, someone he hadn't seen for years, came up on the porch and sat with him. It all seemed so perfectly natural. Campion Honeywell—he was down on a visit from Boston town, winding up the matter of a contract for army candles with the quartermaster at Carlisle. And a good thing, too. Campion Honeywell was as direct and incisive in his talk as he had always been. You would scarcely think that they hadn't seen each other for eight years. Why, Campion didn't even know that Mrs. Glen had died. And he'd known Marie so well. They exchanged reminiscences briefly. Honeywell did most of the talking; he managed to convey that he was pretty well off, and both his daughters had married well. Mr. Glen began to complain a little languidly of his widower's loneliness at the mill. The boys were away—and all that. But he didn't feel like talking very much.

But Mr. Honeywell's face lighted with sudden interest. Maybe he could help make things less lonely at the mill, he said. He'd brought a townswoman of his along with him from Boston, it appeared. A competent old lady, poor, but she'd sold her house to get to Carlisle to try to find her captivated grand-daughter. And, in a way, Mr. Honeywell was interested. He'd provided her a passage down, and more important, he'd found her a place in Carlisle for a few days. But he was going back to Boston tomorrow, and he was worried about Mrs. Larned—Mrs. Theodosia Larned—a nice old party, well connected in Boston. But where could she go, what would she do after he left? Could Mr. Glen take her in? Why wouldn't it be a good idea for him to take her back to the mill with him and let her be housekeeper there, while she was waiting for her grand-daughter —and the Glen boys were away. Mrs. Larned was respectable. She would like to earn her keep. Why not?

Mr. Glen thought it over. Not very clearly, to be sure—but carefully. He could see no serious objections and several advantages. And Honeywell was quietly insistent. He had a brisk Yankee way with him when there was something he wanted to get done. Mr. Glen *was* still a bit faint. But, why not? Still, he would like to see Mrs. Larned and talk to her first. He couldn't introduce just anybody into his dead wife's cherished house.

Naturally, of course not!

But Mrs. Larned was staying only four houses away down the street. Mr. Honeywell would go and fetch her. It would be no trouble, no trouble at all.

Mr. Glen was left fanning himself again, while the baby sucked its thumb, seated on the floor before him. The coloured girl had been called in to help Mrs. Williams ready the bed-chamber. No one, least of all Mr. Honeywell, had any idea that the last pinch of sand in the bottleneck of Mr. Glen's hourglass was running out.

Presently, Mr. Honeywell was back again with Mrs. Larned. He also brought Jim Fergus along. Fergus had just delivered Mrs. Larned a letter from Fort Lyttleton, and Mrs. Larned held it in her hand, trembling, almost tearful, with joy. Her face shone with inward delight. Everybody was pleased. It seemed providential that the old lady's grand-daughter had been preserved and that she might soon hold her in her arms.

Mr. Glen became now simply a third party to aid Providence. He liked the old lady. He was even touched by her justified faith and preternatural neatness. While Jim Fergus sat on the steps, and despite Mr. Glen's feeling of exhaustion, he made the final arrangements with Honeywell and gave sensible directions for taking Mrs. Larned home to Boiling Springs.

It was all quite simple. He explained he had had a touch of heat and would have to stay the night at Carlisle. But if Jim would find the wagon, "hitched nigh to the fort gate across the square", the German boys could get Mrs. Larned's luggage and drive her back to the mill with them that evening. They would have to come back for him with the wagon next day. But after a night's rest, he would be feeling much better, he thought; and he could get all his errands done next morning. Meanwhile, Mrs. Larned could be making herself at home. The German boys would show her about the mill house and tell her where the house keys hung. She might keep a little eye on them. Would she? Mr. Glen smiled. The two old people nodded to each other. He liked the way she brushed her bright silver hair back from her forehead. Their understanding was peacefully complete.

Would Jim Fergus please find the German boys and tell them?

"Why, sartin," Jim smiled; and said he'd know now just where to direct the people who'd bring Mrs. Larned's grand-daughter to town. He'd sure remember. "The mill, Glen's mill at Boiling Springs."

Mr. Glen and Mrs. Larned shook hands. With a simple expression of deep gratitude, she departed to pack up the few belongings that she still cherished in this world—for Bridget. The wagon would doubtless call for her soon. Mr. Honeywell said he would see her off.

For a few minutes Mr. Glen was left alone again with the brown baby. The excitement and emotions of the past few moments had been intense. He had admitted a stranger to his house. Too easily perhaps—but he was *so* tired of being alone.

Alone, alone!—he sat pondering. The world seemed to be withdrawing to an indistinct distance. Alone! Why, he'd never felt so completely alone as he did now! He seemed to be sitting in the centre of some vast deserted vacuum, abandoned, left suddenly entirely to himself. It was hard to fill his lungs in this breathless silence. Lord, this was what he had worked all his life to prevent. To die all by himself, and not a soul to bend over him! No one! Where was Marie? Where were the two boys? Where was he? Oh, the everlasting silence! All he could do was see now. The blood whispered in his ears. It made a noise like darkness coming on.

He looked out into the light to the very last.

The Negro baby squatted in a narrowing circle of sunshine before him. It was crying. He could see its face and mouth move. There were ants on its hands, and it was trying to lick them off. That was the way it was. Little things worrying a body. It was terrible, unbearable. Somebody must tell the baby. Why didn't its mother come? He would call for her, cry out . . . *M-o-t-h-e-r* . . . But he had no breath. He struggled for it. He tried hard. The ants were still crawling. Let me out of here! Let me go! Jesus! Enough . . .

Godamighty . . .

Mr. Glen's tired face fell forward and rested on his quiet breast.

23

The Sound of Flowing Water

THE BLUE MILL WAGON and the German boys called for Mrs. Larned and her luggage, a horse-hide trunk and three pitiful bundles, about the same time that Mr. Glen was making his final observations on the irritating characteristics of ants. The two redemptioners, although outwardly respectful, were both inwardly quite sullen. For Jim Fergus, on finding them sparking in the wagon with the two girls in the public square, in a manner which he considered wanton, had withered the budding flower of a double romance with the black frost of his invective. He spoke powerfully and directly. The girls decamped—and the wagon was at Mrs. Larned's door almost before she could get the hairy lid of her scuffed portmanteau closed.

Mr. Honeywell and Jim Fergus saw her off. Jim put an old rush-bottomed slat chair in the wagon for Mrs. Larned to sit on, with admonitions to the boys to return it promptly next morning when they called back for Mr. Glen. And after final instructions to Johann to stop upstreet at Mr. Williams's and get his master's last orders, they waved the old lady a cheerful good-bye and strolled across the square together for a pipe and a nip, with the fellow feeling of a good deed well done, and a charitable account edifyingly closed.

Johann did exactly as he was told. He stopped at the Williamses' door, and while Mrs. Larned and Karl sat waiting in the wagon, he went in to speak to his master, who appeared to be dozing on the front verandah.

The baby had finished satisfactorily with the ants and was now quietly sucking its thumb again. But on approaching his master more closely, Johann stopped in his tracks. Something in Mr. Glen's attitude told him that the good miller was not dozing, not dozing at all.

This was a shock even to the oxlike Johann. But he did not nervously betray himself. He stood stolidly pondering. He could not think quickly, but he was cunning. And it was quite plain, even to him, that here was an opportunity which, if properly utilized, might save him two years' further service and cancel his articles profitably. He stood thinking over the situation carefully, item by item. Then he glanced at the wagon. They were just sitting there, waiting. Ja, py Gott, he would do it! But he would have to be careful; and what was even more difficult, be swift.

Just to make sure, he bent over and spoke his master's name.

But there was no reply. The brown baby removed its thumb and looked up at him.

Before it started to cry, then.

He leaned down as if he were carefully and respectfully listening to instructions from Mr. Glen, and detached his tasselled ring-purse that was wound twice about his leather belt.

Then he backed away a few paces, his face still towards Mr. Glen, and said quite loudly, "Ja wohl, sir, ve vill do it—ve coom back *tomorrow.*"

Mrs. Larned was looking at him as he walked back, but he managed a bit of a swagger, as he climbed onto the wagon. Probably she had heard what he had said. He hoped so. He had never flinched, not even with the dead man behind him. He just climbed up on the seat with Karl and began talking to him softly in voluble German.

The wagon rattled off rapidly in the direction of Boiling Springs, and Mrs. Larned with her bundles gathered about her, seated comfortably in the borrowed kitchen chair, began to enjoy the late-afternoon ride. It would have been helpful if Mr. Glen had come out to speak to her again, she thought. But she knew he was tired, and there would be plenty of time to talk things over with him more fully *tomorrow*—wasn't that what he had said?

The bound boys on the driver's seat continued to converse in German, the louder and more confidently as they left the town behind them. They seemed shortly to have arrived at a satisfactory conclusion about some important matter. Johann finally clapped Karl on the back. Once or twice they looked back at her. Doubtfully, she thought. Perhaps they wondered how she was getting on? But she nodded reassuringly at them. And at that, they looked at each other and laughed.

A half mile or so beyond the fort gate, they stopped to pick up a couple of barefoot girls picking their way along the road towards LeTort's Springs. Evidently the boys knew them. There was some whispered conversation, giggles, a guffaw or two; and then Johann explained in broken English that here were a couple of neighbours' daughters, and he would like to give them a ride back home.

Mrs. Larned had no objections, of course. She was even pleased at having been deferred to. The girls did look unkempt, slatterns, no doubt. But, then, this was Pennsylvania—and the manners of the back-inhabitants were no doubt primitive.

Mrs. Larned rode the rest of the way to Boiling Springs with the German boys on the seat before her and the two girls sitting together, looking out behind. They never even glanced up at her. As twilight came on, she gathered her precious bundles closer about her. The mill must be farther out in the country than she had realized. The drive did seem to be a long one. It was twilight by the time Johann led the horses carefully over the water at the little ford, and black night fell as they trotted on down the road through the forest. Mrs. Larned could see nothing at all. She had no idea now even in what direction she was going. At last they drew up in a starlit open space before a dim building. Karl went in to fetch a lanthorn. They sat waiting. No one spoke.

The first thing she was aware of was the sleepy noise of continually falling water. Insistently, the quiet music of the place began from the very first to sing itself into her ears. It was a peaceful sound, a constant bubbling as though a great domestic kettle were forever boiling away, singing a lullaby to itself of hearth and home. *Boiling Springs—*

Why, this must be Mr. Glen's mill! They were home!

Lights in the windows of the mill house began to shine. An approaching radiance poured out of its open door. Karl came with the lanthorn to lead her in; Johann handled her luggage.

Afterward, when it was too late, she began to think that the behaviour of the two bound boys that evening *was* a bit strange. But at the time it all seemed, as far as she could see, right enough. The only thing that impressed her as being odd was that the boys seemed to be in a terrible hurry about everything Still, they took care to treat her courteously. And who was she to complain or to give directions in Mr. Glen's house? Doubtless, the boys knew exactly what their master wanted. Yet how they did rush about!

Karl gave her the house keys. Johann with her luggage showed her forthwith to what evidently must have been Mrs. Glen's own bedroom. Karl had had to unlock the door for them. It seemed to have been locked and closed for a long time. The key worked with difficulty and the door complained. Had Mr. Glen really wanted her to sleep in his wife's bed-chamber? she inquired.

"Ja, ja," replied Johann emphatically. Mr. Glen himself had told him to take her there. Also to show her where everything was: the buttery, the storeroom, all the kitchen cupboards. She toiled after him.

He unlocked them rapidly for her. Sometimes he took an article out and gave it to Karl. They were loading the wagon out there in the dark. She could hear the girls chattering. "Hurry," one of them kept calling. "For God's sake, you Dutch fools, get a move on!" Yet the other girl came in and kindly built up the fire for her— between running in and out to the wagon, carrying various things.

Mrs. Larned offered to get supper, but the girl told her not to mind. This was the boys' evening off, she explained. They would take both the girls home and spend the evening together. It was bell-snickelin' time. They were in a hurry to get going, "before their off was all".

Mrs. Larned pieced this together as best she could. Well, she would get her own supper, then, after they had gone. She didn't exactly relish being left alone in a strange house. But it was natural, she thought, for the hired help to spend their evening together at the neighbour's. She hoped they wouldn't bundle all night. But probably they would—and what could she do about it?

Nothing indeed—that was quite evident.

The boys continued to load the wagon, probably for going to town tomorrow, she thought. They certainly had a heterogeneous assortment of articles to take back to Mr. Glen. At the last, they put in several bags of flour and horse feed that they carried out of the mill. Ah, probably *that* was it! They were going to barter at early market tomorrow in town. Still, as moonrise came on, she stood in the doorway watching them doubtfully.

Finally, they all clambered into the wagon together and drove off rapidly, without even saying a civil good night to her. They left her standing there in the moonlight, alone and listening to . . . what was it? . . . oh, yes—the sound of flowing water . . .

My gracious though, what was that? Only some little owls? She remembered them at home. They made a melancholy liquid bubbling sound, too. She shivered, drew her shawl closer; and going in, closed the door behind her and locked it.

As she stood watching the slow play of firelight on the walls and low ceiling of the room, and the black shadow down the hall from the single candle left burning in the bed-chamber, she clutched her old hands together in a sudden access of apprehension. The house was so deathly silent. It came upon her that she had been left strangely and fearfully alone.

She stood listening, her heart pausing. In the breathless silence there was nothing; nothing but a faint windy stir from the fire and an occasional crackle from the burning sticks, like a wicked chuckle.

And then, gradually, she became aware of it again. It penetrated the room from the outside. It seemed to saturate the log walls of the place, the mill house and the mill itself with an occasional dripping note from a subterranean harp and a low scarcely audible musical undertone; secret, confidential, soothing . . . the sleepy noise of ever-falling water . . .

She wakened slowly to hear the same music next morning. She scarcely knew where she was at first. She lay awhile like a child with her eyes closed, listening to the harp. It was a bit uncanny. Yet there were liquid runs on it that were positively cheerful. She smiled at her sleepy fancy that she was being welcomed home. The notes slipped one into another, soothing her. She lay for a long while, resting. It had been a long journey. But she had slept *so* soundly, she felt renewed and refreshed.

Also she had slept unconscionably late. It must be—why, to judge by the outside shadows, it must be well after ten o'clock! Good heavenly gracious!

She wondered if Mr. Glen had come back yet. That would put her in a pretty pickle. Her first day as housekeeper—and she a sluggard lie-abed like this. She hadn't slept like that for years. She sat up, listening. Except for some squirrels scampering over the roof, and the water, there wasn't another sound.

Yet it was cheerful in the daytime. The bedroom was cozy, dusty, to be sure, but the sun streamed in through a big window, reflected from the mill-pond. The light on the ceiling rippled. The house felt warm. She got out of bed, said her prayers in gratitude, prepared a bite of breakfast at the hearth, and went calmly to work.

Work, in fact, hard work, was Mrs. Larned's sovereign remedy and prime way of overcoming the difficulties of earthly existence. In her seventy-three years of experience, most of which she could vividly remember, she had seldom found work to fail. She had met reality in some of its more grisly aspects, previously, and was not easily to be fooled into a panic, even by an unexpected quirk of Providence. In short, she was prepared to carry on under almost any circumstances, so long as her body lasted. Nor did she at first regard the absence of the miller and his two bound boys as anything more than an unavoidable delay, one which their return would shortly explain. She simply turned in to make things ready for them. She had long been a widow, and being alone in the house was nothing new to her.

Besides, the house itself was a positive delight. Outside, it was a substantial and ample log structure leaning up against the big stone mill; inside, it had been sealed with smooth chestnut boards, wall and ceiling, and it shone with a smooth grey silver light. Mrs. Glen's old French furniture lent a lightness and grace, even a certain frivolity to the mill house, which was astonishing—to Mrs. Larned, almost immoral—yet pleasant. And there were hooked rugs on every floor, which at least displayed industry.

Despite some inevitable qualms, she was soon forced to admit to herself that, log walls or not, here was a "hawnsome residence" within, and a pretty tribute to the dead woman who must have made it. For as she first went about the house that morning, Mrs. Larned everywhere came across dainty posthumous traces of the miller's wife in every nook and cranny; her thin white china on the painted shelves, her thick silky linens in chests, beautifully marked, and some ingeniously embroidered bedspreads bespattered with scattered spring wildflowers and gay, faded butterflies.

Yet it was also equally apparent that no woman had been living in the mill house for a long while. Recent traces of the practical and somewhat ascetic life of the miller and his two sons concealed as with a useful disguise of contemporary masculine disorder the original more fragile and exotic character of the establishment as initially arranged by Madam Glen. A leather hunting jacket hung from the gilded wreath around the portrait of a Huguenot ancestor, evidently a minister; a porcelain shepherd and his shepherdess on the mantel had been pushed aside to make room for a bullet mould, clay pipes, and brown earthen jugs for snuff and tobacco; a small library of calf-bound French polemics was buried under Philadelphia newspapers, *Poor Richard's Almanacs,* and the tracts of the times.

Here was a fertile field for Mrs. Larned's earnest New England housekeeping proclivities. She saw that instantly, and set herself determinedly to putting everything to rights. She dusted, scrubbed floors, shined windows and the brass candlesticks and andirons. She turned the rugs, made up the beds with clean covers, moulding the bolsters like fine pieces of bakery. She hung up all the men's clothes, after brushing them off, in the closets where they properly belonged.

Thus it was that the morning and the evening of the first day slipped away rapidly. Mr. Glen did not return. And then it was another day, and still another. The sound of falling water sang a soothing dirge for time. Mrs. Larned let the steeple-shaped clock on the mantel shelf stop.

Between short intervals of preparing her own meals, which were essentially simple and mostly of a gruel-like consistency, for she had lost her teeth, she fairly flew about the house. As time went on, she planned her tasks to suit the brief morning or the long afternoon hours, and her own strength. She was conservative in her renovations, yet she was Yankily thorough about everything.

In four days' time, if Mr. Glen had returned, he would have

found his mill house shining, restored within to the comfortable and quaintly elegant state of the early days of his French marriage; but with a certain upright primness and sense of righteousness conferred upon it by a pair of precise, old Boston hands. The harp, slack strings and all, Mrs. Larned still left standing behind the door, where she found it. When she swept the cobwebs off it, the feathers of her duster made it complain softly.

But Mr. Glen did not return, nor the German servant boys either. Mrs. Larned remained completely and entirely alone. Not even a wagon rattled past the door. Apparently not a soul lived in the neighbourhood, if neighbourhood there was. There was nothing all day long; nothing but two cows that came home every evening to be milked, and the pervasive and interminable sound of flowing water. The cows were a welcome difficulty. Her old hands tired easily, but she managed to milk them.

As day succeeded day, rapidly but monotonously, and still no one came, it would be idle to say that Mrs. Larned was not concerned about it. She certainly was, but she was more puzzled by the event than alarmed at its possible consequences. Undoubtedly, Providence for its own reasons seemed to be playing a sorry trick on her. But the ways of the Lord were always mysterious, she reminded herself. And then, she was much too much a fellow-townswoman of both the Lord and Mr. Honeywell to suspect either of them, even for an instant, of having collaborated in a joke. No, no, there was some entirely reasonable and serious explanation for her having been left alone that would eventually be vouchsafed her, probably by Mr. Glen himself. Patience rather than panic was called for.

Panic and loneliness indeed were neither of them likely to prevail against Theodosia Larned. She had inner springs of strength that sang to her like the everlasting waters that flowed by the mill. Ever since the edifying, although apoplectic, demise of her husband during the late Great Awakening of only twenty years before, she also had been definitely convicted that she was one of God's own elect. His Word, which she read every night, was always of infinite comfort to her as the inspired confirmation of her unavoidable salvation. Any worldly circumstance in which she found herself was, therefore, only another earthly step towards assured heavenly bliss. And this faith, more than anything else, accounted for a certain simple complacency of contentment in Mrs. Larned, even when she was in great adversity, which might otherwise have seemed foolish. Sustained by it, her lonely hours at the mill became, in fact, periods of grace in her own estimation, beads which she told, not without a certain penitential relish, on the stout thong of daily labour.

And then, almost equal to the comfort of the Holy Word itself, pregnant perhaps with a warmer earthly hope, was Mr. Patton's letter from Fort Lyttleton, which she kept in her Bible and read every evening, too. Bridget, the grandchild whom she had never seen, the last of her blood, was coming home to her arms. So the good Mr. Patton had written, and there was no reason to doubt him.

Indeed, Mrs. Larned was now as much convinced of Bridget's return as of her own divine election. The letter, too, was a confirmed article of her faith. She knew now, she was positively informed instinctively and directly, that Bridget would undoubtedly come driving up to the mill-house door, and that she had been sent there to prepare a place for her. That was what sustained her as the days went on. When, or whether, Mr. Glen and his family returned, or not, was merely an accessory circumstance before the miraculous fact of Bridget's certain arrival.

So—after the house in general was all rid-up and even given an extra lick and polish in every corner, as she felt her bounden duty first required—Mrs. Larned concentrated on getting ready for Bridget, and in particular on the bed-chamber where she knew the child would soon be sleeping. She cleaned it meticulously, wiping down the painted dado and the wooden walls. She disposed her own things there along with the presents she had long been preparing for Bridget, as favourably as possible.

On a small dresser, which she took the liberty of removing from another room, she laid out a set of hand-carved wooden combs, brushes, and toilet boxes before a small mirror not too much the worse for wear. There was also a neat sewing-case with needles, scissors, a child's silver thimble, and skeins of bright-coloured thread. These were the chef-d'œuvres of her offerings, things she had had bought in Philadelphia with some of the last shillings of her small stock of coins.

On a marbled French table in the middle of the room she placed one of Mrs. Glen's finest embroidered covers, a tall shining candle-stick, and the Larned family Bible. She drew up a convenient rocking chair close by. The big bed in the corner she made up with double bolsters, after starching and smoothing the ruffled flounces overhead that had been drooping and turned faintly yellow from neglect. From underneath the big bed she pulled out the trundler, mended its sagging cords, and pounded its long-unused child's mattress into shape. It could not be made soft or white enough to suit her, even with fine linen. Bridget was to sleep there, next to the big bed, close beside her at night.

It was on the trundle bed that she laid out the doll that had once belonged to her own daughter, 'Dosia, and an outfit of tiny dresses she had made for it. There, too, reposed the new clothes for Bridget;

dresses, knitted jackets, a red-ridinghood cloak, stockings, several petticoats, and small woollen underthings flounced with linen lace. All these she had made or restored herself with needles hard to thread; with faltering but patient hands informed by love and the skill of seventy years. She arranged and rearranged them now, bedewing her handiwork with secret tears and the fond smiles of hope deferred.

For the window that looked out over the mill-pond, the window that was always so cheerful in the morning, she washed and rehung Mrs. Glen's fine lace fensters and tied them in with broad smiling bows. On the window-sill she placed her only and cherished treasure of the painter's art, a small picture of a lamb done in tempera on olive-wood. It was carrying a churchly gonfalon on a spear, with one leg twisted coyly about it, while pausing on its other three, to baa, "IN HOC SIGNO VINCES." The lamb, an eternal one, had been brought over from England by Mrs. Larned's great-grandmother, and had survived, although with difficulty, for three generations at Waltham, Massachusetts. There its Roman origin was Protestantly suspect, and the cross over the gonfalon had been carefully erased.

Nevertheless, Mrs. Larned loved it. She and the Agnus Dei had innocently gambolled through the pagan meadows of childhood together, lost in each other's mild virginal dreams. And it was the lamb that now transformed and illumined the late Madam Glen's erstwhile rather too worldly bedroom with his long-sustained ecclesiastical gesture, so firmly fixed in tempera, and his mildly childlike but soft and comfortable Christian smile.

Yes, it was the Lamb of God, strayed innocently out of the catacombs by way of a vanished British monastery into America. It had come almost as far west as it could get. Only the cross had been lost during the journey, and its destination on the window-sill now looked final.

For the lamb was now the first thing that Mrs. Larned saw in the window when she came into the room. And she kept coming back through the doorway again and again just to admire him, and to be sure that everything was ready to the last item for the child she should soon be leading in there by her hand. What would Bridget do? Where would she pause to admire? What would she say? Mrs. Larned clasped her aged hands in youthful anticipation.

It did seem a long time that the Lord was requiring her to wait. After everything was ready, after she had explored and set to rights every part of the house, and even carried in some extra firewood, which gave her a lame back—still nobody came.

Perhaps, if it had not been for the misery in her back and her painfully stiff limbs when it came to walking, she might have tried to get back to Carlisle. For after a week, or was it a week, had gone by—she wasn't sure—her greatest worry was that she couldn't be certain when the Sabbath day would fall. And even in a Pennsylvania town someone could tell her that. She had hoped her own marker in the Bible might still tell her. But she often read more than one chapter at one sitting, in the rocking chair, and she couldn't be sure any longer. She might be three days ahead of herself in I Samuel now. A bad error, a lapse partaking of the fall of Adam, she thought. But when *they* came, she could rectify it.

Certainly someone would come, sooner or later. Common sense insisted that the big mill and the mill house, all the furniture and all the property, could not be left abandoned for too long. No, someone must come soon. And yet—how many days had she been there alone now, harkening to a dream-harp and the sad sound, the eternal whispering rush of ever-flowing water?

The evening before the weather changed and the storm came down, she ventured out of the house at last and hobbled painfully down the road. It was a sudden untimely impulse that had driven her forth, one which she soon began to regret. She couldn't even remember in what direction the town lay. It had been so dark that evening when they came from Carlisle. But she would try to see; she would try to trace the wagon by its wheel ruts and hoof marks. There were many of these old wheel marks in the road, however, and they told her a confused tale. Afterwhile, it was nearing twilight, she came to a swift ford in a muddy river. It was not so far from the house, but it had taken her an hour to limp there. She now sat down to rest. To her terror, night began to fall.

How foolish, how lacking in faith she had been to leave the house. Bridget might come while she was away! And this was wild country, Pennsylvania! She sat on a log waiting, waiting for something, she didn't quite know what. She must have dozed. She came to herself again shivering and realized it was getting late. What should she do? She was frightened now, frightened to the bone.

The moon rose and those little owls began. Down the muddy river around its first but distant bend, firelight was glinting redly, reflected across the yellow water. A faint high singing floated on the wind. It was some time before she recognized, between the splashes of night-feeding fishes, the garbled melody of a familiar hymn. The firelight on the water became wider. Around the bend of the river stole the black shadow of an Indian canoe.

Mrs. Larned got up from the log and fled wildly back to the house. She tottered through the door, all but finally exhausted, and forgot to lock it behind her. Thank God, the fire was still burning. She had had her lesson. There were savages near-by. It was a sign. She must not go out of the house again. She must wait.

Next morning a cold wind came pouring through the thickets while snow and sleet pattered against the window-panes. She prayed anxiously for strength to endure. Winter had come, and she was all alone. Also—she was running out of flour in the kitchen crock.

Well—at least there was plenty of *that* in the mill loft. Bags of it were stored on a platform between the rafters, high up away from the mice, she remembered. It was only a question whether she could climb the ladder. But probably—for flour she must have.

She got a saucepan and a spoon from the kitchen, and hobbling back through the hall to the big door that led into the mill, she opened it with much difficulty, went up a few steps and peered into the place.

It was comparatively dim there, a wide stretch of empty floor. The windows were small, and the arabesques of the mill rafters, beams, and wheel shafts crisscrossed the dusty gloom. But the ladder was there, just as she had last seen it, still in its place, and only twelve rungs high. Above it, the flour bags lay like fat swine flopped on the planked platform between the beams of the loft. She could hear the water gurgling away under the mill floor and the mice scampering. A gleeful run of harp notes dripped under her feet as though a finger had muted the liquid strings. Gracious! But she was no silly girl to be frightened by . . . by mice!

She limped to the foot of the ladder and looked up. Finally, after putting the handle of the saucepan in her mouth, and the spoon in her apron pocket, she began to climb. It was painful. But with both hands she held on hard, and resting between rungs, she slowly dragged herself up. The last rung now, all but one . . .

It did seem terribly high up there. The shadowy floor lay miles beneath her. And how was she going to get the flour out of the bags?

At last she pushed the saucepan onto the platform with her mouth, and pulling the spoon out of her apron, she began to jab with it at the side of the nearest bag.

Eventually a small hole appeared. She dug at it some more and flour began to stream out. She shifted the saucepan under it. It soon overflowed. My! This *was* going to be wasteful.

But at that instant her hands were frozen by terror; the blood in her veins stopped. From the gloom of the depths below her a sepulchral voice said:

"*How.*"

She poised there lightly, precariously clinging like a grey moth on a slanting leaf. Her flour-dusted skirt hung still and drooping behind her like a quiet wing. Her blood no longer whispered in her ears as she listened . . . listened . . . even the sound of flowing water seemed to pause . . .

"*How, mizzy.*"

The guttural voice boomed dismally to crack the silence again. She looked behind her now. She looked down.

In the shadows at the foot of the ladder stood an Indian holding up an empty bowl . . . holding up a pot . . . There was one white feather in his hair . . . it gleamed.

Mrs. Larned tottered on the ladder and lost her grip. She gasped, and threw up her hands . . .

The flour reached the edge of the platform, poured over, and began to waste into the air.

But Doctor Scarlet did not stay to fill his usual weekly bowl. He left instantly, flitting back through the silent house by the same way he had come.

The door closed furtively behind him, and the mill house stood waiting. There was no one there now to tell whether the harp notes dripped in the silences or not. Afterwhile, the mice came out again to scamper over the wide millroom floor. Now and then a squirrel frisked across the roof. It was Sunday afternoon, but Mrs. Larned had forgotten. Only the sound of flowing water babbled on.

24

"Grandma That Art in Heaven"

IT WAS TUESDAY morning when the wagon and the trundler passed through the gate by the artillery gardens without question and took the road for Boiling Springs. Jed drove, and Salathiel rode on Enna happily beside.

They were following the same road that Manoah Glen had covered in the opposite direction only a short while before. But, of course, Salathiel knew nothing as yet of the good miller's fatal journey to town, nor of anything else that had followed. And it was this state of an as yet happy ignorance that had permitted him, as he rode along, to look forward with such confident anticipation to a prompt arrival at Boiling Springs. It had been part of a streak of his best luck to have run into Jim Fergus, he thought.

Inside the wagon, Bridget sat wide-eyed but demure, swinging her feet nervously. She hoped her Grandma Larned would be like Mrs. McCandliss, soft-voiced, calm, lady-like. She kept putting her hand up to her new bonnet to straighten it. They were *so* near now. Frances was smiling contentedly. She, too, had hopes and cherished dreams of what Boiling Springs might be. But the possibility of her being parted from Bridget was not among them. Jed did seem to be cracking his new whip unnecessarily often, she felt.

But, as a consequence, and in less than half an hour, they were rumbling across the stout log trestle that carried the road over the branch at LeTort's Springs. There they were forced to pull up to watch a heavy military convoy of four and twenty wagons turn off the highway for the camp at that much-frequented spot. The main camp of the garrison lay only a few rods down the stream below the log bridge where they were stalled. The engineers were busy there, he observed, filling in swampy places, a pet aversion of Bouquet's, and pegging new sods down on the bare glacis. There was a good deal going on at LeTort's that would bear watching.

"Get to it, men," he muttered, not without a twinge of nostalgic envy. "Fly to it before Buckey gives you hell."

The camp had long been nearly empty of troops, but was being put in meticulous condition for the return of the units absent with Bouquet. It was now being given some final spit and polish against his return. Its streets of white tents, the tall painted flagpole and new whitewashed barracks for the non-coms; its bright brass cannon and precise entrenchments all seemed to have been laid out as an ironical rebuke or severe moral reprimand to the fiddling riot, squalid confusion, and frank abandon of restraint that went on day and night about the old stockade at LeTort's Springs.

Before that sorry place, the road to camp and the road to Carlisle parted, or joined, according to how you looked at it, and, by the passing and repassing of wagons, cavalry, artillery, farm vehicles and strings of pack horses, the cross-roads for a full half acre in front of LeTort's were churned and rutted into a compost of half-frozen yellow mud.

About this infernal tarn, a sad rookery of a village had grown up. In dwellings that were compounded of everything not nice, those who wished to be as near as possible to the protection of the garrison had squalidly congregated. Waiting, wandering, and idling like lost souls in limbo, gathering in ragged, unkempt groups, these people picked the last shreds of meat from every bare bone of rumour that was thrown to them from the western wagons at the cross-roads.

Immediately before the gate of the old stockade yard itself, and facing directly on the main road, one Ferdinand, a high yellow of West Indian origin, had set up a shack roofed with bark, old bottles on sticks, and streamers of flapping cloth. Every wind raised the hair on his emporium. Before it, an old kettle hung from a striped barber's pole with a signboard beneath announcing in illiterate and drunken script the presence of

The Barbadgeon Apathakerry

Ferdinand was sparse-bearded, had jaundiced eyes, and lived in a gentleman's ancient red velvet dressing gown with a rampant gold crest on it. Apparently, there was almost nothing Ferdinand could not do for, or to, you if you would let him. He told fortunes by reading palms; the future, with two coconut shags. He pulled teeth, cured inflamed eyes, sold love philtres, delivered mares, and bottled herb medicines for man or beast, etc., etc.

All this was not to be gathered from his sign. It was to be heard, however, if you could understand the strange gibberish in "Delaware-

English" from the mouth of his old squaw and woman, who droned out from morning until night the gifts and merits of her lord and master, the father of her five children. They, too, helped loudly, and the combined sound was like that of wind through the knot-holes of a withered oak. It rose and fell. In the evenings, by the light of two pine-knots, a fiddler took the family's place. Ferdinand's was merry after the sun went down. In the day, though, there was nothing so efficacious to drum up trade as an ocular demonstration of the master's skill.

The convoy had made the turn into the camp, and the wagon had started to move forward again. But just as they drove by LeTort's, one of Ferdinand's notable demonstrations was in progress, and Jed drew up by the kettle on the painted pole to let Frances and Bridget see. Salathiel turned back and waited.

It was Ferdinand, the dentist, who now emerged from his den. He had a young white girl with him, wrapped in a meagre blanket. He rang a bell and began a talky-talk in "Spanish". A haggard crowd rapidly gathered. The bell stopped. A pair of pliers emerged from the dirty folds of the red velvet gown. The girl screamed. The old squaw grabbed her from behind and hugged her like a squat bear. Ferdinand violently twisted out a tooth and held it up for all to see. The bell rang. The girl staggered over and leaned against the painted pole. The tooth was tossed into the pot. Ferdinand came forward and, bowing low before Frances at the back of the wagon, offered to read her palm. She shook her head violently.

" 'Twill be an onlucky day for ye, me foin lady," he shouted after her, as the wagon pulled out, scattering mud and the crowd at the same time.

She thought he had an Irish accent. But how, with such a yellow face? She knew nothing of Barbadians. The wagon rolled onward. An English officer rode up and stopped to look at the girl sobbing convulsively against the painted post. Finally, he dismounted.

"Here, you damned scoundrel," he shouted at Ferdinand, "give me your forceps! You've drawn the wrong tooth!" He opened the mouth of the girl, who gaped up at him. He pulled hard. Pus gushed out. She began to try to eat handfuls of snow, which rapidly turned scarlet. "That'll do," said the officer. He mounted, and trotted up the road to the camp.

It was Surgeon Boyd. He was on his way back to England via Philadelphia. He was going to retire, and he was glad of it; he was going to retire on a legacy. Ferdinand tossed the second tooth into his pot on the pole above him. It clinked. The crowd laughed. It had been a good show. The wagon continued in its own direction. By such narrow margins do old friends fail to meet . . .

They were soon out in the very middle of the open fields between the town and the forest. On every side small hovels of sod, chinked logs, and fieldstone shouldered up like beavers' huts above the weeds. Mud-and-stick chimneys leaked smoke. Yellow brush fires with forlorn people gathered about their leaping flames dotted the landscape. Even in the fresh winter breeze, the place reeked. Here and there, men or women squatted shamelessly over shallow trenches. They were long past caring. A few thin cows, their bells clanging funereally, grazed along the road. How many people were living thus in the ground, waiting dismally, it was hard to tell. There seemed to be miles of them. But all of these places were not inhabited. Scars and pits of former encampments pock-marked the fields everywhere. The nearer the forest the less of them there were. Salathiel was glad of that. It would be more decent when they came to the woods again.

They took the south fork at the next cross-roads. In a few moments the forest closed over and behind them. The silence smelled sweet. The road to Boiling Springs was quite good, considering it hadn't been used much lately. The wheels rolled silently now over deep leaf mould. The harness bells chimed secretly in the solitude. Salathiel felt better and rode straighter in the saddle. Just ahead the water of a small stream glinted through the trees. They must be coming to a ford. Probably a shallow one . . .

Goddam . . . what the devil . . . ?

All the horses seemed to be going crazy at once. Enna reared and walked about on her hind legs, pawing the air. She "trumpeted" with nervous fright. The lead team of the wagon was trying to tear itself out of harness. The others backed and filled. They swerved violently, and the big ash single-tree cracked. Jed had disappeared, and the devil was in all the horses playing merry hell . . . Judaspriest . . . where could he ever get another single-tree like that? And Jed?

"Hey, Jed!"

Jed arose from a ditch full of leaves where he had been neatly catapulted, but with enough sense left in his dazed head to snatch at the lead team's bridles and hang on. He began to batter them in the face with his old hat. Salathiel forced Enna to the rear of the trundler, tied her fast, and then racing forward on foot joined Jed in his battle with the frantic teams. It was hard, swift struggling for a minute or two. Finally, he shouted to Frances to toss him out some blankets, which he wrapped around the horses' heads. They stood quiet at last, sweating and trembling, looking like a procession of blind, bandaged invalids halting in the road, but breathing tranquilly.

It couldn't be something they had scented, then. It must have been something downwind, or something they saw. But what the devil was it? A painter stretched out on a limb? He walked down the road cautiously. Damnation! That was it—nothing but a white lightning blaze on an old thunder-tree. Horses were the durndest fools, and the single-tree was cracked. Then he saw what Karl and Johann had seen, and began to laugh. To think that *that* had nearly wrecked them.

He ran forward, and leaping the stream lightly, began to cut some young cedars and pile them against the sprawling white blaze on the thunder-tree. It was not long before the thing disappeared. Only a stack of green trees stood there now.

"Come on, Jed," he shouted. "Just keep 'em blinded and lead 'em easy. There's nothin' to be skeered of but an old wagon, and it's lyin' wheels upward in the ford."

Nevertheless, he was quite relieved and happy when "the hul consarn", including Enna, finally stood breathing easily as usual, safe on the other side. He took the blankets off the horses' heads and comforted the women. They had taken it commendably well. Frances was more anxious about the cracked single-tree than scared at what had happened. Would the single-tree last, did he think, as far as Boiling Springs?

"Probably," he answered briefly, after inspecting it, but Jed would certainly have to drive slow. He himself would ride ahead now, at quite a distance. The "tree" wouldn't take any more surprises. Mounting Enna thankfully, he trotted ahead. It was not long before he left the wagon well behind him.

The forest road stretched before, curving away easily through the sunny woodlands. There were no fresh wheel marks, he noted. It would be hard to tell how long it had been since the last wagon had passed. The storm had come that way recently. Presently, between the nervous *clip-clop* of Enna's hoofs, he began to hear a sound like a breeze stirring through the forest. Yet what autumn leaves remained hung stiff and listless. It was the sound of ever-falling water. The mill-dam—Mr. Glen's mill-dam at Boiling Springs.

Before him, down a stretch of smooth road covered with tamped river gravel, lay the open space in the forest that was Boiling Springs. A patch of sunshine glinted brazenly on the troubled ford at the far end of the vista, where Yellow Breeches Creek rolled through the trees. The noise of falling water now seemed to accentuate rather than to lighten the silence. The place seemed totally deserted, eerie with the absence of any human noise. On one side of the road stretched a shingled horse shed that ended against a log house. The house in its turn was part of a large mill, stone underneath, with logs in the story above. On the opposite side of the road, a considerable two-story dwelling slept in the cold sunshine, its porch sagging and covered with sodden leaves. A dry bush of many seasons past hung like the skeleton hand of dead hospitality withering above the door.

A fox trotted across the road and stopped to look at him. Boiling Springs, eh? He scratched his head doubtfully.

The falling water seemed to be complaining about something. The mill-pond trembled slightly, reflecting a wavering picture of the mill with icicles hanging from its wheel. The bare trees that surrounded it were upholstered in white rime-frost from roots to tips. There was no wind in this sequestered vale. A thicket of sumac blazing with red candles hemmed in the race. Enna stamped uneasily.

There was only one sign of life, a blue haze hovered over the top of the chimney of the mill house. Salathiel rose in his stirrups. "Mrs. Larned," he shouted. "Are you there, Mrs. Larned?"

There was no answer. Perhaps he should have called for Mr. Glen?

The wagon came in sight. He waited for it to draw up and told them to tarry for a minute. He'd like to look the place over himself first. Bridget sat quiet but tense, holding her basket with the kitten in it on her knees. She hoped her grandma would like cats. She looked preternaturally neat and vividly expectant. "Granny can't be far away," Salathiel said, patting her hand.

Frances looked up apprehensively. He winked at her, conveying a sense of caution.

"We'll wait for ye," she said.

"Put the horses in the shed, Jed," he ordered, as he tied Enna to a post and crossed the road towards the mill house. "Liken we'll be staying here for quite a spell."

His remark encouraged Frances and Bridget greatly. They already liked the quiet of the place, the cheerful splash of the water.

"Like home," sighed Bridget. "You know, Lissa, I'd almost forgot." Her eyes shone. Frances put an arm about her.

Salathiel walked over to the mill house and knocked at the front door. He waited. He knocked again—and then trying the latch, he found the door opened, and stepped inside. The door shut behind him. A small flurry of ashes lifted in the fireplace. There were still some living sparks there. A newly shined brass kettle stood on the hearth.

The room was bright. Two large windows overlooked the mill-pond at its far end. The light reflected ripples on the silver-grey ceiling, and the whole place swam. But it was certainly comfortable. Alive. Mrs. Glen's old-fashioned furniture, nicely covered with faded green cloth, looked luxurious to Salathiel. There were books on a hanging shelf. Jars for tobacco and snuff were arranged on a tray with several long-stemmed clay pipes. On the mantelpiece, a shepherd and a shepherdess smiled in gold and blue at either end. A small clock stood between them. It was silent. In a rocking chair, two bone needles thrust upward from a pile of new knitting were still caught in the last stitch. But the room was growing cold.

He went over to the hearth and laid a few sticks of light-wood on the fire and stood waiting. . . .

"Mrs. Larned," he called again. "Mrs. Larned, your Bridget's here!" A squirrel scurried over the roof. . . .

He went down a hall leading towards the mill and looked into the various rooms that opened off it. There were two rooms on each side. The first one was undoubtedly the old lady's. An embroidered counterpane covered the bed in the corner; and a crazy quilt, the little trundle bed next to it. No matter which way he turned, a silly lamb on the window-sill followed him with its smile. A bureau and a small dresser stood with feminine things, waiting. A small table with an embroidered linen cover held a big Bible. It lay open before a half-burned candle that had been neatly snuffed. It looked like an altar, he thought, but there was a rocking chair drawn up next to it.

He walked to the table and glanced at the back of the Bible. Yes, there could be no doubt of it . . . the whole Larned family tree was there—and Mr. Patton's letter! Very carefully he laid the Book back where it had been, still open at the same place. It was somewhere in Samuel.

He looked at the trundle bed again. It was covered with things that, quite evidently, Mrs. Larned had made for Bridget. They were all too small for her, he thought. But pretty damn dainty, too. And there were some toy clothes and an old doll. There was also a faint stale odour like old white people. He wrinkled his nose and backed out, closing the door.

The other three rooms all had men's clothes in them. One seemed to have been recently lived in. The miller's own, he judged. A pair of wrinkled flour-dusty gloves lay on the stand. That room didn't smell so good, either. Mr. Glen, if it were his, undoubtedly took Swedish snuff. He closed that door, too.

The silence of the house against the sound of water was suddenly overpowering.

No one at home! Maybe the old lady had gone for a visit to the neighbour's to borrow something—or? She couldn't have been gone long. Well, there was one more door.

It was at the end of the hall, heavy and massive, closed. He walked to it and rapped. A scurrying of innumerable small feet on the other side came to him faintly. . . . It ceased. He opened the door and went up five steps.

It was a big place filled with twilight from some windows high up, fogged with flour dust. He was in the mill itself. The half-visible shafts and wooden beams of mill machinery, the strange shapes of flumes and hoppers studded the darkness under the high roof. Mice squeaked, and the water gurgled away underneath the floor. Sometimes it dripped musically. He turned suddenly.

Something dead was close by.

There it was!

He first saw her silver hair shining in the semi-darkness. She was lying at the foot of a ladder that led up into a half-loft on the beams above, where many bags of meal were piled. There was a small saucepan at the foot of the ladder and a high cone of loose flour that must have run out of a sack. Also mice dirt.

She lay crumpled on her left side, her head twisted under her arm, her neck broken. There were no marks on her that he could see. One thing now stood out above all else, the intensely neat part in her smooth silver hair. Her back comb was broken. She was cold, stiff. She had been dead for a long time, he judged. He went hastily and got a candle to see better. It was then that he saw the moccasin tracks in the flour dust on the floor.

They led from the door, where he had come in, to the foot of the ladder. One pair of moccasins, one person. Whoever it was had turned around in them and walked back to the door again, stepping exactly where he had stepped before. He could see the faint double trace. There was no doubt of it. Whoever had come had gone some time ago, and through the house. There were mice tracks over the big trail. The saucepan was half full of flour from a hole in a bag above. He climbed up. A spoon was caught in the threads about the hole.

He thought he could tell now what had happened. Mrs. Larned must have been standing on the ladder, digging into the bag, when she heard moccasins behind her. She must have looked back and seen an Injun. He couldn't be sure of that. Other people wore moccasins. But probably, probably it was an Injun. And ladies from Boston were not used to seeing Injuns at the bottom of ladders. She had fallen? Maybe? He would have to go into that carefully. If it had been old Doctor Scarlet, it would not be so easy for him to keep his fine promise to Jim Fergus, just to say "how". But he would have to look into all that later. He rose from his knees and blew out the candle. Just now there was Frances to think of first— and Bridget! God ease her little soul! He would have to manage it quickly, somehow or other, now! They were waiting out there in the wagon.

He tied the mill-room door behind him with a thong and a knot that would have to be cut. It was the "death knot" that Kaysinata had showed him.

When he got back to the room, the fire was blazing up brightly. It crackled and talked. That was what really settled the matter for him. He went to the door and called them. "Come in, sweethearts," he cried. "The place is all warm and waitin' for ye. Granny's away, I guess. But she's been expectin' ye. Come and look!"

Frances' eyes veiled with a mist of pleasure as she entered and looked about the room. The fire leaped cheerfully, the brasses glinted.

"Take your bonnet off," she said to Bridget, who had been rushing around examining everything and was now rocking in the chair before the hearth. "I want your grandma to see your pretty brown hair." She combed it back and smoothed it, and looked anxiously at her man. She saw something was wrong.

"Bridget, go into that room and see what Mrs. Larned has made for you," he said. "She'll want you to know."

The child got up and tiptoed to the first door down the hall to which he pointed. "Grandma," she called.

"Go in," he said.

They stood listening to the child's ecstatic cries. "The lamb, oh, the dear, dear lamb . . ."

He took Frances' hands and held them tight.

"Keep her close here. Keep her happy in this place until I can git back."

"What is it?" she demanded.

"Can you bear it?" he asked.

"Yis," she said. "Is it so bad?"

"Terrible," he whispered.

She stood waiting.

"Grandma fell off a ladder and broke her neck. She's lyin' stark and still out there in the mill room behind the house. Can ye keep Bridget here until Jed and I can hide her?"

"Yis," she whispered, and sank down in the rocking chair. The tears sprang out of her eyes now. "Mother of God," she whispered, and crossed herself. She sat looking into the cheerful crackling fire, in misery. A few seconds ago it had seemed to be warming her heart. Now . . .

"Look, Melissa," he whispered, leaning down over her, "I'm not goin' to leave here for a while. We've got no other place to go. And yon is the hearth fire she laid for us. I was just in time to save the flame alive."

"Let it burn then," she said. " 'Tis God's will. I'll beguile the child. You go out and do what must be done, and say a prayer," she said. "Do ye know one?"

"I'll make one," he answered, and left her before the fire. Bridget was calling to Frances as he closed the door.

"Bring two spades from the side-box, Jed," was all he said.

It took small time to dispose of Theodosia Larned. He and Jed got her out of the mill by the back way. He picked a high dry site quite a distance back from the road. They dug a deep grave in the soft red soil, lined it with fallen leaves, and laid her in it, with her face looking east at the house. Jed was not badly frightened. It was bright daylight, and he thought of Bridget's sad case, and wept copiously. Mrs. Larned smiled behind a veil of autumn leaves. Her eyes were half open as though she were quite sleepy. He closed them with two silver shillings, and said a prayer. Jed said "Amen" over and over again, and then prayed himself. They covered her quickly and quite deep. Then they dragged some heavy logs over the spot and went back to the wagon.

Salathiel cleansed himself carefully and changed into his decent blue clothes before he went back into the house.

He nodded to Frances and sat down before the fire. Bridget was nursing her new doll. The kitten lay stretched out, purring. He called to Jed to get some heavy wood for the hearth. Melissa had taken up the knitting where Mrs. Larned had left off. A sleeve on the little jacket was growing longer. She had even started the clock.

Stolen time in another man's house, he thought. He'd explain it, nevertheless. He'd make it right with the miller. Mr. Glen would just have to bear with them. Surely he must have a good heart, if he'd sheltered the old lady. Surely he would understand.

But Mr. Glen did not return. No one came.

It would have been a hard afternoon to pass if they had not turned in to put all to rights in the wagon and the house for staying. Frances made much of it and kept Bridget busy. They were cheerful enough for a while. It was only as the late afternoon wore away towards evening that Bridget became subdued and silent. Everybody was hungry and eager for supper.

They had it on a small table drawn up before the fire. There were three candles. And Jed was proud to show that he knew how to wait on them. He set three places with blue plates and a white cloth. Frances looked at it before she sat down, happily. Bridget went over in the corner and began to drag out another chair.

"It's for grandma," she explained.

Then she stopped. They were all so silent. She saw tears in Jed's eyes.

"Ain't she coming?" she asked finally, and looked at Salathiel. He shook his head.

"Liken she's gone to be with Mrs. McCandliss," he said huskily. "That's the way it is." He didn't know it, but it was the best way he could have put it.

"Oh," said Bridget, drawing her breath in sharply. She left the chair and came over and sat down, round-eyed. Salathiel said Colonel Chambers's grace. They ate quietly. Melissa began to talk afterwhile about the fine things she was going to make, now that there would be time and a spell free from travelling. There would be a new dress for Queen Alliquippa, paduasoy, with a dash of royal scarlet. Bridget considered this. She listened solemnly.

After supper Salathiel sat smoking before the fire, watching Melissa's scissors snip at the cloth patterns she was laying out. Jed slumbered heavily in a corner. The cat walked about with her tail in the air.

Presently, Frances took Bridget into Mrs. Larned's room. She looked at him significantly as she went out. He heard them undressing together. Then there was a moment of quiet murmuring. He couldn't hear what Bridget was saying. But Frances did.

The child was on her knees and had laid her head in Frances' lap as she always did now. She folded her hands and looked up with tightly closed eyes, but the tears came through.

"Grandma," she began, "grandma, that art in Heaven . . ."

Melissa comforted her as best she could. They cried it out together in the rocking chair. They went to bed afterwhile and left the candle burning. Frances held Bridget close. It would have been too much to try to go to sleep in the dark the first night. Not in the old lady's own room. She looked at the lamb and crossed herself. . . .

Salathiel sat late before the fire pondering. He waited up, expecting Mr. Glen. Time passed with the ticking clock and the sound of rushing water. He whittled, and did a good deal of thinking. He sure was in for it now. How mysterious things were, how unexpectedly they turned out! It was enough to daunt a man. Up there with shillings on her eyes! Did she know? Anyway, they'd *have* to keep Bridget now.

What was that?

Only Jed slipping out to crawl back into the wagon. He didn't blame him. The house surely was kind of . . . kind of strange.

He saw that the candle was still burning in the women's room. Could it be that Mrs. Larned's open Bible might have a message for him? She might have meant it that way. The Word of God! Well, he would see. At any rate, he would outen the candle before it burned to the socket.

He slipped to the door of the bedroom and looked in. Melissa and Bridget lay asleep in each other's arms. Melissa's dark hair streamed down over her shoulders to mix with the brown locks of the child. They were both unearthly beautiful in the candlelight, he thought. White as angels.

Oh, Lord, now *who* had done that? Now wasn't that just like the women! It must have been Frances.

The Bible on the stand was closed.

25

The Triumph of Brigadier Bouquet

THE MUSIC was coming down the great western road, military music. The dull single drum tap of the long tired marches that had marked the weary forest miles all the way back from the Ohio country still ticked off the final paces of Bouquet's veterans returning to Carlisle, like a space clock, while the gaitered legs of the regulars swung in pendulum.

But these single taps were only reminders now, heartbeats out of the embattled past that seemed to return as memories will, with a plaintive throb between wild bursts of louder music. The skirl of bagpipes and the shrill whistling of fifes alternated, only to be overwhelmed by the rolling of massed snare-drums; topped by the light high lilt of happy bugles. When the trumpets glinted in sound, sunlight seemed suddenly reflected from dark water. And then the single drum taps would resume.

A warning gun boomed solemnly from Fort Lowther.

The music was coming down the great western road, drawing nearer every minute, the music of Brigadier General Bouquet.

All Carlisle bestirred itself instantly. Like the Shawanese towns on the Muskingum, it, too, was being taken by surprise. It was like Bouquet to do the unexpected; to steal a march even on his friends in peacetime. He strove to be his own harbinger. It was good strategy at any time. It served to discover the incompetent and disconcert the complacent ones. It saved a deal of official tomfoolery. It amused him, and—after all—he was only ten hours ahead of himself today.

However, that was the reason the commandant at Fort Lowther had fired an alarm gun. *He* was alarmed.

Lieutenant Colonel Asher Clayton had had a beautiful plan to receive the general in right military style and full regalia, every

324

button, even on the goddamned militia, bright and in place. When the news of Bouquet's having reached Shippensburg came in only the night before, he had immediately begun to issue orders. He had even conferred with the Reverend Mr. Duffield and Mr. Tilingham, the schoolmaster, about the erection of a triumphal arch of evergreens with the general's name and *"Ante Tubam Trepidant"* worked in with goldenrod and mountain laurel. Twelve little girls from the Presbyterian congregation were to scatter oak leaves and daisies, if there were any. And now! Now, all this was spoiled, cancelled. The arch, the noble Latin sentiment, the twelve maidens —none of them would be there. The general's music was coming down the great western road, and the devil was to pay.

Boom!

Actually, it was only the commandant who was alarmed. Everybody else was delighted, and they could hear the music for themselves. The best Colonel Clayton could do was to line the square immediately on all four sides with the regulars of the garrison, and even some of his invalids, drawn up in single rank; and to mass the militia by companies at the entrance to the square and down the great western road. And it was well he did so, for the brave news had spread like wildfire. The commandant might have saved the king's powder. Long before the alarm gun was fired, some people had heard the music and begun to stream in from the fields and down the roads from every direction, and to crowd into the square. Soon there was a solid mass of them between the houses and the thin line in scarlet and white cross-belts that fenced off the rectangular open space kept in the middle of the square. People crowded every doorway and hung out of the upper windows. Even the low shingled roofs were packed with spectators, and the few scraggly trees that rose here and there from dooryards dripped with boys.

The place reverberated with a clang of wild talk, shouts, and a resurgent hum of eager expectation. But to Colonel Clayton's relief, the noise was all good-natured. It was a fine sunny, winter afternoon, and for once the crowd seemed inclined to govern itself. There was a rare feeling of common interest and enthusiasm abroad, a spontaneous undercurrent of satisfaction and loyalty. That was a novel experience for the colonel. It was the first, and, as a matter of fact when he came to recollect it long afterwards, it was the last and only time during his long service in the colonies when all the people seemed to behave like fellow Britons—loyal subjects of the crown, as he phrased it—all at one with themselves. Even the backwoods characters in buckskins seemed less sullen than usual. They stopped pushing people aside rudely, and actually stood lost in cheerful talk, waiting quietly, apparently willing to join the majority in giving Buckey a good rousing welcome.

Whether it was Bouquet's personal popularity, the thrill of victory, or the return of the captivated that most moved the various individuals composing the crowd made little difference. In any case, long-deferred hopes were about to be satisfied, and both citizens and soldiery were alike in their enthusiasm. The happy surprise of Bouquet's early arrival was intensely gratifying. That, indeed, was the common interest and uncommon excitement which drew everyone to the square, for there were few residents of Carlisle who would not have some poignant private interest in the spectacle of the brigadier's return. Everybody who was not an invalid, and not a few of the wounded, crippled as they were, managed to be there.

All LeTort's Springs had poured itself into Carlisle. The hovels in the surrounding fields were left entirely deserted. The numerous employés and clerks of *Boynton, Wharton & Morgan* and the other merchants and contractors had left their various posts and hurried into town. The lucky householders contended with their boarders and throngs of eager strangers for a place at their own windows, doorways, or front porches. Turbanned house servants, and the humbler coloured denizens of the place, even field hands, managed somehow to be inconspicuous, but present. Their excitement, in fact, was greater than anyone else's and harmonically contagious, for from time to time they broke into shouts of "Glory be", rhythmic shufflings, and snatches of gospel hymns.

By the time the music coming down the road could be heard clearly, as the returning regiments emerged from the forest and approached the town across the open fields, the commandant himself was inclined to feel satisfied. The general's reception seemed to have arranged itself by general consent. Authority, mysteriously, no longer seemed to be needed. There would be no evergreen arches or female children in white scattering posies—but that was not *his* fault. And there must be between six and seven thousand persons present in and about the square, he figured, probably inaccurately. He and his staff, the mayor, the burgesses, Colonel John Armstrong, and other military and civil notables and worthies were gathered together waiting, either on horseback or on foot, as a kind of hastily arranged reception committee, before the west gate of the fort. On the whole, Colonel Clayton felt, the brigadier was bound to be pleased. But like everyone else, as the drums and music came nearer, his gaze and attention were soon entirely detained by the corner of the stockade wall and High Street, where the van of Bouquet's column might now at any moment be expected to appear.

To say that the centre and cause of all this excitement and

interest, Brigadier General Henry Bouquet himself, was not interested in how he was going to be received at Carlisle, after his exemplary campaign in the wilderness, would not be accurate. Undoubtedly he was interested, but he was highly intrigued rather than deeply concerned. Being of an intensely practical and far-seeing, if not prophetic turn of mind, he was never indifferent to what properly concerned him and his officers and men. But at the present moment, for various reasons, his thoughts were projected into the future rather than amused by the present or bemused by the past. In short, as he rode along with his tired adjutant and a couple of mounted messengers who comprised his modest staff, splashed with mud, and in a faded uniform frayed by a long campaign, he was not in that vainglorious and self-gratulatory frame of mind, which, it is said, has at times been known to accompany victorious generals returning home. Such a mood and such an attitude could not be entertained by a man of Bouquet's genius and depth of character. Despite years of professional service under many flags, Henry Bouquet remained an essentially modest, kindly, and devoted man. He was a professional Swiss soldier who had frequently outfaced both death and defeat in hard-won battles, and was therefore inclined to bear his laurels as he had borne intolerable responsibility, patiently, and chastened by an ironic sense of humour.

Oval- and olive-faced, taller than most, he now rode forward about the middle of the column, upon a borrowed government nag, shaggier perhaps than was necessary, and with stirrups too near the ground, but competent and convincing withal; a big man upon a little horse, whose choice of the best, if not the most impressive means of always arriving successfully had won him first the grudging respect and finally the devoted affection of all his veterans, regulars and colonials, who now trudged before and behind him. His and their immediate destination was a rousing and grateful welcome at Carlisle, he hoped, but that is not to say he was preoccupied or intended to be overwhelmed by it.

In several ways things might, and in his own opinion, *ought* to have been even better than they were. The balance of his successes and of his disappointments was, he felt, entirely too nice. His cup was full, but it had never run over. And it would have been gay, he thought with a Gallic grimace, to have been able to thank the gods lavishly by spilling a few extra drops even of sour wine. As it was, there was wine, but there was none to spare.

He had won all his battles, but in the process lost his only lady love. His promotion to brigadier had arrived unexpectedly, for the crown was slow to recognize merit in foreigners, and how long, O Lord, how long, had he not sustained as colonel of the Royal

Americans the condescension of cultivated British generals and the defence of the savage frontiers? *Now* he was brigadier and the applause and affection of the Pennsylvanians and Virginians were his; and *now* he would have to leave them all forthwith. For he had also been appointed to the command of the new Southern Department. Headquarters would be at Pensacola instead of at Philadelphia or New York. Another world to conquer, he thought ironically. At a little higher salary, he might soon become the Alexander of Louisiana, the conqueror of innumerable barbarian tribes, the Twigtees, par exemple. There would be fatal fevers, but no Babylons to die in. Heigh-ho, c'est la guerre! "Oh, Richard, oh, mon roi!" He whistled through a few staves of the old tune, his brown eyes widening with speculation on the future, and then narrowing with regret.

Now there would be no settling down on the plantation near Frederick. Peggy Willing would not come home with him as a bride to be mistress there. Ecuyer was gone, that plucky little devil. No hands of whist and no bottles of Burgundy before the fire in the evenings together. Those capable of conversation always died first, exhausted by trying to explain the obvious. And he would have liked to talk it out with S. Ecuyer as a neighbour. In Maryland they might both have cultivated adjoining gardens. But silence would sit before the fire at Frederick now. Silence was coming on! He shivered with an uncomfortable premonition. . . . The Alsatian girl could have the place. The land he had left her ought to be enough to close her mouth, although she could talk in three languages.

Land! He had plenty of that. Land about Bedford, land in Maryland. What good did it do him now? It was the fault of the War Department in promoting him and transferring him, too. Or it was the fault of English generals, red-faced, stupid, corpulent, spawn of the Horse Guards and a Hanoverian Bellona; bellicose, pampered cupids sent to fight Indians! Sacrebleu, how had they ever prevailed? It was inscrutable that the same country had given birth to Marlborough. A little more and they would lose what the great duke had gained. Probably he had lost Peggy Willing just from the necessity of having to correspond with them. It was a fatal epistolary style to acquire. He must have addressed her, that charming girl, as though she were an adjutant, in the same vein he had written to Jeffrey Amherst or to the late Duke of Cumberland. Name of a dog, that *must* be it! No wonder she hadn't waited for him. No wonder she'd married her Philadelphia beau. Yes, his love letters had been fatal! Nothing less than official—and so—

Peggy would not be waiting for him at Carlisle. She would not be watching for him when he marched in. None of her family, not even Ed Shippen, would be there. Colonel Burd, as a dutiful son-in-law of the family Shippen, would be dutifully sulking at Lancaster, glad of an excuse to stay away. A triumph—but no place to lay his head afterward, and no pretty head beside him on the pillow. Well, it would be headquarters again, a military family. But, by God, he'd set himself up well in Philadelphia for a while before he left for Florida. He'd get some help in that. He'd hold his head high, despite Peggy. He'd entertain. Let the men be received with acclamations, they certainly deserved it. But the poor rescued captives would need something more sustaining than huzzas. And he'd see the people he had liberated taken care of. They'd remember him for that. Yes, he'd look after them; see that every last one of them, orphans and all, found work or a place they could call home. After that, for him— Pensacola. Ah, quelle magnifique dispensation du ciel!

He brought the column to a halt and for the last time rode up and down it, with his hat off, while the men closed up. Another quarter of a mile and they would be entering the town. There was a certain military pathos in thus seeing an army, his small but victorious army, all drawn up in familiar formation for the last time. Never again! They understood. They began cheering him as he passed. It was good-bye. He sent the 42nd Highlanders forward. The honour of the first acclamations should be theirs. They deserved the van. Allons—forward now. The bagpipes struck up "When All the Blue Bonnets Came Over the Border," the drums danced. The column stepped out like one man. A thousand times they had all dreamed of this. In the square at Carlisle the crowd began to roar.

It was due to sheer blind luck, and a little more, that both Salathiel and Frances were in Carlisle the day "Gineral Buckey" marched in. Jim Fergus had come back from Lancaster only the morning before, and, happening to meet Mr. Williams on the square, he had heard, much to his consternation, about the death of Mr. Glen. Mr. Glen had then been buried but a few days, a hasty funeral attended by some friends but none of the family. For both the Glen boys were known to be away, and so far as Mr. Williams or anybody else knew, there was no one at the mill but two German redemptioners.

"A sad case, quite perplexing and totally unexpected," explained Mr. Williams. "He just passed away on our front porch and Mrs. Williams went out and found him sitting there."

No, the wagon had not come back from the mill next morning to get him. Nor had Mr. Williams, or anyone else, had time yet to ride out to Boiling Springs. He and his wife had had their hands quite full. Something had to be done with a dead man pretty quick. Well, they had done the best they could. No one even knew where Mrs. Glen was buried. The commandant had "loaned" them a pine coffin, whatever that meant. How could you "lend" a coffin? Who would pay for it? Mr. Glen had been a man of property. But where were his heirs, and who was his lawyer? At least the interment had been Christian. Mr. Williams would not listen to what Jim Fergus was trying to say. He was out of pocket two pounds ten and was not to be interrupted. It was a serious matter for a small grocer like himself, these days, when even dying came so high. He shook his head and, before Jim could make any further remarks, went on his way still looking puzzled.

Beyond saying that at least one of the Glen boys would soon return with Bouquet, Jim Fergus had not been able to offer Mr. Williams much comfort. He thought he would not add to the good man's perplexity by mentioning anything about Mrs. Larned, the Albines, and all that. But, good Lord, what *had* become of the old lady? Doubtless, Mr. Honeywell had departed for Boston as he had said, and Jim strongly suspected the German boys had cleared out, too. Had they left the old lady alone or had they fixed her? Had the Albines found her yet? A hundred questions ran through his head. Jim was genuinely concerned. He was a good friend of the Glens'. Also he'd liked Salathiel. What an unexpected mess it all was. He was tired after the trip to Lancaster, but he'd ride down to the mill that evening and find out, just as soon as he could get his mare's off-shoe tightened.

So, ride down he did, and arrived about suppertime. The Albines were there, and he soon heard all about Mrs. Larned, or all that there was to hear. It seemed bad. He was inclined to blame the German redemptioners. He didn't take much stock in the moccasin tracks at the foot of the ladder. Maybe old Doc Scarlet had come in for some meal and found her lying there. Like enough, agreed Salathiel. But the doc had lit out for the mountains. He wasn't camped on the stream any more. He'd just naturally do that, insisted Jim. Well, there was no way of finding out immejit. They'd have to wait and trace down the redemptioners. Maybe they could? But it would take time. Meanwhile, the Albines were much confused and not a little embarrassed at finding themselves, and no one else, at home at the mill.

Jim Fergus was not so much concerned about that as were Salathiel and Frances. It was a lucky happenstance for the Glens, he argued. Otherwise the mill and the house would have been left deserted. They'd better stay on until one of the Glen boys came home. He'd take it on himself to say he thought both the brothers would be pleased. Any drunken fool might come along and burn the whole place down. No, no, they must stay until they heard. All he knew was that either John or Martin would be back sooner or later,

and that the old man had made a will by the advice of a smart
lawyer. "A man by the name of Ed Yates, practises out of Lancaster,
when he ain't ridin' the borders on Penn family affairs." They could
get in touch with him if they wanted to. Mr. Yates would be in Carlisle on a land case tomorrow, he'd heard him say only last Tuesday up
at Lancaster. Yates had asked him to get him a place to stay at the
Williamses', and, by God, he'd forgotten to do it. He was that
flustered when he met Mr. Williams, who talked all the time, that
he hadn't said a word about it to the old man. "Doggone it"—he
smote his knee with vexation.

"Well, I'll be damned," said Salathiel. "I'll be double damned!"
He and Frances looked at each other. Frances laughed.

"Sure, and it's fate," she said. "I'll be after makin' up one o'
the Glens' bedrooms for ye, Mr. Fairgus. Ye're the most welcome
body with a soul in it I've seen for many a long day. And it's a koind
heart ye have, too. I was beginnin' to think that the rest of the world
had been destroyed intirely, sittin' here listenin' to the sound of fallin'
water. But it's a snug, sunny little house, and Sal has shot a turkey
for supper. Bridget, put your dolls to bed now and do up yer hair.
We have company."

Jim Fergus was favourably impressed. The house shone. The
supper was excellent. He listened to the murmur of prayers after
Bridget went off to bed. Sal Albine had found himself a mighty spry
young wife. The Glens were lucky. He'd drop in this way again.
The ford was a short cut to Shippensburg. He'd remember. Poor
old Mrs. Larned, what a fall she'd had! He yawned, had a nip, and
went to bed.

Next morning they were up bright and early. Salathiel put Enna
in the Glens' two-wheeled cart and drove off to town with Frances
beside him. Jed and Bridget were left to keep house together. It
couldn't be helped. They hoped to find Yates at Carlisle and persuade
him to come back with them. That, Frances suggested, might not be
so hard to do. But what she needed was another woman in the house.
A lawyer would not be much help in having a baby, she opined.
Salathiel agreed, but drove on steadily. Enna made a good cart horse,
he observed.

When they got to LeTort's they heard the general's music coming
down the great western road. And, as if they didn't know it themselves, Jim Fergus kept riding up behind them shouting out what it
was. They were caught in the crowd rushing to town, and if Salathiel
hadn't turned Enna off the road and driven the little cart directly
across the fields, they might never have got into the square at all. As
it was, they were stopped just at the corner of High Street and the
stockade by a sergeant of the guard, an old Fort Pitter whom

Salathiel recognized, and forced back against the wall. It was within a few feet of the place where Mr. Glen had tied up his wagon for the last time. It was Salathiel now who stood up and looked across the heads of the crowd, hemmed in by the lines of redcoats, and the empty space in the middle of the square. The commandant and his staff were only a few rods away to his right. Good enough, he thought. Luck was still with him. He could see the whole show from here.

The sergeant, however, was by no means so well satisfied. A two-wheeled country cart, begod, just where the column would have to make its first turn into the square, the first bloody thing the bloody general would see! His remarks finally became too notable to be ignored. Being an Irishman, the sergeant involved the entire Holy Family in his profane view of the situation.

"How be the Sweeney twins over at Pittsburgh, sergeant?" asked Salathiel mildly. "Or do ye ever hear from there any more?"

The sergeant came closer, making his way through the crowd. "So, it's yourself," said he, "the little captain's Injun boy turned country gintleman—and the captain's mare, too!" He looked at Frances appreciatively. He winked. "All right, keep your big mouth and your little harse quiet, and I'll niver ask ye how it is ye've lost an ear."

"Now, how *did* ye lose it, Sal?" demanded Frances, throwing herself into the spirit of the occasion.

The sergeant withdrew satisfied with the harm he thought he had done. Salathiel tied Enna firmly, climbed into the cart, and waited. Up the road the bagpipes and drums broke out with "All the Blue Bonnets Came Over the Border." The crowd roared and stared at the corner—where the cart was tied.

The general's music marched into the square first. The combined snare-drums of the returning regiments rounded the corner, rolling a wave of sound before them that drowned out the shrill fifes and squealing bagpipes behind them, and the roars of the delighted crowd. The drummers were ragged, hatless, and mostly boys, but they were veterans; and they knew they were good. Their elbows all lifted together while their drumsticks shivered in a rhythmic mist. They stopped. The brass trumpets tossed, shouted triumphantly, and the drums resumed.

The crowd in the square was lifted clean off its feet. Some people began to try to dance and holler where they stood. Handker-chiefs were waved and fluttered at open windows all the way around the square. A happy breeze of feminine voices seeemed to breathe through the place. Even little men began to bellow, and the staff horses pranced. The complicated rigadoon continued as the music, drums, fifes, bugles, and bagpipes, marched across the square to the south border, countermarched, and stood playing—more softly now —but ready to burst into new tunes and appropriate flourishes as each regiment or unit turned the corner of the stockade to march in review across the square.

The massed weather-beaten, shot-torn, faded colours of the 42nd, 77th, and 60th royal regiments and Royal Americans and the flags of the Pennsylvania militia battalions appeared next. They were met by a respectful, but an eager and expectant silence, for everyone now craned his neck to see what came next. The drums flourished, the pipes squealed, and the 42nd Highlanders, white knees flashing, kilts and tartans flaunting, marched into the open space and passed before the commandant. The crowd cheered them wildly as one company after another flowed past to mass and ground arms at the north end of the square, where the music played. There were many people at Carlisle who remembered the Highlanders, the forlorn hope of the frontier, leaving lonely and in the midst of terror and silence, with Bouquet at their head, only two summers before. The general's compliment to the Highlanders was well understood and taken kindly. Even the backwoodsmen were vociferous, remembering how they had charged at Bushy Run.

"What a pity it can't always be like this," sighed Colonel Clayton, who had never found gratitude associated with buckskins before —"what a pity!"

It was only when the Highlanders began to march past them at the corner that Salathiel came fully to appreciate what a nice point of vantage accident and the Irish sergeant had conferred upon him. Sitting in the high-wheeled cart, he and Frances could look directly down into the faces of the men in the marching ranks as they turned the corner. Now and then he recognized someone familiar. Ensign Erskine, a lieutenant now, and the four surviving Alexanders replied to his happy yell. Then the Royal Americans began to pass, the old companies from Fort Pitt. His hands and voice were kept busy. Even the captains gave him a pleasant nod. Well, well . . . they seemed to say, as they smiled and marched on. And now the general was coming. Yes, there was Buckey himself.

He was riding a shaggy-looking little horse. He looked faded and war-worn. It was Captain Ourry who was acting adjutant. Bouquet must have brought him along from Bedford. But Ourry was never much on a horse, either. Why, the crowd didn't seem to realize who the general was! Salathiel stood up in the cart and began to roar his name.

The crowd caught on, the place rocked with cheers.

Bouquet passed within ten feet of the cart. He looked up at the tall fellow waving a hat and roaring his name, with an amused smile. That terrible ragged ear—where had he seen it before? . . . but yes! His expression flashed into one of pleased recognition. He made a wide cordial gesture, he took off his hat and bowed in his saddle to Frances.

The crowd began to cheer her. It was the proudest and happiest moment of her life. "Oh, Sal," she gasped, "oh, Sal, he really knew ye. Ye'll be after takin' me now to see him at headquarters, won't ye, Sal? The grand, good man! To think that we might have missed him! Oh, I think I'm really married to ye now. Now won't ye . . ."

"I'll take ye," he said.

After that the rest of the procession was bound to be something of an anticlimax to the Albines, but not to the rest of the crowd. What they were most eagerly expecting was the captivated.

Over there, a few rods away, Salathiel saw Buckey being welcomed by the commandant. There was a deal of saluting and hat-raising. People were stepping up to shake hands with the general: Colonel Armstrong, Mr. Craighead in a black skullcap, two or three other ministers, Mr. Arthur St. Clair, a string of well-dressed gentlemen, Mr. Edward Yates. . . . My, my, what a powwow! Mr. Tilingham, the schoolmaster, pulled a paper out of his pocket and began to try to read a Latin address he had composed but had not had time to memorize, and against the bagpipes, too. Buckey finally patted him on the head like a big dog, and the committee and staff dissolved in laughter. The drums and bagpipes took over. The remnants of the 77th Royal were passing, veterans of campaigns from Cuba to the Ohio. But few people remembered that now.

The big ovation, naturally enough, fell to the green-coated, brown, and buckskin-clad Pennsylvania battalions, especially to the Rangers, and the Light Infantry with bucktails in their hats. The town went wild over the "country troops". Only *they* were really coming home. Friends and relatives began to break through the line of redcoats that held the sidelines, and there was no stopping them. Wives, mothers, and sweethearts found their men. Lieutenant Pomeroy and his diary, his mother-in-law, and *her* daughter were there. But others were forever absent, and there were screams, cries of anguish mixed with cheers and laughter, and few dry eyes. With the return of the home troops the culmination was reached, and the military precision of the occasion began to disintegrate.

At the corner of the square a hostile roar turned all heads in that direction, and rapidly bore down the din of cheering with a welcome of another kind. Three open ammunition wagons surrounded by a company of the 77th with fixed bayonets entered the square at a slow walk. A threatening silence gradually grew, and accompanied them. Why was it, Salathiel wondered, that Indians in wagons always rode standing up?

But so they did, packed in solidly, all standing up and looking straight ahead: chiefs, warriors, squaws, and a few children. Their eyes glittered. So did their beads and wampum finery. They held their coloured blankets close about them. There were a few cocked hats, red turbans, and turkey- and eagle-feather headbands among them, and these, together with their red wooden faces, all snapped forward or jerked backward together like turtle heads when the wagons jolted, stopped—and went on.

A furious tempest of catcalls, laughter, jeers, threats, and imprecations burst out from every side and accompanied the end of their stolid progress across the square. These were the Indians who would not be separated either by threats or cajolery from their beloved adopted captives. Despite all that Bouquet could do, they had followed them and the army downcountry. Now, for their own protection, the general had loaded them into wagons, surrounded them by a hedge of bayonets, and was sending them to jail.

Here and there lank-haired men in buckskins ducked under the arms of the much-harassed line guards and ran out to menace the wagons, yelling insults vociferously, and threatening to combine for mischief. But they were stopped cold by the hedge of bayonets. And the helpless contents of the wagons, despite roars of ridicule and protest, were safely lodged in jail. The grenadiers of the 77th immediately surrounded the building and prepared to camp there. Bouquet was taking no chances of another Paxtang massacre—and the renewal of the Indian war.

Even at that, snatching so succulent a bone out of the jaws of the mountain wolves, as Bouquet put it, might have been a more serious matter than it proved, had it not been that there was no time left for the pack to gather about the prison, or for the snarling and growling of those who considered themselves balked of their natural prey to gather head.

The captivated now began to arrive amidst enormous tumult and excitement at the south end of the square. There was a universal rush in that direction, and the "children of the forest" were left temporarily forgotten to gaze through the iron bars of their conquerors' windows in stony peace.

A line of seventeen wagons interspersed with men, women, and children walking, or in a few cases mounted on the sorriest of nags, forced its way slowly into the crowd at the bottom of the square. They were preceded by the remains of Bouquet's Virginia Rangers, whose use of rifle-butts on the toes and corns of the too curious, or frantic friends and relatives of the long expected Indian captives, caused them to be remembered vividly for many years*—but also cleared the necessary space for the liberated to continue to breathe in, unload their dunnage, and encamp. The detachment of Royal Americans that had marched beside them, a file on either side of the ragged and motley procession through the forests and over the mountains all the way from the western Ohio woods, was now withdrawn. But not without many tearful good-byes, blessings, and the clinging and howls of the young pets of the red-coated soldiers, many of whom had been "fathers" and "uncles", rather than guards. Captain Morgan of the Virginia Rangers now took charge.

The scene that ensued transcended the powers of several gentlemen of noble sentiment who afterward tried to describe it. Sentiment was not historically adequate; basic emotions were involved and poignantly manifested. Ecstasy, pathos, tragedy, and dumb disappointment were epitomized. For a few poignant hours, about the seventeen wagons, all the emotions attributed to heaven, hell, or limbo found their genuine earthen mix. The long lost, the supposed dead returned. Children rushed screaming to throw themselves on the breasts of parents, whose features renewed themselves in life again out of the dwindling images of exiled dreams. Small daughters grown to be young women in the wilderness laid their cheeks darkened by far-western suns against the pale cheeks of their mothers and begged them to repeat the cherished music of their half-forgotten names— was it Jane or Annabelle or Sue? The beloved tones of voices from the past renewed themselves. Shy orphans with scraggly feathers in their hair, their naked legs trembling under ragged blankets, were tearfully examined by hopeful relatives, claimed ecstatically and borne off. Or they were patted on the head sadly and left to stand waiting, trying to say something in English, muttering in Shawanee or Algonquin who they thought they were. Would Uncle Ed come? Would Aunt Jessie know them? What was the colour of mama's hair? "Me Smitty, me 'itty Yon Smitty," one Saxon-looking child kept shouting. But none of the English Smiths, and, of course, they were there, knew him. Little Smitty eventually went home to the valley of Virginia with a big Ranger named Ed Tredigar. Old people, captured many years before, for the most part stood together. Time as well as war had lessened the chance of their being found again by kin. Most of their surviving friends they now saw amongst themselves. It was not likely that grandchildren would know them. And

---

* Most of the Virginia riflemen who had accompanied Bouquet in the Ohio campaign had been dismissed at Fort Loudon and gone home to the "Valley", taking many of the rescued Virginia captives along with them. A "remnant" accompanied him to Carlisle, *probably* on account of difficulty in paying them off, an harassing affair for Bouquet.

not many young people did stop to inquire. Only Lillian Johnson of Grand Island found her grandpa. She already had two children of her own holding onto her skirts; but she had kept a small wooden fox grandpa had once whittled out for her. He hobbled off with her without looking back, a warm fireside before him and the cold misery of the forest behind. God, what a little wooden fox could do!

But the babies, the babies with Indian beads around their necks and small moccasins with porcupine quills in starry patterns on their small feet—there was a whole wagonful of babies—some standing up and some crawling around, under the care of two Scotch matrons and a couple of Shawano squaws. Bouquet had seen to that.* But the babies? It was hard to know who and whose they were. Indeed, some of them never found out. There was a crowd of women about the wagon. But not so many mothers. They had been scalped. Other women came around the wagon, crying, silent, talking together, wondering. People kept coming up and looking into the baby wagon, and then going away again. Some of the two- and three-year-olds were plausibly claimed. Gaunt women looked bloody death at the nursing squaws they envied, and walked away.

All this for an hour or two in the late-afternoon sunlight, and then suddenly, for the fortunate, the era of captivity was over as early twilight came on.

The claimable were claimed. They had gone on their way; on their way home rejoicing. By twos or threes, by couples and families. Husbands and wives together again, strange with each other but shyly delighted, vouchsafed another honeymoon perhaps, or prayers again, kneeling down at the same bedside together. And there were lovers who walked away silently hand in hand, fond hope justified at last. A widow who had not found her husband came down off a porch on the West Walk that evening and thrust a bouquet of homemade paper flowers into the hands of a slim girl dressed like Pocahontas. She was passing by on the arm of a young farmer, whose face was exalted with happiness. Mrs. Judith McCormick, the widow in the black dress, threw her arms about Marigold Cooper, the girl in deerskins, kissed her, and left the paper flowers in her hand. They were pathetic little fly-specked mantel blossoms. But they glowed there in the winter sunset, clutched in the fingers of lovely destiny, with the authentic radiance of undying fire.

Up and down the tramped-out "streets" between the lonely wagons of the captivated that still waited glimmering whitely in the public square, those who had *not* found what they had come so hope-

---

* These "matrons" were specifically allowed for in the general marching order for the organization of the expedition before its leaving Fort Pitt. Other women were excluded. The "nursing-squaws" were added as a necessity on the Muskingum.

fully looking for still stood talking together softly in dejected groups, trying to take what comfort they could from one another out of desperate rumours of prisoners that were still to be returned from Canada or captives said to be gathering at the DeTroit. A few still wandered alone, or searched in desperate couples afraid to look at each other, hunting amid the wagons, peering into the faces of half-savage children, asking questions, hoping against hope. A continual wailing now came from the baby wagon, one which was not easily to be assuaged. A number of forlorn-looking people, both men and women, stood about silently, crying dejectedly, watching. Captain Morgan now had the supper fires kindled and rations issued, after ascertaining that upwards of seventy people still remained unclaimed. He and his men, tall fellows in fringed buckskins, went about, unexpectedly helpful and gentle, carrying what comfort they could, and explaining with bashful embarrassment why it was necessary to tie up some of the captives, especially the younger ones—"jist for the reason that as soon as yer back gits turned, they slip off like wild deer into the woods ag'in and run back to the Injuns that be waitin' fer 'em. Hit's orders, and until their people come or somebody kin work on their speerits, a light leg-iron at night's the only answer."

"Now, son, hold yer feet still. This ain't goin' to hurt ye none." The lock snapped. "Eight years with the Munsees, fer that young'un. He kin understand now, but he won't talk no English. He's got the wilderness taste in his mouth and the forest look on his face. He's jist plumb sullen. He won't be no good no more to nobody but himself, will ye, Tommy?" The boy grunted. The Virginian passed on, the light irons and chains over his arm jingling. "Whar's that sloe-eyed gal now?" He stuck his head inquiringly into a wagon. "She's talkin' to her buck over at the jail window," replied a woman's voice. "They've allowed her." The man passed on. The supper fires began to dance, and the shadows wavered on the wagon-tops. A Quaker brought two buckets of fresh foaming milk still warm from the cows, and gave them to an attendant squaw.

"Thee will find it helpful," he said.

"Heap heap good," grunted one of the nursing Indian crones. The babies began to quiet down. The Quaker stood watching the proceedings in the wagon contentedly. The small greedy noises he heard pleased him. The bucket yoke now rested lightly across his neck. There should be more milk in the morning, but he would take the two buckets home tonight. It was hard to get iron hoops in Carlisle.

"A very sensible thing, Friend Tavistock," said a quietly contained voice just behind him.

The Quaker turned slowly. He remembered just in time to keep his hat on. "Thee has a firm memory, Friend Bouquet," he said.

"I seldom forget those who come to help the men in the hospitals," replied the brigadier. "They're not so numerous as to confuse me. It was at the City barracks in the Northern Liberties, if I remember right."

"Yes," said the Quaker. "Not many came to help there, 'tis true. But then the smallpox is always so catching—and that was many years ago."

"Nevertheless . . ." said Bouquet. They stood talking while Friend Tavistock waited for his buckets.

The news that the brigadier was come amongst them spread rapidly. The unclaimed captives, the disappointed people who had not found their lost children or relatives, all who still lingered about the seventeen wagons and were waiting for supper, gathered about the big fire that crackled near the baby wagon, looking at the general, and the Quaker in the brown coat he was talking with, curiously. The children and young people gradually edged forward. That was Buckey there, that was the great man who had brought them back over the mountains. They had seen the chiefs, the terrible fierce warriors, humble before him. He had made them smoke the peace pipe, squatting in the green arbours before him by the river-bank in the far Ohio woods. The long wampum belts had been laid across his knees while the soldiers stood behind him. Many fine speeches had been made. Buckey was strong and powerful. The king had sent him. But standing in the warm light of the dancing supper-fire he looked different. He looked tired and had a sad smile. Maybe he would help them now, if somebody would only ask him.

Bouquet felt their eyes upon him, and turned. They were all looking at him. Bon Dieu!

Heaven knows he had not meant to make any speeches at Carlisle. Of Indian oratory and formal mouthings he had had a bellyful. For the past three months in particular, he had had to be nothing less than an oracle; male Fate in a red coat. These people—he would have to *talk* with them.

He beckoned to them to draw in closer about him, with a familiar personal word here and there for some of the captives he knew. Tomorrow, he said, they would all be moved out to the camp that had been prepared for them at LeTort's Springs. It had been a heroic march they had made over the mountains from Fort Pitt in the depth of winter. They had done well. Things would be better in the new huts at the camp. There they would no longer be exposed to the open weather. Let those who had not found their own dear people take heart. They might still find them—let them hope on and be patient. To those who had no place to go, and for the orphans, he would see that they were taken care of. There were many good people in Philadelphia, at Lancaster, and in other towns and on farms, who would open their hearts and their homes to the captivated. Good men in the assembly and the governor himself had them in mind. Before he left the province he would promise them that everyone, great and small, should have a decent place and honest work to go home to. He had laid that upon his honour and upon his soul. For those who had been beguiled by their Indian captors and would return to the ways of the wilderness, he asked them to consider well what they were doing. They ought not to endanger their souls or repudiate their own people that way. Let them be patient and try to learn. He would ask them to do that for the sake of the brave men who had risked and lost their lives to bring them back.

His voice ceased, but they still stood looking at him standing alone with drooping epaulets in the red firelight, the shadowy Quaker behind him.

"Be ye goin' to leave us, gineral?" asked an old woman in a cracked voice, leaning on a stick.

"The king hath commanded me to far southern parts," he replied. "But I shall still be with you for a while."

A sigh went up from the circle. "God bless you, Buckey," someone said. There were a number of amens. But still they stood looking at him. It was indecently poignant, uncomfortable. What more could he say?

A five-year-old in ragged deerskins and the fragment of a trade blanket walked out, sensing the feeling of general gratitude, and gravely shook hands with the general. He then presented him with his chief treasure. "Blow it, general. Blow it," the boy said, seeing the general was puzzled.

Bouquet looked at his gift gravely. It was a long white willow whistle with two red-robin feathers tied on little strings at the end.

"It blows," insisted the child.

"Thank you, my boy," said the brigadier. He put the whistle to his lips and blew hard. He puffed out his cheeks. A splendid squawking squall emerged from the thin tube. The red feathers danced forward in his breath. The crowd was delighted. They laughed and clapped happily and began to disperse for supper. The child retired, satisfied, and with the cherubic dignity of innocence resting proudly upon him.

The general stood pondering in the firelight. What was that sententious phrase the schoolmaster had tried to repeat in his Latin speech, poor fellow? A notable sonorous tag . . . *Ante Tubam Trepidant* . . . They tremble before the trumpet. A smile of exquisite ironic enjoyment twitched the great general's lips. This, then, was the great moment of his triumph.

He blew on the willow whistle long and hard. . . .

At the bare and quite unprepossessing headquarters in the camp at LeTort Springs, Captain Ourry already had all the marching orders for the regulars laid out on the table, ready to be signed. The Royal Americans and the 42nd were to march early next morning for Lancaster. Some of them were to go in wagons, and it was time to get the orders to the colonels. Also, it was long after suppertime. Captain Ourry was hungry. The clerks sat looking at him vacuously. Jesus, where in the name of the fifteen colonial governors was the general?

There was a rout at the new town hall that night and the brigadier must be there to answer the speeches. Under no consideration was Ourry going to do *that* for him.

At that moment the thin sound of a shrill whistle commenced to sound outside the barrack door. The three clerks sat up, and sat still like a lot of silly rabbits, with their plumes behind their ears, listening. The whistle continued.

Now, there are *some* things which even an adjutant doesn't have to stand for. Captain Ourry arose, upsetting his desk stool, and strode furiously towards the door. He flung it open indignantly. . . .

Salathiel and Frances had not joined the crowd in going to look at the captivated. For many reasons it would have been more than Salathiel could bear. Also he was afraid Frances might want to bring some babies home. They sat in the cart after the captivated passed and the crowd broke up about them, rather doubtful just what to do. It was in that way they saw what nearly everyone else had missed. Long after the rear-guard had passed and the music had stopped playing at the north end of the square, a lone farm wagon appeared, pulled by a single sway-back nag. There were no less than five ministers seated in it. The Reverend James McArdle and the Reverend Charles Puffin, the chaplain at Fort Bedford, were on the front seat, with the light of missionary inspiration playing about their devoted countenances. They looked over the heads of the crowd in the square and into the future with a fixed and enthusiastic expression.

Salathiel ducked. He found it necessary just then to be sure that Enna was firmly tied to her post. The wagon with its holy freight moved slowly forward and disappeared up the road on the other side of the square. Salathiel thought it just as well not to tell Frances who and what had passed.

A few minutes later, while they were discussing whether to go back to the mill immediately or not, they were interrupted by the familiar voice of Yates, who stood with his hand resting on the side board and looking up at them quizzically.

"I've just had a good talk with your friend Jim Fergus," he said. "Don't you think it would be a good idea to come across the square to the Williamses' and spend the night there? Mrs. Williams says she'll make room in her own bed for Mistress Albine. You and I, Sal, can roll up in our cloaks in the back hall. It won't be so bad, and I really think you'd better come and talk over the Glen affair. Besides, this will be a memorable night in Carlisle, you know. Bouquet has come home—and the war's over. I suppose you'll be wanting to make plans for moving to the City now."

"That's about the size of it," replied Salathiel.

26

Applewood and Sealing Wax

IT IS DEFINITELY a pity that the title of "counsellor", rather than that of "attorney-at-law", was not the usage of the bar of the Province of Pennsylvania before which Edward Hamilton Yates, Esquire, had the honour to practise; for while he was very much an attorney and constantly at law, in one way or another, it was as a counsellor in the art of conducting life's more serious affairs in general rather than arguing legal cases in particular that he most shone as a lawyer.

And Yates's success in this advisory and admonitory capacity, by far the larger aspect of the legal profession's relevancy, was due not alone to a technical knowledge of the law and statutes which applied in any given case or situation, but also to a fine sense of justice both innate and cultivated, a professional instrument which at best he sharpened by practice and employed with ever hopeful tact, and at worst applied with a merciful politeness. Add to this, the peculiar flavour of his amused and amusing charm, his discerning and disarming smile, and his singular eye; and it was difficult for most people not to accede to, or at least to acquiesce in, any points of law, equity, or logic which he undertook to defend or promote by his dapper and fearless personality.

Not a little of Yates's success was due to his subtle method of clearing the primrose path of his opponents of any minor obstacles that promised to hinder them in going their own determined way to the Bonfire, so that the snares that they had rigged for others frequently engaged their own feet; while several learned judges and numerous ignorant juries were from time to time persuaded into the opinion that if God and the legislature were not *both* on Mr. Yates's side, it could only be due to the fact that the wisdom of the

Former was superhuman by definition and the acts of the latter known to be fallible.

As a friendly adviser then, rather than as an advocate, Mr. Yates was like a compass whose true north was the opposite·pole of folly. Not occasionally it did take both courage and intelligence to follow his counsels, but few who took his advice were ultimately disappointed. All of which might be summed up in Salathiel's homely remark the morning after Brigadier Bouquet's arrival at Carlisle, to the effect that Ed Yates was a damned good man to have on *your* side, and his cleverness a kind of friendly virtue.

Certainly, the results of the morning were good warrant for Salathiel's assertion, for the affairs of the Albines, which to themselves at least had lately seemed confused and entangled, were straightened out in a manner that seemed little short of magical to Salathiel, and finally forced even Frances to revise her estimate as to the practical value of having a lawyer and a good friend actually in and about the house.

Even while they were washing together, stripped to the waist, under the frosty water that fell from Mr. Williams's pump, early that morning, Yates had after a manner cross-questioned Salathiel. And while they were having their bacon, eggs, hominy, and small beer together later on, he had arrived at certain conclusions as to the exact items which, in his opinion, it was advisable to cope with in order to relieve Salathiel's perplexities and settle the Glen estate. The neatness and economy of two birds at one shot appealed to him. Most of his legal cogitations took place while Mr. Williams and his wife kept repeating in a kind of matrimonial chorus the, to them, still perplexing and expensive details of Mr. Glen's mysterious demise. But while Yates picked over his victuals he also, without anyone's noticing it, picked over what brains there were present, and arose from his breakfast refreshed by certain salient points in an otherwise trivial conversation. These he reserved for further consideration.

For it was Yates's custom, after breakfast, to retire to his chamber and, after locking his bedroom door, to go through a bit of physical and mental ritual there which had to do with two worlds, this and the other one.

First, he cleaned his teeth with a furred sassafras stick and Eccles' Powder of Desiccated Pearls. Then he carefully attended to his left eye, washing the empty socket and the smooth stone Surgeon Boyd had given him to keep in it, in an emollient elixir. After which he tied a fresh black eye-patch securely in place. After that he shaved and did his hair, usually without powder, unless he were pleading a case, and dressed himself carefully, keeping in mind the visible weather and the probable business of the day. He then pulled all the bed-clothes into the middle of the bed, provided he was staying overnight, so that the servant would have to make the bed up new. After which he knelt down, usually over a chair, and addressed a prayer to the Father of Mankind, which somehow, to his own mind at least, although it was often wordless, embodied a plea for continued mercy, an act of gratitude and contrition, and a hope for the continuance of a sound body and a clear mind. In all of this it must be remembered that out of set habit he moved with the greatest celerity and economy of motion.

His mental preliminaries for the day, on the other hand, were more leisurely. They usually consisted in setting down in a diary in brief Latin sentences the events of the day before, together with such items of accounting and other factual reminders as he deemed essential. He then pondered the total result, noting keenly the probable effects of the events of the previous day upon the one which lay immediately before him, and thus having summed up the past and anticipated the immediate future as well as he could, he made his final preparations for the campaign of the next twelve hours, accordingly. These always consisted in putting into or taking out of his leather trunk, which invariably accompanied him, such articles, books, documents, and notes as the exigencies of the current day required, and transferring them to his portfolio which closed with a silver hasp engraved with the ducal arms of the House of Hamilton. He then put his watch, his keys, and the necessary change to see him through the day into his waistcoat pockets, and assuring himself he had *not* left anything behind or anything of value loose in the room, he locked his trunk, put on his cloak and neat cocked hat, opened the window to air out the chamber if the weather permitted, and descended the stairs.

On the particular morning in question Mr. Yates varied his matutinal program slightly. Instead of going downstairs immediately after locking his trunk, he sat down at a small dressing table, and extracting some foolscap from his portfolio, carefully sketched in and then wrote out in fair-hand three formal statements which he felt would hold good in law, to wit: a lease embodying a waiver as a preliminary agreement, a form of indenture for a minor child, and an agreement between certain parties for the hiring and subsistence of a slave. Having checked these for correct phraseology against a volume that always accompanied him, *Cunningham's Law Dictionary,* he placed that useful tome back in the trunk together with *Blackstone's Commentaries* and *Taylor's Elements of Civil Law,* etc., etc., and again locked the large leather travelling valise, for such it was, and returned the key to its ring. His plans for the day thus thoroughly in mind, and the documents he had completed and certain other writing materials in his portfolio, he then descended the stairs.

In all the plans Yates had made for the day and for the immediate future, it would not be precise to say that he had been entirely and professionally aloof or even averse to considering his personal interests, since he had decided to include himself in the temporary establishment that he now foresaw, for various reasons, it would be advisable to set up at Mr. Glen's mill. Unexpectedly, he found he had to stay for some weeks at Carlisle in connection with certain of St. Clair's land warrants, the petty litigation over which had held up for the nonce the immediate forwarding of emigrants to Ligonier. But what could be more pleasant or convenient, he thought, since he now had to stay at least in the vicinity of Carlisle, than stopping with old friends and in good company? And since by doing this he could also accommodate both his friends and clients, and protect the property for which he was an executor under Mr. Glen's will, he had decided to try to perfect the arrangement.

Frances Melissa and Salathiel, he felt, were probably the only ones who might prove inimical. They were always talking about moving to Philadelphia. But after a short conversation with Frances, she proved unexpectedly pliable and was soon herself pleading with Salathiel for a delay at the comfortable mill, while the child was coming on.

Having thus opened the campaign for the day hopefully, the only other thing that remained for Yates to do was to get Mr. Glen's son, Martin, and Arthur St. Clair together with the Albines and Williamses in order to accomplish the rest of his plan. And he was moderately sanguine of success, for upon this, as upon many other occasions, Yates's tactics consisted in making it convenient for everyone to profit at the apparent concession of somebody else. To that end he now acted immediately, and putting on his grey cloak, he made his excuses and departed down the street, portfolio in hand, to call upon Mr. John Byers. It was at that gentleman's residence that he confidently expected to find Arthur St. Clair.

Nothing, in fact, was more certain that morning than finding Arthur St. Clair. He was stopping only a few houses down the street with his good friend, the wagon commissioner, and, as Yates well knew, few people slept sounder and no one liked better to linger in bed a little longer when circumstances permitted than Mr. St. Clair. He was, therefore, very much at home but not yet up, following the hearty town hall rejoicings of the night before, when Yates sounded his ardent reveille on Mr. Byers's bright brass knocker—and who should come to the door but the Reverend Mr. Muir Craighead, with his bald pate wrapped in a home-made turban fashioned from an old red curtain—and his features in a cordial smile.

There was a bright applewood fire going in Mr. Byers's snug little parlour, where they were all having breakfast that morning on Mrs. Byers's only and best marble-topped table, which *still* has coffee stains on it. But despite the fire, the minister was taking no chances of catching cold even in the warm parlour. He continued to wear his turban like a Turk, but for a Christian reason. For above all clerical errors, Mr. Craighead deprecated croaking out the sacred words of Holy Writ like a frog. Next to coughing amongst the congregation, he feared a cold in the head most as the Nemesis of good preaching; so that the loss of his wig, impossible to replace at Carlisle, had been the incessant topic of his conversation for many days past and was the immediate theme of his salutation to Yates, whom he began to question as to the whereabouts of Salathiel almost as soon as he had opened the door.

"The Lard be praised," said he, leading Yates into the parlour, while he explained his predicament and the crimson turban all in one breath. " 'Tis now over a week since John Byers delivered your friend Albine's message to me that he'd found my best bag, and now you tell me Salathiel's biding practically next door. Well, well, *that's* good news! I wonder if he brought the wig with him?"

"I wouldn't guarantee that," replied Yates. "But I'm sure Sal will be able to put it in shape for you soon."

"Will he now?" mused the clergyman. "What a help that'll be! I shall drop in on him immedjit. At the Williamses' you say?" He again touched the faded crimson stuff on his head thoughtfully, while Mr. Byers tried to stifle his laughter in a large blue bowl of coffee.

"Sal will be glad to see you again, Mr. Craighead, I'm sure," continued Yates, suddenly struck by a notion. "But if you *are* going over to the Williamses', kindly be sure to rouse St. Clair first and take him along with you. Tell him it's quite important and urgent, please. There's to be a bit of a meeting, and he'd best not oversleep himself. Sal will be all the happier to see you if you take St. Clair along."

"Now, I'll *do* that," cried Mr. Craighead emphatically, and departed upstairs hot-foot, where he was soon heard banging at St. Clair's door lustily, and getting sleepy replies.

Thus having assured the reasonably prompt attendance of St. Clair by the aid of a third party, Yates was about to depart, explaining his necessity of finding young Martin Glen. But Mr. Byers would not hear of it. Mr. Yates must sit down. He must have a dish of coffee. It was a cold morning. One of the coloured boys could be sent with a note to young Glen's captain. His company was camped just outside the town. Certainly, certainly, Mr. Byers would see to it. He would guarantee young Glen would get to the Williamses' in a jiffy. Pompey could leave now. "Martha, pour Mr. Yates a dish of mocha."

So it was that, while Reverend Mr. Craighead roused St. Clair, no small effort, and the coloured boy went riding to fetch young Glen, Mr. Yates sat quite comfortably in the Byerses' snug parlour and discussed a dish of steaming mocha with his host and hostess, as congenial a pair of morning gossips as sat happily at their own board for many miles around. And it would have been surprising if amongst the lively small fry of town gossip with which they regaled their visitor, one or two convenient minnows of information had not lodged in the meshes of Yates's net, which he had learned to make small and fling wide.

It was in this way, indeed, that he learned further enlightening details of Mr. Glen's death and burial, his host's concern over the disappearance of Mrs. Larned, the pertinent fact that *both* the Glen boys had been courting the same girl at Conestoga, and, of course, all about the loss and finding of Mr. Craighead's wig. After which, Mr. Byers could not refrain from telling in his most finished, and in what he considered to be his best, humorous manner what *he* had heard had happened at Stottelmyer's stable the first morning after the Albines came to town. There were many versions of the affair going about Carlisle, but Mr. Byers guaranteed that he *knew,* and that his own was by far the best story.

Hence it happened that about half an hour later, when St. Clair and Mr. Craighead finally did come downstairs, they descended into a gale of laughter. They were even able to join in themselves heartily, once Mr. Byers repeated his story and they discovered that the merriment was not at their own expense. Mr. Craighead was touchy about his wig; and St. Clair was as usual in the morning, touchy. But a dish of hot coffee and a bowl of porridge soon tended to settle his stomach and his apprehension of being the butt of a joke, all at the same time. Mr. Craighead was now fully dressed in his decent black suit, with a starched clerical stock, Yates observed. And he also held a respectable black chapeau under his arm, ready to clap it down on the India silk handkerchief swathed about his shaven poll, as soon as he went out.

"At least," Yates remarked, "it will prevent you from being taken for a tonsured papist in disguise, Mr. Craighead. I understand there are several priests of the old religion, out of Maryland, running loose amongst these hills."

"Shocking," said Mr. Craighead, looking suddenly nervous. It had never occurred to him he might be taken for a Roman priest. "I'd be consternated if any such report ever got about." It made him all the more anxious to see Salathiel, immediately. But it was only decent to let St. Clair finish breakfast, he felt, and to wait for the return of the coloured boy with young Martin Glen. So the talk went on while the applewood burned smoothly, and Mr. Craighead's only sop to his impatience was a rather doubtful twinkle in Mr. Yates's single eye. Perhaps it was only a reflection of the fire?

Yates for his part was quite content to delay a little. Breakfasts were proving important to him that morning. He was picking up a deal of minor information that would stand him in good stead in the meeting at the Williamses' that was soon to follow. He thought he saw the way now to settle the affairs, not only of the Albines but of his several clients and other friends, quite satisfactorily and in the round for some months to come—with certain personal comforts in view as his own reward. And it also occurred to him that Mr. Craighead's wig was not the only one at Carlisle that might need attention. And that Mr. Albine, if he cared to, might profit considerably thereby. There were all the regular officers, for instance, whose false hair had been so considerably disarranged by the exigencies of an Indian campaign. Yates chuckled aloud, and he might again have had to explain himself to Mr. Craighead had not the breakfast and St. Clair's second dish of coffee just then been interrupted by the return of Mr. Byers's boy, Pompey, with the news that young Martin Glen had been excused from morning drill by his captain and was even now waiting in the Williamses' parlour, a few doors upstreet. "An' he done take de news ob his pappy's death hahd," said Pompey.

"No doubt, no doubt," murmured Mr. Byers. "Poor fellow, I thought he might have heard of it before."

"No, sah, no, sah. Missy Williams done buss out wid de news when he fust come in. An' she up an' arsked him straight out if he gwine fer to pay fer his old man's coffin."

"Lord!" exclaimed Yates. "I think we'd better adjourn to the Williamses' without further delay." And thanking Mr. Byers and his spouse for their morning hospitality, he and St. Clair and Mr. Craighead walked hastily up the street, scarcely taking time to note on the way that it was a bright frosty day with a touch of powdery snow blowing about, and that the square was comparatively deserted.

Mr. and Mrs. Williams, the Albines, and young Mr. Martin Glen, who had quite evidently *not* yet been introduced to anybody, received the newcomers in the Williamses' best front room with the wagging clock on the wall. There was no fire there and the atmosphere was not only frigid but sadly constrained; although tempered, Mr. Yates noted, with precisely the proper lugubrious respectability on the part of the Williamses, which only an English origin and life in a small Pennsylvania town could achieve. Mr. Craighead, for one, was so much impressed by it that he sat in his kerchief resignedly, watching his frosty breath hang in the air, and forbore for more than half an hour to say anything about his wig, although he did nod hopefully at Salathiel and received an encouraging wink in return. Nevertheless, and despite the fact that St. Clair called for a fire immediately, and got it, Mr. Craighead always remembered the occasion as one which required the exercise of considerable Christian forbearance and patience on the part of a certain clergyman.

The truth was it was a legal rather than a clerical occasion. And Yates moved so skilfully and so tactfully into the arena of action that it was soon a nice question as to whether he or the fire was the more efficient source of the light and warmth that now so rapidly pervaded the frigid gloom of the cold front room.

Young Martin Glen was, of course, rejoiced to see his father's attorney, and to find somebody on his side, as he bluntly put it, looking a bit vindicatively at the Williamses. But Yates put an end to that, and to all other taking of sides whatever, by immediately expressing with a plaintive twist of funereal eloquence the immeasurable sorrow and horrid sense of shock felt by the united company at the untimely and unexpected departure of so virtuous and kindly a man as the late Mr. Glen. How he would be missed! So phrased, Yates's gentle opening of the case amounted to an elegant bit of threnody, and all who had not actually been moved by the event were now deeply touched by the attorney's kindly and deeply poetic words.

For the first time young Martin fully realized from what virtuous loins he must have sprung. Tears of natural pride rather than a mist of indignation now suffused his eyes and veiled the strangers before him in a more charitable and friendly light. Mrs. Williams herself was not able to refrain from letting fall the damp overflow of a neighbourly heart into the conveniently absorbent lap of her apron. Nor was this aquid tribute to the virtues of the deceased at all diminished, rather it was increased, when she heard the charitable and sensible offices of herself and her spouse celebrated with an unexpected and tender applause. The small expenses which the Williamses had so generously incurred in burying Mr. Glen were now guaranteed to be forthcoming immediately from the miller's estate; and, in addition, as a kind of mortuary bonus and just dividend of appreciation, two fine jet mourners' rings, worth not a whit less than a pound apiece were apportioned to herself and her husband. To which proposition, since Yates looked at him so fixedly, young Martin was compelled to nod an immediate and solemn acquiescence.

Thus oiled, the rusty flood-gates of Mrs. Williams's unconsciously venal soul were now opened fully, and the course of her sorrow ran in flood. Almost—almost, she could see glimmering, even through her copious tears, these jet bands of fashionable sorrow like double links in the chain of respectability, shining in dark elegance on the fingers of both the Williamses, moulds of virtue in the round, from the best jewelry shop in the City.

Thus having, as it were, paved the floor of his rostrum with a mosaic of auspicious design, Mr. Yates now swept aside the death of Mr. Glen and the ancillary tragedy of poor Mrs. Larned as misfortunes, sad indeed, but inevitable in the unrestrained course of Nature. And he then began, with a kind of movement to the right oblique, which shifted ground without changing front, while he marshalled his arguments, to prove to Martin Glen what an essentially fortunate young man he actually was. For, granted, that death was bound to come to everybody, and no man could tell the hour, averred Mr. Yates, lowering his voice appropriately, had not the passing of both Mr. Glen and Mrs. Larned, strange and unexpected as the circumstances of their demises seemed to be, occurred in a manner which was as merciful to them as possible, and more fortunate to their heirs, assigns, and survivors than *they* had any right or reason to expect? How much worse and sadly otherwise it might have been!

Mr. Glen might have died alone·at the mill, deserted by his unfaithful servants, and left to be devoured by rats. How would either of his sons have liked to find him like that? Martin, indeed, was not able to stifle an unsoldierly sniffle at the thought. Instead of which, continued Yates, it had been vouchsafed to Mr. Glen to depart this life on the front porch, nay in the very arms of pious and kindly neighbours, who out of the native generosity of their charitable hearts had provided him with a Christian burial. And old Mrs. Larned, too, Yates insisted, skipping rapidly along, might she not also be said to be only the devoted victim of a wise Providence? She seemed to have been providentially sent to replace Mr. Glen at the mill, a faithful caretaker *ad interim*. And scarcely had she been removed, by the mysterious will of God, when those whom she had manifestly been preparing to receive providentially appeared to continue her good offices. How could it be deemed that there was not more than chance at work in all this? Was not the benign hand of a merciful Providence plainly discernible? "And," said Yates, waiting solemnly long enough to look everybody significantly in the face —"is it not the best part of our childish wisdom to take hold of the hand of Providence, which seems to have been so happily extended to us, and to continue to walk in the direction in which we are manifestly being led?

"To that end I thought it well this morning to prepare certain papers to be signed," he added, and turning to open his portfolio, he set out on the table before him an ink-horn, a couple of plumed pens, sealing wax, a sand-box, and several sheets of legal paper with blocks of his small but clear professional script on them, each paragraph of which began with a capital made with a shaded flourish.

So that's what he was doing upstairs this morning, thought Salathiel. But whoa! Isn't Ned going a bit too far? The next thing, he will be trying to show young Glen that his father's death was a special act and favourable dispensation . . . that we ought to be glad. Salathiel, however, was to learn that his friend did not make serious mistakes like that.

Yates was simply putting new points on the quills with his gold penknife, as if there were no doubt that the pens would soon be used and should, therefore, be usable.

"You see," said he, "young Martin here finds himself in difficult circumstances in regard to taking immediate possession of his father's estate. He is only one of two heirs. The other, Mr. John Glen, his brother, has probably not yet learned of his father's death, since he left some time ago for Conestoga, in order to get some wrought-iron work done for the mill machinery, I'm told—but I fear he has been detained there for softer work on even more malleable metal."

"Oh, the foxy old polecat!" exclaimed young Martin, and began to sputter. "The last thing John promised me was he wouldn't go poking around Clara over at Conestoga, until the war was over and I came home. No, sir, that was the bargain between us, if I went to war, and I was the younger."

"*H-m-m,*" said Yates, "I fear your affectionate brother has anticipated the calendar slightly, although the war may be said to be over."

"But *I'm* still in the service!" exclaimed Martin. "Now look here, Mr. Yates, you've got to help me, sir. If Clara . . . if that derned skunk . . . !"

"I've anticipated your natural feelings under the circumstances, Martin," said Yates. "Mr. Byers has already showed his good offices, and I'm sure Mr. St. Clair, whose influence with the authorities is so considerable, will be pleased to aid in expediting your discharge. Your captain, I believe, is a Scot."

"McCalister, Captain McCalister," mumbled Martin without any enthusiasm. "But maybe he'd give me a furlough to Conestoga. Even a couple of days would help, before my discharge."

"I'll do you the service if I can, young man," said St. Clair. "And I know Don McCalister."

"Oh my, oh, sir, if you *only* will," cried Martin. "I'll never forget it, I promise you."

"Meanwhile," continued Yates, smiling a bit in spite of himself, "since both of Mr. Glen's heirs will probably be at Conestoga for some time to come, there is the matter of the care of the mill property. It would be most inadvisable to permit it to stand empty and unguarded."

"I don't give a damn—" began Martin.

"No, but as executor of your father's will, and your and your brother's attorney, I must and do," insisted Yates. "And it seems to me that you could not do better than make an arrangement with the good people who are already providentially occupying the premises to continue to do so, and to look after the place and continue the business of the mill, while you and your brother are settling your, *ahem*, mutual affairs at Conestoga."

"That's just elegant, but what'll John say?" cried Martin.

"I've drawn the lease with an agreement to take care of that," said Yates. "Under your father's will, our two signatures will be sufficient, since it is a matter of preserving the property."

Martin extended his hand for a pen eagerly and would have signed forthwith if Yates had not cautioned him to read the paper first.

"You see," he pointed out, "this not only takes care of the legality of Mr. and Mrs. Albine's present occupancy of the mill property, about which they have been greatly concerned, but also gives them tenancy for the full quarter beginning New Year's Day, 1765, they to take all care of the premises and such runs of the mill and other items of business as may come up concerning it during your and your brother's absence. The ten shillings a month rent is merely nominal to be sure about the value-received clause. As I expect to board with the Albines for some weeks to come," he added, looking at Frances, "you and your brother can be well assured that the property will be looked after until you settle your difficulties. By the way, Martin, it's about time you formally met your new tenants, I think," and he motioned to Salathiel and Frances to come forward. Frances made a grave curtsy to her young soldier landlord, her face solemn, but her eyes snapping.

Thus, with all due formality, shaking of hands, bows and mutual politenesses, the lease on the mill property at Boiling Springs, which was to prove such an important item in all their lives, was duly signed and sealed, Mr. and Mrs. Williams being greatly flattered and much pleased at being called up to act as witnesses. The ink on the lease was scarcely dry, however, before Martin Glen was making his excuses and bouncing down the street to be sure Mr. Byers was going to go with him to see Captain McCalister—and would Mr. St. Clair be sure, please, not to forget his promise?

"Not where a lady's concerned, Mr. Glen," said St. Clair, "provided she's one of the truly fair."

"Oh, she's lovely, she's the toast of all Conestoga," shouted Martin. "Clara? My God!" Then he blushed to the roots of his curly red hair and rushed out.

" 'Pon my word," exclaimed St. Clair, "I hope that young cockerel does win his girl. I'll see McCalister today. You have my promise, if that's all you wanted with me," said he, rising.

"There's something that concerns you much more nearly, Arthur," replied Yates, motioning him to sit down. "As for young Martin, freshest advices from Conestoga have it that John is not faring so well. But what'll concern you more is the suggestion you made to me at Lancaster that we make a definite arrangement about Jed."

"Ah!" said St. Clair, taking the paper that Yates handed him. "Good! I simply can't have that rascal on my hands any more when I ride the western road, and Mrs. St. Clair is at her wit's end with what to do with him in the City. He's the black Lothario of the second ward. All the neighbours with maidservants in the block are complainin'. Yet I don't want to sell him. I never like to do that, *hmm,* yes. This will do well enough, if Albine here will agree. I might rent Jed out to the stone-cutters, but like enough he'd run off. No, on the whole, this is better, I suppose." He passed the papers to Salathiel.

It was an agreement by which Salathiel was to provide Jed with board, shelter, and clothes for the next six months, and to receive his services "as a house servant" in return. If Jed ran away, Salathiel would be responsible to the extent of fifty pounds, but not if he died in the course of nature.

Both parties being willing, the bill of rental for a chattel was signed, witnessed, and sealed.

Frances long remembered Yates that morning, sitting before the fire behind the little round table, turning about to melt the stick of sealing wax in the fire, and dropping it precisely in the right place upon the papers, while the wax sputtered and flamed. Yates managed always to cast a certain air of dignity, of humour, and of natural drama over what he did, and yet he never overdid it. What he did seemed to have to happen his way. It was just right, she thought, just right! But she couldn't exactly fathom his secret of how it was he knew precisely the moment to spring a smile or to conjure a laugh.

How could anybody be so precise, and yet so deft and neat and gracefully mysterious all at once? Perhaps it was the black patch, or the large grey pupil of his other eye that looked through you? Or was it the always unexpected and swiftly changing expression of the mobile mouth, the keen flash of white teeth timed to the pleasant and yet dangerous voice. Was that it? Yes . . . no! Something more than that, a man essentially lonely, yet amused, constantly amused at something—something mysterious in himself and in others. Who could tell? But she decided that morning for good and all that she liked him. There now—the eye was gazing directly at her.

"One thing more," he was saying as he picked up the last of the written sheets and looked at Frances and Salathiel. "You young folks who have just come out of the woods into the realm of legal papers, this concerns you both deeply, I'm sure. You know, since Mrs. Larned has gone, you are going to have to do something definite about Bridget. Now, legal adoption is a rather involved matter, and not much indulged in in these parts. Later some of Bridget's relatives may show up, after all. But meanwhile, you won't want to let her remain a waif, and to save trouble, I have drawn up an indenture here, binding her out to you, Sal, until she's eighteen. You'll have to produce her before a magistrate and swear to the provisions for her nurture before this can be registered, but you can easily do that any day now, and meanwhile I'd advise you to sign the paper."

"She'll belong to me, too, won't she?" demanded Frances, her colour mounting and then growing pale. She knew that Yates was avoiding a certain marriage difficulty.

"In fact she'll be a child of your household," he answered. "The indenture is a helpful formality."

"Sign it then, Sal," said Frances eagerly. "And I'd like to see anyone that durst try to take her away from us now." She gave Salathiel's arm a squeeze.

Yates smiled, and Salathiel signed—the most important document he ever laid pen to.

"Ah," said Yates, shading his good eye with one hand, "a proper morning's work, I take it. And now—Mr. and Mrs. Williams!"

He shook out some guineas on the table from his ring-purse. "These will reimburse you, my friends, for your expenses in burying your neighbour, and perhaps a little more. The mourning rings will have to come later. It will take some time to probate the will and settle Mr. Glen's estate."

"Naturally," mumbled Mr. Williams, "of course." He cleared his throat as he signed the receipt that Yates extended to him, and turned the money over to his wife.

A warm atmosphere of general satisfaction and mutual gratulation suddenly pervaded the room. Everybody but Mr. Craighead got up and shook hands with one another.

"Bejasus," whispered Frances, going up to Yates, "if iver I find me in a pickle, 'tis yourself I'll be after askin' to pull me out of the brine."

"I accept the tribute—and responsibility too," he added. He took her fingers that showed out of her black knitted half-gloves and pressed them lightly to his lips. "It's a bargain," said he. She nodded, looking pleased.

"Here, here, Ned, what's going on?" called Salathiel. "If you're thinkin' of takin' my gal for the retainer, it's too high a fee." He put his arm around Frances possessively. "Not that we're not beholden to you more than I can say," he blurted out. "I can't think of a single thing that you've overlooked . . ."

"My wig," said Mr. Craighead, coming forward. "You've forgotten my best Sabbath hair."

"That," said Yates, laughing, "is something you and the good minister will have to settle between you, Sal. I refuse to intervene in so delicate, and naked, a matter. And besides," said he, "I'm long overdue at the courthouse to file Mr. Glen's will." He gathered up his papers rapidly, and putting everything meticulously into his portfolio, he started for the door.

Salathiel now found himself fully engaged with Mr. Craighead. Before he could hoist his colours, the minister was pouring in his broadsides. The Williamses took the opportunity to leave the room. It was Frances who saw Yates to the door. In the hall he managed to put a bee in her bonnet about the fine prospects at Carlisle for anyone who could and would mend wigs . . . "And I'll see you at the mill day after tomorrow," he said, raising his eyebrows.

"That'll be all right—and any day after that, too," she said. "But board, kindliness—and no more! Is that what ye mean, Edward Yates?"

"Precisely that," he answered.

"Then that's what it will be!"

He lifted his hat to her and smiled as he went down the steps. In the parlour she found Salathiel reduced to making all but abject promises to the minister. "Before next Sunday, the wig I must have. It's that, or invite McArdle in to preach."

"I'll tell ye what, *father,*" said Frances, causing Mr. Craighead to blanch, "Sal will fix your wig for you, if you'll tell everyone who did it."

"Now, what's all this?" demanded Salathiel.

"Never you mind, I've got my own good reasons." She then addressed herself directly to Mr. Craighead. "Just tell them who done it, and how well it's done. That's all we ask, but that's a bargain, or is it?"

"Why, certainly, madam, certainly," replied the minister, looking puzzled. "I'll do anything to get my hair back." He shook hands then and left hastily. *Father!*—did he really look like that? It was not until he thought it over at the Byerses' later on that Mr. Craighead began to see the sense in Frances' remarks. "So that's it!" he suddenly said at dinner to Mrs. Byers, causing her to regard him doubtfully. Mr. Byers had just served him the *next* to the largest mutton chop. Was that *it?* she wondered.

In the parlour at the Williamses', where the fire had almost burnt itself out, Salathiel and Frances sat down on a sofa together and held hands. Presently she leaned against him and sighed happily. He put his arm around her. The clock on the wall kept wagging its pendulum, like the tail of Happy Dog Time, thought Frances.

"Wal," drawled Salathiel, "I reckon we can go back to the mill house now. Yes, ma'am, we can just about go home!" He took a deep happy breath.

"Not for a little, not yet," she said.

"What?" he exclaimed, and this time he was genuinely disturbed.

She pressed closer to him. "Let's call on your best friend first," she whispered. "The brigadier will be after expectin' you. Oh, Sal, let's not neglict the opportunity."

27

A Day at Great Headquarters

Morning

IN THE PERMANENT CAMP near LeTort's Springs, the morning at headquarters had been a busy one, and not without its peculiar irritations. A number of officers, of both the staff and line, had hangovers from the night before. The new adjutant was among the severer sufferers, since rum punch in quantities always gave Captain Ourry what he called an "echo", next day. That is, when anyone spoke to him in even a medium loud tone, the words seemed to bounce back from a sore and inflamed spot and reverberate inside his head. With an echo aboard, Captain Ourry tended to repeat what had already been said. Fortunately, the brigadier understood his adjutant's sad case and didn't think him stupid. Even when he repeated his orders verbatim like a sentry, Bouquet only grinned.

Colonel Haldiman, however, roared. And there had been a terrible lionlike interval just before morning mess over a minor mix-up in the marching orders for the 60th (R.A.) and 42nd regiments. But then the colonel, too, had been up most of the night before, drinking and dancing. And no doubt, being notified shortly before dawn to start marching for Lancaster, with the snow flying and no coffee, was something few officers could endure quietly.

Ah well, mused Ourry, the colonel and his gallant men were gone. By this time they were probably trying to ford the icy Susquehanna, horse, foot, and guns; wagons, wounded, and all. Regimental headquarters for the Royal Americans would be at Lancaster after this and for some time to come, Colonel Haldiman commanding. The Highlanders would eventually go to Philadelphia into their permanent quarters at Camptown in the Northern Liberties.

358

Captain Ourry thought of this arrangement with considerable satisfaction. The brigadier was mortal afraid of the smallpox, and always made a point of scattering the troops as soon as he could. Incidentally, it relieved department headquarters at Carlisle of a lot of trouble that, in Ourry's opinion, was purely regimental. Also it gave the adjutant, whose head was still ringing after the merry rout of the night before in the half-finished and drafty town hall, a chance to clean up his headache, a bottle-cold—and various other odds and ends of military troubles that remained after the long western campaign.

It was surprising to Ourry to think that Carlisle was now head-quarters for the entire new Southern Department; that he, Ourry, was the brigadier's adjutant and aide, responsible for the military affairs and correspondence of half North America, most of which, to be sure, was unknown. But it was quite a change, a sudden wrench indeed, from being a deputy quartermaster, and running the com-paratively simple affairs of the garrison at Fort Bedford.

Ourry often wondered just why Bouquet had chosen to promote him. He was not so sure it was not a dubious compliment. As aide to the brigadier, he would be responsible not only for departmental administration, but for the general's official military family, too. And that certainly was *not* doing so well. Bouquet was a Frenchman by nurture, and he liked to live well when he could. Hardships might be condoned in the wilderness, but it would have to be different when they moved to the City. The brigadier would have to live there as befitted his rank. Yes, it would have to be *very* different. Well, he would try to improve headquarters mess first, and brighten the aspect of the general's table later. But he was a bachelor—not apt in domestic affairs. Also there was the serious matter of personal finances, his own and the brigadier's; laundry, the general's badly tattered linen; and his own sorry clothes.* It would never do to be called "Captain Lazarus" by the damned macaroni subalterns. Smart-ness and some display at headquarters were now called for.

Ourry rested his chin on his hand and tried to gaze into the future. It still appeared, however, to be quite foggy from the effects of the immediate past, and he fell to cogitating gloomily. Probably they would stay for some weeks at Carlisle, closing out the campaign. The brigadier would have to go to New York to report, and then

---

* To be promoted to the grade of "brigadier" (general) in the British Army, circa 1764, and for many years after, was often tantamount to being kicked upstairs into bankruptcy. A colonel, on the other hand, *owned* his regiment and had fees, perquisites, and "drawbacks" on the men's pay and subsistence. Not so the brigadier. Bouquet had made certain stipulations, but was none the less financially harassed and faced with a greatly enlarged expense to meet the new scale of his official living. Cf. *passim*, Fortescue, Hon. J. W., *The British Army 1783-1802.*

come back to Philadelphia to set up temporary headquarters there
for some months at least. After that Pensacola in the new colony,
West Florida—*Lord!* But all that delay might give him a chance to
look about a bit; to perfect arrangements and domestic details.

Meanwhile, he took a surreptitious drag out of a bottle of
schnapps. Schnapps was his drink. He always carried it well. It was
the damned Jamaica rum that got him. Rum required a powerful
antidote. He took another good swallow of schnapps. The sore place
at the back of his head began to heal miraculously. Almost immediately he felt better. The echo effect, he noted, was greatly relieved.
It was about time! Noon mess call would sound presently, and there
would be a deal of conversation at the general's table which he
wouldn't necessarily desire to repeat like a parrot. What a morning
it had been!

Not that the brigadier had not arisen cheerful as usual, calm-
voiced and self-contained. It was Colonel Haldiman who had done
all the roaring. The brigadier had shown no ill effects of his reception at the town hall last night, none whatever. He had gone to the
hall, drunk a toast to the king and another to "the ladies"; answered
the speeches of welcome and thanks most affably; complimented the
new schoolmaster on his Latin; shaken hands all around cordially—
and departed for a good night's rest. Ourry, of course, had had to
stay; it was the part of a faithful adjutant and aide-de-camp to do so.

The rout, the wild dancing and fiddling, the innumerable toasts
to every local personage and every magistrate's lady in Cumberland
County; the noise and confusion of the small hours had gone on,
without the general. The adjutant had managed it alone as well as
he could. And it was not until the punch bowl had been emptied five
several times that any real trouble had started.

That damned fool creole, Monsieur Molyneaux! He *had* been a
sad case, absolutely insufferable! What was he doing at Carlisle,
anyway? Lieutenant Frazier's challenge, quite inevitable under the
circumstances, would have to be withdrawn just the same. How had
the brigadier ever heard about it? The very first thing he said when
Ourry came on duty that morning was "No duels in the militia,
captain. Let them learn to dance without quarrelling. We can't permit
the scandal of duelling and get military grants from a Quaker legislature, too. Let the officers fight the savages, and no one else. Arrest
both the young coxcombs who made that trouble last night. If necessary, prevent their meeting."

That was the way the morning had begun, if you disregarded the
trouble before dawn with Colonel Haldiman.

The next thing was a delegation of the evangelical clergy come
early to protest about public dancing. Scarcely had the last troops

marched when the ministers drove in. There were five of them, all in one old oval-wheeled wagon, headed by that crop-eared fanatic, James McArdle. As if there hadn't been enough trouble with *him* at Bedford. Why, he'd devilled poor Ecuyer into his grave. The brigadier, nevertheless, had received them quite courteously.

As far as Ourry could tell, the Reverend Mr. McArdle desired to drive a sharp bargain with the general. The protest about the dancing at the town hall the night before proved to be only a means of introduction. McArdle's proposition was that he would drop his complaints about dancing, gambling, and other more delicate affairs, provided the brigadier would lend him some tents and a few engineers to help put up prayer-booths for a big field preaching, one which all the ministers had come to Carlisle to attend.

A visitation of the Holy Spirit was about to occur, Mr. McArdle insisted, and he would like to have the loan of some military equipment suitable for the occasion. The brigadier had demurred. There was no warrant, he said, for lending the king's stores, men or matériel, for what he was pleased to call an "evangelical revel". Mr. McArdle was not only shocked at the expression, but indignant at being refused so small a request. And he proceeded to try to argue the case with the general.

McArdle was angry that two regiments had quietly been sent away to Lancaster that very morning. He felt *he* should have been consulted. He had counted on preaching the Word of God to them. "When many sinners are gathered together," he said, "the work of the Spirit is bound to be more efficacious. I have waited long, and prepared patiently for this occasion." The four other clerical gentlemen, whose mouths were potent fountains of the Spirit, according to McArdle, also considered themselves much aggrieved.

It was the duty of the secular authorities to further the Kingdom of God, McArdle then proclaimed. If the brigadier was genuinely interested in furthering the work of the Spirit, he would order the troops back to Carlisle to attend the field preaching. After all, it needed only a scratch of his pen. The Reverend Mr. Puffin, the official Church of England chaplain to the garrison at Fort Bedford, agreed. In Captain Ourry's opinion, Mr. Puffin was more zealous than respectful. And it was he undoubtedly who had provoked McArdle to drop to his knees and ask God to touch the general's heart to return the troops to Carlisle.

Two *hallelujahs,* both premature as it turned out later, accompanied McArdle's fervent petition to heaven; and a rolling chorus of *amens,* apparently meant to influence the divine decision in a manner adverse to headquarters followed. Owing entirely to the phenomenon of the echo, Captain Ourry contributed an inadvertent *amen* himself as a final remark, much to his own chagrin, the general's secret amusement, and the excitement of the ministers. After this Bouquet permitted a short interval of silence to elapse to restore order, during which Captain Ourry suffered; and Mr. McArdle, who now felt the loss of his ears severely, leaned forward and cupped a hand on each side of his wig.

"*Ahem*," resumed the brigadier a bit dryly, only raising his eyebrows slightly, for he was quite used to dealing with the unconscious self-righteous effrontery of the frontier—"you seem to forget, gentlemen, the different stations in life to which it has pleased God in His mysterious wisdom to call us."

"I, for one, fail to see the application of any such text, sir," said Mr. Puffin stiffly.

"Ah, *you,* in particular, have failed notably there, Mr. Puffin," continued Bouquet. "I shall take that up with you later. But, meanwhile, permit me to explain myself in my own house. I refer to these humble headquarters." This the brigadier said hurriedly, raising his hand in anticipation of the protests which his assertion about Mr. Puffin now obviously threatened to bring down on his devoted head. "If you please, gentlemen, if *you* please . . ."

Another moment of hard-won silence, not entirely respectful, since Mr. McArdle could be heard muttering something about the "House of Rimmon", ensued.

"My point," resumed Bouquet, disregarding Mr. McArdle's Biblical innuendo, "is that while it may be your office by divine commission to shepherd souls towards the realm of the hereafter; it is mine by the king's commission, and sundry acts of Parliament, to dispose of the bodies of fighting men in the sinful kingdom of this world, according to my best, although admittedly fallible, judgment. Now, I do not propose to interfere with or enter into your field of the divine, and you should not rashly presume to advise me in my worldly rôle. In my judgment," he continued, taking a small pinch of snuff, "it was expedient to march two regiments to Lancaster this morning, and the orders stand. Frankly, I am not convinced that marching them back to Carlisle would cause them to enlist en masse in the service of the Kingdom of God, even with the advice and assistance of you gentlemen. A visitation of smallpox is as likely to occur as that of the Holy Spirit, and it is my duty to consider the former contingency."

For a moment or two the self-appointed delegates from Beulah Land sat digesting this thought as well as they could.

"He that is not with us is against us," shouted the Reverend Cadmus Thurston, a thin man with a horse face and inflamed red hair. "*Henry Bouquet,* you are an atheist!"

"Tut, tut, *Cadmus*," replied the brigadier, who was long familiar with the Reverend Mr. Thurston's strict Calvinistic doctrine, "I was baptized at the very fountain of our mutual faith in Geneva; and you will not, I presume, have the effrontery to deny the efficacy of baptism by the Mother Church. I," said the general, leaning forward and pointing inward towards himself with his thumb, "I, *too,* am a certified Child of Light, *Mr.* Thurston."

Mr. McArdle snorted in a manner which conveyed at once his indignation and doubt. "Be that as it may, general," he said, "and *if* so, as a Child of Light, you might well lend us a few tents to help erect the tabernacle of the Lord in the wilderness."

"I concede your point, Mr. McArdle, since it is now sensibly and respectfully put, and you shall have your tents, a whole dozen of them. Captain Ourry here is authorized to lend them to you. See that some of the less mouldy of the condemned marquees are issued to Mr. McArdle, captain."

Captain Ourry, since he was still subject to the echo, repeated the orders verbatim, while the ministers looked both impressed and pleased.

"But on the same reciprocal basis, Mr. McArdle," continued Bouquet, "you should aid headquarters in checking the lists of the returned Indian captives. Your work as a missionary beyond the frontiers is well known; a great credit to you. No doubt you have saved many souls. Will you not, then, help me in seeing that the bodies of these poor souls are now rescued from the savages? It is the Shawanese especially who are to be watched. They have agreed to bring in to Fort Pitt all those who remain in their hands, by next spring. But I should like to be certain none are being secretly withheld."

"I'll not refuse ye," replied McArdle, "but, tell me, what have ye done with the list written upon bark that Albine carried into Fort Pitt at the risk of his young life, when Ecuyer was besieged there? My memory is no longer so keen, but that list, I know, was complete. It was gathered at fearful risk, sir, and with much ingenuity. 'Twould be a pity were it lost. Like enough it has been despised and mislaid by your military clarks for not being written upon official paper."

"Have a search made for the bark list, Ourry," said the general. "If it isn't here, send Fergus for it to Fort Pitt. I do remember now of Captain Ecuyer's speaking of the 'bark roll of the captivated'."

"Aye," groaned McArdle, "*Ecuyer!* Gone where no further questions can be asked him. Gone! And beyond hope!"

"A godless, obstinate little man," interpolated Mr. Puffin, "without marcy on others or upon his own soul. It would be just like him to have destroyed the list to hinder further the work of salvation."

"It would *not* be like him," said Bouquet, the icy calmness of controlled anger smoothing his voice dangerously. "It would be more like *you*, Mr. Puffin. And I will not have the revered memory of such a devoted and loyal officer as Simeon Ecuyer traduced before my face. Saving your cloth, sir, your assertion is a stinking calumny. Permit me to elaborate:

"It is you who have been neglecting *your* duty, Mr. Puffin. As an ordained priest of the Church of England, you have deserted your appointed cure of souls, that of chaplain to the garrison at Fort Bedford, and gone gadding about this howling wilderness, spouting cataracts of evangelical nonsense and irresponsible sophistry, all of which you are pleased to denominate the 'Word of God'.

"Now, loud, unauthorized, and wilful preaching hath ever been the ignorant hand rashly extended to rock the cradle of rebellion and eager to undo the swaddling bands of paternal authority in an infant state. 'Tis a heady yeast with which ye brew, sir. One that foams upon your lips to begin with. 'Bethink ye, Mr. Puffin, bethink ye—in the bowels of Christ you may be wrong!' Aye, it may take another Cromwell yet to convince ye. For you invoke lawless force. Consider—

"Already you are become the boon companion of Anabaptists, Pædobaptists, Antipædobaptists, arrant busybodies of shouting Methodists, and zany Old and New Light ranters; the happy ear-waggling brother of every enthusiastic little independent ass who hee-haws from forest stump stocks in the name of gentle Jesus. The avid cockroaches of disorder escape from the gaping pockets of such itinerant godsters. They are spreaders of the dirty biting bugs of impudence. And you, sir, their cozy new bedfellow, are now infected with such, and crawling. Authority and respect are no longer within you, or due you. This morning you, an ordained chaplain, had the gall to begin by advising me, a commissioned general, as to the proper disposition of the troops; and the insolence to end by attacking the memory of a man whose stoic virtues you cannot even comprehend. Well, it *shall* be an end. You think I do not know how you harried Ecuyer over the steep verge of the world? By the Eternal, have a care, Mr. Puffin, have a care, or I'll throttle your puffin' down to a wheeze." Here Bouquet squeezed his fingers together into tense fists, which he smashed on the table before him, and paused to take breath.

No one had ever seen the brigadier so angry. The veins throbbed in his temples, and he was red with wrath. True, he was surprised and chagrined at having permitted himself such an outburst. But the attack on a dead comrade had outraged him to the soul, and sparks seemed to leap from his eyes, and the tension in the room was intolerable.

A pretty mess, a fine kettle of fish, thought Captain Ourry, who was standing at rigid attention just beside the general's chair. He was flabbergasted. So were the ministers. They sat staring with white faces; all except McArdle, who had gradually been turning brick-red.

That Mr. Puffin should undertake to reply to the general was, therefore, a matter of no little astonishment. Secretly, even his colleagues felt he had gone too far. But they had not supposed he durst undertake to defend himself. At first he was scarcely audible. They leaned forward to try to catch what he was saying.

"A week ago come Thursday," Mr. Puffin began in a half-whisper, while his voice trembled, "in the middle of the afternoon at Mr. John Inman's house by the Arched Spring at Aughwick, there was a visitation of the Holy Spirit. We had all been engaged in prayer and fasting for many days in preparation for the coming field preaching at Carlisle. Our prayers were notably answered. At three of the clock that blessèd afternoon, the Spirit of God overshadowed us. Mr. Thurston and myself were both vouchsafed the gift of many tongues. Mr. McArdle prophesied in a tremendous voice. All of us rejoiced loudly together in a new Pentecost. I received a call, a direct revelation that my work lay in the missionary field. In a holy trance the heavens were opened to me. I heard the voice of my Saviour, the very Voice of God," whispered Mr. Puffin, sweating. "Can you understand what it is to have the call? Oh, what is ordination compared to it! I have heard the Voice speak that spoke to Paul. I have been called to the mission for the saving of lost souls. I am no longer a member of the Established Church of England. I renounce the laying on of hands, sir. I denounce all worldly and ecclesiastical restraints. I am made free, and subject to the Voice of the Spirit alone. What is the dim light of tradition compared to direct revelation? Oh, Lord Almighty, oh, Christ in Heaven!" He checked himself, for at this point his voice threatened to achieve the shrillness of a feminine scream. Also, the Reverend Cadmus Thurston had begun to mutter and to show signs of internal excitement. He cried *amen* loudly, and rose up to address the meeting.

"Sit down, sir," roared Bouquet. "This is not a conventicle." Mr. Thurston sat down, instantly. The general kept looking at Mr. Puffin.

"Have you notified your superior, the Bishop of London, of the step you have taken, Mr. Puffin?" asked Bouquet.

"Not yet, sir, but I shall. That is now only a worldly formality."

The brigadier considered him carefully again, and arrived at a reluctant conclusion.

"Let me relieve you of that formality," he said, "—and your appointment as chaplain at Bedford as well. I shall also save you the trouble of writing the venerable Society for the Propagation of the Gospel to cancel your stipend as a missionary. You can rely upon me to relieve you of *all* such minor mundane affairs, Mr. Puffin. In fact," continued Bouquet, leaning back and regarding the company almost genially, "since *all* you gentlemen are in more or less direct communication with the Almighty, I can see small advantage in your conversing any longer with a mere brigadier general like myself. However, permit me, before you go, to offer you a glass of inspiration." He sniffed—"Now, Captain Ourry appears to have a distinct odour of the working of the spirit within, or somewhere about him. Captain?"

But no one took advantage of the offer. They sat as though confounded, staring. Finally Bouquet waved his hand affably.

"Show the clergy out, then, captain. Perhaps some of the more inspiring examples of divine handiwork outdoors will interest them. We are greatly favoured here, you know. There is a noble view of the mountains from the outer barbican."

"We can see the mountains without your assistance, sir," replied Mr. McArdle in an acidulous tone. The general waved his hand again, indicating his release of all claims on the landscape, whatsoever. "But the tents?" exclaimed Mr. McArdle, struck by an afterthought on the very verge of the threshold.

"They are yours as I promised," answered Bouquet, and bowed him out.

Somewhat mollified by this concession to shelter religion, Mr. McArdle followed Captain Ourry to the door of headquarters more cheerfully, and, without pausing to observe the mountains, clambered into the muddy wagon after his four colleagues and rattled down the road towards LeTort's Springs. The progress of the evangelical mission along the roads of this world was dilatory, since neither hickory nor prayers had much effect upon either the stern or the spirit of the steed that gave motion to their chariot. As the horse was a gift from the pious Mr. Inman of Aughwick, no one felt inclined to complain. Still, there was ample time, before the company reached Carlisle, to discuss the finer shades of meaning in the general's remarks, and to indulge in a bit of mutual chiding.

Thus it was that the day at headquarters got under way—or bogged down, depending on how one considered it. In any event, since the next hour or two was taken up exclusively, and almost violently, by the removal of the remaining unclaimed captives from the square at Carlisle, and settling them in the huts at camp vacated by the 60th only that morning, there was nothing sedative about it. Quite the contrary. A large crowd of putative relatives and not a few of the curious followed, and insisted upon staying. It was impossible to separate the sheep from the goats without making scenes, and Ourry had capitulated. The wailing from the baby wagon was now transferred to a room in the log barracks. But for a bachelor with an echo, it had been hard to take.

However, time and the hour sees through the longest day—and even runs through a bad morning. And, it was almost time for the noon mess call when Captain Ourry finally sat down at his desk to fortify himself with his antidote for rum, and take further stock for the future. The schnapps had just begun to get in its good work and to convince him that the crisis of the day was really over, when he was confirmed in that opinion by what he ever afterward considered to be a distinct stroke of luck, both for himself and for the brigadier.

"There's a lidy and gen'leman outside in a two-wheeled country cart, sir," announced the sergeant major, saluting. "The man says as 'ow 'e 'as business with the general." Captain Ourry grimaced. "Rather a decent sort, sir. Drivin' a neat little mare," added the sergeant encouragingly.

"One of the town shopkeepers come to protest sending the troops off before pay-day, I suppose," sighed Ourry. "We'll have the lot of them here by tomorrow."

"No, sir. They don't look it," said the sergeant.

"Show 'em in, show 'em in," sighed Ourry resignedly, reaching for his bottle under the desk—but too late.

The next moment as fine a looking woman as he had ever seen came proudly into the room, and the frame of the door was familiarly occupied by Captain Ecuyer's man; by that ragged-eared ranger, Salathiel Albine!

"I'll be everlastingly damned!" exclaimed the captain, blinking. "*You!* Rat me, if you're not one huge piece of luck come in the nick of time." He took a deep breath and shouted, "What became of the bark list of the captivated?"

Salathiel smiled, and shook hands more calmly with the captain than the captain did with him. "I thought you'd be askin' that question," said he. "You see, we met McArdle and his friends drivin' out. Oh, yes, *quite* an encounter. I'll tell ye about it later. Yes, I've got the list—here," and he pointed to his breast, which Ourry took to mean his pocket. "But I want you to meet a lady, someone who lives with me now. Happened recently."

"My word, madam, headquarters are greatly honoured. The brigadier will be delighted. You can scarcely imagine how fortunate is your advent this morning." Ourry bowed deeply.

"Oh, I have an idea how it is, captain," replied Frances, after her best curtsy. "When the gineral bowed to us yesterday, I urged Sal not to fail to call upon him. Sal's always talkin' about old days at Bedford."

"And well he might," cried Ourry. "This is an auspicious reunion. Permit me to mark it. Orderly, two chairs and three glasses. An old military custom, madam. I hope you'll not mind." Frances did not mind at all. From underneath the desk Ourry produced the bottle of schnapps. Alack, it was only half full! The captain had to send to his quarters for another bottle, immediately.

Now, Ourry admired a lady who drank heartily and daintily at the same time, a girl who became softly radiant at the first glass. After the second, his impression that the difficulties of the day were entirely surmounted was confirmed.

His amiability soon extended to the whole force on duty. They, in fact, were already agog. Beautiful ladies at headquarters were rather more unusual there than elsewhere. The clerks sat watching the doings at the adjutant's desk, and exchanged winks at the unexpected transformation of Captain Ourry. Human after all, eh? The big hawk-faced man was Captain Jack's chief ranger, whispered the sergeant major. A dangerous customer, no doubt. He must be pretty sure of himself to let the captain carry on with his girl like that. All writing had ceased. Listening was apparently in order. No one pretended to do anything else. They idled openly. It was almost mess time, anyway. The unexpected treat of what remained of the second bottle, just before the adjutant took the visitors in to see the general, capped the climax.

Meanwhile, a hundred ideas and surmises had been chasing themselves around in Captain Ourry's suddenly clarified head. In the fortunate presence of the visitors before him he thought he saw the possible solution of many of his difficulties in organizing the new department headquarters. The matter of the bark list was only one item. Salathiel, he remembered, had been a combined "secretary and valet", as he now optimistically phrased it, to Captain Ecuyer. And no one had ever been so letter-perfect in running a command or a detached post as the little captain; and a tailor's model for the regiment, too. Now, perhaps Salathiel could be persuaded to come back and apply what he must have learned from the captain, for the benefit of the new brigadier. In some way or other, he must be attached to headquarters, or personally employed by Bouquet. Yes, it might, it ought to be, arranged. As for Frances, she might bring that missing touch of feminine elegance into the domestic arrangements of the general's official household which no bachelor aide-decamp could ever accomplish. Perhaps it was because he could grasp a situation like this so quickly that he had been made an adjutant. Maybe *that* was it? At any rate, the first step was to detain and to get on famously with his visitors. Details could be laid before the brigadier and perfected later. All of this, he, Ourry, saw in a flash, and in less than two glasses of schnapps.

After all the pleasantries and amenities he could think of were applied—and all the liquid hospitality which seemed advisable— Captain Ourry responded to a sigh and a hint from Frances that they ought to be going, and deprecating any such untimely thought, led them both into the other room to present them to the general.

Bouquet grasped instantly the advantages of having the Albines appear so opportunely. He took the words of explanation out of Ourry's mouth by congratulating him on being freed now of any dependence on McArdle. And he was much amused at Salathiel's explanation that he could "sing" the list from memory, whenever required. "That'll be music to my ears, whether you're off key or not," insisted the brigadier.

As for Frances, he was charmed with her. Her refreshing combination of careful elegance, tact, humour, and dewy rawness caused him to think of her as a European rose gone wild in the American wilderness, a self-cultivated flower whose origin must be romantically mysterious.

Bouquet was a soldier-courtier with a Gallic flair for clever conversation, the scion of an age when witty talk was the golden key to the casket of success.* With a merciful heart, an amiable disposition, and a careful shrewdness, he also combined a politician's talent for names and faces and the capacity to listen with a warm understanding. In brief, he was instinctively and sympathetically adroit. That morning for over a quarter of an hour he provided a prime example of how to be the most popular and respected man in the colonies.

In five minutes they were all talking with him as with an old and tried friend. Captain Ourry was reassured; Salathiel carefully consulted and his advice honoured; Frances complimented in a discerning way. For the first time, even through the fumes of juniper berries and spirits-of-wine exhaled by all but the general, Frances sniffed the keen air of those higher altitudes to which she aspired. Her laughter conveyed a hint of rapture, and her eyes shone like twin stars twinkling in the lacy haze of her cloudy black bonnet.

Bouquet, on his part, had soon learned as much of the story of his visitors, from coal caves to Mr. Glen's mill, as he thought he needed or ought to know. He pondered Salathiel's progress as something to be noted for future reference, and appraised Frances as a beautiful young female, who *might* go far. Time for a while seemed to relax or be cancelled, and the interview might easily have con-

---

* Bouquet had served in various military capacities at several European courts : in Germany ; in Savoy ; at The Hague ; and he was familiar with St. James's.

tinued if the bugle announcing noon mess had not put a natural end to it.

However, the general's invitation to his table also followed naturally. He laid Frances' hand over his arm gallantly, and her great moment arrived—and passed swiftly—as she emerged from the door of headquarters with the "gineral", while the sentry presented arms.

Melissa was walking on air, Salathiel observed. But he did not begrudge her the triumph. A little cloud-walking was good for her, he figured. His chief concern was that she should walk steadily. But she was doing that. She was even being whimsically sedate. Yet his concern was only natural under the circumstances, for Captain Ourry, he noted, tended to deviate from a straight military line of approach. And whether he tottered or simply marked time at sharp corners was a question too nice to be asked. There was no doubt that his tongue wagged more than was required of an adjutant.

That at least was Salathiel's opinion. It was only a few hundred yards across the parade from headquarters to the old log building where the general's mess was temporarily installed, although Captain Ourry did follow a rather zigzag course. But in that short distance, he managed to spill his plans for annexing Salathiel to headquarters, with a completeness and amplitude that a more sober and less sanguine view of the future would have prevented. Not that Ourry was a bottle-slave, he had simply succumbed to the unusually fervent rejoicing incident to the brigadier's return. For the most part he was circumspect as an adjutant should be, but the walk to the general's table that afternoon did constitute a long slither rather than a mere slip of his tongue.

Salathiel listened intently but made noncommittal replies. He took a much less enthusiastic view of an opportunity to return in some vague capacity to work at headquarters than did Captain Ourry. He would be helpful where he could, for the sake of old days and out of admiration for Bouquet. That much he felt was due the memory of Ecuyer. But he also remembered that when he had left the captain's service, he was through forever with being anyone else's man. He would be neither servant nor subject, apprentice nor hireling again. Whatever he did now must receive its equivalent reward, and that implied a transaction between equals. So he was no more to be persuaded to return to headquarters as a clerk or a minor assistant than an escaped panther can be lured back to its cage by the remembrance of kindly keepers and the safety conferred by iron bars. What he would do, he reserved for time to unfold. He listened to Ourry and replied with smiles. If the captain took them at more

than their face value, that was his affair. Frances, he knew, would
not fail to make hay in the sunshine, and he was going to leave the
reaping of opportunity largely to her. A steady hand on Captain
Ourry's elbow proved helpful as he negotiated the porch steps of the
mess hall.

Ten officers, and the two visitors, for whom chairs were hastily
brought, sat down to luncheon at the brigadier's table. Frances, of
course, sat next to Bouquet and on his right. As the only woman
present, Frances was naturally the centre of constant attention, which
she enjoyed greatly and managed to cope with, without neglecting
the brigadier. He was delighted with her salty and naïve anecdotes,
her quick responses, and her witty replies. If some of the broad
attitudes of a former establishment in Cork affected her social technique, it was well calculated to intrigue a company exclusively male.
The anecdote of Mr. Craighead's wig, which everyone leaned forward to hear, convulsed the general and brought down the house.
It was a good story, fetchingly told. The result later that afternoon
was a pile of wigs left at headquarters with fervent prayers on paper
for their repair. Salathiel was right. He knew that somehow Frances
would make hay.

Soup, fishballs, boiled potatoes, and a huge pumpkin pie having
been sent to their proper destination, the brigadier proposed a toast
"to the frequent return of our fair and charming visitor". The wine
was a clear honey-coloured Madeira, in the bottle. But to Captain
Ourry's horror, the Negro attendant dumped it into an earthen
pitcher, lees and all. Every glass, as it was filled up, swam. No one
said anything, of course, not even the general. It was left to Frances
to endear herself to him by remarking, as the company broke up,
that the sediment would settle and the sentiment remain.

There was no time for lingering at the table that day or for the
customary formalities of leave-taking. The brigadier explained with
a hint of embarrassment that, what with the departure of two regiments that morning and the moving-in of the Indian captives from
the square at Carlisle, the camp was in a turmoil, and everyone frantically engaged. The officers were no exception.

"But there is something more interesting in camp now than the
usual drill and parades of soldiers," Bouquet added. "Let us go and
have a look at what Ourry here has managed to do with his unfor-
tunates. I think it will be something for you to remember having
seen. Captain, you know where you have disposed them, suppose
you lead the way."

Thus, with Frances leaning on the brigadier's arm, and Ourry,
who was now much himself again after a full meal, leading the way

with Salathiel—they all set forth on an afternoon's stroll about the camp, one that was to have momentous consequences for several people.

Afternoon

Frau Anna Lininger was a figure of woe, a member of the Lutheran parish of Tulpahocken, and her troubles were so notable, even in a troubled age, that Henry Mühlenberg, pastor, patriarch, and chronicler, made permanent note of them. Governor Hamilton in his time, Richard Penn, Justice William Allen, Colonel Burd, and a score of other prominent Pennsylvanians had had to listen to her story. And she had also taken to haunting the headquarters of various generals or colonels, whenever a hopeful expedition westward was getting under way. In certain ways, Frau Lininger was annoying, for she lived on all the multitudinous rumours that afflicted the frontier, and seemed to know the plans of the authorities even before they had any. Possibly she was a bit touched with grief; certainly she was tragic.

She was a dumpy little German peasant woman with moles on her face and scraggly grey hair by the time she took to haunting Colonel Bouquet in the early months of 1763; and after he marched west she stayed at Carlisle through the desperate summer of Pontiac's Rebellion. Time could not wither nor old age abate Frau Lininger's infinite capacity for tears. They ran down between the several moles on her apple-cheeked face as between islands of grief overwhelmed in a spate of sorrow. The trouble with Frau Anna Lininger was that she expected someone to *do* something about her tragedy. She never ceased to hope. Bouquet, among others, came to know her story well. But he not only listened, he heard.

In the great immigration of the 1740's Frau Lininger had come from the Palatinate with her sturdy young Bavarian husband and settled in Berks County, Pennsylvania. In due course of time, three fine children and a profitable farm were the rewards of their mutual labours. Then in the days of the French and Indian troubles, on an afternoon when Frau Lininger was visiting a neighbour, the hatchet fell.

Her husband and eldest son were horribly murdered while ploughing. The house was burned down, and her two daughters dragged off into the wilderness. Their mother heard about them afterward from a man who escaped with scars of fire on him. The older daughter, a girl in her teens, died while on the march westward; the younger, a child of six, had survived. Her name was Regina—Regina Lininger.

Owing to her mother's dedicated labours in beseeching anyone and everyone who she thought could possibly help prevail on the Indians to return her child, Regina's name was remembered by many at home long after she had forgotten it herself in the damp shades of the forest on the distant Maumee.

Among those who remembered, but who had planned to try to help Frau Anna, was Henry Bouquet. Even in the desperate hurried spring of 1763 he had found both time and sympathy to listen to the pathetic old German woman, who had trudged all the way from the Lehigh valley to Carlisle to tell him the sad things that had happened to her ten years before. Perhaps it was because Bouquet understood and spoke a little German, in a Swiss way, that she had put her complete trust and founded her final hope on his success. He remembered her prayers, and her blue tear-soaked apron waving him godspeed as he marched westward with the forlorn hope of the faithful Highlanders.

Frau Anna had remained at Carlisle. She went to live at Captain William Rainey's log house on Pomfret Street, where she helped the family in the kitchen and the garden. As the rumours of Bouquet's victories were brought back to Carlisle, she seemed to grow younger and to blossom with hope renewed. And when she was shown the name of her lost darling on the list of captives returned by the Shawanese to Bouquet, posted on the gate at Fort Lowther, she became hysterical and had to be led home by one of the younger Raineys.

Now a curious thing had happened to Frau Lininger. The images of her hope were those of a fixed idea; and it was the slim towheaded little girl of ten summers before that she was still expecting to return to her arms. Bouquet was the child's saviour. In her dreams, it was *he* who was leading Regina back to her by the hand. She saw him walking through the green forest in his red coat with Regina hanging onto his arm. And she dreamed this a number of times and awoke with tears of joy on her face. Frau Anna was a very simple old German woman.

It was not until the afternoon when Bouquet and the army returned to Carlisle, and the captivated were brought into the public square to be recognized, that it occurred to Frau Anna that she might not find the little girl she was looking for. Instinctively she had gone first to search amid the smaller children, and it was only the fact—as she scanned their strange little faces hopefully one by one, and over and over—the fact that Regina was *not* there that shook Frau Lininger out of her static dream and forced her to face the reality of fleeting Time.

That she would never find her little girl again was her first realization, the equivalent to her mind of having lost her. It was only comparatively slowly, only as the afternoon wore away while she sat miserably stricken and unable to explain herself, that hope began to burgeon again and to renew itself in the reasonable expectation that Regina had not died; that she had grown up and was waiting for her somewhere amongst the wagons, a young woman of sixteen. It was only after Frau Anna had counted over all her fingers several times, and *so* slowly, that she was able to understand and to face the conclusion. She was aided in this more by the sympathy than by the logic of one of the guardian Virginia Rangers to whom she appealed. He made out her broken English and German only with difficulty, but was easily touched by her pathetic appearance and floods of tears.

Sunset was near when the tall Virginian finally understood her difficulty and led her to where eight or ten maidens under twenty were sitting protectively together, undergoing the baffled inquisition of uncertain relatives and the curious inspection of the crowd. Some of their companions had already been claimed, and it so happened that those who remained, scared and bereft of their recent friends, were Shawanese captives who had been carried away many years before; girls, who, in effect, were young squaws so far as their habits or their language were concerned. Most of them felt a dread of and an ill-concealed hostility towards the palefaces, and despite the honey-coloured hair of several amongst them, they looked and acted like the sullen savages they were. Questions brought nothing; kindness elicited scared tears; and prods resulted in indignant grunts.

It was to such hopefuls as these that the tall ranger had led Frau Lininger and then stood waiting expectantly, while she called out the name of "Regina, Regina Lininger" again and again. She stood before them, took her shawl from her head and smiled, making soft German noises persuasively. But nothing happened, except sloe-eyed glances of shy fear or secret contempt from most of them, or at best sullen unintelligible replies from the girls with yellow hair.

This went on for some time, and it was then that Frau Anna suffered a second terrible shock that awful day. It was almost like a physical stroke, the stunning realization that Regina might never be able to recognize *her*. It affected her speech, at least temporarily, for she stood at last with her arms crossed, folding-in her shawl over her breasts, and could not even moan. Old Captain Rainey found her thus and led her back to the comfort of his warm hearth and family; and it was in that way that she missed Bouquet when he spoke to the captivated that evening, standing before the supper fire.

Frau Anna remained up late that evening, restless, staring across the square at the dim figures moving in the firelight about the wagons. No one knew what she thought, for she said nothing. But she must have been certain in her heart that Regina was somewhere there, so near and yet so far!

There is a proverb about hope and the human breast, one which Frau Lininger well personified. For next morning when the captivated were moved from the square to the camp at LeTort's Springs, she followed them, trudging along beside the wagons desperately. At the camp itself she continued, but dumb and dry-eyed now, to haunt the precincts of the huts assigned to the girl captives, and to walk up and down the grassy street before them, moving her lips silently. No one prevented her, and when questioned she mumbled something unintelligible in German about General Bouquet . . .

It was towards the middle of the afternoon when Frau Anna looked up and saw a tall hawk-faced man and the adjutant, Captain Ourry, turn the corner of the log barracks where the babies were. Behind them came Bouquet in his red coat and faded epaulets, with a lady leaning on his arm.

The next thing Frances Melissa knew, an old woman, her grey hair tousled in the breeze, came running up to the general and started to beat her hands frantically on his breast, while she made uncouth noises. Then she tried to put her arms around his neck. Captain Ourry turned with an oath, fearing some crazed or savage fanatic with a knife.

"Now, now, Frau Lininger," cried Bouquet, catching her hands firmly between his own and trying to quiet her, "so it's you! Has our good Father Almighty not been merciful to you?"

"Ja, ja, gracious lord general," sobbed the old woman, who seemed now to regain her powers of speech, "she is here; she is near, but she is forever verloren. She does not know me, her mother, nor do I know her. Thou alone canst help, thy august self alone. Have pity on me, serene and exalted sir."

"Come and sit down on the steps awhile, Frau Anna," replied Bouquet, leading her towards the porch stoop before the log barracks. "You are tired. Ah, I can see that!"

"Bitte," said Frau Anna, wiping her eyes. Trotting over to the steps like some subservient domestic animal, she sat down.

They all gathered about her. Bouquet stood directly before her, looking down patiently into her face, one hand twirling a small walking-stick nervously behind his back.

"Now, tell us," said he, "tell us slowly, Frau Anna. Perhaps I, or this lady here, can help you."

At the mention of the lady, the old woman looked up at Frances' face to see if there was any help for her there, and so forlornly that Frances impulsively sat down beside her and put an arm about her. Thus reassured and comforted, she managed to speak more clearly, and at last made her predicament clear.

"Good Lord!" exclaimed Bouquet, looking stumped. "That girl is probably even now within a hundred yards of us, sulking in one of those huts down the street. But how to trace her, if she doesn't know who she is; there's the rub."

"I'm sure she's here, sir," said Ourry. "I distinctly remember her name being on the lists, and of your speaking to me about her at Fort Bedford. Yes, yes, *Regina, Regina Lininger*."

"Ja!" interjected the old woman, "*Regina,* mit der flaxy hair."

"If she's among the Shawanese captives, maybe *I* can talk with her and find her out," suggested Salathiel.

"Do so by all means," replied the brigadier, pleased at any helpful suggestion. "Suppose you go along with Albine, Ourry, and show him where you've put the young females."

Accordingly, Captain Ourry and Salathiel started down the camp street hastily. Presently, they could be seen going into and then coming out of one hut after another.

"Ach, du Lieber Gott, my poor baby!" exclaimed Frau Anna, and burst into tears again. "Ten years, ja, it is a long time." Frances strove to console her.

"But she must remember *something* of her childhood," muttered Bouquet, striking at the grass with his cane, "something that you often did together, Frau Anna: a game you played; a pet she played with, a family dog or cat. The Injuns don't keep 'em, you know."

"No use to bark or meow," muttered Frau Anna despondingly, "no use . . ."

"No, but you can sing, Mrs. Lininger, you can sing!" exclaimed Frances in great excitement, seizing the old woman by her shoulders and holding her at arms' length, while she looked into her face. "A lullaby! A song you used to sing Regina to sleep with at home."

"By God, it would take a woman to think of that!" cried Bouquet. "Do you understand, Frau Lininger? Do you see . . ."

"Ja," she cried, leaping up, hope dawning in her eyes again. "Ja, I remember. I vill sing, *sing!*"

She ran away from them down the street a piece, and then stopped.

"Now pray heaven!" exclaimed Bouquet. "Ah!" Frau Anna had started to trudge down the street, and she was singing, singing with a kind of desperate urgency and tender appeal in her soft old voice, the words of an ancient German hymn:

"Alone but not alone am I,
For in this solitude so drear
My Saviour always is near-by,
My lonely hours come to cheer.
While I'm with Him and He with me,
I cannot solitary be."

She trudged on bravely, looking to neither right nor left, holding her shawl wrapped tightly about her, singing ever more clearly. As the plaintive voice continued, faces came to the doors of the huts and peered out. Soon a number of the captivated came outside to watch her. Captain Ourry and Salathiel emerged from the fifth hut down the street and stood watching, too. They had not found Regina. At the bottom of the street Frau Anna turned and came back again still singing; singing the words as she remembered phrasing them long ago. She was now half-way back, coming up the street. The brigadier stopped twirling his cane and waited tensely.

Suddenly there was a piercing scream, and from one of the huts a young woman in a deerskin skirt, with a snood of blue wampum over her light-brown hair, ran out into the street, and falling to her knees clutched Frau Anna frantically about the waist. "Kleine Mutter," she cried in a strange thick accent, "Mutter, Mutter, kleine Mutter."

"Du, mein liebchen, du," whispered her mother, leaning over her and half covering her with her drooping shawl.

People down the street began to shout in various Indian tongues, and to run from one hut to another as the news spread. Bouquet turned away from looking at Frau Anna and Regina. He was not immune to emotion. He saw Frances sitting on the steps with a far, far-away look in her grey eyes and tears trembling on her lashes.

"Well done, madam," said the brigadier huskily.

Frances dried her eyes and smiled at him. "It's like this, sir, I'll be after remimbering *you* in times to come," she said.

"Ah, the days to come," said Bouquet more to himself than to her, "I wonder? But better a soft heart like your own than letters traced on granite. 'Tis the living quality of remembrance that lasts. Will it be hearts, marble, brass, or bronze that is chosen—who knows? Fate is a weird engraver. Children are the best of all remembrancers, I suppose . . ."*

* Save for the letters of his name and a date on the old "Blockhouse" at Pittsburgh, not a single monument exists to this truly great and benign soldier in all the lands that his genius preserved for posterity. His statue has lately been removed from the old State House at Philadelphia, and the legislatures that sit so comfortably at Harrisburg have probably forgotten his name. Bouquet died miserably of yellow fever at Pensacola, Florida, late in 1765, and his grave was washed away

" 'Twas hard remindin' Regina Lininger," said Frances.

They both laughed.

"True," he said—"but here come Ourry and your long-legged ranger. We stole a march on them this time, my dear. Let's rally 'em about it."

"*Well,* captain," he said, with a mock severity, as Ourry and Salathiel appeared, "how now?"

"Oh, quite as usual, sir," replied Ourry. The adjutant was getting nowhere, when he saw that the general had solved the difficulty. "But Albine at least had a certain success."

"I found someone I wasn't looking for," explained Salathiel.

" 'Tis a talint you're much afflicted with," cried Frances. "What is it you'd better be after tellin' me?" she added anxiously, for she saw he was serious.

"Come, and I'll show you," he replied. "It concerns you more than anybody else, I guess."

Salathiel had now said enough not only to arouse Frances' curiosity, but also to alarm her. A mystery was what she most abhorred.

The brigadier laughed. "Sounds like something you had better investigate, Mistress Albine," he said. "I shall count on hearing about it before you leave camp. But the captain and I *must* be getting back to headquarters now. You will not forget, Albine, to see me before you go?"

"Lord, no," said Ourry; "the list, you know, the list!"

Salathiel promised, and after the bows were over, and the clicking of rapier scabbards on boots had died away up the street, he turned and put Frances' hand over his arm precisely as Bouquet had done at headquarters. "Madam, permit me," he said ironically, "only a brief stroll . . ."

"Oh, Sal," she said apprehensively. "Howly Mither, what is it now?"

"Do you remember, yesterday, when we were driving into town from the mill, you said that what you needed was another woman in the house?"

She turned pale under her bonnet. "Oh, my dear," she said, stopping to look at him, "you'd not be twisting the words out of me mouth the wrong way like that, all for a little jealousy over me passin' the time of day and a bit of blarney with the brigadier? All that I meant was . . ."

"Yes? What was it you meant?"

"Why," she cried, "all I meant was after havin' a bit of help in

---

by a hurricane. Although the Pensacola library is housed in what was once the church of the old English garrison, on a recent visit to Pensacola the author found no one who had ever heard of General Bouquet. *Sic transit gloria mundi.*

the house, an old woman with a latent talint with a broom and for makin' beds, or cookin' in the kitchen. Now that Mr. Yates is comin', and Mr. St. Clair, and God knows who else, and we'll be after keepin' house at the mill for another five months at least, before we git to the City, and the baby comin' on, the baby, Sal, *your* baby . . ." Then she saw he was laughing at her. "You rogue, you miserable rogue, to twit me like that!" she exclaimed.

"Come on, me love, I've found the very woman you're looking for. An old friend of the Little Turtle. I hope you'll not be jealous of her for that."

"Some squaw, I suppose," she said, tossing her head.

"Come and see," he replied. "She's as Irish as you are."

It was at the fifth hut on the left-hand side of the street that they stopped. He motioned for her to wait and went in. She heard him talking in guttural Shawanese. The voice of an old woman replied. The conversation went on for some time, and then the woman's voice said, "Howly Saints, you big awkward spalpeen, have you left her tied outside like a colt! Ask her to cross the threshold, and twice tin thousand blessin's on her little fate." At that, Frances waited no longer.

Inside, the hut was filled with twilight; there was only one small dusty window and the slanting streak of sunshine falling through the open door to light it. Salathiel towered upward into the gloom of the room, and before him, squatting on the mud floor, sat an old woman in dirty deerskins.

"Frances, this is Malycal," said Salathiel. "She says, since you're not a cold-hearted Englishwoman, she'll go home with you. She had an English mistress once."

"The wolves et the hard obstinate face off her," said Malycal, "and her proud daughter's, too. I foretold them so."

"I hope I'll plaize you, Malycal," said Frances, and filled the hut with a tentative ripple of laughter that shuddered slightly towards the end.

"Stand ye in the sunlight, mistress, and throw back your bonnet over your shoulders," said Malycal. "I would see what betides between us."

Frances complied, and the old woman rose stiffly from the ground and came towards her, crouching a little and making a small sign of the cross with her little finger.

"Are ye there, Sal?" asked Frances apprehensively.

"Yes," said he, with his head still in the gloom.

"Don't ye be scared," said the old woman. "My Christian name's Mary Calahan, and I was baptized at Cashel. I'd niver overlook ye. 'Tis only a dear Irish face I want to see again."

She laid her hands on Frances' shoulders and looked at her with her small intensely blue and finely wrinkled old eyes. Frances quietly returned her gaze without flinching.

"Ah, the blessèd wild soul and the sweet fey face of ye, mistress! 'Tis a wanderin' angel ye be; and I see the bright sunlight beyond ye, and the glory of it catchin' in your raven hair."

"Come home with me, Mary Calahan," whispered Frances. "The house is full of men, and the sound of lonely water. I've only a Presbyterian child and a hathen black boy to help me. And there's a new baby under my heart."

Malycal laid her head on Frances' breast and said so low that Salathiel could not hear her, "Why, I'll come home to ye, mistress, and brew white magic and hot cups of tay before the fire. 'Tis comfort I need in a lonely land, and comfort I'll bring ye."

Frances slipped an arm around her, thinking it was the second old woman she had comforted that way in one afternoon.

Salathiel was so pleased, he couldn't help showing it, which meant that he was very pleased indeed.

"It takes the women to fix things up," he asserted twice over, and claimed thrice that it was a wonderful day.

". . . which is five times as much as ye ginerally say," laughed Frances. " 'Tis the influence of Edward Yates turnin' you into an orator. But the wonderful day will soon be over. And Bridget's alone at the mill with Jed. We must get back now, get back to her!"

"So we must," he agreed. "Malycal, put your plunder up in a bindle. We'll call for ye with the wagon. Dang it, I wish we could skip goin' to headquarters now."

"But ye can't," said Frances. "You promised the brigadier, and besides the wagon's hitched there with Enna gnawing the painted post. I'll wait here with Mary Calahan till ye git back. I've got many a thing to talk over with her, now that she's comin' to live with us at the mill. Give the gineral me affectionate remimbrance, and for God's sake sing them lists to Captain Ourry, or he'll be after pestering us all to death. And fix it up about takin' Mary home with ye— and hurry! I guess that's all."

The last items she had to call after him, for he was already striding away up the street. He felt like running, but the captivated might have wondered. He was all in a sweat now to get out of camp. He'd forgotten about Bridget, and his heart smote him.

Too many things had been happening today. Everything was working out much too well. It was being too nicely wound up. If it hadn't been for that meeting with McArdle, he'd be downright superstitious about being so happy. Maybe that was where his luck would begin to turn. Maybe that's the way it would be from now on. McArdle gave him the shivers now. He couldn't help it. The way he'd looked at Frances when they stopped in the road to talk. My God! Did McArdle think he'd ever leave a woman like Frances for a girl like Jane? Just let him try to bring that up. But he'd like to get back to the mill now. He'd like to be sure all was well there. He wished he hadn't come to camp after all, just at Frances' behest. Now that they had a house to go home to, he wished . . . well . . . he wished he'd gone home. He'd get over with it at headquarters in a jiffy. God, what a life the military led. He was sorry for the brigadier. A lonely man. In many ways he reminded him of Ecuyer —but a truce to all that. He was in a hurry now. How much faster a man could get things done, when he didn't have a woman along!

None the less, it was a good hour, or more, before he finally got through at headquarters. He copied the lists out himself for Ourry and only had to hum a little now and then, even if it did bring the brigadier to the door, grinning to see him singing to the adjutant. There was no trouble about Malycal. He just signed for her; and Captain Ourry countersigned, without question. "Just for the record, you know." So much for that. But the brigadier called him then and had quite a long talk with him. He'd had to admit it was a reasonable proposition that Bouquet asked him to consider. Also that he was tempted by it. Good pay. He'd promise to come back after he'd thought it over. He didn't see how he could do less than that. Besides, Bouquet was so understanding and sympathetic, and a great man! Of course, he could not refuse to repair his parade wig for him. Who else could do it? So he'd brought it along with him—and the six others, including Ourry's, that were waiting for him in a bundle of brown paper. Ourry had certainly been grateful, no doubt about it, but too hopeful, he thought. Well, he'd see. He'd think it over. But home now!

Frances and Malycal were ready when he dashed up to the hut with the two-wheeled cart, but they were alone. None of the captivated came to say good-bye to Malycal. Her reputation for being a weird-woman had come along with her. She climbed into the back of the cart with her bundle and sat there cross-legged in the straw. "Sure and it's like gintry you are with a low-backed car and a fine little harse," she said.

"Hold on, for I'm drivin' fast," he warned her.

"I've no teeth left to rattle in me head no more, drive on," she flung back at him, and showed her toothless gums in a happy grin.

He drove fast. It was about an hour before sunset, he figured, when he turned Enna's head eastward at LeTort's Springs. But he'd forgotten the mountains, and the sun sank behind them sooner than he'd thought. It was twilight when they splashed through the little ford where the turned-up wagon lay; its wheels looked like huge spiderwebs with their dim tracery of spokes in the half-darkness. He was glad now that he'd piled those cedar boughs against the scar on the thunder tree. Enna didn't even snort. Darkness began to fall as they struck the silent leaf-covered road through the woods.

"We'll be home about candlelight at this rate," he said, breaking a long silence. "I hope Bridget *will* have the fire lighted for us. She's got too much sense to wait in the darkness, or to think we'd leave her alone for another night, don't you think?"

"Yis, I do," Frances replied. "She's wiser than *you* think, Sal—wiser than her years. Belike she's been havin' a foin time playin' mistress of the house and orderin' Jed about."

Frances had been silent all the way through the dark woods; and as usual he'd said nothing, either. Something in her tone now, as she spoke about Bridget, disturbed him. But it was only for a moment. She leaned nearer him, laying her cheek against his shoulder. He slipped an arm about her and drove with one hand. Enna knew the way back, anyway.

"Oh, I'm terrible happy tonight, Sal," she whispered. "I want to thank ye for bein' so good to me." She felt him tremble, as her arms crept about his neck. "I love you—and now we'll be at home togither at least for a while."

"That's how I figured it," he said. Their lips met in a long kiss, as the dark boughs slipped past over their heads and a new moon looked down.

"God, but I'm a lucky orphan," he said hoarsely at last.

"Hush, niver say it," she whispered. "Who knows what's leanin' over us now in the darkness, listenin'? Hear that!"

"'Tis the sound of runnin' water at the mill," he answered, "water talking peacefully. And I see a light!"

"*A* light!" she exclaimed, sitting up and peering ahead over Enna's ears. "Lights, you mean. Bejasus, 'tis an illumination. There's a candle in every window. Now, what did I tell ye?"

28

The Labours of Hercules

IT IS ONLY in retrospect that the full flavour of a period in personal experience can be roundly savoured and evaluated. Yet most people's lives, even very haphazard and quite humble ones, tend to fall into distinct epochs. For, besides the trilogy inevitable in the book of *Everyman,* of Youth, Middle Age, and Senescence, there are both chapters and paragraphs in the volume of life which take on in perspective an emotional or dramatic unity of their own; some unique quality that Time, Place, and Character or, if you will, Accident and Fate seem to have conferred upon them. It is as if there were an invisible Scrivener who arbitrarily rules lines across the blank foolscap of eternity, or a Grand Editor of the Great Almanac of time. Signs, portents, weather and seasons—sun, moon, stars, and people are the very stuff of his quaintly illustrated calendar, and a steady wind from nowhere keeps turning back its leaves.

This, or something similar, is the general impression of the majority of mankind about the passing of days; and Salathiel and Frances Melissa were no exceptions to the rule. Looking back at their experience together in the mill house at Boiling Springs, it took on for them in retrospect the form of a distinct and memorable chapter in their volume of mutual adventure.

It was not a long chapter from the standpoint of the calendar.

In a diary which Salathiel kept in a calf-bound ledger in his round, carefully shaded, and all but juvenile script, his several entries at *Glens Mills* (*sic!*) run from the sixteenth of November 1764 to the twenty-eighth of March 1765, N.S., closing on the latter date with the remarks:

Leaving this pleasant place of Glens Mills near Boiling spring this morning at half after five by Capt E his watch, intending for the city of Philadelphia by way of the town of York at E Yates behest, he awaiting us at Lancaster, & the latest advices from the brigadier—with 1 wagon, 1 cart, 6 horses, myself, Frances, Bridget & our people, Maly & the two black boys, along. We being heavily laden & a long muddy haul by way of John Wright his ferry, of which some qualms by last report, & a slow trip expected with Frances growing big now & oft-times queasy.

£184-6s-5d in hand, with £4-2s-6d due Stott'l'myr for harse hire. But he will owe me £80 str upon final del'v'y of wagon & return of the teams to him at Carlisle. Therefore—have this day to touch or in just expectation 260£s sterling plus 3s & 11d, with 18£s drawn at sight upon Japson in the City, being the first advance from the Brigadier sent lately by Capt Ourry in his last letter. Fair enough, with coins scarce as hens teeth.

A.o.h. X libra r.g. cast bullets; XVI libra bird shot, but small powder. (6 scalps), pelts new and left over 32, fair to mid'l'n. Now farewell to the country, may the good Lord prosperous us in the City.

> "My burdens upon Him I cast
> That shelters lambkins from the blast,
> And hears the new born coddlins peep
> To Him from out the murky deep."*

& & &

Here endeth *all* the entries under "Glens Mills", with a grand shaded flourish in the form of a bow knot and a few inky splutters from a worn quill; indicating perhaps great haste about half after five that morning of departure (if one may guess) accompanied by the loud ticking of S. Ecuyer's indomitable watch.

From which entry, with careful reading, and some scanning between the lines, a fairly accurate idea of the material condition of the *familia Albine* upon their eventual departure for the City at the end of March 1765 can be puzzled out.

* From Vol. 2, 2nd leather-bound ledger of Major S. Albine's Diary & Accounts, found *circa* 1829, with Mr. Yates's papers in a deerskin bag at Gunset Hall, Richfield Springs, New York. There are in all eight ledgers, the last watersoaked and partly illegible. The next entry after the one above occurs in the ledger marked Vol. 3, "City Entries 1765-'67," and is headed as follows: "Slate House, Second Street, City of Philadelphia, 4th of April 1765, arrived this morning and civily met by Mistress Graydon." Also see *Bedford Village*, Chap. 11, pp. 115-116.

The entry "A.o.h.", or ammunition on hand, was probably made merely from old habit and the natural solicitude of a frontiersman over such matters; since it is scarcely to be supposed that ten pounds of ready-cast rifle-gun bullets, etc., etc., was a necessary precaution for taking up residence in the City of Brotherly Love, even then. Probably the ammunition was left over, and therefore "on hand"; and lead was valuable.

The "6 scalps", in parentheses, might be more disturbing and give rise to speculation as to the continued health of Doctor Scarlet and his wandering family, if it were not known that two years later the doctor and his flock returned with Martin Glen's permission to dig roots in the woods along the course of Yellow Breeches Creek, and that "Mrs. Robin Scarlet" and two fledglings helped young Mistress Clara Glen in and about her kitchen.* So we can exonerate Salathiel there, although his record in regard to the unfortunate accident that overtook another itinerant is not so clear. But of that later.

Three facts stand out from Salathiel's entries: the stay at Boiling Springs was a comparatively short one; it was happy; and it was memorable out of all proportion to its length. The rest can be gleaned from Captain Ourry's orderly book; from his letters to Salathiel from Philadelphia; from Yates's cryptic Latin entries in his "Daily Reminder", and the known course of events in and about Carlisle.

But "the rest", handy as facts are, is actually *not* so relevant to this chronicle of character and feeling; and the time at Boiling Springs could better be expressed for its emotional and inner meaning in terms of a sustained and quiet piece of music rather than in the faded and silent entries in old accompts and diaries. They, to be sure, do betray the past into the future, but are at best voiceless notations, toneless and unharmonic pot-hooks that can seldom speak. Yet some unwritten music vibrates sympathetically through time. All is not lost. And phrased in terms of moonlight, falling water, the lilt of applewood fiddles, candlelight, tree shadows on mossy roofs, departed footsteps, and vanished voices—the themes, grace notes, overtones, dissonances, and harmonies of the Mill House Symphony must have been something like this:

It began with winter, a quiet season, clear, cold, and dry. The streams froze. The sound of water was much hushed under the ice. Only now and then beneath the mill floor the water-harp tinkled with frosty tones, more like icicles being struck by a stick than the fingering of strings. All about the Boiling Spring, which now sang to itself a more subdued and snow-muffled monody, stretched the silent, sunny woods and unfrequented roads of the deserted neighbourhood—only fitfully disturbed as yet by some solitary messenger

---

* Martin Glen to John Glen at Conestoga, August 4, 1767.

spurring to Carlisle or by a creaking farm wagon returning with a family to their long-abandoned home. Snow fell occasionally, but fine and dry.

Beneath the powdery drifts the woodcock looked for winter berries; along the streams the coon left his midget hand-prints in dainty patterns; under the moon the wild turkey roosted higher in a leafless tree. Foxes barked madly in the distance, and no hound replied. The brief sunny days blent slowly into the long darkness of constellated nights. But day *and* night the wood-smoke drifted from the chimneys of the mill house, and red sparks died over its frost-rimed roofs like falling stars.

Once that season the rare Northern Lights came far southward. Hanging on the northern fringe of the horizon one December evening, they smouldered with the cold fire of diamonds in a black vault. Then shaking with sidereal palsy, they died out; only to flash again into distant lightnings like the reflected sword play of Frost Giants behind the crouching mountains; steely white, cobalt, wonderful!—flaming up at last into a climax of S-shaped glory, twin green and lilac curtains trailing faint dripping fringes of pale icy blue, as though a thought of spring stirred already in the convolutions of the brain of heaven, or the dreaming of innumerable acres of sleepy coiled arbutus filtered through covering snowbanks to tinge prophetically the frosty pastures of the sky.

Frances and Malycal, Bridget and Salathiel saw the Lights. Standing before the open door of the mill house, with the warm heart of the hearth fire in the vacant room beating behind them, they watched the show and went in silently afterward, touched by awe and the hint of some unrecoverable memory that hung and flickered like the iris of a watchful eye just beyond the horizon of the mind, cold and fearful—but that closed with the house door—and left them happy and rejoicing together in the shelter of the roof-tree and the warm leaping of the familiar chimney flame.

Jed had seen the Ghost Lights, too. Out in the wagon, where he slept, he lay peeping under the canvas and shuddering under his blankets, while the Great Northern Snake with the Pole-star for an evil eye coiled and squirmed and looked down upon him. That night the comfortable remembrance of the hot suns of Africa withered like flowers blackened by frost-bite and ceased to warm his hope. He knew now he would never get back. He gave up even the unconscious hope. The cold secret power that he now saw overarched his exile, quietly prevailed. "I don't know what you've done to him," said St. Clair to Salathiel not so long afterward, "but Jed's a different nigger. He seems somehow to have been toned down."

"I reckon he's jes' wintering through. We ain't teched him," replied Salathiel.

But something had.

Thus, mysteriously for everybody, the winter nights at Boiling Springs began. But the days were quite different. There was nothing mysterious, overpowering, or silent about them. They were cheerful. They seemed to slip away one into another rapidly, smoothly, and timelessly. Everybody great and small was fully occupied. Salathiel, for one, was busy as a beaver with two tails.

There was firewood to be cut and hauled, whole carloads of it. And Jed was not skilful with the hand-axe yet. But he soon learned, for they burned stacks of logs that winter; great logs in the chimney place, until the fire-back glowed white hot and beat a genial wave of summer clean down the long hall; and piles of kindling and pine faggots in the kitchen where Malycal revelled in simmering August heat in January, as if her bones could never be warm enough after the icy draughts and aching ground-cold of Kaysinata's gloomy forest hut. And with the mill full of flour, an eternal baking went on in the Dutch oven that also glowed genially with wooden fuel and sent a continuous stream of hot breads, piping meat pies, muffins, corn puddings, and honey cakes smoking and steaming to the table.

So the sound of the wood-axe was frequent. It rang cheerfully in the thickets near-by, and there was a perpetual chopping and splintering of kindling on the big stump just outside the kitchen door. There, too, the bucket yokes hung: yokes that fitted equally well, and so naturally and so often, across both Jed's and Malycal's shoulders, as the numerous pails full of spring water, or "waiting" milk smoking in the inside entry, proclaimed.

Jed was leary of Malycal at first. Gradually he came to like her, but he never dared take liberties. She said her prayers on beads, charmed away warts with burnt feathers, and muttered sight-unseen, while the bread was rising, to somebody who wasn't there. So Jed fetched and carried, waited on the table, plucked fowls, cleaned fish, and drew rabbits diligently—and kept his mouth shut. But above all he chopped wood. All Malycal had to do was to turn the northern lights of her blue Irish eyes upon him, and the hand-axe began to ring.

Chopping, however, was not the only sound that broke the silence of the forest. Many an afternoon, or in the first light of morning, Twin Eyes's sharp bark as a rifle bullet went home; or the brief cough under a light charge of powder, when a cluster of swan shot burst from an old bell-shaped fowling piece of Mr. Glen's, one which Salathiel had "borrowed"—both could be heard near or far along the banks of Yellow Breeches Creek or in the woods and abandoned fields near the mill.

It was small game, "varmints," as Salathiel called them; rabbits, squirrels, and an occasional coon or possum that he was after, and the waterfowl in the quiet back-reaches of the creek. There was no lack of them.

For that matter, ducks and wild swans came down regularly on the mill pond just behind the house. And the deer particularly frequented the lonely farm lanes, where they fed upon the short "English herbage" that was there so plentiful. It was amazing how less than two years of an abandoned country had brought the game back into it again. The wolves came back, too. They could be heard howling across the river, and ran boldly in packs of from four to six. Foxes were careless, even curious; and he shot a good many, for their pelts were worth something.

All in all, it was easy pot-hunting. There was always plenty of fresh game hanging from the rafters in the mill. The turkeys were getting leaner towards middle winter; but the deer were still unusually fat and lazy, after the long succulent feeding of the prolonged fall. Except for a family of merry otters that lived craftily under the mill house, there was nothing that particularly required Salathiel's cunning. All that was necessary was ordinary common wood-sense and powder and shot. Yet he enjoyed it beyond expression.

Driving the wagon had been small exercise, and to be back in the forest again in the cold sweet air and solitude, with the crisp leaves under his feet, was balm to both his body and his soul. He soon looked the better for it, leaner and more hawk-like and keen; more himself. And he went back to moccasins, keeping his boots and shoes for trips to town or when company came.

Jed tended the night fish-lines faithfully, and every morning there were chubbs, suckers, or catfish with bacon for breakfast, even when the ice grew thick. What with wheat, grist, oats, corn meal, and fine flour, with which the mill loft was bursting; with fish, game, barrelled salt meat, venison, and wild-fowl, they lived high, wide, and handsome at Boiling Springs that winter. And Mr. Glen's cellar was provided with sundry cider kegs, liquor barrels, and a minor stock of wine bottles; to say nothing of potatoes, carrots, onions, and turnips buried in straw away from the frost. It was Bridget's task to keep the mother of yeast alive and growing in a warm crock covered by a damp cloth in the kitchen. But that was only a small part of her daily round. It no more covered what Bridget was doing than did a few excursions into the woods pot-hunting suffice to explain Salathiel's innumerable activities.

The truth was he had never been so busy and so happy before. And it was all his own work, work which possessed a genuine importance, because it was naturally essential; tasks for the hand, heart, and head. He now got out and set up all of Johnson's valeting and wig-making kit and machinery, things which he had inherited from Ecuyer. He set them up in a shed with a forge in it, next to the mill. All the mangles, curling and smoothing irons; the polish, pomade, starches, dyes, and combs and brushes; all the wig forms and head plates for five different sizes; the canvas web for bases; the flax, the false and real hair; and the needles and hooked draw-pins were there. Some of these he had never used before, but he soon surmised their application and went to work.

Mr. Craighead's "best Sabbath hair" was soon a happy replica of its pristine self, washed, starched, curled, and stiffened with lime-bleached horsehair. The brigadier's parade wig was a simple matter, for Salathiel was used to the regulation military set for perukes, and the other officers' wigs were in the same case. All these when returned, powdered and in new stow-bags made up by Frances, were samples that generated a surprising and all but clamorous patronage. Yates had been more than right in foreseeing it. Nearly every officer, most of the lawyers, and many a war-prosperous merchant and rising clerk in Carlisle needed professional revamping to their wigs, something hitherto available only at Lancaster or in the City.

Salathiel charged all that the traffic would bear, from a guinea to five shillings, depending on the state of the wig and its owner's apparent solvency. And there were then more wigs in the county than he could have mended or retrimmed in a year. It was a veritable lode of rich ore he had accidentally struck, and he worked at it hard. If some of his repairs were amateurish, they were at least ingenious; and if the exact set of his customer's head toggery lacked something of the latest cast or curled flair affected by the bucks in London coffee-houses, it would have required a voyage of several months to make the comparison. Also, venting falderol vapours and minor macaroni complaints upon a "wig-maker" who frequently delivered his wares with an axe dangling from his belt was something to cause even a peevish personage to ponder gravely. It was better on the whole to look pleased—and to pay promptly.

For Salathiel, it was the beginning of what became for him later a profitable side-line. He brought to it, besides Johnson's initial instruction, a natural aptitude in the use of his hands and a certain ingenious cleverness of invention. Also his skill in the preparation of skins, pelts, and hides, in connection with wigs and in a hundred other ways, was of infinite service and profit to him as time went on.

The aptitude for using tools and weapons that he had picked up and come by naturally during his years of life with those who, even Frances allowed, must have been "ingenious savages" now proved invaluable. If he lacked some article or item, he generally made it. He could copy almost anything in wood or iron, if he put his mind to it. He had patience and the inherited knack of seeing *how* things were to be done. In the wagon he had accumulated a raft of peaceful tools and a small armoury of lethal weapons. With the former he now went to work in various ways.

It was this manual capacity in Salathiel which Yates could never admire enough. He liked to think that in his own head was the same *kind* of latent cleverness which Salathiel found in his hands. The alliance of head and hand in their friendship was, Yates felt, the chief advantage of it; "highly expedient". But he went further. He was also given to speculating upon whether the combination of the two capacities in one personality was not the ideal of proper character for success in the New World. He even thought he could detect signs of such characters developing about him, and he liked to hunt up and talk to men who he thought best exemplified it, even if he was reproached for being "democratic".

So work, and work of many kinds, now went on in the forge shed at the mill. It was soon the shelter for all kinds of minor crafts, some of them curious ones. Jim Fergus, for instance, who had not failed to keep his resolution of stopping off at the mill often, brought a curious and, in the end, a dangerously lucrative suggestion. It was for nothing less than the counterfeiting of scalps. And Salathiel was found equal to the occasion.

Fergus traded whisky and new scalps for old with some of the warriors still living in the hospitable protection of the jail. He then turned in the old ones for bounty money. Thus the chiefs retained the replicas of gory trophies to sew back on the fringes of their breeches and lost none of their glory, while Jim profited considerably, and Salathiel shared. The trick, of course, was to copy the old scalps so passably that they would pass muster even when the "chiefs" returned to their own people. And to copy Indian scalps only, for it would not do to have turned in scalps of the inhabitants to the authorities. Some carefully tanned and shaped rabbit hides mounted on willow rings, horsehair tied in the proper knots indicating various tribes, some ink stains, dyes, and a little smoking accomplished the design. Yates laughed heartily, but opined that this was going a little too far. He finally managed to put an end to the episode after only a few transactions, and before any embarrassing questions were asked.

But all this activity at the mill required numerous trips to town —and to headquarters—for Salathiel had succumbed and made certain arrangements there. In particular, he undertook to look after the personal comfort and kit of the brigadier. He also managed to get things done and to see people who could oblige headquarters in various local but important personal matters. Bouquet paid him decently, and Captain Ourry proved grateful in various ways. Salathiel came twice a week to camp, and Ourry and the brigadier occasionally rode back to the mill with him for an evening of good company there, a game of whist, and a supper that was always worth going eight miles to get, even in bad weather. On several evenings the gathering was notable, and the company rode back to town next day. Undoubtedly the brigadier appreciated the good fare and the cheerful domestic atmosphere. And this was especially true after the "French cook" came. The manner of his arrival and the disastrous aftermath of his unexpected and unsolicited advent were essentially as follows:

It was a Saturday, and Salathiel had hitched up the greys to the big wagon, and with Jed driving, had taken Frances along with him to make the usual rounds at Carlisle. He had a good deal to do that day and quite a few calls to make. There were no less than six resuscitated wigs to be delivered to various persons at camp and in town, and Frances herself had three bonnets to return after retrimming them. Inspired perhaps by Salathiel's success with perukes military, Frances had already begun to do a little "head-work" in millinery, confining herself at first to the refurbishing of hats, a field, or rather a garden, in which she afterward became famous in the City. Then, that day, there were some imported groceries to be bought, such as pepper, coffee, tea, and spices; and the injured single-tree was to be repaired at the blacksmith's, since the forge at the mill had not yet had its bellows repaired. Last, and most important, a final arrangement about the team horses was to be made. Stottelmyer had returned to Carlisle and sent a message to Salathiel about them. With such a calendar of business before them, Frances and he started early and expected to be gone all day.

The advent of the French cook must have occurred during the time when the wagon was waiting at the blacksmith's and the new sleeve for the singletree was being forged. In fact, Salathiel learned afterward, although the smith would never admit it, that the man had been working concealed at the forge for almost a month. Probably Jed knew it.

At any rate, it was Jed's fault, Salathiel figured. Perhaps there was a bit more work at the mill now than one boy could well be expected to do, since Yates had come, and St. Clair was a frequent visitor, and others too. The firewood proposition alone was—well, it was admittedly quite considerable. And he had heard Malycal driving Jed hard. Maybe that was it. But even then Jed ought not to have let the man persuade him; or did *he* persuade the man? Both probably. It must have been what Yates called "a meeting of minds". And it must have happened at the forge. There was plenty of time to have arrived at an understanding. And, as the *devil* would have it, it turned out that both Jed and this other black fellow spoke the same African tongue. It put a white man at a great disadvantage.

So while he, Salathiel, was out at the stables settling the delicate matter of the "horses", while that great oaf, Schmidty, kept trying to ooze out under the door like a barrel of spilled molasses—and while Frances was calling on Mrs. Williams with a new jet-trimmed mourning bonnet to learn all there was to know, and a little more, about how the Glen boys were faring with Clara Garber at Conestoga —it had happened. That was the way it must have been—and now there was another mouth at the mill with about twenty stone of man behind it to feed, and what was much more difficult, to keep shut.

That was the way Salathiel thought about it at first. And it wasn't until some time later that he began to think that, as *God* would have it, it was all a great blessing in disguise.

But as they drove away from the smithy late that afternoon neither of them had an inkling that anything was in the wind; and the simple fact that he had decided to take the reins himself and Frances sat beside him all the way, as they drove home under a glorious winter sunset, was what made it so easy. The man must have just climbed in the back of the wagon as they left, and sat grinning at Jed all the way to the mill, with his outlandish plunder on the seat beside him. Neither he nor Frances had thought of looking behind the canvas. Why should they? It had been a long and satisfactory day, and there was a lot to talk about.

All the errands were done and the new purchases piled in the wagon behind them. Frances had three good Portagee joes for herself, and ten shillings still coming, for her trouble with other women's bonnets; he had collected for all the wigs, and the settlement with Stottelmyer was easier than he had thought.

He had forgotten that he and Stott had fought that passel o' scum together at Bedford. That helped now. And, of course, he didn't say anything about taking the whip off Schmidty. Nor did Schmidt. No use complicating matters! So the teams were his now for a pound a month apiece, as long as he needed them. And Captain Jack's nag was to be sent back to the mill at the first opportunity just for the cost of oats consumed. He didn't know just what he'd do with that extra horse now, but there was plenty of feed at the mill. The surprise came when Stott had offered to *buy* the wagon! He evidently wanted it bad. They'd argued a long time over that. It was worth at least a hundred pounds, Salathiel thought. But Stottelmyer wouldn't pay more than eighty.

Well, he'd chew the proposition over. He hadn't thought of selling the wagon. But when they moved to the City it would be of small use there. And he could never keep four horses. Probably, he couldn't keep even one! Still he hadn't said "yes" yet; and he hadn't talked it over with Frances. Stottelmyer had agreed to let the offer stand for a while, and so he'd let it go at that . . .

It was half an hour after dark when they got back to Boiling Springs.

Bridget met them, jumping up and down in the doorway, and with all her dolls and the cat sitting before the fire in a solemn company waiting for supper. He just left it to Jed to bring in the plunder and put up the wagon and teams, and thought nothing more of it, since Jed had had an idle day in town loafing at the blacksmith's—and half a bit for drink. They sat down to dinner before a clear fire and three candles, with the comfortable feeling of a day well spent. Bridget was merry as a grig.

So was Jed. He spilled the peas porridge, ladling it out on the hearth, and instead of being contrite, made trouble afterward in the kitchen, where Malycal could be heard remonstrating with him in a high-pitched voice for turning handsprings past the milk pails in the entry.

"What the divil's got into him?" exclaimed Frances, annoyed at the sense of mysterious elation with which potatoes, cabbage, and other unexciting dishes were served. "A bit of blackstrap, no doubt," surmised Salathiel. "I think tuppence will be enough next time Jed goes to town. You're like to spoil him, Melissa, with your constant indulgence."

But the shindy in the kitchen continued, and Malycal finally came in to say, with tears, in her eyes, that an elegant corn pudding had just disappeared.

"Jed, you black rascal, come here!" roared Salathiel, whipping off his belt.

"Where's that corn pudding?" he demanded, when Jed appeared, his chin trembling. "I want the truth."

"Yas, sah, yas, cap'n, I gwine tell ye gospel. De lil ole conjure man, him done et um spang up." There was an uncomfortable pause while this news sank in . . .

"Git a lanthorn," said Salathiel.

"Him already done got 'em now," sighed Jed, holding up two fingers.

Bridget giggled.

"Lead on!" commanded Salathiel, putting his belt on again and slipping Kaysinata's axe into it—at which Frances sat quite still with her palms down on the table, and Bridget's eyes grew big and round. "Lead me to the conjure man, Jed."

They went out through the kitchen, and Salathiel now saw a telltale crack of light under the forge door. He strode ahead and flung it open.

In the light of the two best brass wagon lanthorns set on the floor conveniently near his feet; and seated on the anvil, with the bowl of smoking corn pudding in his lap, which he was devouring with a large iron spoon, sat probably the mightiest Negro then in North America. He was simply stupendous, not so much in height as in width, and he was black as night.

He laid the bowl and spoon at his feet when Salathiel and Jed came in, and stood up. He showed neither fear nor surprise. He simply stood there, bulking, in the circles of the two lanthorns. He stood calm, and looked Salathiel in the eyes. Then he bowed civilly and said, "Bonsoir, monsieur."

Salathiel examined him slowly, holding up one of the lanthorns to do so . . .

A decent blue fustian coat, not so decent now. *A fine cambric shirt,* frayed and filthy. *Good black silk breeches,* still passable. *Red worsted stockings,* badly darned and muddy. *Stout Copenhagen boots,* out at the toes. *One silver earring . . .*

"What have you done with your master's gold watch, Herquelees?" demanded Salathiel.

"Jed, him got um," replied the newcomer.

Salathiel did not make the mistake of taking his eyes off the man. He simply held out his left hand behind him until Jed laid the watch in it. He then slipped it into his pouch. The man muttered something in French. But Salathiel shook his head.

"What do you want here, my very big friend?" said he.

"Amis, oui, *grands* amis!" exclaimed the big Negro, flashing his white teeth in a fine grin. Then he pounded his chest. "Me, Hercule. Me work. Me cook, très bon chef! Make ze hammair go." At which he turned suddenly and seizing the smith's hammer, which stood handle up near-by, made it ring on the anvil mightily.

Something in the sound of the clanging hammer and the dull answering bell of the anvil moved Salathiel, and settled the business forthwith in his mind. He held out his hand to stop the demonstration.

Hercules dropped the hammer and grabbed the hand. He began to shake it up and down in a kind of ecstasy of animal delight at being accepted. He seemed to have read Salathiel's mind. Gradually Salathiel closed his grip on the Negro's fingers.

And then, for the first time in his life, he felt fingers as strong as his closing over his hand, and the muscles of a tremendous arm replying to his own. They stood man to man for some moments in the lanthorn-light, testing out each other's strength, arm against arm. They neither swayed nor spoke, but their ligaments cracked. Jed's eyes bulged while he watched. Neither of them gave. Hercules finally grunted. Salathiel suddenly let go, but the man did not fall.

"Ye can stay," said he. "Understand? Savez? *You,* you Her-quelees, stay. *Freeman. Work!*"

"Oui, monsieur," replied the Negro huskily. "Vous, grand ami." He slowly made a fist out of his half-crippled right hand, patted it with his left consolingly, and blew on it.

"You, me, verra fine people," he said.

Salathiel grinned. Hercules resumed his bowl, and sitting down on the anvil again, began to finish his supper with the big iron spoon.

When Salathiel turned to go out, he found Jed doing cartwheels in the shadows, and was forced to take him by the collar to shake a bit of sense into him. With a lanthorn in one hand, he ended by hoisting him through the shed door with his foot, although since he was wearing moccasins, it was not too serious. But he didn't enjoy having huge surprises brought home to him, even if they turned out to be useful ones. Jed understood.

"From now on, I guess you'll be working for Herquelees instead of Malycal," mused Salathiel. "And you may have noticed he's a powerful man. I jealoos you didn't figure it quite that way, did ye, Jed?"

"No, baas," said Jed sadly, "no, ah see ah ain't figured it jes' right. But hones' to Jedu 'twarn't de goold watch brat me to it. No, sah, baas. Not dat tic-tic. Hit war de *mnungee* bird!"

"Bird?" said Salathiel. *"What* bird?"

"You come see um," said Jed, showing excitement again. "Please, sah, jes' hab a look at um."

They went hastily to the wagon, and holding the lanthorn before him, Salathiel looked in. There were two raggle-taggle bundles on the side seat, and between them was a wicker cage of curious and obviously foreign design. It looked like a miniature hut from some heathen tropical land, and the "native" who inhabited it was of a blue-black complexion. It was a large raven. His eyes burned coal-red as the lanthorn-light flashed upon him, and he fluttered and croaked dismally at having his sleep disturbed. At the sound of the sepulchral voice from the depths of the wagon, Jed retreated several paces and put his hands over his ears. None the less, he was forced to take Hercules his plunder, prophetic bird and all, and make up a shag mattress for him in the forge shed, which from that night onward became the home of "de lil ole conjure man".

Satisfied with these proceedings for the time being, Salathiel returned for a pipe by the hearth and to discuss with Frances the rearrangements of the household which the arrival of a black Hercules obviously implied.

At first blush, these complications appeared to be more serious than they proved in the end. Frances instantly saw an opportunity to take Malycal out of the kitchen, where indeed the old woman was being overworked, and to install her in the house for her company by the hearth while sewing and weaving, and for a thousand other small tasks, which her comforting and motherly companionship so cheerfully undertook and so faithfully supplied. Malycal's being an Irishwoman and a Catholic was a boon to Frances and a firm bond between them. And there was also a certain mystical understanding that underlay and cemented their feminine friendship far deeper than all else.

It was something out of the past that they shared with instinctive understanding and subliminal sympathy. If Malycal was a weird-woman and knew what was toward with both people and the weather, in a frequently disconcerting and apparently irrational way, Frances Melissa also had her moments, indeed whole hours sometimes, in which the world and immediate surroundings were lost in a suddenly expanded awareness and exquisite sensitivity; times when she became conscious of whole realms and areas within herself where it seemed to her that the past and the future were both present and a fearful swiftness of incalculable activity was going on, going on; swiftly and vastly and overwhelmingly going on.

It was true that Frances' new-found happiness and her pregnancy seemed greatly to have relieved and lessened these "spells", as she called them—or so she thought. For, on the whole, the winter spent at Boiling Springs was calm and lit with a quiet happiness and the sense of growth and self-accomplishment, a completion, for which she said prayers of gratitude before Mrs. Larned's holy lamb—but there were also certain other moments. And then, oh, then it was balm to have Malycal in the house. Someone who could understand, and could help her get out of that "other place"—and keep the bottle out of her hand! At the mill house she drank hardly at all. What she did take had little effect. For the time being it was body drink only, and had no inner meaning. And she was never sick with her baby, until almost the very end of her time.

But that evening that Hercules came—she saw her opportunity. "Sure," said she after Salathiel had finished explaining, "sure 'twill never do to be after havin' an African wizard and an Irish witch all in the kitchen at the same time. Belike the praties would sprout legs and start scramblin' out of the pot like crabs—or the eyes of spiders start lookin' at us out of the fire. So, I think I'll just move Malycal into young Martin's room, for that will put her right across the hall, if I want to call her nights. And I'll be wantin' to call her.

"For I'll be askin' her to drop a few beads with me when we say our evenin' prayers, whither Miss Bridget likes it or not; and maybe Malycal knows a few prayers backwards, too, and the right kind of herbs to 'cense the house out, a smoke that will keep poor Mrs. Glen's harp quiet behind the door, and the old woman with shillin's in her eyes for spectacles from sittin' in the rockin' chair and readin' her Bible in the moonlight. Aye, it will be a fine thing for me. And the two black boys and yourself can have the run of the kitchen entirely. Whist! I'll have someone besides Bridget to talk to and help me make clothes for me own baby, instead of ilegint fairy costumes for Miss McCandliss' dolls."

These remarks, of course, settled the matter with Salathiel. Indeed, in some respects Frances' eager consent and unexpected reply had been flooring, for he could not remember ever having told her that he had put shillings on Mrs. Larned's eyes, and it had never occurred to him that there was anything but affection between Frances and Bridget. How curious, and how deep, and unexpected, and unreasonable women were!

So it was that the coming of Hercules altered and revealed many things in the household to Salathiel, and brought him to a fuller realization of the nature of her who was going to be the mother of his child.

As for Bridget, she had already observed that Malycal said her prayers in the same elaborate and peculiar way that Melissa did. This, for all that it meant, troubled Bridget greatly. And because of it, she had also suffered a secret shock which, childish as it was, affected, although unbeknownst to them, all the grownups in the house then and in times to come.

With the coming of Malycal, and especially after she had moved into the room across from Frances, Bridget had decided to "find Mrs. McCandliss" again, and have a word with her about the correct manner of saying prayers. The blow came when Bridget discovered that she could no longer find Mrs. McCandliss. She skipped, she sang, and she spun around until she was dizzy. She went out into the thickets at dawn and tried her old game again and again, but no one in a white nightgown with a hole in her head and her mother's voice came to answer her. No, Mrs. McCandliss was dead, and she, Bridget, was alone. That was quite evident. The way back to Mrs. McCandliss was lost.

As a consequence, the child turned to Salathiel. Frances had Malycal now, and Frances was having a baby, too. Now, Yates was very fond of Bridget and was forever bringing her presents back from town, and he had also complicated matters by trying to clarify them. He had explained to Bridget how and why it was that she "belonged" to Salathiel, because it was "papa Sal" rather than "mama Lissa" who had to take care of her. This seemed right and natural to Bridget, who had felt so from the first time she had found Salathiel that night at Patton's, and their mutual sharing of the terrors of an Indian past was a great secret between them. And so Bridget now began, in her own mind at least, to keep house for Salathiel and to regard all her dolls, especially Queen Alliquippa, as his children. But Bridget was enormously competent, a fearless and practical little soul; and gradually as time went on and slow changes in character shifted people by natural stresses and strains and mutual gravitation into their fixed orbits in the household—Bridget did what she always did; she put her dreams into actual practice. And it was she who ended by really keeping Salathiel's house, while Melissa's children gradually took the place of the dolls. Unto him that hath, much shall be given—and the rest, of course, inevitably follows.

But equally, *of course,* nobody at Boiling Springs knew this in the calm winter months of 1765, while Melissa sat in her chair sewing things for her baby, Salathiel smoked his pipe, and Malycal drew tay at the hearth. Then Bridget only *played* with her dolls, and the cat looked into the fire.

What Malycal sometimes saw in the bottom of teacups, for the most part, being a wise-woman, she kept to herself. It was enough to intrigue Mr. Yates and to get a shilling from him by being able to tell him what the weather would be a day in advance. He often asked her, and he was a pleasant gentleman to have about. Malycal was secretly afraid and very respectful of "the bright shining thing" that lived in Mr. Yates's head, and looked out at her through one eye. It might be something Protestant, she suspected, but let be! To her it was not inimical. As for Salathiel, Malycal loved him as only an old woman could love the broth of a boy she had once mothered in Kaysinata's hut in the days of their dismal captivity on the Beaver. Now he had grown into a fine man, and by God's grace she had come home to live with him, as seemed right and natural. Let him smoke his pipe before the fire in peace, then—and never mind what the tea-leaves said.

Consequently, Hercules and Jed had full and undisputed run of the kitchen. Or at least Hercules had. Salathiel supplied fresh game with Twin Eyes; and Jed, the fuel for cooking, with his axe. The other viands, potables, and comestibles Hercules had a knack of assembling himself by dint of his own acumen and unheroic labours. That is, either he asked or he took. In any event, he "procured". And so it was after his arrival that the "card-suppers" at Glen's Mill began to prove more and more attractive to certain officers and gentlemen, and a few others, in and about Carlisle and LeTort's Springs; Brigadier Bouquet and Captain Ourry amongst them.

Amongst those who can definitely be traced as frequently present were Edward Yates and Arthur St. Clair, esquires; the Reverend Mr. Craighead; Messrs. Byers, Tilingham, and Williams; Jim Fergus; and both the brothers James and Martin Glen with their ever-memorable friend, "Colonel" Cornelius Vandercliff—to say nothing of various minor local worthies merely occasional, whose shadowy faces, shady anecdotes and reputations, low jokes and tallest stories have all alike been swallowed and digested in the maw of time. As to still other friends, neighbours, and travellers, who merely paused for refreshment or news at the mill door, there is no saying. Only the savoury rumour of the notable card-suppers at Glen's Mill remains to trouble the memory of a more crowded, less leisurely, and far hungrier epoch.

Yet behind the misty curtain of the years, in the honey-coloured glow of the mill-house parlour with all the candles lit, and the brasses and pewter glinting with cherry lights to the leaping flames, the amiable gaiety of the brigadier, Captain Ourry's appreciative snorts, Mr. Yates's genial sallies and ironical asides, the Reverend Mr. Craighead's anecdotes of *Aburrdeen* and theories on infant baptism; even Mr. Tilingham's mild speculations as to the Etruscan origin of the letters in the Oscan inscriptions recently disinterred near Capua— all of this—with the wheeze and bubbling of Salathiel's stone pipe and the tapping-throb in the next room of Frances' spinning wheel can still be overheard, if you listen—listen carefully. But that is all, gentlemen, that is all.

Meanwhile—and that meant the time when February had commenced to roar like March, but not a single bleat of spring had yet been heard—there was many an undisturbed winter night when Salathiel and Frances had the hearth-fire all to themselves while a wig or a bonnet was under way, the wind sang in the chimney, and Bridget, to her dolls.

It was then that they seemed most to be living with and for each other, while Malycal drew endless cups of tay, and in the kitchen Jed's feet could be heard shuffling to the weird wailing of Hercules's nose flute, and the raven croaked its harsh thanks for small gobbets of red meat or its even harsher prophecies about the end of the grey kitten, from its hutch on the beam above. These were the nights when Frances stopped the steeple clock on the mantel from ticking, as though she herself would arrest or prolong the flight of time. "And no wonder," she said, clasping her stomacher, "with two hearts beating happily together under here, *what* would I be after listenin' to a clock for, too?" And Salathiel smiled and nodded proudly, but with a curious sense that in time to come he might long to be able to turn the clock back; that they would never be so happy again as they were now.

"When happiness mates with time, they both fly away together."

The verity of which saying was soon made evident, for it was about this time that M. Henri de Molyneaux was released from his bond to keep the king's peace at Carlisle, and having been cruelly prevented by the brigadier and the unfeeling Quaker magistrates from meeting up with Lieutenant Frazier and spitting him on a small sword, began to pursue in earnest his runaway servant and his unfortunate creoline intention of carrying Hercules in chains back to Martinique.

Anyone *might* have told M. de Molyneaux that taking one Hercules away from another even stronger, on the verge of the lawless Pennsylvania frontier, was not a matter that should be gone about lightly. But no one *could* tell M. de Molyneaux that, or anything else in English. Bouquet had remonstrated with him in French about his madcap challenge, and had eventually been forced, after listening to an impudent tirade, to send him to cool off in the town jail, which in January was awfully cool for a gentleman from Martinique. *Mais, n'importe.*

For "butterfly" was the name for Henri. He fluttered. He did. His coat was wired out from his waist in a graceful Parisian manner. He minced when he walked, and his delicate little behind twinkled in tight doeskin under the wiry tilt of his coat-tails like the nose of a white rabbit under a leaf—it wrinkled and twinkled. And no man who spoke English could possibly take the polite Latin threat which M. de Molyneaux's jewelled rapier so daintily conveyed, or his character, seriously. Even in the saddle he was unsubstantial as thistledown, and almost as easily blown off. He lacked gravity both in fact and in demeanour. In fact, there was not enough of Henri to carry any weight at all.

He chattered English like a wren, but never understood its serious import. He danced like a sylph in mothy satins. He was rich, and richly adorned. And he had come to Philadelphia to arrange for the smuggling of sundry cargoes of Martinique molasses up the Delaware, with himself and his tropical estates thrown in as a kind of amatory bonus. For, in addition to profiting sweetly on sugar, he also fully expected to return to Saint-Pierre with a lily-white and, if possible, a fertile daughter of one of the affluent merchants with whom he did business.

Now there were no major difficulties with the merchants over the molasses. It had started to flow north promptly without *any* customary delays. And M. de Molyneaux had also promptly been bidden to flutter in some of the best drawing rooms in Philadelphia. In fact, he was finally invited to the Assembly, for the sweetest of reasons. But even belatedly virginal daughters of his mercantile hosts were forced to reflect, while he ardently languished before them, on what going to bed in Lilliput might be like, if they returned with him to Saint-Pierre; and to ponder discreetly on what must be the quite minor and yet principal difficulty of mating with a humming-bird. For such a little thing the better half of M. de Molyneaux's northern mission eventually failed.

Thus with a far heavier sensation in both his purse and his heart than when he had arrived, M. de Molyneaux had been forced to stay longer than he had expected at the London Coffee House on Front Street. But even he was at last convinced of the permanent aloofness of northern Dianas; and he was really "intending for Saint-Pierre", as his handbill afterward announced, when his stay was unexpectedly and, as it finally turned out, permanently prolonged, by the exasperating disappearance of his valet, cook, and general factotum, Hercules.

What life would be like at the "Morne d'Espérance" near the slopes of Pelée without his valet—to return minus the lily-white bride he had come for and without the famous black servant he had taken away with him—all this was more than the proud little creole plantation owner could face. And he had set out to pursue Hercules with a determination as strong as its object.

Actually, Hercules had not run away at all. At least, he had not intended to. He had liked his indulgent and carelessly generous little master well enough. If he sometimes wore his master's jewellery surreptitiously, there had never been any complaint about it. And grooming a butterfly was small labour for a Hercules. But he had been left idle in Philadelphia, and had spent his time loitering a good deal along the water-front, picking up an odd job here and there for sixpence or a shilling or two. It was in this way that he had been inveigled one day into loading some especially heavy military chests being shipped westward by wagon-train; and having proved himself a mighty man at the task, he was further indulged with a ride as far as the barracks at Lancaster, and no questions asked. Once at Lancaster, where he had tarried for a few days tasting the delights of freedom, and picked up the raven for his conjuring tricks from an old German woman, it was no great shakes to repeat his wagon performance and get a lift with another convoy as far as Carlisle.

Hercules had enjoyed all the excitement he found under way there, and profited by it. He had no trouble in getting enough small change together to ensure his living. Rumours of feats of strength with a crowbar in quiet corners; his fortune-telling bird; and the eerie reputation of a West Indian wizard come into their midst spread like wildfire amongst his fellow-blacks, always numerous in that vicinity, had kept him safe. Shortly before the brigadier's arrival Hercules had decided to let M. de Molyneaux return without him to Martinique. And he had about made up his mind that this welcome departure must have taken place, when he was warned one day that his master had come to town looking for him, and that a great reward was posted at the town hall for his apprehension and return.

This, indeed, put another face on affairs, and he was forced to disappear promptly even from the purlieus of slave quarters where he had frequently lurked, for fear that he would be betrayed for the five pounds offered. He determined, nevertheless, for his own and several feminine reasons, to remain in the neighbourhood of Carlisle. Besides, it was winter, the first out of the West Indies he had ever seen, and travelling was doubly difficult. So he made careful overtures to one Josiah Loften, the blacksmith, who hid him by day in his barn and allowed him to work at night by the warm forge fire, as often and as long as he could.

Matters had thus strung along for some weeks, and Hercules might eventually have emerged at Carlisle as a successful Vulcan, had not M. de Molyneaux also lingered dangerously in the vicinity. And it was for that reason that Jed had finally been cajoled by watch, bird, and mumbo-jumbo to smuggle Hercules out to Boiling Springs.

It was the "borrowed" gold watch that eventually caused all the trouble. It, and Captain Ourry's mischievous curiosity. Salathiel's sense of property was a strict one. It was still tinged with the colour of Indian customs, but he had his own code, and he stuck to it.

Thus Hercules had come to him as a fugitive asking shelter, and he had made a certain bargain with him and shaken hands on it. It was not only that he had decided he did not like to have people working for him as slaves. Hercules he had come to regard in the light of a chief of his own people, one who had escaped, much as a prisoner of war might escape, and been given shelter at his fire. That Hercules was black had little to do with it. He might have been red, and a Delaware escaping from the Mohawks. Furthermore, Salathiel now regarded Hercules as a friend, one whose giant strength and primitive but indomitable self-respect he greatly admired. All this had come to pass in a few weeks' acquaintance at the mill. They had been working and out hunting together. That Hercules trusted and liked him, and in much the same way, Salathiel had no doubt. Almost from the first it was thus understood. He would no more have betrayed Hercules for a reward than he would have turned in Bridget's scalp for a bounty.

But the watch was different. It was a piece of property like an item of trade goods that had been made away with unfairly. In fact, it had been accidentally filched from M. de Molyneaux, and brought to Salathiel's house. He had no quarrel with the Frenchman, and he had instantly decided to return the watch when he could. That was the reason he had taken it from Jed and kept it. So one day towards the middle of February, when he was working at camp, knowing that the brigadier had locked up M. de Molyneaux over the matter of a duel and the Frenchman's impudence, he had given the watch to Bouquet and asked him to return it to the Frenchman when he was released.

He thought no more of it. Both Bouquet and Ourry knew Hercules was at the mill. They had seen him there, but they had said nothing. Their silence as guests was taken for granted. The watch would be returned, thought Salathiel—and thought no more about it.

His perplexity, disgruntlement, and eventual indignation were, therefore, considerable when a few evenings later Yates returned from town with what he described as a "missive and masterpiece of coxcombry", written in French in an exceedingly minute but engraved hand, on a tremendous piece of paper. Upon being read in quite literal translation, and obviously with an all but ribald enjoyment by Yates, what Salathiel heard was this:

Monsieur Henri de Molyneaux de la Morne d'Espérance de Saint-Pierre en Martinique, these, at Carlisle in Pennsylvania this 13th day of February in 1765 by the courtesy of the advocate, Edward Yates, Esquire.

To the very large Gentleman of the Forest who now infests the vicinity of the late Miller Glen's establishment at Boiling Springs.

Monsieur,—Our mutual acquaintance, the Adjutant of the Brigadier, Captain Ourry, would not condescend to enlarge your name to me. But since it is you, I am otherwise informed, who has returned to me the watch of my revered male parent, so barbarously purloined by my valet, I have arrived at the tentative opinion that I address a man of honour, and at the certain conclusion that it is you, sir, who must be harbouring my escaped servant and personal property, contrary to the laws of this province and the lately concluded notorious treaty of peace between The Most Christian and His Britannic Majesty. Nevertheless, in view of your meticulous return of the watch of my father, I am supposing, as a man of virtue, that it is an excess of humanitarian rapture rather than the ignoble passion for gain which has led you thus, rashly, to give shelter to my poor Hercules.

But in any event, very large sir, since Monsieur Bouquet, the Brigadier, has this day recalled the letter of cachet with which he has seen fit to restrain my burning ardour for the vindication of my aspersed honour, while removing the object of my just resentment hence—be it known to you, that it is my resolution *not* to suffer the further indignity of leaving my valuable servant behind in this barbarous country when I depart for Martinique, and to the end that I may recover him promptly, it is my irrevocable intention to call upon you, sir, at your mill about mid-day tomorrow on the 14th of this month, when I shall expect you to take such measures as will secure the custody of the said Hercules into my charge.

Do not concern yourself, my dear Gentleman of the Forest, as to the return of Hercules with me to the City, I shall do myself the honour and you the compliment of coming fully armed with a dag in either holster, one to insure your compliance with my request and the other to watch over Hercules as we ride along happy in our reunion and in returning so amicably together to that beautiful Martinique.

Receive, Monsieur, the assurance of my continued and peculiar regard,

Henri de Molyneaux

M. de Molyneaux's seal, firmly impressed, disclosed two cupids romping in an infantile but abandoned manner with a crescent moon that was advisedly hiding behind a cloud.

Yates finished reading and handed the letter to Salathiel, who received it without comment. None the less, he was considerably annoyed.

It was not so much that the visit of the little Frenchman announced for the following day threatened to disturb the happy tenor of the satisfactory life they were now leading at the mill; there were a hundred ways of dealing physically with such a man as M. de Molyneaux. But it was quite apparent that both Yates and Captain Ourry had collaborated to bring this coxcomb down upon him out of a purely mischievous and humorous curiosity as to what might happen when the little Frenchman set out to capture a giant with a butterfly net. This, Salathiel thought, discovered a certain surreptitious superiority in Yates and Ourry, and a humorous conspiracy on their part to perpetrate a practical joke for their amusement at his expense. Side-splitting, no doubt! But, then, of late he was getting pretty tired of just that kind of thing on the part of several people.

So he let Yates laugh alone as he read the letter; and laugh alone all over again as he returned to it to repeat its more memorable passages. "Very large Gentleman of the Forest"—after all, what in hell was so funny about that? He determined to take care of M. de Molyneaux, Ed Yates, and Captain Ourry all at the same time, and to teach them a lesson about what was funny and what wasn't.

When Yates had stopped laughing, therefore, Salathiel quietly took the letter again, thanked him for his trouble, asked him to say nothing about it, and put it in his pocket without comment. He simply did nothing further about it, and he was aware at supper that night that Yates was uneasy and all but consumed with curiosity. They had a pipe together afterward, and everybody went to bed as usual.

Next morning Salathiel saddled Enna and rode with Yates as far as the ford with the upturned wagon in it. There he parted from him, for Yates was going to town, and for the first time alluded to the letter. "Tell your *new client*," he called out, while Yates was in the middle of the stream, "that you delivered his letter to me, and that I await his arrival *at the mill*." Yates nodded, nonplussed for once, and continued on to Carlisle, where, happening to meet M. Henri on the street, he delivered Salathiel's message, and hastened on to argue a case that had just been called up.

Salathiel waited at the ford for some time after Yates had left him; a good half hour at least. A fine sunny day, a little misty so early in the morning after a thaw, but the forest was quiet and the water gurgled about the sunken body and through the wheels of the overturned wagon cheerfully. One of the wheels occasionally moved a little, spinning slowly between the current and the wind.

After he was quite sure that Yates was not coming back, Salathiel dismounted, and tying Enna well back in the thicket, went over to the thunder tree and removed the cedar boughs that he and Jed had so carefully piled over the broad white lightning blaze, on another occasion many weeks before. The tree was damp underneath, and the white blaze, bared again to the sunlight, glistened. After that he rode back. But M. de Molyneaux did not appear at the mill at noon. Indeed, no one was expecting him—not even Salathiel. Work went on quite as usual.

About four o'clock the same afternoon, however, both the horses which M. de Molyneaux had hired that morning returned sweating, and with empty saddles, to their owner's stable at Carlisle. Some inquiry was aroused, but the little Frenchman had not seen fit to leave word as to his destination or errand—"he would return that evening," he'd said. Doubtless the horses had escaped him. Such things would happen even with good mounts.

It was already twilight when Yates and Captain Ourry, who were making a point of returning together for a merry supper at the mill that evening, had a decidedly grim experience just as they attempted to cross the little ford. Their horses suddenly went crazy. Ourry was thrown headlong into the mud as his horse tried to bolt, and he was dragged by the bridle. Yates's fine big grey swerved and made a desperate attempt to start back to Carlisle on his own. After a considerable interval of swearing, racing confusion, grabbing of bridles, and scraping off of mud, they soothed their trembling horses and managed to force them, rearing and bucking, across the stream.

It was while crossing the water, and thus busily engaged, that Yates first noticed the man lying in the water face down, with his head thrust through the spokes of the wagon wheel. From the very first he had small doubt as to who it was and what had happened. Further examination disclosed that it *was* M. de Molyneaux, and that he had been pitched forward so violently that his head had broken one of the oaken spokes in the wagon wheel. Yates then ascertained for himself that the big white blaze on the tree, which he had never noticed before, was a genuine freak of nature, while Captain Ourry dug clay out of his features and swore.

Much chastened in spirit and somewhat further matured in experience, Yates and Ourry brought the news to the mill long after supper that night. Nothing was said about it to Frances, at Salathiel's earnest request.

"Why, of course not," said Ourry, trying to look gallant and knowing all at the same time, even with muddy epaulets and a caked wig. "I simply can't understand it."

"Act of God," suggested Salathiel, looking gravely at Yates. "I waited here all day for your client, Mister Attorney, but he never turned up."

Yates nodded sagely and said nothing about the legal aspects of collaborating with the deity. It was his fault, too, he felt. He would not underestimate the Very Large Gentleman of the Forest again.

Hercules was given unexpected instructions by Salathiel next morning, and buried his master on a small hillock in a sumac thicket overlooking the ford, while Salathiel cut down the thunder tree, blaze and all.

But the gold watch, and sundry other small pocket trinkets of M. de Molyneaux, had now returned to the mill. These Salathiel gave to Yates, as the effects of his late client, and suggested that he dispose of them *properly*.

Mr. Yates did so. The watch was water-stopped but still of some value. He gave it to a stone-cutter at Lancaster with instructions. The other trinkets, a diamond pin, some gold buttons, keys, and the cupid seal ring, he sent to the governor of Martinique on the same ship that was to have conveyed M. de Molyneaux home, with a discreet statement of the tragic circumstances of his late client's demise. The stone-cutter, after a month or two, carried out Yates's instructions, and for over a century afterward it was well known to certain farmers and hunters in the neighbourhood of the little ford that in a small thicket overlooking the water stood a neat stone with the inscription:

ORARE
H de M

A native of Martinique
who
being of slight presence
both
of mind and body
but
of overweening determination
here
departed this life unexpectedly
under
tragic circumstances
on
postridie Ides of February
1765
A stranger in a strange land

RIP

The conciseness of this, if nothing else, served to soothe Yates's conscience as the discreet memorial of an affair which he wished to remember only as a restraint upon his rash sallies of humour, an earlier instance of which had cost him an eye. But the less said about it the better. Salathiel even went him one better. As in the case of Taffy's hand, he smoked over the letter thoughtfully, preserved it in confidence, and as usual, said nothing. Nor did Hercules, whose freedom was founded henceforth on silence.

All this was tacitly understood amongst those involved. And it was not long before it was as though the incredible little Frenchman had never been. Even his minor virtues worked towards his oblivion:

he left no debts to draw the interest of memory; his hired horses had returned themselves; at Carlisle his absence was scarcely noted. There, as in the City, his departure for Martinique was taken for granted. At home the news of his passing became the unexpected solace of collateral heirs. And there were no further accidents at the ford.

Life at the mill house continued happily in its undisturbed domestic round. Before the end of February, Bouquet departed for New York and Captain Ourry, to set up new headquarters at Philadelphia. Spring showed vernal signs of coming in early. The inhabitants of the country about Boiling Springs began to return confidently to their long-abandoned farms. Business at the mill gradually resumed. The ice was broken and the wheel turned.

Only the preparation for the colossal field preaching under way at Carlisle prevented and delayed a major exodus from that still much thronged and troubled borough. James McArdle and his inspired colleagues were preparing the town and the countryside for miles around for a visitation of the Holy Spirit. They prayed and preached fervently, with the twelfth chapter of Isaiah like fire on their lips, proclaiming "a joyful thanksgiving of the people for the mercies of God". As February began to turn into March, the spiritual excitement mounted—and "Colonel" Cornelius Vandercliff rode into town on his famous white horse.

29

The Fifth Horseman

NOW, THE WHITE HORSE of "Colonel" Cornelius Vandercliff was greatly feared in all that part of Cumberland which marched on the west with the mountains; and from Ephrata on the north to York on the south, and down into the borders of Maryland, as the sign of evil and a portent of disaster to the Shepherds of the Lord and the bleating sheep they gathered into pinfolds amongst the hills, against the Day of Judgment. For, to them, the horse was like a steed come smoking out of the pit, his neck clothed with the threat of thunder; and he who rode upon its back was a priest of Baal, whose delight was to tempt the lightnings and to call down the fiery wrath of the Almighty.

The name of the horse was Mahar-shalal-hash-baz, or Baz for short, and his master, Cornelius Vandercliff, was an atheist whose geniality was stentorian; a son of Belial, who prayed negatively with a mighty voice that was at once the envy and despair of every itinerant evangelical roarer from Philadelphia to those valleys called the "Shades of Death" amidst the Alleghenies, which was about as far west as you could lift your voice loudly in favour of salvation, or anything else, without losing your hair.

The horse was tall, white, narrow, and bony. He was ribbed like a skeleton; and his countenance was zebraic, with yellow teeth and fawnlike eyes. A mane like blanched seaweed waved behind him; but he shaded off into yellow towards his hocks, beneath which the mark of evil was plainly laid upon him. For the hoofs of Baz were not as the hoofs of the nags of Christians. They were spatulate like the war-horse of Julius Caesar; and when he trod in the dust he left the marks of two toes behind him, sinister as the cloven trace of the Devil himself.

Nevertheless, Baz was the bad apple of his master's evil eye, and he paced off the parasangs between camp meetings with a soft padding sound, instead of the healthy *clop* of iron shoes, which lent his abhorred approach a stealthiness, especially over pine needles, that some held to be unearthly. Indeed, even a rare advance glimpse of Baz with his black-cloaked, spade-bearded master, slipping along through the sumac thickets shortly after twilight, making towards the red glow in the sky and the shouts and songful clamour amongst the hills, which marked the site of some hopeful preachment, was about as welcome to the pastors of a mountain flock as a cockroach scuttling amidst the sprays of a bridal wreath is to a bridegroom— and almost as disruptive of the ceremony. For the arrival of Cornelius Vandercliff at a stump preaching in the forest was so nicely timed and so precisely managed as to take the ministers at the height of their own demonstrations of the power of prayer, and turn the rough scale of their previous success into the exact measure of their undoing.

Colonel Vandercliff prided himself, after some years of trial and error, upon two major ways of timing his disruptive arrival successfully. There was the appearance dramatic, and the approach subtle. But for small affairs, it was the former that he had found more effective.

The appearance dramatic consisted in riding Baz directly out of the night of the forest into the smoky ring of torchlight around the pastors at the very height of holy enthusiasm. When the bench was full of mourners, and moaning sinners were beginning to sway and press forward to take shelter in the outstretched arms of ministerial grace, then the bony white horse and his black-cloaked rider would appear, usually from somewhere behind the pulpit.

After allowing a few seconds for the silence that inevitably occurred to sink in, the colonel would rise in his stirrups and shout, "Lost! Lost!" with the voice of a siege cannon, while he pointed to sanctimonious pillars of the congregation who had already testified eloquently as to their heavenly future, and quoted horrid prophecies from Scripture as to the wrath in store for such tall Pharisees and hypocrites. And if this artful dodge, quite humanly popular even amongst the godly, did not suffice to break the spell of holy oratory and start bitter personal controversies in profane prose, he would himself dispute with the ministers, attacking the orthodoxy of their faith and the authority of their particular brand of salvation. These theological arguments were both raw meat and manna to the crowd. And he would end by challenging all the ministers present to a test of their faith in the efficacy of prayer. Let them pray, and let him pray; and let the Lord judge between them. This was the colonel's top offer. "And I'll kiss anybody's white tail if it ain't a fair proposition," he would sometimes add, fishing for sisterly giggles.

Now, in this bare but provocative offer lay the devilish cunning and the demoniac strategy of Colonel Vandercliff's attack. For the crowd was always eager for a contest, even though they were on the side of the ministers; and the ministers durst not refuse without denying the sincerity of their own belief in the power of prayer. There the colonel took them at their own word as to the power of it; and they were thus automatically reduced to the rôle of the defensive.

For it was only the mercy of the Lord that the ministers could invoke; at most they might ask that He should forgive all their enemies, and for Christ's sake save Colonel Vandercliff. Only thus by innuendo could they indicate he was bound for hell's fire. While he, when his turn came, he prayed for lightning, *now*.

He called down brimstone and the vengeance of the Almighty, and pleaded with God to assert Himself and purify the world. The colonel asked for the total wiping out of the putrid sinners now gathered at one spot so conveniently for the execution of electric justice; a just end for all of them—including himself. His voice seemed to anticipate the latent thunder, until, if there were a lazy echo slumbering in the vicinity, it was violently awakened and forced to go to work. Fearful blasphemies smoked from the square end of the colonel's spade-beard that dug dangerously at the heavens, and his hands at the end of his long arms threatened to pull down the electrical fluid out of the hole he made in the clouds, by the sheer magnetism of their writhing appeal. Until even those who had said in their hearts secretly, "There is no God," began to think, "What if there is one?"—while his voice gained in volume and eloquence, praying for lightning, beseeching to be struck down and damned now, on the spot, daring and tempting the Lord to do it.

Naturally, it was those nearest to the colonel who usually began to leave first. But this was not always so. Sometimes mere spectators on the outer verge of the gathering early took advantage of their open line of innocent retreat. As the first fervent requests for lightning ascended on high, they could be seen by ones, twos, and threes sneaking for the hitching-trees on the edge of the camp-ground, untying or cutting their horses loose, and making off into the country beyond as anonymously as possible. Nor could their judgment be seriously impugned. For it is one thing to occupy a valuable piece of real estate with a noble view overlooking the tabernacle and the holy proceedings in the streets of Zion, and quite another to be found standing on a piece of ground that might at any moment prove at best to be only a parcel of the outer rim of Gomorrah. In any event, here was a moving doubt.

And in the end it made small difference whether parties vitally interested in personal salvation were ranged inwardly amongst the chosen sheep or outwardly amidst the doubtful goats. At the first suggestion of fiery destruction as the unexpected solution of their spiritual difficulties, a rift ran through the entire assembly. Here and there frantic believers would begin to push through the crowd, bound for a safer neighbourhood. As the voice continued, the smell of ozone and singed flesh became imminent. Pauses, waiting for the lightning to fall, were horrible; the sound of hoofbeats receding into the distance, suggestive. Panic would generally ensue. And in the course of a few minutes Colonel Vandercliff could usually pray an entire congregation off its own feet and camp-ground, under the sorrowful eyes of the ministers. The firmer their faith in prayer, the faster they ran.

If, in the end, no lightning actually followed, still the triumph of the ministers who stood to abide the result was a lonely one, since there were few save the most obstinate of the elect who cared to remain to give praise to the Lord that it was His mercy rather than His vengeance that had finally prevailed.

Most exasperating of all was the colonel's sudden and humble concession of his defeat, while standing upon the field whence all but him had fled. After which, and disregarding the bitter anathemas that followed him, he would blithely turn the head of Baz towards pastures new, and ride off into the sheltering night.

Yet behind him lingered the fear, likewise the anticipation that his fearful prayers for levin might still be answered. In this sense, the colonel's dreadful reputation stretched into the past and extended witheringly into the future. The great moment of his life had been experienced on the borders of Virginia, when during a preachment that had shaken the spiritual foundations of the lower Valley itself, thunder had gathered behind the mountains, red lightning had flowed along the Blue Ridge, even while the colonel was intoning; and the assembly had been scattered by a furious shower of pelting rain and hail. This incident was long and vividly remembered.

That there might be something to it, and to the colonel himself, was the private consensus of lay opinion up and down the frontiers. And so, whatever were the mysterious motives that moved so strange a man to such eccentric performances—the causes of his conduct may well be left to the sequel and their dire effects temporarily taken for granted.

One thing is certain; nothing caused the Reverend James Mc-
Ardle or his inspired assistant, Mr. Puffin, more serious thought in
the spring of '65, when the great field preaching was getting under
way, than the sinister news that Colonel Vandercliff and his apocalyptic steed, Mahar-shalal-hash-baz, had undoubtedly been seen
passing through the streets of Carlisle.

That was in late February after Bouquet and Ourry had both
left Carlisle. But as nothing more was seen there of the man on the
bony white horse, and there was no further rumour of his immediate whereabouts, the anxiety of the ministers was gradually al-
layed, and the fervour of their exhortations mounted.

Meanwhile, the north wind switched into the south and became
a kind of gulf stream of the air, a balmy, sometimes a sultry zephyr,
day by day. Winter vanished like the receding memory of a white sin.
Save for the groanings and travailings of minor spirits in preparation for the coming of the Great One, the season advanced happily,
rapidly; and proved a peculiarly lovely and peaceful one. The Indian
war was over. March came early, imitating May. Spring arrived
lushly and all at once.

Suddenly the aisles and porches of the forest were hazy with
misty sunlight and lit by a million exultant tree-candles. On the
pines, locusts, catalpas, and horse-chestnuts, the altar lamps of Mani-
tou untimely bloomed. The dogwood veiled itself in lacy memories of
snow. Tall virginal maples lost their lacquered sheaths and blushed.
The perfume of deserted apple orchards haunted the wilderness. In
abandoned clearings the greedy hum of bees gone wild welcomed the
returning settlers back to burnt cabins lost in the midst of mounded
blossoms. The sound of axe, and saw, and adze resumed. From
Albemarle to the Susquehanna, from Chesapeake to the mountains,
the forest flushed through tender reds to misty green.

Up from the still unvisited fountains of life far to the southward,
out of the warm beating heart of the mysterious continent, came
wave after wave of birds, many of them as yet without European
names, but alive for all that, in their American myriads: first the
shy-coloured brown ones following the retreat of snow flurries; then
the bluejays, robins, scarlet cardinals, and the oriole glory of the
House of Baltimore. The sun smote against and reverberated warmly
from a thousand miles of rolling mountain walls; the snow-flushed
rivers leaped and sang. Erect tails of deer rocketed across the glades.
Northward up the valleys passed the clanging flocks of waterfowl
with far high trumpetings and quaint vibrant flutings underneath

the moon. All night frogs rang their Virginia-bells in the swamp
lands. By day the sun was speckled and the cloud shadows of incalculable flocks of passenger pigeons flowed across the land.

Salathiel had never seen anything like it. Spring along the Ohio
had come in less abundantly than this; more reluctantly. There the
winter chill died slowly, with snowbanks lying long and dank underneath the gloom of ancient trees. Here the very skirts of the Season
herself seemed to swirl overhead as she strode swiftly northward,
her ivory ankles flashing briefly amidst the dogwood as she passed.
Boiling Springs was in the direct path of the great bird migration
from the Atlantic coastal swamps up the valley of the Susquehanna.
The sky overhead was alive with restless music; the earth beneath
replied with rustlings and snatches of delirious song. Everyone at
the mill house heard it.

Indeed, they were not *in* the mill house any more. The doors were
now thrown wide and the windows propped open. The fires died down,
and they leached the piles of white ashes in the yard. The smell of
new leaves—and a lost fawn wandered in through the open door.
The child began to move faintly under Melissa's heart. There were
six new kittens in Bridget's basket. Malycal grew plumper and less
inclined to predict unpleasant things. The water-harp was touched
with new fantasies of melody, and Frances washed her black tresses
in vinegar and soft spring water and sat in the beating sunlight to
let them dry.

No man can keep any promise as fully as every woman would
like him to, but Frances Melissa felt for a while that Salathiel had
more than lived up to his word about bringing her "home". There
was one week of quiet living in pure ecstasy, with the sound of wings
on window sills and a stir of life within and without her, when she
understood why a plant struggles through all its other stages just to
bloom. That was before many people and the farm wagons began
to pass by.

Salathiel and Hercules were much afield together that early
spring. The muscles of strong men answered to such weather. They
hunted with bow and arrow and with guns. They were both good
with both. The larder lacked for little. They ploughed five acres to
keep the horses fit and last year's seed wheat from moulding. They
cleaned sedge and cress and water-weeds from the race and sluices.
They sludged down the wooden engine that turned the mill. The
stone house shook and shuddered now to its muttered thunder. The
raven fluttered and ran croaking to the end of his pegged string. He
squawked and made clacking noises with his beak; and it was
thought that he would have gone back to the forest again, if he

could. Jed would have liked to let him go. Perhaps there was a black
she waiting for him in the woods, he speculated. His mind ran much
upon such matters that spring. He hoped they would all be going to
the City soon. He was sorry for the *mnungee* bird. The country, for
all its new-born beauty, which he dimly felt, irked him.

Not the least lovely aisle in that still unconquered and unspoiled
forest was the tree-arcaded strip of sandy and river-gravelled road
that led past the mill-house door down to the ford over Yellow
Breeches Creek. In the summer the road was like a long tunnel with
the yellow waters of the river streaming past the end. It was overarched with tall red maples that Mr. Glen had planted, and in the
spring, when the trees sloughed, the lacy shade along its red-velvety
duff-littered floor was intricately wonderful.

There Bridget danced now in her new moccasins and took her
dolls out for promenades, while cardinals whistled at her down the
lane. There the empty inn on one side of the road had long stared
silently at the face of the mill house just across the shadowed way.
The porch of the old tavern was sagging in, but a change now came
across the resigned expression on its weathered face. Wagons began
to pass up- and downcountry, splashing across the ford, with chiming bells. The old place seemed to listen. The wheel ruts in the red dust
of maple buds grew frequent. Farmers' carts came to gather before
the mill door. About the time that violets nodded over Mrs. Larned's
secret grave, Conklin Drake, the erstwhile proprietor of the deserted
ordinary, returned, sniffing business in the warm southern trade wind.

He swept the leaves of two autumns off the porch floor, opened
the doors and shutters on their screaming hinges, and hung a new
bush over the door. In another week cross-eyed Jenny Greentooth
was back serving beer over the bar, and stronger liquor if you asked
for it. And it was just about this time that John and Martin Glen
with their fascinating new friend, Colonel Cornelius Vandercliff,
came riding along under the new maple shade and put up temporarily
at Mr. Drake's badly weathered establishment, pending the lapse of
Salathiel's lease on the mill.

The Glen brothers had compromised their mutual difficulty over
Clara Garber in a way that was perhaps more complimentary to them
than to her. They had tossed a coin one evening to decide who should
have her, and young Martin had won. Whether this was more satisfactory to Clara than if tails had come up for John, being a sensible
girl she would never say. Indeed, it was her reticence that had
brought about the coin tossing, combined with Colonel Vandercliff's
advice. For he had been staying in the same ordinary at Conestoga
with the Glen boys during the time of their double wooing. And he

hated to see two such fine fellows, as both the Glens undoubtedly were, embarked on what he considered to be a gratuitous quarrel. The world was full of pretty girls waiting to be wived, but where would either of the boys get another brother?—that was the string he had harped on, well or long enough, at least, to get them both to consent to trial by lot.

Fraternity having been thus, on the whole, happily restored again by the toss of a coin, and the course of true love made clear, it had been settled that Martin and Clara were to be married in June at Conestoga. Meanwhile, both Martin and John had come back home to advise with Mr. Yates as to the final disposition of their father's estate and the equitable division of the mill property between them. Whether this would imply selling it or not was at first a moot question.

Colonel Vandercliff had included himself in this happy return of the brothers to the vicinity of Carlisle almost inevitably, or so it seemed to them. As a man of considerable, albeit somewhat mysterious means, who always paid in coin, he was deeply involved in several schemes for western trade and settlement, amongst them, St. Clair's "colony" at Ligonier. Both he and the Glens, therefore, had business to transact with Mr. Yates. And what could be more practical and natural than to find him riding back with them from Conestoga and taking rooms at Mr. Drake's ordinary at Boiling Springs, with bed, board, bar, and stable; with Mr. Yates, the Penns' land attorney, just across the road, and with Arthur St. Clair himself a frequent visitor?

Why, it was convenience in a nutshell, the colonel told himself, even if the inn *was* a bit unsound in its upper story. But surely Mr. Yates had not meant any more than exactly what he had said in recommending its upstair's chambers as "quarters perfectly suited to a gentleman like himself". No, no, ambiguity was an inherent quality of English which every good lawyer must abhor. And Mr. Yates was an attorney whose opinions were always delivered gravely. Clever, no doubt, and a bit of a wit, too. But it was not to be supposed that even *he* could as yet suspect the compelling reason that actually brought Colonel Cornelius Vandercliff to board at such a place as Drake's ordinary—or the unparalleled opportunity for the exercise of his peculiar talents that was about to be afforded him at Carlisle.

And in this feeling of rational security, the colonel was at least reasonably correct. For no one, unless he were as privy as was Cornelius himself to all the underlying causes of his conduct, could possibly or at first blush begin to understand:

THE CURIOUS AND NATIVE STORY OF
CORNELIUS VANDERCLIFF

First Generation

More native than many others, even in 1765, Cornelius Vandercliff's story already stretched four generations back into the
American past. Perhaps the chief difference between him and
any of his stock who may be alive now is that Cornelius could
"remember" vividly and still enter into the lives of his immediate
forebears with a completeness of understanding, a feeling of
warmth and unity, which made him not only himself, but consciously the compound and the living exponent of the men and
women of the years behind him, who ran in his blood and
walked in his brain.

Nor was this by any means the *curious* part of his story. He
lived in the same house on the Rancocas River in New Jersey
where his people had dwelt for nearly a century before him. He
felt them there. He heard them spoken of by old people. Their
portraits, their books, their letters and old clothes, and their
weapons and domestic implements and furniture were his by
inheritance and familiar use; and he felt both the sunshine and
shadow of their presence as companions of his own personality
and components of his character. That was the *native* part of
his story, one which he himself and most of those about him
at that time took entirely for granted. It was what being a
Vandercliff of Swansdam meant.

"Memory" did not run so vividly back into the old country
in Holland, where his saga may be said to have begun. It grew
dim there. A few names of people and of places, a latent sentiment of loyalty and obligation to the House of Orange; several
old pipes, a large Dutch Bible, and a heavy mace, whose, he
knew not, were about all that remained. At Bergen op Zoom
there were relations. His father knew them, but his father was
the last who could write "home" in Dutch, and who probably
still thought in it sometimes. For Cornelius, Dutch no longer
made a noise in his head. At Swansdam now everybody but a
few of the blackamoors spoke English, and they spoke bastard
Arabic.

No, it was quite impossible to imagine himself across the
Atlantic. There, the curtain fell. And he was more familiar with
ancient Rome than he was with Amsterdam, or London, for that
matter. Philadelphia was the only city he had seen, and if he
was a citizen of anywhere, he was a citizen of that place. But

he was certainly not a subject of any man or state, and it is more likely that in reality and in a peculiarly contemporary and North American way he was the free hereditary colonel of Swansdam. Swansdam was *his* in a way that no one could possess it now, and few even then. It was his father and grandfathers who had seen to that.

Hendrik Vandergrift—Vandergriff—Vandergreeft—Vandergriffen—for so the name at various dates and places appears, Cornelius's great-grandfather, had come to New Amsterdam from the Low Countries in the days of the old peg-legged governor, Peter Stuyvesant, and made a place and some small reputation for himself there.

Whether he was a gentleman by descent or by achievement is not quite clear, but he seems to have had some Greek and Latin, gentle friends at home, a few gulden and an acquisitive instinct that soon made him respectable and acceptable even among those who coveted in a patroonish way.

He early went up the Hudson to Fort Orange (Albany) in a clerking capacity, but soon turned from sheepskin to peltry. And his ability as a fur trader must have been considerable and have had free rein, especially during the first English occupation of the province, for upon the return of the Dutch, the new governor complained bitterly to Amsterdam of the loss in profits to the West India Company which Vandergrift's free trade in furs on the Delaware was causing. That is a significant mention and not the last gubernatorial complaint in the course of family history, by any means. But it does show that quite early, probably a good many years before, Hendrik had shifted the scene of his free enterprise from the Hudson to the valley of the Delaware, and that he was doing well.

Probably he was connected with the Dutch Fort Nassau on the Delaware, which was built right across the river from where Philadelphia was later to stand, in the days of troubles with New Sweden. At any rate, he operated in that vicinity, probably from Nieuw Amstel (New Castle) to the Watergap and almost certainly around Cape Charles and up the Chesapeake as far as the Susquehanna. For he seems to have had some dealings with Kent at his island, and his ship, the *Catkin,* is mentioned, without blessing, as being a nuisance to the English "with its cheap Dutch goods carried to Virginia planters" against the acts of Parliament so provided, and the letters of instruction from the indignant Lords of Trade. The ketch *Little Puss* is mayhap the same ship that did a thriving business with Williamstadt in Maryland, "the Thrid Haven", and thridded up the two Choptanks, without so much as a waft of its ensign to the proprietors of those parts. References are not many, but enough to sketch in the outlines of a genre portrait of Hendrik Vandergrift as a very free trader indeed. He traded with the Dutch, the English, the Swedes, the Indians; and the French and Spanish, too, later, down into the Indies, with a talent for avoiding the customs' regulations of any governments whatsoever, which implies a certain mercantile genius, good seamanship, a loose political allegiance, and a safe base of operations.

It is the last, the base and locus of his enterprise, that most concerns this story and the history of the Vandercliffs. It bears the stamp of Hendrik's freebooting genius and was actually already extant at the time of Governor Andros, whose sicretrary (*sic*) was entertained at "ye trading marineer's stockado on ye Rancockuss in Jarsey next ye coast of ye South River"— and was apparently sent away in a merry mood, for no further visits or visitations from authorities are on record. But by this time Hendrik must have been doing a roaring little business quietly at "ye stockado". He was probably one of the many and now rather dim Dutch traders, proprietors, and adventurers who held land and traded in one way or another, and mined and farmed all up and down the east bank of the Delaware from the Watergap as far south as Swannendael (Lewes) down the bay, on the opposite shore. The indications are that they were some of the most enterprising of the sons of New Amsterdam, for the entire Hudson Valley having been pre-empted by patroons in a highly successful and permanently feudal way, gentlemen who were not to the manor born, and less *persona grata* than others with their High Mightinesses in Holland, turned westward and tried to achieve their fortunes in one way or another along the Delaware.

Such have largely been forgotten, for much of their success depended upon avoiding notice or mention in official documents, as far as possible. With the final fall of the Dutch régime and the taking-over by the English of New Netherlands, the Dutch along the South River found themselves, in sentiment at least, political orphans. But there were few signs that the disappearance of their High Mightinesses from the scene caused the men of the South River to sit idly by in sack-cloth and ashes.

On the contrary, the lax period of English establishment that ensued, while the claims of the Duke of York were being transferred to William Penn, while Governor Andros vanished hence with his threat of strict government along with his obstinate master, James—this was indeed a period of "glorious revolution" from several standpoints; and cheap Dutch goods were plentiful and much appreciated by the English planters in both the great bays and the numerous rivers of the Chesapeake and the Delaware country.

The long and fatuous quarrels of the proprietors of the Jerseys helped to prevent the riveting of any but the loosest shackles on the feet of trade, and there were not a few colonists who at that time drew the apt conclusion that freedom and the absence of government were synonymous, and acted accordingly. Hendrik Vandergrift was one of them, and the golden age of "ye marineer's stockado on ye Rancockuss" was undoubtedly before and during the coming in of William Penn and his followers.

A century of prosperity for the family that Hendrik founded testified to the penetrating quality of his glance into the future, and nothing was more indicative of it than the situation of the family seat, which in the next generation came to be known as "Swansdam". As for Hendrik, he seems to disappear sometime early in the new century, without exact date, but with the genealogical data that he had married one Anna Swanson from the Swedes' congregation at Southwark. She brought him a dowry of numerous bales of beaver skins, counted amongst her moral virtues, and, in the course of the last two decades of the seventeenth century, three children: Cornelius, the first of the name, and two daughters, Anna and Katie. The latter married an officer in the garrison at Fort George in New York, while the former died of smallpox. Hendrik seems to have been buried in the family graveyard in the stockade on the Rancocas. He was succeeded by his son, Cornelius, who about 1709 was signing his name "Vandercliff". And it is he who is first referred to with the title of "colonel".

Second Generation

This augmentation of style and shift of nomenclature in the second generation undoubtedly deserves notice, for it throws considerable light on both the fortunes and the social status of the Vandercliffs. "Colonel" is the only title, besides the less honourable one of "doctor", that still finds favour and lingers naturally on American lips. In the colonies, where no feudal titles were conferred by the crown, the desirability for honourable terms of address in communities striving for recognition and social self-respect was deeply and keenly felt. "Colonel", for many intricate linguistic reasons, was the word. It had all the right feeling about it. It was used to designate a man of courage, abilities, and estate sufficient to raise, own, and lead a regiment. He might never be called upon to do so, or he might be appointed by the royal governor as a colonel of militia. But he was *that* kind of man to begin with, a colonel. All the governor could do was to make it official.

Now, it is not likely that in the Quaker parts of Jersey the first Cornelius would have been appointed a colonel. And for other reasons, it is all but impossible, for he was by no means at that time a favourite with the authorities in any colony. Indeed, they were obliged to wink at him, if they regarded him at all. Yet it appears from certain ships' papers, family letters, and dockage leases that Colonel Vandercliff was a "colonel", and that the title was completed when "of Swansdam" followed his name, as before long it always did.

This much is certain, if nothing else, by 1711 the first Cornelius was regarded as a man of courage, attainments, and property. And that there was good warrant for his status appears later. As for the change in the spelling of the name, it was as the English authorities would have it, for they early became alarmed at the influx of "German foreigners and landless Dutchmen" into Pennsylvania and to adjacent parts, and it was doubtless good policy for Cornelius to assume as indigenous a spelling for his name as possible, and to speak the English tongue. At any rate, "Vandercliff" the name became and remained. And with "colonel" before, and "of Swansdam" after, it must have been more than merely respectable.

"Of Swansdam" there is much to be said. It was a realm rather than an estate, and he who held sway there was the master of many—of ships, slaves, land, and merchandise. It was something at Swansdam to be "the man of the house". It must have been the first Cornelius who built it.

The old stockade disappeared, and the thick-walled brick house with narrow windows and high corbie Dutch gables and terra-cotta chimney pots, all in a row at either end, took its place. It was three-storied and gambrel-roofed, peg-floored like the decks of a ship, and with large comfortable rooms. But it was so Dutch that Dutch William himself might have been at home there, if he could have rowed up the Rancocas in his royal barge and stepped ashore. The blue tiles in its chimney places came from Delft, and the place might well have been called "t'Huys ten Bosch", for it was hard to find, lost behind a wall of forest on the river-bank, and on an island in a sequestered backwater of Rancocas Creek, where several smaller streams led off into the swamps.

Take a very crooked stick, a marshmallow; take the thumb and pointer finger of your right hand. Make those fingers into a circle and place them against an angle in the crooked stick. Now pull your thumb back just far enough to open the circle, and drop the marshmallow in the center—and you will have a "map" of Swansdam before you—with the crooked stick for Rancocas Creek, your forefinger and thumb for two wooded points of land, and the circle a deep pool with a marshy island in the center. The wooded points overlapped each other slightly; the entrance was narrow, but in those days it was deep. The island was diked and the house built high on a mound—which shows that there must have been a good many hands at Swansdam to begin with.

It was swampy country to the east and west of Swansdam, Jersey swamps; an unbroken forest to the north and south. Unless you were a bird, or came up the Rancocas in a boat, you could not come to Swansdam at all. The place lay about four or five miles up the Rancocas from the Delaware, and when a small ship or schooner slid between the wooded points into the pool before the house and anchored in about three fathoms, all that had to be done was to douse topmasts, and the ship disappeared. Apparently it had sailed into the woods.

This was a feature that must have greatly appealed to Hendrik. The *Little Puss* cannot be traced after his time, but Colonel Cornelius I built three ships in his day at the east end of the pool, launched them, and sailed three or four of the seven seas. The ships' names were *Thetis, Ariel,* and *Ariadne,* the first two topsail schooners, and the last, a snow. All of them must have been capable seacraft, for it was Cornelius I who began to trade extensively across the Atlantic and down into the West Indies, with probably a bit of sketchy privateering, and even some freebooting, when occasion served. There was a good deal of freebooting in the first two decades of the century, and the Delaware and its creeks were neither averse nor immune.

Of Colonel Vandercliff's connection with airy commercial transactions, the following can be traced. He was hand-in-glove with one Dickon Brown, a son-in-law of Deputy Governor Carl Markham of Pennsylvania, when Brown was denied a seat in the Assembly for dealing with pirates. There was also a Miss Beulah Jacquet who tended store on High Street in Philadelphia at No. 77, a little west of Second Street. She saw Captain Teach (Blackbeard) there frequently. "He bought freely and paid well. She knew it was him [*sic*] and so did some others. But they were afraid to arrest him lest his crew, when they should hear of it, should avenge his cause, by some midnight assault."

That must have been the year Captain Teach wintered in the Delaware. And about the same time, as near as the observant Beulah could afterward recall, Colonel Vandercliff of Swansdam bought freely from her master, "with gold moidores", and also sold him a couple of bales of East Indian shawls and silk falderols, with several other curious items, obviously not manufactured on the Rancocas. Also Crane, a Swede of the upper Schuylkill ferry, went regularly in his boat to supply Teach's ship when she lay anchored off State Island, and he also plied monthly to Swansdam. Crane may have been one of the colonel's men. Finally, at Marcus Hook, where Teach's crew and the people of several other doubtful craft rendezvoused for winter fun, the "House of Revels" there was kept by a Mistress Margaret Swanson, a cousin of the colonel's mother. Perhaps that is how the falderols got to the respectable shop on High Street. All this, of course, is not enough to place the colonel in the prisoner's dock, or—

"Hang him by the neck, or brand his hand
As a black member of the buccaneering race,
The dregs and feculence of every land."

He was doubtless too discreet ever to be a principal, and kept his mouth shut as to any little agency business that he may or may not have been an agent for ashore, as were many others up and down the river, who gained in purse without suffering in reputation.

At length it was rediscovered that force need not be the monopoly of rascals. And after some clanging sea fights, and a number of select hangings, after 1705 that particular era of bloody revelry on the high seas and blackmail on the coasts came to the end of its rope, too. The continuing inability of the authorities to enforce the Navigation Acts acted as a kind of inadvertent compromise to make the continuation of trade bearable. But the pirates had been found only less tolerable than lawful authority.

There still remained, however, between outright piracy and strict conformity with mercantile restrictions, a twilight area in which, by the exercise of ingenuity, daring, bribery, and superb seamanship, a general commercial intercourse, international and intercolonial, could be carried on. It was within this margin between black and white that Colonel Vandercliff continued to operate, much assisted by more profitable interludes of privateering, but certainly with greater profit than applause. In 1709 he managed to achieve both by a lucky coup on the high seas.

In August of that year on a voyage back from Cork, his snow, the *Ariadne,* encountered an Algerine rover off the south coast of Ireland, and in a brilliant and daring boarding operation by moonlight captured the corsair, crew, and cargo. It proved to be an enormously rich haul, as the rover also was returning home, to Algiers, after a long and successful cruise in which an English East Indiaman, two tall Frenchmen, and a small Spaniard had been plundered and scuttled.

Colonel Vandercliff's only embarrassment seems to have been what to do with the Christians of the enslaved crew, a difficulty he solved forthwith by liberating them at the lonely Scilly by boatloads, despite the all but hysteric protests of the deputy governor, who, however, under the guns of the *Ariadne,* was forced to roar like a dove. The colonel then sailed for the Delaware with the *Ariadne* and his prize, named the *Scourge of Jesus,* and he seems to have taken both ships direct to Swansdam without troubling either the guard-ship at New Castle or the Philadelphia authorities.

Nevertheless, the capture of the "Sallee rover" made some noise not entirely unfavourable at the time. Traces of the affair are to be found chiefly in the earnest efforts of John Company to recover at least part of the cargo of the East Indiaman, *Charles,* which the *Scourge of Jesus* had taken off St. Helena. But no one at Philadelphia knew anything about it. No doubt the captain had avoided that abode of ignorance and virtue, and come home by night. We can be fairly certain that if the assurers paid the loss to John Company, the colonel pocketed the only profit.

In short, the fortune of the Vandercliffs was now permanently made. The house at Swansdam was bursting with fabulously valuable Oriental merchandise, silks, teas, spices, china; and the luxurious and exotic furniture, which for nearly a century afterward continued to intrigue and astonish all those infrequent visitors who were lucky enough to be guests. And from then on the Vandercliffs paid in coin, gold and silver, of a variety and date of mintage that was astonishing.

But the most permanent item of cargo in the *Scourge of Jesus* proved to be a dark crew of twenty-one Arabic-speaking Moors or Negroid Berbers whom the colonel evidently brought back and settled as a kind of garrison at Swansdam. They took wives from the Negro slaves already on the estate, and as time

went on intermarried with squaws of the scattered Indian families who still lurked along the banks of the Rancocas. It is
possible that their progeny could still be traced in the vicinity
by a discerning eye. For three generations they were known as
"Vandercliffs' people", and bastard Arabic was spoken in the
servants' quarters at Swansdam. It was no small advantage to
the head of the house that he alone could communicate with them
in what became a private language and secret jargon, in the
small realm surrounded by swamps. They were certainly not
held as slaves. They were fanatically devoted to the "colonel"
and his successors, and were superb seamen, fishermen, and
skilled workmen. Fire at Swansdam, and the rapid changes and
growth of the nineteenth century finally scattered this people
over the southern face of New Jersey.

All in all, the first Cornelius was probably *the* great man of
the family. It was he who brought the black swans to swim
in the harbour pool, which must have given the name to the
place. Perhaps the times helped to make him outstanding, but
neither his talents nor his strength of character can be denied.
He coped well with the world as he found it. He married comparatively late, apparently during an extensive voyage to England, in 1711, a Miss Margaret Lightfoot, sister of one Matthew
Lightfoot of St. John's, Wapping. As this family were members
of the Society of Friends, and Margaret's brother, a cordwainer,
this may be taken as an affair of the heart, for in rank and
fortune the colonel at this time might have aspired higher.
There is curious confirmation and legend later that the women
of the Lightfoot family were beautiful enough to attract the
notice of princes. And then there may have been Quaker connections in Philadelphia, of which we know nothing. There were
two children born of this union at Swansdam, Cornelius II in
1713, and Mary in 1715.

For the rest, the colonel seems to have continued and increased his mercantile activities to the French islands in the
West Indies but especially and directly to Holland, where his
interests were mainly centered at Leyden and his credits there
at one time, large. He may have found blood relations in the
adjacent countryside. At any rate, his connections with Leyden
account for the fact that his son, Cornelius, was entered there
at the university at the age of sixteen, the start of his somewhat
callow intellectual adventures on the Continent as a rich and
brilliant young American, one who spoke Dutch and French
pedantically well. Mary married into a patroon family on the
Hudson, with a portion of four thousand pounds, which is a

gilded comment on the state of the family fortunes about 1732, and maybe a final tribute to the *Scourge of Jesus*. In brief, Colonel Cornelius continued handsomely and in handsome style until 1731.

A portrait painted in England, said to have been by Knolles, a fine library of the classics, various works on the art of ship-building, and theological tomes in French, Dutch, and English, perhaps disclose both the practical and the ghostly nature of his tastes. He annotated carefully some volumes of ante-Nicene Fathers, wrote a polemic against Pope Gregory for destroying the works of Sappho, hated the Arian heresy, to judge by his notes, and altogether seemed more obsessed by theological questions than even the spirit of the age required. And this is all the more surprising in view of his, to say the least, worldly career.

He was remembered in the City for his rich and elegant attire, for the shady but salubrious nature of his mercantile dealings, and for the turtle soup dinners "with wines from the Greek islands", which towards the end of his life became notably frequent at the inn kept by Wilcox Phillips at the east end of the Kensington Market Bridge, while his eight-oared barge with the blue uniformed "Arabs" waited nearby in Cohocksink Creek to take him back to Swansdam. It was noted that he seldom invited anyone from the City to accompany him home. Consequently, it was not until some three months after he and his wife were carried off by yellow fever in August 1731 that, some of his drafts falling due in Philadelphia, it was learned he was dead, and that the "young colonel" was in Leyden. One "Mustaf Suliman", who violently resented being taken for a nigger, and described himself as the mate of the *Ariel,* paid the drafts in Turkish coin.

Third Generation

Young Cornelius II was at the University of Leyden when in December 1731 the *Ariel* brought him the news of the death of both his parents, and he found himself the Colonel of Swansdam and the master of a comfortable fortune. He must have been a cool young hand, for he claimed possession of his father's credits at Leyden forthwith, dispatched the *Ariel* back home with a fourteen-page letter of instructions to one Mr. Robert Jenkins, his factor at Swansdam, which is a model of pedantic English mercantile prose, keen accounting, and economy. In fact, it is hard to escape the conviction that at this stage of his career at least young Cornelius was a prig. The *Ariel* was given instructions to come back and meet him at London in December of the following year, after which the new colonel drew a large sum in gold, a larger letter of credit, and set out on the Grand Tour in a post-chaise, apparently in company with some young English noblemen referred to only as "my Lord and cousin Harry" —and their tutor, Dr. Kenneth Simcoe, a Scottish Jacobite doctor of divinity of considerable learning and expensive tastes.

The party saw the two Germanies, crossed the Alps, and visited Italy: Milan, Padua, Florence, Rome, and Genoa. From there they took ship for Marseille and then posted to Paris, where they evidently had letters to the British Embassy and some French families of note. One suspects that the Englishmen supplied the letters and influence, and the American the funds for the tour, which was fabulously expensive. And towards the last, the post-chaise with the young gentlemen was followed by another in which reposed Dr. Simcoe and the rare books and other items he had collected en route.

At Versailles they saw King Louis and Queen Marie dining in state, and visited and conversed with "philosophers and female conversationalists", at least Cornelius and Dr. Simcoe did. We are also informed that "cousin Harry catched the itch". How matters were going can be generally inferred from the fact that my Lord and cousin Harry returned to England, leaving Cornelius and Dr. Simcoe in Paris to continue their philosophic conversations. Cornelius did not get to London until April, where he found the *Ariel* "eaten up by expenses and port bills, for having waited since December, and three of the crew pressed, for which I did severely take my father's agent to task and find me another with better connections for the future".

The *Ariel*, we learn, was finally freed of libels, attachments, dockage, and boarding-house bills and sailed for America late in May. The Grand Tour had cost the grand sum of £4,230 18s 6d, which "fretted me like the devil to think upon, and various devices to recoup myself", writes Cornelius in a letter home to Jenkins, sent in April. The most significant result of the Grand Tour was that Dr. Kenneth Simcoe and all the books returned together with Cornelius in the *Ariel* in May. Evidently Kenneth Simcoe had seen where ease and his future most hopefully lay. And Cornelius also must have done some earnest thinking upon the devices to recoup himself, for the *Ariel* took him to New York, and there in October 1733 he married Susan, a daughter of the Heathcotes of Pelham Manor, who brought him a dowry "that did comfort my heart almost as much as her person".

Of this convenient and well-heeled marriage there were two

children, Mary, born in 1737, and Cornelius III, a year later, but the mother died having her son. She was an inveterate horsewoman and brought riding horses even to the swamp country at Swansdam and had ridden them regularly every day about the yard on the island. It was this for which she was chiefly remembered by the Vandercliff people, for the place was one of ships and boats and maritime things, and riding horses was regarded as something strange, useless, and sinfully exotic, especially for a woman.

It was said that the mistress paid a fatal price for it by having great difficulty in bearing children. Mary had arrived only after painful labour, and the child Cornelius, a baby with a big head, at the cost of his mother's life. He was given to a wet nurse in the servants' quarters. She tried to bind his head into shape with strips of cloth, and left them on for some months, until the colonel could bear to look at his son, and had him brought back into the house and left to sleep with his sister in the nursery.

But it was also said that the colonel never cared much for either of the children after his wife died, and that he seldom saw them. He was the first of the Vandercliffs who spent most of his time away from Swansdam. Perhaps this was only the small talk of the servants' quarters, but certain it is that the hardest thing in the life of the third Cornelius was his getting born, and that he and little Mary seldom saw their father.

They were both lonely and strange children and were noted by Dr. Simcoe as being prone to spasms and having the jerks. Most of his notes about this time, however, were strictly confined to a comparison of the doctrines of St. Augustine and Athanasius, and in Greek. For Dr. Simcoe had realized the ultimate limbo of scholarship in a nirvana of annotation, and a luxuriant living without effort, in a paradise of books to which he added others as he saw fit.

The colonel evidently liked and trusted him. He left him to his own devices for about ten years of textual pedantry, by the end of which Dr. Simcoe was greatly feared and thoroughly disliked by almost everybody at Swansdam, including young Cornelius; but with the exception of Mr. Jenkins, the factor, who luckily for the estate was not apprehensive of Dr. Simcoe and was immune to Greek and Latin epigrams, albeit sensitive about English oaths, which he repulsed in a vulgar, forceful, colonial manner.

Such was the status of affairs at Swansdam when Colonel Cornelius II died suddenly after the lancing of an impostume

on the back of his neck at St. Vincent in 1748. It was said the
colonel's head had swelled to the size of a bucket and his face
turned black. Whatever the details are, he died, and the snow,
Ariadne, came back with his body preserved in spirits of wine
in a lead coffin. He was buried beside his wife, the equestrienne.
The funeral, with Dr. Simcoe in full canonicals, and some gentlemen up from Philadelphia, was one of the first things that
young Cornelius III could remember as a genuine piece of
reality. He was about ten at the time; and Mary, a little past
eleven. The colonel was buried by torchlight, accompanied by
the weird chanting and singing of the Vandercliff people. The
merchants and lawyers went back to Philadelphia. Despite Dr.
Simcoe's canonicals and liturgy, it had not been a Christian
ceremony.

As the City gentlemen left early the next morning, with the
sun rising through the mists of the marshes behind the long
shuttered house; with the black swans gliding on the smooth
pool before it, which reflected them and the surrounding forest
and the anchored ships like a Claude Lorrain mirror, several
of the gentlemen, as they pulled out into the river, had the sensation of wakening out of a sinister dream. And there were few
of them who did not disembark on the noisy water-front at
Philadelphia without a sigh of relief.

Fourth Generation

So the two children were left alone at Swansdam with Dr.
Simcoe in the house, and Mr. Jenkins in the counting-house.
And very much alone they were. By the terms of the colonel's
will, Dr. Simcoe was left as guardian and tutor, with his living
and the use of the house, until Cornelius should reach his seventeenth birthday; while Jenkins, under the executors of the
estate, was in charge of the mercantile operations of the establishment and the running of the plantation at Swansdam. As
there was little love wasted between Dr. Simcoe and Mr. Jenkins,
the arrangement worked out in practice that Simcoe was master
of the library and Mr. Jenkins of everything else: ships, people,
plantation, and revenue. The saving grace in this provision
proved to be the sterling character of Mr. Jenkins. He was able,
upright, and honest; a Yankee from Plymouth, Massachusetts.
But it was a good many years, and those the most formative of
life, before the little boy, who slept in the same room upstairs
with his sister at Swansdam, grew old and wise enough to
appreciate the comparative merits of Mr. Jenkins. As Cornelius
was a curious young specimen, it will do no harm at least to try

to understand him and the strange world in which he now found himself.

Whether consciousness is a dream, a reflection of reality, or a combination of both is too involved a piece of metaphysics to pursue here. But it can be truthfully stated that, to Cornelius, the years of his childhood and those immediately following the death of his father always seemed to him to be a beautiful, vivid, and terrible dream. The reality which he came to savour later always lacked the poignancy of the dream. Also he was constantly under the impression that some kind of gigantic practical joke had been practised upon him. And it was a constant temptation, one which he was not always able to resist, to repay the world in kind.

The room in which he and Mary slept overlooked the stretch of lawn and the pool before the house, where the black swans swam and the forest was mirrored upside down in the water. The scene was forever engraved upon his memory, and it was out of it that he later sallied forth into the world, and to it that he returned from time to time to refresh himself in the fountain of dreams. But if you, reader, could have looked through young Cornelius's eyes like a pair of spectacles, you would have been immensely startled, for you would have seen that the trees in the pool were pointing earthward, and the swans upside down. In fact, to Cornelius, the pool was the sky. Cornelius, of course, didn't know it. That was the way the world was hung for him, with everything fitted into it quite nicely.

He was also left-handed, and was a handsome child, subtly misshapen if you looked closely. For his head was set a bit on one side, favouring his left shoulder with a kind of cockiness not unpleasant, but disturbing. Cornelius and his sister both had large deep blue-black eyes that examined the world and other persons with a candour of curiosity that was disconcerting to most people. For their gaze was almost expressionless, and their faces gave back no hint as to the conclusions which might have been reached behind the dark pupils. This gaze made the servants uneasy, and the two were often referred to in the quarters as "the young owls".

Mary was certainly beautiful, both in face and contour— gay, mischievous, completely feminine, and all but diminutive, which last probably accounted for her being alive at all. For she had been the first child of the mother neither of them could remember. She was proud of her handsome father, but her whole affection was centered on her "baby brother", for so she always regarded him; and his, on her. Cornelius was a moody child, and it was only through the bright gaiety and mischievous sallies and interests of his sister that he was lured out of the shady cave behind his eyes into the full sunshine. At times when they played together, he achieved this. She wakened him in the morning, for she was always up first. They played together all day, and they went to bed at night romping and talking and whispering together.

The first thing he could remember was Mary as a little girl getting up in the spring and summer mornings and dancing naked in the sunlight streaming into the room. She was ivory, dainty, and delicate; beautiful, with burning blue-black eyes and fair flying hair. And it was this vision he always held in his soul of what he loved most and never found again.

Add to this, that both children were constantly together day and night and saw hardly anything of the children in the quarters, who were forbidden to play on the island about the big house, and that, except for the servants, whose ministrations and affection they both took for granted, they were left to their own devices—and it is no wonder that they shared not only the outside world as a mutual experience, but also each one the life and mind of the other. Possibly Mary saw the world as Cornelius did. Afterward he could not be sure. But he was certain she understood, for she seemed to find her way about in it in the same way that he did. And not like all the other people. Neither of them had any idea that this state of free adventure, that the eerie and all but changeless childhood, which lasted only a few years, was not permanent. That was what made it seem like a happy eternity to look back upon. Indeed, Mary did not go on when time began for Cornelius. She died—but she was still there. She remained with him in the house. She was permanently a part of Swansdam. And she was seen looking from the windows of the house fifty years later when it burned down.

Time, life, and misery began for Cornelius with Dr. Simcoe.

Scholarship as a vice, and pedantry as a sedative have never received the comment under those aspects which they deserve. Like the aimless reading of history, they can become a form of intellectual debauchery in nirvana. For two years after Colonel Vandercliff died, Dr. Kenneth Simcoe was enabled by the provisions of his late employer's will to indulge himself in an orgy of scholarship and a dream of pedantry, only to be described as notable. Since the era when Maximus withdrew the Legions from Hadrian's Wall, there were few Caledonians who had lived so comfortably or had had such an undisturbed opportunity to examine the records of the proceedings of the early church fathers; to estimate the dogmas which they had promulgated and to sniff at the heresies they decried, that of Arius in particular. The canny doctor had himself assembled the remarkable theological and classical library in which he now sported alone like a bachelor porpoise playing in the salubrious ocean of the past about the galley of learning. There were the rare books that had accompanied him in the post-chaise from Italy to Paris, and those which he had had brought over in every ship's cargo to Swansdam since, at a cost that had caused Mr. Jenkins to pale under his tan.

Now that the indulgent colonel was no more, Mr. Jenkins had sadly limited the field of the doctor's collecting. But the library in bulk was already there. The doctor's comfortable bedroom was upstairs immediately above it; the house from cellar to garret, with its nine domestic servants, was at his disposal. And time, illimitable time. Consequently, Dr. Simcoe, shortly after the colonel's obsequies, began to annotate the sources for every clause and phrase in the Athanasian creed, including the articles definite and indefinite, and to lose himself in the ancient world which had once been familiar to, and chattered with shrill controversies about, Athanasius himself and the great Bishop of Hippo. Alexandria, Constantinople, Carthage, and Rome itself were dreamfully re-erected in the doctor's brain, on the banks of the Rancocas.

To the contemporary world about him, Dr. Simcoe became as oblivious as though he were addicted to opium, the equivalent of which he had indeed found. He was, in holy orders, an archdeacon of the Nonjuring Episcopal Church of Scotland, a church without cathedrals, chapels, or congregations, which by this time existed only in theory and was embodied solely in the apostolic succession visible in the persons of its priests.* Yet at Swansdam Dr. Simcoe had now attained the ultimate in conducting a chapel of ease. Dinner in the evening was his sole contact with the world of men and the flesh. The two children sat with him at the table, but he seldom spoke to them; and for the most part he did not see them at all, but sat behind a wall of candle-shine, thousands of miles removed in distance and centuries withdrawn into the past. For, if the church which Dr. Simcoe belonged to was disestablished, disembodied, and

---

* It is the apostolic succession through the bishops of this church from whom all bishops of the Protestant Episcopal Church in America have received their consecration through the laying on of hands. The Rt. Rev. Samuel Seabury, D.D., bishop of Connecticut, was consecrated at Aberdeen in 1784, after being refused in London.

disallowed—the fields of thought and theological cogitation into which he had withdrawn were even more tenuous and ghostly. Indeed, it was with some difficulty, and only by dint of earlier habit, that he was now able to convey soup from his plate to his mouth without spilling it. Dinner was served. The doctor said an aftergrace and evening prayer. The children fled. Two bottles of port were brought, one of which he consumed at the table, and took the other into the library. At about midnight, if he could not get upstairs himself, he was carried to his bedroom by one of the Moors, with a book in his hand.

For two years the doctor continued his recension of the creed of Athanasius, while in the pool before the house the black swans swam. His notes on the procession of the Holy Ghost were interrupted by the death of little Mary. The child died late one night in a blue convulsion, and was buried beside her parents. She died and was buried, but she did not leave the house.

A few days afterward the formal education of young Cornelius began.

The matriculation of Cornelius in the field of learning was due to the annoyance of Dr. Simcoe at having been interrupted, and the protests of Mr. Jenkins, who, upon finding that the boy had not yet been taught to read, threatened to complain to the executors of the late colonel's will in the City. This, some latent genuine remorse, and a few shreds of conscience in the doctor aroused him at last to the bodily presence of his ward, who presumably had a mind. On a memorable August morning, when the mosquitoes were biting viciously and the heat and stench lay upon the marshes like a sigh from the entrails of hell, young Cornelius was called into the library and had his reluctant attention called to the twenty-six letters of the Roman alphabet and the ten Arabic signs.

The doctor was at first nonplussed and eventually thoroughly enraged at the obstinacy of his pupil in writing the alphabet from right to left and upside down. This initial difficulty having been overcome by a week or two of patient explanation and the application of a bootstrap, the boy eventually learned to place his letters and to pretend to see the page as the doctor insisted he should. So serious a stumbling block having thus been surmounted, his education proceeded from there by the same means and in the same way. That is, by heads up and tails down, which was Dr. Simcoe's sovereign method of striking fresh coins in the mint of learning, and fixing the design deeply in the blank rounds so that their value would be instantly recognized and pass current without weighing.

Consequently, Cornelius was spanked through his Latin primers and arithmetic, thrashed through grammar, slapped through logic, and banselled into Euclid; he whimpered over Caesar, wept with Virgil, and screamed and roared with Tully. But he advanced precept by precept and stroke by stroke. He learned well, and he remembered. For what was imparted to him was engraved in his head with the same force with which it had been incised upon his tail, and being thus fundamentally acquired, became a firm basis for the future. Even Mr. Jenkins, who now had constantly in his ears the painful evidence of Cornelius's progress in the things of the mind, was concerned, and in the end even a little more than just satisfied that Dr. Simcoe was not neglecting his pupil. Jenkins finally had mercy on the boy, after a year or two, and took him off from time to time on ships—voyages to the islands or on coastal ventures, during which he installed Cornelius in the best cabins, as he thought that the young owner of the fleet and the master of Swansdam deserved. And these voyages, infrequent as they were, were also a part of the boy's education as a gentleman of ample fortune in the ways of the world.

As to how Cornelius lived; what was his state of being; and how he grew in stature and in favour with men and women, that is a much more difficult thing to trace, lacking the notes of Dr. Simcoe. The death of Mary might well have been the end of Cornelius so far as his progress went, if Dr. Simcoe's impact, both mental and physical, had not come to the boy as a shock about the same time, one that drove him out of his dreams and into reality, painfully, it is true, but effectively. And then he soon discovered that his sister was still with him in the house.

Not long after she died, he had been sent to sleep in the great room in the big bed that had belonged to his father and his grandfather, but at night he would get up and slip back into the nursery where he and Mary had been brought up together. There he would lie in the darkness on his old bed and talk to her as he used to. Afterwhile he became aware that she was near him, lying on her bed in the dark. So they talked together again in whispers. Then he began to see her from time to time about the house. In fact, she followed him about, and he was conscious of her presence even when he could not see her.

Now, all this might be explained as an hallucination on the part of young Cornelius, from causes not hard to surmise. But the trouble is that other people saw Mary in the house, too. They said so, they thought so, and they acted as if they saw her. In short, if testimony, oral and written, is ever evidence,

Mary was "there". The servants saw her, and that made the conducting of the household at times extremely difficult. Mary also meddled with Dr. Simcoe's things in the library. He reluctantly became aware of it after eliminating Cornelius and the servants, whom he suspected. From time to time he was ingeniously harassed, however, and at last he saw Mary, too. It was just the day before the catastrophe of his lifetime overtook him, when young Cornelius had him thrown out of the house.

It was a little before midnight, and he was going upstairs from the library to his bedroom—up the front stairs, with one candle in his hand, when, as he turned on the landing, he was aware that another light was coming up behind him. It was a bright light, and he felt it before he saw it. But the thing that raised his hair was that it cast no shadows of the banisters or anything else whatever. It was a light altogether unto itself. Despite that the doctor turned, holding the candle in his hand, and looked down.

Standing halfway up the stairs just below him, ready to follow him again, and looking up at him with an incredibly malignant and yet beautiful expression was a face so ethereally lovely and so devilishly mischievous and ruthlessly innocent that the clergyman knew he was looking on something from another world. It was a naked and palely luminous figure of a sprite-like girl-child. All the rest that he could remember was the two deep wells of blue-black darkness like windows into eternity that looked up at him, and an effulgent brush of hair burning with an intense sea-green light. The sister spirit of the soul of the boy he had ruined chuckled with the tone of an echo and started to come up the stairs. Dr. Simcoe gave a harsh scream like a tormented horse, and galloping down the hall to his bedroom, managed to stumble in over the threshold and lock his door.

This strange occurrence took place on the eve of Cornelius's seventeenth birthday. The doctor had long forgotten the exact provisions of the old colonel's will. The habitude of his daily round, his concentration on his books, the ease of living, and even the hours of tyranny over his pupil had taken on for him the status of something ordained in the order of nature, until the manner of his life seemed to be an intangible that he possessed of right and thought of as if it were an item of indestructible private property. For the past six months he had been leading Cornelius into the necessary historical and biographical vestibules to theology, and leading him by the nose, he thought. He even flattered himself that a certain amount of respect and mutual affection was bringing him and his pupil closer together, and over a year had gone by since he had resorted to apostolic blows and knocks in support of his theological views.

But Cornelius had not forgotten that on his seventeenth birthday he was free, and, under his father's will, the master of Swansdam. He had long looked forward to the event as a criminal might who sees the days of a sentence slowly expire and determines what he will do first when his prison door finally swings back.

When Dr. Simcoe came downstairs late the next morning fortified with brandy, but still shaken to the core by the vision of the night before, he found Mr. Jenkins, two of the Moors, and all of his small effects, except those still in his bedroom, packed into sea chests, awaiting him in the hall.

"The *colonel* no longer requires your services, doctor," Mr. Jenkins casually informed him. "He asked me to give you this, have you sign a receipt for it, and to tell you that the barge is waiting to take you to Philadelphia."

The doctor in one moment felt his world crumble silently about him. But he was in no condition to protest. He signed the receipt, scarcely noting the weight of money in the bag that Jenkins gave him. He was then led down to the dock, where he sat in the barge and waited until his bedroom effects, his clothes, and a few books that were his, were brought from the house. The day was a hot one with no breeze, and the barge drifted slowly on the tide towards the narrow entrance. As it slid between the wooded banks, the doctor stood up and looked back. "My notes!" he said. "All my notes!" The familiar house on the mound gazed back at him across the wide silent reflecting-glass of the harbour pool. A procession of five black swans imperceptibly glided across it. It was the seventh of July, but a wisp of white curling smoke ascended high into the air from the library chimney. Dr. Simcoe sobbed and sat down. "I saw Mary last night," he said to Mr. Jenkins, who did not reply.

It being a glassily calm day, the barge proceeded slowly down the Rancocas and drifted leisurely out into the Delaware. It was after nightfall when Dr. Simcoe was landed with his chests, and left sitting on one of them, on Clifford's dock at Philadelphia. "I saw Mary last night," he said, looking down into the barge. None of the uniformed oarsmen even stirred. "Good-bye, sir," said Mr. Jenkins. "I always thought you were a learnèd fool."

Dr. Simcoe watched the barge rowing slowly down river

towards Swansdam; saw it diminish to a dot and disappear into the moonshine on the water. A few days later he became an usher at William Milne's night school in Aldridge Alley at the sign of St. Andrew, the only sign of the past that he now cared to recall.

Thus began the majority of the fourth and last colonel of Swansdam. He was now at liberty to see the world turned upside down, if he chose. But he did nothing of the sort. Indeed, he continued to try to improve the most generally acceptable view of it. For two years he toiled with head, heart, and hand under the direction of his devoted factor, Mr. Jenkins, to increase the volume and profits of the intercolonial and interisland trade in the West Indies, which they were now mainly engaged in, long voyages to Europe under the restrictions of convoys having been given up during the French war.

Although trade directly from one colony to another was also for the most part forbidden by the Navigation Acts, it was now practically more feasible and implied fewer risks and more certain profits. But it also required smaller and swifter ships. The snow, *Ariadne,* was sold, the two old topsail schooners were sheathed with copper and refitted with more sail. Three new, smaller, and swifter sloops were built at Swansdam in the late fifties and early sixties and employed to the islands for rum, molasses, and slaves, and for running the French, Spanish, and Dutch goods picked up in the Indies into various quiet and snug harbours, not provided with the facilities of his Majesty's customs, from the Carolinas to Long Island.

Much was also made of the fine pine and white oak forests about Swansdam for naval stores. And tall masts, spars, and ships' knees were sold extensively in Philadelphia. Young Cornelius and Mr. Jenkins were not making the great coups that Cornelius's father and grandfather had managed, but they were learning new tricks of the trade with every voyage. Cornelius had agents and friends from St. Augustine to Long Island Sound, and he was especially well provided with them, thanks to Mr. Jenkins's able endeavours during his minority, about the coasts of Chesapeake and Delaware. He now undertook to cultivate and visit these people personally.

As the Moors and Negroes at Swansdam had now increased beyond his capacity to employ them profitably, he began at this time to permit certain of them to scatter and settle along the banks of the creeks and in vacant pine lands in the still empty land east and south of Swansdam. He lost ownership over these people, but he also lost mouths to feed. And for a generation at least they felt a proud loyalty to serve the colonel. Thus Swansdam, the estate, and earthly affairs. But what of the ghostly? They were indeed taking a strange turn.

Cornelius continued, in fact, he might now be said to have first really begun, to read in the library which Dr. Simcoe and his ancestors had left behind them. He read intermittently and feverishly. He came across the tomes of philosophy that his father had brought back with him from France. A vision of the Age of Reason opened up before him. He felt himself being set free from the religion and theology of Dr. Simcoe.

Gradually, in the course of several years' time, after constant cogitations, even when away on voyages, he elaborated the plan of freeing his fellow men from the bonds of religion and superstition. It was a youthful, a utopian, and a quite American enthusiasm, one that gradually assumed in his mind the form of a mission to liberate mankind. Cornelius did not differ in this so much from other young "patriots" of his era, except that he thought in theological instead of political terms. It was with this high, and perhaps mad prospect in view that from about 1760 on he began to make more and more frequent visits to Philadelphia and eventually to spend much of his time there alone.

The executors of his father's will, and what few friends the family still had in the City, could make neither head nor tail of young Cornelius Vandercliff. He was not interested in routs and assemblies, and he was not even interested in women. He lived comfortably enough, as a rich young man could, at various of the best inns and coffee-houses. The rest of the time it was rumoured he spent in going to various Quaker meetings, making the rounds of the several churches, and above all attending camp meetings and field preachings in the country and the small towns around about. It was put down that he was a religious enthusiast in quest of salvation, and although it was thought a pity by several of the late colonel's more convivial friends, this was nothing new in Philadelphia, and it might wear off. As a matter of fact, Cornelius was listening, sampling all the sects, and elaborating his method of attack.

One day at a blacksmith's shop just across the street from the school where Dr. Simcoe now had the honour of being usher, Cornelius found Baz. The farmer who owned him was having an argument with the smith as to how or whether or not a cloven-hoofed horse, which attracted a small crowd and some idle curiosity, could or should be shod. The white horse was the catalyst that precipitated the elements of Cornelius's long-elaborated but not yet cohesive plan to deliver mankind from the bonds of religious superstition. No sooner did he lay eyes upon him, than he saw it all in a flash.

He bought the horse from the farmer forthwith at a price that made the countryman whistle, and it was soon afterward that Baz and his rider began to make those shattering appearances at field revivals, of which there was so much angry discussion at the time. It was not long before Cornelius began to ride farther afield and into the western woods on his mission. As to whether the mission was really accomplishing its object—that grew fainter and fainter in Cornelius's mind. He found a curious and profound satisfaction in the confusion that he produced. It could best be understood as it had been revealed to Dr. Simcoe in the impishly innocent, devilishly malignant, and yet ethereally lovely smile on the face of Mary's ghost as it looked up at him from the stairway that night at Swansdam and gave the echo of a chuckle from somewhere else.

The news of the great field preaching being prepared at Carlisle had as inevitably attracted Colonel Vandercliff to the vicinity as honey does a fly. He and Mahar-shalal-hash-baz had come a-riding. In this case, however, owing to the size of the assembly, Colonel Vandercliff had decided when the day came to try the approach subtle, rather than the appearance dramatic. At Boiling Springs he now awaited only the time appointed for the descent of the Holy Spirit.

30

Retrograde Procession of the Paraclete

Preliminaries

EDWARD YATES, who was in many ways an epitome of the Age of Reason, was, because of that, peculiarly sensitive even to a slight haze of bats flying about the loftiest of belfries. For him, one leather-wing spoiled the harmony of many a melodious high-hung set of chimes. Also, Yates was a close observer, and from the very first he had sensed in Colonel Vandercliff a something extraordinary. He was, therefore, quite content that the colonel had taken his recommendation of the shaky upper story of the inn as a fitting place of abode literally rather than figuratively, for he opined that the whimsical Cornelius had thus been prevented from becoming another guest at the mill house with the Albine family, for whom Yates now felt a high moral responsibility, since he lived there himself.

But that is not to say Yates was not considerably intrigued by Colonel Vandercliff, or that he did not take the trouble to find out, while the colonel was boarding just across the road at Drake's tumble-down ordinary, in what particular direction his obliquity lay.

His conclusion, after an evening or two as *amicus curiae* before the bar, with Jenny Greentooth assisting spiritually behind, was that the colonel and the Reverend James McArdle were both afflicted by the same kind of bats, although by hostile varieties. And since Cornelius finally became confidential and eloquently outlined the nature of his mission to liberate mankind, with emphasis upon his plan for scattering the coming field preaching at Carlisle, Mr. Yates began to view that evangelical occasion from another standpoint, and revised his decision not to be present at what now promised to be a diverting and informative scene. As usual, his reasons were nice and several.

The chances of the colonel's drawing down lightning at any given time and particular spot were, he felt, negative, or at most constituted a risk which he might cheerfully take as a purely passive spectator of the event. For this time he was determined to remain purely neutral, and in no way to supervene. The colonel might prove to be the prince of harlequins and a past-master of divine fooling, but Yates had had his lesson with the little Frenchman as to just how tragic comedy can sometimes be; and God, lightning, and Mr. McArdle were a triumvirate which he thought it expedient that the colonel should undertake to try to tease all by himself.

In this sentiment he found himself completely at one with Salathiel, who, on his part, desired nothing less than to bring down on himself and Frances the meddling or indignant attention of James McArdle. That day when driving out to headquarters he had encountered the angry ministers in the wagon, Mr. McArdle had addressed him in the tones of an ancient Hebrew prophet, and it had been all that he could do, for old times' sake, to restrain himself. Another time, and he might not be able to do so. After all, there were distinct limits to what he could take quietly. And so he, too, had determined to stay away from the field preaching, when the arrival of Jim Fergus and Arthur St. Clair for an overnight stay on their way to Philadelphia caused him to change his mind. Fergus had brought him a letter:

> Carlisle, Pennsylvania
> 20 March '65

My dear boy,

This will be carried express to you by that excellent newsmonger, James Fergus, who intends for the City in company with Mr. Arthur St. Clair, and tells me he will pass the night at your mill. Were it not that I am detained here about Our Father's business, and the things of the spirit must be paramount, I should long ere this have paid you a visit and had from your own lips the resolution of certain perplexing and conflicting reports about you, from which, I pray that you and my own heart might be at once absolved and delivered.

For oh what is it that I hear—on the one hand, from all your friends from Carlisle into the western borders, and they be men of nice repute I do allow, praises of your strength of mind and limb; courage, honesty, gentleness of heart and worldly skill. Yea all of this and more! I hear of the great trust that the Brethren of the Sign and the Square have laid upon you— until I know not what to think, and have so far sealed my lips, when I consider that all this is amerced and brought to nothing by still other praises, pleasant and well meant for you and her, the woman you let men reckon as your wife.

Only this morning, meeting Fergus in the street, did I hear that you have added to your deeds of mercy by giving shelter to that poor lost pagan, Irish Malycal; and when I think upon times past and darkling days so dangerously spent in evil happiness amidst the heathen host, and sweetest converse 'round the winter fires in dismal huts together in those days, needs must I seize my pen and even in the tumult of these streets that shadows forth the coming of the Lord, pour forth my agitated soul to you, Salathiel, my sometime son and erstwhile student of the Word 'midst forest shades.

This bodily frame of mine I do avow, to you I owe its life and all the days since added from the time you plucked me forth at midnight from the Ohio's stream. But did not I in gratitude and by the Word of God lead you, from even darker waters yet, up to the sunny heights whereon your soul might glimpse the high and distant city of its Home, those rainbow battlements and golden bastions of the Faith, beyond which mirth resounds, and music rings forever, made to God? Have you forgotten this—*then all is lost!* Better that you had lain with Indian maidens in the tasselled corn, and tasted of the hearts of savage chiefs, in pagan ignorance, and died with darkness in your soul and in your eyes—gone to the unfranchised sleep of wakeless things, than thus to wake, to glimpse, fall off—and *then* to die! Consider what awaits.

The Lord forgive me if I hold your soul more precious than a thousand other brands, meet for the bonfire, I snatch back for Him who judges all alike. But 'tis dear as my own child might be, for by me you were begotten of the Spirit out of darkness and 'twill not be like me to stand by and let you be drawn back to the fires by the silken strings of the Devil attached to your vitals, through the temptations of yon Romish Jezebel.

Therefore, there are some things that you must know that you may enter into a state of repentance with a whole heart and an informed mind: first, the woman I married you to, Jane Sligo, hath gone back to Redstone Old Fort and tarries there again with Madam Cresap; taking care of the children in her household; second, she has remained true to you, and she is still alone, save that she is comforted by numerous of her relatives on her mother's side who have also removed thither at Captain Cresap's behest to settle. She awaits word from you. Third, what shall I tell her? Or will you come yourself?

Now if I do not hear from you directly, my dear boy, it will be my painful duty to descend upon the establishment which I hear you are maintaining as a kind of Hell's Kitchen for the revels of the ungodly as well as a snare for the respectably innocent, who know not that you are living in sin—face your Romish Irish sweetheart with the proof of the shame she shares with you, and publish abroad that you are nothing, if not a whited sepulchre. But all this I *beg* you will spare me, yourself, and her by a timely repentance, the sign of which I shall take to be your appearance at the great Beseeching to be holden here three days beginning Friday, and your sharing with me in the descent and benefits of the Holy Spirit to lay hold of righteousness and have a part in salvation, after which all else shall be added unto you, as the promise goes, and between me and thee all shall be as it was before. I shall, therefore, eagerly expect you and look for your face first and before all others, and trust to be forgiven for so natural a partiality on the part of your

sometime preceptor and spiritual guide,

James McArdle

Salathiel's indignation upon reading this unexpected and unwelcome effusion was unbounded. McArdle alone could strike at his happiness so nearly; and what gratitude he felt for his former "preceptor and spiritual guide" was now cancelled by the unbounded claims of the man himself and his fanatic and pious threats. It would now be necessary to take immediate measures to see that Mr. McArdle minded his own business. Plainly, in one way or another, here was an end of peace and quiet home-keeping at the mill; and equally plainly, this letter could not be answered in the direct and practical way in which he had "replied" to that of M. de Molyneaux.

Mr. Yates also was alarmed, not at the letter, but for fear that Salathiel would resort to some simple violence. He was soon relieved of that apprehension by Salathiel himself. But his sympathy for his friend, and his natural repugnance to meddling fanatics, prompted him to sit down the same evening that Jim Fergus brought the letter and go into a careful conference over what he now called their mutual affairs. Both of them now admitted it had come to that, and they now for the first time put their heads together as partners to work out a solution of their difficulties in a partnership that was to prove perpetual.

They both agreed that in view of Frances' delicate condition, it would never do to have McArdle come and make trouble at the mill. In that event it was plain that Salathiel would take violent measures. After a long talk, and a careful weighing of means of defence and offence, and all the possibilities involved, they determined to act in advance upon the advices in the letter, and so take McArdle at the disadvantage of his own terms. "Nothing," said Yates, "is so disconcerting to those who undertake to disturb the repose of whited sepulchres as to find them occupied by wasps."

So it was arranged that he and Salathiel should both ride up to Carlisle together and appear in the field at the great intercession—but take Colonel Vandercliff along with them.

"Of course, we shall all have to avoid being converted," said Yates, "but the chances of that do appear to be small. And this will let Mr. McArdle see the face of his belovèd pupil, as he says he desires, and thus prevent his coming to the mill. If the colonel and Baz scatter the ranks of the faithful, we can then suppose that the Reverend James will be provided with sufficient troubles of his own to detain his attention; if not, we can still outface him, deny the validity of the marriage, and threaten him with the law of slander if he talks. It is one thing to be a preacher of the truth, and quite another to purvey slander.

"As to the alleged marriage," continued Yates, "I'll be frank: McArdle might make his contention good as to the legality of the ceremony. It is unfortunate that your girl has that piece of bark with the signatures on it and her ring. But I do not think there are any living witnesses left. And in any event, we can contend that this marriage was never consummated and that you did not and could not understand at the time what the ceremony implied. Therefore, no consent and no consummation. That might be our case. But I hardly think it will ever come to trial. Having lost his plea to your emotions, Mr. McArdle, if I know him, is not the kind who will take an appeal to the law. I think I can shut his mouth, since he is not able to shout 'bigamy'. That could be nasty. You see now why I always felt it best to let your living with Frances remain a matter of common law. After the child comes, you can both consider further. But meanwhile, only the girl herself, now at Cresap's, could make real trouble. And you will always, unless she dies or marries, have to abide that chance. But we'll meet that when it arrives. Mr. McArdle we can outface now on his own ground by pulling it from under him. If nothing else, we can certainly admonish him to keep away from the mill."

Salathiel agreed, although he did not care much for Colonel Vandercliff as an ally. He also felt it a good opportunity to tell Yates that he thought it high time to arrive at a final understanding with the Glen boys, to tell them that he would not enter into any further arrangements with them as to occupying or running the mill. "I intend for the City," he said; "I always did, and Frances is content as soon as I can make decent arrangements there."

"I'm glad to hear it," Yates replied. "I was diffident of trying to persuade you to leave, since we've been so snug and comfortable here. But it so happens that many things, and, as I see it, your best advantage all point eastward again. Both the reason and the convenience of your stay in your journey to the metropolis are now over. And, 'tarry not too long in Wittenberg', has always been, I thought, the best of worldly advice." Here Yates reached down and knocked his pipe out on the hearth, where the fire was beginning to burn low.

"That is literary, but this is practical," he continued, refilling his pipe and drawing on it comfortably. "Your arrangement with St. Clair will soon be over, and I'd advise you to terminate it. I happen to know he'll not be able to start any new settlers westward until well into the summer. Also, let me remind you of a certain promise you made one evening at Patton's to help me in settling people on *our* land."

"*Our* land?" inquired Salathiel.

"Yes, yes," insisted Yates. "For I'll tell you what, if you'll come in, I'll make it amount to that. I haven't had a chance so far to go into the result of that little card game with Lieutenant Grant, but we came off well. Yes, sir," cried Yates, smacking his knee, "damn well! I've put Wully's papers through, and seen to all those important and nasty legal details, and the result is two considerable tracts of land, one in the province of New York and the other in East Florida. But we'll have to occupy them both some way or other in the near future. Now, I've plans under way to do that; if you and your former acquaintance, Friend Japson, can get together in Philadelphia and undertake to work with me, 'thee will profit in a worldly way'. It's a grand scheme, 'my dear boy', and you'll be needed at first in the City to help see it get under way. It's nothing less than our mutual fortune, mayhap!" Yates snapped the patch on his eye.

"Now, that's one thing. The other is that I think you do well *not* to try to enter into business with the Glens. Martin is going to bring his bride home to the mill house this summer, and you wouldn't want to board Frances and have the child born at Mr. Drake's ordinary, which, as I pointed out to Colonel Vandercliff, is infirm. No, I am sure you wouldn't want to do that. Milling isn't your permanent career. And if you do move, move to the City.

"Ourry is mighty set on having you and Frances come over to Philadelphia to help conduct domestic headquarters for the brigadier. If I were you, I'd settle *his* mind about it. So far you've avoided saying yes or no, but it would be, if nothing else, a fine chance to get started in the City, and provide Frances respectable quarters to settle down in for having the baby. To be sure, Ourry hasn't thought of that. But let be! You would have at least a stipend to start on, and the helpful influence of the general. I'd not delay. St. Clair and Fergus are going to the City tomorrow. Why not send a note on with them to Ourry? You could write it tonight. I'm due in Lancaster on land business, and later to go on to the City myself, but I'll stay over and help outface the Reverend James McArdle on behalf of a client. You and I and the colonel can all ride over and watch the spirit descend. As far as that goes," he added, "if you can get ready in time, you could come by Lancaster and pick me up on your way to Philadelphia. Why not?"

Salathiel sat considering all this for some time, his feet outstretched in the glow of the midnight fire that was now falling to ashes before him. Finally he reached over and knocked his pipe out on the hearth, too.

"I'll do that," he said. Yates nodded.

That was the reason that shortly afterward on a Friday morning five horsemen, the two Glens, Salathiel, Edward Yates—and Colonel Vandercliff, all set out together, bound for the great field preaching at Carlisle.

The Event

The natural scene, human strategy, and the divine event of the great field preaching at Carlisle took place essentially as follows: Inwardly, within the minds and hearts of the multitude who had been drawn to the spot; outwardly, upon a level field about a mile outside of town with the trade sheds of *Boynton, Wharton & Morgan* along the road at one end and a clump of high and still noble pine woods at the other, which last provided a convenient grove for the retiring cabins of the ministers, and a place to tie innumerable horses.

Between the woods and the sheds, along two sides of the approximately square area kept free for the grand congregation for mass preaching, Mr. McArdle and Mr. Puffin had erected the marquees which they had begged from the brigadier, six on a side, to be used as prayer booths and rallying points for the flocks of the twelve ministers who were "joined together as members in Christ for the revival and reawakening of religion along the western borders in a great beseeching of grace to be holden at Carlisle". Although the total number of the ministers, or "managers", as they were often called, was purely accidental, it had not failed to receive some arch comment, and was the cause of professional persiflage even amongst the ministers themselves as to which one of the "twelve apostles" would prove Judas.

The canvas marquees, however, were not the only shelters along the east and west sides of the grassy square. There were also booths roofed over with green boughs in a Biblical manner, rustic sheds for the purveying of meat and drink, pits for roasting whole, hitching bars, and the lines and stone-marked spaces for covered wagons, all laid out and provided with a forethought and wisdom of experience on the part of the ministers that caused the cleverness of the managers to be much praised, and lent the scene of the great preachment a bowerlike and pleasantly rustic yet prepared appearance, which the assembly of God's people in a tabernacle in the spring woods might justly be expected to show.

But there was no altar here provided either for sacrifice or for oblation. That, in the course of ages and several migrations, had been left behind. Instead, and consequently the center of all pious comment and attention, was the mighty pulpit and platform for the divine oratory of the ministers, erected in the heart and center of the field. It was six feet high, eighteen feet wide, and thirty feet long. Stairs ascended to it on every side in the center. It was built of strong logs and rough-hewn planks and meant for mass exhortation. As many as four ministers could exhort from it at the same time, each facing his own cardinal portion of the listening crowd. A choir of the faithful sat upon it in the middle to lead the multitude in psalm and hymn singing. The newly converted climbed the steps to testify. It was surrounded at a little distance by poles with iron baskets for cressets and rings for pine torches, lit and renewed frequently during night preaching. And day or night, the pulpit was a mighty instrument to be played or danced upon by the ministers, even as David played and danced before the Lord—albeit with more attention to raiment.

With its tents, its bowers, its open square about the pulpit, and the lines of crowded wagons all looking one way at the pulpit with so many oval eyes; with the smoke from its camp-fires rising heavenward, crowds of people, the voice of exhortation and the sound of hymns and prayers, there was something impressive and memorable about the scene itself; a sense of fitness and of apt design with purpose for the matter in hand, as though a modern Moses had pitched God's tabernacle in the wilderness and paused in the years of journeying to rest and refresh the people of the Lord. The mountains looked at it, the sky overarched it. And quite suddenly it was indubitably there.

Like many other things, however, this impression of ease of achievement of the miracle of being was apparent rather than real. In one sense the tabernacle was the culmination of the life-work of the Reverend James McArdle, who, if anybody, was looked upon as the Moses, if not the St. Paul, of the occasion. And it was he who was now expected to strike the rock of indifference with the rod of inspiration and bring forth the gushing waters of salvation. It must be remembered, however, that James McArdle had spent many years in both the location and the preparation of the Rock. And in the end it was his devotion that had gathered about him, and in some cases converted, a band of inspired apostles for the preaching of the Word to the multitude at Carlisle. He was now regarded by many as a prophet, and in some sense a martyr to the faith, although a surviving one. All this, however, had not come about immediately.

The mission of James McArdle to the people and the savage tribes of the Alleghenies, "God's country", now entended backward into time for well over a quarter of a century. He had started preaching to the Indians before Salathiel was born. About 1742 old Garrett Pendergass had noted in his diary,

> Sab'th—We five to hear the Reverend Jms McArdle at the Cona-
> dogwinet log meeting at McCombs' in the vale. A pert young
> minister, he, has a call to preach to the Indians like a mad
> Moravian. Dissuaded him . . .

But James McArdle had not been dissuaded. He was firmly persuaded that Indians were the lost tribes of Israel, ignorant of the coming of the Messiah. And he had tried valiantly to bring them the news of salvation and gather them into the Christian fold. In the process he had lost both ears by an unfortunate misunderstanding; but in compensation, the power of making other people listen had been added to his tongue.

Bitter experience in having his Indian converts murdered by the white settlers, who had indignantly rejected his thesis that their mortal enemies were the remnants of the chosen people of God, eventually gave Mr. McArdle pause, although it never changed his opinion. He had gradually, during his own captivity, changed the object of his ministrations from the Indians themselves to the white captives he had found amongst them; and upon his deliverance and coming eastward, he had continued to preach the Word and to hold revivals and prayer meetings in the settlements along the frontiers.

Gradually, he had gathered about him the ministers of certain mountain flocks, the rude disciples he had most impressed. The accession of the Reverend Mr. Puffin at Bedford, by conversion, had given him a Joshua to match his Moses. And it was this group of devoted ministers with whom he had worked and held pentecostal meetings, until they were all as one, fanatically enthusiastic and irretrievably inspired.

It was their great ambition to hold a mighty mass prayer meeting, or "Beseeching", as they called it, at Carlisle. The example of the doughty Whitefield and his like in the recent Great Awakening of the forties was hopefully in mind. McArdle, for one, had long felt his powers were being wasted in working with single converts here and there, or in small meetings lost amidst the hills. He was now for conversion en masse and by multitudes; for the bringing in of the millennium, if possible, at one stroke. And in the state of mind to which he and his colleagues had attained, almost anything seemed possible.

For whatever had been the minor difficulties of sect and dogma that had hitherto contrived to hold them apart, they had now all joined together in one band of convinced apostolic evangelists. The central tenet of their faith was no mere dogma, but a mutual and overwhelming personal experience. They held that where two or three are gathered together, what they ask shall be given, as the Scripture promised—and what they asked was the descent of the Holy Ghost.

Such a boon was not, of course, lightly to be asked nor easily obtained. Long and arduous preparation had marked their early meetings together: searchings, repentance, and open confession; abstinence, fasting, and days and nights of continuous prayer. At last, a final beseeching for grace by all of them praying aloud together.

Then, at last, the moment would arrive. Often it was late at night, usually when it seemed that the weak flesh could stand no more—a power would shake them as the wind shakes leaves. It would come pouring down upon them. Mr. Puffin would be laid low babbling of and like the brooks in Paradise; Mr. McArdle would prophesy tremendously of the judgment to come; Mr. Elijah Jeremiah McCandless would be given visions of the exquisite torments of unrepentant sinners; Mr. Irwin spoke with his brethren in the golden accents of angels, and in unknown but seraphic syllables his brethren replied . . . Mr. Jeffrey saw a napkin snatched back up into heaven with all his sins wriggling in it, and knew they were taken from him to be used as temptations for others. He fell into a relieved trance. Afterward, a divine peace and silence would fall upon them all; and Mr. McKelvy, the oldest, would lie on his back, his eyes open without winking, watching a great wheel whose spokes were double-headed seraphs with their hair on fire revolve on the ceiling.

It was this enormous experience which bound them together, in faith confirmed by the event. And it was this supreme moment which, as good evangelists, they strove to repeat in bringing down the power of the Spirit on a crowd.

After the success of their own meetings, they had held Beseechings with each other's congregations. Then they had ridden about in groups of three or four to larger assemblies. Finally, after several years, they had all combined for one culminating meeting at Carlisle in which the whole countryside was to receive the baptism of the Spirit en masse. That, at least, was the ambitious goal of James McArdle, who was now in such a mood of high exaltation that it prompted him to think he might be capable of hastening the date of the millennium all by himself.

He was now completely surrounded by followers who regarded him as the coming Whitefield and often hinted of greater things to come. And he would no longer tolerate anything less. But he was also beginning to receive the punishment for his sin of enormous presumption by unconsciously engendering in himself spiritual arrogance to a corresponding degree. His manner was now so lofty that it brought about an opposition which he could no longer understand.

To him, it was now a matter of indignation, or at best mysterious chagrin, that many of his regularly ordained brethren held aloof. And if they did not openly denounce, at least passively opposed him. The Reverend Mr. Craighead was one of them. Also many of his brother Masons were not to be moved. Mr. Byers, who was of high degree, gave him the gate. As for the gentlemen and the gentry, lawyers like Mr. Yates, and the conservative members of the old churches, with a few exceptions, they were plainly not with him at all. Messrs. Boynton, Wharton, and Morgan had all been heard to say they wished the spirit would descend at Lancaster. Only a few of the merchants contributed. In short, there were two minds at Carlisle as to whether the Great Beseeching was good for trade or not. People who came in wagons and camped, usually brought all their "fixin's" with them.

All this, for a man of James McArdle's spiritual sensibility and exalted state of mind was, of course, hard to bear. Wheedling contributions in kind from the faithful was also a sordid and difficult burden. During the preaching, he and the other apostles would live in plenty; but afterward, he and Mr. Puffin would be reduced again to Mr. Inman's oval-wheeled wagon and the tired old horse, for the gathering of country tithes.

It was a combination of these petty anxieties and annoyances that had prompted the letter to Salathiel. For James McArdle had not only met Jim Fergus on High Street one morning, and had to listen to his gossip about how well Salathiel was doing at the mill—a few minutes later he had also run into Dr. Craighead, trim if not elegant in his newly restored wig, and had to listen all over again to the merits and talents of Salathiel and Frances, as well as to Mr. Craighead's scarcely veiled menaces about tampering with his flock. They were, he claimed, already in "a reasonable state of Grace" and had fully accepted the Atonement. Did Mr. McArdle *not* think the Atonement sufficient?

Now, this was quite a poser, and in the heat of the ensuing argument Mr. McArdle had found great difficulty, among other things, in refraining from telling what *he* knew about Salathiel; and his somewhat fiery vein at parting from Mr. Craighead had been continued into the letter, which he sat down and wrote immediately afterward, so that Fergus could take it to the mill.

Such considerations were purely minor and quite personal, however. Even Mr. McArdle realized that, when he cooled off. And he did not permit any small opposition to abate the fervour of his preparations and exhortations preliminary to the final event itself. He and the other eleven had continued to preach and to visit and exhort in all the countryside about. The news had spread far. People now began to pour in from all sides, even from distant towns and hamlets; from north, south, and eastward. On the Sunday preceding the Beseeching there were almost as many people in overwhelmed Carlisle as there had been a few months before when Bouquet marched home. Some thought there were more. Day after day family wagons and lone horsemen continued to arrive.

At last the great day dawned, Friday morning. Before sun-up McArdle gathered his "managers", and in a cabin in the pine woods next to the tabernacle they prayed together, asking strength and inspiration for the three days' ordeal to come. The rumour that the white horse of Colonel Vandercliff had been seen stabled at Boiling Springs was more like fuel to their enthusiasm at this point than water on the fire. Promptly after breakfast a drum sounded solemnly from the platform. The Welsh choir began singing, and the people gathered in from all sides. Looking across the fields still hazy with the mist of morning, the multitude now saw the twelve ministers advancing towards them from the woods. A loud exultant shout went up to heaven. The preaching and praying and beseeching began.

* * * * *

No, there had never been anything quite like it. And long afterward those who followed the progress of evangelism westward, in what were later on called "revivals", harked back in memory to the great original Beseeching at Carlisle. It was James McArdle's genius and devotion, his very fanaticism that had brought it about; set the standard, and provided the form. There were more people gathered at other places later, but never a greater fervour, never so profound a preparation, such loud hosannas or more overwhelming excitement. Excitement, excitement, excitement—it began in the morning; it mounted and climbed and reached minor crests through the afternoon. It attained a delirium of repentance, a triumph of conversion, and a peak for the Spirit to descend upon in the wild fiery hours of the torch-lit night.

It was a warm spring morning. The breeze kept blowing softly from the south. Even by ten o'clock the ministers and the congregation were sweating. The heat of the noonday began to wear them down. It had been McArdle's plan to spend the morning in thanksgiving for the blessings of peace restored, the afternoon in repentance, and the night in purifying prayer. The beseeching itself and the hopeful advent of the Spirit had been planned for Saturday. But the rising tide of emotion now began to overwhelm and outrun the schedule of Mr. McArdle's plan. This was plainly apparent even before noon. But he was too sagacious not to let his ark float home on a spring tide, when the current was with him.

After a morning of hymns, songs of thanksgiving, and an outpouring of praise and gratitude, ending in an acclamation of universal joy and a storm of hosannas, time was taken out for the noon meal. Buckets of boiled meat and potatoes were passed around, chunks of bread, and certain liquid refreshments.

During this mundane interlude Mr. McArdle imparted to the other apostles that it had been revealed to him that the Spirit would descend that night, instead of Saturday. This apocalyptic news flew from lip to lip, while the holy excitement mounted. Sinners realized that they now had less time than they had counted upon in which to procrastinate; the joy of the elect was unbounded. And the entire assembly, which was constantly being increased by newcomers, gathered about the pulpit platform to hear the clarion call to repentance from the ten ministers, who succeeded one another without pause, except for the intermittent singing of the choir.

Mr. McArdle and Mr. Puffin were saving themselves for the great and final beseeching in the evening. They had carefully planned the strategy of the night attack between them. Mr. Puffin was to hold forth upon the mercy, the love, and the free fountain of salvation. He was to preach his great sermon, now perfectly memorized with appropriate gestures, upon the unparalleled sufferings of the Lamb of God. It was a tragic poem, a masterpiece of forensic rhetoric, which he had been practising and revising ever since the days of his long-past but inspired youth. With it he had brast many a brazen heart in twain.

That night there was to be a middle moon. It would appear about meridian at sunset and glide slowly down into the west. Mr. Puffin was to preach it halfway down the sky. Mr. McArdle was then to take up the tale of God's mercy and paint the horrors of the pit, for those who refused to accept what was freely offered; limn them in the original incandescent horrors of a paint pot of fire. When the moon dipped, that was to be the crucial moment. Then would go forth the call for the Spirit to descend and lighten the darkness.

Meanwhile, neither of the two leaders was idle. During the afternoon, while the preaching went on and on, they divided and visited between them the twelve tents, where for the most part bands of women awaited praying, preparing themselves for the great event. Some were already torpid from their long vigils; others were hysterical from apprehension. The former the two ministers roused again to a sense of spiritual crisis, the latter they calmed with extended promises of hope.

Outside, the tumult of continuous preaching, shouts of glory, and shrieks of despair, wild psalm singing and uncontrolled weeping marked the afternoon hours, as they swiftly unrolled with ever-mounting excitement, until the shades of evening began to fall. As the moon appeared directly overhead and looked down with half-averted countenance upon the frenzy of the crowd below, the twelve bands of women emerged from their tents on either side of the square and were marshalled by their pastors towards the platform, while the crowd burst into glad hymns and hallelujahs of welcome. The torches and cressets were now lighted, while Mr. Puffin waited in patient dignity for a calm moment in which to begin.

It was just at this juncture that the five horsemen from Boiling Springs approached the assembly. They had waited in town during the afternoon. Evening, they knew, would be the height of the holy spectacle. They rode their horses quietly along the dusty South Road through the dusk of growing twilight and tied them under the platform of the trading sheds. There Baz could be well concealed, and a modest fee of sixpence assured the others from being lifted by sinners anxious to flee too rapidly from the wrath to come. Without attracting any particular attention, they took their places, standing upon the outskirts of the crowd. Gradually Yates and Salathiel worked themselves forward until they stood close under the platform. Mr. Puffin arose, and quieting the multitude with a prayer, began to preach.

The great appeal, the original reason for Christian hope and sympathy went home. Mr. Puffin employed an ancient but effectual and catholic device. He related the suffering of the Saviour Himself. He detailed the scenes at the stations of the Cross, and the great defeat and triumph at Calvary. No one who was not feeble-minded remained unmoved. Mr. Puffin was sincere; the devices of his rhetoric had become natural. He suffered. The crowd suffered with him. Tears ran down from the single eye of Edward Yates. Salathiel stood transfixed with amazement that all this had been suffered and borne patiently for him. Mr. Puffin preached the moon halfway down the sky. He ended with the despairing words of the Divine Man on the Cross, "My God, my God, why hast thou forsaken me?", and held out his arms to the multitude, begging them to accept the salvation so dearly bought.

Oh, if it could only have been left like that! The crowd sighed as one man, and moved forward unconsciously two or three steps as though to receive the boon. Many were weeping, many distraught. It moved forward—and found itself, almost magically, it seemed, in the flaring shadows of the torches, confronted by the grim earless countenance of James McArdle.

Here and there arose shrieks of startled and anticipatory terror from the women. A great groan went up. In the midst of this, Mr. McArdle began.

"And He descended into Hades" was his text and theme. Steadily, unrelentingly, and convincingly, he pictured the obscene horrors and writhing torments of the pit. He quoted Scripture, line by line. The lava-heated vistas in the murky caverns of endless melancholy, the unavailing cries of never-ending despair, the just indifference of God, an immortality in the living moment of death at the stake forever prolonged and suspended, unsocketed all but the firmest souls with a sweeping nausea of terror, until the field of McArdle's labours gibbered and seethed in ripples of fright. He was not Dante, but he transcended Edwards, and the breath of vengeance seemed to strike down and wither the crowd in wilted spots, where the people writhed and lay moaning on the ground.

Thus it was that James McArdle preached the moon down to the western horizon. He was transported by his overwhelming success and the sound and roll of his own periods. The great moment of his lifetime was now at hand. As the branches of the distant forest began to finger the silver bottom of the moon, he paused. Darkness was rapidly coming on. The noise from the multitude before him, as the shadows deepened, was like the sound of a herd of buffalo caught fatally, and wallowing in a bog. Men bellowed, and women shrieked to be saved. In another moment the time for the universal beseeching would have come. But at that instant the man on the white horse rode down the aisle of terror, which opened before him, and dismounted before the platform. The horror was so great that it seemed the Devil in person had come. In the universal and overwhelming silence, the spade-bearded and black-cloaked figure climbed to the platform and stood outlined in the smoky red glow of the sputtering pine knots.

He threw his cloak back with a confident gesture, and stepping to the low rail of the platform just as the moon finally sank and darkness swooped, he roared, "Lost, lost!" like a sudden double clap of thunder from the surrounding murk.

But the effect was quite different from what the arch-atheist expected. Mr. McArdle had already been so successful that terror could do no more. And it was the minister alone who responded. He came forward and laying his hand familiarly on the colonel's shoulder, leaned out over the rail and shouted, "See, good people, here is the great doubter himself come to be saved. Oh glory! Glory be to God in the Highest! Let us pray!"

The revulsion came. A babble of indescribable relief, a shout of joy at this visible miracle of mercy, rose from all sides. The stricken leapt to their feet with new hope and began to prance. The colonel's prayer for lightning went unheard. Indeed, those who saw him praying thought he was giving thanks. A vast and wallowing excitement ran in waves through the crowd. Colonel Vandercliff realized that he was undone. His failure weakened his knees and struck him like a blow somewhere in the back of the neck. In fact, neither he nor McArdle had control any longer over the crowd roaring below.

A wizened little fellow, a discharged militia drummer, with a head shaped like an eggplant and small burning eyes turned back in his head, emerged with a line of rocking and swaying people, arms on shoulders following behind him, beating an imaginary drum with flailing hands, and roaring over and over again in a harsh voice:

> "A rat-a-tat-tat, the dog and the rat,
> A rat-a-tat-tat, the dog and the rat."

To this fascinating rhythm the crowd now began helplessly to respond. It swayed to and fro; it trembled and it stamped.

> "A rat-a-tat-tat, the dog and the rat."

Some people leapt high into the air. A Samson of a man howled exultantly that the Spirit was upon them. On the edge of the encampment, boys rocked back and forth in the boughs of young maples and whooped to one another gleefully. Women were mowed down in windrows. They lay gasping on their backs with their legs apart and their eyes turned back into their heads. Mr. Yates, who went to the assistance of one of them, who was obviously having a fit, was sternly repulsed by the girl's husband.

"Leave her lay where Jesus flanged her," the man roared, and then rising, tore his handkerchief loose from between her teeth, and went jigging off after the little drummer, beside himself with spiritual glee.

> "A rat-a-tat-tat, the dog and the rat."

James McArdle, with his hands before his face, was now kneeling on the platform and praying earnestly that God should not mock him, that this cup of gall and stupendous failure should be removed from his lips. His prayer was answered. He looked up from where he was kneeling and saw that Colonel Vandercliff was being converted. He looked upon him in the very throes of the act. The colonel began to prance to the roaring chorus of the crowd. He could not prevent himself. The drummer's song lifted his feet into the air one after the other. He bowed and swayed. And then the miracle occurred.

The Spirit descended, and the gift of tongues was upon him. To Cornelius the power seemed to be coming from behind. It rained down into the crowd. He could see in the wavering torch-light patches in the crowd before him that seemed to be struck as by puffs of wind on the surface of water. The power poured into the people, and everywhere they ceased shouting about the dog and the rat and began to gibber in a new, a holy dialect, and a hundred strange languages. Each was given his own heavenly tongue. Colonel Vandercliff was lifted by his neck to the rail of the platform. He stood upon it. He meant to pray for lightning. But he felt Dr. Simcoe's hand on his collar, shaking him. He began to prophesy. The Scriptural words came straight into his mouth but emerged backwards:

"But these two things shall come to thee in a moment in one day, the loss of children, and widowhood: they shall come upon thee in their perfection for the multitude of thy sorceries, and for the great abundance of thine enchantments. For thou hast trusted in thy wickedness: thou hast said, None seeth me. Thy wisdom and thy knowledge, it hath perverted thee; and thou hast said in thine heart, I am, and none else beside me. Therefore shall evil come upon thee; thou shalt not know from whence it riseth: and mischief shall fall upon thee; thou shalt not be able to put it off: and desolation shall come upon thee suddenly, which thou shalt not know. Stand now with thine enchantments, and with the multitude of thy sorceries, wherein thou hast laboured from thy youth; if so be thou shalt be able to profit, if so be thou mayest prevail. Thou art wearied in the multitude of thy counsels. Let now the astrologers, the stargazers, the monthly prognosticators, stand up, and save thee from these things that shall come upon thee. Behold, they shall be as stubble; the fire shall burn them; they shall not deliver themselves from the power of the flame: there shall not be a coal to warm at, nor fire to sit before it. Thus shall they be unto thee with whom thou hast laboured, even thy merchants, from thy youth: they shall wander every one to his quarter; none shall save thee."

As he ended these words he tottered, threw up his hands with a great cry, and pitched forward from the rail, diving head-foremost into the crowd. Someone had hamstrung Baz, and the tormented cries of the white horse rose above everything, until the wild clamour of those who had found salvation drowned his moaning in a prolonged gurgling and chortling of the peace that passeth understanding. . . .

Aftermath

Hours later Cornelius Vandercliff came to in a tent, surrounded by triumphant ministers. As their prize convert and chief exhibit, they now ministered tenderly to his extreme bodily wants. He looked about him. He remembered. He understood what had happened. But he said nothing. He was sick in soul and body, and he slept intermittently for two days and nights.

Yates, Salathiel, and the two Glens returned together to the mill. They had not waited after the fall of their friend, Colonel Vandercliff. They emerged from the babble of tongues without making any comment themselves, mounted their horses, and came home in the early morning.

"Thank God for the cleanness of the dawn," said Yates. Salathiel agreed. He felt that he had escaped from a foul quagmire, but still felt the mud caked upon him. He took a swim in the mill-pond, and at breakfast began to talk to Frances about getting ready to move to the City. He said nothing about what he had been through at Carlisle. Such things were not for a sweet woman like his common-law wife to hear. He had kept trouble away from her. McArdle, he knew, would never come to the mill now. He would be too busy with his converts and other plans. Whether Colonel Vandercliff returned or not, he didn't care. They were all crazy, he thought.

At Carlisle the Reverend James McArdle's triumph was complete. His cup ran over. He had seen the face of his pupil stricken with repentance in the midst of the crowd. It was enough. He was now preparing, in the light of his unparalleled success, to carry the message of the gospel westward; to call down the power of the Spirit in remote and benighted vales amidst the mountains. He hoped to take Cornelius Vandercliff along, and regretted the loss of the white horse.

At Boiling Springs all was haste and hurry in the days that followed. Captain Ourry had sent back a note by Fergus urging that Salathiel and Frances be on hand to meet the brigadier when he returned to Philadelphia from New York. Convenient quarters in one of the most respectable boarding-houses in the City had been found. General Forbes had been buried from that house, after being laid out in the parlour. And no better assurance of convenience and respectability could be desired. Yates laughed; and left for Lancaster, where he would wait to be picked up when the wagon came through. He would be at Colonel Burd's house, he said—not the one that Colonel Burd was building at "Tinian" in the country, but the big one on the square. At which Frances pricked up her ears. Perhaps Bridget could see that house after all. It was the mansion which Mrs. Patton had thought of at Lyttleton as being so "very, very genteel".

Heigh-ho, who could tell? Respectability, gentility, and possibly affluence now lay before them. Frances Melissa hurried about her packing in the old mill house contentedly, while Malycal and Bridget excitedly helped. Whatever else it might be, Frances was certain a move to the City was a move in the right direction.

Let the rest happen as it might.